CHILD OF SHIVAY

CHILD OF SHIVAY

VEILS OF TERR

J R CATHERS

Book Cover by Arkadiusz Andrzejewski
Interior Formatting by Mariska Maas, Rubre Art
Mariska Maas (chapter art)
Anastasia Pionkovskaia (character art)
Gerralt Landman (Cartographer)

ISBN (special edition): 979-8-9989749-0-8
ISBN (hardcover standard): 979-8-9989749-2-2
ISBN (paperback): 979-8-9989749-1-5

First edition 2025

To my editor, Lindsay Hause. For the love and friendship grown from this project and for the magic she poured into this story with her passion. Your incredible voice echoes within these pages.

To my Smutty Buddies, Ame and Kenz. For the patient and persistent love they pour into my life and for the encouragement that spurred this tale into print. Your light is radiant, piercing even my darkest days.

A'KOR

LA'TARI
GERRALT

GLOSSARY OF TERMS

A'KORI (ACK-O-RYE) – The northern continent. Home of the A'kori.

DRAKAI (DRUH-K-EYE) – Elite assassins of the La'tari crown

FEA (FAY-UH) – Creatures closely linked with nature and connected to the life force of Terr.

FEA DIEN (FAY-DEE-EN) – The beautiful death. An organization of female assassins within the Drakai.

FEYN (FAY-N) – A species of fea, most similar to humans in appearance.

LA'TARI (LA-TAR-EE) – The southern continent. Home of the La'tarians.

SHIVAY – The soul of Terr, the light of all life.

TERR (TEER) – The world.

THE SUNDERING – When the ancients divided the soul of their world into five parts, known as the veils of Terr.

THE VEILS – The five realms formed by the sundering. Five realms living side by side, each unseen to the other.

PRONUNCIATION GUIDE

Awri — (Ar-ee)

Bagya — (Bog-yaw)

Felias — (Feel-ee-us)

Kishek — (Kish-eck)

Media — (Muh-dee-uh)

Mi'ajna — (Mia-jh-na)

Muri — (Mew-rie)

Niya — (Nai-uh)

Nurai — (Nur-eye)

Riah — (Ree-ah)

Riesh — (Ree-sh)

Shivaria — (Sh-i-var-ee-a)

Siserie — (Sis-err-ee)

Tha'haynah — (Tha-hay-nah)

Vakesh — (Va-kesh)

Valtoura — (Val-tour-ah)

Vatruke — (Vat-rue-k)

Xeyvian — (Zay-vee-an)

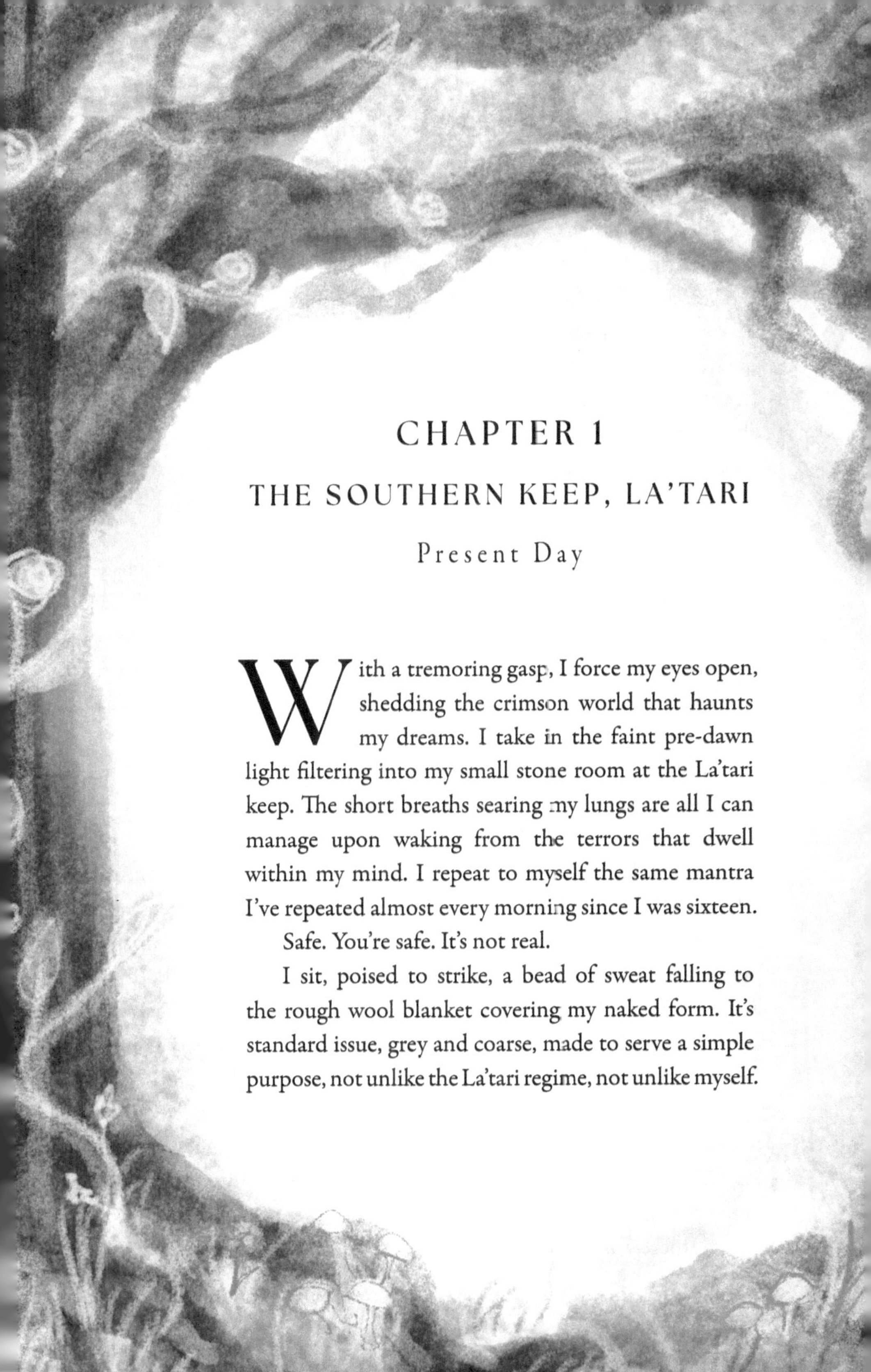

CHAPTER 1

THE SOUTHERN KEEP, LA'TARI

Present Day

With a tremoring gasp, I force my eyes open, shedding the crimson world that haunts my dreams. I take in the faint pre-dawn light filtering into my small stone room at the La'tari keep. The short breaths searing my lungs are all I can manage upon waking from the terrors that dwell within my mind. I repeat to myself the same mantra I've repeated almost every morning since I was sixteen.

Safe. You're safe. It's not real.

I sit, poised to strike, a bead of sweat falling to the rough wool blanket covering my naked form. It's standard issue, grey and coarse, made to serve a simple purpose, not unlike the La'tari regime, not unlike myself.

My knuckles are strained white from gripping my obsidian daggers. Blades I hold defensively, shielding my face, as if the nightmares that consume my mind could somehow follow me into the waking world and deal a fatal blow.

The darkness that wells within me as I sleep every night has at least afforded me my own room. Few women are selected and trained to be Drakai, and all refused me as a bunk mate after an unfortunate incident years ago. Avanjelin, an exceptionally beautiful young woman, had roused me from a fitful sleep, taking one of my daggers to the side of her face for all her efforts. The girl lived, but the thick, jagged scar left upon her porcelain skin stripped from her the life she'd been intended. She will still be Drakai, an elite assassin of the crown, but never again Fea Dien, the beautiful death. There will never be room in our ranks for the flawed.

My racing heart finally begins to slow, and I sheath my blades beneath my pillow, forcing a deep breath into my lungs, puffing it out in a haze. The grating burn of the cool spring air against the tender flesh of my throat is all I need to tell me that I've been screaming in my sleep. Again. Years of the same taught me that no one ever hears me. The walls of the keep are far too thick for my terror to reach the ears of another or, if it does, no one cares to investigate the sound.

I don't blame them. Even in the middle of the largest stronghold on the southern shore you have to think twice about risking your neck for a stranger. The same deadly skill and brutality the La'tari drill into their ranks seems to come with a lack of discernment as to the difference between friend and foe. Still, what is within the keep is safer by far than what lay outside its walls.

Peeling my sweat-soaked body from the bed I make my way toward a small metal jug by the window. Taking a long drink of the icy liquid within, I ignore the trickle of water rushing past my lips and down my chin. The room is plain, bare of excessive furnishings, save for the small, uncomfortable bed and the simple wash station beneath the window. It is more than most La'tarians would dream of having. I'm lucky, a fact I'm reminded of every day.

My mentor, Leanna, found me as a child, hours after the treaty had been signed, bringing an end to the war I'd been born into. But news was slow to reach the small border towns and by the time her contingent arrived at my village, there was nothing the woman could do but pull me from the burning wreckage of my home. She's never been much of a mother, not in the way I'd heard them described by others who'd been gifted with lives surrounded by family. But she's given me a life, a purpose, and a way to avenge all that was taken from me that night.

I fill the small basin beneath my window and wash myself with a cold, wet rag. The chill of the water draws a sharp inhale from my lips as a stray bead of liquid drips down my side. It's still early in the spring thaw, and just last week I was breaking ice from the surface of the jug every morning. I remind myself that in the blistering summer heat I'll be happy for the relief offered by the cool water and suppress a shiver as I pat myself dry and reach for my uniform.

My fingers deftly lace up the black fighting leathers I've worn since I was a child. They are a stark contrast to the demure lady that Leanna spent the last twenty years training me to be. It hasn't been for my sake that she's spent so many painstaking hours molding me into a consort fit for a king, it has only ever been for the good of the realm. I live to serve, and these precious moments alone in my small, modest quarters are the only moments that will ever be truly mine. I push away the thought that even those are quickly coming to an end.

Wrestling the knots out of the thick, raven spirals falling to my lower back, I plait them into a long braid. Despite my best arguments, Leanna always insisted I not cut my hair any shorter. Most La'tari women go through great lengths to maintain their hair and display it as a source of pride, woven and curled or otherwise adorned with all manner of jeweled embellishments. Perhaps I would do the same had I been gifted the golden honey tones that are considered so desirable. As it is, the color of my hair feels like a stain that will never wash away. A sure marker of the feyn blood in my veins, however distant that blood may be.

I glance toward the door, pushing down the darkness writhing inside me. I should never have allowed Leanna to distract me from my sparring lessons with Bront the day prior. It is one of the few ways I have found to quell the demon that plagues my sleep.

I puff out a small misty laugh at the thought that I could in any way manage Leanna. My entire life has been subject to the woman's demands, and nothing I ever say or do will dissuade her from the trajectory she has set me on.

Through squinted eyes, I peek out the small window above the water basin. Judging by the light, I still have an hour before the rest of the keep begins to stir. Most everyone is still sleeping at this hour of the morning. Most everyone.

"You look like *hisht*, Shivaria."

"Well, Bront, at least the days *I* look like *hisht* are few and far between. Don't you wish you could say the same?" I smirk.

Bront laughs, the grizzled old soldier spitting on the freshly groomed sand of the sparring ring. Leaning against the wooden border fence, he swipes a dirty blonde lock of hair out of his eyes. He's been growing it out since his retirement last year and can now proudly pull it back into a thin leather tie, tucking the few remaining strands behind his ears. His face and hands are heavily scarred, the jagged pink lines only mildly obscured by his fair freckled skin. They have been like that as long as I have known him, though I've never gotten enough ale into the man to hear a single story behind any of the white lines marring his flesh. He's never been keen on sharing his war stories, unlike many of the cocky soldiers who served under his command.

"Leanna know you're here?" His eyebrow quirks up in an awkward angle, pulled by a fresh, bruising cut above his eye.

"You know she doesn't," I say, "I just need to let off a little steam."

I've counted on my morning sessions with the old general for years. He hadn't hidden his surprise the first day I'd come to spar while the rest of the keep slept, but he never asked questions and he'd always been happy to oblige. After weeks of sparring, he came to expect me in the early mornings. After months, it seemed that he craved the ritual of it. I'm not his favorite student, I'm not anybody's favorite, but after all these years, I am his best.

He smiles and shakes his head, a few loose strands of hair falling into his face. "Not today."

"Bront—"

He cuts me off before I can argue. I'm not even sure why I try, I've never won an argument with the man. Every part of him is cut from steel, from the

muscular form of his body to the unbreakable will that made him a general. Even his retirement hasn't softened that.

"Big day today. Can't ship you off to A'kori with a split lip," he says with a knowing smile.

Leanna may have forced me into the service of the Fea Dien, but I have always been most at home in the ring, in battle. If I am, one day, fated to die a warrior's death, I'd prefer it be on the battlefield, and not tangled up in the silk sheets of a failed seduction.

I'll never know what Leanna was thinking when she made me what I am. I'm not cut out for it. I have spent my life around women who revel in the chase, the hunt, the trickery, but I've never cared for any of it. I have always been, will always be, a sharp blade hidden in a vase full of lovely flowers.

I pin Bront with a taunting smile. "You would have to actually land a blow on me to accomplish a split lip, *old man.*"

It's too easy to bait him, and he shifts his weight off the fence, the smile falling from his face as his fists clench at his sides. He takes a step toward me, and I shift my feet, preparing for his advance.

Good.

The release I seek in the ring each morning is a selfish need. The adrenaline it shoots through my veins has always been the quickest purge of my mind and the bloody visions it conjures at night. Of course, the need that drives me also helps to hone my skills. At the age of twenty-four, the hours I spend sparring with the general every morning have molded me into an efficient weapon, and now, I can count on a single hand any in the La'tari ranks who stand a chance at besting me one on one.

My back stiffens when Leanna's voice floats through the air, caressing my ears like lethal silk. "Shivaria, I'm glad to see you up early this morning."

Bront quickly resumes his lax position against the fence, as if he hadn't been seconds away from an attempt to prove just how quickly he could out-maneuver me. He hasn't managed it for years, and I have serious doubts he would have been brave enough to actually split my lip, no matter the taunting that had preceded. If the man is afraid of anyone on this side of the continent, it's Leanna, and no one who ever met the woman would blame him for that.

"Good morning, Leanna," Bront replies with a smile as he watches her

approach, his eyes drifting up and down her form appreciatively.

Her dark eyes dilate like a large cat sizing up its prey. The man has balls, I'll give him that. In the twenty years I have known the woman I have never seen her take a lover, though I suppose it is entirely possible she simply killed any who displeased her. That being every single one.

Leanna, my tutor, teacher, and tormentor, glides across the courtyard in a painfully graceful stride. Her honey hair is striking against the fawn tone of her skin, tumbling down her back in unnatural spirals, strands here and there held back by small combs. Her eyes burn with clear satisfaction at having found me here. I'm not surprised to see her. She has the uncanny ability to know my mind, often long before I know it myself.

I hate the relief that washes over me that she hasn't discovered me in the midst of a match with the old general. She may have ended the man for leaving a single mark on my body today. And, if I displease her, the woman is perfectly capable of inflicting her own kind of brutal punishment without leaving a single trace upon my skin.

"Getting your goodbyes out of the way?" she beams, halting by my side, before taking in my black leathers with a frown. "No need," she says, flicking her wrist dismissively, "just follow my instructions and you will be back within the year."

"As you say." I dip my head slightly. It isn't quite a bow, but life with Leanna is always easier when deference is supplied regularly.

"Come, Shivaria. Your ship leaves on the morning tide," she says flatly, turning on her heel and making her way toward the keep without so much as a glance back.

A cold spike of fear runs down the length of my spine and my eyes meet Bront's for what might be the last time, despite her reassurance. He smiles encouragingly, and I wonder how many soldiers he's given that same smile to. Soldiers he had never seen again.

"Until we meet again, my lady. Courage and Strength."

"Courage and Strength," I repeat his motto numbly before rushing after Leanna.

"I was told my ship left on the evening tide?" I say as we make our way through the quiet stone halls of the keep.

"You know better than many that we take what fate provides and make the most of it. Conditions have changed and our plans must be adjusted accordingly," she says simply, as if that explains anything. I know better than to press for answers.

My mind is a scattered mixture of violent dreams and visions of an equally violent future as I follow her back to my room. She closes the door behind us and pulls the laces of my leathers until they loosen and fall to the floor. Rounding me slowly, her gaze wanders across every inch of my ivory skin, eyes creasing with annoyance when she finds any imperfection. She no longer comments on the pale slate grey of my eyes, or the raven spirals that speak of my unfortunate ancestry. All flaws that I am well aware of but cannot remedy. Only once when I was young did she speak approvingly of my full lips and shapely figure. Though I've known enough Fea Dien without either who still brought men to their knees in a torrent of blood.

"No more of this," she says, pulling my hair loose from the braid and smoothing it down my back. "Here, it may not be a desirable color, but you will care for and adorn it as if it were the color of the sun. Once you arrive in A'kori, it will be a boon to your cause."

La'tari women are nothing if not vain, and as much as I've always seen my hair as a liability on the battlefield, Leanna always insisted that the benefit of its beauty far outweighs the potential risk it poses.

"As you say."

She pulls a silk gown from my wardrobe; she'd had a handful of them crafted for my mission. The cost of each, I'm sure, could feed a large family for months. My stomach twists at the thought of it. Only if I am successful in my mission will the cost be worth it.

"Are you ready?" she asks.

"Yes." It is the only answer to give her, true or not.

Since I was four years old Leanna raised me, training me to be exactly what she is, beautiful death. For as long as I can remember I'd known that one day, when she considered me ready, I would receive my first mission in service of the crown. For years I watched enviously while the Drakai who trained alongside me received their letters. None were more equipped to fulfill any given task than I. Some returned from their missions, many did not.

My letter came only days ago. Leanna handed it to me stoically, despite the king's seal adorning it. She had not asked me what it contained, I suppose she already knew. Her question had been the same then, 'Are you ready?' But who is ever truly ready for a mission that requires ending the life of a king in a foreign land? A feyn king no less, ancient and powerful.

"Good." Leanna cups my face and kisses my forehead. It is the gentlest, most unsettling thing she's ever done. "I always knew you were born to be a blessing to our people. Just remember where you come from." She smooths my hair, her voice sweet. "They will lie to you, use their gifts on you, try to sway you, attempt to convince you to turn on your own people and join with them. Don't be weak. Complete your task and come home. The day you return victorious is the first day of a new life on Terr, for all of us."

She looks me over one last time, unable to hide the full measure of her disapproval. "Go with death, child."

I board a large ship waiting outside the keep, heavy-laden with cargo for trade, swaying upon the tide of the northeastern shore. Large planks of roughly milled lumber are stacked high on the main deck with small walk-ways between.

I run my hands along a large, rough-sawn board. It is all we have to trade, and with every shipment that crosses the sea our lumber becomes less valuable. We've over supplied every continent in Terr, harvesting our lumber as quickly as our groves are dying.

The captain is a short, plump man, nose and cheeks speckled pink from the harsh breeze of the open ocean. He boasts a barrel of a stomach and a white, neatly trimmed beard contrasted by the deep red of his pressed uniform. He ushers me below deck before the crew boards. Every witness to my voyage across the sea is a risk and, despite my profession, I do want to live.

"If you should need anything, my lady," the captain says, and points to a small rope by the door that undoubtedly rings a service bell.

The man leaves without another word, and I listen to the heavy fall of boots as his crew begins to board the ship above. The room is large enough for a cot and table with a small wardrobe beside it, but little else. I don't need much, but I can't help the dread that wells inside me when I consider the many days I will be confined here during the crossing, with no outlet for my demon.

I eye my flesh suspiciously when goosebumps spring up along my arms, and my gaze darts to the wardrobe standing opposite the door. A small smile curves at the edge of my lips and my stomach dips as I take a step toward it, reaching for the handle. Even before I open it, I know what I will find inside.

"Does Leanna think I needed a babysitter?" I ask, arching an eyebrow.

The thin, wooden door swings open, revealing Vakesh leaning against the side lazily. I can't recall ever seeing him without a simple pair of black leather pants, and a white tunic. Though many of those days had seen the white of his top stained and torn, he never seemed to mind.

A mischievous smile I haven't seen in far too long breaks across his face. Where it is not bound, the ends of his stark white hair brush against the umber skin of his strong jaw and his brown eyes sparkle, framed by faint, joyful lines. Despite everything, I can't help but return the smile he offers me.

"Leanna has every confidence in your abilities, but I have business of my own in A'kori, and I couldn't help but stop in and see *the lady perfection* that Leanna created for his majesty."

His eyes rake lazily across my form before he brushes past me and collapses onto my cot. Pushing one arm behind his head to support it, he produces an apple from the pocket of his tunic and tosses it into the air repeatedly, catching it with ease though his eyes never leave me.

"Lady perfection?" My mouth twists around the term distastefully.

"Don't you like it? I named you myself." His eyes glint as his smile grows.

Only Vakesh would think to hide all my flaws in a title claiming perfection.

"If anyone hears the title, it will certainly put them off my trail." I give him that.

His eyebrows pinch together as he frowns.

"And? Does the master of shadows approve of Leanna's creation?" I ask, unnecessarily smoothing the thin fabric of my gown.

"She might as well have sent you naked." His eyes narrow on the fabric as if he is actually disapproving of the choice.

"Perhaps you should suggest that to her," I say, fluttering my eyelashes

and lowering my voice to a breathy whisper, "Though I hear that the males of A'kori do like to unwrap their gifts."

He nearly fumbles the apple, the smile vanishing from his face. It takes everything I have not to grin wildly at his sudden lack of composure. Before I have time to register the movement, he's standing before me, lifting my chin with a single calloused finger until my eyes meet the rather unexpected glower he is leveling at me.

"Never let it get that far," he warns, "You always strike the first moment you have the chance. If you hesitate, you die, or worse."

In light of my mission, it is the *or worse* that truly concerns me. Though the thought of death can be a frightening prospect to ponder, there is something in the finality of it that offers some small semblance of peace. Rumors of the gifted feyn across the sea have always been in abundant supply at the keep, and for years I have listened on bated breath to the tales spun by soldiers who lived through the war, never sure of what was true and what was pure fabrication.

Throughout the years I'd heard it claimed, often enough that I suppose it to be true, that the king of A'kori is the last of the reavers. A rare gift, capable of invading the mind and warping the will of any man.

All my life I have weighed the validity of those stories. Really, there is very little I am sure of, and I will be walking a fine line between my ignorance and what knowledge I can glean along the way. I only wish my life did not hang in the balance of the two.

"Vari," Vakesh hisses, bringing me back to the present moment. "Promise me, you never hesitate."

"You almost sound concerned." My lips pull up at the edges mockingly. "Since when does the master of shadows care if one of his fledglings makes it back to the nest? As long as the mission is accomplished, right?"

His jaw tenses, a subtle twitch indiscernible to anyone but me. "You know better than that, *mi'ajna.*"

My brow creases at the strange term, and his eyes flick between my own before he drops my chin with a sigh and makes his way toward the door.

"We should make the crossing in four days. Leanna had some things delivered before your arrival." He points to the wardrobe. "I've added a

thing or two myself. Settle in and I'll be back to keep you company for meals. You're not to leave this room."

"As you say." I smirk.

He returns the smile, shakes his head, and leaves, closing the door behind him. He will never admit it out loud, but I have known him long enough to have recognized the pride in his eyes when I received my assignment from the Drakai conclave. And despite everything we have been through, the look nearly brought me to my knees.

Vakesh is as responsible for my creation as Leanna, perhaps more so, and though I always feel that there are still parts of me that completely unnerve the man, there are also parts of me that slip right through all his carefully constructed defenses. It is a heady feeling, disarming the master of shadows. Or it had been, before I'd felt the fearsome sting of Leanna's unrelenting disapproval.

I push down a swell of emotions I thought I'd buried deep and begin rummaging through the assortment of goods Leanna sent. It's all very unsurprising: hair combs and other adornments, four flimsy dresses, and a small variety of lethal concoctions. I smile when my eyes land on the obsidian daggers sitting at the base of the wardrobe. A small favor left by the master of shadows himself. I loose a breath when my hands slide across the familiar form of the blades, and some of the tension leaks out of my body.

Stars above, grant him their favor.

I may not be able to take the blades ashore in A'kori, but I sleep fitfully without them, and they will at least serve their purpose throughout the voyage.

Sitting on the edge of the bed I turn the daggers over in my hands. Lately it has begun to feel as though there was never a time when my nightmares did not plague me. Over the years, I have managed to keep Leanna in the dark about them, but there was no hiding them from the shadows. Vakesh knew the moment they began.

I am suddenly all too aware of the images I was unable to chase from my mind this morning. Four days without sparring, perhaps weeks or even months if I fail to obtain an immediate audience with the king. I've never had to make a concession like it and have been quick to find my release each morning in the ring with Bront. What others perceived as diligent practice I use to hide a great weakness. One of the first lessons Leanna ever taught me: perception is the greatest strength of any Fea Dien.

I assure myself that Vakesh will have ideas on how I can manage my demon after the crossing. I just can't afford to let him know how bad the dreams have become in the time since he last witnessed them.

He's been gone for years, tying up loose ends on the never-ending bombardment of missions Leanna crafted for him. If I thought my life was hard before knowing Vakesh, the last four years have been the hardest yet. I haven't felt whole since we've been parted. Not that there is a single soul on the continent I will speak those words aloud to.

I pinch one of the obsidian blades between two fingers and with a quick flick of my wrist throw it into the air. It spins in a timing I know well, and I catch it by the hilt when it falls back toward my hand.

I can't help but wonder how Vakesh managed to obtain a mission that put us aboard the same ship. The decision couldn't have been Leanna's. She would never allow us to be out of sight together for so long. If she knew, I wouldn't put it past her to ensure the shadow master never makes it to port. I only hope that the years of superficial greetings I have exchanged with him are over and that, finally, we can settle back into the ease we'd once had with each other. In this moment, I know that there will never be anything I want more.

CHAPTER 2

THE SOUTHERN KEEP, LA'TARI

Eight Years Earlier

"**Y**es, Shivaria, you *must* meet the new master of shadows *and* train with him. Don't ask me again."

Leanna has never been a patient woman and though I hadn't actually repeated myself, I'm not surprised when she responds like I've drawled the question at her eight times. I hate my shadow lessons, almost as much as I love my sparring lessons with Bront.

The previous shadow master was a slip of a man with thin, oily, black hair and a face so pocked it somehow distracted from the intense crook of his nose, though that wasn't why I hated him. He had no business being the master of anything. He was prideful, arrogant, and never willing to train me beyond what *he* considered adequate.

Years before, I made the mistake of besting him at a task in which he himself had trained me. The man had no idea just how many hours I spent on my own perfecting the skill. It was something I would later consider simple, but at the time, with a horde of onlookers and my palms sweating out the adrenaline shooting through my veins, it seemed monumental.

I sat on the ground before an intricately locked chest, the shadow master doing the same beside me. My tools barely entered the lock before the lid sprung open with a loud pop. It was a warm summer day, and a small crowd gathered to watch. Even serious Bront had thrown a fist in the air and whooped for me while others clapped and some laughed. It was the laughter that earned me the withering glare of my instructor.

For the remaining time I knew the man, he simply trained me to fail at everything. He would gloat and mock my botched attempts, louder when anyone was present to hear. Frustrated, I complained to Leanna. I'm not sure why. I knew better by then to expect any help from her. She only scoffed at my plight and told me that managing people was as much a part of being Fea Dien as mastering the shadows.

I would never be Drakai if I failed to pass my shadow training. I started skipping meals, the only breaks in my heavily scheduled days, and spied on the shadow master as he taught the students he found worthy of his so-called skill. I gleaned what little I could and practiced late into the night, all to barely keep up with Leanna's exacting expectations.

I was glad for the break in my training when the shadow master was sent off on a simple, low-risk reconnaissance mission and never returned. There seemed to be some debate as to what might have happened to him. But I am sure he was found out by our enemies and killed, probably by a well-trained house cat.

This morning marks a month without shadow lessons. And though I know I need them, nothing on Terr could excite me less than the new master of shadow's unannounced arrival. Leanna's face holds its usual mixture of lovely and brooding storms as I follow her across the deadwood yard. A cascade of long yellow hair tumbles down her back, and she's wearing her pristine fighting leathers, the ones she usually reserves for special occasions. I doubt anyone else will notice, but it's a fact that certainly piques my interest.

Following Leanna's gaze, I find a tall man leaning nonchalantly against an old, decaying oak, his arms folded across his chest, full lips tugging up at the corners as he eyes me expectantly. I expected him to look older, though the hair that frames his strong jaw is pure white, a sure sign that he shares in the disgrace of my feyn heritage. Physically, he is nothing like the previous master. The man who stands before me is broad in the shoulders and, even below the loose, white tunic he wears, his muscles are well-defined. His leather pants could be tighter. No, really, they can't be, and I can see from the corner of my eye that Leanna is appreciating the sight.

I roll my eyes.

Stars above. I hope these two don't find it necessary to complicate my life by falling into bed together.

A cheeky smile adorns his face, and he has an eyebrow quirked at me when I look back as if the man can read every petulant thought in my head. Schooling my features, I settle myself next to Leanna when she stops in front of him.

He breaks the quiet of the deadwood and says, "Thank you for coming to meet with me on such short notice." I like his voice, it's deep and soft, falling on my ears like a gentle breeze. My skin prickles at the sound and goosebumps rise on my arms, hidden beneath my dark fighting leathers.

"There is no need to thank me. I am happy to come whenever you choose to summon me," Leanna says sweetly, suggestively.

Did she just say that? Gross.

It takes everything I have to keep my face placid and suppress the bile threatening to rise from my stomach. I'm surprised when the smile falls from the man's face, not cruelly or dismissively, it's just gone. Leanna stiffens beside me when she notices the same, then places a hand on the small of my back and pushes me forward.

"Shivaria, meet the new master of shadows, Vakesh." All the sweetness is gone from her voice as she turns on her heel. "I'll leave you two to get acquainted."

I chance a glance behind me as she makes her way back to the keep on pointedly wrathful strides. I don't envy the man the ire he's provoked in her.

"Come." He issues the command as he turns toward the trees, and I follow him into the forest.

For twenty minutes we walk in silence. Well, he walks in silence. The man doesn't make a sound when he moves. His feet glide beneath the leaves fallen to the early frost, and I try to mimic the movement as we pass beneath the sparse growth above. He stops occasionally, listening and observing the forest surrounding us. By the time we approach a small stream I have become determined to perfect the skill on my own, already having granted myself the title, *the silent death*.

A thick leather sack waits against the base of an ancient maple, and I watch quizzically as the master of shadows plops down beside the water, casts his boots aside, and lays his back on the ground, sinking his feet into the crisp water. He sighs contentedly, eyeing me through a squinting wink. Sunlight shimmers across his face, filtering through the canopy of bright yellows and deep reds as the leaves flit about on a light breeze.

"What would you like to learn today?" he asks, sounding almost bored.

If I've learned anything over the last twelve years training as Drakai, it's that there is a correct answer to his question. He is attempting to draw something out of me; I just need to figure out what it is. Rolling my shoulders, I search my mind for the reply he seeks. He takes me in curiously, the corners of his mouth tugging up ever so slightly. My cheeks begin to heat under his gaze, and I loathe that he seems to be enjoying my discomfort.

"Well?"

"I would be happy to learn whatever it is the master of shadow would like to teach me," I answer blandly.

"Hmm." He sounds thoughtful. "That doesn't really answer my question, does it?"

My brows pinch in, and I scold myself. Of course, it's a trick question. I've already failed the first task he's given me.

I ponder my possible answers, first considering picking something I am already well versed in to show him my skill, then quickly discard the idea. No one likes a show-off. I consider picking a skill for which I've never been trained, though those are few and far between at this point in my life and I'd rather not make him immediately aware of my flaws.

"I've been told you are an exceptional student, and a quick study too. I'm honestly a little surprised it's taking you so long to answer such a simple

question. But, by all means, take as long as you'd like to consider it." He smiles and it almost seems genuine, but I know better than to believe it.

"Teach me to walk silently, like you," I blurt out without thinking, but it's a safe choice.

If he chooses to, I am sure he will be able to improve upon my technique, but I'm also confident enough in the newly acquired skill that I won't risk utter shame and embarrassment attempting it under his scrutiny.

"Excellent!" He smiles, bounding to his feet. "Though after the progress you made this morning, I expected you to have nearly perfected it by the time we made it back to the keep."

My face falls and I eye him suspiciously. He scowls at the change, and uneasiness twists my stomach. I hadn't noticed his attention on me as we made our way through the forest. My cheeks begin to tingle as I consider just how aware he must be of every fault I made in my attempts to mimic his movements.

His mouth forms a thin line as he observes me, before quickly settling back into the relaxed smile he seems to favor. "Shall we begin?"

The master of shadows settles his stick on a flat piece of wood and spins it between his flattened palms, brows pinched with intense determination. The sun has just begun to sink beyond the horizon, casting an ever-brightening display of orange and purple hues onto the thin layer of clouds buffeting the mountains to the east. In no time at all, his efforts produce a curling strand of smoke, rising from the small bundle of dry moss at the base of his stick.

It's been six months since I was brought before the master of shadows. Six months since he taught me to walk along the forest floor without making a sound. Six months of teaching me anything I've asked to learn, without question or hesitation. Months of his patient tutelage and kind smiles, things he never seems to be without.

I squint my eyes suspiciously as his lips curve up at the edges, his gaze never wandering from the task at hand. In the deepest part of myself I know, it won't be long now. Someday soon he will break. The cheerful mask will

fall from his face, and the truth of the monster he keeps hidden away will finally be revealed.

Picking up the bunch of smoking moss, he cradles it close to his lips. Blowing gentle streams of air into the heart of the ember, he encourages it into a spurt of tiny flames. His eyes flick up to mine and he smiles, depositing the fire into the center of a bundle of kindling waiting by his side.

"Would you like to try it?" he asks.

He always asks, even though he must know by now, there is nothing I do not want to learn, to perfect. I nod, wrapping my long hair into a knot at the nape of my neck. His smile grows as he hands me my own bundle of moss and a tall, narrow stick to work between my hands.

"What did Leanna teach you yesterday?" Every day the same question. I'm not sure why he wants to know, and, for some reason I don't understand, answering always puts me a little on edge. There are plenty of skills that Drakai must learn, and while each of us will inevitably differ in those we become proficient in, we are, for the most part, all taught the same things.

"She is teaching me about poisons this week." I keep my eyes on the base of my stick when I reply.

"An entire week for poison? How many lethal herbs does that woman know?" He whispers the last just loud enough that he knows I'll hear.

"Thirty-seven." I know because I asked her the same thing. Though I was sincere in my curiosity, unlike the man sitting before me, a sarcastic lilt coating his tongue.

"Thirty-seven?" he balks. "Well, if anyone on the continent knows how to kill a man with as little as a blade of grass it's Leanna. Tell me, has she asked you to poison me yet?"

My head snaps up from my work and my hands falter, the stick nearly falling from between my palms. I open my mouth ready to defend her, to defend myself. If the man thinks I'm likely to end him, I have no doubt I will never leave this lesson alive.

The shadow master meets my budding concern with a cheeky smile and waggling eyebrows. Blinking back at him, I encourage the pit in my stomach to settle, a small huff escaping my lips before I turn back to my task.

"Stars above. Was that a laugh, Shivaria?" I've never heard him sound quite so intrigued.

"No."

I don't laugh. Not that I need to tell him that. He knows. His attempts to provoke a chuckle from me were irritating at first, but throughout the months I've become accustomed to them. Though I've never seen him bristle at his failure on this front, the longer it goes on, the more power I've begun to feel from my stoic nature.

I hate to admit, even to myself, that recently his jokes and quick wit are becoming a bit of a problem for me. I almost laughed last week when in the middle of an exercise on stealth he decided to do a studied imitation of Bront. His lack of grace and clumsiness as he moved through the shadows was spot on. He had obviously been watching the general closely and knew just how to exaggerate his movements to paint a perfect picture of a failed attempt at subtlety. I feigned a tickle in my throat and coughed over the giggle that bubbled up unbidden, rather than allowing my true amusement to surface.

Maybe laughing wouldn't be the worst thing but it's gone on so long that at this point I would feel like I lost a battle, like I'd given something up. Thanks to Leanna's careful tutelage, I am always thinking about my interactions with others in terms of trade. It's a safe stance to take and helps me maintain a powerful position in most social situations. If the shadow master seeks my laughter, then my laugh is the commodity, it is the thing I have that is of value to him. Nothing of value should be given away without price, another of Leanna's lessons, and yet everything I want from the man he gives freely and in abundance.

My little bundle of moss finally begins to smoke, and I quicken the pace of my palms, rolling the stick with fervor. At last, a tiny flame springs up in the midst of the loose bunch of tinder sitting at its base.

"Shivaria. Come with me," the shadow master says sternly.

"But I have it," I insist, bristling at the demand.

The inflection in his voice is one that I am unaccustomed to hearing from him.

"Now." He is deadly serious, his voice barely more than a whisper.

My head snaps up in annoyance. I haven't done anything wrong, and I

stiffen under the weight of his murderous tone. But when my furious gaze lands on him, his eyes aren't on me, they are on the forest, a darkening glower creasing the lines of his brow.

A tingling mass of nerves skates through my body. I didn't hear him unsheathe any weapons, but he fists a dagger in each hand and my skin prickles as I note the coiled tension throughout his body. Abandoning my dying ember, I slowly rise to my full height, the top of my head barely cresting his shoulder. I scan the edge of the clearing where his eyes are narrowed on a dense patch of trees.

"It's too late to run," he whispers, "Say nothing and do not interfere."

I nod once, even as a foreboding chill runs through me. I have no idea what he is talking about or what I have just agreed to. What in all of La'tari would the master of shadows run from?

He moves like the wind, swift and silent, until he is positioned in front of me, as if to shield me. I strain my ears but hear nothing. I will my eyes to focus on the shadows cast by the ancient oaks surrounding us but see nothing. It occurs to me that this may be a simple test, and I find myself wondering if I am searching for a nonexistent threat in the quickly darkening woodland. Some of the tension begins to leak out of my body.

And then, I hear them. Masculine voices filter through the trees—I count four that I can tell apart. They haven't realized we are here, or they would have quieted their voices as they move toward us. My brows pinch together. It doesn't make sense.

Tension radiates from my companion. Surely, he would have removed us from their path if they were unaware of us. And what threat would dare venture so near the keep? My skin tingles, dread saturating my veins, when one simple word skits along the forest floor like a flat stone atop the mirrored surface of a lake and lands on my ears.

"...*durah*..."

I will my breathing to steady and the muscles winding in my shoulders to relax while my mind grasps at any possible reason for hearing the feyn speak. The strange voices and the word alone may not have put me on edge, we are supposed to be living in peace after all, but the posture of the man standing before me reeks of violence.

A deep laugh echoes through the trees before the voices fall into abrupt silence. The moment is unmistakable and my subconscious tucks it away as vital information. It's a simple mistake on their part, their voices faltered the moment they realized we are here. Their quiet, a simple unintended acknowledgement that they've become aware of *us*.

Long before I see them step out from under the dark canopy, I feel their eyes on me. Five males emerge from the shadows. They are the first of their kind I have ever seen, far from the nightmarish monsters I conjured in my mind as a child. Their features are almost human, but sharper and more defined with an odd and unmistakable otherworldly beauty that, despite the danger, beckons me. I have always assumed the pointed tips of their ears would be the easiest way to tell them apart from humans. I understand now that there is no veil in Terr in which they could be mistaken for mortal, tipped ears or no.

There is a deadly grace in each step they take toward us, and I have never felt more like prey. Even with their pinched brows and the deep lines accentuating their scowls they are lovely, and I have never felt less worthy of the title Fea Dien than I do in this moment.

"*Shivay lathrek.*" These words coming from the master of shadow startle me.

Even the feyn falter in their approach, obvious in their discomfort as he speaks to them in their own tongue.

"*Shivay thien,*" the large male leading them replies, his scowl deepening.

They exchange a look among themselves before their leader tips his head in our direction, and as one, they continue toward us. I suppress a tremor as a bead of sweat drips between my shoulder blades. There is no mistaking the intent on their faces. As easily as I can tell that these are battle hardened soldiers by the way they move across the small clearing, I can tell that they have no intention of letting us leave this place alive.

"*Ma'hi vey'ruh lie'an ca'var di'esh na'vey,*" the shadow master says in that unfamiliar tongue. It takes every bit of willpower I possess not to shift my gaze and stare at him as he speaks.

This time there is no hesitation in the males' steps when the large feyn at the front of their procession replies with a sneer, "*La'tari durah, vie'di thiara vey'na en valtour.*"

My mind tumbles over itself, and I quickly wrangle it back into the peaceful comfort of the space it occupies in the sparring ring. I will myself to calm and examine the situation, but there is no time to think as they fan out, strategically positioning themselves around us. They are careful to remain outside of striking distance as they surround the master of shadows.

My heart threatens to rupture within my chest as the world slows. The shadow master lunges forward, shifts to the right, and lands a crippling strike to the chest of a tall, broad male. The body crumples to the ground with a thud and all haliel breaks loose around me.

At once, they strike at him in a rage, all but one. The large male leading them skirts the skirmish despite the shadow master's attempts to stop him. He's taller than I am by more than a foot, broader, and stronger to be sure. But Bront hadn't spent years teaching me how to overcome an enemy by means of strength alone. I learned early on that there will always be those I cannot match by force.

Shifting my feet beneath me, I prepare for his attack. His eyes flick down, a puzzled look on his face as he studies the movement, but it's hardly enough to dissuade him. He levels me with a cocky smile. It's one I've seen on every Drakai that Bront pit against me for years, each of them learning that their brawn is no match for well-refined skill. Every lesson I learn in the ring is hard won, and maybe I should feel bad that this lesson will cost the male his life.

I don't think about it when he strikes at me, and I deflect the blow. Grappling his arm, I let my weight take me to the ground and hook his leg with my foot, striking at his knee with the full force of my leg. I'm already on my way to my feet when the male goes down with a roar of pain, the hinge of his leg bent at an awkward angle beneath him.

His cry is enough to garner the attention of one of his allies. A scarred male with a crimson mark banding his forearm. In his moment of distraction, the shadow master unleashes a deadly series of strikes at another male. His body tumbles to the ground, just as I deflect a blow from the scarred feyn whose attention is now firmly set on me. His downed comrade issues a flurry of what I can only assume are curses as he points at me from the ground, unsheathing a blade at his hip.

I should have moved faster, I know I should have. Should have ended

him before my focus was taken by the other. Another lesson I learned the hard way, the danger of a desperate and wounded opponent. A lesson I have apparently not learned well enough.

My years of training with Bront have sharpened my reflexes and turned each studied movement into unadulterated impulse, but if I think I am prepared for battle, my failing attempts to land a single blow on the feyn before me prove me dreadfully wrong. It is a near impossible task to focus on the fists he throws my direction. My attention divided, between the male before me and the male on the ground, hefting the end of a dagger between his fingers, waiting for an opening that will allow him to sink the blade into me from a distance.

I take a staggering blow to the face and my lip cracks open wide, a small trickle of blood running down my chin. There is no question in my mind that in this moment, I have let myself become too vulnerable. It takes everything I have ever learned to simply defend myself against the barrage of fists he throws at me while keeping his body between that of his friend and my own. When I imagined what war must be like, this is not the picture of battle I conjured. There is no blow for blow, no blood for blood.

Relief is the only thing I feel when the shadow master dodges an attack, rounds the male he's facing, plucks the blade from the hand of the grounded feyn and sinks it into his chest. The feyn grunts as his body goes slack, and for a moment the attention of my attacker snaps to the now lifeless body, leaving him wide open.

It's a grand mocking gesture that says everything without a single word being uttered. I am nothing for him to fear, not worth the effort it takes for him to keep his eyes trained on me.

I learned early on in my training with Bront that arrogance can be a death sentence, and I won't waste his. I take the moment to prove to him the mistake he's made by turning his back on me. Lunging, I thrust out my fist, aiming a blow at the center of his throat. It is a simple strike, one that doesn't require much strength to bring a larger opponent down. My fist is halfway to meeting his flesh when my heart shoves itself firmly into my throat. I see it, my error. It is *my* arrogance I should have been conscious of, not his, and he played me like a fool.

He smirks when he catches my arm, whipping me around to pull my back against his chest. He secures my arm behind my back, positioning it with a twist that threatens a break. My eyes fall to the shadow master's when the male behind me pulls a dagger from a leather sheath strapped to his thigh, raising it in a white knuckled fist, high above his head.

I'm aware in some distant part of my mind that all I am is a distraction right now, nothing but a liability. The shadow master lands a blow on his last opponent, one that makes the male curse and stagger, a spurt of blood gushing from his nose, coating the lower half of his face in a thick sheet of crimson.

The shadow master takes the short reprieve to look back at me, and I feel the male behind me shift as his body tenses against mine, and he winds up to bury his blade deep into my chest. I have no doubt he will leave me with a fatal wound, and I do my best to offer an apology by way of my eyes to my teacher. I should have been a better student.

The injured feyn facing the shadow master collects himself, wiping a slick layer of blood from his chin, flicking droplets onto the forest floor. He's claimed one of the master's obsidian daggers. I'm not sure where the other went, no doubt it is buried in the body of one of the fallen. The male moves to strike him, just as I feel my captor commit to the swing of his blade.

I can't help the frown that falls upon my face as I watch the shadow master run toward me, leaving himself open to the male at his back. The male's eyes gleam at the opportunity he's been given, and the shadow master takes the dagger to his shoulder as he lunges, quickly disarming the male that holds me. I'm not sure which of us is more surprised when the shadow master turns the dagger aimed at my neck on him in one swift motion and he topples to the ground.

Whipping around to face the male charging his back, the shadow master slides the blade between the feyn's ribs, puncturing his heart.

The world around me stills, and the silence is deafening. The weight of the moment fully sinks down upon me as I watch the last of them collapse onto the forest floor, the light leaving his eyes.

I can hardly believe I'm alive. My entire body trembles and I attempt to draw shallow breaths as I follow the shadow master back to his smoldering fire. He sits cross legged, his wounded arm pinned to his side, the other pulling his pack toward him from where it rests against the base of a decaying tree.

He quickly produces a thick coil of gauze from within its depths, blood flowing down his shoulder when he removes the blade with nothing more than a grunt. There is no question he will survive the wound, as long as it doesn't become infected. The blade landed far from any vital organs.

Tearing the gauze with his teeth, he clumsily packs it with a poultice of herbs and attempts to bind the wound. My stomach twists with guilt as I watch him struggle, first with the herbs, then with the binding. This is my fault. Falling to my knees beside him, I take the dressing from his hand and start the process over, binding the wound snugly, making sure to stanch the bleeding with as much pressure as I can apply.

I study the injury as I work the gauze into a binding that will hold. Based on its position the feyn undoubtedly intended for the dagger to find its mark in a more deadly part of his body. I can feel the scowl forming on my face as I wrap the gauze around his chest to fully secure it. There was no way for him to know that the male would miss something vital. He turned his back on a deadly threat, utterly accepting of his fate, on the chance he could save me. It doesn't make any sense.

"You did well," the shadow master says, raising himself to his feet, slinging his pack over his good shoulder the moment I've secured a knot to hold the bandage.

"He was going to kill me," I say, pulling the pack from his shoulder and slinging it over my own. "Don't treat me like a child."

I may have been useless in the skirmish, but I can at least carry his pack when he is wounded.

"Shivaria," he snaps, grabbing my arm and whipping me around to face him. "You. Did. Well. I have known grown men who were full Drakai for years who still fell to feyn warriors in seconds. Sometimes, doing well is simply surviving."

I cross my arms over my chest and roll my eyes.

"That was no random group of wandering feyn. They were battle trained," he says, confirming my suspicions.

"What were they doing here? And why would they attack us? I thought we were at peace."

"There are plenty alive, both feyn and human, that were never in favor of the treaty," he explains. "The La'tari may not like to talk about it, but even the humans are willing to turn a blind eye when a brutalized feyn body appears in the middle of a village without explanation."

I should feel bad about it, an innocent life is an innocent life, but everything I've ever been taught tells me that most feyn are like the ones we encountered today. I can't help but feel that one less means the world is a safer place. It is the only thought I allow to occupy my mind as I survey the bodies lying scattered about the small clearing.

"Thank you for saving me." I roll my shoulders, adjusting the weight of the pack on my back when I say it.

He frowns down at me. "You didn't expect me to intervene. I saw it on your face the moment you met my eyes."

I shake my head and look away, wishing to vanish under the weight of his stare.

"Look at me," he demands.

I choke back a whimper as I do as he says, biting my lip to still a rising quiver, my nerves catching up to me.

"You may feel otherwise, but your life *is* worth saving, and I would take that blade again a hundred times over to see you walk away unharmed."

"Why would you?" I don't mean for it to sound like an accusation.

"Because that is what friends do." He sounds so sure of himself.

"We're not friends," I remind him.

"You're right," he sighs, and I nod as if that will be the end of it. "But I would like to be your friend," he adds.

I roll my eyes again, along with my whole head, and begin back toward the keep. "Nobody wants to be my friend."

"I do, and who cares about anybody else? Anyone who doesn't want to be your friend is just afraid of what you are."

I manage three more steps before reluctantly taking the bait. "And what am I?"

"Enviable," he says with a grin, "No one wants to spend their life alongside the sun when their own light only appears like a dull flame beside it."

I have no idea what he means but I am done arguing. He's probably lost

too much blood and has become delusional. Hopefully he won't remember any of this tomorrow.

It takes two hours to walk back to the keep, and I spend half that time pondering what friendship is between Drakai. It's a foreign concept that I can't fathom. There is too much competition, the risk of betrayal far too high, and the cost of that betrayal even higher. How then can I possibly imagine a friendship with the master of shadows, and why would he want such a thing, with *me*? The thought nags at me long enough that I finally give in and ask the question, not that I will ever actually consider the friendship.

"What would it mean if we were friends?"

The shadow master tries and fails to look nonchalant as he answers. I can tell he is giddy about my inquiry, and the fact that I've pleased him in any way chafes at me.

"Friendship is different for everyone," he shrugs, "but I suppose what friendship looks like for me is this. I trust you and you trust me and if you need me, I'll be there no matter what, and if I need you, I know you'll be there for me too."

"So, you could just summon me any time you want?" I scowl.

He chuckles. "You don't summon your friends, but you *can* depend on them."

I hum thoughtfully, grateful he doesn't press me as we continue on. I glance over at him every now and again to check that the bleeding hasn't resumed. He saved my life, and I tended his wound—is that friendship? It really doesn't sound too bad the way he explains it, and I can always change my mind when he inevitably fails to live up to the title.

Once we arrive at the edge of the deadwood surrounding the keep, I plant my feet, ignoring the anxious palpitations in my chest as I turn to him.

"I think I'd like to try and be friends," I say, and he smiles at that, "but I don't trust you."

The smile stays plastered on his face. The only sign that he's heard the last of my declaration, a small shrug. "Then let's be friends, and we can find our way through the rest as we go."

I nod and offer him the thing I know he wants, the thing I know he values. A smile.

If I think I have ever seen the man smile before, I am wrong. The smile he offers me in return is like coveted rays of sun on a dreary spring day, when winter left the land barren and you yearn desperately for the promise of summer. I don't know where we go from here, but I make it my personal mission to find out how to make him smile like that again, as often as I can.

CHAPTER 3
OUT AT SEA
Present Day

Midday, there is a knock at my door. When I open it, I'm not surprised to find Vakesh standing outside with a sly smile on his face, a tray of cured meats and cheese in hand. He said he would join me for my meals, and in all the years I have known the man he's never once gone back on his word.

He shoulders the door open and saunters into the room, dragging a small wooden chair behind him. Most of the space is already taken up in my cramped quarters, but I don't complain when he sets the chair across from the bed before moving the small table in between the two. I smile, glad for his company, and settle myself on the cot, his chair directly across from me, the small tray of food between us.

"Do we know how many ladies have traveled from La'tari to A'kori for the season?" I ask around a mouth full of cheese.

"The last report we received said no more than thirty-five," he says, taking a seat.

"Thirty-five," I repeat under my breath. "So many."

He laughs and when I look up, he is examining me incredulously.

"You have absolutely nothing to worry about, Vari. Despite what Leanna drilled into you; the king would be out of his mind not to notice you."

I snort my disbelief and Vakesh rolls his eyes with a shake of his head. I don't need the king to notice me in that way, not really, but it could make it easier to get close. Leanna's beauties are known for nothing if not for completing their missions by less obvious means.

My stomach knots as I wonder how so many women can think themselves tempting enough to entice such a male. It pits further when I imagine the quality of women I will be surrounded by. Each of them competing for those attentions.

I've never been confident in my beauty, not growing up alongside the Fea Dien, boasting the golden honey toned hair that claims purity of blood in La'tari. Though I can't help but wonder if a feyn king might be more partial to the black locks that spiral down my back.

"I've never understood why any woman would throw herself at someone who could bend her will," I admit.

Vakesh leans his chair against the wall and laces his fingers behind his head, popping his elbows out on either side, and he shrugs. "Power, money, security, family influence, desperation. I suppose they do it for all the same reasons anyone has for doing anything dangerous."

No matter their reasons, I am surprised any of them still try. It's no secret that despite the growing number of ladies willing to sacrifice their maidenhead to the king he hasn't had a consort since long before the war. A fact I argued when Leanna first suggested his assassination would be simplest by means of seduction.

I was born into that war, four years old by the time the treaty was signed,

far too young to remember it myself. My only memories from then, the brutal visions that haunt my sleep. A woman falling to the floor in a bloody heap, tears streaming down her face as she reaches toward me. A man's voice screaming in anguish and the gurgling sputter of that voice as he drowns in a torrent of his own blood.

These were the atrocities of the A'kori kingdom, of the feyn, and the violence they rained down on my people had been for nothing more than greed.

"It only takes one death to change a course set by the fates, Vari," Vakesh says softly, as if he too is witnessing the histories that play in my mind.

I smile grimly. "Have you forgotten one of the first lessons you ever taught me?"

"Remind me."

"Death is never sated."

The corner of his mouth quirks up at the edge and he stands, grabbing his sack from the ground and slinging it over his shoulder.

"Then make sure the souls you send to haliel are souls upon which he can feast."

With a promise to join me for dinner he leaves me alone with only my thoughts for company. Thoughts that shift from the bloody woman reaching for me to Leanna. She was traveling with an armed force the night she pulled me from the burning wreckage of my home. The luckiest families were slaughtered in their sleep, before the fires had been set. But not everyone was so lucky, and many perished by flame, or worse.

A single line of gifted males has ruled the feyn, far longer than our written history, and always favoring those born gifted. Those who draw power from our world, the power of Terr. To the feyn those of us born without that connection have no value aside from what we can produce by labor. *Durah,* they call us, and though I have never taken the time I should to learn their tongue, every La'tari child born understands the meaning of the word. *Worthless.*

Leanna took me in the night the war ended. She pulled me from the blood-soaked floor of my home and brought me back to the keep, raising me the only way she knew.

Per the treaty, the southern territory across the sea was cleaved off and given to the La'tari to be ruled by the mortals of our world. Now a safe haven

for those who would otherwise be oppressed, our laws keep La'tari safe for all who choose to seek refuge here—or so it was intended.

With the end of the war, and the departure of the feyn across the sea, an ever-growing blight began to spread across our land. First, the forests began to die, followed by the fields. Vast rivers became trickling streams, and even well-tended soil will never yield enough harvest to feed the families that labor over it.

While the rest of Terr remains free of the blight, our people continue to starve, with no question as to why. It was agreed that if the La'tari ever left their homeland, it would once again fall under feyn rule. What might have seemed a small requirement of the treaty at the time had surely been the excuse they needed to finally end every mortal life on the continent. Now our only hope of survival, a small caveat written by our leaders. Should the ruling line end, the treaty installs the La'tari king to rule over A'kori. The one man alive who will set the continents on a path toward true peace.

Through the years tensions continue to lessen. Trade is reestablished, and though rare, I've even heard of unions and children born of them. Of course, my own life is evidence that such unions existed throughout our history. The tell-tale black or white hair paired with the brightest of blue eyes being a clear marker of feyn blood.

While peace seems tenuous at times, it works, for the most part. Though in the years leading up to this moment it has become clear to us all that we can't afford to wait to end the line of their succession. One life to save thousands.

I lay back on my cot and sigh, trying to imagine a world in which being born powerless does not mean you spend your life fighting off starvation. My day is consumed by a maddening spiral of dark thoughts of the life I am soon to end, until Vakesh arrives with two small bowls of bland soup and fresh bread for supper.

He puffs out a breath, pushing past me to set a tray on the table.

"You'd do well to leave those thoughts on the ship when you disembark. That look on your face screams of vengeance. Leanna may have been over-confident in your ability to mask your true feelings."

I bristle at the assumption. "I like you enough not to suggest to Leanna that you are second guessing her choices."

"Thank foc for that," he laughs, tearing off a piece of bread and shoving it in his mouth as he motions for me to take a seat opposite him. "All jesting aside, I have no doubts about your abilities. There is no one in all of Terr better suited to accomplish this task than you."

"So I have been told." And I have been, my entire life I have heard exactly that from every soul that had a hand in my training. "Care to expound on that?" I ask dryly.

"No," he replies flatly.

No one ever has.

We eat our rations in silence, likely each pondering the future and the many possible outcomes of the next few weeks. I wonder about the mission Vakesh is on, knowing it will do no good to ask him about it. Such things are never discussed. Vakesh, however, is privy to all missions under his purview, including mine.

My eyes wander to the daggers sitting at the head of my cot.

His eyes track my gaze to the dark obsidian blades, and he sighs. "I shouldn't have given them back to you. They are a crutch. One you are soon to be without."

"Then why did you leave them for me?" I ask curiously.

"Maybe I like watching you fight against the darkness inside you." He shrugs and looks up with a sad smile.

I can't help but wonder about his own personal demons. Demons he keeps from me, secreted away beneath his tranquil surface. I lift the blades, turn them over in my hands once more, then offer them to him.

"Don't ever give me a crutch again," I say, trying to temper the anger in my voice. "What good are you to me if you have nothing left to teach me?"

His head shifts back as if I have struck him, and he raises an eyebrow thoughtfully. He has only ever encouraged me to be completely honest with him, unfiltered and raw. I've always wondered how he endures it.

Still, I can't bring myself to tell him that his friendship means more to me than any lesson he will ever teach me. That even when there is nothing left for me to learn, he will always be valuable to me, simply because of the man he is.

"Tell me about them. Your dreams," he says around a mouthful of bread.

He's never asked before and I can't help but debate just how much I want to share. I know he won't push if I tell him I don't want to talk about it. Vakesh always made it abundantly clear that he will respect whatever boundaries I choose to set between us.

Sighing, I sit back in my chair. "The dreams have always been the same."

I tell him of the woman who reaches for me and the man who mourns her before following her into the afterlife. I conveniently leave out that the dreams have begun to worsen, occasionally spilling over into my waking life.

As I tell the tale, the loss of the blades beneath my pillow nags like an itch on a booted foot. I know I can't take them with me when I leave the ship. That knowledge continues to haunt me more than any other part of my mission. Though I know they cannot fend off the terrors that plague my mind, they have always been an anchor when I fear my demon might pull me out to sea in a torrent and crush me beneath the raging waves.

"These people in your dreams, do you know them?"

"It feels like I do," I admit, "Like with each of their deaths a piece of me is torn away and I'll never be whole again. Then I wake and every bit of that emptiness fills with a growing darkness that I can barely contain."

It is the closest I will allow myself to get to telling the full truth of it.

"But you do keep it contained." He tries and fails to sound comforting.

I nod my head, a reassuring lie, though I am sure it is a rhetorical question.

"And the daggers calm you down?" he asks, puzzled.

I shake my head again. "Not really. I just feel better when I have them. Sparring helps. It takes off the edge and burns off a bit of the lingering darkness."

He huffs a throaty laugh and leans forward, scratching the back of his neck, hesitating to say all that is on his mind.

"Out with it," I encourage him.

"It may be hisht advice, but you'll never outrun whatever haunts you. So, fight or drink or foc. Do whatever it is you need to do to keep it under control. If you let it get away from you, you're as likely to be the cause of your own ending as you are someone else's."

"You are right," I say with a sarcastic smile, "That advice is hisht."

"I *did* say that." He smiles as he stands, slipping my daggers into his sack as he heads toward the door. "I'll see you for breakfast."

As soon as his footsteps fade, I stride across the room and pull the small rope that hangs by the door, ringing the service bell. The captain appears shortly after, his face twisted in annoyance due to the hour.

"Ale," I say through a crack in the door, "Lots of it."

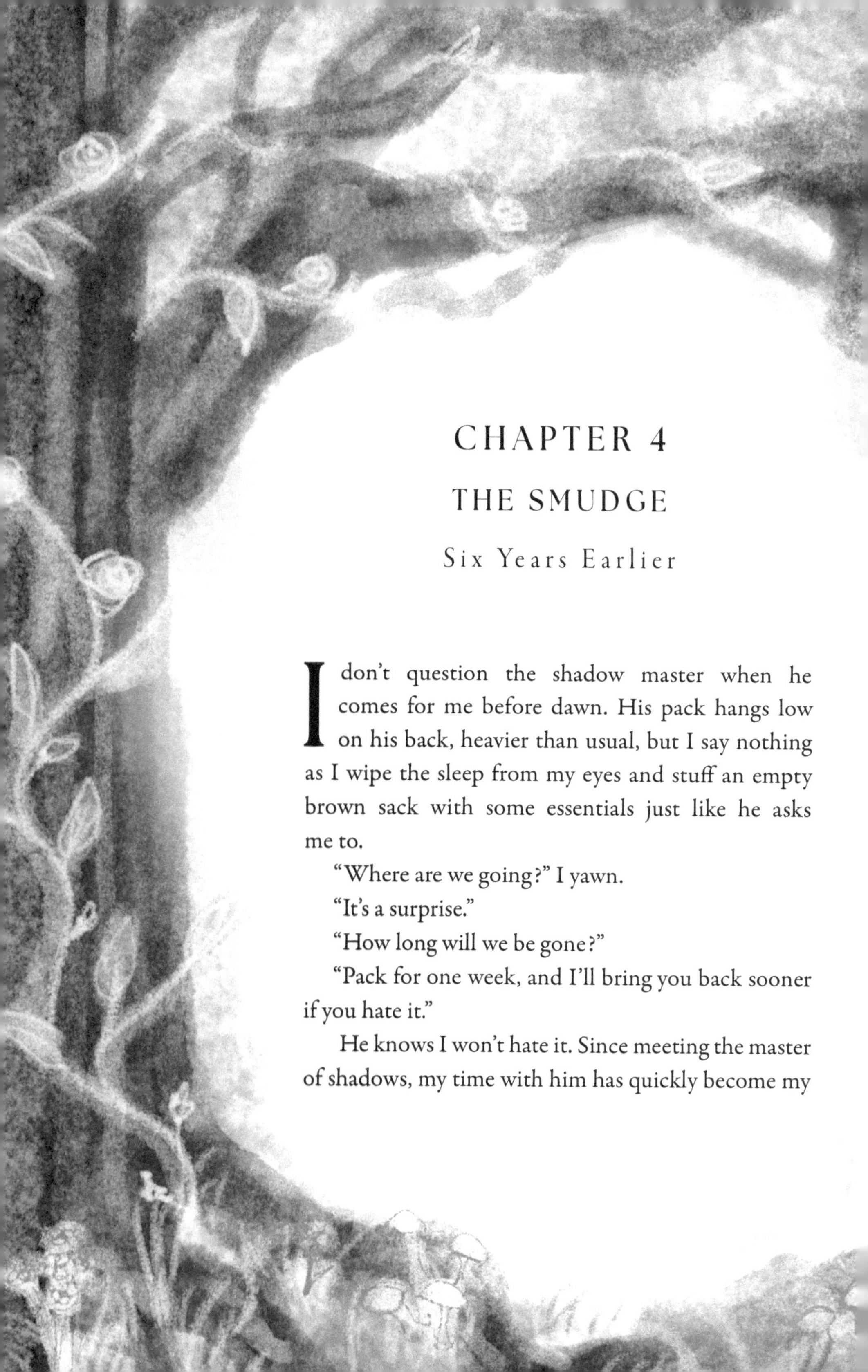

CHAPTER 4
THE SMUDGE

Six Years Earlier

I don't question the shadow master when he comes for me before dawn. His pack hangs low on his back, heavier than usual, but I say nothing as I wipe the sleep from my eyes and stuff an empty brown sack with some essentials just like he asks me to.

"Where are we going?" I yawn.

"It's a surprise."

"How long will we be gone?"

"Pack for one week, and I'll bring you back sooner if you hate it."

He knows I won't hate it. Since meeting the master of shadows, my time with him has quickly become my most valued commodity. Not that I will ever tell him that. Not that I need to.

I follow him into the forest, the sky still tinged with darkness where the faint light of dawn has yet to reach its western most reaches. He doesn't say a word, but I don't mind the silence. I take the time to get my bearings, becoming increasingly alert as he leads me south. By the time we stop midday under the shade of a cottonwood I'm full to bursting with questions.

Setting my pack against the tree, I open my mouth, snapping it shut again when the shadow master hands me an apple and a wedge of cheese with a sly smile. Of course, he knows I'm curious, but I won't give him the satisfaction of breaking and asking him where he's taking me.

I throw myself onto the ground gracelessly, the movement sending a small puff of silt into the air around us. Crossing my legs, I bite into my apple, giving my mouth something to do other than rattle off the list of growing questions in my mind.

He laughs heartily at the display and his eyes gleam. "What I wouldn't give for one day inside that brain of yours."

"It isn't that interesting," I argue.

"If you say so." His eyes sparkle with the high sun as it shines through the canopy of the deadwood.

Like much of the woods surrounding the keep, these trees have been dead for many years. Their branches dried and fallen, bark stripped to reveal the smooth surface beneath. Little remains but the skeletal frames of once great stands reaching toward the sun in the graveyard of our forests.

I take another bite and decide on a different approach. "We are heading south."

Not a question.

"We are." He smirks.

I hate the way he looks at me like he's won something. My brow pinches in and then the tension leaks out of my shoulders as he gives me answers to all the questions I'm too proud to voice.

"I told Leanna I wanted to work on your survival skills. Foraging, hunting, tracking..."

He told me months ago that I perfected these skills, and I couldn't help the pride that had welled within me at his approval. To hear now that he

is second guessing that decision lands like a blow, and that he voiced that opinion to *Leanna* makes it so much worse. If the master of shadows finds me lacking, I will spend the week proving to him just how wrong he is.

"I lied," he says around a mouthful of cheese, "Your survival skills are flawless."

"You lied to Leanna about my training?"

My eyes grow wide. If Leanna ever finds out he lied to her for any reason, I sincerely doubt I will ever see the man again.

"I did, and I'd prefer that you didn't tell her that." He mock scowls.

And there is my leverage. His smile falls when mine begins to grow and I relax exaggeratedly against a fallen log behind me, sighing contentedly and popping a small piece of cheese into my mouth.

"I can see why that might make you nervous. It's bad enough that you smuggled me out of the keep right before the gauntlet, but you lied to Leanna so that she would go along with your request." I whistle, long and low. "She has high hopes that I'll win this year."

In fact, she is ready to break me pushing me beyond my limits to see that I do. One week in the woods means we will return just in time for me to compete in the challenge but for the time leading up to it I will be granted a reprieve from Leanna's torturous training regimen. Even the master of shadows was unimpressed by the fractured arm I received by her hand two months ago, and that was only the beginning of it. Where Leanna is concerned, there is no room for weakness.

"While Leanna is hopeful that you will win, I brought you out here to make sure that you do. Leanna is a battle-axe, and you need to learn to be the wind. Not everything in this world can be overcome by force."

I can't argue with that. Leanna is an effective weapon but not one suitable for every task.

"Fine. You teach me how to win the gauntlet, and I won't tell Leanna you kidnapped me."

He quirks an eyebrow at my demand and offers me a lopsided grin. "I'll help you refine the skills, but the winning will be entirely up to you."

We continue all day, stopping only when the sun sinks to the horizon, its rays brushing a thick patch of dark rain clouds a lovely shade of pink. It's the farthest south I've ever been. For good reason. I don't know what those reasons are, but below the southern border of La'tari, on every map I've ever seen, it is smeared ominously in a thick layer of dark coal. *The Smudge.* That is the name I gave it years ago, when not one of my teachers would tell me what it was called.

Though it is impossible to know exactly where we are, I knew the moment we crossed the border, and that was hours ago. There was no marked crossing, no drastic change in the land save for a growing abundance of healthy trees, but I had known. Just as I know with utter certainty that there is no veil in Terr in which Leanna would allow the master of shadows to bring me here. I begin to wonder just how many lies he told Leanna to orchestrate this trip. If she ever finds out that I've kept his secrets and gone along with them, she will have me whipped right alongside him.

The shadow master drops his pack and produces a hidden batch of tinder from the crook of a healthy tree branch. I raise a brow as he scans the ground nearby, brushing his palm across a thick layer of fallen leaves strewn across the forest floor. Within seconds he removes strategically placed leaf litter, revealing a shallow fire pit. My eyes widen and I survey the area. He's been here before.

I'm not surprised that he's scouted the area before bringing me, or rather, I wouldn't be surprised were it not for where we are. Never in my life have I considered that anyone would intentionally spend time in The Smudge. There is only one thing I've ever been taught about it—it is the most dangerous place on Terr. And those who venture beyond its borders rarely return.

"Get comfortable. This is home for the next week."

No matter how hard I try I can't seem to relax as we sit by the fire. By all rights this forest should be teeming with life, every tree alive, vibrant leaves fluttering in the wind that weaves through the canopy. It isn't a rustling in the bushes or the snapping of twigs that keeps my attention on the dense forest surrounding us. It is the eerie quiet and unnatural stillness that prickles my skin and keeps me on guard late into the night.

I sleep like hisht, tossing and turning all night. I can't blame the rolling thunder in the distance or the roots that dig into my back, barely buffered by the thin bedroll beneath me. It's the image my mind keeps conjuring of the black void of the south on every map I have ever laid eyes on. The void in which I now find myself. And I can't help but wonder, what would cause the La'tari to wipe every map clean of this place?

I'm relieved when, just as dawn breaks, the torrential downpour brought in by the wind ends abruptly before reaching our camp. The clouds quickly burn off and the weather shifts into an unseasonably warm, fall day that I welcome with a weary smile.

Though he promised me training, I don't complain when the master of shadows puts a fishing pole in my hands, ushering me to a nearby game trail that leads to a winding stream. There is an absurd abundance of fish, and I've never seen anything like it. I doubt anyone living on La'tari soil has. At least none born in my lifetime. Animals had become scarce, driven from our land, when our depleted soils could no longer support life. Though salted fish, pulled from the northern seas, is a staple at the keep, I have never in my life eaten fresh meat.

With a little guidance from the shadow master, it takes no time at all for me to procure our breakfast. He busies himself, starting and tending a small fire at the edge of the water and we spend a lazy day along its bank, each content with the other's company and the long stretches of silence we share.

I'm nodding off late in the afternoon with a belly full of fish, decadent and rich, unlike anything I have ever tasted. A warm breeze rustles the colorful leaves above me when his voice comes from the quiet.

"I will cook our meal tonight if you catch one with your bare hands."

I crack open a single eye, taking him in where he sits perched on the edge of the water, watching the fish swim by lazily. A taunting smile spreads across his face and my eyes fully open, fists balling at my sides. Perhaps my greatest weakness, I've never been able to walk away from a challenge. It's a fact the shadow master has exploited since he became aware of it early on in my training.

"You'll cook meals all week, or no deal," I bluff.

I'll accept the bet either way and we both know it.

"All right, it's a deal," he laughs.

I slide into the water and settle my feet on the smooth stones littering the streambed. The fish dart about warily at the first sign of intrusion but quickly become accustomed to my presence and settle into the current swirling around my legs. I wonder if these fish have any natural predators. Every one of them is fat, tails swishing slowly back and forth as they idle contentedly in the flickering sun breaking through the leaves above.

This is going to be easy.

Two hours later I'm soaking wet from my many failed attempts at fish wrangling. I've managed to wrap my hands around two, both sliding through my grip with frustrating ease. Now, most of the trout have taken to hiding from me under cover of a nearby rock ledge where they watch from the shadows, mockingly. I'm about to give up for the day and go back to using the pole, preferring a shameful surrender to that of starvation. Whether it's tonight or another day this week, I will catch a fish with my bare hands. It is now my single purpose in life.

A lone, portly trout flicks his tail lazily between where I stand and the shore. Unperturbed by my attempts to seize the others, he seems happy to ride the current and simply exist as though I do not.

I glance up to find the shadow master watching intently. His brow drawn down, as he surveys my target with great interest. I suppress the shame of my imminent failure even as I narrow my eyes on the water. Shame that promises to send me down a minor spiral of depression for the evening.

I move slowly at first, lining my hands up behind the fat fish, whispering near silent prayers to the stars. I lunge, noting the flick of its tail the moment he spots me. I'm too late. The plump trout makes a break for the obscuring shadows of the rocky overhang only to be swept into a strong eddy that slings him toward me nearly sliding him right into my hands.

My mind fumbling the line between shock and utter exhilaration, I latch onto it like my survival depends on this single act. With a *whoop* and a wide smile, I throw it onto shore where it thrashes about, covering the shadow master's cheeks in a smattering of water droplets that catch the waning light of the day.

Wiping his face dry, he claps his hands cheerfully, meeting my smile with a wide toothy grin of his own.

"Was it worth the effort?" he chuckles.

"I suppose that depends on how good your cooking skills are," I snark, tipping my chin toward the fish.

My quip has the desired effect and I'm practically drooling over the mysterious smells coming from the firepit. The sun casts out a wide array of orange and red hues across the horizon as it sinks below the mountains to the west. While Leanna may have taught me about other, more deadly herbs, she failed to mention the herbs that the forest provides for flavor alone. I tell myself that I will make the shadow master promise to teach me about all of them, just as soon as I have eaten my hard-won prize.

With a self-satisfied grin, he hands me a large, folded leaf containing my dinner, and I dig in. It is, by far, the best thing I've ever tasted, and I can hardly slow my eating enough to make sure I'm not swallowing any tiny bones.

Oh well, if I die, it might be worth it.

It only takes three bites for all my well thought out plans to change. My only goal for the rest of the week is to eat as much as I can while he is still bound by our deal and forced to cook for me. A luxury I highly doubt I will ever receive again.

His eyes sparkle as he watches me eat, clearly smug about how much I'm enjoying his cooking. He is less enthusiastic when he starts in on his portion, but I suppose he's become spoiled by a lifetime of savoring his own meals.

I suck the tender meat off every frail bone I find, licking my fingers clean of the buttery herbs until there is nothing left. The moment I'm done my eyes grow heavy and I slip into my bedroll with a satisfied moan. One sleepless night and a belly full of fish and all I can think about is how good the fire feels on my face and how life would be perfect if every day were just like this.

My eyes don't open again until the sun breaks the eastern horizon the next morning. I yawn, glancing across the fire to find the shadow master still sleeping deeply. My lips quirk up at the ends. It appears I'm not the only one who'd fallen into a fish induced coma.

Content to let him sleep a while longer, I stretch my legs before quietly pulling myself from my bedroll and making my way to the stream to wash. The forest is eerie in its stillness. The only sounds as I trudge back to camp, the swish of my pants rubbing against my thighs, and the occasional crunch of my leather boots upon a fallen leaf.

My feet still at the border of our camp, the hair on the back of my neck stiffening. Eyes squinting warily when I find the shadow master still asleep. I check the sun, telling myself it's still early, but for reasons I cannot understand my nerves begin to fray and all my instincts wail that something is wrong as I approach him. I've never known him to sleep past the sunrise.

Eyes narrowing across the fire, I suppress a gasp. His skin is slick and lightly tinged an alarming shade of yellow. Every hoarse breath he draws is shallow and his body is far too still.

I stop myself from reaching for him when my eyes flick to a glint at his side, my breath catching in my throat. A small viper sits coiled above his hip, green scales refracting hues of purple and pink under the light of the rising sun. I don't take my eyes off it, and, in a similarly wary fashion, the serpent watches every movement I make.

I crouch down and slide a blade from the shadow master's pack. The viper flicks its tongue, scenting the air, as I take aim. Exhaling a deep breath to steady myself, I lob the dagger at the beast, severing its head from its body with the solid *thunk* of the blade as it sinks into the earth. The tail of the creature coils and writhes, bumping and pitching it's still very alive and lethal head closer to the shadow master's side. I lunge, carefully snatching the head from the slithering mass and throwing it into the forest.

My stomach twists as I kneel beside him, my eyes falling on the angry bite on his forearm.

This is bad, really, really, bad.

My mind reels, grasping for anything I've ever been taught about surviving the venom of such a strike. These are lessons I was given long ago. Lessons I've had no cause to use in the many years since. Clenching my jaw, the muscles in my arms strain, my fists balling at my sides as if the physical effort my body exerts might somehow summon the long-buried memories I seek. My brow draws down in frustration as I search the deep and dormant caverns of my mind.

"Latrice." I suck the word in on a thin breath, nearly tripping as I throw myself to my feet and run into the dense overgrowth of the forest.

Leanna taught me about the herb when we first began to venture into the deadwood surrounding the keep. I was young, with many years still to pass until my courses came to claim me as a woman. Leanna reached into a viper's den, allowing a strike to her wrist that should have been fatal; it would have been fatal, if not for a small patch of Latrice growing nearby.

Of course, the lesson hadn't ended until Leanna forced my arm into the same den. The herb worked as intended, and had I not taken three strikes before she allowed me to withdraw my arm from the pit, the herb would have kept me from the week of purging and bedrest that followed.

Digging into the recesses of the memory, I conjure an image of what I seek. A slender shoot with a plethora of dark, waxy leaves and small snow-white bells to adorn it. It is the leaves of the plant that nullify the toxin, but only if they are ingested soon after the bite. Without knowing when he was bitten, there is every possibility I am already too late. I smother the terror that skirts across my veins in icy waves, willing my pace to quicken, weaving through the trees with a deft grace I hardly recognize as my own.

My frantic pace only slows when I find a dense stand of ancient oaks with wide arching branches. I curse the moments that pass as I squint, my eyes adjusting to the low light. The world turns on its head as thin shafts of flickering light make it through the thick canopy above, each ray pattering the mossy ground beneath my feet to resemble a star flecked night sky.

I search for signs of water flowing beneath its surface, stumbling when my toe catches on a thick layer of lichen underfoot. My heart stutters hopefully as I follow a trail of darkened moss like a map, searching the northern base of every tree for the sprig I seek.

Heart plummeting, my throat burns, and I push back the pitifully useless tears of frustration that threaten to come, when finally, I find what I am looking for. Kneeling on the soft mat of green beneath me, I inspect the herb growing at the base of a gnarled and heavily knotted oak and frown.

Though I was taught of the many herbs that could heal, for each of them there are a dozen that can end a life. I nearly choke on the knowledge that latrice has a deadly cousin, a look alike. The only way I've been taught to tell the two apart are the tiny, bell-shaped flowers that adorn Latrice in the spring. The two are otherwise identical, at least to my eyes.

I examine what I've found, turning the leaves over in my hand, crushing them between my fingers, taking in their pungent aroma. I will myself to recall more, to remember a scent, a feeling, any small detail I've locked away that can help me differentiate the herbs. These stems have long been bare of the tell-tale flowers that proclaim the healing properties I seek. But there is nothing more to recall, no memories, no hidden sign, no way for me to be sure. If I feed this to the shadow master, I'm just as likely to assist in his journey to haliel as I am to heal him.

I throw the crushed herb to the forest floor and scream in a fit of rage. Every fiber of my being demands that I bring the entire forest down around me. If this land cannot help me save him, I will burn it to the ground and extinguish its life in kind. My voice continues to come unsummoned in a broken wail.

Pushing to my feet, I strike the tree, leaving a small crimson stain where my knuckles split against the jagged bark. I hardly notice the sting as an ache in my chest begins to form, promising a new, excruciating type of pain I've never known.

Pressing my forehead to the trunk, I close my eyes and try to slow my breathing. There must be some other remedy, some knowledge still tucked away in the recesses of my mind that will save him.

Though the land has been oddly quiet since we crossed the border, a deeper stillness settles in the surrounding brush. Goosebumps spring up along my arms and icy tendrils lick the tender skin between my shoulder blades as the heavy weight of awareness grows thick in the air and my lungs deflate.

After a single deep, shuddering breath I spin myself around, fists held up in front of my face as I squint into the darkness, ready to face whatever monsters have found me in the depths of the forest. Swearing under my breath, I nearly trip over my own feet in my fearful spinning rush. I stagger back, my spine slamming against the oak.

Graceful.

My head whips toward a low cackle coming from a small patch of deeply darkened shade. I will my eyes to focus on the form of an old, decaying crone sitting atop a large, mossy boulder a few feet away, chastising myself for not bringing a weapon into the strange and unfamiliar woods.

A long, tattered cloak hangs draped around her shoulders, its large hood pulled low over the crown of her head. Her hands and eyes are bound by an abundance of frayed rags. She tips her head to the side, observing me from behind the moth-eaten cloth as I shift my feet into a defensive stance.

Unperturbed, she smiles, a near toothless grin pulling at the corners of her thin, colorless lips. The few teeth she has are blackened by decay much like the fingernails protruding from her bindings; these she taps rhythmically on her thigh. Every nail is caked in filth, split into the bed of her fingers, and broken in a jagged array along the tips.

With a long, slow sweep of her head, she takes me in from foot to head curiously, each of us weighing the other.

"Who are you?" I demand, forcing strength into my voice.

"Does it matter?" she rasps in an unnaturally high pitch that raises the hair on the back of my neck.

I guess it doesn't, but her answer is in no way relieving, so I try another approach. "What do you want?"

"I came to ask that question of you." She grins, pointing a crooked finger at me. "Your need called me. It drew me from my home and brought me here. So, tell me, what is it *you* need, child, and let us strike a bargain."

I weigh my reply, only hesitating for a second before telling her about the herb I seek. The shadow master is running out of time, and I doubt there is danger in the small truth I offer her. I would rather not end the life of an old hag living deep in the forest, and even as that thought attempts to pass through my mind unexamined, I can hardly bring myself to believe that she is not more than she appears.

"Such a simple request," she crows, "I can give you what you seek."

Her hand disappears beneath her cloak and when it reemerges, she holds a tall sprig of latrice between her fingers. Unlike the herb littering the forest floor, this sprig is abundant in the unseasonable flowers declaring it to be exactly what she claims.

I step forward, reaching out my hand to take it, stumbling, my back slamming into the tree again when her face quickly transforms into a darkening mass of pointed teeth. I tense when an inhuman growl rips out of her chest in warning. When I don't make another move for the sprig her face settles back into the haggard, wrinkled crone I'd first seen.

"You may have it, for a fair price," she coos, with what I think must be a sad attempt at a warm and reassuring smile.

"I have nothing to trade," I explain, trying to keep the desperation from my voice.

A guttural cackle rolls from her lips, and she clicks her tongue.

"Grant me a piece of the lie that binds you, and it is done. A small sliver, hardly noticeable. And make your choice quickly, child, before the venom reaches his heart."

My blood runs cold, a knowing grin splitting the crones face.

How does she know? And what in all of Terr is she asking me to trade for his life?

"Will it hurt me?" It's the only thing I can think to ask, the only thing I really need to know, and no matter what her answer might be, I'm not entirely sure I can be dissuaded from accepting her offer.

"No. But once the thread is removed it's only a matter of time before what remains begins to unravel."

Good enough.

"It's a bargain then."

She reaches out to me, and I assess the threat that she could easily become as I step toward her reluctantly, grasping her outstretched hand. My eyes widen in shock. A familiar beat brushes over my skin, like the cool waves that drift up and down the La'tari coast when I would lay in its deep sands as a child. A push, and then a pull. Something foreign and yet so familiar that some deep part of me calls it home. It's as if the very pulse of Terr is rushing out of her, caressing my skin, beckoning me to join in the rhythm of all who have come before me and all who will come after.

"It is done," she says simply, dropping my hand and offering me the herb she pinches between two knotted fingers.

Regret, longing, want, more emotions than these play in my mind as the beat of my world dies without her touch. She examines me curiously and I school my features, pushing any lingering questions far into the back of my mind.

Moving slowly, I gauge her reaction. When she makes no move to shift into the toothy creature she had before, I snatch the herb from her grasp and shuffle back, out of her reach. My heart thunders within my chest, out of relief or fear I cannot say.

I risk a glance behind me, my eyes narrowing toward the clearing where the shadow master still lingers on the precipice of death. When I turn back, the crone is gone, and my heart falters a beat as my head whips around, eyes searching for any sign of her.

I break, running as fast as I can, stumbling over an exposed root, scraping my arm against the sharp and uneven stones protruding from the forest floor. Cursing under my breath, I push back up to my feet and vault into a run, turning the surrounding forest into a blur of shadowed leaves.

I cradle the herb against my heart, as if it is the most precious cargo I will ever possess, unwilling to lose a single stem. The action in direct contrast to the ferocious determination and wild desperation building inside me.

I don't slow until I reach the clearing. My knees wobble as I skid to a halt, falling to the ground beside the shadow master. Wrinkling my nose, I snatch the now limp body of the serpent and throw it into a nearby bush. Hands shaking as my fingers pluck the dainty leaves from the slender shoot, I crush them, turning them into a thick paste of deep green. This I add to his waterskin, shaking it violently until it dissolves, before tipping it against his lips and massaging his throat, encouraging his body to swallow the bitter tonic.

Once I've emptied every drop onto his tongue, I dump the contents of his pack on the ground, offering up a silent prayer as my hands shoot to the gauze he thought to pack. I pick through a variety of poultices, sniffing and discarding each one until I find what I am looking for. I slather a thick violet paste onto the bite, binding it tightly. It will help draw out the venom. That is, if I'm not too late.

There is only one thing left to do, wait and ruminate about the day. It's sure to be the longest day of my life, a day that will shave years from the end of it, and it will all be worth it if he lives.

When the sun begins to reach its height, I drag his body into the cool shade of the trees, emptying the contents of my own waterskin into his

mouth. Fear and frustration take turns vying for my attention as the hours pass. I can do little more than dry the perspiration from his brow and remain by his side, unwilling to leave him alone, even to fetch water for myself. I've never felt more useless.

I've never been more useless.

His breathing remains shallow long into the night. Only with great effort do I turn from him long enough to strike flint to kindling and start a fire, sending up a prayer that the rolling storms in the distance keep to the mountain tops. It will be no small task to craft a shelter to keep him dry, and I'm not sure I have the strength to pry myself away to go in search of materials. There is no use trying to sleep, I can hardly blink as I watch in vain for any sign of improvement.

The minutes that pass take on new meaning as they drag on in a tauntingly sluggish fashion. I now measure time by the faint tick of his pulse where his wrist rests below my fingers. Finally, with hours yet before dawn breaks the horizon, his breathing shifts. His chest rises high with the first full breath he's taken since I found him unconscious, and a burdensome weight falls from my body, the tension unspooling from my shoulders.

Never again do I want to feel this way. Never again will I allow myself to be helpless when I can be strong, to be at the mercy of the fates when I can control my own destiny.

I haven't taken time to wonder what I'd given up in the forest, but it doesn't matter. I can't bring myself to regret it, and I know that whatever it is I would give it again without a single thought, reckless as it might have been.

Late into the night, or perhaps early the next morning, the shadow master's pulse becomes strong. Color returns to his cheeks and the unnatural, quiet stillness of his body turns to that of a deep and restful sleep.

I glance at my bedroll and discard the thought before it fully takes form in my mind. Despite the weight settling over my eyes, I won't risk falling asleep and waking up to find him dead. I shake the fog from my head and sit by his side, pulling my knees against my chest and resting my cheek upon them. The warmth of the fire soaks into my bones and the stars blur in my eyes even as the sun dims their glorious light with the rays of its promise to rise.

I rock on my heels as the subtle light of dawn falls across his eyelids and they flutter awake. It is, by far, the most beautiful thing I have ever seen.

"Vakesh?" It comes out as a croak.

My stomach pits when a low moan is his only reply. His face twists with uneasiness as his eyes shutter in rapid succession, focusing on my face. I will myself not to cry, flicking a single rebellious tear from my cheek. I have cried before, out of anger and frustration, but this is something else altogether. Something about it weakens me, and I can't help but hate it.

His brow creases and he shoots upright on his bedroll. I suspect the motion makes his head spin when his hand flies to his forehead, cradling it as he wobbles, struggling to regain his bearings.

"What happened?" he demands, his eyes tracing the wet skin on my cheek with a frown.

I haven't prepared the story that tumbles from my lips. It is just the raw and unrehearsed truth of the last day. The first part he takes fairly well, considering he seemed nearly dead when I found him. He tenses, his eyes narrow and his brow drawn at my first mention of the crone. His stiffening spine and the rapt interest with which he regards me at the mere mention of the woman in the woods hollows my gut.

He lets me finish my tale, from beginning to end, without interruption, before asking pointedly, "Tell me again. What did she say? Her exact words."

He makes me repeat myself three times before he's satisfied that I have neither left anything out or forgotten a single word that was exchanged between us. He doesn't ask me about the bargain or to explain what it was she took from me. Surely, he'd seen enough of my own confusion when I told him that part of the tale.

After my story has ended and he is finished asking his questions we both grow silent, losing ourselves to thoughtful contemplation. My stomach growls late in the morning, and though I try to demand he stay off his feet, he insists on joining me to catch a fish for breakfast and on cooking it after. His joke, that he is still obligated to cook my meals after losing our bet, falls flat. With every step he takes along the riverbank, I see the strain in his smile and the coil of his muscles. He is no longer at ease here.

By the time the sun sets and I've eaten an entire herb encrusted fish by myself, the last two days begin to feel like a dream. The shadow master is fine and whatever the crone took in our bargain, I can obviously live without. My lids finally close over my eyes and I'm lulled to sleep by the crackling fire and the knowledge that everything is going to be fine.

Blood. There is so much blood. My hands fly to cover my ears, and I scream, willing away the sound of the blade as it's dragged across the flame licked floor.

A woman lies before me, unmoving, her hand stretched out toward me. Her beauty is striking, even beneath the wet, crimson ribbons adorning her cheeks. Though the light is gone from her eyes and her lips do not move, she calls to me.

"Shivaria." The ghostly whisper chills my blood and my screams begin again in a key of true horror.

"Shivaria!"

Eyes flying open, my shaking hands clawing at my neck, I gasp for air. Bile creeps up my panicked throat, and I throw myself out of my bedroll into a nearby bush as I begin to heave uncontrollably. I lose my dinner to the knots in my stomach and the turmoil of my mind.

My nerves do not easily settle, nor do the tremors that wrack my sweat-soaked body. Once the constrictions of my gut have ceased, I wipe my mouth and take a seat by the edge of the woods. Keeping my back to the fire, I face the forest, closing my eyes, as I draw long, calming breaths through my nose.

Vivid images of the bloody woman threaten to replay in my mind. I've had nightmares before, but nothing like this. Even after waking it all feels too real, like I am still in that room, gripped by fear and screaming at the carnage surrounding me.

Wrapping my arm around my stomach I heave again, struggling to push my dark thoughts into the farthest reaches of my mind.

You are safe. It was just a dream.

I find the shadow master atop his bedroll, poised to sprint across the fire to my side. Plucking my waterskin from the ground, I empty half of it, rinsing out my mouth as I observe him.

"It must have been something I ate," I lie.

His face is pale with no hint of the smile he usually graces me with. His mouth forms a thin line as he shakes his head.

I fall back onto my bedroll with a graceless thud. "It was just a bad dream."

His eyebrows hit his hairline. "*Just* a bad dream?"

"Yes. *Just* a bad dream."

Rolling onto my side, I turn my back to the fire and my friend. I have no interest in going over the gruesome details with him. It takes hours to rid my body of the tremors I woke with, and I don't find sleep until the night sky begins to grey with the faintest light of the coming dawn.

When I wake, late the next morning, the shadow master looks as if he hasn't moved since I last laid eyes on him. Still crouched with a deadly scowl, he appears to have at least regained some of his color.

"Why do you look like you're about to end someone?" I huff, trying to lighten his mood as I pull myself to my feet.

He blinks twice, eyes flicking from my bedroll to my face, as if he hadn't noticed me rise. He loses a small bit of the tension in his body with a deep breath and a shake of his head, his face softening.

"I'm sorry. What?"

"Never mind." I shake my head. "I'll catch us some breakfast."

The rest of the week goes by too quickly. I settle into our lazy routine of fishing and laying in the sun. The shadow master even teaches me to forage fresh herbs from the forest and which ones to combine to make the most delicious foods. I imagine this is what a perfect life would be like if it weren't for one thing. The dreams.

The nightmares persist, and, though I don't wake violently ill again after the first night, I continue to be thrown from the bloody visions in a full panic during the early hours of each morning after. Every morning is the same, I wake to find the shadow master watching me, poised to launch across the fire. A thread of something unknown to me lingers deep in his eyes. Eyes that hold dark and weary circles by the time we pack our bags on the last morning. I can't help but wonder if I look the same.

"Here," he hands me two obsidian blades as he slings his pack over his shoulder, "Keep these."

"Why?" I don't mean to argue, but the daggers are a curious gesture.

I am allowed to have weapons, but the Drakai custom has always been that we earn our blades in battle.

"To fend off the demons." It's the only answer he gives me before turning north and starting toward the keep.

I don't ask what he means as I throw my pack over my shoulders and follow him. I don't want to know what he observed in our time in The Smudge, or what demons he's seen that have kept him from his sleep.

I fist their hilts tightly, fearing nothing in the waking world and feeling silly that the cool, smooth stone at my fingertips somehow eases my mind. They may not be suited to fight the darkness that plagues me, but I feel my shoulders relax as I will that darkness into the blades for safe keeping.

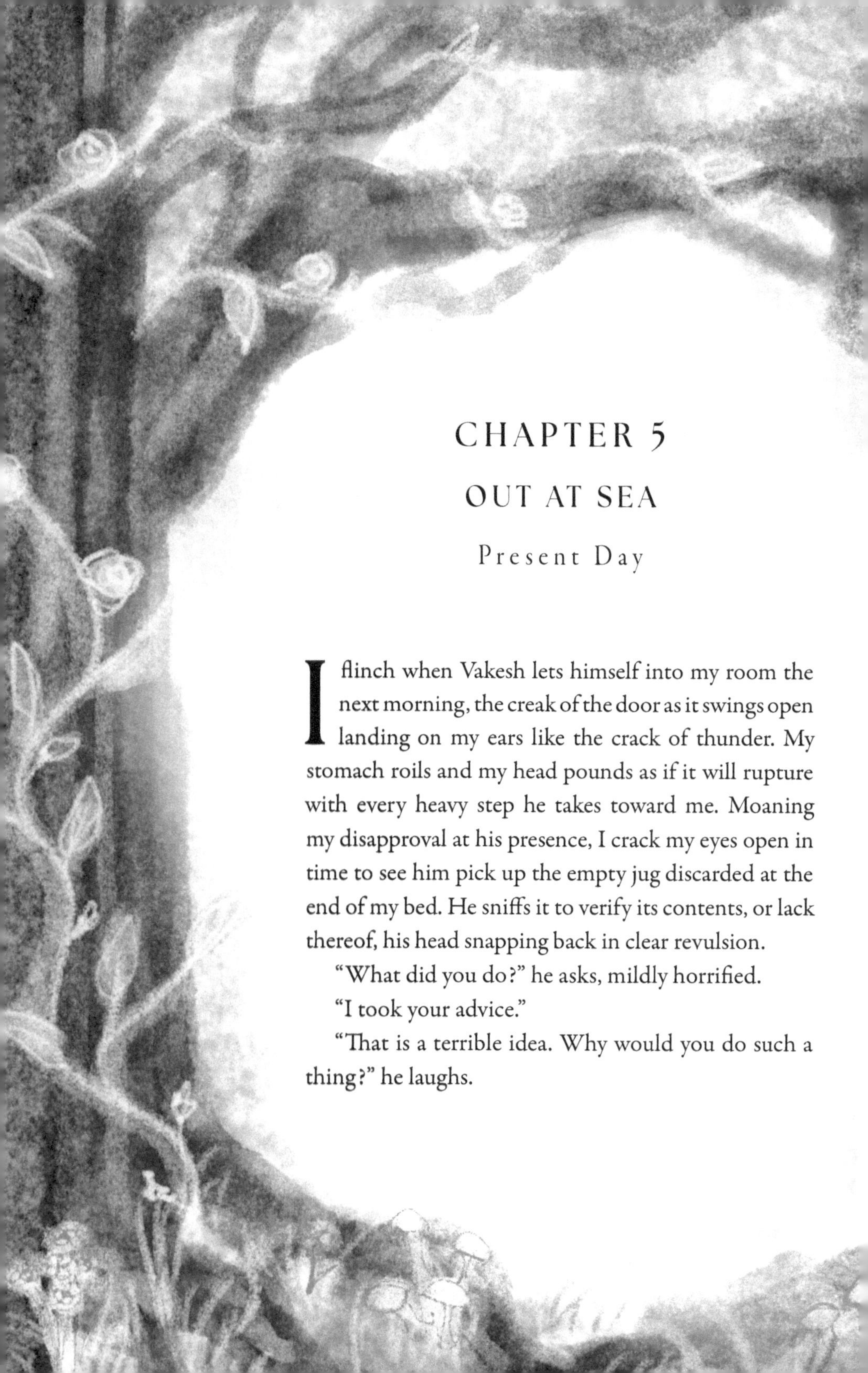

CHAPTER 5
OUT AT SEA
Present Day

I flinch when Vakesh lets himself into my room the next morning, the creak of the door as it swings open landing on my ears like the crack of thunder. My stomach roils and my head pounds as if it will rupture with every heavy step he takes toward me. Moaning my disapproval at his presence, I crack my eyes open in time to see him pick up the empty jug discarded at the end of my bed. He sniffs it to verify its contents, or lack thereof, his head snapping back in clear revulsion.

"What did you do?" he asks, mildly horrified.

"I took your advice."

"That is a terrible idea. Why would you do such a thing?" he laughs.

I try my best to glare at him, but it only makes him laugh louder, the sound causing my head to split painfully and earning him a flimsy punch to the thigh.

"That was entirely uncalled for." He smiles, rubbing the leg where I struck him. "I've brought you breakfast. You could at least sit up and thank me like a lady."

"Kesh," I groan, closing my eyes, willing him to disappear.

I want ten more hours of sleep, followed by a greasy meal and a hot bath, and I am in no mood for any of his cheeky sarcasm. My body pitches toward him as his weight settles on the edge of the bed beside me. His thumbs work magic, circling the tight muscles at the base of my neck.

"Kesh," he purrs into my ear. "You haven't called me that in years."

I groan, my muscles becoming more pliant with each stroke.

"Why did you stop?" he asks, his hands turning to the muscles along my arms.

"Leanna," I admit, my mind taking me back to painful moments I remember all too clearly.

"What a harpy," he chuckles.

"She said that '*Kesh*' was far too familiar a name for the master of shadows," I groan out as his fingers press into the tight muscle between my shoulders.

"If it was anyone else, I would agree with her, but you," he says, rolling me onto my back, waggling my nose mockingly with his finger, "are *mi'ajna* and you may call me whatever pleases you."

"Incessant." I smile. "Obnoxious." I quirk an eyebrow. He clutches his heart feigning injury. "Obtuse." I chuckle lightly, as he rolls his eyes, and I raise my hand to my forehead to comfort the pain.

"As I said, you may call me whatever you please, though I really would prefer you'd choose one nickname and stick with it. Or perhaps it would be easier if I simply respond to every insult you shout in my direction?" he pouts.

I can't help but laugh, my head throbbing painfully as he swings himself off the bed, stretching his broad shoulders as he stands.

"I've brought you enough to last until dinner." He gestures to the small basket of food he set on the table. I want to complain about his pending absence, but I won't. It isn't his job to entertain me for the duration of the crossing. Still, I will be bored out of my mind before midday and we both know it.

"We are at port today and I have work on shore," he says, as if he already knows every question I leave unvoiced. "I'll join you for dinner."

He makes his way toward the door and my eyes fall on the obsidian daggers he left by my side. Stretching lazily, I pinch one of the blades between my fingers, letting the cool stone soothe my psyche. They are the same ones he gifted me years ago. I know the look and feel of every notch and groove from the leather wrapped hilt to the tip of the blade. Long after I've forgotten my name and the few fond memories I carry are ravaged by the thief of time, I will remember these.

"You said they are a crutch," I say to his back as his hand reaches for the door.

"They are only a crutch if you need them, and I'm only leaving them for the day."

He stops in the doorway and leans against the frame, picking at invisible dirt beneath his nails when he says, "Can I ask a favor of you?"

"You know you can."

I push myself into a sitting position, my eyebrows drawn together as I ponder what possible task I can perform for him in the stifling room I am confined to. Whatever he asks, if it is within my power, I will grant it. After all we have been through together, even after the time we've spent apart, there is nothing that could persuade me to break the bargain of friendship we made years ago.

"Good. That's good." He nods solemnly, and I begin to worry. "In that case," he sighs dramatically, "I'll have the captain bring down a basin of warm water along with some soap, because Vari, my lady perfection, you smell like a cheap tavern on Sunday morning."

My spine stiffens and my cheeks flush with the heat of my embarrassment. With one hand I clutch the thin sheet to my chest, with the other I hurl a dagger toward the door. It strikes its mark, embedding itself in the wood directly next to his jaw. He doesn't so much as glance up from where his eyes are still firmly glued to his hand. He simply stands there, unflinching, a satisfied smile tugging at the corner of his lips when he turns to leave.

The dagger wobbles, clattering against the floor when he closes the door behind him. I'm sure my cheeks are still crimson when the captain delivers a steaming pot of water with a small sliver of jasmine soap not long after.

Every layer of sweat disintegrates beneath the floral lather I work across the planes of my body. As I cleanse my skin of an entire jug of ale's worth of sticky perspiration, I silently thank Vakesh for the kindness though they are words I will never voice aloud.

I let my hair dry into its natural spirals, and I'm surprised to find that I do not immediately miss my fighting leathers when I put on one of Leanna's silk dresses. The thin fabric cocoons my body, caressing it with each step I take. If I am to be confined to my small room, bored out of my mind for the duration of the voyage, I can find no reason not to be exceedingly comfortable.

Smoothing the dress idly, I recall just how badly I balked when Leanna presented me with the first of the gowns she'd commissioned for my assignment. As Drakai, I am privileged to have the promise of three hot meals a day, a roof over my head, and fighting leathers. Drakai are not paid for their service to the crown, and the only other possessions I will ever own will be gifted to me or acquired by means of mission or challenge. Fea Dien often return from their missions with all manner of rich and handsome gifts they receive along the way, though I don't personally know of any missions that began with the crown's endowment.

I will not, under any circumstances, acquire a taste for silks.

It is a mantra I know I will have to repeat often if I intend to remain unspoiled by the fabric.

I spend the better part of the day practicing with my daggers. It's a comforting pastime I've been encouraged to pursue for years. I will never claim to be the most beautiful of the Fea Dien, and though I surpassed both Bront and Leanna in the ring long ago, there are other Drakai with proficiencies I can't even fathom. But when it comes to blades, there isn't a soul in all of La'tari that can come close to besting me. At least, none that I've met.

Hours pass, and finally our departure from port is marked by muffled shouts overhead. The ship sways, rolling upon the waves of the open sea. I glance at the table, my stomach growling at the sight of cured meats and what remains of the thick wedge of cheese I enjoyed for lunch. I find myself pacing the small cabin as I wait, picking at the leftover morsels until the late hour settles a weight upon my eyes.

Finally, I succumb to my body's bid for sleep. Turning down the wick

of the lantern by my cot and hanging my gown in the wardrobe, I settle in for the night. Despite what I expect, sleep does not come easily, my mind grasping at every possible reason he hasn't come.

Perhaps business kept him ashore. Maybe he's been killed. Drakai aren't known for their exceptionally long lives.

And I prefer these options to the nagging voice that says he is as bored in my company as I am without his.

Eventually the sway of the ship lulls me to sleep. The torment from a maddening array of worry, self-pity, and loathing gives way to the more familiar bloodbath that dries my throat and leaves a gaping hole in my chest every night.

She is so lovely, the woman reaching for me. A thick, dark braid is draped across her shoulder, dragging along the floor as she pulls herself toward me. A dark trail of blood follows her, staining the wooden floors a sickening shade of red.

"Vari," she whispers.

Bile surges in my stomach, burning the soft tissue of my throat as the woman collapses onto the floor at my feet. Her eyes are fixed on me, and I watch them dull as her breath leaves her.

"Shivaria."

"Wake up."

Some incoherent, distant part of me thrills at the rasp of my blades sliding against one other as I pull them from under my pillow. I draw a ragged breath, my lungs refusing to fully expand, my chest roiling with the demon I can never fully expel.

"Vari stop!" The voice is a harsh whisper in my ear, and I will my eyes to focus in the low light. I struggle beneath an unfamiliar weight, my demands for release muffled by a hand over my mouth, my arms pinned above my head.

Dark eyes peer down at me through a tangle of white hair, flicking from my face to the blades I fist in a death grip.

Just a dream. I'm safe.

I relax my grip and Vakesh looses a sigh, shoulders tense as he slides

his hand off my mouth, easing the daggers from my grasp. He gives me a single terse nod. Only after giving him a reassuring nod back, does he pull his weight from me and sit on the edge of the cot, pinching the bridge of his nose and exhaling sharply.

A moment later he collects himself and stands, removing his cloak, handing it to me while his gaze flicks to the door.

"Put this on and come with me."

I dip my chin in agreement and let the silence I'm accustomed to with the shadow master fill the room as he turns his back to me. Savoring the stormy scent that lingers on his cloak, I drape it over a silk dress pulled from my wardrobe and follow him out into the night.

I'm relieved to find that the deck is empty topside. There is no doubt in my mind that he knew we would have it to ourselves. He has never been dismissive of any risk where I am concerned, not when he can help it. The captain alone stands at the wheel, looking past me as if I am merely a phantom.

Smart man.

Leaning against the bow of the ship, I pull in a lungful of fresh crisp air, then another, and another. With greater effort than I will admit aloud, I manage to still the slight tremor of my body and let the cool sea breeze have a go at dampening the beast that roils inside me.

"It's gotten worse," he says, his eyes on the sea.

It isn't a question, but I nod once.

"Leanna doesn't know?" he asks, but he already knows the answer.

I just look at him skeptically and shake my head. She would never grant me a mission if she did. I would have been cast into her minor collection of broken Drakai who never quite made the cut.

"Of course she doesn't," he sighs.

I try to keep my mind off the bloody woman that haunts my dreams. I focus instead on the way the moonlight ripples across the waves. Lulled by the sound of the sea being cleaved apart by the ship as the wind pushes it through the open water. The early spring air is even colder out at sea. It fills my hood, spooling around my cheeks and whipping chilly tendrils across the back of my neck.

I watch Vakesh from the corner of my eye. His jaw feathers and relaxes, his body following suit. His lips form a thin, hard line, disrupting the masculine beauty of his normal jovial smile.

"We can disembark in Daidron. I will come up with an excuse for our delay. Perhaps there is someone there that can help with—"

I whip my head around to face him. "Absolutely not. There is no need."

"Don't be prideful, Shivaria."

I pinch my mouth shut, unsure if I am more offended by the implication that I am too prideful or the fact that he used my full name.

"You don't simply walk into the north and find yourself accepted into the king's presence. It could take weeks or even months before you are accepted to court and if anyone witnesses this in the meantime—"

"You think a fitful sleep will disqualify me?" I challenge weakly, knowing the answer.

"A fitful sleep?" he balks, and when I roll my eyes, he grabs my arm and brings me to face him fully. "A fitful sleep?" he repeats in a harsh whisper. "Call it what you want but remember that *I* have seen for myself what you call a fitful sleep. You might have gone unnoticed if you only woke fearful, but you wake as if you are in the middle of an eternal battle raging around you, ready to send haliel every soul within reach."

"I can control it," I lie.

"How?" he demands but he does not wait for an answer before holding up a finger. "Fighting, which you will *not* be doing in A'kori." He holds up a second finger. "Drinking, and while I don't altogether disagree with an occasional numbing of the senses, you can't go to bed drunk every night and expect to be considered suitable for society." He holds up a third finger, faltering, and I quirk a brow.

"Focing?"

He swallows a lump in his throat and his face falls into a perfectly placid mask.

"Also, not an option," he says lamely.

The child in me wants to argue about perceived moral virtue but I understand why he protests. If it comes to it, the king will find me more appealing with the assurance of my virginity. Though, I have no doubt I will have to find another way to end the male. Falling far from the standard of beauty does not lend me any favors as Fea Dien.

Frustrated, my eyes shift back to the sea, the edges of the water now barely contrasted by the grey light of early dawn. I push off the bow and take myself below deck into my cramped quarters. Vakesh follows closing the door behind us before leaning against the wall to observe me.

"I'm not abandoning my mission," I insist, pacing the small space.

"I am not asking you to abandon it, Vari. I am simply suggesting that you delay it. I, more than anyone, want to see you on the shores of A'kori, accepted into the presence of the king so that all of this might end."

"You know as well as I do that a delay could set us back years. Help me find another way," I beg.

"Other ways are not for you," he says.

"But there are other ways?" I stop my pacing and sit on the edge of my cot, looking to him for the answers I desperately seek.

"Pitch." He shrugs. "But it would take too long to find you a supply and even then, if you were caught..."

Pitch. The drug is illegal on the whole of the southern continent and widely used by battle worn Drakai to assist in a dreamless sleep. It is highly addictive, and I have known more than one who died after overindulging in the teeth blackening substance. Though the more common death associated with the drug is starvation. While oblivion has its appeal, it can quickly become all-consuming. Hours on the drug can easily turn into days or weeks of caring for nothing but the promise of the void.

"The fact that you are actually considering pitch concerns me," he says, pulling me back into the conversation with a worried frown.

"A small amount, to sleep through the night," I argue.

"Put it out of your mind. I shouldn't have suggested it."

"If not pitch, then what else?"

His eyes survey the floor, and he clears his throat. "Pitch, drinking, fighting, they all offer a similar *release*," he nearly chokes on the last word, "an oblivion that all Drakai come to desperately crave. Can you think of nothing else that might offer you the same ... reprieve?"

I think for a moment before answering. "No. Nothing. What else is there?"

He curses and rubs the back of his neck. Squeezing his eyes shut, his

head falls back against the wall with a thud. "Leanna should have been the one to teach you."

"Teach me what?" I laugh uncomfortably at the uneasiness he is so obviously feeling.

It has never been this way between us, and I do not care for his parsing of words or the invisible wall he's built with the mask he wears. He eyes me from across the room, exhales sharply, and turns to go, stopping just before his hand grasps the lever on the door. His hand flexes and he spins on his heel, striding back across the room and pulling the chair to the edge of the bed before depositing himself in it.

"Surely," he says, running his fingers through his hair, "Leanna taught you something of what to expect should you find yourself alone with a man in his chambers?"

I roll my eyes and huff a laugh. "In fact, she did *not*. Leanna is of the opinion that I am more appealing to men if those things remain somewhat of a mystery. And she has every intention of utilizing that naivete in whatever way she can."

Even I can hear the bitterness in my voice at my admission that Leanna continues to mold me for her own ends. Perhaps leaving me lacking in a way that I never expected.

Vakesh buries his face between his hands and shakes his head.

"I'm not completely ignorant," I reassure him. "I do understand the … act." I flush despite myself.

"The *act?*" He blanches.

"The expectation," I say, hoping it is an appropriate correction, as I throw my arms in the air.

"Stars above," he swears, looking up as if he is offering a silent prayer to the heavens.

"Why are we even talking about this?" I sigh deeply, rolling my shoulders and willing the muscles in my neck to relax.

"I'm not sure you want me teaching you this lesson," he says without looking me in the eye.

"You said Leanna should have already taught me—"

He falls into a fitful laugh before I can finish, and soon his eyes begin to

water in the fashion of true humor. A laugh bubbles up within my chest to join him, though I have no idea what he finds so funny.

"Leanna should have, though I expect she would have a much different way of going about it." He shrugs thoughtfully. "Though, for all I know she would go about it in exactly the same fashion."

His eyes glint with thoughts unknown while they fully take me in.

"All right," he says with a look of determination.

"All right?" I say, brows pitching low.

"I shouldn't have to say this, but it needs to be said." He unclasps the cloak I wear and pushes it off my shoulders. "It's hard not to take some lessons to heart, and this is one you can't afford to take personally. Understand?"

"Yes," I answer easily.

In the years I have known him he's taught me many harsh lessons and never have I taken any to heart. Resilience, for all my failings, is a skill I have in abundance. He pinches my chin between his thumb and finger, drawing my eyes to his.

"You don't understand," he says flatly. "But you must, so just don't forget it."

He stands, dropping his hold on the cloak and motions for me to stand with him. I don't hesitate and as soon as I am on my feet, he wraps a hand around my waist, pulling me close. My breath hitches as my cheeks flush and I freeze under his gaze. I look up at him through thick lashes, and his jaw bounces at the end just before he spins us around with the abundant grace he's always possessed so that the back of his legs are touching the cot.

"Say stop and the lesson ends, no judgment and no explanations required. There is no expectation here." His voice is so serious that I repeat what he said in my head trying and failing to make sense of it.

"All right." I choke on the breathy whisper and I'm suddenly only aware of just how close he is.

My nipples pebble as the silk that binds them brushes against his tunic and I recall the hot summer day when we had last been this close. A day I have wished a hundred times to relive so that I might correct the error I made that split our paths and sent him so far from me.

His eyes don't leave mine as his hands glide to my hips. He gathers the fabric of my dress until it is high enough to expose my core to a gentle breeze snaking in below the cabin door. My skin prickles with goosebumps and my breath shudders out in a whisper as I begin to tremble. My entire body tenses and my hands ball into fists at my sides. His eyes take in every minute reaction to his touch, studying the effect he has on me.

"Relax," he says, "This won't work if you don't."

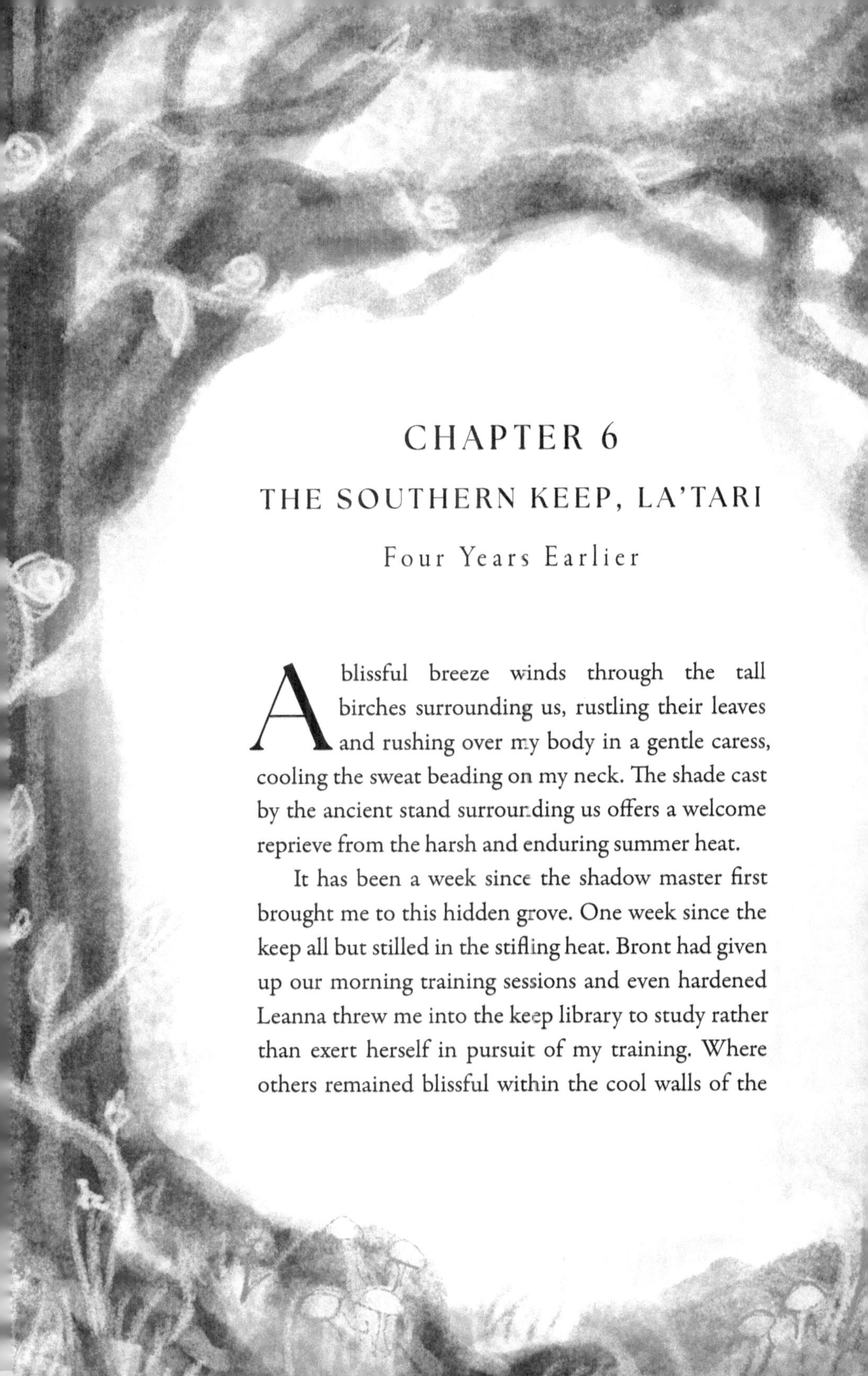

CHAPTER 6
THE SOUTHERN KEEP, LA'TARI
Four Years Earlier

A blissful breeze winds through the tall birches surrounding us, rustling their leaves and rushing over my body in a gentle caress, cooling the sweat beading on my neck. The shade cast by the ancient stand surrounding us offers a welcome reprieve from the harsh and enduring summer heat.

It has been a week since the shadow master first brought me to this hidden grove. One week since the keep all but stilled in the stifling heat. Bront had given up our morning training sessions and even hardened Leanna threw me into the keep library to study rather than exert herself in pursuit of my training. Where others remained blissful within the cool walls of the keep, I'd quickly grown restless. A dark cloud settled over me as my dreams began to leak into my waking life.

Vakesh alone noticed the change in me and pulled me from my sleep early one morning without explanation. It was a testament to our friendship and the trust we share that I followed him without question, through the forest and down the precarious scree field littering the face of the valley.

When we emerged from the dense foliage of the forest at the edge of the winding river in which we now train, my eyes lit up and our plans diverged. While the shadow master thought my darkening countenance might be lifted by more leisurely activities, I'd been quick to wrangle him back into the lessons that distract from the nightmares that plague me.

The current is still swift despite the time of year. As if it works in tandem with the wind, the water wraps around my calves gently stroking the fatigued muscles, while the cool breeze caresses my dry extremities. It is heaven.

Vakesh has, at my request, been happy to train me to move silently in the water. After failing miserably for two days I've only become more determined to perfect the feat. It is my singular focus and despite my best efforts, it isn't going very well.

The shadow master stands two strides before me, the light fabric of his white tunic fluttering against his abdomen as the leaves overhead mimic the sound of the sea. His eyes are closed behind the black length of fabric he tied over them. I told him it wasn't necessary; I trust him. He is the most honest man I have ever met, but he continues to insist, tying it on every morning without fail.

Slowly, I raise my foot off the rocky floor of the riverbed and take a step forward with my left foot. Vakesh points to the foot, and I return to my starting position. I begin again, careful to move with the current where it weaves around a large boulder. I rest the pad of my foot on the teetering rock beneath it and hold my breath. When he doesn't move, I press my weight onto it fully, willing the rock to stay in place. A single shift of the slate will give away my position.

My next step brings me within reach of him, it's taken me days to get this close, and I'm afraid to loose the breath in my lungs until I strike him and claim the title of *master for the day*. I'm sure Vakesh regrets the game he invented by now. Every time I win, I make him hunt and cook me a fresh meal for dinner. He never complains.

I steady myself on the loose rocks underfoot, striking forward as quickly as I can. My stomach hollows the moment I commit to the jab, noting the smirk on his face. I never stood a chance. Not only does he block my blow, he grapples my arm and I pitch sideways.

"Hisht." The curse comes out just as the slate stone rocks beneath my foot do, sending me tumbling into the water.

He pulls the black cloth from his eyes and fails to stifle a laugh while offering me his arm.

"I'm sorry, I didn't mean—" he says, but the rest is lost amidst his growing laughter.

A chuckle escapes me, and I take his arm. He pulls me from the water, the slate rocks shifting beneath my feet as I rise and careen into his chest. His hands move to my waist, holding me upright while I regain my footing.

I flush as his eyes track the droplets falling from my face, down my neck, and over my peaked nipples. The pink flesh at the center of my breasts made obvious by the cool water drenching the thin fabric of my tunic. When his eyes find mine again, I lift an eyebrow and the corner of my mouth quirks up. The blush that rushes to his cheeks is exquisite, though I regret the absence of his hands at my waist when he removes them abruptly.

"For the love of the veil, Vari," he says under his breath as he moves his eyes over everything but me.

I laugh. "I never imagined the master of shadows would share the same weakness as every other man on the face of Terr."

I feel like I've won something when he only heaves a breath, still unwilling to meet my eyes. It's not every day the shadow master is thrown off guard.

Checking the sun's placement, I begin to panic. Today is the first day I am to resume my training with Bront since the heat wave set in, and I'm going to be late.

"Kesh," I twist my braid, wringing the water from it, "let me have your shirt."

Finally, he looks at me, but his brow is drawn as he surveys my outstretched hand, puzzled by my request. I know he heard me, but I become worried when he doesn't immediately move to give me his tunic.

"Please, Kesh. I'm going to be late for my morning training with Bront, and I can't go back to the keep like this, and anyway, it's your fault I'm soaking wet."

I don't like to beg but I've found Vakesh to be particularly susceptible to it.

"Stars above, Vari. Fine, take the shirt." He gives in with a sigh and pulls his mostly dry tunic over his head.

It's hard not to notice the tumble of hard-won muscles adorning his abdomen or the definition of those distracting dents on his hips, lost below the line of his pants.

I spin around before he catches my eyes on him and teases me as I've just teased him. Pulling the drenched tunic off, I toss it onto the shore to dry then reach over my shoulder and wait until I feel him place his tunic in my hand. Sliding it over my head I take in a lungful of Kesh's comforting scent. It smells like home, like a wind that brings with it the promise of a coming rain.

"See you for training," I yell as I rush off through the forest with a grin, imagining the shadow master walking through the keep in my sopping wet tunic when he returns.

I regret every step I take away from him, dashing through the forest, toward the keep. Something has changed, though I can't put my finger on exactly what it is or when it happened. A tension has settled between us, not altogether unpleasant, but it has stripped away some of the ease we've shared for years.

I no longer feel entirely settled in the shadow master's presence, and he has begun to move around me like I am a doe on one of our hunts. As if I might be spooked away at the snapping of a twig. It is something I don't understand.

Things I have endured for years have begun to chafe. A month ago, I sent one of Leanna's beauties to the infirmary after baiting her into a sparring match. No one asked questions when I set aside my usual restraint and dropped her to the floor of the ring with a single well-placed blow.

I overheard her whispering to a girl in her class, dark promises about what she would do to the shadow master when she slipped into his room that night. The conversation bristled me unreasonably, though I'm not sure why. I have heard my share of similar comments over the years, even laughed when a group of ladies wagered a year ago about which would be the first to take him to bed.

I push the stray thoughts out of my mind as I break from the deadwood, jogging toward the ring, looking for Bront. I will puzzle it all out some other time. I'm already late, but I know he'll give me time to change into my leathers before we train. Only it isn't Bront I find waiting for me today, it's Leanna.

I try not to cringe when I ask if she has seen the general. Being late for lessons has never been an option with the woman and I have no doubt she will make me regret my choices fully before the end of the day. My skin crawls when she doesn't mention my tardiness or my attire, though I am all too aware that she notes both.

"Bront is otherwise engaged. I will be stepping in to assist in your war lessons until he returns."

Foc.

Bront has never missed one of our scheduled training sessions and Leanna is the last person in all of Terr I would choose to replace him. Not that I would ever be given a choice.

I school my face into a placid mask, straightening my back when I say, "All right. I'll just go and change into my leathers."

"No need. You will remain just as you are."

She turns and makes her way toward the sparring ring and my brow furrows as I start after her warily. There are lessons in war that do not require the use of steel or armor, but Leanna is no tactician, at least not that I have ever seen. The sparring ring is eerily vacant for this time of day, despite the heat, and it does nothing to help the sudden disquiet I feel when my tutor pulls a long leather strap from among the weapon racks.

"I will be testing your proficiency with your off hand," she says, pulling my right arm behind my back and fastening it against my spine.

"I attack. You defend." She barely finishes her sentence when her closed fist lands a blow to my jaw, sending me staggering to the side.

I shake the fog from my brain and my eyes snap to hers. I see it now, the anger behind her eyes, and it hollows out my stomach.

"I heard something interesting today," she says, just before she swings again.

This time I dodge.

"You remember Avanjelin, don't you?" she asks, running a finger along the side of her face. As if I will ever need to be reminded of the girl I accidentally scarred with my blade years ago. "She was in the woods this morning and claims to have stumbled upon the strangest thing."

I can feel the wrinkles between my eyes deepen as I try to ascertain what this is all about. She lunges toward my left, but I see the feign for what it is and block the fist that swings in from the right before rolling out of her reach and resuming a defensive position on my feet.

"Tell me, Shivaria. What were you doing in the woods this morning with the master of shadows?"

"Training." I can feel the crease in my brow deepen as I answer.

"Without your clothes on?" She jerks her chin toward the too large tunic I wear and when my eyes flick down to it, she lands another jab.

This time her knuckles land as if they were stone, splitting the tender flesh beneath my left eye. I suck in a curse, partially in pain but also furious for allowing myself to look away from the threat before me.

"I've often wondered why you have always been his favorite student. I suppose now the entire keep knows exactly how you've gained your marks. I only hope you've enough sense to have kept yourself intact."

Her eyes wander across my cheeks, taking in the blush rushing to the surface of my skin under the weight of her accusations.

Before she can misinterpret my rage for embarrassment, I hiss, "We've never—It isn't like that."

She barks a laugh, a hideous and bitter sound. The wind picks up, stirring the dry dirt beneath our feet and, as if inspired by the weather, Leanna kicks a cloud of dust into my face. I reel back, trying to blink away the grains that scrape beneath my eyelids, and take another devastating blow to the jaw. The strike is precise, sending me to the ground with a bright flash of light that swallows up the world.

Before I can get my feet under me a fist slams into my side and I yelp just as the crack of my rib claps in my ears.

"I hear you even have a little nickname for the master of shadows. *Kesh,* is it?"

I grip my side with my loose arm, protecting the broken rib, sucking a

punishing breath into my lungs. Leanna stands over me with a self-satisfied smile.

"Get up," she demands.

I take another shallow breath, carefully maneuvering onto my feet. I feel like a fool as Leanna rounds on me again. She hasn't beaten me in a sparring match in months, thanks to my training with Vakesh. No wonder she bound my arm and told me to stay in the flimsy fabric of the tunic. She never intended for this to be a lesson, not in the way I perceived it. This is a beating.

I throw my arm out to block another of Leanna's blows, only to expose my ribs to a rounding kick. Even as her knee slams into me, the sharp, brutal pain ripping a shriek from my lungs, I feel her restraint. The rib floats in my chest like a dagger. While I'm not altogether convinced that she won't strike it toward my heart, I hope that her control is a sign that she values my life too highly to end it now.

Before I can recover from the pain, she sends me to the ground with a downward blow that splits my lip. A warm trickle of blood mixes with my sweat, slicking my chin before it drips to puddle on the silty floor of the ring. I stay down. This was never a fight I was going to win—she's made sure of it.

A summer storm begins to roll in, flicking Leanna's braid in its turbulent winds as she stands over me, victorious.

"I never took you for one of those silly girls who would give a man the power to break her. I thought I taught you better than that. Now, get up," she spits through gritted teeth, taking a step back, waiting for me to do as she commands.

My arm trembles beneath me as I push myself off the ground, peeling my bloody face from the dirt, leaving a crimson stain on the floor of the ring. I have nothing left in me that I can call on to defend myself and she knows it. But I learned long ago that the punishment for disobedience will always far outweigh the momentary discomfort of my submission.

I'm not yet on my feet when the back of her hand slams against the side of my face, throwing me down to the ground. The jab is well-placed, landing high on my temple, and the world spins beneath me after another blinding shock of white takes over my vision.

"Your shadow lessons are over. The shadow master has already been sent away on a lengthy assignment. I've seen to it." Thunder rumbles in the distance, hiding the sound of the whimper I fail to suppress upon hearing the news. "You are more than proficient in the way of the shadow, so there will be no need for your lessons to resume if he returns."

My throat tightens around a strangled choke that burns as I suppress tears of rage. My mind reels, cradling that single phrase that threatens to undo me completely. *If* he returns. I can't tell if it's a threat or if she's simply stating the obvious. He is Drakai after all, and that means wherever she has sent him his life will be in danger.

Leanna crouches down and swipes the blood from my cheek with a painful stroke of her thumb.

"Do you see how weak he's made you? This is where trust gets you, Shivaria." She motions to my broken body, still bound and at her mercy. "Don't let anyone compromise you ever again. Not even me."

Her finger brushes the fine whisps of loose curls off my face, sending a fearful tremor down my spine.

"Cling to this lesson, hold it close. Because when you do forget it, which I have no doubt you will, and you decide it might be safe to let someone in, that person you choose to trust with your heart or your life, or something else precious to you, that person *will* betray you."

She reaches around my back and with a tug on the leather strap my binding sags, releasing its hold on my arm.

"Go change. Then come and find me. It's obvious there are some gaps in your education that need to be remedied."

She hovers above me, and though I don't meet her stare, I can feel her eyes burning against the side of my face.

"Kesh." Her mouth twists distastefully. "If I ever hear you use such an informal endearment with anyone again, I'll make sure they regret ever having met you."

Rain begins to fall as she turns toward the keep and makes her way inside, leaving me alone to stem the pain of every poisonous word spilled from her lips. It isn't the tender bruising I can already feel setting in on my cheek, or the sharp pain in my ribs that holds my attention. It's the wrenching of my heart as I contemplate life without the shadow master.

Rain patters my face, pooling in the crevice of my eye, running through the streaks of blood that paint my cheeks a shameful shade of red. The rain

is a welcome mask, hiding the evidence of the sorrow spilling from my eyes that I cannot control.

Leanna isn't wrong. The shadow master is a weakness, a distraction. One I selfishly keep because in my life that is only cold and desolate winter, he is the promise of spring.

I have no doubt he will regret knowing me after Leanna is finished with him. I tell myself I can handle his loathing, as long as he makes it back alive.

Looking to the keep, I force myself to my feet, bracing the rib I will need to have bound before finding Leanna for our next lesson. I don't let myself ponder what the lesson might be. As I slowly make my way out of the rain I swear to the stars that I will do whatever it takes to keep Vakesh from her fury, even if that means I will never live through another of the shadow master's springs.

Six Months Later

"Vari!"

The shadow master has been back from his mission for a week, and I have done everything I can to avoid him since his return. I'd managed to slip into the shadows the few times he'd gotten close to cornering me. I curse myself for letting my guard down as I venture into the snow-covered forest surrounding the keep in the early hours of dawn.

I turn to greet him. I won't be able to avoid him forever. My stomach twists at the sight of his perfect smile. A smile he only ever wears for me.

"I've been after you all week. I heard you passed the trial of shadow and wanted to congratulate you."

"Thank you." My voice sounds forced, even to me. "I appreciate all the time you put into my lessons. I didn't miss a single mark, and I'm sure that speaks more to your efforts as a teacher than to my own innate skill."

The smile shrinks from his face and his brow dips as he takes in my posture and the distance between us.

"Give yourself some credit, Vari. You have always been an exceptional student."

I dip my head. "I'm sure, now that you are back, you will find many exceptional students who are eager for your time."

In fact, a great many students have suffered in his absence. Leanna's vendetta against the shadow master caused many young Drakai to fall behind in their training. That she is willing to allow her precious Fea Dien to become weak to keep the man away speaks volumes about the lengths she is willing to go to distance him from me.

"I'm sure I can still find time to meet with you in the mornings," he says hesitantly.

"Thank you, but I have other studies that require all of my attention right now."

He studies me, his lips forming a thin line as he does. But the things I keep from him I've buried too far beneath the surface for him to expose.

"The offer is always there if you change your mind, Vari."

There is a palpable tension in his voice, but I know he won't press me. He never has.

I offer a half-hearted smile and a nod before he breaks into a run back the way he came. He doesn't look back and I don't blame him. He spent the last five years patiently breaching all my defenses and I've just slammed up an invisible battlement between us without explaining why.

I take a deep breath, the frigid air spearing my lungs, and I remind myself that this is all for him. Since Leanna sent him away, there is no doubt in my mind she will do whatever it takes to keep me away from the shadow master. If time and the missions she kept hurling at him did not prove to be a solution to her problem, she would take it into her own hands.

Despite the bitterness I felt when she sent him away so abruptly, she could never know the gift she had given me that day. For as much as I ached to say goodbye, I would never have wanted him to witness the wrath she laid bare upon my flesh because of our friendship. I know him too well to think he could let it go.

I will never tell him the full truth of what I endured that day. If I can spare him the guilty conscience that is sure to stem from that knowledge, I will. If it were ever in my power, I would do far more to spare him from even the slightest hurt.

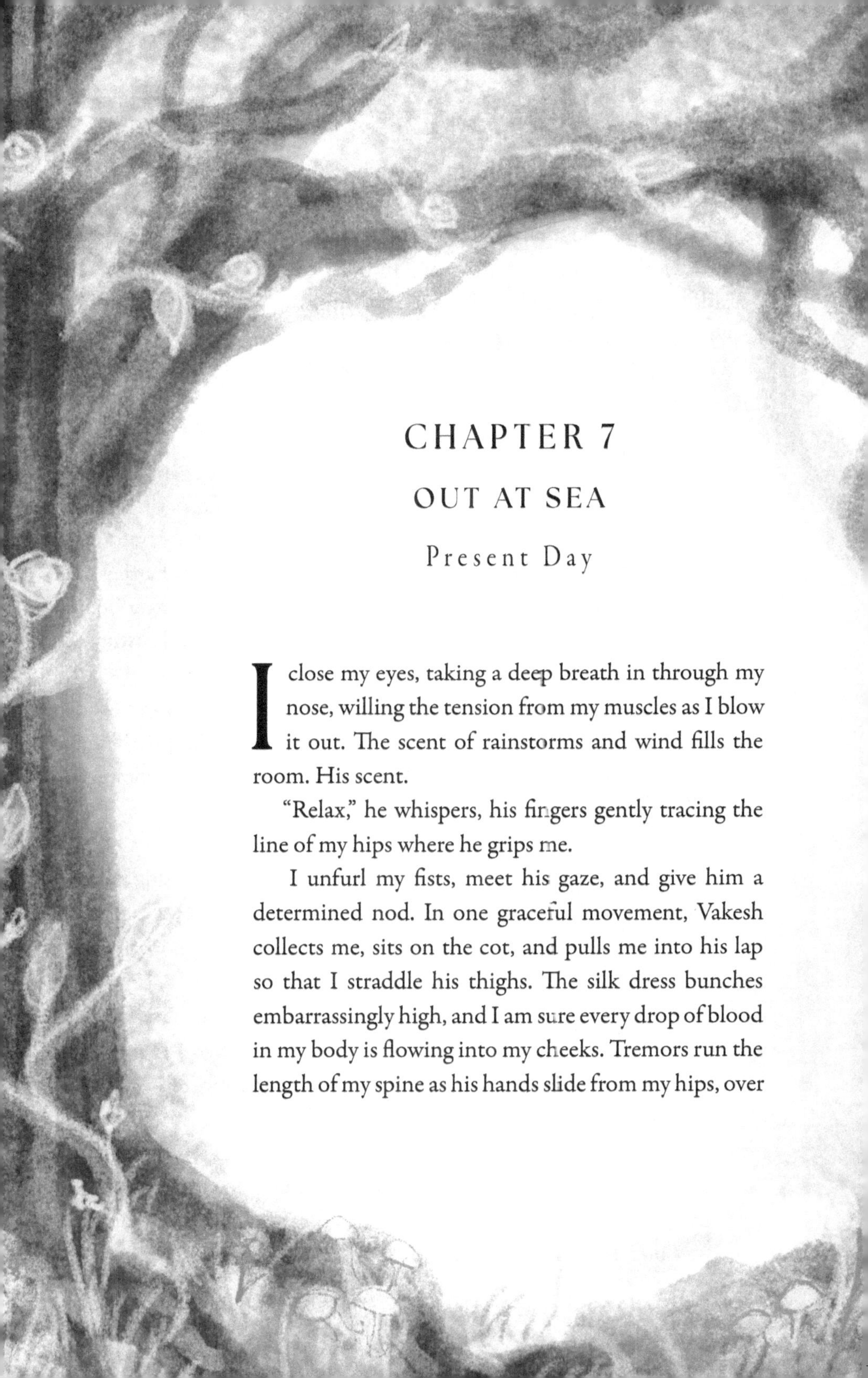

CHAPTER 7
OUT AT SEA
Present Day

I close my eyes, taking a deep breath in through my nose, willing the tension from my muscles as I blow it out. The scent of rainstorms and wind fills the room. His scent.

"Relax," he whispers, his fingers gently tracing the line of my hips where he grips me.

I unfurl my fists, meet his gaze, and give him a determined nod. In one graceful movement, Vakesh collects me, sits on the cot, and pulls me into his lap so that I straddle his thighs. The silk dress bunches embarrassingly high, and I am sure every drop of blood in my body is flowing into my cheeks. Tremors run the length of my spine as his hands slide from my hips, over the bunched fabric, and onto my bare thighs, his thumbs stroking softly.

His dark eyes are locked on mine, pupils blown so wide that it feels like if I lean in, I can follow those dark pools straight into the depths of his soul. I want to run from the room and beg him for more all at once. I am a tangle of nerves, teetering on the edge of the unknown with a man I trust with my life. Countless questions bubble to the surface of my mind and there isn't enough air in my lungs to form a single one.

Adjusting himself beneath me, he pulls me close until his lips brush the shell of my ear.

"Stop thinking about it," he says.

Before I can argue, before I can think, his fingers sweep against my core, buffered by the thin swath of fabric beneath my dress. He drags a single finger across my center, swiping up until it brushes that tender bundle of nerves between my legs. My breath catches in my throat, and I swallow hard. A vain attempt to dislodge my voice. He grins like a fool, hooks his finger behind the delicate barrier between us and pulls, tearing the seams and casting the garment to the floor.

His hand follows the length of my thigh until he sweeps against the wet evidence of my desire, now bared to him. He inhales sharply the same moment I do, his mask slipping almost imperceptibly, his composure regained so quickly that I question what I've seen.

Why does he hide from me?

His fingers slowly glide across my entrance, teasing and parting me only to retreat and begin again, both taunting and promising. His eyes take in my breasts as my nipples peak against the taut fabric holding them in, brushing against him with every heaving breath I take.

"Kesh." It comes out in a breathy plea as I close my eyes, resting my forehead against his.

With a slow caress he parts me, his fingers gathering the slick need between my legs. I want more and, without thinking, press my hips forward, my desire, my very nature, urging him inside of me.

He hisses and withdraws his hand. "None of that."

I hold my breath, wishing I hadn't pressed for more than he is willing to give. That breath releases in a sigh when he pushes his hand back between

my thighs. His finger strokes in lazy circles, drawing up and rounding that tiny bud of sensitive nerves like liquid silk.

I can't help the moan that escapes my lips as my eyelids flutter closed. My stomach clenches with every stroke of his finger, and his grip tightens around my waist. The darkness within me dampens, replaced by a need that quickly builds into a single blinding focus. It threatens to overwhelm me, but I ride it as it grows into a shuddering climax, the sweetest release.

"Well done," Kesh whispers as every muscle in my body goes slack.

He releases my hip, gently brushing stray hairs off my flushed cheeks, tucking them behind my ears as I sway in his lap.

"Why don't you try to get some sleep, and I'll come back in a few hours?" he says softly, lifting me off his lap, smoothing my dress back down to the floor. "If it keeps your monsters at bay, you can do it yourself next time."

The smile he offers me before he leaves seems forced, but maybe he simply feels as awkward as I do. Sleep doesn't come easily, though I feel like it should. Every unasked question plays on a loop in my mind but only one really worries me.

Will this change everything? No. I don't think so. It can't.

Because there is nothing in this world I would take, nothing I wouldn't keep if it meant he will never look at me the same way again. Not even my demon. I will keep it without question and fight it gladly every night for the rest of my life if things can only stay the same. I just can't help the feeling that it's too late and that I've just sacrificed the most precious thing I have in this world on the altar of my own stupidity.

"How were your dreams last night?"

Vakesh sits across from me, a variety of fruits arranged thoughtfully on the table between us. He arrived late in the morning, wearing his usual cheeky smile, filling my heart with promises of normality. Though he seems to be unchanged by last night's lesson, I eye him skeptically.

"Muddled?" I sip the hot black tea he brought with him, tilting my head to the side thoughtfully. "The dreams were the same, only less—"

"Violent?" He quirks an eyebrow.

I smile and shake my head. "They were just *less*. I'm not sure how else to describe it."

"And if you were home, would you be heading for the sparring ring this morning?"

"Absolutely." I grin.

He frowns at that.

"But only because I love reminding Bront that he hasn't bested me in years," I say.

A beaming smile followed by his beautiful laughter causes his eyes to sparkle in the dim light of the room. "I'm not sure he needs to be reminded. You were barely eighteen when I realized you'd already outgrown most of your teachers."

"When did I outgrow you?" I ask slyly, eyeing him over my steamy mug.

"If I'm still teaching you things, you haven't outgrown me yet."

The air in the room seems to still around us and I swear I hear his muscles creak under the tension.

"I suppose you're right," I laugh, trying to lighten the mood. "Though I admit, I'm glad it was you and not Leanna who taught me my last lesson."

His laugh booms into the room, his eyes watering, and just like that, the tension dissipates from his body and the weight that had settled between us evaporates.

Us. We are just us. We are happy, and nothing will change.

I spend the entire day reminding myself of it. Every time he laughs, every sarcastic comment and cheeky smile he graces me with, I tell myself we are fine.

He stays through the day, and we reminisce about the years I was his student.

"You were always my favorite," he admits, as if I don't know.

"And you were always mine," I assure him with my sweetest smile. And my heart aches because for some reason I can't quite understand, the words feel a little too much like goodbye.

He stays for dinner, leaving shortly after with promises of returning in the morning. Two more days at sea and the following dawn will see us at port in A'kori, forcing us to part ways for stars only knows how long. Too many unknowns exist in each of our futures to make promises of days to come.

I hate that it bothers me, and I hate Leanna for tearing us apart years ago. 'You were always my favorite.' The words play over in my mind. Leanna knew it and thought his favor made me weak, in more ways than she would ever say. Leanna always had her reasons, and I have lived alongside her long enough to know that she is usually right in her decisions. Just one more thing I will never admit to her.

I hang my dress in the wardrobe and settle into my cot for the night, leaving the lantern low. My thoughts turn to my lesson early that morning and once again, questions flood my mind. Is this something I will have to do every night? Not that I mind, but it could prove difficult if ever I have to share a room. Would Leanna approve? Do I care? Can I even do this on my own?

It is the last that stops the torrent of questions flooding through my mind. None of the others matter if I can't accomplish for myself what Vakesh had so easily done for me. I roll onto my back, exhale deeply, and, with my brow furrowed in determination, shove my hand between my legs. I mimic his movements exactly. A circling here, a swirl there, light dip, and glide. My stomach clenches and my body jerks away from my hand in clear disapproval.

Too much pressure. Try again.

Twenty minutes later I growl in frustration. If Vakesh can call my release within seconds, there is no reason I cannot do the same. I debate trying again. I debate letting the dreams take hold and trying again in the morning. I debate *pitch*.

How quickly can I find a source in A'kori?

I decide on pulling the service bell rope. Five minutes later a knock sounds, and I open the door to be greeted by a rather sleep rumpled captain wearing a tired glare.

Clutching a sheet to my chest, I simply say, "Ale, lots of it."

He grunts as he leaves to procure my request. I will hide the evidence and bathe before Vakesh comes by in the morning. What he doesn't know won't hurt me or lead to potentially embarrassing questions about my own inadequacy.

I leap across the room gleefully when the knock sounds, announcing my late-night delivery. The smile quickly falls from my face when I am met with

Vakesh on the other side, half brooding, half cheeky smile. He raises the jug of ale, swinging it on his finger as he quirks a brow.

I pull my shoulders back, raise my chin defiantly with a simple, "Thank you," and reach for the jug.

He only snatches it away before pushing his way into my room.

"I didn't realize the captain was one of your spies," I say sweetly, adjusting the sheet wrapped around my body. Closing the door, I mentally prepare for the disappointment that is undoubtedly about to spill from his lips.

"A small piece of advice, *mi'ajna*?" He smiles. "Simply assume for the rest of your life that everyone you ever meet is one of my spies and you will never be caught off guard again."

It's good advice, but I'm not about to tell him just how seriously I'm going to take it.

Vakesh settles into the chair opposite my cot, so I make myself comfortable on the edge of my bed. He sets the jug on the table, tauntingly, and pushes it slowly toward me.

"Want to talk about it?" he asks, crossing his arms across his chest as he pins me with a stare.

"Not really," I admit.

"You and I had a deal. Get it under control or I put you off the ship before we reach A'kori."

I want to scream that we hadn't made a deal, that he is being a domineering ass, and that he needs to mind his own business. But he's right, and we both know it. I can't drink myself into oblivion every night, and all it will take is one episode, a single morning where I wake fighting for my life, and no one will ever let me near the king.

"Was it not—" Vakesh sighs, and I watch, puzzled, as he tries to gather his thoughts. "Did the lesson not have the desired affect?"

"I told you it did," I answer, my brow pinching in confusion.

"But you didn't care for it?" he guesses, nodding his head as if that is the only reasonable conclusion. "You really should at least attempt it yourself. It is an entirely different experience."

I swallow the lump in my throat and will my cheeks not to flush. I haven't felt like such a child since I rounded the stables at the age of twelve and found a boy of my year with his pants around his ankles and a hand full of himself. After demanding the boy's name, Leanna had drawn me a rather crude anatomical diagram to explain what exactly it was I'd seen, and I never saw the boy again.

"Or don't try it at all," Vakesh quickly adds, with a dismissive flick of his wrist, unwilling to bring his eyes to mine. "It isn't for everyone and if it isn't something you enjoyed—"

"I did," I say, and his eyes shoot to mine. "I did enjoy it."

"But?" he asks, raising an eyebrow.

"But..."

How on Terr does he expect me to have this conversation with him without humiliating myself?

I cross my legs, and his eyes traverse my skin as the sheet falls to the side, baring me to the hip. I have never felt the need to be overly modest around him before, but now, for reasons I'm still trying to devise, the small ribbon of flesh on display feels vulnerable. Yet there is an undeniable sense of power in it as well.

"Do you remember when we began my dagger lessons?" I ask.

He smiles and chokes out a small laugh that he quickly hides behind a horrendously fake cough as he schools his features. I squint my eyes at him in mock anger. He promised never to laugh about it again. I suppose he is doing his best, and all things considered, I can hardly blame him.

"You made it look so easy," I continue, "You stood in the yard and threw dagger after dagger, each crowding the other at the center of the target."

His eyes gleam and I can see that he is lost in the memory that we share.

"You were so sure of yourself, you never hesitated, never faltered. As I watched you, I remember thinking for a moment that I could be just as good as you, if only I had your confidence."

His mouth cracks into a genuine toothy grin, it's glorious.

"You never told me that," he says, choking down another laugh. "I always wondered what you were thinking when you plucked a dagger from the rack and looked me in the eye as you threw the blade across the yard without so much as a glance toward the target."

His entire face turns beet red as veins begin to bulge in his neck and forehead.

</p>

"All right, you can laugh, but just this once."

I smile as he gives into himself, a beautiful chuckle tumbling from his lips.

"Stars," he gasps, "I thought Petron would murder you when your dagger found it's mark in his arm."

I can't help myself and let loose a laugh at the memory as well. My dagger struck a full ten span off the mark, lodging itself solidly into the arm of the general's favorite son. He was a cocky bastard of a man and even Bront had forgiven me for it, saying that anyone who stood close enough to a target to be struck by a blade deserved what they got. Petron had taken a few months off to recover, and the incident had been quickly forgotten by all but Vakesh who needled me endlessly about it.

"It took months before I learned to strike the center of the target," I continue.

"It took you less than a week," he corrects, and I roll my eyes.

"My point is, I did learn a valuable lesson that day. There is no substitute for practice and no honed skill that comes without the investment of time."

"So," he says, his brow creasing, "you need time?"

"I need practice," I say, "And, maybe some instruction?"

He seems a little surprised by the request but nods thoughtfully and agrees. I admit to him that I failed miserably at my earlier attempt, and he doesn't laugh or make any quips, he just listens until I'm finished talking.

"You said you did it *exactly* how I showed you?" he asks curiously, his brow arching ever so slightly.

"Exactly," I say.

He nods, as if I've just confirmed something he suspects.

"This isn't like sparring, Vari. Routine won't help you. It isn't so much about the movements as it is the feeling, and I can't teach you to feel it. That's all you."

"That is utterly unhelpful." I smile dryly.

He returns the smile, rises from his chair, and points to the bed.

"Lie down and practice."

I do as he says, adjusting the sheet over my body as I get comfortable, fully expecting him to leave me to it. My skin prickles when Vakesh settles himself by my side and observes me. I remind myself that I did just ask the man for instruction and will my nerves to settle as I lay beneath his gaze.

Like before, I push my hand beneath the covers and between my legs. Before I reach my core his hand snakes down the sheets, following the path of my arm and settles like a vice around my wrist. He pulls my hand out from within the sheet and rests it on my breast.

"Start here."

"You didn't," I argue.

"I didn't need to. The first is always..."

"Easier?"

"With the right person, yes. Now, focus on the feeling."

I close my eyes and keep my hand on my breast, kneading the soft tissue. Maybe he's wrong about this part. I know men have an odd fascination with them, but they don't have to manage them the way women do. Does he touch his own when he does this to himself?

No. Absolutely not. I am not thinking about this.

But it's too late and the image is already in my mind. Just like the boy I found, holding himself. Before I can shake the image, the featherlight touch of Vakesh's nimble fingers swirl along the rosy skin that surrounds my nipple.

"Like this," he whispers and my stomach clenches as he lightly pinches the peaked flesh and my back arches off the bed.

My breath quickens and his fingers move to my side, tracing the curve of my figure until reaching my hip. I sigh contentedly.

Why do his hands feel so much better than mine?

I hear him smile and he removes his hand, grabbing my wrist and guiding my own hand along the same sensitive lines of my body he traced moments before.

"Practice," he says softly, "I'll see you in the morning."

He snuffs out the lantern before leaving me to it. After what feels like an eternity, my hand starts cramping between my thighs. I tear it from within the sheets, grumbling under my breath as I slam my head back against the pillow in frustration.

I give up and my eyes wander toward the jug of ale that I'm sure is still sitting on the small table in the pitch black of my room, beckoning. I reject the idea before really considering it and settle in for a night of terror and a morning of bloodlust.

The woman falls to the floor reaching for me. She's so pretty, even when the light leaves her eyes.

A tall man with broad shoulders and strong arms bellows. His face is a mask of rage as a blade pierces his neck. The gurgling spurt of his agony makes my eyes burn, but I can't make myself look away as his blood runs like a river down his chest and onto the floor. He falls to his knees and my eyes take in the demon towering behind him. Black flames lick off the dark scales that adorn it. It steps toward me, reaching, a bloody blade marring the wooden floor as it drags it behind.

Its fist closes around my throat. I can't scream. I can't even breathe.

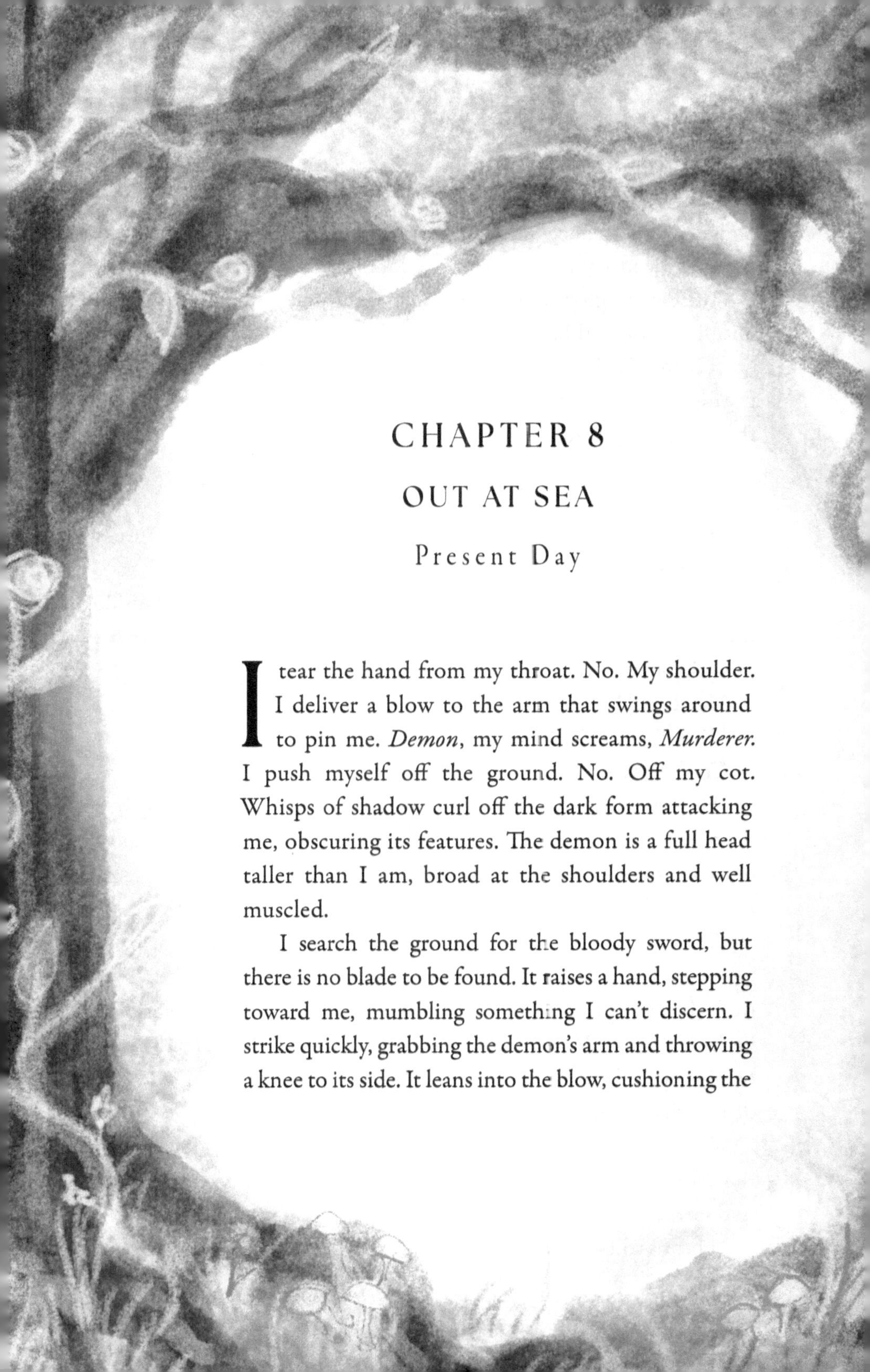

CHAPTER 8
OUT AT SEA
Present Day

I tear the hand from my throat. No. My shoulder. I deliver a blow to the arm that swings around to pin me. *Demon*, my mind screams, *Murderer.* I push myself off the ground. No. Off my cot. Whisps of shadow curl off the dark form attacking me, obscuring its features. The demon is a full head taller than I am, broad at the shoulders and well muscled.

I search the ground for the bloody sword, but there is no blade to be found. It raises a hand, stepping toward me, mumbling something I can't discern. I strike quickly, grabbing the demon's arm and throwing a knee to its side. It leans into the blow, cushioning the impact, and holds my leg against its side, moving forward to tip my balance.

I push off the ground with my free leg, letting it bear my weight on the leg secured at its side, throwing the force into a spinning kick that it barely dodges. My leg glances off its head. It is faster than I am, stronger too. I am going to die in a bloody heap on the floor just like them. I know it.

The demon growls, an unintelligible, guttural sound, shifting its weight until I am truly off balance. I begin to fall, and it hooks an arm around my waist before I collapse onto the floor. It throws me against the wall, pinning my hips with its own, before catching my wrists in one hand and securing them above my head.

Breathe, I demand of myself, *Breathe.*

But it isn't my voice I hear.

"Breathe. Vari, wake up. You're all right. It isn't real." The voice turns gentle.

Safe. You're safe. It isn't real.

A familiar scent fills my lungs, calming the demon that roils inside me. I lean into him, taking a deep breath, resting my head in the crook of his neck. His grip on my wrists slackens.

"I'm here," he murmurs.

"Kesh?" My voice breaks.

"Yes," he says.

He wraps his arms around me and pulls me close as my body begins to shake. This is about the time I would normally be letting Bront land a blow or two in the sparring ring, to refocus my mind.

"What do you need?"

What do I need? I need to start wearing a night dress to bed.

With that thought, I peel myself out of his arms and take a step away from the man, pressing my back against the wall as I will the world to come back into focus. Vakesh keeps his eyes on my face as I stand before him baring more than my naked body. The man just witnessed a sliver of the demon that torments me.

A dim candle sits on a small shelf by the door, its warm glow highlighting the sheen of sweat on his bare torso. I wonder when he came, how much he'd seen, and how it is that he always seems to know when I need him.

"I heard you screaming," he says, as if he can read my every thought.

"I'm sorry."

"No," he says, sternly, "*I* am sorry. I shouldn't have left you the way I did. I should have stayed. Made sure you…" His jaw feathers as his lips draw a thin line.

He takes a step toward me and leans against the wall. Towering over me, he braces a thick well-muscled arm on either side.

He takes a deep breath and gently repeats his question, his demand, "Tell me what you need."

I press a hand to his chest and puff out a breath. "I need to spar."

"I think we already tried that." He smiles, placing his hand over mine reassuringly. "But I'm not opposed to another round."

I eye the small space and consider it. I'm shocked when I find that nothing was broken in our skirmish, but I seriously doubt the rickety furniture adorning the room will make it through another bout.

I check on the darkness inside me, finding it coiled like a snake. It isn't sleeping but it isn't roiling either. It waits, for what I have no idea. The feeling is unnerving.

"Where do you find your release when you spar?" he asks. "Is it your control in the ring?"

"No." I shake my head. "It's when I let that control slip, when I let go and lean into the chaos."

His brows shoot up and he smiles his understanding. He knows the feeling, every Drakai does. Control is life and to lack it often leads to one's demise. To embrace the chaos is to go against our very nature but to be at ease in that space, to be settled when you lack control, is also necessary and a far more difficult lesson to learn.

"No wonder you are struggling with your lessons." He smiles wickedly, wrapping a calloused hand around my throat. "Tell me to stop and it ends," he whispers, giving me a moment to end it before it even begins.

I hold his gaze, saying nothing, willing myself to let that control slip. His hips press against mine, pinning me to the wall of my cabin. I consider that this is the same lesson he taught me when he settled me onto his lap. It is, but it isn't.

This feels … different. Almost as if we are sparring, but not quite. His hips roll against me, his hard length rocking against the sensitive nub of nerves above my core. I moan at the friction and his hand tightens around my throat.

My fingers tangle in the locks of his hair. He lets go of my neck and collects my wrists, pinning them above my head. I'm vaguely aware that this is the same position he was holding me in when I woke from my bloody vision, but its meaning is altogether different. He leans into me, his chest pressing against mine, his lips brushing against the ridge of my shoulder in featherlight sweeps.

Closer, I need him closer.

He pushes a hand between us, and the friction of his pants is replaced by his palm. He snakes a single finger against my core, parting me, and my stomach clenches as his breathing quickens against the tingling skin of my neck.

"Kesh," I whisper, "I want more."

His body stills against my own, rigid with hesitation, a low rumble forming deep within his chest.

"There is only so much I can give you right now, *mi'ajna*," he says, his voice tinged in regret.

I push him back until I can see the dark pools of his eyes then lean toward him with an offering of parted lips, my gaze dipping to his mouth. He tenses, his eyes flicking to my lips then back to my eyes as the rumble in his chest grows. I can feel the heat of his breath on my skin along with all the hesitation spooling in his body. I see the moment he holds himself back from me, and I bury the loss before it snags on the threads of my heart, unwilling to let it spoil what he is willing to give me in this moment.

"I want everything," I say softly, wholly aware that I have no idea what I am asking for but wanting all of him, nonetheless.

"You ask for too much." I watch a silent battle rage in his eyes.

"Don't think about it," I say, offering him some of his own advice, and before he can protest, I hook my legs around his waist, settling the heat of my core against the thick length beneath his pants.

He presses into me, pushing my back against the wall to hold my weight as his hands hook my thighs right below my ass.

Resting his head against mine he whispers, "You're already going to hate me for this."

I don't want to think about all the ways this can end poorly. I want to tell

him there is nothing he could ever do to make me hate him. But right now, I just need him to stay.

"Say stop and it ends," I tell him, the words fleeing my lungs in a breathy whisper. I push my hand down, grabbing a handful of the hard shaft between us.

Even buffered by the fabric of his pants he shudders at the connection and his hips buck against my arm. With a growl, he spins us around, dropping me onto my cot and draping himself over me. His eyes are ablaze with something akin to the darkness I fight within myself. I wonder what demons haunt the master of shadow.

He drags my hand from between us, bringing it to his lips. Brushing my knuckles against them, he sucks my thumb into his mouth, swirling his tongue around it. My core tightens when he pulls it out with a wet *pop*. He presses his thumb against my bottom lip, my mouth opening at his silent command. My tongue works its way around the digit, just as his did mine. His chest vibrates with a rumble as he watches, before pulling his thumb out with a satisfied smile.

"Good girl," he says, and those two simple words begin to unravel me.

He circles the sensitive nub above my core with the same thumb, warm and slick, as he presses himself against my entrance. My body clenches and my hips rise to meet him. Frustration frays the edges of my pleasure when I feel the press of the thin fabric of his pants between us.

He lightly flicks that tender nub before soothing it with another caress and the demon roils inside me. My body begins to shake beneath him as my hands wind their way down his sides. They steal memories of the hard lines of his body, tucking them away for safekeeping, before my fingers slide beneath his pants, pushing them down his legs.

He catches my hands and pulls at his pants until they rest securely around his waist again, before he fists my hair, pulling my head back to expose my neck. He grazes his teeth along the lobe of my ear, the heat of his breath teasing fine whisps of hair when he whispers, "So greedy."

I whimper as two fingers spread the entrance of my core and another slides right down the center. His thumb strums my sensitive nub and his fingers dip inside me, shallow and taunting as he issues a near silent demand, "Come for me, *mi'ajna*."

With that simple command I come undone. His lips brush the crook of my neck, and he sighs deeply when my back arches, pressing my breasts against his chest, his body shuddering as if he too found his release. His fingers sweep over me through the duration of my peak. Slowly, when my shattered soul settles back into my body and I collapse fully onto the cot, his attentions cease.

He pushes himself off me unceremoniously, plucking the sheet off the floor, where I assume it landed earlier. Draping it across my body, he examines my face, struggling to school his own features.

"It's still early. Sleep if you can. I have business on shore today."

He lingers by the edge of the cot, his eyes sweeping over my body as if the sheet fails to hide what lay beneath. His eyes land on mine and his face dissolves into the blank mask worn by the master of shadows before he makes his way toward the door.

"Tell me I'll see you again before we reach the northern continent." When I voice my request, his stride falters mid step.

"You'll see me again," he says without looking back, and then he's gone.

I don't know why I ask but if he says I will see him, I know he'll keep his word.

As hard as I try, sleep never comes. Vakesh took the air out of the room right along with him when he left. I lay in bed pondering my future as well as my past. Tonight will be my last night aboard the ship and then I will be lost to the northern kingdom until my mission is complete. I will return home a hero, with the blood of a king on my hands. I just have to get to him first.

I never met a single soul on the southern continent that would not see the feyn king dead. Each would have ended him if they had been capable of completing the task themselves. There are plenty of war-torn orphans just like me, willing to seek vengeance at any cost. The king of A'kori knows it, and I have long suspected that it is this simple fact that keeps him hidden away.

Not a single La'tarian has seen the male for more than eighty years. My own king may have even suspected him dead had it not been for the steady stream of men and women beckoned to the court of A'kori. While most of my people would never take a bride from across the sea, it seems there is something the feyn find appealing about our people.

I try to remember if I've ever been told how old he is. Had I ever thought to ask? I suppose it doesn't really matter. As far as I know, all feyn were immortal before the sundering. While he may not be immortal like his ancestors, they continue to have unnaturally long lives compared to that of a mortal like myself.

He is gifted, that much I am sure of. Which means he at least has some feyn blood in his veins, though how much feyn blood qualifies someone for the gifts of their kind I have no idea.

I ring the service bell for a basin of water, soap, and a small amount of food which the captain is happy to supply. He says nothing when I hand him back the full jug of ale he'd provided me with the night prior. I can't help but laugh when he lugs it toward his quarters rather than returning it to be stowed.

I wash in the small basin and stuff what remains of my jasmine soap into a small leather pouch. The floral scent is like nothing I have ever used before, and, despite my best efforts not to care, I love the way it clings to me.

I work my hair into its usual spirals as it dries, then set out the dress Leanna selected for me. She had been quite particular about the cut of it and what jewelry I should wear to adorn it upon my arrival. I have no doubt that the king receives a full report of every lady that makes the journey across the sea.

The day goes by in a blur of contemplation, but the ships withdrawal from port bristles me. Heavy footsteps sound on deck, and I shoot to my feet, head tilting to the side in an attempt to understand the muffled shouts from the crew. The ship pitches to the side, throwing me to the floor. I land with a heavy thud and a curse on my lips, scrambling to my feet seconds later.

The cacophony from the deck above quickly fades. The chaotic sounds replaced by a muffled shout into the bowels of the ship. I stand close to the door, poised to strike for quite some time, both waiting for my small room to be raided and ready to burst out from within to enter the fray if necessary. But no one comes. The shouting is replaced by the lulling drone of the creaking ship as it rolls across the waves on the open ocean.

Long after the commotion ends, I pace uneasily. I hate being left in the dark. The small rope by the door begs to be pulled, summoning the captain so that I might demand answers, but I can't bring myself to do it. If there is a problem, I will only be drawing him away from his duties and if not, I can wait.

I plait my hair only to take it out again ten times over as I sit on the edge of my cot. My stomach growls. Still, I make no move to pull the rope.

I know it is only a matter of time before Kesh comes and explains to me what happened. He will laugh about the fact that I have been worried and tell me a story of when we first met that he thinks I've forgotten. It's what he always does to soothe me. I never stop him to tell him that there isn't a single moment of the years we've spent together that I have forgotten, because I love it when he tells those stories.

Late into the night, my stomach is a twisted mess of knots. I rest my head against the lumpy pillow on my cot and sleep finally wins out over worry. I only stir when a familiar weight settles down beside me.

"Sorry to keep you waiting," he says, brushing a finger against my cheek.

My eyes focus on the man sitting before me and I will myself not to cry, not to make for the door and turn the ship back to port so that I can level that town under the weight of my fury. His skin is pale, and dark circles stain the flesh around his eyes. Some of it is bruising, some of it is something else entirely.

I sit up and clutch his jaw, tilting his head to examine his face from every angle, my brow drawing down as I ask, "What in haliel happened?"

"Just a little tussle with some of the locals," he says, wincing under the attentions of my hand.

It isn't the broken flesh on his knuckles or the fact that they are caked in dry blood that stirs the demon inside me. It is the hand wrapping his waist and the pressure he keeps on his side, obscuring an injury.

"Show me," I demand coldly.

"It's nothing," he says.

"I said, show me." My voice doesn't falter, and he concedes, standing and letting his hand fall so that I can inspect the wound beneath.

I rise to my knees on the cot, carefully lifting the fabric of his tunic, swallowing a gasp. A long gash runs horizontally across his side, and given the placement, he is lucky the blade struck a rib bone and not the vulnerable flesh between. It isn't life threatening, barring infection, and has already been stitched shut. My throat bobs as I lay the fabric back against his side.

"How did this happen?"

In answer, he settles a small leather pouch in the palm of my hand. I

untie the leather strap that binds it, nearly dropping the small bundle onto the cot when I look inside.

"Pitch?!" I hiss, in shock.

His brow creases. "There is no veil in the sundering in which I would ever give you pitch, Vari. It's an herb, a sedative. It will help you with the dreams. Use it sparingly. Try another way to find your release if you can manage. You're not likely to find more of this, so when you run out, you are on your own."

I can feel my blood heating beneath my skin as my hands begin to shake.

"You let them beat you, for this?!" I yell, shooting to my feet to glower at him closer to eye level.

I have no idea who 'them' is but nothing this man could give me would be worth risking his life.

"I got you what you needed," he bites back.

I can't let myself think about what he went through to get the herb. It isn't simple thugs that did this to him. This isn't some deal in a dark alley gone awry. Who on the whole of Terr could come so close to ending the master of shadows with only a blade?

"I don't *need* this," I spit out as I throw the pouch to the floor. "I *need* you, in one piece."

"You've never needed me, Vari," he says flatly.

"Fine." I ball my fists at my sides and swallow, shoving down every survival instinct beaten into me over the years. "I don't *want* it. I *want* you."

"In one piece," he adds, matter-of-factly.

I swallow hard, forcing myself to step forward despite every instinct I possess rebelling against the action. I rest my forehead against his chest and breathe in his scent.

My stomach twists as a truth I have been unwilling to admit, even to myself, tumbles from my lips unbidden. "I just want *you*, Kesh."

There is a moment, I think I feel him lean into me. I imagine his arms wrapping me up and pulling me against him, as he whispers every promise my heart yearns to pry from his lips. When he does speak, my blood runs cold.

"You're letting your guard down, Vari."

My back stiffens and he takes a step back, out of my reach in so many brutal ways. Every muscle in my body coils as I prepare for the blow he is about

to land. He's said it hundreds of times throughout the years, always during our training. It's the way he's always told me I am about to lose. A small mercy in his own way, so that I can observe the mistake before he ends me.

My eyes reluctantly rise to his face. He wears his mask so well, his eyes void of all emotion, making me feel every bit the student as he looks down on me.

"Don't," I beg, nearly choking on my plea.

"You are never to trust anyone with knowledge like that again."

"Except you," I argue.

He has always been the exception.

"Not even me," he growls, "Everyone is dangerous, those you trust and let into your confidence even more so."

"But you would never—"

"Stop!" he shouts. "Whatever it is you are about to say, I would, I have, and I will again. You are going to get yourself killed if you continue to believe anyone is the version of themselves they show you. It's all the dark hateful bits we keep tucked away that truly make us who we are, and no one is ever going to trust you with those."

"Stop it, Kesh. You sound like Leanna." My voice is weak, my mouth dry, but there is still venom when I hurl the words at him.

"And you," he says pointing a finger at me, unable to stop his hand from shaking as his words rush out in a torrent, "sound like a petulant child on the verge of tears because she's been told she can't play with her favorite toy."

I take every word he hurls at me like the soldier I am. Back stiff, chin high, eyes nailed forward. All while he breaks apart the most fragile parts of myself, pieces I trusted him to keep safe when I laid them at his feet.

Once he is sure I won't talk back he stalks toward the door, stopping with his hand on the lever.

"I hate to be the one to break it to you, Shivaria, but all your toys are broken. And if, by some cruel twist of fate, you are ever handed something pristine I recommend you discard it before your own damage infects it, turning it into something you could never adore."

I don't flinch when the door slams shut behind him. I don't fall to my knees and cry. I just feel sorry for her, the girl standing alone in the room. The girl I was before.

I try to map out a memory of that girl, knowing in the deepest recesses of my mind I will never see her again. There are parts of her I will have forgotten ten years from now, parts of her that I'm sure important people in my distant future would have liked to meet and will now never know—parts I wish to preserve and parts I wish to forget.

I snatch the small leather pouch from the floor, spend an hour teasing my curls into perfection, and artfully place a plethora of jewels into my tresses until the silky black spirals sparkle like the heavens under a new moon.

Leanna chose well when she packed the dress I wear for my arrival. The neckline sweeps high and wide across my shoulders. The thin fabric covers every part of my body, and yet somehow the ivory of it blends seamlessly with my skin leaving nothing to the imagination.

I pull a light cloak over my shoulders, the shade of grey a perfect match for my eyes. The small leather pouch, left by the master of shadows, I place inside a well-hidden interior pocket, wondering if the substance is even legal. Best to keep it out of sight, just in case.

I wait on my cot, and it isn't long before the ship drops anchor in port. When the captain comes to collect me, I follow him without hesitation, leaving behind the Drakai woman I was only hours before, in the small room where she was broken apart.

"Lady Shivaria." The captain offers me his arm and puffs out his chest as I survey his dress uniform and nod my approval.

Hooking his elbow with mine, I seamlessly slip on the mask of the woman I was born to play. The captain makes a show of parading me around the upper deck. His crew take me in, whispering amongst themselves. No doubt they have all been wondering about the secret lady brought across the sea hoping to tempt the king. Locals working the dock eye me and fine carriages slow as they make their way past, their passengers peering out curiously.

A simple but elegant carriage pulls up to the bottom of the gangway and the captain escorts me down to the pier. The door swings open and out saunters a somewhat plump, tall man with dark eyes and meticulously groomed golden hair that exquisitely contrasts his rosewood complexion. He's dressed in an ostentatious purple velvet suit with diamond crusted buttons. Plucking a colorful handkerchief from his pocket, he glares down at a fresh pile of manure. Waving the fabric in front of his face, he skirts the pile with practiced grace, smiling when he looks up at me.

"Ah, my lovely niece!" he says when he reaches me, kissing each cheek before pulling me into a warm embrace. "It is so good to see you. How is my dear brother? Oh my, how you have grown!" he beams and gestures toward the carriage. "Come. I am sure you are tired after your long journey."

I let the captain pass me off to the stranger, taking the arm he offers. The moment my foot touches the carriage step my skin prickles as a gentle breeze glides across my cheek, bringing with it the scent of a storm. My back stiffens involuntarily and my step falters. I already know what I will see if I turn around. So instead, I thank my uncle for his arm, and step into the carriage without looking back.

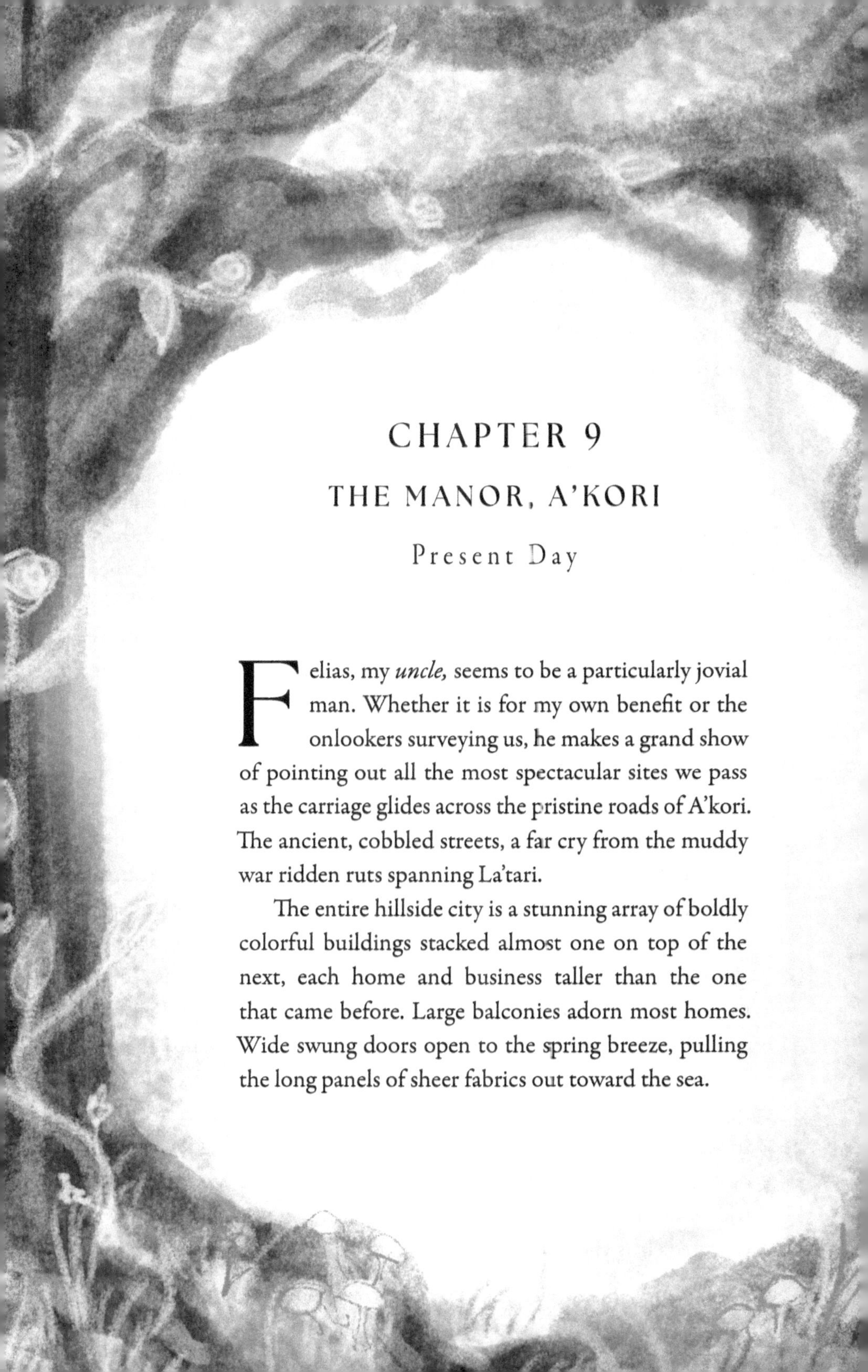

CHAPTER 9
THE MANOR, A'KORI
Present Day

Felias, my *uncle,* seems to be a particularly jovial man. Whether it is for my own benefit or the onlookers surveying us, he makes a grand show of pointing out all the most spectacular sites we pass as the carriage glides across the pristine roads of A'kori. The ancient, cobbled streets, a far cry from the muddy war ridden ruts spanning La'tari.

The entire hillside city is a stunning array of boldly colorful buildings stacked almost one on top of the next, each home and business taller than the one that came before. Large balconies adorn most homes. Wide swung doors open to the spring breeze, pulling the long panels of sheer fabrics out toward the sea.

Thoughtfully designed cliffside parks are decorated with large copper statues, long patinaed by the salty sea air. Many look out toward the open waters of the ocean, so lifelike in their crafting it is as if they once stood watch only to become frozen in their form after centuries of guarding their homes.

A gentle gust tickles my nose, teasing it with the scent of fresh baked sweet breads, and my stomach betrays me with a loud gurgle. Bells hung over the doors of the local shops ring cheerfully as patrons come and go, blending into the quiet hum of greetings and goodbyes. It is a far cry from the dark city I expect to find.

The main boulevard feels as if it will continue to wind endlessly north until, at once, the city ends, breaking from the colorful walls and parting into an open expanse of lush, wild greenery. In the distance, the palace sits nestled against the base of many high snowy peaks. Its dark spires reach hundreds of feet high, puncturing the clouds as if they were built to adorn them like a crown. Rays of the early morning sun refract off the windows of the tallest spires, casting out light in a glittering array, like jewels among the heavens.

"Is it not grand?" my uncle says on a sigh, clearly enamored with the sight, and I can't argue; it's breathtaking.

Only once have I been to the La'tari capital. It was there that I'd been selected to serve as Drakai, though Leanna trained me for five years before presenting me to the king. Since the day she found me, at the tender age of four, every waking moment was spent instructing me.

I doubted my acceptance into the fold when Leanna took me before the king. It was no secret I was Leanna's least favorite student; I had never been enough to satisfy her need for perfection. Never quick enough, agile enough, clever enough, and certainly a far cry from the beauties she was accustomed to granting the title Fea Dien. But nothing I'd seen at the La'tari capital could have prepared me for the opulence of the A'kori kingdom.

The carriage slows as it makes its ascent toward the palace grounds, the size and grandeur of every estate we pass increasing the nearer we come to its well-fortified grounds. The palace sits behind high, thick walls of dark granite, at the top of a steep incline, beyond a beautiful forest with a wide sweeping river at its base. It's clear to me now why it has never been captured. It is the epitome of a tactical nightmare for anyone who would dare to attempt to breach it, and I can't wait to ask Bront how he would go about taking it.

Distracted by the beauty of the kingdom I hardly notice when the carriage stops in the courtyard of what is to be my new home for the foreseeable future. It is clear by the size and condition of the estate that Felias is an incredibly wealthy man, and I can't help but wonder what portion of his funds come from the La'tari crown. His estate sits on a small rise directly across from the palace grounds, bordered on its eastern side by a dense old growth forest. Every inch of his home not occupied by a window or door is covered from ground to rooftop in a robustly flowering vine boasting the most exquisite red flowers I have ever seen.

The carriage door swings open, and I take in a deep lungful of floral air, the breath leaving my lungs on a sigh. I'm glad to be free of my confinement on the ship, somewhere I can stretch my legs, somewhere ... else. I bury thoughts of the ship the moment I summon them, suppressing a tangled minefield of memories that I do not care to relive.

"You've grown into quite the young lady since I last saw you at your birth right." Felias's voice draws me out of my darkening thoughts, and I realize I've taken his arm and allowed him to lead me into the house.

Servants dash by with bundles of cut flowers in purple and blue hues, their trays stacked high with small, ornately decorated cakes. I wonder how many of his men can be trusted. Not all of them, if even inside the privacy of his home he continues to keep up appearances.

His eyes follow mine to a silver tray piled high with letters boasting his golden seal—a small, leaping fox. It seems a fitting crest for a spy, perhaps a little too on the nose, but who am I to judge? The man has done something right if he's been trusted with my care for the duration of my assignment. It's impressive that all while working this closely with the La'tari he managed to remain so close to the court of the feyn king.

I can't control the deep pit that forms in my stomach when a slight feyn male with rusty colored hair rushes past me, hurrying the letters out the front door. While he boasts all of the ethereal beauty of their race, he holds none of the lethal grace I witnessed as a child. Becoming comfortable in the presence of the feyn is both necessary for my mission and the greatest threat to my life. I watch as he disappears around a tall hedge bordering the yard, curious what his gift might be, when my uncle's voice breaks apart my ponderings.

"I've decided to host a party to celebrate you, niece," Felias says, leading me up a grand staircase. "I'm sure you will be well rested and ready to receive my guests by tomorrow night."

"Thank you, Uncle. It will be an honor to meet your friends," I reply when we step onto the second-floor landing. While meeting his *friends* may not be the honor I claim it is, I am eager to make the connections I need to fulfill my mission.

"I'm sure you'll make many of your own soon enough." He smiles and winks, seemingly satisfied with our little show for the time being.

It takes every ounce of self-control to school my features when he opens the door, leading me into a corner room with a view of both the palace and his own expansive gardens.

"I'll have your luggage brought up along with some food. I'm sure your palate is in desperate need of something far more refined than ship fare."

"That is very kind of you."

"Not at all," he says, with a wave of his hand. "I do hope you will make yourself at home. If you need anything at all, there is a service bell just here." He points to a long swath of golden cord by the door.

I dip my head in thanks, and he graciously excuses himself.

Never in my life have I seen a room so large, surely no one person requires this much space to simply sleep. Not that I'm complaining. The bed alone could fit me eight times over and I moan as my hand brushes across the dark silk sheets tumbling to the wood floors. I can't wait to slide my body into them.

Beyond a set of gilded doors is a separate room for the bath. Dark stone floors of green shine under the light cast through the tall leaded glass windows. A large tub sits at the center of the room next to a lever that summons water to fill the basin. I've never seen such a thing, and I chastise myself over my excitement. I can hardly wait to try it. Leanna warned me about the way the nobles hoard their riches in the north, but nothing I ever learned about the A'kori has prepared me for what I am seeing.

Back in the main room I hang my cloak and crack a window overlooking

the garden. The sweet floral breeze permeating the grounds wafts through my chambers, rolling the light floor length curtains in its wake. I settle into a large, velvet-lined chair with a beautiful view of the estate and let my head rest against the high-cushioned back.

My throat burns as my eyes begin to water. I tell myself it must be the flowers, an allergy, a small inconvenience and nothing more. A small quiver of my lip and I tell myself I am exhausted. I am. I hardly slept last night. I'll feel better after a nap. My eyes slip shut as a chittering of dainty laughs drift through the window on the breeze and flit past my ears. Voices, snatched away by the wind, lull me to sleep just as a single traitorous tear falls down my cheek.

I am jolted awake by a knock at the door, my entire being protesting the absence of my daggers as I rise to answer it. It is likely far too early in my stay to have garnered any real attention, and I remind myself that anyone here to harm me would hardly be knocking. It's difficult to be completely relieved when I find the slight male with rusty hair on the other side of the door. He proffers a large plate of home-cooked fare, the scent alone making my mouth water. He only stays long enough to shuffle my trunk into the room and extend a dinner invitation from Felias before leaving me to my meal.

The hours of sleep I missed last night begin to wear on me as the food settles in my stomach, but I can't let myself sleep anymore. I spend the day exploring the home. I mark the exits in my mind, the quickest path to each, objects throughout the house that can be used as weapons should the need arise. The usual.

A mixture of feyn and human work alongside one another, preparing for tomorrow's festivities. I routinely remind myself that not all feyn are like the ones I encountered in the forest years ago, and that living under the rule of a corrupt king doesn't make them evil. The humans here seem at ease around them despite the hardships their people suffer in their true home across the sea. I wonder if they are even aware of the state of La'tari. Of its people. Their people.

A striking feyn with silver hair catches my eye. She stands by a large

window on the first floor, open to the gardens. A vine like those that adorn the exterior is wrapped around her hand and at first, I think she must be trimming them back. My body goes rigid, eyes widening as the vine writhes in her hand and produces a tiny bud that blooms into a crimson flower right before my eyes.

My skin tingles like I'm caught in the middle of a thunderstorm, raising the hair on the back of my neck. I can't pull my eyes away from the scene before me. I watch, dumbfounded, as the vine grows, first by inches and then by feet. She speaks to it, encouraging it to take hold until the interior wall before which she stands is covered from floor to ceiling in a mat of twisted vines, thick with heavy, fragrant blooms.

She leans out the window and offers a quiet "thank you" to someone standing beyond my line of sight. Perhaps she is talking to the vine again. I find myself wondering if the plants speak back to her and decide that until I know for sure, it's best to act as if they can.

I catch small glimpses of more gifted A'kori throughout the day. Some use gentle bursts of air to dust, others light fires with the flick of a wrist when the house begins to cool in the evening. I have done my research and know as much about their abilities as any Drakai. My resources may have been limited at the keep but I've been taught enough to know that gifts used in the open are mere parlor tricks compared to the rarer gifts, which have always been heavily guarded secrets.

The manor house lacks no form of richness. Much of which I've heard described in vivid detail by Leanna but never seen. When I find myself in the library, I can't help that my jaw loosens, threatening to hang open as I survey the titles on the lower shelves. Windows stretch from floor to ceiling, illuminating two stories of leather-bound tomes in soft, waning light.

My fingers are brushing the spines reverently when the rusty haired male comes to collect me upon dinner being served. Felias keeps me company with his easygoing conversation, inquiring first about his brother, my *father*, then about the weather in La'tari, and so on.

Throughout a lavish meal of savory meats, spiced breads, and trays of seasoned vegetables I've never tasted and can hardly describe, we discuss those who have been invited to attend my reveal tomorrow. He makes a point of noting a handful of young females it would benefit me to befriend, giving me the names of those the king holds in high regard. These, I must convince to receive me and persuade that I am worthy of an audience with their king.

"I'm afraid the king himself will not be in attendance. I've just learned that he had business outside of the capital and left only yesterday to attend to it. My source couldn't say for certain when he will return."

It's less than ideal but I hardly expected him to be fatefully drawn into my orbit upon my arrival.

"How unfortunate," I say, "I hope his business doesn't keep him away for the duration of the season."

"I think it unlikely, but I have no doubt we will learn more at the party. My guests are sure to supply plenty of splendid gossip on the subject."

He winks at me over a crystal goblet full of a deep red liquid, and I think at some point I am really going to have to find time to talk to this man about his stealth techniques.

After dinner and a decadent dessert of black forest cake and frozen sweet cream, Felias sends me off toward my room. He reminds me to make myself at home, promising to come by in the morning before his duties as host undoubtedly overwhelm his attention. I'm exhausted by the time I make it back to my chamber and as excited as I was earlier, I don't so much as glance toward the tub. A bath sounds amazing, but I just might fall asleep and drown if I try to take one now.

I head to the wardrobe and pluck the small pouch of herbs out of the interior pocket of my cloak. I untie the sack and give it a sniff, wrinkling my nose when it's met with the pungent, bitter smell of earth and citrus. Experience tells me it must taste as bad as it smells. I pinch a tiny bit between two fingers and place it on the back of my tongue preparing for the worst.

I'm delighted when the herb dissolves almost immediately, leaving a faintly sweet taste behind. I will have to find out what it's called. If it works as well as I suspect it will, the knowledge of the herb will be a valued addition to my already abundant list of homemade concoctions.

After returning the pouch to the hidden pocket of my cloak, I hang my dress and crawl into bed. I moan as my body slides under the silk duvet.

Nothing should feel this good. Stretching my body out between the sheets, I wiggle my toes.

I will not become accustomed to silk.

But I might as well enjoy it while I'm here.

My eyes grow heavy, and my mind follows soon after into a blissful void of dreamless sleep that I've sought for years. The last thought skipping across the surface of my mind before I fade—him.

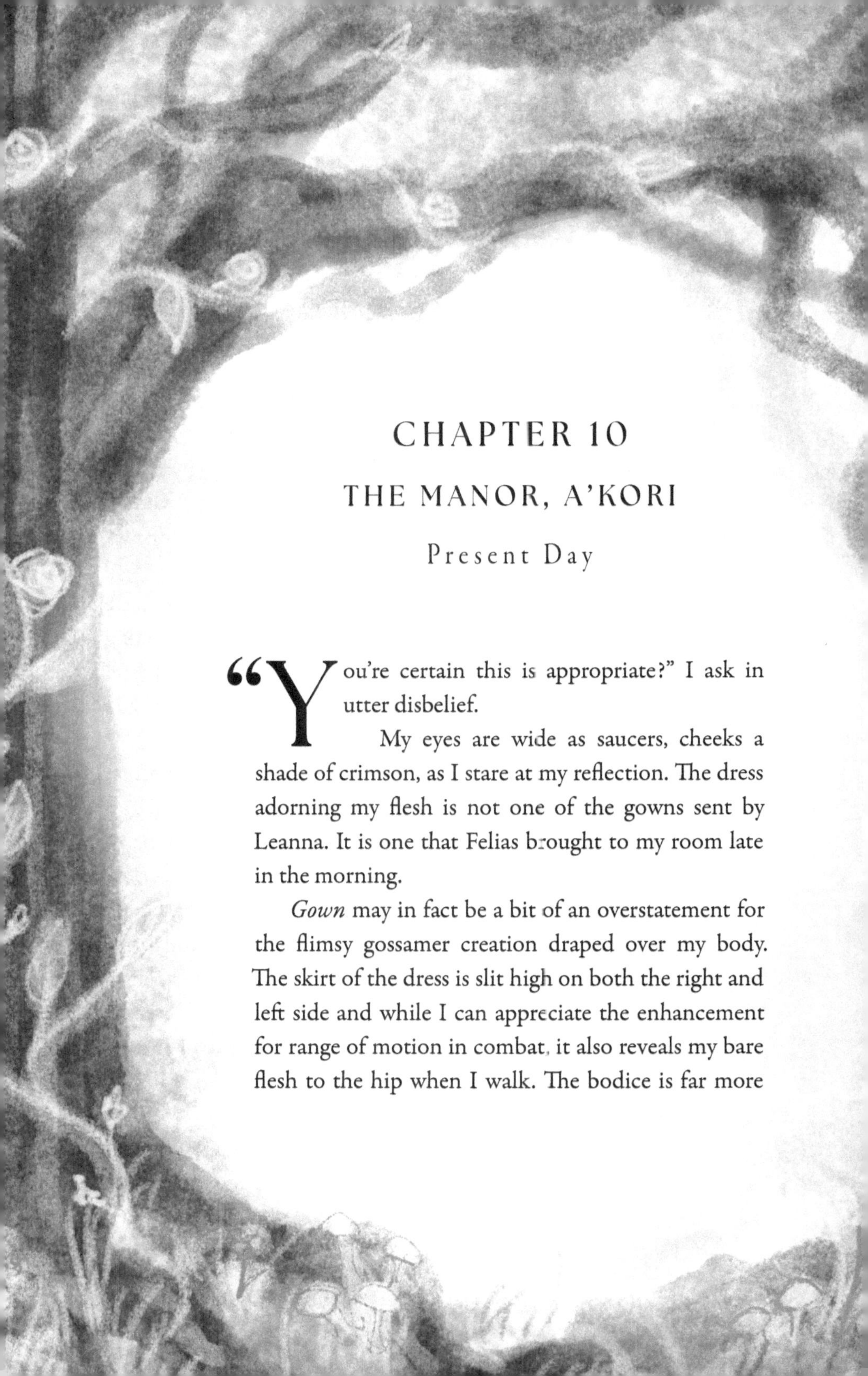

CHAPTER 10
THE MANOR, A'KORI
Present Day

"You're certain this is appropriate?" I ask in utter disbelief.

My eyes are wide as saucers, cheeks a shade of crimson, as I stare at my reflection. The dress adorning my flesh is not one of the gowns sent by Leanna. It is one that Felias brought to my room late in the morning.

Gown may in fact be a bit of an overstatement for the flimsy gossamer creation draped over my body. The skirt of the dress is slit high on both the right and left side and while I can appreciate the enhancement for range of motion in combat, it also reveals my bare flesh to the hip when I walk. The bodice is far more modest, yet not modest at all. It is cut wide across the shoulder, the neckline low, exposing the gentle slope of my breasts before they are hidden within the pale, too-thin fabric that might as well be sheer for all it hides. Its sleeves are blessedly long, tapering at the ends where they extend beyond my wrists to cover half my hand, though too tight to conceal any weapon.

"Quite appropriate. I had them made so that you wouldn't feel out of place. It is a typical A'kori design. You will see many in similar fashion at the party tonight."

Felias had in fact had my wardrobe filled with dresses sewn in like design. He had forcefully batted my hand away when I reached for one ensemble that offered the comfort of a loose pair of pants that fit snuggly at the ankle. Those were apparently only worn during activities that risk exposing too much skin. I hadn't asked how much was too much. It is obvious we have vastly different opinions on the subject.

My uncle has a light breakfast brought to my room and we sit by the window overlooking the garden discussing his plans for the evening. The man has no idea what manner of Drakai they sent him when he tells me that I have a simple task for the night. Be charming, and he will make all the appropriate introductions.

Charming has never been my strong suit. One of the many reasons I was shocked to receive my mission. It is clear the La'tari king feels that my feyn looks will endear me to the nobles of A'kori. All I can do is hope that it's enough.

Felias resupplies the names of those he deems important enough for me to befriend, worried I've somehow already forgotten. Abruptly, the rusty haired male comes through the door, out of breath, forehead boasting a thick layer of sweat, rambling something about a fire in the foyer. While both he and my uncle hurry from the room, there is an overall lack of surprise that makes me wonder what sort of peculiar incidents must be commonplace when you live your life alongside a gifted race.

The large tub in the washroom calls to me and I grin like a fool when the simple pull of a lever has it filling with steaming water. I draw the sliver of jasmine soap from my cloak and step into the tub, reveling in the scent of it as it glides over every surface of my body. My nipples pebble when my hands slide across them, now acutely aware of the pleasure that can be derived by a nimble set of fingers. There is an ache between my legs, an emptiness that mirrors the vacancy in my heart, a feeling that I bury before it can be fully recalled.

I set the soap aside in a small tray and step out of the water, leaving my thoughts to empty down the drain along with the last of the dirt that clung to me from my previous life.

The cushioned chair overlooking the garden has already become my favorite place to exist within my expansive suite. Shelves stacked high with all manner of thick and ornately bound books line the windows. Small pieces of art hang on the walls, speaking of the stories contained within the pages nearby. Blustery voyages across turbulent seas. Foreign lands with colorful markets and vibrant cities. Every image and tome a harsh reminder of how little I've experienced of our world.

I open the window and let the temperate breeze assist in drying my hair. Leaning into the wind I tilt my head to the side, straining to hear more of the soft feminine voices coming from the grounds below, but they are snatched away before I can discern them. I prop myself up on the window ledge and lean out to survey the garden, finding not a soul among the flower lined paths below.

Curious.

Leaving my hair unadorned, it cascades down to my lower back in a plethora of dark spirals. Pulling on the dress Felias gifted me for the party, I make my way outside to explore the grounds for any tactical advantages they might hold. The entire estate is bursting at the seams with feyn and human alike, all bustling about in festive attire, working hard to complete their tasks before the first guests inevitably arrive early.

The quiet solace of the garden is a welcome reprieve and a welcome distraction at that. I've never seen so many flowers in bloom and suspect Felias may have a healthy supply of gifted feyn to assist in the exquisite floral displays throughout the estate. Slinking under the shade of a tall oak, I close my eyes, breathing in the living bouquet that surrounds me.

If only I could bring a piece of A'kori back to the La'tari. How long has it been since my people had fertile soil to plant in? The smell of the flowers sours when I think of their gifts being wasted on something as trivial as a garden party while children starve across the sea.

It is clear the feyn king will let every human outside of his rule waste away into nothing before sending a single one of his subjects to help my people. And for what reason? Power?

He deserves to die for the atrocities he committed during the war, and he deserves to die again for his indifference to suffering that he has the power to end. I've never taken a life, his will be the first, and I will relish each and every one of his dying breaths. Watching the light fade from his eyes will be the one memory I will live happily on for the rest of my life.

"You!" A deep voice booms across the lawn and straight up my spine, stiffening it as my eyes fly open.

A tall male with broad shoulders and an icy glower stalks toward me, the black leather of his pants creaking with every agitated stride he takes in my direction. The breeze flutters the black fabric of his tunic and loose strands of midnight hair fall over his stormy blue eyes. A long silver scar, stark against the olive tone of his skin, runs from his right temple to the back of his head and there is a small nick in his pointed ear where a blade must have clipped him. His full lips are drawn into a tight, thin line that does nothing to amplify his natural feyn beauty.

His posture tells me everything I need to know about the male. He moves like a soldier, deadly and precise, and his glower reeks of violence. A glower he directs at me.

I blink, and my mind sifts through its darkest recesses, dredging up a memory I've struggled to subdue since arriving. I'm taken back to a bloody scene years ago, where five feyn bodies lay dead at my feet. I suppress a shudder as my eyes open again, bringing me back to the waking world.

As subtly as I can, I shift my leg behind me, muscles in my arms coiling as I prepare to strike or defend. He stops two strides short of where I stand and tips his head, observing me. I wonder if I've already given too much away and will myself to relax, unwinding the tension in my body.

"I don't know you," he says through gritted teeth, his voice deep and commanding.

Is he telling me or asking?

When I make no move to reply he takes another step toward me, and his brow draws down.

"This is a private event. I'll escort you off the grounds," he grumbles and moves to grab my arm.

"Who in haliel do you think you are?" I snap, stepping out of his reach.

His legs are longer than mine and in one stride he's closed the distance, wrapping his entire hand around my arm in a vice-like grip that threatens to bruise.

Leaning over me, he sneers, "That dress might make you look like a lady but those are the words of a low born."

"I see that you are familiar with the tongue of your own kind," I snark.

It's a shot in the dark but by the look on his face it seems to find its mark on a deep wound.

"What did you just say to me?" he growls, jostling me closer, leering down at me.

I tilt my chin up and meet his glare defiantly. If he thinks he can remove *me* from the grounds that are to be *my* home, he will soon find out that he is sorely mistaken.

"Niece!" Felias bellows across the lawn and I chance a glance behind the brooding male clutching my arm.

His grip slackens and after a brief hesitation, he glances over his shoulder, laying eyes on my uncle. I shouldn't be insulted that he takes his eyes off me, he has no idea what I am, but I can't help the thoughts that tumble through my mind. I could have him on his knees with two well-placed blows.

"I see you've already met the general." Felias forces a smile as he hurries toward us.

"Niece?" the male huffs as he returns his gaze to me, looking me over more thoroughly.

"General?" I quip back, making sure to sound just as surprised by his rank as he apparently is by my family ties.

He glowers at me, and I suppose if I can't break his hand for touching me, I'll settle for knocking him down a peg. Though, I'd much prefer the first option.

Felias arrives out of breath, his eyes flicking between the general and myself, noting the male's unrelenting grip on my arm.

"General Xeyvian, it's my pleasure to introduce you to my niece, Shivaria."

The formal introduction further loosens his grip and when he finally relinquishes his hold it takes every ounce of willpower I have not to snatch the arm away and break his nose with the elbow he's just freed.

"I didn't know you were feyn born, Felias." The statement drips with skepticism.

The general's eyes fall upon the cascade of ebony hair flowing down my back then land on my grey eyes, features that speak to my lineage.

"She takes after her mother, General." Felias manages to plaster a sweet smile on his face as he looks me over, every bit the doting uncle.

The general tears his eyes away from me with a dismissive grunt and I take my uncle's arm when he offers it.

"Are you satisfied with your sweep of the grounds?" Felias asks.

The general nods. "Thank you for allowing me access to your home, Felias. You have quite the guest list this evening."

"It's Shivaria's first season and I want to make sure she has every opportunity," he says, patting my hand affectionately.

The male looks me over dismissively, as if I am completely unremarkable. Nothing more than a simple blade of grass among a million of the same.

"I'm sure she'll be the talk of the town tomorrow." There is nothing genuine about the male's tone when he says it, and the smug quirk at the corner of his lips tells me the comment isn't meant to be kind.

"If you'll excuse me, I simply must get back to my preparations and send my niece off to ready herself for her reveal. I do hope to see you in attendance this evening."

The moment the general dips his head in dismissal, Felias is quick to lead me off toward the manor. He doesn't explain himself as he walks me straight back to my room, obviously rattled, and apparently under the impression I need hours to prepare myself for the party. He looks as though he might chastise me for my run-in with the general, but instead, he simply puffs out an exasperated sigh, closing the door behind himself as he leaves.

The day drags on and my irritation with the general fades from my mind, lost to the low hum of preparations out in the yards. Even in my chair overlooking the garden, watching fire lights strung from tree to tree, as a small army of feyn coax every bush into an early bloom, I become restless.

The day passes by at a painfully slow rate and despite my natural aversion to large crowds, I quickly become eager for a reprieve from my solitude and any engagement the evening will offer.

When guests finally begin to arrive, I slip on a pair of daintily embroidered silk slippers to match my gown and wait for my uncle to collect me. Despite Leanna's demands, or perhaps in spite of the woman herself, I leave my hair down without any adornment.

The sun has fully set and most of the guests have already arrived by the time my uncle comes to my suite. While I may be annoyed that he left me alone to suffer in boredom all day, I quickly learn that the man is nothing if not a masterful tactician, at least where social events are concerned.

Feyn mingle with humans in the crowded halls. Tall golden trays of exotic fruits and bubbling refreshments are stacked on lavishly decorated tables lining the walls. Men and women, male and female, all in blue uniforms, weave about the throng with trays of delicious smelling foods, offering them to every guest they pass. Lace-clad dancers fall from the ceiling in a cascade of bright ribbons, twisting overhead among the tinkling din of the crystal chandeliers.

"What do you think?" Felias's voice breaks me from my reverie.

One glance at the smug look on my uncle's face is all the motivation I need to suppress the awe that must be visible on my own. He must know I've never seen anything so grand. Even my wildest imaginings couldn't conjure a fraction of the spectacle surrounding me.

"It's incredible," I admit.

I'm not sure the word is enough to describe what the man accomplished. I'm not even sure there is a word that exists that could do it justice.

He smiles, obviously pleased with himself. He brings me to a halt in the middle of the large room where I'd watched the female grow the wall of crimson flowers the day I arrived.

"Wait here. I would like you to meet a few of our close neighbors."

Felias makes a hasty retreat through a large set of ornate doors, vanishing into another room overflowing with laughter. One moment, I'm surprised he's left me alone, the next I understand all too well what my uncle accomplished. Every eye in the room sweeps over me. Eyes that hadn't dared linger so long while my chaperone remained at my side.

The man truly is a genius.

I do my best to avert my eyes in an attempt to appear completely unaware of the display he's made of me. The pink that blooms on the apples of my cheeks is entirely genuine and cannot be helped. I catch small glimpses of males baring their fangs with sly smiles as they look me over, the females by their sides appraising me for completely different reasons. It is no secret they are a wild race, and it wouldn't surprise me in the least to find a set of fangs at my throat, should one of the females decide I am a threat to her position with her chosen partner.

It takes no time for the first male to approach me, offering to lead me in a dance. The subtle hue of red in his hair and flecks of green in his eyes declaring that there is human blood in his veins. The ancients of their kind are known for their striking blue eyes and full heads of either white or black hair. The very features that mark me as impure in La'tari.

I take his arm, and the music lulls, a long chord played on the violin transitioning the quartet into a slower and more intimate dance. He hooks my waist, pulling me closer than the steps require. It takes everything I have to glide across the floor with a smile, just as Leanna had instructed, and not throw a fist at his jaw when he spins me.

I can feel the flush of my cheeks as the panels of my dress part in time with the graceful movements. He smirks, his eyes following the line of my leg appreciatively until the dance comes to an end and I'm swept up by another eager male waiting on the sidelines.

I decide that, brilliant or not, I will end my uncle for forcing me to endure this. There is no doubt in my mind that his overly long absence is intentional, though what he expects me to accomplish with these males is entirely beyond me. While worthwhile connections are at the forefront of my mind, it is clear to me that the only thing they seek is a companion to warm their beds this evening.

Only after my fourth dance do I make my excuses and journey to the other end of the room to find a cool glass of water and a much needed breath of fresh air. The chilly spring breeze nips at my ear as it brushes a curl over my shoulder. The hair on my neck stands on end, a wave of ice rippling along my spine the next moment. My heart seizes and my lungs deflate when I lock eyes with a tall male standing by a large window covered in a plethora of vibrant blossoms.

His short white hair and light bronze skin are a stark contrast to the wall of red floral behind him. His icy blue eyes rest beneath a pinched, puzzled brow, and they are fixed on me. A painfully beautiful female stands beside him, her hand draped across his arm informally. She is his exact likeness in female form, with a long swath of silky hair falling below her waist.

She smiles, politely excusing herself from the midst of a conversation when her eyes fall on her companion. His brow furrows further as the chill in my spine grows, stretching around my rib cage. In the depths of me, the demon stirs, unfurling lazily as if to examine the male itself.

Foc.

His gaze breaks from mine, taking with it the icy veins spreading through my body, and I inhale a breath so deep it feels like the weight of the entire La'tari keep is taken off me. I whisper a silent prayer to the stars when the demon recedes, resuming its fitful slumber. I stifle my surprise at its response to the male.

The stranger leans down, whispering to his companion with a deliberate nod in my direction. Her eyebrows shoot up and she turns toward me, surveying me curiously.

She smiles when her eyes meet mine, and I try not to back away when she begins gliding toward me, pulling the perturbed looking male in her wake. My stomach pits.

She moves through the crowd as if there were not a single obstacle in her path, like silk floating on a gentle breeze, never hesitating in her stride. With every step she takes toward me, her bronze legs shimmer under the flickering light of the chandeliers as they breach the yellow panels of her gown.

Planting herself in front of me, she offers me a kind smile. Her pale blue eyes pin me in place, taking in every inch of me. The female doesn't so much as dip her head as she makes her introductions and a hush sweeps over the room.

"You must be Shivaria. My name is Awri and this is my brother Riesh."

Outwardly Awri seems every bit as cheerful and sweet as her brother seems despondent and troubled. Here, among the feyn, I don't have to remind myself that looks can be deceiving.

"Lovely to meet you both," I say.

I don't recognize the names and assume they must have fallen short of Felias's exacting standards as to who he personally deemed worthy of an introduction.

"La'tarian?" Riesh's brow dips further when he says it.

I can't help the pit in my stomach and wonder what small slip in the cadence of my speech gave me away or why it should matter to him. I'm far from the first La'tarian to grace the northern shores in pursuit of alliances.

"Awri! Riesh! I'm so pleased that you could make it this evening," Felias beams as he ambles up beside me.

The male offers his hand to my uncle who takes it eagerly with a growing smile. They exchange pleasantries and Felias makes his excuses to the young female he brought in tow, sending her away with a quick apology.

"Remind me," Riesh says to my uncle, "who was your brother's wife?"

"She was called Thaliana."

Felias had indeed lost his sister-in-law during childbirth, and I know that there is no pretense in the sad smile that slips onto his face when her name passes his lips. It was the rarest of couplings when his very human brother took one of them for his bride. Though I can't stop the twinge of pain in my heart over Felias's loss, I will never understand why any mortal would willingly bind themselves to a feyn.

"That's right," the male says. And I'm not sure his brow can furrow any deeper, and then it does when he asks, "Ungifted?"

"She was, yes," Felias says with a series of short nods.

I debate making my exit when the siblings exchange a troubled look, and it becomes clear that there is something outside of my understanding taking place. My mind rushes to piece together every facet of my brief interaction with them, struggling to make sense of it. I've never been strong in the delicate art of social grace, much less the tactical scheming and manipulation that comes with those who are proficient.

Awri leaves her brother to come along side me, hooking her elbow with mine. "Will you show me the grounds, Shivaria?"

Felias nods his approval before I answer, "Of course."

I force a smile and let her lead me into the quiet seclusion of the outdoors.

It's a calm night with a full moon that blankets the earth in a pale, shimmering light. Star flowers litter the grounds, their pearlescent white petals unfurled. They reach toward the sky, refracting the moonlight, glowing like a multitude of stars fallen to settle upon the surface of Terr.

"Are you enjoying A'kori?" she asks absently as she turns us down a narrow path, rounding a bushy maple.

"I really haven't had much time to explore, but what I have seen is exceptionally grand."

She glances at me with a sly smile and sweet chuckle.

"You certainly haven't seen enough of the capital if *grand* is the only word you use to describe it. I insist you let me enhance your view of the city. I'll have a carriage sent in the morning if you like?"

I nearly lose my footing on the perfectly flat, well-groomed path beneath my feet when she asks, and she suppresses a small laugh. I only hesitate for a moment. Despite my uncomfortable introduction to the siblings, Felias seemed pleased enough by their presence. And I don't want to risk giving up an opportunity that might prove beneficial.

I plaster a grateful smile onto my face as I regain my stride. "Thank you. That would be—"

"Awri!" The general's voice booms into the night and I suppress a cringe when I glance up and find him on the path before us. "Thank the stars. What did I say about running off when I... What are you doing with *her?*" he barks, pointing a long finger at me. Leveling me with a menacing glare, he tromps toward us.

I am at least happy to see his demeanor hasn't changed around someone he's obviously familiar with. I'm beginning to think there is a good chance the male is simply grumpy all the time.

"You've met?" Awri's brows creep up her forehead before drawing down in confusion as she notes his determined stride and the crease in his brow.

Or maybe it is just me.

"Oh, yes. Xeyvian and I are old friends," I say sweetly, with an obnoxiously innocent smile.

"Xeyvian?" Her eyebrows rise once more, thrown by my lack of formality when I exclude the general's title.

He inserts himself between us, parting Awri's arm from my own as he does. Crossing his arms dramatically, he glares down at the top of my head.

Stars, he is tall.

I lean to the side, peering around him until I catch Awri's eyes, noting the confusion on her face. I smile. My annoyance at his rudeness and his unreasonable disdain for me is overwhelming, and I can't help but let a little of my natural sarcasm slip.

"The general and I like to play a little game called 'who's the more sullen child.'" I sigh exaggeratedly and thank the stars when Awri smiles at my quip, choking back a laugh. I continue, "I'm extremely competitive and I hate to admit that I've yet to beat him at the game."

"Do *not* speak to me like that," he hisses.

"I wasn't. I was speaking with Awri before you interrupted. We were just discussing our plans for tomorrow."

He turns a delicious shade of red when I deliver the news, and I smile up at him. The male is far too easy to rile. The smile quickly falls from my face when I consider exactly who it is I'm vexing and just how much of an impediment he could be to my introduction to his king.

His lips quirk up at the edges like he can tell exactly what I'm thinking, and I decide that I don't really care to be in his presence, not now or ever again.

"General, perhaps you could give us a little privacy," Awri says sweetly, and I wish I knew how to make my voice as placating as she so easily can.

I make a mental note to practice her exact tone and the gentle flutter of her lashes.

"I think I'll stay," he says through gritted teeth.

"I'm not asking, General. I will be with you shortly." She tips her chin toward the end of the garden path, and just like that, he puts twenty paces between us without so much as a harrumph. Though, he does seem like the harrumphing type.

"I didn't realize you could command the general," I whisper, making sure to lock eyes with the male just to irritate him, before reminding myself again why I do not want to annoy him any further. "That might come in handy."

"Only if you intend to start a war," she laughs, and I join in, hoping it doesn't seem forced.

Awri is quick to set a time for us to meet in the morning, before appeasing the general by allowing him to escort her back to her brother's side. I catch her smiling at me throughout the evening, just as often as I catch her brother and the general brooding with their heads together, casting occasional sideways glances in my direction.

My uncle does his duty well, spending the rest of the evening making important introductions. Though he informs me that he is set on me fostering a friendship with the siblings above all others. It isn't until late in the evening that I realize there are a handful of beautiful young women scattered throughout the party, their singular task to make similar connections. I wonder how many of them have traveled to A'kori for the same purpose I have—a moment alone with the king. I imagine, should they succeed, their plans with the male differ greatly from my own.

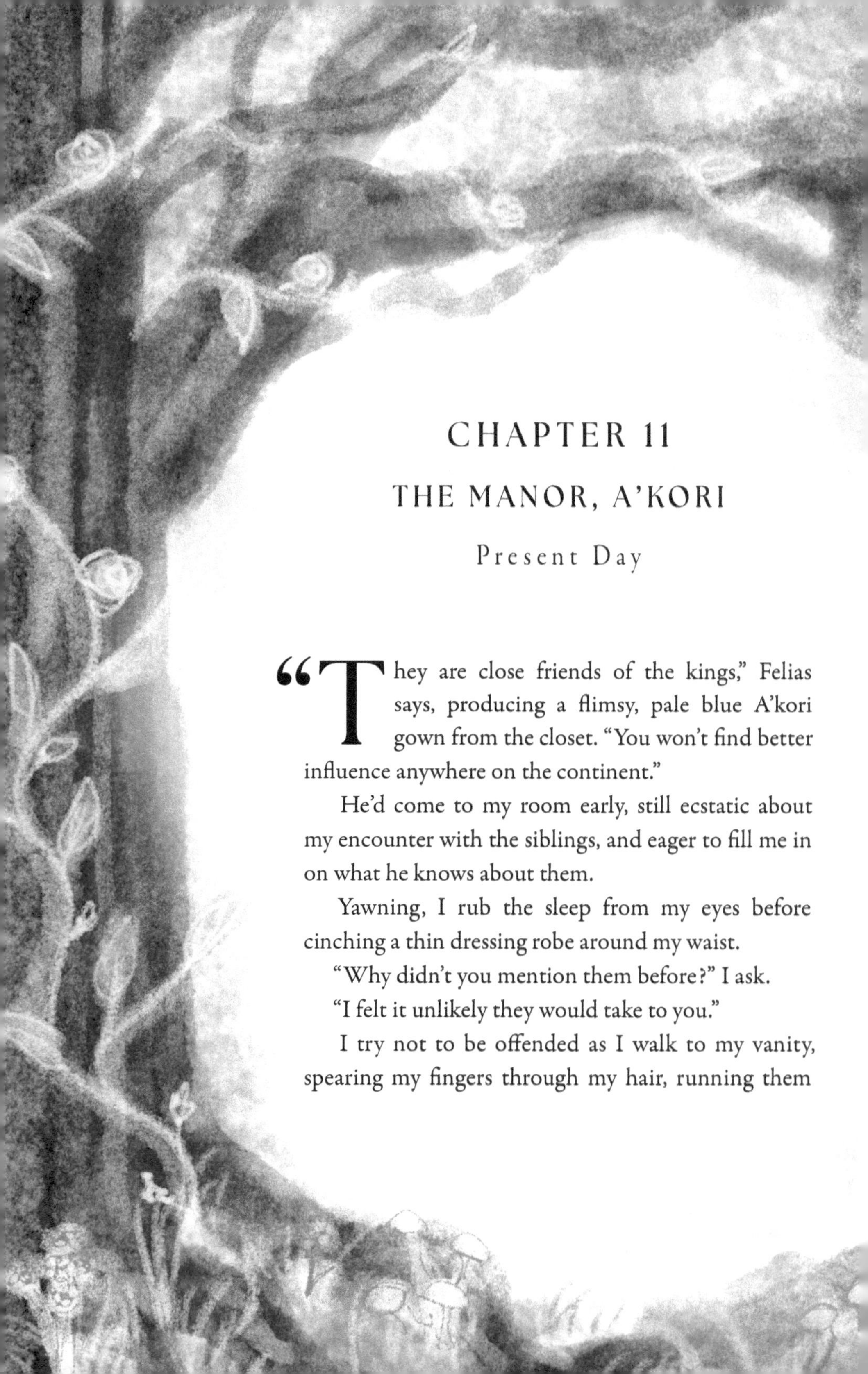

CHAPTER 11
THE MANOR, A'KORI
Present Day

"They are close friends of the kings," Felias says, producing a flimsy, pale blue A'kori gown from the closet. "You won't find better influence anywhere on the continent."

He'd come to my room early, still ecstatic about my encounter with the siblings, and eager to fill me in on what he knows about them.

Yawning, I rub the sleep from my eyes before cinching a thin dressing robe around my waist.

"Why didn't you mention them before?" I ask.

"I felt it unlikely they would take to you."

I try not to be offended as I walk to my vanity, spearing my fingers through my hair, running them through the hefty tangles I have accumulated in my sleep.

"Sit," Felias says, all but shoving me onto a heavily cushioned bench behind a dark wooden desk below a colorfully stained window.

I frown at my sleep rumpled face in the mirror just as my uncle does the same, though his attention is fixed on my hair. He runs his fingers through it, freeing the tangled strands with ease, then selects a gold comb from the table, twisting half of my hair into a knot, and pinning it to the back of my head.

"They must be powerful if they are close to the king," I say absently.

It is the thing that occupied my mind until I fell asleep last night, and the first thing in my head upon waking. Getting close to the wrong type of feyn, in my profession, would be a death sentence. What if they can read minds? Influence emotions? Provoke desire?

"They are, but not in the way you might expect. Awri is a *Glier*. She has the ability to change the appearance of something or someone."

That would be a handy trick for a Drakai on an assignment to end the life of a king.

"Her brother, Riesh, is a *Brek*." His tongue skips along the "r," rolling it along the roof of his mouth. "He can amplify another gift or block it altogether."

"Any gift?" I ask, startled.

"You are aware that feyn are quite private about their gifts and the extent of their power?" he says in clear admonishment of my curiosity.

I suppress a flinch at the bit of chastisement that deepens his tone. Of course, I don't expect him to know all their gifts or the extent of their power.

"I've heard rumors that he's quite powerful," he admits, "Though, I'm sure you know by now, a feyn's gift is only as strong as their opponent is weak."

In fact, it isn't something I've been taught. I'd like nothing more than for him to explain further but decide against telling my uncle how woefully unprepared I am when it comes to any real knowledge as it pertains to their species. Another of Leanna's earliest and most brutal lessons, never expose a weakness.

"And the general?" I ask hurriedly, before he decides to change the subject.

"For the love of the stars, just stay as far away from that male as you can. You will never be allowed in the same room as the king if the general decides otherwise."

I'm not surprised, after all, it is unlikely he became a general without

good instincts. I don't press Felias for more information, not today. If he'd been born feyn he would never have disclosed another's gift to me, much less hinted about the strength of their power. He may be on the side of the La'tari but after living his life in A'kori, it's reasonable that he maintains some of their customs. Customs that likely dissuade the man from revealing the full depth of his knowledge about the gifted.

My uncle leaves me to dress and the moment he's left the room I pull out a pair of the billowing pants that cinch at the ankle. My host may not approve, but the entire upper echelon of society on this side of the sea has already seen me from toe to hip, save for a few small shreds of flesh that weren't on display last night. I have no intention of being on display like that again, regardless of what their society says.

Awri's carriage arrives early, and I run down to greet her before I've managed to procure something to eat. She doesn't get out to greet me, she just flings the door open the moment she sees me, waving me over with a smile as she makes a perusal of my choice of clothing. I cringe, rethinking my decision to wear the comfortable pants under my dress, when my eyes land on the striking cobalt fabric of her own.

"Oh good. I was worried you'd overdress," she says.

"Haven't I?" I wonder aloud, splaying my arms and making a show of looking myself over.

"Not at all," she beams, "Get in."

The moment I'm seated, she taps the roof of the carriage, and the driver snaps the reins, the wheels clinking against the stone as they roll across the cobbled street beneath.

"I know I said I'd show you the city, but Riesh had a new bow commissioned for my birthday and it just arrived. I've been dying to see it. Would you mind terribly if I made a small adjustment to our plans?" she asks, as if I have any choice in the matter. How could I even begin to say no to such a request? Not that I would. Not that I care. My only task is to convince her that I am a worthy companion.

I plaster on my most convincing smile. At least she's taking me to see a weapon. It occurred to me that the female might force me to spend my time with her shopping for ribbons and lace. To have the opportunity to examine

a bow of feyn design far exceeds any expectations about how I imagined we might spend our day.

"I would love to see it. What kind of bow is it?"

"A long bow." She tips her head and eyes me thoughtfully, the points of her ears breaking free from her silky hair. "Made of Osage."

"Do you hunt?" I ask curiously.

"I do. Yes. My father taught me when I was young."

I can't help but wonder how long ago that was. For all I know about the way their species ages, the female across from me has been alive hundreds of years.

"Though I couldn't stomach it for years after the war ended," she says in a pained tone.

She doesn't look much older than me, but if she fought in the war, she is at least twice my age. A *Glier*. That is what Felias called her. A feyn with the gift of illusion.

I find myself wondering how many different faces she wore during her time in the war, deceiving men into thinking it was their comrades who killed them. Perhaps she took a less direct approach, cloaking mortal men in the guise of the feyn, letting them kill each other. At least she has the decency to look ashamed for all the lives she ended. Melancholy at the least.

"I can only imagine," I say, twisting my face in a portrayal of sympathy.

A jostling bump draws my attention outside the carriage and my eyes widen. Awri giggles, clearly pleased with my surprise.

"Where did you think we were going?" she asks, a coy smile turning up the edges of her lips.

We've made our way deep inside the palace grounds, the carriage turning east to follow a wide river.

"You live at the palace?" I gape.

"I live on the palace grounds, in my own home," she says, "There are a handful of us that do. My brother and the general among them."

"Which house is the general's?" I ask dryly.

"Why?" She grins wickedly. "Would you like to visit? I assure you, it would be no trouble at all to arrange that."

"I'd like to know which house to avoid if I ever need to borrow a cup of sugar," I answer dryly.

She laughs, the noise annoyingly dainty and charming. Once again, I begin to think better of mocking her … friend?

"I'm sorry, I shouldn't have said that."

"Please don't stop on my account." She laughs again. "It's been an age since I've seen anyone ruffle Xey's feathers so easily. It is very entertaining."

"How long have you known each other?"

What I really want to know is how old they are, but I assume it's rude to ask. Over time, a few well-placed, leading questions should get me closer to the answer I seek.

"I came to know the general well during the war, but he's been a friend of my family's since long before I was born."

The carriage bounces again and when I look outside, I feel as though I've been taken to one of the beautifully depicted cottages in the fairy books I read as a child. Thick beams of dark wood support a thatched roof. Every window is patterned in a diamond leaded glass, bordered by stone. The home abuts the river, wildflowers melding with the herb garden, a simple stable out back.

Awri directs the driver back to the stables where, to my utter disappointment, Riesh waits for us with the general at his side. Her brother wears a cheerfully colored set of linens with a long, thin coat and a small, forced smile. He offers me his hand, helping me down to the mossy ground, before turning to offer the same to his sister. She bounds out of the carriage without taking it and the general places himself between us, a completely ineffective gesture as Awri darts out from behind him, seemingly oblivious to his disdain for me.

I'm not surprised to find that his demeanor continues to match his dark attire. He looks every bit the villain, though not even his black attire nor the scar he bares at his temple detracts from his lethal feyn beauty. I do my best to plaster a pleasing smile on my face, and perhaps more irritating than his ire is the ease with which he dismisses me as he glances toward his companions.

Awri practically skips around her brother clapping her hands as if she were a girl no more than five years old. He beams at her. It's clear by the look on his face, she holds his heart in the palm of her hands.

"Happy birthday, sister," he says, sweeping his arm toward a tall wooden box laid out on a long table.

She squeals, pulls off the lid, and drives her hands deep into the straw bedding. Her eyes gleam as she pulls the bow from the box with a reverence I know well. It's the same look I'll give my daggers when they're back in my hands.

The bow is carved with gilded leaves—it's as much a piece of art as it is a weapon. She pulls the string taut, testing it, before knocking an arrow and repeating the motion. Bringing the string to her cheek, she lets her shoulders become accustomed to the weight of the bow and the tension in the line. I think she's about to let the arrow fly when she puts it down and pulls her brother into her arms.

"It's perfect," she says, her words muffled by his shoulder.

"You deserve nothing less," he says into her hair.

She's holding back tears when she looks at me, perhaps remembering that she has an audience.

"What do you think of it, Shivaria?" she asks, holding out the bow.

I take it reverently, marveling at the weapon as I run my fingers down its length. Never have I seen its likeness. Though it is imperfect, I find that the right type of flaw has an uncanny way of making something more exquisite.

Tracing the etched shaft with my finger, I can't help but think back on the first time I held a bow, my traitorous mind wandering to the man who taught me. I discard the memory, as I discard the bow back into her hands, forcing a smile.

"It's beautiful," I say.

The general scoffs at my perfectly genuine compliment and I scowl at him.

"You disagree, General?" Awri asks with a quirk of her brow.

"Not at all. It's just—only a woman would describe a weapon in such a way."

"How would you describe it?" I ask.

He shrugs. "I might describe it as accurate."

"Have you already tried the bow then?" I ask.

The general balks at my question, taking it as an accusation. Looking over my head, he rushes to assure Awri, "Absolutely not. I would never take the liberty. The first shot is yours."

I hum thoughtfully.

"What?" the general demands with a sigh.

"I just find it interesting that you would condemn a woman for describing the simple truth of a thing, while you, as a male, will only comment on your assumptions about it."

A wide grin breaks upon Awri's face as the general struggles to school himself.

"Awri, why don't you take a shot and settle this for us? I believe you will find my *assumptions* to be quite accurate," the general says, handing her an arrow.

"I'd love to," she chuckles, walking to a nearby tree laden with pink flowers the size of my palm, and takes aim.

She looses the arrow, narrowly missing her mark, fluttering the petals as it flies by. Her mouth twists as she eyes the bow.

"May I?" The general extends his hand, and she relinquishes it to him reluctantly.

His arrow misses the flower by a smaller margin, taking one of the petals with it when it tears past. He frowns, hardly waiting before knocking another. He takes his time, making minor adjustments to his position, offsetting the arrows trajectory. I have little doubt he compensated correctly for the flaw, a minute curve in the shaft of the weapon. This time, he will strike his mark.

The pink petals flit about in a light breeze, the creek of the general's leather vambrace the only sound to permeate the silence as he draws the string against his cheek. I suck in a sharp breath, my hand flying to his arm, a plea in the form of a gentle squeeze. The words won't come fast enough, and I don't expect him to stop. I'm shocked when he loosens his hold on the string, following my line of sight.

"What is it?" he asks quietly.

"There." I point. "In the tree."

Just below his target, a pair of bright violet eyes stare back at us from within the thick foliage. He nods once, signaling that he sees it, and hands the bow back to Awri. The siblings survey the tree curiously, searching for whatever dissuaded the male from his shot.

When I look back, the violet eyes have vanished. A strong gust of wind sweeps up from the sea, churning the petals into a vortex as they are pulled from the tree in a cascade. If the general hadn't confirmed what I'd seen, I'm not sure I would have trusted my own sight.

We make our way toward the cottage, Riesh and Awri at the front of our party. She's still thanking her brother for the bow, and he continues to tell her how deserving she is. I can't help but wonder if all siblings are like this.

"What was that thing?" I ask, looking over my shoulder toward the tree, hardly expecting the general to answer.

"A wood sprite."

"Really?"

He nods, and I whip my body around, trying in vain to find the creature once again.

"She'll be gone by now," he says.

I sigh in disappointment and turn back, taking a few quick strides to catch up to my party.

"I thought all the fea creatures fled this veil in the sundering."

"Not all of us," he assures me.

"I didn't mean the feyn." Obviously.

"But we are *fea creatures*. Are we not?" he sneers at my unintentional slip.

He isn't wrong. The feyn are in fact fea creatures, but while they live alongside the humans of Terr, the rest of the fea largely belonged to the forests and rarely interacted with the human race, or so I was taught. I want to yell at him for being intentionally difficult, but it occurs to me that it may be my own fault that he hasn't warmed up to me at this point. If Awri is inclined to like me, there is no reason the general can't learn to as well.

"I'm sorry," I say, "I didn't mean it like that."

He huffs in disbelief. "Don't worry. I've rarely met a La'tarian who consider feyn more than mere creatures. Your particular flavor of disdain is entirely unoriginal."

Well, foc him.

In this moment, there is little else in this world I'd like more than to tear the general apart bit by bit, starting with his mind, moving to his body, and finishing with his soul. For all I know, he is the oldest feyn on the face of Terr, and if that's true, it's no wonder they left him behind in the sundering. He probably started the great war all by himself, with his hisht personality.

"Is everything all right, Shivaria?" Riesh stops to open the cottage door for me, wearing a rather concerned look as he examines us.

His eyes flick to the general and I'm not sure what he sees, but he frowns at his friend.

"Everything is perfect. Thank you, Riesh," I say.

My murderous thoughts of the general fade away the moment my feet pass the threshold, landing on the heavily knotted wood of the cottage floor. The home is every bit as charming inside as it is outside. An array of colorful, heavily cushioned chairs litters the room by the stone fireplace. A large table carved from the roots of an ancient tree sits at its center.

"I didn't expect you back so soon," says an unfamiliar voice. A tall male with green eyes and a mop of dark brown hair rushes down the stairs with a wide grin, gripping the banister that's been carved to resemble the gnarled branches of a tree.

He rushes to Awri and pulls her into an embrace, resting his cheek on her head.

"She was never going to make it an entire day with an unwrapped gift waiting for her," Riesh says, smiling.

"It wasn't just that." She pushes out of the male's arms and looks from me back to him. "I wanted you to meet the new friend I was telling you about. Kishek, this is Shivaria."

He dips his head and offers me a warm smile, dimples forming in his olive tone cheeks, and I smile warmly back. Awri hands the male her bow, a proud smile plastered on her face as he looks it over, nodding approvingly. Riesh makes himself at home, swinging a kettle over the crackling fire, and the general simply stands in the corner exuding his perpetual gloom.

The table is littered with papers and a variety of books, beneath which sits a map of Terr. In its entirety.

My stomach flutters with anticipation as I walk to the table, perhaps a little too quickly. The general tenses in the corner, the floor creaking as he shifts his weight off the wall to hover at my back. I lace my fingers behind me, bending over to examine what little of the map is exposed beneath the piles of papers and books splayed on top.

Not wishing to appear too forward by moving anything on the table,

I drink in the details that are visible below the southern border of La'tari. Where I have only ever seen *The Smudge,* this map boasts colorful depictions of mountain ranges and countryside in a land so vast A'kori could fit inside it five times over.

"I've been told that the La'tari censor Brax from their maps," Riesh says, and I startle, not having noticed him settle against the table beside me.

"Brax?" I wonder aloud.

"That is the name for the land between La'tari and the southern sea."

"It's true." I hate admitting out loud that I've been kept ignorant about something that is clearly common knowledge in the north. "I always called it The Smudge. It's nothing more than a dark swath on our maps."

"Why do you suppose that is?" he asks.

My brow pinches when I look at him. It's clear by his tone that he has his own ideas about why that would be.

"To keep us safe," I say, simply because it is what I have always been told.

The smudge—Brax—is incredibly dangerous. I have known many Drakai over the years who'd gone on missions into its unknown wilds and disappeared without a trace. If I ever had any doubts about the danger that exists beyond the southern border, they all vanished the day I met the crone in the woods.

"What other reason would they have?" I ask, letting him bait me into the debate he is apparently eager for.

After all, if we agreed on everything, we wouldn't have teetered on the edge of war my entire life. Riesh glances behind me, lifting his chin toward the general. When I turn to look, I find the male resuming his lax position against the wall, arms crossed over his chest, eyes nailed to the map before me.

Without lifting his eyes, he says, "Awri, would you like to show Shivaria your fea drawings?"

My face contorts in confusion, but it seems I'm the only one thrown by the general's sudden change of subject when Awri nods, turning to dig through a large wooden trunk beneath a rain pattered window. A moment later a thick leather-bound book is dropped with a resounding thud on the table, fluttering the edges of the map.

"If I recall correctly the wood sprites are somewhere near the center," the

general says, offering me access to the tome's pages by way of raising his chin toward it.

I've seen pictures of the creatures before, but it was long ago in a children's book, and at the time Leanna assured me they no longer existed here. When the ancients used the lifeforce of Terr to split the veils in the sundering, most fea creatures fled before the gateway between veils was sealed off forever. I was taught that the few who remained behind died long ago.

I have to wonder how it is that the La'tari have no idea of their continued existence. While Awri and Riesh seemed curious about the creature, neither appeared terribly surprised to see it. Despite all the budding questions in my mind, I can't help but feel a swell of pride that I have uncovered one more piece of valuable knowledge to bestow upon my king when I return. Though I have no idea what he is likely to do with the information. What use is a wood sprite to my people?

I crack the book open near the center and flip through the pages until Awri's hand shoots out, to halt the motion.

"Is that what you saw?" she asks excitedly.

"I didn't really see it," I explain, "Just it's eyes."

"Her eyes," Riesh corrects me, and there is a sharp bent to his tone. I peel my eyes away from the pages to meet his, as he explains, "All of the wood sprites that remain after the sundering are female."

"She's been alive since the sundering?" I say in little more than a whisper as my eyes return to the pages.

"It's possible. Though fea biology is quite a bit different than that of a human," Kishek says as he leans across the table and turns the page.

Drawings of beautifully depicted wood sprites rest beneath the tips of my fingers. Despite the fact that every drawing is colored black and white it is impossible to mistake them for anything but fea. Their sharp features and pointed ears are similar to that of the feyn, though these sprites boast a leaf-like serrated edge along the shell of their ear that remind me of the leaves that fell from the tall oaks surrounding the La'tari keep when I was young. As if they sprouted from a closer form of nature than the feyn, they are draped in vines rather than gowns and small branches protrude from their hair, most adorned with budding flowers or berries.

An unending barrage of questions forms in my mind. So many that I could easily spend the entire day learning about nothing but the little woodland sprites, but my gluttonous eyes are glued to the sheets and my hands work of their own accord. They continue to flip through the tome, hungrily drinking in all manner of fea. Countless images of the creatures line the pages, drawn in vivid detail, and well over half of them are species I've never heard of.

"You drew all of these?" I ask Awri.

She dips her head and a blush blooms on the apples of her cheeks.

"They are incredible," I tell her, "I've never known anyone who could put such an image to paper."

The flush of her cheeks deepens, and I can't help but feel a little bad that I've embarrassed her, though Riesh stands a little taller at her side and smiles proudly down at his sister.

"Did you copy their likenesses out of picture books?"

"Oh no. These are only the fea I have seen myself. There are still a great many I'd like to find and add to the pages," she says, smoothing a thick strand of hair over her shoulder.

My mind reels delightedly at the thought. How is it possible I've lived my life alongside these creatures and never known? Another flip of the page and my breath catches on the dark image at its center.

"I've seen one of these," I say.

Awri and the two males bracketing her share a surprised look among themselves. The floorboards creak as the general takes a step toward the table. He peers down over my shoulder, his eyes sweeping across the intricately detailed drawing of the crone that found me in the woods many years ago.

"Bagya?" He sounds as surprised as the others look.

"Is that what they are called?" I wonder, my fingers tracing the lines of her robe.

"*She* isn't a species of fea, she is just … Bagya," he says.

"How did you find her?" Awri gapes, and the males beside her look to me expectantly.

"She found me," I say.

An odd, strangled sort of moan leaks out of Kishek's lungs.

"You made a bargain with her," Awri says matter-of-factly.

"How do you know that?" I balk.

"She would never have sought you out unless you needed something desperately, and even then, not unless you had something she greatly desired."

I suppress a shiver, struggling to tamp down the memories of my past life, memories that still feel like a punch in the gut whenever they threaten to surface. To this day, I have never been more afraid, and not for reasons I am willing to admit. Perhaps the crone should have frightened me more. I can tell by their faces she should have, but I suppose my fear was occupied elsewhere. And even after everything, if I had it to do all over again, I would give the creature anything she asked, if it meant he would be safe.

"You made a bargain with her too?" I ask Awri, trying to break free of the downward spiral of my memories.

It's written all over her face. She knows all too well what it means to encounter the crone.

"I did. She asked me to fashion a mask that would belie her face. The mask was the payment she required to save a life, that was the bargain."

Just as I had, Awri seems to tumble down a deep well of her own memories and the air thickens with a gloom that I feel entirely responsible for.

"She must have misplaced it," I quip, in an effort to lighten the sudden dreary mood. "The drawing is a true likeness, but I do recall her having sharper teeth."

My sad attempt at humor is lost in another of Kishek's mournful groans and some of the color drains from Awri's face. The water in the kettle begins to boil, and Awri jumps when it whistles behind her. Our eyes meet, we laugh, and I turn the page.

The mood lightens over a cup of tea and Kishek busies himself in the kitchen, coming out with trays of seasoned butter, fresh baked rolls, and all manner of sliced cheese and fruit. He lowers a clattering stack of plates to the table, just in time to hide the growl that comes from my stomach.

An early spring rain sets in and once Awri's sure I'm content to stay and wait out the storm, she sends a messenger to inform my uncle. I'm pleased, if not a little surprised, when the female settles in beside me on a large chair by the crackling fire. She hands me the heavy tome of fea, offering to answer every question I ask about the creatures contained within its pages.

My entire life, I've been taught that the fea who remained in our veil died out long ago, and I can't say that I'm sad that my tutors had been wrong about that. It feels like my entire world tripled in size in the span of an afternoon, and I begin to wonder what other secrets might be revealed to me before I complete my mission and return home.

Late in the afternoon a thunderstorm rolls in with a dense covering of dark clouds. The rain comes down in a sudden deluge with not a single break in the clouded horizon to promise its end.

"I have more than enough rooms for us all. You are welcome to stay here tonight," Awri offers sweetly as Kishek brings a cake to the table, cutting into and plating it before passing the thick chocolate slices around.

"I really shouldn't. My uncle will worry," I lie.

In reality, the man is bound to be thrilled by the proposition, but I left my cloak in my wardrobe like a fool and the contents of my little pouch in its pocket. My need for the herb is something I can hardly explain to the female without being firmly cast out of the inner circle I've somehow managed to find myself in.

"I insist. My letter said you would stay until the rain has ended, so he shouldn't worry. It's far too muddy for a carriage now and I won't have you walking back in the storm."

She squeezes my arm from where she sits beside me. "It's no trouble, Shivaria. There really is plenty of room. Just think of it like the sleepovers we had when we were young. It will be fun."

Her warm smile is full of expectation and all I can think about is the look of horror on Avanjelin's face when my blade sank into her flesh, forever depriving her of her flawless beauty. I smile and nod, even as my stomach clenches with nerves, threatening to expel my dinner.

Late in the evening, Awri shows me to a room tucked back in the farthest corner of the cottage. The general is given a room directly next to mine, and I have no doubt the decision is purely tactical on his part. I will have to pass by his door to make my way into any other part of the house.

My room is every bit as quaint as the rest of Awri's home. Pink ruffled sheets tumble to the floor, falling from a bed that looks as if it was carved from a large bundle of thick roots. A small window looks out over the river

and once I've made sure it opens without a sound, I mark it as my quickest escape route.

I've folded my pants and laid them on top of a wooden dresser painted in sprigs of lavender when footsteps sound on the stairs overhead. The rest of the party settles in for the night and I tip my ear toward the ceiling curiously when only two doors close above.

I have no idea how many rooms are at the top of the stairs, and I chastise myself for not asking Awri to give me a full tour of her home when I had the chance. While it is entirely possible there are only two rooms above me, and one is being shared, I won't be able to sleep until I've done a sweep of the ground floor and made sure I know where everyone is sleeping tonight. I am already uneasy about sharing a wall with the general and having another unaccounted-for body isn't an option. Every instinct I have tells me to know where my enemies are.

I open my door as slowly as I can, blessing the stars when the hinges don't make a sound. I move into the hall and take six blessedly silent steps before I'm buffeted by a gust of air from the general's door as it flies open. It's obvious he was getting ready for bed, like me he is absent his shoes.

My gaze wanders up from the floor, lingering above his waist. He's a few buttons short at the top of his tunic, and it's splayed wide revealing a dangerously chiseled chest that I'd rather have remained oblivious to. I'm not surprised to find the male glaring down at me when my eyes meet his.

"What are you doing?" he manages to somehow bark, even in a hushed whisper.

"I was just going to the kitchen for some water." The lie slides off my tongue.

"Then why are you sneaking?"

"I am *not* sneaking. I am trying not to wake everyone up." I glare back. "It's called being polite. I'll explain the concept to you another time."

He frowns and takes a step into the hall, wrapping his hand around my arm and shuffling me back toward my room. His shoulders are wide enough that he's effectively created a wall barring me from the rest of the cottage.

"You stay here," he says, clearly annoyed when he points at my door. "I will bring you a glass of water."

"Don't be ridiculous," I whisper, trying to tear my arm from his grasp. "As

I must apparently explain myself to you at every turn, I also have to relieve myself, or are you planning on doing that for me as well?"

He stops in his attempt to push me back through the hallway and into my room but makes no move to let me pass. The line of his jaw tenses and I wonder if he is seriously debating whether he's going to allow me the privilege. His eyes narrow and his grip tightens but this time he pulls me out of the hall and toward the bathing chamber next to the kitchen. He lines me up in front of the door, drops my arm, crosses his own over his chest, and waits.

"You're just going to stand right outside the door and listen?" I ask.

When he makes no move to answer or step away to grant me my privacy, I puff out my irritation and slip inside, pulling the lever by the sink to give him something to listen to. I've no actual need for this room but I do a quick sweep, nonetheless. I'm unsurprised to find that it's empty and the small window by the tub is far too narrow to make for a convenient exit if I should need it.

The moment I step out, the general's hand clutches my arm in a bruising grip and he's hauling me right back toward my bedroom. I plant my feet, not that I can stop him unless I plan on breaking his arm.

Tempting.

When he turns to see why I'm resisting him, I just smile sweetly and say, "Water?"

With a sneer, he drags me toward the kitchen, and I wonder if the male is trying to pull my arm out of the socket. He parks me in front of the sink and hands me a glass. I fill it to the brim, take my time sipping it, and fill it once more, his disposition growing darker by the minute.

I have no doubt he will interfere in any further attempts I make at leaving my room this evening, so I decide to make the most of my current freedom. If it can even be called such a thing with my gloomy guard in tow.

My eyes land on the kettle sitting on the countertop among a clean stack of cups.

"You know what I really need? A cup of tea to help me sleep."

"I'm not making you a cup of tea," he says through gritted teeth, his patience with my game obviously coming to an end.

"That's fine. I'll make it myself."

I snag the kettle off the counter and turn toward the fireplace. He latches

onto my bicep once more, pulls me close so that he's looking down on me and I can feel the heat of his breath when he growls, "You've had your water, now go to your bed before I drag you there."

He has no idea just how many men I've known just like him. Men who would try to command me, expecting me to cower and jump to meet those demands the second they are uttered. They are all the same, and I'm sure, just like every other man and male on the face of Terr, his bravado doesn't run as deeply as he'd like me to think.

I soften my face and look up at him through long, dark lashes, taking a step toward him rather than pulling away as I breathe out in a whisper, "Sorry to disappoint you, General. But that's one place I'll never let you drag me."

His eyes widen and his head reels back as if I'd attempted to strike him. He clenches his jaw so hard I think I can hear his teeth begin to crack under the pressure. Finally, he releases my arm.

A quick glance around the main room tells me there is no one else sleeping downstairs.

Interesting.

I tuck the knowledge away and swing the kettle over the flames before picking Awri's fea book off the table and falling into a large comfortable chair in front of the fire. I don't have to look to know the general is standing in the doorway between the kitchen and the room I now occupy. A hefty dose of gloomy melodrama is billowing out from that direction.

"Once you've had your tea will you go to your room?"

I can't help but grin at the plea as I flip through the pages before me. "Perhaps," I say, and the general scoffs at my answer. "I don't sleep well in strange places."

I give him that much. It's an honest answer, though I don't intend to elaborate. Without the herbs to keep my demon at bay I'm beginning to seriously consider staying up for the duration of the night. If any of my new companions witness a single one of my episodes, I will never make it into the king's presence.

"Fine," he says.

I turn, shocked he's allowing it without throwing a fit. By the time my

head whips around, he's already gone. I frown when he emerges from the kitchen with a jar of loose tea in one hand and two cups in the other.

"You're a guest in my friend's home. It would be rude of me not to keep you company," he says.

I hate the taunting quirk at the edge of his lips.

Then again, it isn't the worst thing to have an opportunity to put the general's mind at ease about me. He has made his distrust of me clear since our first encounter at my uncle's estate. I've begun to wonder if I've let my guard down unwittingly and he's seen glimpses of the Drakai lurking beneath my surface. Though, given his nature, I suspect he is highly distrusting of everyone upon first meeting them. Either way, he is just one more obstacle I'll need to overcome before his king returns.

I settle into my chair and flip to the next page. The crone stares back at me.

"You're frowning," he says, his voice gravelly with want of sleep.

"I'm not," I say.

He puffs out his disbelief and I school my features, softening the fine lines that pinch my brow when I ask, "Have you ever seen her?"

He leans over to look at the page. "Happily not. I hope I'll never need anything so desperately that she seeks me out."

"I wouldn't wish that type of need on anyone," I tell him.

It's true, I wouldn't. Not even on him. It's the memory I hate reliving more than any other. Even after all these years, the fear and helplessness of that day are too potent and easy to recall. Like a wound that will never fully heal. Easy to forget at times, easy to learn to live with, but all it takes is a small jab in the right place to be reminded of what I nearly lost.

I startle when the kettle whistles. The general pulls it from the fire, pours two cups of hot tea and hands me one, before taking a seat in the chair beside me.

"Thank you," I say.

He only hums under his breath and blows on the steam rising from his cup as he stares into the fire. Thunder continues to roll overhead, lightning imbuing the night with its flickering arcs. A thick sheet of rain batters the roof and windows, obscuring the view outside, until all that can be seen is the bright, blurry globe of the moon hanging in the night sky as it breaks from the clouds.

"What did you bargain for?" His voice comes out in little more than a whisper and my eyes dart to the ceiling, remembering our sleeping companions overhead.

The memory feels private. Something I've only ever shared with one other soul. But maybe I can give a small sliver of my story to the general as an offering of peace. Perhaps a small bit of truth will put him at ease.

"I bargained for a life," I say quietly.

"No small request." He ponders my answer as he takes a sip of steaming tea. "What did Bagya ask for in return?"

"I don't know," I admit.

His eyebrows shoot up. It's not the most handsome face the male has ever worn but I'll take it over his brooding frowns.

"You gave her a future favor?" he guesses.

"No. She took something, I'm just not sure what it was. She wasn't particularly clear in her request, and I lacked the time it would have taken to ask the right questions."

Though what I would have asked her I still ponder to this day.

He hums and continues sipping his tea. I take a careful drink of the steamy beverage and when my tongue is met with the most deliciously sweet combination of herbs and spice, I pull in a few more greedy mouthfuls. The male certainly knows how to make a cup of tea.

"She didn't tell you what she wanted?" he asks.

I shrug as if it was nothing, but I've replayed that moment in my mind thousands of times, desperate to understand what the female took from me.

"She said the price was a piece of the lie. I was young," I say, worried he will call me a fool for giving up something I still don't understand, "and desperate, and I only thought to ask if it would harm me. The moment she said it wouldn't, I agreed and that was it."

His face converts back to its typical glower, only this time I'm relieved when it's directed at the fire. Even the flames seem to shrink a little under his gaze.

The crackle within the hearth melds with the patter of rain overhead, lulling me into a sleepy haze. The moment my eyes slip shut I snap them open again, giving myself a shake as I stifle a yawn.

Unbidden, the general remarks, "Trust me when I say you should never strike a bargain with a fea. The price will always be far too high."

"You're wrong," I say, and he turns to look at me speculatively. "Sshhe could have asked me for anything, and I would have given it to her. Even now, in that sssame moment, I would do it again."

Did I just slur?

"If you truly feel that way," he says as he puts down his cup and stands to look down on me, "it's only because you haven't begun to understand what you traded for that life."

I want to argue but I've forgotten how to use my tongue. My neck suddenly refuses to support the weight of my head as it lolls back against the chair, and then, there is nothing but the void.

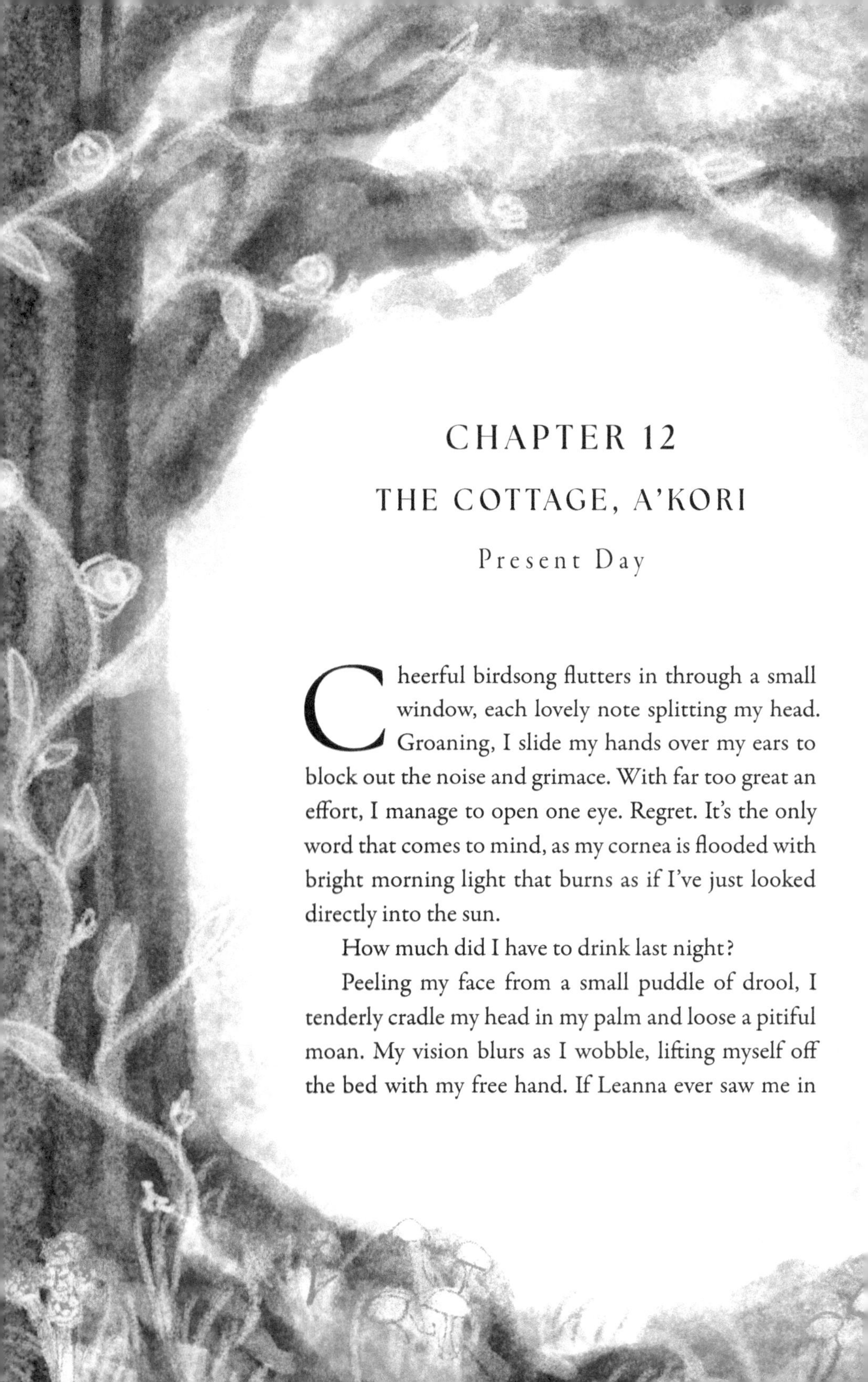

CHAPTER 12
THE COTTAGE, A'KORI
Present Day

Cheerful birdsong flutters in through a small window, each lovely note splitting my head. Groaning, I slide my hands over my ears to block out the noise and grimace. With far too great an effort, I manage to open one eye. Regret. It's the only word that comes to mind, as my cornea is flooded with bright morning light that burns as if I've just looked directly into the sun.

How much did I have to drink last night?

Peeling my face from a small puddle of drool, I tenderly cradle my head in my palm and loose a pitiful moan. My vision blurs as I wobble, lifting myself off the bed with my free hand. If Leanna ever saw me in such a state, she would all but end me just to prove how vulnerable I made myself. She wouldn't be wrong.

Forcing my eyes into focus, I prop myself up on my arms and take a moment to look around the room. My gaze settles on the dresser painted in sprigs of lavender and I'm thrown from my stupor when I remember exactly where I am.

My feet hit the floor, followed by a small throw I've been sleeping under. Rushing to pull my pants on under the dress I still wear from the night before, I glance in the mirror hanging on the other side of the room. I groan and drag my fingers through the ratty nest of hair. Cursing under my breath I give up and weave it into a somewhat manageable braid.

As my fingers deftly work the length of hair, I replay the events of the previous evening. I don't recall coming back to my room. Apparently, I hadn't even crawled under the covers before I'd fallen asleep. I frown, glancing at the thin throw on the floor. My mind feels like a dense cloud of fog has taken up residence. I remember sitting by the fire and ... the tea ... the general's smile. The bastard.

I tie my braid off with a small strand of hair and march toward the door. He is lucky the sedative he slipped me kept my demon at bay during the night. I'll have to ask him about the herbs he used. And I will. But first, I am going to kill him.

The moment I open the door I hear murmurs coming from the kitchen. By the sound of it, I'm the last one to wake. Riesh's voice carries farther than the others, or is it Kishek's? I haven't heard either male speak often enough to tell them apart at this distance, though neither has the depth of the bastard general's deep booming tone.

"I didn't say I can't. I said it will take time."

I take a few stealthy steps down the empty hall, recalling that not a single floorboard made a sound when I snuck down them the evening before.

From the end of the hall, I can hear Awri's voice clearly as she says, "Listen to him, Xey. This isn't something we can rush without risking harm. Not only to us, but to the girl as well."

"You think it is the Vatruke?" the general asks.

One of the males answers, "More likely one of the Vatruke than any of

the other feyn working with the La'tari. Nothing like that has been born into Terr since before the sundering."

An icy chill spreads throughout my veins and my stomach hollows. The La'tari would never work with the feyn and what in haliel is a Vatruke?

"A relic perhaps?" Awri suggests.

"No, Kishek would have sensed it," the general says thoughtfully.

"It can only—" Awri's voice cuts off abruptly.

A silence I know well sweeps over the cottage. It is the same silence I experienced when I'd first seen the feyn as a child. The deafening quiet that screams that they are aware of my presence. I don't waste a second before walking out of the hallway, making sure that my steps can be heard as I make my way into the kitchen. I tell myself that if they've only just become aware of my presence, there is a good chance they won't suspect I was eavesdropping.

I smile when I meet Awri's eyes across the kitchen. She smiles back. It's a genuine smile, but she looks tired, they all do, and I wonder if they have been up all night discussing—whatever this is.

Kishek in particular looks like sleep may have eluded him entirely. Dark circles stain the flesh below his eyes, and he braces himself on the stone counter as if he might need the support to remain on his feet.

"Good morning. I hope I'm not interrupting." I try to sound as cheerful as possible.

"Not at all. Have a seat and I will make you some tea." Awri grabs the kettle, but I stop her before she leaves the room.

"Thank you for the offer, but I should really get home to my uncle." It's not a lie, but more than that, the idea of another cup of *tea* sours my stomach.

"Of course." She smiles. "In fact, I've already called for a carriage. I hoped you wouldn't mind. I have some things I need to take care of in town this morning. We've just received a letter from the king."

That piques my interest, and I stand a little straighter, quirking my head to the side with genuine curiosity.

"He has high hopes of returning in time to host his yearly masquerade. It's quite the event, and I'm afraid he's asked me to plan it in his absence."

"I've never been to a masquerade," I say absently.

In fact, I've never been to any sort of formal party before landing upon

these shores. Though, Leanna was thorough in my education of such things and ensured I was well trained in dance, proper dinner etiquette, and every other social nicety required for attending.

"Well, I do hope that won't stop you from coming to ours," she says by way of invitation.

I smile and nod. If I'm able to reach the king by no other means, the party may be my best chance at ending him.

"How long do I have to prepare my costume?" I ask. What I really want to know is when the king will finally be within striking distance.

"The party will be held in little less than a month," she says.

"So soon?" I don't try to hide my surprise, and Awri giggles, clearly amused by my shock.

"Don't worry. I will introduce you to the seamstress I use for these events. She will have your gown ready in time."

We all turn to the window when the carriage comes into view and Awri takes my arm, leading me through the door, the others following close behind.

"I'm so sorry the storm kept you from your own bed last night. The general told me you don't sleep well in unfamiliar places."

I feel the flush of my cheeks and wonder if he told her exactly how he *had* managed to get me to bed.

"Please don't be sorry," I say, "I had a wonderful time. Thank you for sharing your drawings with me and for answering my questions about the fea. I still have hundreds, and I fear many of your answers will only lead to more."

"Well, I hoped to tempt you into helping me with my preparations for the masquerade. If you are willing, it would certainly give you plenty of time to ask those questions." She smiles coyly.

"It would be my pleasure," I tell her, even as I realize that Leanna's efforts in my tutelage may have fallen flat when it comes to event planning.

It certainly isn't a request typically made of a Drakai. But I have little doubt that my efforts on this front will surely gain me an audience with the king upon his return.

"Wonderful. I will be in touch." She kisses me on the cheek and her brother helps me into the carriage. Kishek stands at his side, his hands clasped behind his back, brow drawn into a thoughtful dip.

Even the general comes out to see me away and as the carriage lurches down the road I wonder if his glower will lift the moment I am out of sight. Not that I care.

"Oh, dear girl. I'm so glad you've returned," Felias fawns, as if he hasn't seen me for months, pulling me into a warm embrace in the middle of his courtyard.

The servants don't stop to stare, but I'm not fool enough to think they aren't paying close attention as they dart around the grounds, busily performing their tasks.

"I'm sure you'll want to freshen up. Have you eaten? No matter, I'll have an early lunch prepared for us. I want to know absolutely everything about your night away."

The man is too convincing for his own good. If I have to put up with another month of this, even *I* am going to start believing we are related. He shoos me up the staircase toward my room. The moment I close the door to my suite I loose a breath that's been trapped in my chest since I walked into the cottage hallway this morning.

I open the window overlooking the garden and inhale the gentle breeze that stirs the hairs framing my face. Lilac. Today the air is laden with lilac and lilies. I sigh, as the delicate bouquet permeates my lungs.

As I roll my head from side to side, the wind caresses my cheeks, spooling at the base of my neck and stealing away some of the worry that plagues me. Voices flit across my ears and I lean over the windowsill casting my eyes across the expansive grounds below. My brow pinches curiously when I find only birds flying between the trees and a small rabbit with a bushy tail eating a small patch of clover.

Strange.

The giant tub in the washroom calls to me, promising to ease some tension and soothe the knots in my shoulders. I flip the lever above the tub and strip down as thick steam wafts into the air, fogging the mirrors and the tall glass windows that line the walls of the room. I settle into the water inch

by inch, sucking air into my lungs between pursed lips. The water is near scalding, perfect in fact, and I ride that fine line between pain and pleasure as I slowly submerge my body up to my chin.

Most of the baths I've had throughout my life have been taken in the rivers and streams surrounding the keep. They'd been painfully cold in winter and early spring. I always enjoyed the temperate summer swims that served to wash the filth from my body after my early morning training sessions.

I had, on rare occasions, managed to sneak a bucket of warm water into my room and reveled in the luxury of washing with a rag, but Leanna made it clear it was an unnecessary indulgence and would only serve to make me soft. Though her warning, at times, went unheeded, I have no doubt the woman would have flayed me alive if she'd ever known.

So, I let the heat from the water sink into my bones, willing to take this moment and enjoy the pretense of the lady I claim to be. I may not care for the dresses, the parties, or the antics of social climbing. However, I will take whatever time I can secret away for myself, wholly aware that even upon returning as a hero to my people, I will once again be placed back into a humble life.

Thoughts I've managed to push aside since the morning settle into my mind as the water begins to cool. I wonder why they hadn't seemed suspicious about my eavesdropping, but I expect they would have been speaking somewhere more discreet if they had concerns about being overheard.

They hadn't said anything I couldn't repeat to the crown in A'kori. No secrets of state were whispered. No dark plots against my king. Still, my mind churns.

"Vatruke." I test the word on my tongue.

Perhaps Felias will know what it means. How they can possibly think the La'tari would work with the feyn is beyond my scope of imagination. I have never been taught much about the A'kori perspective as it pertains to ... well, anything. I have no doubt it is by design that I was never taught these things. Though, what benefit my ignorance is to my mission I cannot fathom. But soldiers don't ask questions, we simply do as we are told.

I reluctantly pull myself from the tub when a chill sets into the water. Drying off with an absurdly soft towel, I wrap myself in the silk dressing robe

hanging on the wall. As I lean down to pull the drain at the base of the tub, my attention snags on a flicker of movement at the corner of my eye.

My head whips toward the large double doors leading to my bedroom and my breath catches in my chest. Two slight fea creatures stand in the doorway. Well, one stands in the doorway, the other peeks out from behind the wall, pulling on her companion's arm as if to tug her out of my line of sight.

I should be afraid. I know enough about the creatures to know that many are gifted, just like the feyn. I'd grown up with tales of the vicious monsters that tore children apart with their bare hands and devoured them with their sharp fangs. As a child I was relieved to learn they no longer lived in our veil. Every fea that fled in the sundering was one less beast to haunt my dreams.

But the faces I see before me are not those I'd conjured in my mind when I was young, these two are feminine and soft. Thanks to Awri's detailed drawings they are also easy enough to recognize.

"You're a wood sprite," I say, curious if they will even understand me.

The sprite in the middle of the doorway cracks a toothy grin, points to her chest and nods eagerly.

Stars her teeth are sharp.

I should definitely be nervous, they managed to sneak into my room while I remained unaware, but their posture isn't threatening. If anything, they seem as curious about me as I am about them.

My eyes rove over their features. Even Awri's beautiful drawings could not capture the unearthly loveliness of the fea. I should have suspected as much, considering the feyn themselves are so startlingly ethereal in their own right. It only seems natural that other fea should share the trait.

Their features are similar. Both barely reach the height of my hip, heads covered in wisps of green hair that resemble fine grass wafting about in a light breeze. Small branches protrude from their hair, each holding a number of delicate buds and colorful flowers among waxy green leaves. Their skin is bronzed, the color of golden wheat with a small pattering of brassy freckles beneath their eyes.

The bold sprite in the doorway stares back at me, her vivid green eyes scouring every inch of me as I'm embarrassingly aware I've just done to her.

Blue and green meld over the lids of her eyes in a shimmering pattern that reminds me of the colorful wings I'd once seen on a pinned butterfly in a glass display box. Her friend stares at me from a pair of beautiful, but nervous, violet eyes with the same shimmering gilding behind a thick sweep of lashes. A large flower on top of her head is absent a magenta petal. I suck in a breath.

"That was you, up in the tree yesterday."

It isn't really a question but the brave sprite nods enthusiastically once more, pointing at her companion.

"I'm sorry. We didn't see you." It feels right to apologize even though I hadn't taken a single shot with the bow.

She takes a step back, gesturing for me to come out and join them in the main room. An uneasy shiver skates up my spine, and I hesitate. It's possible I've misread them completely and if they are upset about being shot at, which would be perfectly reasonable, I'm unprepared for what it might entail to fight one off.

Walking into the bedroom, I decide that if they are more fearsome than I realize I'm not likely to win a fight no matter where it takes place. Still, I head toward the vanity, eyes on the sprites as I stealthily grab one of the longer hair pins, just in case.

The shy sprite skitters away in retreat, hiding on the far side of the wardrobe as the other laughs at her, shaking her head. The hair on my arm stands on end when I hear it, like a laugh in the distance, brought on the wind only to be snatched away before it can fully settle on your ears. It's a familiar sound that I recognize immediately as the ghostly voices I've heard in the gardens of the estate.

The entire moment is too odd to convince myself it's a coincidence. Every word they speak skips off my ears like a small rock skipping across the surface of a lake to land upon the opposite shore. It looks like they are arguing, but it's hard to be sure.

The bold sprite stomps an angry foot on the floor, pointing a demanding finger, as the shier of the two steps out from behind the wardrobe, keeping her eyes on me. She begins rummaging around inside it while her braver companion points me to the chair in front of the vanity, ushering me over with a wave of her hand. I don't ask questions. I'm not sure it will help.

I sit as instructed, knuckles white under the strain of my grip on the large pin hidden in my fist. The sprite takes hold of my hair and inspects it, tapping a dainty finger against her chin. She proceeds to twist and braid it until she's crafted a rather whimsical masterpiece out of my tresses. Eyeing herself in the mirror, the sprite plucks a soft white flower from her branches before tucking it into my hair.

"Please don't do that."

She quirks her head to the side curiously when I speak.

"Doesn't it hurt?" I wonder.

The sprite smiles and shakes her head, plucking another flower from her branches, weaving it next to the one she placed behind my ear.

I watch through the mirror as her bashful comrade tumbles out of the wardrobe in a flurry of colorful silks, her cheeks flushed when she finds her feet. She directs a wheezing snarl at her friend as she hands her a pink gown, standing as far from me as she can, while still reaching the sprite standing by my side.

The brave sprite ushers me off my chair and stands on it. Now that she's nearly my height she raises the gown, dropping it over my head. I can dress myself in less than half the time, but each time I attempt to help and hurry things along I find my hand slapped away unceremoniously.

I resign myself to letting her have her way with my clothing and study the drape of leafy vines that seems to be a part of her skin, covering every intimate area below her waist. Her breasts are covered in a similar fashion, though there is a swell of flesh behind them, and I find myself wondering if those vines can be removed like clothing.

Her tiny fingers wrap around my jaw and lift my eyes to hers as she quirks an eyebrow. My cheeks flush when I realize I've been staring at her breasts from inches away.

"I'm sorry."

She drops my chin with a huff and a firm nod.

Hopping off the chair, she ushers me toward my bedroom door. Her shy friend shuffles across the room with a squeak and hides behind the bed the moment I move toward her. I glance at the garments strewn about the floor and risk snagging a pair of pants that match the dress, quickly pulling them over my legs.

The decision spurs the timid one to rush out from behind the bed and shower me in her displeasure. Fists at her sides she stamps a foot and glares across the room, her windy voice brushing past my ears in clear annoyance. Her friend waves her off with the sweep of her hand and pushes me out the door, into the hallway beyond, pulling it closed with a loud thunk and click.

What in the veil?

The rusty haired male crests the top of the stairs before I've had a single second to process what just happened.

"Your uncle sent me to collect you. He's had a lunch prepared in the gardens."

He leads me deep into the midst of countless heavy blooms artfully placed at the center of a winding maze of stone pathways. A rather ornate lunch is set out among a display of vases, overflowing with clusters of cascading flowers. Tall ornately carved crystal glasses sit among the array, and porcelain plates painted in delicate floral designs are heaped full of mouthwatering foods.

If I didn't know any better, I would say the man is preparing for a garden party, but there are only place settings for two. He's already told me he wants to know everything that happened yesterday, and I take note of the isolation the garden will offer. I wonder if I will finally have an opportunity to ask some questions of my own without fear of being overheard.

Felias saunters across the lawn just as I arrive, his voice carrying across the yard. "Don't you look lovely, Shivaria." He waves a hand at the rusty haired male, dismissing him. "Thank you, Enrik, I will handle it from here."

I've begun to expect his warm embrace and the light kiss he plants on my cheek but this time he lingers before pulling away. His eyes glimmer as they catch on the flowers woven into my hair.

"I see you've met Tig and Eon," he says with a knowing smile.

I hadn't had time to consider whether or not to tell Felias about the sprites, and I'm shocked to learn that he is more than simply aware of them.

"You know them?"

"All my life." He draws a chair out from under the table, offering me a seat with an outstretched arm.

I expect my uncle to seat himself across from me, but he pulls out a chair to my left, settling in beside me. It only takes a moment to understand why.

147

He wants to talk candidly, without risking our voices carrying into prying ears.

He holds a finger up to silence me before I can release the torrent of questions he surely sees bubbling up to the surface.

"First," he says, "You tell me everything that transpired yesterday, then I will tell you everything you want to know about the sisters."

"Sisters?"

His eyes gleam and I scold myself for allowing him to read me so easily. He's dangling a carrot, and I want it like I've never eaten a meal in my life. I make quick work of my story, careful not to leave out a single detail no matter how irrelevant it may seem. The man has known the players in my tale much longer than I have, and I would be a fool not to allow him total transparency, in case there is something I've missed.

"I told you to leave the general alone." He frowns.

"I'm sorry, I think you misheard me," I say, "It was the *general* that drugged *me*, not the other way around."

"I must say, I've never known the male to be quite as unpleasant as you make him out to be. Though he's never been a particularly jovial sort of fellow."

I exhale a small sigh of relief. It does feel good to know that I'm not entirely responsible for the general's consistently foul mood.

"Still, you know as well as I do that you are going to need his favor if you have any intention of meeting the king when he returns," he says, as he sweeps a thick smear of butter across a slice of berry sweetbread.

"I am acutely aware of that fact." I frown. "He is just so disagreeable about everything."

"Everything?" He raises an eyebrow at me disbelievingly.

"Everything," I say, taking a small sip of lavender lemonade.

"Well, the male must enjoy something," he insists, "You'd do well to find out what that something is and acquire an immediate and healthy appreciation for it."

I nod. He is right and at this rate I can't get on the general's good side fast enough. Awri is sweet and appears to be abundantly generous with her friends. If she likes him, he must have good qualities. Right?

"Any other questions?" I ask.

"No. The floor is yours, my dear," he says with a wide and theatrical sweep of his hands.

"I honestly don't know where to start... Can you understand them? The sisters."

"Of course, and you can as well. It's a simple matter of learning to listen."

"I have listened," I say.

"And do you understand them?" he asks with a coy smile, obviously aware of what my answer will be.

"No."

"Then, learn to listen better." He smiles over his glass as he takes a sip, holding his pinky in the air daintily.

"Which is Tig, and which is Eon?"

"Tig has green eyes, she's a bit more outspoken and the older of the two. She came to me the night of your arrival announcing that she was to attend you." His brow pinches a bit. He seems as perplexed by the sprites' actions as I am. "I thought it wise to wait, but it seems she's taken matters into her own hands."

"Attend me? Why would she want to do that?"

He shrugs, as if it isn't the strangest thing he's ever heard.

"Fea rarely explain themselves to mortals, but I do not doubt she has good reason for it. Though, what *good reason* is to a fea often alludes me," he chuckles to himself.

Felias takes my hand and his face grows serious.

"It's not often their kind are bold enough to reveal themselves so fully to a stranger. To other fea or human alike. You'd do well to treat that trust like the honor it is. There is a reason the fea fled this veil, and a reason the ones that remain are still in hiding.

I mean no offense when I say that if I had it my way, you'd have left A'kori without ever knowing of the sisters' existence. But as it is, all I can do is ask you to keep it to yourself. There is power in the friendship of a fea, and power in the secret of that friendship as well."

Some of what he says puzzles me but the last of it I understand in a deep primal part of the Drakai I was fashioned to become. Knowledge is power, and the right secret is powerful indeed.

"You trust them?" I wonder aloud.

He's clearly anticipated my question when the answer tumbles out of his mouth without a second thought, "With my life."

"With *my* life?" I ask deadly serious, because those are the stakes, and that is exactly what I forfeit if he's wrong about the sisters.

Awri didn't speak as if the fea worked closely with the feyn, she'd even made the fea sound allusive, but I'm not about to make assumptions that can jeopardize my mission, or my life.

"Especially with *your* life," he says.

I open my mouth to ask what he means just as my head snaps up to investigate a quick movement out of the corner of my eye. Enrik darts across the lawn at a pace far too hurried to be considered casual. He arrives out of breath, delivering a letter to Felias who pales upon reading it.

"If you'll excuse me, Shivaria. I have some things to attend."

The man rushes off before I can speak a word, and the hundreds of questions I still have about the fea sour on the end of my tongue. I immediately regret that I hadn't asked him about the Vatruke while we still had time to speak privately. Standing, I brush an invisible crumb off my dress, resolved to make sure we have another opportunity to speak, soon.

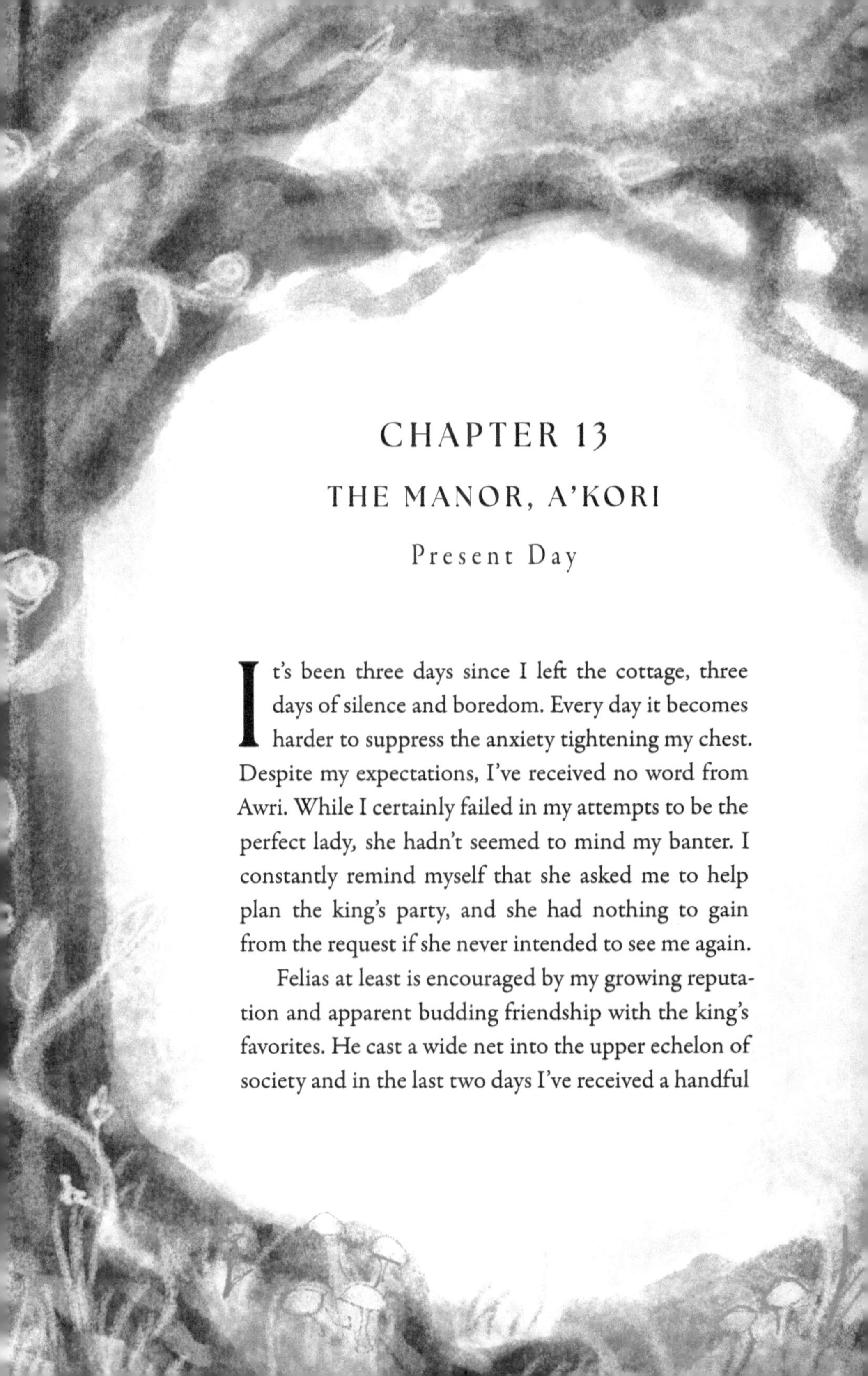

CHAPTER 13
THE MANOR, A'KORI
Present Day

It's been three days since I left the cottage, three days of silence and boredom. Every day it becomes harder to suppress the anxiety tightening my chest. Despite my expectations, I've received no word from Awri. While I certainly failed in my attempts to be the perfect lady, she hadn't seemed to mind my banter. I constantly remind myself that she asked me to help plan the king's party, and she had nothing to gain from the request if she never intended to see me again.

Felias at least is encouraged by my growing reputation and apparent budding friendship with the king's favorites. He cast a wide net into the upper echelon of society and in the last two days I've received a handful of friendly visitors that would like the benefit of my newfound connections. The social luncheons are tedious, and I find that my favorite times of the day are when Tig and Eon come to attend me. Unlike the social climbers, the sisters are entertaining and easy company to keep.

Lounging on a soft velvet chaise, book in hand, I watch the sprites and chuckle as they argue amongst themselves. Eon, while still timid, has stopped hiding behind the furniture, and I'm beginning to think Tig might have preferred her when she still acted shy in my presence. It hadn't taken Eon long to devise that I preferred the comfort of the silk pants beneath my dresses. Though it seems the sprite may have become bored with color coordinated fabrics as she is currently in the middle of a heated debate with Tig that I assume has something to do with the blue dress and green pants she tries to offer me.

A light skid along the hardwood floor has both sprites snapping their heads toward the hall, a wary growl escaping Eon's lips. I glance past them to find a letter, slipped beneath the large doors. Tig takes advantage of the distraction, pulling the colorful silks out of Eon's arms, as she points her sister toward the letter with the stomp of her foot. Eon lets out a string of windy words that flit past my ears as she walks to the door, snatching the sealed envelope off the floor despondently.

I'd taken Felias's advice seriously when he told me to listen harder and spent the last two days straining to understand the sprites. I find them in my suite every morning and night and while I still don't understand them, they do not lack for conversation among themselves. It wasn't until last night that I'd finally managed to grasp a single word as it attempted to glide past my ears. It was an enchanting sound, a breathy echo on the wind, and only made me more determined to listen until I can hear every word.

Eon hands me the letter, her arm stretched as far as she can manage, nearly bending backwards to keep herself away from me. The sprite is fearfully determined to keep as much distance between us as she can. At least she isn't hiding behind the furniture anymore. It's progress.

The moment my hand closes over the envelope she darts to the center of the room, her eyes wide saucers of violet.

"*Tha'haynah,*" the sprite says as she dips her head, and my own head tips curiously at the strange windy word.

I repeat the word, curious about how it will feel on my tongue, and the sisters share a glance at one another as they smile.

"What does it mean?" I wonder aloud.

I can hear the excitement in their voices as they talk over each other, but the words themselves are once again lost in the wind. I do my best to hide my disappointment and tuck the word away so that I can ask again, another time.

My eyes fall to the letter in my hand, and I puff out a breath, relieved to see Awri's seal. I was beginning to wonder if she changed her mind about being my friend. I certainly wouldn't blame her.

The letter is vague, and she hasn't asked for a reply.

"She's taking me to town," I say to the sprites, "and she'll be here within the hour."

Tig puts a hand on her hip and quirks an eyebrow. The sisters are every bit as animated and expressive as their words are elusive.

"I agree." I quirk a brow back at the sprite. "A little presumptuous of her."

Tig puffs out her agreement and selects a pale silver gown and a matching pair of pants to dress me in. As presumptuous as the *invitation* might be I'm nearly as relieved to be free of the manor as I am about furthering my friendship with the female.

I'm not used to being idle and despite the fact that the herb continues to keep my demon at bay during the night, when I dig deep, I can feel the darkness coiled inside of me. It bides its time, waiting for the release I desperately need. The herb won't last forever and that's something I'll have to deal with, but not today.

I shake off the thought and instead watch Tig braid my hair. Her hands haven't stopped moving but her eyes are fastened on mine and she's absent her usual smile.

I hurry into the courtyard when I see Awri's carriage approach. Whatever remains of my trepidation vanishes the moment she flings open the door and I see the warmth of her cheerful face. My mood spoils just as quickly when I take in the general sitting across from her. Another wave of relief hits me when she pulls me into the seat beside her so that I'm facing him, rather than sharing his bench.

"I'm so glad you could come with us today," she beams.

"As am I. Thank you for the invitation," I say, as Awri taps on the roof of the carriage, and it jolts forward.

"I'm glad to see you will be joining us as well, General," I say sweetly.

The male who hasn't so much as glanced at me since I climbed into the carriage whips his head toward me as if I've just threatened him. He looks me over and his lips form a hard line, but he tips his head in greeting before resuming his perusal of the grounds outside the window. I try not to be smug about the fact that I've already annoyed him and without even trying.

"I thought we might stop by Adora's," Awri says, "She is a good friend and by far the best seamstress in A'kori. She isn't taking new clients, but I'm sure she will make an exception for you. I've sent the invitations out for the masque just this morning and she, along with every other needleworker in town, is sure to be flooded with orders as soon as they are received."

"I would love that, Awri. Thank you," I say, biting back a grimace.

"Then why do you look like you're in pain?" the general sneers.

I hadn't noticed his eyes on me, and I think I prefer being ignored by the male. I school my features into a pleasant smile and keep my tongue from lashing out. No need to tell him that if I do look like I'm in pain, it's likely because I'm acutely aware that I'll have to suffer through his *charming* personality for the duration of the day.

"It will be fun," Awri says, taking my hand and wrapping it around her arm. "I normally despise standing for measurements, but I think you will find Adora is particularly amusing." She leans in, whispering in my ear loud enough for the general to hear, "I believe the general is afraid that you and she may get along a little too well."

I have no idea what she means but I can't wait to find out when the general side eyes her, his frown deepening.

A small bell rings when we enter the brightly painted shop near the center of town. I hadn't given it much thought the day I arrived in A'kori but due to the gentle slope of the city there are few areas in town that lack an expansive view of the sea. Behind a small table of sandwiches and cakes, a settee sits below a large window with a sweeping view of the shimmering harbor. Crystals hanging from a small chandelier over the seating area dance and sparkle in the sunlight. Vases of cut peonies adorn every surface, filling the air with the scent of spring.

A slender feyn rushes out from behind a heavy curtain leading to the back of the shop. Her hair is a dark shade of blonde, twisted into a knot at the top of her head. She wears a dress in the typical A'kori fashion, but she's taken the front panels of her skirt and knotted them below her hip, turning it into little more than a tunic and pants. Her dark brown eyes look me over from head to toe before she looks to Awri and opens her arms, her lips breaking to reveal a warm grin.

Awri is quick to wrap her up in a lingering embrace as she says, "It's been too long."

"You always say that," Adora chuckles.

"Well, it's always true." Awri pulls back from her friend, handing her a sealed letter produced from within the cloak she wears.

The seamstress cracks the seal, pulls out a thick, forest green invitation with golden scrollwork and lets out a long whistle.

"I'll make sure my girls are expecting the orders. But your dress, I will sew myself," Adora beams.

"I'm hoping you'll have time for two," Awri says and beckons me over. "Adora, this is Shivaria. She's recently come from La'tari to stay with her uncle for the season, and she's in need of something exquisite that can only be crafted by your magical hands."

I will myself not to look at her hands as I wonder if the seamstress is in fact gifted or if it is only a turn of phrase. Adora's eyes sparkle at the compliment, and she offers me a small, kind smile.

"Lovely to meet you, Shivaria. If you've managed to work your way into Awri's favor, I'm sure I can find the time to craft your gown as well." Her eyes fall back to the invitation. "What is the theme?"

"Fea," Awri says, bouncing on her heel as she claps her hands. "Inspired by my new friend here." She nods in my direction.

"Stars above. You realize my girls will be working around the clock to satisfy the demands for such an event? You couldn't have simply picked a color for your theme? Blue maybe?"

When Adora's gaze lands on the general, she gives him a thorough perusal

as if she has only now become aware of his presence. Her lips curve up at the ends as she says, "I take it you will be wanting a gown as well? I suppose I could work in a third. Something bright and cheerful to cover up that disposition of yours."

Oh, I like her.

The general on the other hand doesn't look particularly amused. Which only makes it better.

I bite down a laugh, twisting my lips to keep the smile off my face. Awri gives me a mischievous wink, and I think just maybe this will be the first time I've ever enjoyed seeing a seamstress.

Adora offers me a seat by the window, encouraging me to help myself to refreshments while she takes Awri's measurements across the room. The general makes himself comfortable in a seat close to mine, careful to place himself directly between us. He still doesn't trust me, though I have no idea why. I should have realized the moment I saw him in the carriage that he likely came for her protection.

"The theme is fea?" I ask, trying to make conversation with the male.

"It is."

He looks content to leave it at that, but I am determined to win him over. So, I press on.

"Any fea?" I ask.

He purses his lips, tapping his fingers on the armrest of his chair before turning to meet my eyes.

"Traditionally, you dress as the last fea you've had dealings with. I suppose since you've only ever interacted with the one, it will be an easy choice for you."

It takes me a moment to track his line of thought. He doesn't know about the wood sprites and the only other fea I've had dealings with...

My stomach pitches at the thought of the crone.

"Bagya." It comes out as little more than a whisper on my lips.

"It's a good choice," he shrugs, "and it will be unique. She reveals herself so rarely that you're not likely to come across anyone else dressed in her likeness."

"Shivaria. I'll take your measurements now."

Awri takes a seat by the general as the seamstress escorts me across the room.

She situates me on a small landing surrounded on three sides by tall mirrors and asks, "Any thoughts as to what you might like your costume to be?"

"What did Awri choose?" I wonder.

"I'll let her tell you if she wants to," she says with a small smile. "Most of the ladies prefer it to be a surprise and being a seamstress is as much about keeping your lips sealed as it is about creating lovely things."

I consider all the closely guarded secrets the female is likely privy to and decide that she might in fact be a *very* good friend to have.

"Bagya," I say quietly.

Her hands still and she raises her eyes to meet mine, a half-smile forming at the corner of her mouth when she says, "I think I'm going to like you."

She is back to work measuring my arms before I can reply.

"Brave choice of costume. I'm going to have a lot of fun with the design. Unless you prefer to design it yourself? Awri usually gives me free reign on her gowns."

"The design is all yours."

She laughs at the clear relief in my voice as she stretches her measuring tape across the top of my arm before jotting a number down in a small booklet.

"Awri tells me you two met recently," she says, "She rarely takes to anyone so quickly. You're lucky. She is an exceptional lady and a good friend."

"I can see that."

"I'm glad to hear it," Adora says, standing to wrap her cloth measuring tape around my chest. "The general is a good male, too. It just takes him a while to warm up."

"I'm not sure I'll live that long," I say.

"You might not," she chuckles, "but if you do, his is a friendship that is well worth the wait."

Adora frowns when my body tenses as the shop door swings open, announcing the arrival of a new customer with the delicate ding of a silver bell hung over the doorway.

"Awri," the female's voice coos sweetly, "How lucky I am to find you here."

Adora rolls her eyes, scoffing around a mouthful of pins but no one seems to notice.

"Sycophants," she mumbles under her breath.

The female glides from the doorway, a flutter of red silk billowing after her. She bows her head deeply as she approaches Awri. There is no doubt in my mind, had she been born La'tari, Leanna would have claimed her as one of her own.

Her dark strands gleam like raven's feathers in the sunlight, shades of blue dancing along her tresses, pulling on the deep sea in her eyes. Her porcelain skin a stark contrast to the deep red of her pouting lips. Lips that can only be described as a mockery of sadness. For nothing about the female would convince me she has ever had a hard day in her life.

Her skin is absent a single scar, her form absent any declaration of mended bone. No calluses or sign of any wear upon her skin. If perfection has a form, it is standing across the room. The feyn blood in her veins is surely responsible for some vast part of her unearthly beauty, but even for one of them she is striking.

Awri smiles warmly, almost warmly enough to convince me she's fond of the female.

"I'm hardly surprised to see you here, Ishara," Awri says, "I expect you've already received your invitation."

Ishara feigns a sweet laugh, her eyes darting to and from the general briefly.

"And so, I have," she says. She produces the invitation from a cleverly concealed pocket, fanning herself with it playfully. "I'd hoped to arrive early enough to secure one of Adora's masterful creations."

"I'm afraid my books are completely full," Adora says, her back to the door, as she measures my right arm for the fourth time since Ishara entered the shop. "I've just taken on my last client."

Ishara looks at me for the first time, her eyes expressing her displeasure as they roam across my form before rising to meet my own.

"The La'tarian?" Her lips pucker in clear annoyance.

"Ishara, may I introduce you to Shivaria, niece of Felias." Awri's kind smile doesn't fade.

"*Durah?*" she asks, and my fists clench at my sides.

Awri glances toward the general, who gives the subtlest of nods, before she confirms with a nod of her own. "Yes."

Worthless.

I tell myself that maybe friendship means something else to them, and even if it doesn't, friendship was never my goal, only a means to an end.

"How unfortunate," she says with an overly sympathetic smile that only I can see.

The ease with which she dismisses me is perhaps more cutting than anything else she's said or done. Her attention turns to the general and I can't help but feel some small amount of pity for him. That is, until she speaks.

"And have you decided what your costume will be, General?" she says, her head tipped down in false modesty as her thick lashes flutter at the male. "I will have mine made to match it, if you would be agreeable to the pairing."

"I am undecided," he says flatly, his hands clasped behind his back.

She steps toward him, utterly unperturbed by his tone. "Then tell me what you would find most pleasing, and I will have it made."

She only stops when the space remaining between them becomes intimate. "Perhaps one of the island nymphs of Kator?"

Adora's hands falter in their movement as her eyes widen, and she glances over her shoulder to survey the scene. Awri tenses and the general stiffly rises to his full height. Though the suggestion would have been lost on me only days before, I had been thorough in my investigation of Awri's drawings during my time at the cottage.

While there were many nymphs, most appeared in the forest, hiding among the bushes, blending with the bark of the trees they favored. Some seemed to prefer the sea, disappearing among the kelp and foam. The nymphs of Kator however, had been notably absent any clothing, and preferred to frolic nude beneath the stars, with an audience no less.

The shop bell chimes once again. The three young females it announces bring air into the room, releasing a small but notable bit of tension.

"Good morning, ladies," Adora greets them as if the conversation taking place across the room is not occurring.

Again, I begin to wonder if I've been seriously under instructed as to the social norms of the feyn.

I startle when I hear the general say under his breath, "Nothing you could add or remove from your form could convince me to consider you, Ishara."

"Xey," Awri issues the warning under her breath.

I know the tone, and I'd seen the tightly wound stance of her body thousands of times in my years at the La'tari keep. Though I'm unaware to what extent, there is danger here.

Had I not seen the mild flush in Ishara's cheeks or noted the quick contraction and loosening of her fists at her sides, I might have missed the subtle chill of anger in her tone when Ishara speaks again.

"Now General, is that any way to speak to a future sister of your king?"

While the general's face remains a sheet of unprovoked granite, Awri's lip pulls up in a near snarl. An odd contrast of beauty and anger displayed across her features.

With the slightest backward tilt of his head and raise of his brows, the general is looking down his nose at the female before him, a smile tugging at the edges of his lips.

"*My* king? Is he not your king as well?" he says.

Though her back stiffens defiantly, Ishara wisely takes a small step in retreat. If such a thing were uttered on La'tari soil, it would mean a death sentence for the one who had spoken it, and a long, uncomfortable life for anyone associated. No matter the continent, there will never be room for questionable loyalties in times of war.

I remind myself that we are at peace, tenuous as it may be, and tuck away the knowledge that even among their elite there are alliances to be had.

"Of course he is *my* king," she says fiercely.

"Then I don't need to remind you to choose your words more carefully. Otherwise, some might think you are in rebellion of the crown. Or worse."

Whispers break out among the audience of females lingering by the front door and Ishara's confidence falters, as she takes another step in withdrawal.

"I will write to the king and tell him of what, I assume, is your mother's request for a match between your house and the crown. Trust that I will explain in meticulous detail every word spoken here today."

She pales at that, and I wonder what her king will do to her upon his return. There is no doubt in my mind that the general will send the letter, happily.

To my surprise, and judging by the look on Awri's face, to hers as well, Ishara falls to her knee in a graceful flutter of silk. She holds her hands above her head, palms up as her gaze falls to the floor. An offering of submission.

I'm not entirely convinced the general will accept her defeat. His face holds no sign of being amused or even satisfied with his triumph. Only a small flicker in the line of his jaw and a hard glint in his eyes give any hint as to what the male might truly be thinking.

"Save your apology for the king," he says in a measured, harsh tone.

Slowly, as if it pains her, Ishara rises to her feet. Her eyes take in the measure of the room, of those who have witnessed her shame. Defeated, but with a defiant stride, she steps toward the door, reaching for the handle.

"Ishara," he says, and her eyes meet the general's once more, "I suggest you disinterest yourself in your pursuit of me."

She stiffens at the command but offers the general a small nod before issuing a command to the ladies who continue to watch nearby, "Forget everything you've seen here today."

Though I can't fathom anyone in the room simply forgetting the spectacle she's made of herself, her threatening tone stands my arm hair on end, a chill rushing up my spine as she departs.

I nearly jump when Adora slaps her notebook closed beside me and with a cheerful smile announces, "All done."

And as if Ishara were in fact the queen of A'kori, the ladies, who had only moments ago been witness to her social obliteration, begin bustling about the shop, examining the thick bolts of delicate fabrics.

Odd.

It seems there will be no end to my surprise when it comes to the social antics of the feyn. I begin toward the door, my feet slowing beneath me as I observe Awri and the general beside her.

Had I met them in this moment, I might have assumed Awri to be the military commander. Her gaze never leaves Ishara as she disappears down the cobbled streets in a sea breeze billow of crimson fabric. Perhaps it is her keen feyn sight that keeps her eyes lingering on the streets long after the female's departure.

"We are done here," she says to no one in particular, before offering Adora a warm smile and a quick embrace.

Somewhere between the shop door and the carriage there is a shift in the mood of my party. The general opens the door for Awri and, by default of my presence behind her, for me as well. Though the male does not so much as acknowledge my thanks as I slip into the seat beside her.

The carriage is in motion the moment the general shuts the door. A wide range of emotions play across the face of the female beside me. Anger. Speculation. Curiosity. When her turbulent features finally settle, she is clearly annoyed, waiting patiently for the general to meet her eyes.

When he does, it is only the tilt of her head and raise of her brows that beg an unasked question.

"Three weeks ago," he begins, "Yshka approached the king, proposing an alliance of houses."

Her brows pinch together. "And he declined," she says with a fierce certainty, a thoughtful look passing over her features before she adds, "And then he left A'kori."

The general nods in confirmation, Awri's brow unfurrowing as she sighs the tension from her shoulders, her gaze growing pensive the next second.

"Yshka is Ishara's mother," she says to me, "Long ago, her grandsire was nearly crowned king of the feyn, and though her family has never expressly spoken out against the king, they remain a great power with a great deal of sway in the kingdom."

"It sounds like a perfect match," I admit.

The general's mood notably sours and Awri chuckles as she says, "If the king wanted to wed a viper, it would be."

"If they are dangerous, why would the king allow them to remain here?" I ask, immediately regretting the question when the general levels me with his disdainful glower.

"Spoken like a true La'tarian," he says, "*We* do not simply murder anyone that doesn't fall in line."

It takes everything I have to school my features and bite my tongue. Leave it to the male across from me to take a simple question and turn it into the most horrific assertion.

 162

As if to alleviate the growing tension in the carriage Awri places a hand on my arm, drawing my attention and asking, "You don't mind if we make one more stop while we are in town, do you, Shivaria?"

"Not at all." I force a smile. How can I tell her if I do?

Thankfully, the general seems content to glower out the carriage window for the duration of our journey. A blissful, if not somewhat tense, silence falls over us. Awri is clearly lost in thought, and in this moment, I am happy to remain forgotten. My own thoughts attempt to unravel all that I have learned today.

I tuck away the knowledge that there are feyn families who would like to see the king dethroned. While I learned many years ago that the enemy of my enemy is not always my friend, there are certainly ways to leverage such animosities. If I play my hand well, I might be able to end the king without lifting a finger.

I lose track of time as we journey toward the outskirts of town, stopping outside a tall building nestled in a large, wooded grove full of playful children. We are greeted by a tall man in a navy waistcoat waiting outside the front door.

"I'll wait here," the general says, handing Awri a large sack before leaning back in his seat.

I half expect the male to demand that I remain with him, but he does nothing more than give me a cursory glance as I follow her.

Awri is quick to introduce me to Lias, the old man in the waistcoat. He has a thick mat of grey hair and a heavily wrinkled face.

"Boys are waiting just inside. Have been all morning."

"I'm sorry to have kept them waiting," Awri answers sweetly.

"Bah," he balks, "Don't you dare tell 'em that. They're like to wait there every week if they think it'll bring ya sooner. Ought to be out back playing with the others."

Awri chuckles. "I think I may have the solution to your problem."

She hoists the bag off the ground and Lias smiles, tipping his head toward the door. Awri glances back to see that I'm following before letting herself inside.

Three young boys chase after one another in a large room littered with all

manner of toys, the walls lined with a colorful display of children's artwork. Their heads whip toward the door in succession, the boys beaming toothy grins when they see Awri enter. Two call her name excitedly and rush to her side. The fond smile on her face as she looks down at them is pure and genuine, adding a heightened beauty to the female that seems altogether obscene.

"Thom, Fandry." She greets them each with a dip of her head and gestures to the thin feyn boy standing behind them. "Who is this?"

"Elian. He's new," says Thom, a young boy with a thick mane of dark brown hair and dark eyes. "He wants to meet the king."

"Does he?" Awri asks, crouching down, closer to the boy's height. "I'm afraid the king had business to attend elsewhere and doesn't plan to return for more than a fortnight."

The boys visibly slacken, their faces crumpling.

Thom scuffs his boot across the floor, sighing despondently, "I told Elian that the king would make him a sword, so that he could practice being a knight, just like us."

"I will take your request to the king myself," she says firmly, and their posture straightens a bit. "I have no doubt that the king will craft another sword for your new friend." Awri loosens the strings at the top of her sack and pulls out two small wooden swords, handing them to Thom and Fandry. "Until then, perhaps you two can share with your new friend?"

The boys nod eagerly as they take hold of their new treasures. The swords are well made, carved from a wood much lighter and softer than those I'd been trained with at their age. Unlike the one I'd been handed as a child, these will not break bone if the boys get too carried away.

"And when the king comes back, you're sure he'll carve one for Elian too?" Thom asks, not the least bit shy.

I'm shocked by his question. Not because of his forwardness but by his assumption that the king himself carves the toys. I may have never ruled anything, but I imagine kings lack time for such things.

"I am sure of it. Now go play with your friends and I'll see you next week."

The boys wave to Awri as they run out the door, their shouts and laughter lost among the myriad playful voices coming from the woodland outside. My feet are moving before I know where I'm going and Awri follows me to the back of the building where a large window looks out over the yard. Children weave between the bases of the giant pines, chasing each other in a game of tag, while others swing on benches tied with long rope to the branches of a wide maple.

"What is this place?" I wonder.

"The orphanage. It is a place where children without families can live until we are able to find them good homes."

"You find them homes?" I say, marveling at the notion.

"We do, and until then, they stay here. The crown supplies them with clothes and food, and they attend school, just like every other child in A'kori."

I feel my cheeks flush. She isn't shocked when it is obvious I've never seen an orphanage in my life, she must know that we have no such thing in La'tari. Not that our parentless children lack choices. They are always welcome to join the military. There they receive three meals a day, a roof, and a uniform, just as I had been given when Leanna found me.

The mixture of both feyn and human children playing with one another twists my stomach. What will happen to the humans when another war erupts between the continents? A war I am likely to start. Will they raise them to fight their own kind or simply slaughter them?

I force a smile at Awri and begin toward the carriage. Every day I spend with this female produces a hundred irritating questions I lack answers for. The general opens the door of the carriage, and I step inside. Awri stops just outside, snatching a heavy sack of coins off the bench and turning back toward the orphanage.

"I almost forgot. I'll be right back," she says, closing the door behind her and striking up a conversation with Lias after she hands him the coin.

I settle back against the wall of the carriage and stiffen when I find the general pinning me with a stare.

"What do you think?" he asks.

"About what?"

"About the orphanage."

Again, my cheeks begin to heat. "It's charming."

"You think it a novel idea to feed and clothe helpless children?"

I can't help but glare at the male. "I think you've never traveled to La'tari if you believe it has the resources to feed and clothe every child orphaned by the rippling impact of the war."

I want to suggest that his king send supplies for the human children in La'tari but I won't gain any favors implying that his king hoards resources.

"It certainly has enough resources to feed its ever-growing military," he says flatly.

"And the military is always an option for any of the parentless children on our shores. They don't turn anyone away," I say.

He sneers, "Such a small price to pay not to be left to die of starvation. Groomed as a child into a life of indentured servitude to the crown."

I laugh at him then. "You would lecture me about grooming children when I've just seen those boys handed play swords sent to them by their king?"

Hypocrite.

"How can you justify the same actions you condemn?" I say heatedly.

His eyes widen and he clenches his jaw, as he growls, "It is not the same thing."

"Because it is *your* king that does it?"

"Because we make no demands on any child in exchange for safety, the promise of a warm bed, and food. Things that every child should have, no matter what they were born as, or what they choose to be when they grow older."

I open my mouth to argue then snap it closed when I find that there is no argument to be had. I don't disagree, and if I had the ability to feed every starving child by simply wishing it, I would have no requirements set upon them in exchange.

"Where exactly in La'tari are you from?" He glares down at me. "It's obvious you've lived a life far removed from the *lower class*."

His words are sharp as daggers as he continues, "How easy it must be to settle that pretty head down upon a silken pillow and fall asleep in the safety of your high tower and not give a single hisht about the suffering of those unfortunate enough to have been born outside your class."

I imagine crushing his windpipe with a single well-placed jab and my neck tingles as all the blood in my body rushes to my face. He has no idea what kind of life I've lived or what I've seen. Yet the venom of his words burns in my veins as if every word were true, because this, this is how he sees me. *This* is why he hates me.

I should be flattered that he's bought so thoroughly into my guise, stars know I haven't given the male much reason to think I'm a lady. I cool my temper, pressing my back against the wall of the carriage, willing the tension out of my body. It's a monumental effort to stifle the rage he riles within me, to calm the coiled demon that demands to be set loose upon him. But I can use this. I latch on to all his assumptions and let them pour into me, refining the mask of the lady, and I slip it on.

As my features turn placid, his own slip, but only for a moment. The anger and assumption flickering to confusion before he regains his composure.

"You're right," I say, "I don't have much experience with those born less fortunate. The orphanage is a good idea, and I can honestly say I wish this wasn't the first I'd ever seen."

I hate every silken word as it slides off my tongue. I actually agree with most of it. It's the lie, tangled in an unfortunate web of truths that I despise. *I don't have experience with those born less fortunate.*

All I have *is* experience with those born less fortunate, and if anyone here is accustomed to laying their head on a silken pillow at night, it is surely him.

The air rushes out of the carriage when Awri swings open the door.

"Sorry to keep you waiting," she says.

Though a taut thread of tension remains between us, if Awri notices, she doesn't say anything.

It's late afternoon by the time I'm ushered out in front of the manor and sent off with a promise that a carriage will be waiting for me in the morning. I watch the carriage cross the avenue, heading toward the palace grounds.

Aside from Awri's remarks that the orphanage was most grateful for the coin left by the king, it was a silent journey home. I can't tell if I'm relieved that he had nothing more to say or annoyed that he never acknowledged my declaration that he was right. Maybe it's a bit of both.

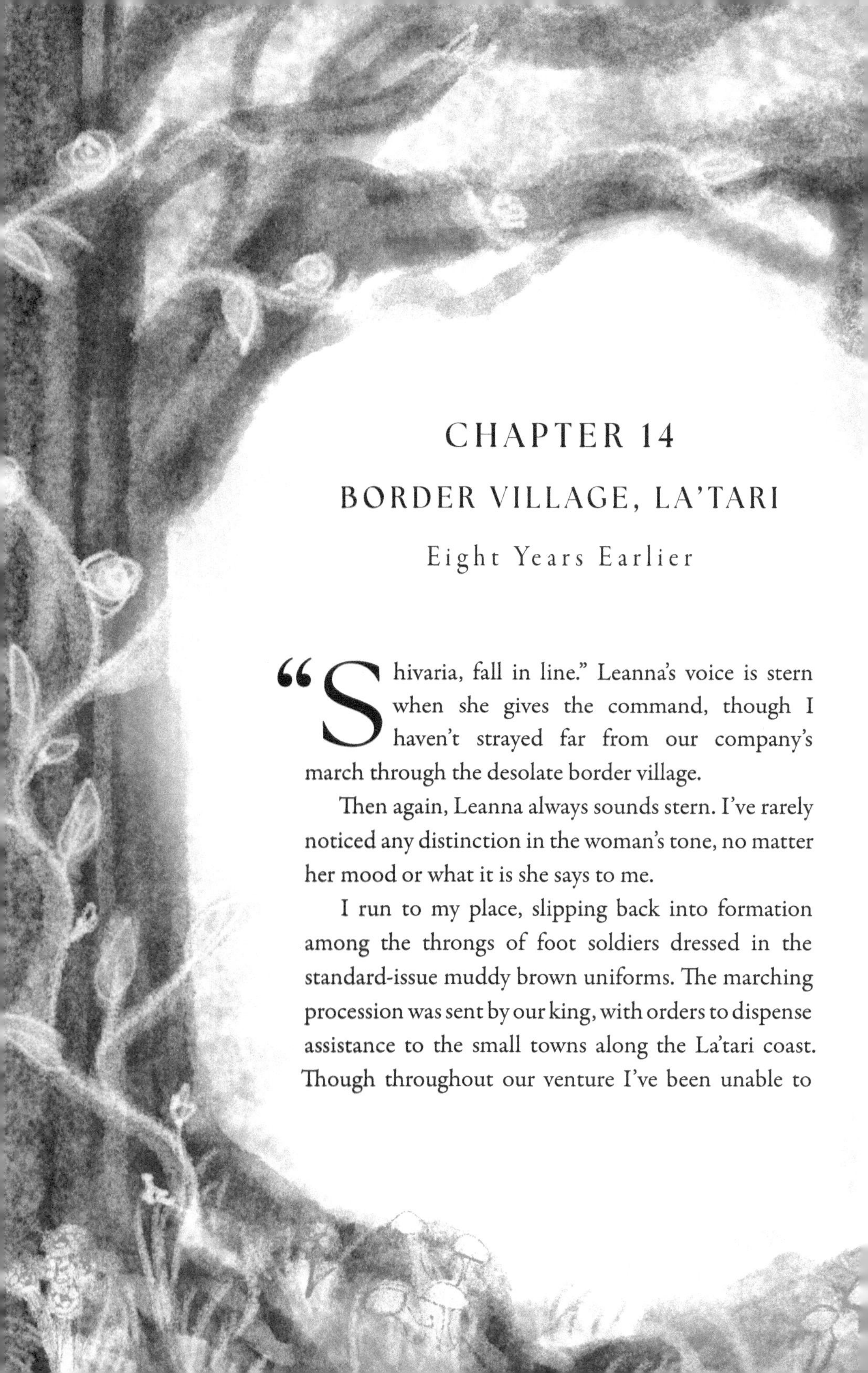

CHAPTER 14
BORDER VILLAGE, LA'TARI
Eight Years Earlier

"Shivaria, fall in line." Leanna's voice is stern when she gives the command, though I haven't strayed far from our company's march through the desolate border village.

Then again, Leanna always sounds stern. I've rarely noticed any distinction in the woman's tone, no matter her mood or what it is she says to me.

I run to my place, slipping back into formation among the throngs of foot soldiers dressed in the standard-issue muddy brown uniforms. The marching procession was sent by our king, with orders to dispense assistance to the small towns along the La'tari coast. Though throughout our venture I've been unable to discern what assistance, if any, we might offer our people. The land remains desolate, dying off a little more every year and with it, the La'tari people.

Every step along the silty, rutted road sends plumes of dust into the air until we are marching in a cloud of dirt so thick, I can taste it. Even the normally pristine, black leathers of the Drakai leading us begin to cake in the debris, camouflaging them among the rest of the legion.

When the feyn came during the war they took more than mortal lives, they took the very lifeforce of Terr from these lands. Bled dry of its essence, the La'tari found that though seeds could still be sown, we would never see another abundant harvest upon our shores. This was the price the feyn exacted upon us for fighting back against their slaughter. If what they stole from the land can be recovered, we certainly haven't found the way.

The homes we pass are haphazardly pieced together. Some made from rotten logs, others mud and whatever drifted scraps their occupants scavenged along the coast. Few structures remain standing from before I was born. They are easy to spot. Blackened boards blistered by brutal fires mark them as remnants of the war. I can't help but wonder how many had gone up in flames with their families still inside. Just like the one Leanna pulled me from as a child.

I eye the remnants of a small garden outside a tilting home built of rotten boards and my stomach drops. It's not the first we've passed. Every small garden started in early spring inevitably ends as a desperate effort in futility. Lands that not long ago produced in abundance beyond anything I've ever seen, are now little more than barren wastelands. Vast expanses of unfertile soil spread out in every direction as far as the eye can see.

It isn't uncommon to find a body lying in the road, bloated in the sun or thoroughly decayed. I'd seen both, stepping over three in the span of two days. I've never been brave enough to look down at their faces.

Through the churning dust I spot a small group of children huddled against a large building, abandoned long ago. They cling to one another in small piles, curled up against flea ridden mutts for warmth. Anything to protect themselves from the chilly air that promises an early winter. I haven't seen a scrap of food outside my rations since we left the keep three days ago, and it is clear by their sunken eyes and distended bellies that each soul we pass hasn't seen a warm meal in much longer than that.

"Halt," Leanna issues the order, throwing a fist in the air to signal the end of our march. "Make camp."

The procession breaks. Not a moment wasted before the mass of bodies around me begins to roil, every soldier confident in the task they have been assigned. That is all it ever takes. One word from Leanna and the entire company would hop on one foot until she told them they could rest.

As a younger child I often wondered how she inspired such dedication and obedience. Now, surrounded by the reminder of where our troops would be if they had not pledged their lives to the service, the choice they've made is a clear one. Service or starvation. I'm relieved that our military at least has enough food to feed its own.

Dropping my pack by the side of the road, I erect my small canvas tent before running off in search of Leanna. It's my first trip with the company and out of all of them, I have by far the simplest task. Watch, listen, and learn.

I find her in a small house that looks like one good windstorm might knock it over. She's standing next to Bront and two other commanders, leaning over a rickety table with a map splayed out on top. As always, everything south of La'tari on the map is smeared with a heavy layer of black coal.

The Smudge. Just once, I'd like to see what lies beneath it. Someone must know.

"Our informants say it landed here," Bront stabs the map with a thick finger, indicating a small swath of land along the coast.

"Sorie, scout the shore. One mile in each direction. Davik, search the homes." Leanna flips her long golden braid onto her back as she gives the command, and the two soldiers break from the rickety shelter without a word.

My eyebrows pinch together. The entire company was told we came to help the villagers, but we'd done nothing but march past them for three days. Leanna hadn't explained the mission, she didn't have to, and I know better than to ask.

Davik and Sorie jog back up to the door and I eye them curiously. There's no way they've run a mile in each direction and made it back so quickly.

"We found it," Sorie puffs, a little out of breath, "In a cellar, by the shore."

She leads us to a small shelter sitting on a sandy rise overlooking the sea. Bending down, she opens a small hatch in the center of the hut, and I gasp.

The large cellar beneath the structure is bursting with food. Fresh and dried, preserved meats and jarred goods. Enough to last five villages through the harshest of winters.

"Excellent." Leanna surveys the abundance, not seeming the least bit surprised. "Have it loaded onto a cart."

The villagers watch from afar as the precious cargo is loaded and taken back to the road. It's settled safely among our ranks and after sunset, when we've all finished our rations, each member of the company is given a fresh apple. My mouth waters as soon as the reddish pink fruit is plopped into my outstretched hand. Rations are little more than stale bread and tough cured meats. I stopped asking what kind of meat it was. I learned long ago that I don't want to know.

Soldiers settle into their tents around me, and I brush the sandy apple against my pants. Bringing the pink fruit to my lips, I inhale deeply, basking in the fresh scent, wishing I had a dozen more just like it.

My teeth graze the peel as my eyes meet the dull gaze of a boy half my age, shivering in the doorway of the rickety house across from me. I've seen a hundred just like him. He won't last the winter if he doesn't take the offer Leanna extends in every village—join the march back to the keep and pledge service to the crown. I try not to linger in the knowledge that, in their current condition, less than half will survive the march back to the keep.

My stomach twists when the boy stretches his hand out toward me. His eyes have fallen to the apple I now hold in my lap and my throat burns. He's too young, too thin, and I know what the dull color of his eyes means. He won't make it. Not to the keep, not through the winter. He's already a ghost, he just doesn't know it yet.

I roll the apple toward him, and he leaps, snatching it off the ground before running off into the night like he's being chased by a pack of feyn. It's a useless act; I might as well be feeding a corpse for all the good it will do him. But maybe the boy will pass into the veil among the stars with a memory of kindness and something sweet on his lips.

His face is the last thing I think of when I close my eyes to sleep, and the last thing I see as we march back to the keep the following morning. His eyes no longer hold the dull hue of those on the precipice of death; there is no light left behind them. He didn't make it far, and I wonder how it was that no one heard as he was beaten on the side of road. His hand lays open in front of him, absent the small morsel of food that I'm sure cost the boy his life.

Guilt twists in my gut like a knife. I take one last look over my shoulder, counting the villagers that follow in the wake of our march, fueled by hunger, or hope, or desperation of another kind. A thin but broad man at the front of the villagers catches my eye as he raises his hand to his mouth, biting into an apple. My apple. The boy's apple. I choke on the sight, forcing myself to face the front and march, like the soldier I've been trained to be.

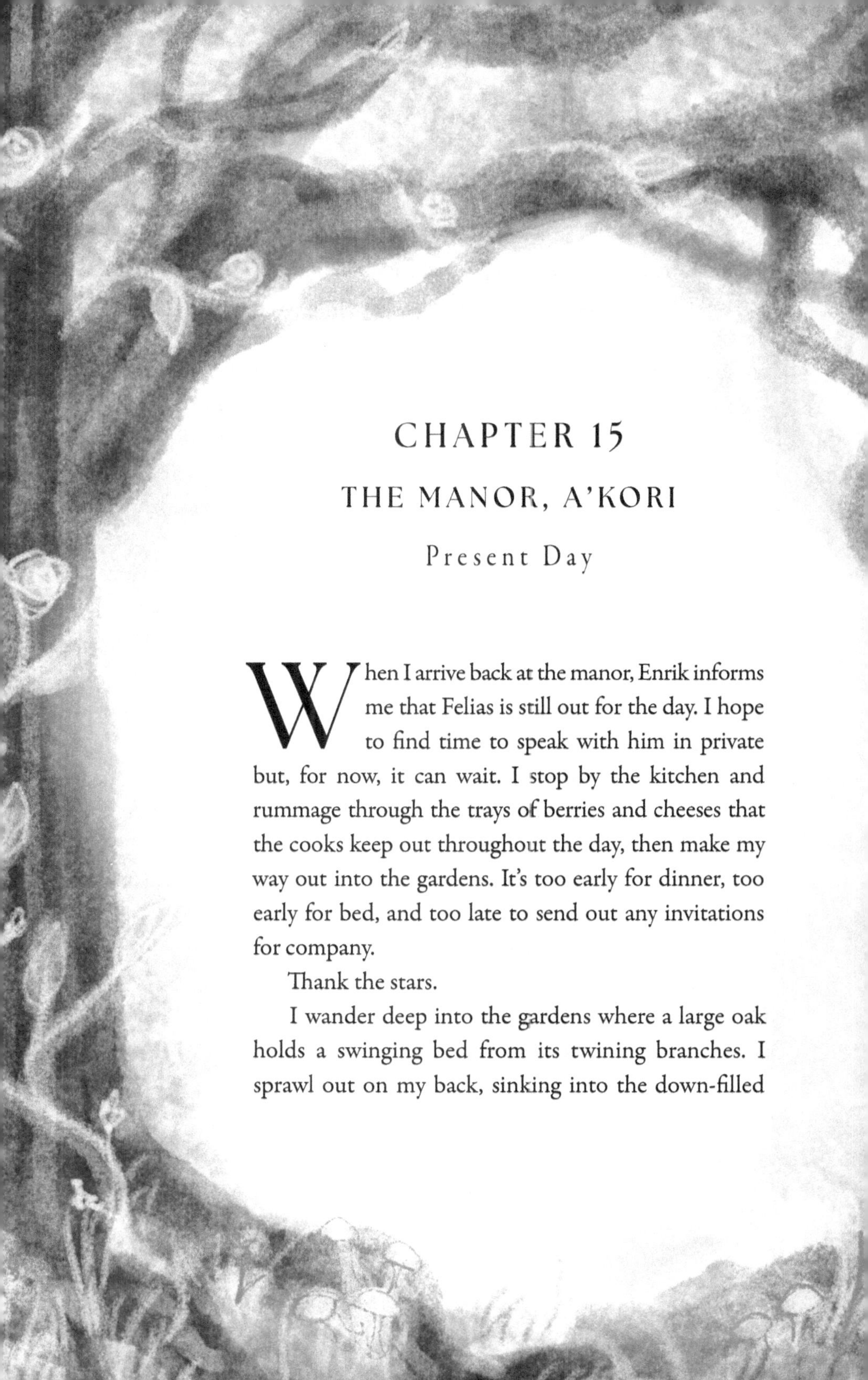

CHAPTER 15

THE MANOR, A'KORI

Present Day

When I arrive back at the manor, Enrik informs me that Felias is still out for the day. I hope to find time to speak with him in private but, for now, it can wait. I stop by the kitchen and rummage through the trays of berries and cheeses that the cooks keep out throughout the day, then make my way out into the gardens. It's too early for dinner, too early for bed, and too late to send out any invitations for company.

Thank the stars.

I wander deep into the gardens where a large oak holds a swinging bed from its twining branches. I sprawl out on my back, sinking into the down-filled cushions. It's impossible not to think of the orphans and my conversation with the general. There are bound to be things in A'kori that don't match up to the horrific image I'd painted of the feyn, but I hadn't expected *that*.

I would have been surprised enough by the sight had there only been feyn children, but that they allowed human children to stay as well makes me feel sick. Not because I feel they should keep the children separate, but because even if such a place for children existed in La'tari, life on Terr would end before they ever offered a feyn child the safety that all children deserve.

I remind myself that feyn children grow to become warriors. But a child should never be punished for what they *could* become. I discard the thoughts that feel like an iron weight pulling me down into the depths of haliel.

A dense gust of wind nudges the bed until it sways beneath the leaves, and I wind a loose strand of hair around my finger. I close my eyes, prepared to let the breezy afternoon lull me to sleep, when a faint feminine voice slips past my ears. I smile, take in a deep breath, exhale slowly, and listen.

Her whisper breaks through the gentle rustle of leaves overhead. "*Tha'haynah*. She sleeps."

I crack my eyes open to find two pairs of bright fea eyes staring down at me from within the dense foliage of the tree overhead.

"Is this where you live?" I wonder, and a gentle laugh flits past my ears.

"Every tree is sprite's home." Their words are a whispering echo and a wide smile breaks upon my face.

I close my eyes, taking another deep breath, worried I will lose this moment, and the sprites' words will fade back into the wind.

"What does *Tha'haynah* mean?"

Another heavy gust of wind rocks the bed beneath me, and my mind begins to drift off. The gentle breeze falls upon my ears as my mind is swallowed by darkness.

"The old blood."

The world is born in a deep shade of red. Streaks of dark crimson smeared across the floor. Lovely eyes, dulled by death, stare out from under a dark mass of hair stained by blood.

A tall man falls to his knees with a sickening thud, drowning in

the gurgle of his last thoughts, thoughts he will never expel. My eyes water and my lungs burn as I choke on a thick layer of smoke rising from the floor.

A demon stands in the doorway. I can feel the noise of its blade along the ridge of my spine as it drags it across the floor and reaches for me.

"Vihi'Valtour." Its voice claws into the depths of my mind, painfully sharp, searching. I scream through the terror and the overwhelming agony.

"Shivaria." My name. The promise of death on its tongue.

"Shivaria." I leap toward the door and do something I've never done before. I run.

I break from the grounds and into the forest. Groves of ancient trees darken the night sky overhead, blotting out what light the waning moon casts into the scarlet hued world. I hear the strike of the demon's heels behind me, the heavy breaths it draws as it gains on me in long strides.

I weave left, skirting the base of a giant cedar when its hand wraps around my arm and I slam against the trunk with all the force of my momentum.

I'm going to die.

Fear triggers my instincts. Everything I've ever been taught about defending myself pushes to the forefront of my mind, taking over my body as if all the years I spent training have a life of their own.

I grip the wrist of the hand holding me and twist until the unnatural angle threatens to break it. The grip slackens as the demon inhales a hissing breath. I don't waste the moment. Using my leverage to pull its shadowed form toward me, I strike with my free hand. My fist lands right below the eye, before sliding off its face in a slick of fresh blood.

"Foc!" the demon yells.

I turn to run, my fear compelling me deeper into the forest where I can more easily lose it in the dark. A rigid arm wraps my waist and pulls me back, slamming me up against the tree.

"Why are you afraid of me?" it demands.

The crimson world shutters around me and I blink, trying to refocus my eyes. I twist out of the arm binding my waist, blocking the hand that flies out to grapple me. I grab the demon's shirt and pull it forward, carried by the weight of its momentum, and I throw out a leg, tripping it. I'm not quick enough when it latches onto my sleeves, taking me down with the force of its fall.

What remains of the crimson world shatters when the air is pushed from my lungs by the heavy weight landing on top of me, pinning my back against the forest floor.

"Stop!" the general growls, gripping my biceps.

I latch onto his sleeves and blink, inhaling the crisp clean air of the forest, the world coming into focus like a punch in the gut.

What have I done?

I will my body to relax and draw in a shuddering breath as I drop my head to the side, resting my chin against my shoulder. I can't bring myself to look into his eyes, to let him see me in this moment where I know I've failed.

"Are you done?" His voice is softer than I expect, and I might have flinched if I had any room to move.

I nod, grasping for any way to salvage this.

"Look at me," he demands gently.

I turn my head to face him, a break in the trees around us letting in a few stray rays of moonlight. The soft light casts a silver glow along the general's scar, a stray sweep of black hair falling in front of his stormy eyes.

"Why did you run from me?" he asks.

Because I thought you were a demon.

"Why did you chase me?" I bite back, though the vicious tone the male usually draws out of me is nowhere to be found.

"I chased you because you ran, and you were terrified," he says.

"I ran *because* you chased me."

"That doesn't make any sense," he growls.

"I just—I had an awful dream, and the next thing I know you're chasing me through the woods."

I will my voice to soften and wish Leanna had been successful in her attempts to teach me to cry on cue. Not that those lessons were very fun.

His grip slackens on my arms, and he studies me. I'm sure he's trying to decide whether he believes me or not and I take a deep breath to steady myself. When my chest heaves against his, my breath hitches and I decide to stop

breathing altogether. The contact peaks my nipples, sending goosebumps across my arms. The moonlight ripples across his jaw as it tenses and he shifts his weight, pulling his leg from between my own and lifting himself off me.

"I'll walk you back," he says, offering his hand.

I take it reluctantly, letting go the moment I'm on my feet.

We walk in silence for quite some time, and I'm relieved that he seems to know where he is going. I likely would have had to wait until morning to be sure of my direction or risked walking further into the forest.

"Who taught you to fight like that?" His question comes from nowhere, but I've had plenty of time leading up to this moment to have considered what my reply will be.

Not that I ever expected this situation.

"My father made me take lessons. He thought it wise to ensure I could defend myself, if necessary," I say.

I glance at the broken skin beneath his eye and wince. It's stopped bleeding but has already begun to bruise.

"He sounds like a wise man," he says, "Awri's father felt much the same way."

"Really?" The shock is clear in my voice.

"Really." He nods. "Though she doesn't practice those skills on her friends."

"Neither do I." The quip slides off my tongue before I can choke it back.

The general huffs. Was that a laugh? And he lets it go.

The woods break around us, revealing the soft lights of the manor up ahead. We stop at the edge of the forest, and I expect him to part ways with me. The evening certainly could have gone better, but it could have been equally worse, and after such a mild reaction from the male, I can't help but harbor some small hope that I haven't ruined everything.

The general kneels by a small stream flowing along the border of the forest and tears a swatch of fabric from the bottom of his tunic. He dips the fabric in the water, wringing it out before handing it to me.

"Wash your face. I can't take you back to your uncle like that, he's bound to have too many questions as it is."

"You tore your tunic for that?" I blot my face with the damp fabric. "That's a touch dramatic. I could have used my hands."

"Do you find it necessary to have a snide remark for everything?" he asks,

clearly exasperated. "You're like a snake when it's being fed, just as likely to bite the hand that feeds it as it is to—for the love of the veil, give me that."

He tears the cloth from my hands and wipes my face like I'm a child. "Better," he grunts.

I rip the cloth from between his fingers just as he'd done to me.

"Your turn." I smile and raise the cloth to his cheek. When he pulls away, I quirk an eyebrow. "You'd rather explain to my uncle that I punched you in the face when you slammed me up against a tree?"

He hesitates for a moment, before leaning forward reluctantly. Despite what he'd said in the carriage about my privileged life I try to be gentle when I wash the blood from his face.

"You were at my uncle's when you found me?" I ask.

"I was," he admits, wincing as I work the dried blood around the broken flesh on his cheek. "I came to apologize for what I said at the orphanage. I spoke out of turn and shouldn't have made assumptions about your life."

The sweep of my hand falters and I wait until he meets my eyes.

"Did that hurt?" I ask.

"A little, but it will heal."

"Not the cut, the apology," I quip.

He glares at me, and I hand him back his torn piece of tunic, now covered in a fine layer of dirt and blood. He shakes his head as he begins again toward the manor, and I pull my braid over my shoulder as I nibble on my lower lip.

"Thank you for the apology," I say quietly as we cross the lawns.

"Did that hurt?" he asks.

"A little," I admit and his mouth quirks up at the end, then falls so quickly I'm not sure I've seen it.

"Shivaria! Thank the stars," Felias calls from the gardens, "And thank you, General." He approaches and clasps the general's hand before rushing to hug me. "Where did you find her?"

My spine stiffens as I prepare for the tale that is sure to be the end of my time in the A'kori court.

"I followed her trail into the woods. It seems she got a little turned around once the sun went down and fell into a shallow pit."

"And you retrieved her?" Felias gasps.

"I did." He nods once, looking me in the eye as he lies to my uncle.

"My boy!" Felias pulls him into an awkward embrace and claps him on the back. "Shivaria, thank the general," he says.

"I already have," I assure him.

"Have you?" The general tilts his head, pinning me with a gaze as he waits expectantly.

"Haven't I?" I tap my finger on the bottom of my chin, squinting my eyes at the sky thoughtfully. "Perhaps when you fell on top of me you hit your head, and it slipped your mind?"

The general's eyes twinkle in the moonlight.

"Thank you," I say with a slight bow of my head. Though I have no idea why he would, if he's willing to keep this secret, so am I.

Felias ushers me inside after offering the general a long and sincere thanks as well as an open invitation to visit again soon, which I'm not sure I personally care for. My uncle leaves me at my door, promising that he will make time for another garden luncheon soon.

I'm a little surprised to see Tig and Eon waiting for me when I enter my suite. They must have seen me coming home, at least, I hope they haven't been waiting here all evening. Eon looks on the verge of falling asleep as she waves at me sleepily from where she lays on my bed. Tig points to the bath and I stumble toward the steaming tub, moaning at the mere thought of hot water soothing the new knots I gained struggling with the general.

I sink into it, letting the scalding water wash over me. I imagine the general will also need a bath once he makes his way home. A small part of me can't help but feel a little bad about the bruise he'll have to explain in the morning. The warrior in me can't wait to see the evidence of my handywork on his face.

I wash my hair before I end up falling asleep in the tub and reluctantly step out before the water cools. Tig hands me a robe and brushes my tangled mop of hair while I swallow down a pinch of the herb that wards off my dreams. I wonder what time it is, then decide I don't care and head for the bed. Eon is fast asleep on top of the duvet. When Tig looks like she's about to wake her, I pull a small blanket from the end of the bed and drape it over the sleeping sprite.

"She can stay," I say, crawling in beside her. "You can stay too, if you'd like."

For a second I think she's about to wake her sister and haul her out into the night. Just as quickly as it came, the moment passes, and Tig rushes to turn out the lights. I close my eyes and the thick cushions of the settee rustle lightly as she settles in by the fire just as I let the darkness take me.

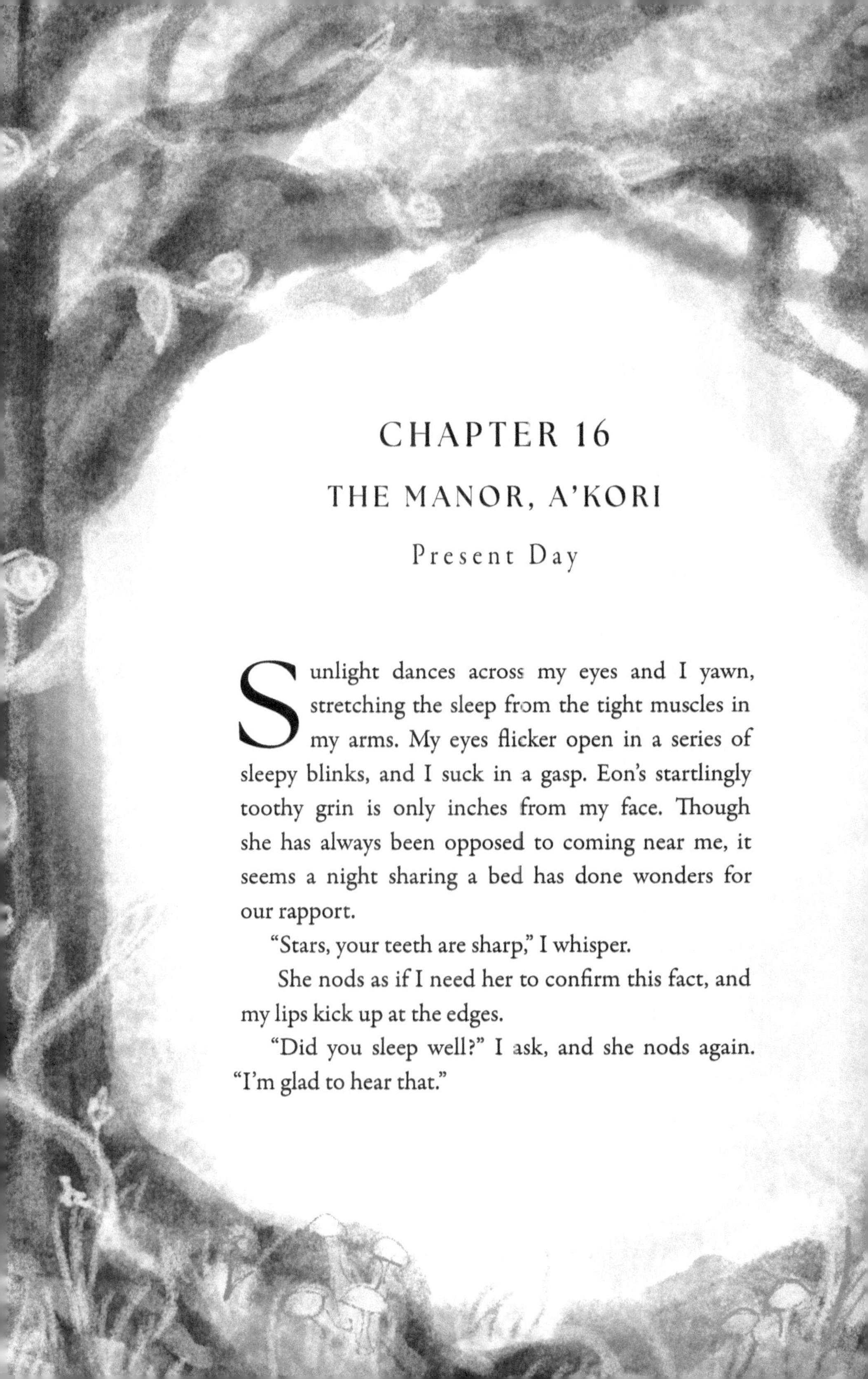

CHAPTER 16
THE MANOR, A'KORI
Present Day

Sunlight dances across my eyes and I yawn, stretching the sleep from the tight muscles in my arms. My eyes flicker open in a series of sleepy blinks, and I suck in a gasp. Eon's startlingly toothy grin is only inches from my face. Though she has always been opposed to coming near me, it seems a night sharing a bed has done wonders for our rapport.

"Stars, your teeth are sharp," I whisper.

She nods as if I need her to confirm this fact, and my lips kick up at the edges.

"Did you sleep well?" I ask, and she nods again. "I'm glad to hear that."

I find Tig waiting at the end of the bed with her head cocked to the side. "How about you? Did you sleep all right?"

She shrugs, then nods, a little less enthused by the sleepover than her sister appears to be. I pry myself from my warm bed and the sisters help me dress for the day before I ring the service bell, asking Enrik to have breakfast sent to my room. The sprites make quick work of my morning bowl of berries, and I tuck the information away in my pile of curious sprite facts. It can't be the only thing they eat, otherwise they would have no need of their pointed teeth. It's not hard to imagine them tearing into flesh as the juices from a particularly plump raspberry slide down Eon's chin in a thick ribbon of red.

"Awri took me to see a seamstress yesterday. The masquerade has a fea theme and she'll be sewing my costume," I tell them.

Though the few conversations I've had with the sprites have been largely one sided, they do seem to enjoy the engagement.

"Would you like to know what my costume will be?" I ask around a small piece of dried fruit.

The sisters nod enthusiastically as I tell them, "Bagya," then quickly shake their heads from side to side and furrow their brows.

"It isn't that bad," I say and Tig quirks a brow at me. "I'm sure the dress will be lovely." I hope it is.

I catch a glimpse of Awri's carriage coming up the drive and give the sprites a quick goodbye before heading for the courtyard. My dark blue dress kicks up in the light breeze wrapping about my ankles as I haul myself onto the bench. The carriage jolts forward the moment I close the door, delivering me to Awri's cottage not long after.

The front door is open when I arrive and I let myself inside, the small act making me feel a little more welcome than I have been before. Awri stands across the table with Riesh on one side and Kishek on the other. The general looms over a thick stack of papers, glaring down from the head of the table, knuckles white where he grips the edges. At least this time his glower isn't directed at me.

"Good morning," Awri says, beaming, and runs around the table to greet me.

Kishek and Riesh share a grin when their heads bob up and they catch sight of me walking through the door.

"Good morning. What is all that?" I ask, pointing to the papers splayed out beneath the general's arms.

"Battle plans," he says, and I wince when he turns to meet my eyes.

The bruise is worse than I expected. But his proclamation of war quickly overshadows the shame I feel for inflicting the mark. I step toward the table, my stomach sinking in on itself.

"Battle plans for what?" I wonder, my stomach pitting.

"He means plans for the masque," Awri giggles.

I try to laugh along with her but when the noise sounds as nervous as I feel, I clear my throat instead. Of course, they wouldn't invite me into a room where they are discussing war.

"I heard you managed to land one on Xeyvian last night when he followed you into the forest," Riesh says. My eyes whip up to him, only to find him boasting a wide smile and a gleam in his eye.

I turn to assess the general wondering what else he told them.

"Is that what you heard?" I ask, a little too amused. "I was under the impression I fell into a shallow pit. As helpless maidens tend to do."

"I told you, your uncle would have had too many questions," the general says.

I shrug as if I'm completely unbothered that his friends have been told his version of events, entirely unsure how that story might differ from the one I would tell.

"I'm just surprised you wanted your friends to know I'm responsible for that." I gesture toward the bruise.

"I was caught off guard. It wouldn't happen again." He says it so matter-of-factly, resuming his position over the table, that I want to show him just how easily it *could* happen again.

"I'm not so sure, Xey. She looks like she's about to prove you wrong," Riesh says from across the table, and I school my features under his annoyingly amused gaze.

My face is settled into a well-rehearsed indifference by the time the general looks up to see what he's talking about. I glance down at the papers scattered about the table. Probably for the best that the memory of last night fades with the mark under the general's eye. Knowledge that I can, at the

very least, defend myself is something I would rather have kept secret until there came a time I needed those skills. I've lost the benefit of surprise to a small degree, if it ever comes down to it.

I spread the papers beneath my fingers, each sheet holding an inky outline of every aspect I imagine makes up a party. Many I never would have considered. Floral arrangements, seasonable flowers, options for the vases to hold them, color schemes, cake flavors, sizes, and shapes.

"You have a baker who can make the cake look like a swan?" My eyebrows shoot up in disbelief.

"We do," Awri says warmly, "Though I think a swan is a little off the mark for the theme. Don't you?"

"I do," I answer, suddenly aware that she'll have a question just like it for every piece of paper on the table and they won't all be so simple.

We spend the day going over several of the mind-numbing party details. She asks for my opinion on everything and though I'm sure I make a fool of myself with a handful of answers, she never lets it show. Despite my assumptions, I do in fact find an advantage in agreeing to assist in the planning. Like those Felias employs to grow his flowers, Awri made a list of feyn with various gifts that will assist with the event. I memorize each name and the gift they were born with. The more knowledge I have about their abilities, the better.

Riesh and Kishek try to offer their opinions throughout the day and Awri thanks them while simultaneously shutting them down completely, yet politely. I don't know how she does it. They give up altogether after a late lunch and vanish toward the stables to spar. If I thought I hated party planning before, the effort of sitting through it while enduring the clash of steel is almost unbearable.

I expect the general to be more on edge after the events of the prior evening. He's somewhat more relaxed and it puzzles me. Maybe he thinks he has a good understanding of my skillset and he's sure he can overpower me in a fight. Whatever the reason, while he still remains close throughout the day, he seems to no longer feel the need to be a physical barrier between Awri and myself.

When the light begins to fade Awri calls her carriage and insists on joining me on my journey back to the manor.

"I would call today a success, wouldn't you?" she asks over her shoulder as the general helps her into the carriage.

"I'll feel a little more accomplished when we've managed to get halfway through that stack of papers," I say, covering a yawn.

She laughs a little manically from inside the carriage, and for some reason it makes me smile. I reach out to pull myself onto the step, and my breath catches when the general snaps my hand out of the air, drawing it close to his face. Me along with it.

"What are you doing?" I wonder.

"Making sure you didn't hurt yourself too badly," he says.

I snort when I realize he's examining the small sliver of broken flesh on my knuckle where it split when I struck him. It's so small I'd hardly noticed it myself.

"Don't worry," I tease, "I've slept on pillows harder than your face."

Awri masks a laugh and I swear the edge of his mouth twitches. He lifts my hand to help me inside the carriage, and I think maybe I hit the male harder than either of us realized if this is the change it has elicited in him.

Awri raps her knuckles against the roof as soon as he shuts the door, and I try not to gape as he disappears into the cottage. He's left me all alone with his friend. It's entirely unexpected.

Despite the fact that he has hardly looked at me since I've known him, I've always felt his eyes on me. He's kept close watch every second, poised and at the ready to interfere in … well, I'm not sure exactly what he expects. While our encounter in the woods seems the likely culprit to his change of heart, it makes no sense. If the male needed a reason not to trust me, a reason to expel me from the good grace of his friend and keep me from his king, he has it.

The ride to the manor is quiet and contemplative, at least for my part. The carriage stops in the courtyard, and I turn to say goodbye when Awri slips past me without a word. I almost fall out of the carriage in my rush to chase after her as she makes for the front door.

"May I come in?" she asks expectantly, standing on the stone threshold of the manor.

"Of course," I say, my brow pinching as I usher her inside.

Nothing about this feels right and my stomach knots. Maybe she has her

own set of opinions on the events of the prior evening. I should have done more to find out exactly what the general told her, but if any of the others were concerned by his tale, they certainly hadn't shown it.

Enrik greets us at the door, looking as unsure of the situation as I feel when he asks, "Will the lady be joining us for dinner?"

Awri sticks me with another look of determined expectation, and it takes me entirely too long to devise what she wants from me.

I stumble over the words as they leave my mouth in a jumbled rush, "Would you like to stay for dinner?"

"How kind of you to offer," she coos, "If it's no imposition, that would be lovely."

She hands Enrik her cloak and glides off beyond the foyer. I share a questioning glance with the male as he takes my cloak as well, hanging them in a large closet by the door before darting off toward the kitchen.

I hurry after Awri and stop her with a light touch on her arm, hopeful that I haven't offended her.

"I'm sorry," I say, "I should have invited you to join me for dinner before tonight. You shouldn't have had to ask."

"I've never enjoyed the nuances of what is considered appropriate in society," she says, taking hold of my hand and squeezing it reassuringly. "Let's make a deal. I will always tell you what I want, though you will be under no obligation to provide it unless you choose to do so, and in return, you will offer me the same."

I'm more than taken aback by her proposal. It seems too easy. Here I am preparing myself for her rejection, and what she's offering me is true friendship. Something I've only known once before. I would be a fool not to grasp onto the offer despite the bitterness that comes with my acceptance. Though she will never know it until it's too late, it will never be real in any meaningful sense of the word. I'll use her and kill her king. Her friend.

"That's a deal I would like to make," I agree with the warmest smile I can muster, shoving thoughts of my looming betrayal deep into the back of my mind.

"Ladies!" Felias beams, bursting into the room in a tailored suit of purple velvet that I'm sure he changed into after Enrik warned him about our

impromptu guest. "How wonderful it will be to have not one, but two, lovely young ladies to keep me company this evening. I hope you are absolutely famished."

He links his elbow with Awri's, leading her toward the dining room.

"By happenstance, the cook has been working on a new masterpiece, and I must have your opinion on the dish," he whispers into her ear.

Awri offers me a wry smile, and I follow close behind. I'm sure neither of us have any doubts that the chef was working on no such thing until he'd been made aware of our arrival.

The dinner is delicious, but I'm not one to complain about the quality of a hot meal. Felias's cheeks dimple when Awri expresses her pleasure upon tasting every dish he presents, and I can't help but wonder if she's just being polite.

I'm surprised when, after dinner, Awri accepts an invitation to sit by the fire and join us for an evening cup of tea. I'm taking mental notes on what I assume is the accepted regimen of invitations, offerings, and appropriate replies, as Felias dotes and fawns over her.

How Leanna ever expected to pass me off as a lady with so many holes in my education is beyond me. But I suppose no one intended for me to remain in A'kori for this long. If the king had been present upon my arrival, he would already be dead, and I would have returned home. The thought of my inevitable return to La'tari is enough to make me savor the warm cup of spiced tea in my hands.

"How are your plans coming for the masque?" Felias asks over a steamy cup.

"Much slower than I anticipated," she sighs exaggeratedly. "I would have liked more time to make everything perfect for our king. There is simply too much to do."

Her eyelashes flutter, and she offers him a sad smile. I have to stop myself from rolling the tension out of my shoulders. I feel as though I'm watching a dance I've never seen, and despite my not knowing the steps I am somehow mixed up in the rhythm.

"I for one, have no doubts about your abilities," Felias says with a flourish of his wrist. "And if I can be of assistance in any way, you have only to speak the word. If it is within my power, I would be honored to grant you your request."

The man sounds like he's swearing fealty to a lord and my stomach knots when I see the satisfied look on my friend's face. I don't know Awri to be a malicious female but every fiber of my being rebels against the idea of giving someone that much power.

Awri's mouth quirks up behind her teacup and her eyes shine a little brighter. I know that look, she knows she's won. She settles her features, tilting her head to the side thoughtfully, as if something just occurred to her.

"I've just had a wonderful idea," she says, eyes gleaming.

There is no doubt in my mind this is something she's been planning, and now her sudden request to remain for supper is becoming clearer.

"It is my intent to take up a temporary residence at the palace in order to facilitate the preparations. What if your niece were to join me? Just until the masque."

I see the moment Felias realizes his mistake in offering her so much, though he hides it rather well.

"She's been such a help in preparing for the event," she says, leaning toward him to rest her hand upon his, "I am sure that with Shivaria by my side, I could accomplish a month of planning in the next week alone. It would be such a relief."

She seems so bright and optimistic I'm not sure how Felias doesn't immediately grant every request as it tumbles from her rose-colored lips.

"I can't say that I won't suffer the loss of my niece, but if Shivaria is agreeable, I would be happy to send her to assist you in your endeavor."

They both look to me, waiting in silence for my reply. If Felias thinks he's left the decision in my hands, he has no idea of the tactical mastery this female possesses. She has offered me a friendship I'd been eager to accept and in the same night asked a favor of me that I have no reason to refuse. How can I possibly decline without it seeming an outright rejection of that bond?

So, I give them the only answer I can, the answer she's placed on my lips.

"I would be happy to."

"Wonderful." She smiles. "Then let's leave your uncle to the rest of his evening and I can get you settled in."

I nearly choke on a lungful of hot tea, as I sputter, "Tonight?"

It's the only word I can force out around the liquid being expelling from my chest.

"Only if you're agreeable," she says, tipping her head to the side expectantly, "This way we can get an early start in the morning."

I'm no longer sure that she's really asking, this seems like an expectation. I have a feeling she had her mind made up about how this evening would play out long before she stepped foot inside the manor tonight. I wonder if the price of this female's friendship is entirely too high.

Felias stands, his voice breaking me from my stupor. "Why don't you go and collect the things you'll need for this evening, Shivaria. I'll have the rest sent over in the morning."

I nod and try not to run to my room like I'm fleeing a predator. I tell myself that this is a good thing. Last night I was worried I'd never have an opportunity to stand in the presence of the king. Tonight, I'm being thrust into the midst of his home. It isn't the destination that bothers me, but how I'll have gotten there.

Awri had this evening planned and my presence at her side assured as if I'd wrapped and gifted myself to her of my own accord. Tacticians win wars, not the soldiers that fight in them, and unlike my newfound friend, I am no tactician.

Tig and Eon don't startle when I burst into the room, though they seem concerned by my lack of composure. I debate asking Felias to smuggle them in with my luggage. Not that I need an attendant, but their presence in the evenings and every morning when I wake have come to be my most treasured times of day. If the king returns while I remain at the palace, there's a good chance that I'll never see the sprites again. A sharp pang of regret strikes my heart at the thought.

I pull myself together and brush off the feeling of loss as I produce a small velvet sack from the closet, stuffing some essentials inside.

The sisters follow me around the room curiously as I explain, "I'm going to stay at the palace for a few days. I hope. Maybe longer. I'm not sure."

Whisps of their voices travel past my ears but I can't settle myself enough to properly listen right now. I walk to the door and take one last glance around the room until I'm sure I have everything I need for the night.

189

"I wish I could take you with me," I say.

And maybe I'm fooling myself, but I think they'd like that too.

When I make it downstairs Awri and Felias are waiting in the foyer. Enrik hands me my cloak and I discreetly brush my hand over the hidden interior pocket, making sure the small pouch of herbs hasn't fallen out. I won't risk being caught without it again.

Felias pecks each of my cheeks lightly. I wish I knew the man better because there is a world of what he wants to say seeping out in the expression on his face, but I don't understand a single thing he's trying to convey.

Awri turns to him. "Thank you, Felias. You have no idea what a relief it will be to have your niece by my side. I'm sure the king will want to thank you both properly for your efforts."

It's the last thing she says before leading me into the carriage and I latch onto the hope that *this* is the act that sets me before her sovereign. We ride in silence, the carriage beginning its ascent toward the palace as my stomach twists itself into knots. It's clear from the smug look on her face that she's pleased with herself and the well-orchestrated outcome of the evening. I can't even blame her.

"You'll have to teach me how to do that," I say.

Her eyes move from the window and land upon mine.

"Teach you what?" she asks, shifting her weight beneath her.

"How to have everyone in the room agree to give me exactly what I want before I've even asked for it."

"That's rather blunt." She smiles.

"I didn't think you'd mind," I say.

"I don't. There is little I appreciate more than honesty."

I don't like the pang her simple declaration sends deep into my gut. There will come a day when the female across from me will hate me, and I won't blame her for that either. It is only a matter of time before she learns from me the lesson Leanna tried to teach me years ago. When you care about others, you open yourself up to wounds you cannot defend against.

"It's a skill that takes time to learn." Her voice brings me back to our conversation.

I huff a laugh. "I'm not sure I'll live long enough to perfect it."

"I wouldn't be so sure," she says quietly, her eyes taking me in fully before they fall back to the window, and I leave her to her thoughts.

I won't live long enough to perfect the art I watched her so easily craft. I suppose she forgot long ago just how short and fragile mortal lives are. What meaning does ninety years have to a feyn? Can they truly grasp the fleeting nature of our mortality? I think not.

The carriage draws to a stop and Awri disappears into the night. I follow after her, slack jawed as my eyes look skyward. I try in vain to discern the palace's black spires from the dark peaks of the mountains looming behind them.

While the exterior of the palace is dark stone, the steps leading up to the grand entrance, and all that I see within, is carved from white marble with thick veins of gold. Ornate pillars span the entry, each one carved uniquely to display rich pockets of gold imbedded in the stone.

Some are carved into protruding flowers. Others into birds in mid-flight. It would take days to study them all. Part of me wishes I could spend the time doing so, because each one my eyes fall upon is more beautiful than the last.

My awe of the grandeur quickly sours when my eyes land on a white pillar wrapped in a trellis of golden vines, and I consider the coin a single golden rose would fetch. I've witnessed children dying of starvation, elders begging in the streets for crumbs. How could anyone reside in such obscene opulence with the knowledge that so many suffer? I remind myself that when the La'tari king takes the A'kori throne these pillars will be destroyed, and the wealth of this kingdom will be dispersed to those who need it most.

I follow Awri, determined to ignore the grandeur of the palace and focus instead on our direction and the placement of the guards. I take note of their numbers, which halls they guard, and which doors they bar entry to. I follow her deep into the recesses of the palace, knowing it will take a handful of scouting missions before I have it clearly mapped out in my mind.

"Here we are," she says, pushing open a large set of tall doors.

My eyes grow wide and my room at the manor suddenly feels every bit as barren and rudimentary as my room at the La'tari keep had been.

Tall windows line the southern wall, stretching from floor to ceiling, topped in a leaded array of glass diamonds. Flowering vines drape wildly across the exterior of every pane. A large bed sits across from the fire with posts carved in the likeness of trees, the high branches of their canopy reaching out toward one another and twining over the center of the bed. Deep blue silks drape from the pillars, cascading into pools of fabric on the marble floor. A small seating area for entertaining sits beside the fire, with another large set of doors opposite it. Awri explains that the doors lead to my bathing chambers, though she doesn't come inside.

After reassuring her that there is nothing I need, she leaves with a promise to collect me in the morning. I walk into the bathing chamber to get ready for bed and groan when my eyes fall on the tub. It sits in the center of the chamber, a giant bowl carved out of a mossy green stone, large enough to fit four more beside myself. Not that I have any intention of inviting someone to join me.

I want a bath, but the day has worn on me, so I wash myself down with a warm soapy rag and crawl into bed. I eat a small pinch of my herbs, looking deep into the sack as I try not to think about the fact that my supply won't last the weeks until the king's return. Throughout my life, there were often nights when I wished I could summon sleep more quickly and tonight will surely be one of them.

A general sense of unease has taken me over. It started the moment I agreed to Awri's offer of friendship. It changes nothing. It can't.

Still, my mind wanders to lessons I learned from Leanna and then to Vakesh. I flinch at the thought of his name—it's the first time I've allowed myself to think it since I set foot in A'kori. Though Leanna attempted to teach me the same lesson long ago, hers had been far less painful. She was never able to reach me the way he could.

Turns out, I'd preferred her method of teaching in the end. After all, bones heal and flesh knits back together. I suppose some lessons require deeper wounds, wounds unseen that take far longer to heal.

Stars, I hope they heal. As much as I hope they scar. It is always harder to break through a wound that scars.

I won't let myself be mad about those lessons, but I can't stop from hating

myself for my willingness to inflict those hurts on another. I tell myself it will be worth it, that her pain is nothing compared to the lives that will be saved. I remind myself that Awri fought in the war and is responsible for inflicting this same pain on countless others.

But nothing I tell myself settles the roiling mass of guilt inside me. After a while, I give in and stop fighting it, letting it wash over me. I bathe in the ugliness, reminding myself that this is what I was made for, and this is what I deserve.

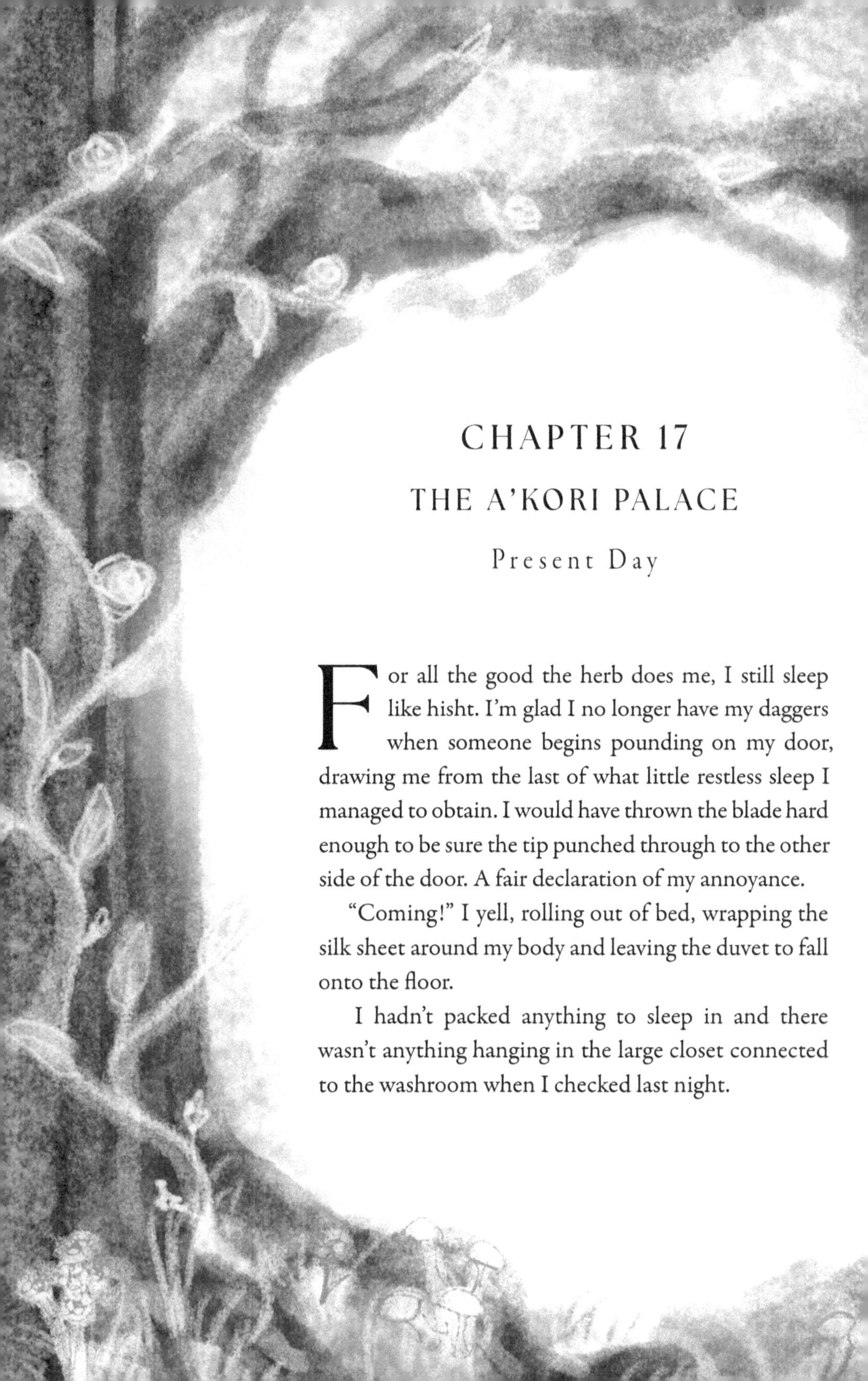

CHAPTER 17
THE A'KORI PALACE
Present Day

For all the good the herb does me, I still sleep like hisht. I'm glad I no longer have my daggers when someone begins pounding on my door, drawing me from the last of what little restless sleep I managed to obtain. I would have thrown the blade hard enough to be sure the tip punched through to the other side of the door. A fair declaration of my annoyance.

"Coming!" I yell, rolling out of bed, wrapping the silk sheet around my body and leaving the duvet to fall onto the floor.

I hadn't packed anything to sleep in and there wasn't anything hanging in the large closet connected to the washroom when I checked last night.

Another bang sounds, and I glare through squinted eyes, still tender in the light of the morning sun. Awri did say she wanted to start early but I wasn't expecting a predawn awakening. I glance out the window as I swing open the heavy door and—all right, I might be exaggerating, it isn't *that* early. Normally I would have been out of bed an hour ago.

A plump woman with a tidy brown bun and mousy nose backs into my room, dragging a large trunk behind her.

"Good morning, lady. I am Tiana. I've been sent with your things and asked to attend you."

I'm about to protest my need for her services when she disappears into the washroom and I'm struck silent by a series of fluttering whispers gliding past my ears. My head whips toward the bed, where I find two angry sprites, hiding half-heartedly behind a bedpost.

I've never considered what one of the sprites might do if she were offended, but I have no intention of finding out. Tiana flips the lever above the bath, the water splashing as the tub begins to fill. The beautiful golden hues of the sprite's skin begin to rapidly darken as they glower in unison toward the woman.

Keeping my eyes on them, I yell, "Thank you, Tiana. That is very kind of you, but I won't need your assistance."

The woman ambles into the main room, and I place my body between hers and the seething sisters, entirely unsure if I'm protecting them from her or the other way around.

"But I was told—"

"Never mind what you were told," I say, grasping her hand and pulling her to the door. "I'll make sure everyone is aware of your efforts and that the decision was mine."

"But—"

"Thank you." I shuffle her into the hall with a hand on the small of her back, shut the door, and pin my ear to it until I hear her leave, grumbling under her breath.

Tig's color is a little closer to normal by the time I turn back, but her eyes are glued to the door. I think she may be debating the logistics of going after the poor woman.

"She was just doing her job," I assure her.

Tig puffs out an annoyed breath and makes for the tub. I exhale a deep breath of my own, thanking the stars that the sprite seems to have given up on whatever plans she had for the woman. I hope.

Eon skips after her sister without a care in the world and the sprites make up my bath like they usually do. Unlike every other day, however, a golden tray of salts and flowers, perfumed oils, and bubbling soaps sits by the sink. Tig picks an oil, the scent of which I can't quite place. It smells of the woods in the spring when the flowers are beginning to bloom and the cottonwoods shed their seed.

Eon climbs onto the marble counter, and I smile as I watch her uncork and sniff every concoction within reach, all but one issuing a sigh of pleasure from the fea. The last she dramatically chokes on, clutching her throat as she holds the bottle as far away from her tiny nose as she can manage.

The rest of the morning is much like every other. Almost. Eon picks an A'kori gown in a greyish blue that makes my eyes brighter against the pale hue of my skin. When she doesn't proffer the usual matching set of pants, I walk into the large closet to find them.

While Felias hadn't approved of me constantly wearing them, I never expected him to go so far as to remove them from my wardrobe entirely. My cheeks heat when I look myself over in the mirror, one part embarrassment, two parts rage. The wide cut of the top exposing my shoulders and the swell of my breasts is bad enough, but the floor to hip slit on either side of the gown is wildly indecent.

Since the night of Felias's party I've understood why the feyn favor this fashion. They have no need to hide behind clothing. It only detracts from their natural beauty. But I am not feyn, and each way the cut of the gown is designed to embellish their loveliness, only serves to expose every one of my flaws.

Thankfully, Tig leaves my hair down and I pull a few loose spirals over my shoulders in an effort to obtain some semblance of modesty. I debate writing Felias and demanding he send the rest of my things but if he doesn't want me to have them what can I do? I can hate and understand his motives simultaneously. Assassination by means of seduction has always been on the table even if only as a last resort. It is, after all, the way of most Fea Dien.

I pause when my hand lands on the lever of my bedroom door, looking back toward the sisters.

"I'm glad you're here," I say.

It doesn't scratch the surface of the relief I feel in their presence, but they look pleased by the sentiment, and I crack a smile before walking into the hall.

"Are you always this cheerful in the mornings?" The general's deep voice echoes down the corridor.

He stands across the hall, his shoulder leaning against the stone. The smile falls from my face when I see him, and he frowns, his eyes falling to my mouth.

"Where is Awri?" I ask.

"Something came up," he says, "and she has been delayed."

He saunters toward me, his bruise looking markedly better. I was taught that feyn heal much quicker than humans but never witnessed it myself.

"I came to offer you a tour of the palace until Awri can make herself available," he says.

"All right."

I'm sure I can decline, and he won't force it. But the rejection won't do me any favors, if I plan on staying in whatever good graces I've somehow fallen into.

He gestures down the hall, and I step in beside him, his heavy boots clipping loudly upon the marble. Blood warms my cheeks when his eyes follow the length of my leg from my hip to the floor.

"You aren't wearing pants," he says.

"How observant," I quip.

He looks at me out of the corner of his eye and asks, "Why?"

"Do I need a reason? I was told this is entirely appropriate." It's impossible to keep the flood of color from my cheeks when I reply, but I breathe easier when his eyes return to my face. The feeling doesn't last.

"It is," he assures me, "It's just that, aside from the day we first met, I've never seen you without them."

I hum thoughtfully, scrunching my face as if I am trying to recall a memory from long ago.

"Oh yes, I remember. That was the day you tried to have me removed from my uncle's home."

"Don't change the subject." He glares.

I look down at my legs when I say, "I thought I would try something new."

Of course, it's a lie, but I hope it's enough to encourage him to leave it alone. His stride falters and he turns to face me.

"Why are you always so difficult?" he growls, his sneer falling away as quickly as it came when realization sets in, and he voices the revelation aloud. "Your uncle didn't send any, did he?" I don't have time to answer before he barks a laugh. "Of course he didn't."

He seems truly pleased with himself as he starts down the hallway once more, shaking his head and looking far too amused, as if he unearthed some great mystery lost to the ages.

I glare at the back of his head. "What do you mean, 'Of course, he didn't?'"

"Are you being intentionally ignorant?" he puffs out, "Or do you truly not know that your uncle has designs on you for the king? For his bed."

I almost trip over myself when his words land a blow on a soft and unfortified piece of my deeper self that I'm entirely unfamiliar with. I laugh to deflect, to make myself feel better, to do anything but answer the question.

Of course, he laughed. I laughed the first time Leanna told me I would seduce their king but hearing it from the male beside me is like a dull dagger twisting in my gut.

"Don't worry, *General*," I say snidely, "I'm well aware I fall far below the standard for even the lowest of the feyn. I have no intention of degrading myself in pursuit of your sovereign."

He has the nerve to look angry at me for speaking the truth. I likely spoiled all the fun he wanted to have at my expense, mocking me based on his assumptions and the unfortunate fact that I was born mortal and therefore somehow *less*. He opens his mouth to argue and is blessedly interrupted when Awri bursts into view from around a corner at the end of the hall. She's a cascade of teal silk as she runs toward us, and I've never been happier to see her or more envious of a pair of pants. I decide it's rude to ask if she'll loan me a pair.

"Sorry to keep you waiting," she says breathlessly, leaning in to peck my cheek. "Did you enjoy your tour?"

The general must have waited outside my chambers for quite some time if she thinks we've had enough time to make it farther than the hall.

"I did." I smile to hide the lie and pin the general with a stare. "I was just telling the general that I know that I am entirely undeserving of the privilege of being here."

"I wouldn't have invited you if I felt that way," she reassures me with a curious tilt of her head.

The general doesn't move. He doesn't blink or say a word as Awri leads me around the corner and out of his view. I wish I could say that the moment I'm out of his sight I shrug off his comment. I'm strong in more ways than he knows, and it shouldn't bother me. He didn't say anything I don't already know. *Nothing* about me is enough to tempt the king.

"Did Xey say something to you?" Awri asks.

I hadn't noticed her eyes on me. I give her a small smile and shake my head.

"Not at all. I just didn't sleep well," I say, which reminds me, "The night we spent at the cottage, the general made a tea to help me sleep. I've been meaning to ask about the herbs he used."

"Xeyvian made you tea?"

Somehow, I think she might seem less shocked if I told her he'd drugged it. Her lack of knowledge about the incident is both disappointing and relieving. I need to find an alternative to the dwindling supply in my small pouch, but it's good to know that she wasn't an accomplice to my sedation.

I decide, for the time being, it's best she doesn't know. There is every chance she'd take the general's side, and it would only drive a wedge between us.

"He did," I say, trying my best to smile appreciatively. "I'll have to ask him for the recipe."

And I will. Maybe.

My steps slow when Awri leads me into an enormous room with a tall domed ceiling painted in ivy and starlight. The ivy twines down the walls, cascading into a dense plethora of leafy ferns containing broken beams of moonlight. An array of colorful eyes are painted among the ferns. I can only assume they are meant to represent the fea. It's as if I've stumbled into the middle of a lush and wild landscape the likes of which I've never seen.

"You like it," she says, beaming, "I can tell."

"It's incredible," I say, my voice low in reverence.

"I'm glad you approve. There are a number of rooms to choose from, but considering our theme, I think this is the perfect place to host the event."

She picks a string of fabric swatches from a table at the center of the room, and I try not to cringe. No doubt she'll want opinions on tablecloths and napkins, followed by a request for my opinion on lighting and music. Today can't be over soon enough.

Hours spent planning drag on, feeling like days, until Kishek comes to remind Awri to break for a meal. The male has always been quiet compared to the others, but today he's surrounded by an aura of lethargy and dark circles hollow out his eyes. My friend schools her face well as we follow him toward a small table set with a late lunch, but her brow creases with concern that she's unable to hide whenever she looks at him.

They dismiss me when I ask if everything is all right, explaining that a matter of the crown kept him up long into the night. My spine tingles under the weight of the possibilities, and I find myself wondering what the male's role is at court. They must be more than close friends to the king. They must be vital in some other way. Another question for Felias.

After the sun is fully settled beyond the mountains and no dusky light remains in the evening sky, Awri walks me to my chambers, leaving me with a simple goodnight. I've never been so tired. I feel like I've gone to battle with tea flavors and party favors, and I never stood a chance.

Prepared to fend off the sprites and fall into bed without any preparation, I let myself into my room. A small fire crackles in the hearth and the lamps have been dimmed but the sisters are nowhere to be seen. A shiver rattles my spine and my senses heighten. I swipe a sharp blade from a nearby desk. It's meant to open letters, but it will serve the same purpose as a dagger should I have need of it.

Rising on the balls of my feet, I stalk silently toward the washroom and then the closet. I'm not sure what I expect to find and maybe it's just the sprites' absence, but something feels out of place. With my letter opener-turned-dagger fisted above my heart, ready to strike, I walk back into the main room. A small knot forms in my stomach when my eyes land on a bundle sitting at the foot of my bed.

There is no note to explain their presence, but I find that I am not in need of a letter to explain who left them. It's a simple pair of black leather pants, most certainly procured from a uniform.

Perhaps it's his way of apologizing or maybe he simply prefers me covered up. It makes no difference to me. It's the closest thing I've had to my leathers since leaving home and even if it's meant as a slight, I'll take them gladly.

I let go of the notion I have about falling into bed. My eyes move from the pants to the makeshift dagger at my side. The night is still young, and there is enough time left before dawn to accomplish something for myself. Something more than party planning and socializing. Something that means ... well, something.

I rush to my closet and change into the darkest dress I find. It is a true black, as dark as the sea on a stormy day. I pull on the leather pants, folding the excess bunching at my ankles. They're obviously made for a male, someone taller but thankfully lean. They fit like a glove along the curve of my legs and when I cinch them at the waist the feeling is nearly the same as the day I'd been given my first pair. I want to squeal.

I drape my dark cloak over my shoulders, pull up the hood, and swing open one of the tall windows lining my room. I'd been given a room with a view of the forest on the western side of the palace, and I thank the stars for my luck as I crawl out the window, setting my feet on the wildflower lawns. A ground floor room isn't ideal for defending against a siege, but in this case, it is perfect for my secret endeavors in the dark.

I manage to skirt the guards patrolling the grounds with ease. It occurs to me that with knowledge of the fea's existence, I should be more wary of trudging through a dark forest in a strange land. But if there is a forest that is safe to traverse it will be the one closest to the palace. I doubt they let malicious fea run wild in these woods.

It doesn't take long to find what I'm looking for. A young birch tree sits amidst a starlit grove, a freshly broken branch hanging at its side. I wrench the branch free, knot the panels of my dress below my hip, and settle in on a small boulder in the center of a clearing.

The small blade carves into the soft flesh of the branch like butter. I make quick work of it, every stroke of my blade shaping and refining it until it no longer resembles a sword; it becomes one. A breeze coils at the base of my neck, licking chilly tendrils along my jaw. The treetops sway and I can hear the noise of the sea in their fluttering leaves. Thick shafts of moonlight break through the forest beyond the clearing and I'm reminded of the domed room with fea eyes.

A loud snap from the dark woods beside me draws my attention. Could be nothing. Another snap and a rustling of leaves brings me to my feet.

I lean the toy sword against the rock and flip the dagger in my hand, studying the weight of it. The noise gets louder, nearer. Whatever it is, it's big. I shift my stance, widening my feet, preparing to be charged.

I'm not entirely relieved when a tall horse breaks from the edge of the forest with the general astride, but I exhale a deep breath and my muscles relax. I might have preferred the wild fea my mind conjured to the male holding my gaze across the clearing, his lips a thin line of displeasure.

I don't owe him an explanation, though I have no doubt he will demand one shortly. I reassure myself that I haven't done anything wrong and retake my seat on the boulder, continuing to carve the finishing touches into the hilt of the toy sword.

Dismounting, he ties his horse to a tree before striding across the grove to study my project.

"Why did you sneak out of your room?" His voice is soft, and if I didn't know any better, I might think he's concerned.

"What makes you think I snuck out?"

He scoffs as if my question is the most ridiculous thing he's ever heard.

"The guards would have told me if they'd seen you leave," he says.

"Then how did you know I left?" I bait him for the knowledge of his reply.

I was sure I wasn't seen but his presence here tells me otherwise. If there is some other way in which the male can be made aware of my location, I want to know what it is.

"That is beside the point," he barks into the night.

Damn.

"I didn't realize I was to be confined to my rooms without an escort. Perhaps there is a small book you'd like me to sign whenever I leave my room, so that I can log my whereabouts?" I regret the suggestion as soon as it slips past my lips. I don't want to give him any ideas he might actually consider using.

"You are not a prisoner," he says, and his voice holds an edge, all hint of softness gone. I force myself not to crack a smile as his temper shows itself. "You are free to come and go from the palace as you please."

I know this, but I also knew it would bristle the male that he felt he had to defend himself, and after his comments earlier this morning I no longer feel the need to placate his ego.

"Then why are you here?" I ask, blowing a curled wood shaving from the carved hilt.

"I should have told you earlier to make yourself at home at the palace. I intended to." He shifts his weight and sighs. "There were also things I wish I hadn't said. Things I hadn't meant." His voice sharpens in annoyance. "Would you stop whittling that stick and look at me?"

I let the stick fall to rest atop my knees and meet his eyes with an irritated sigh and arch of my brow.

"What are you doing?" he asks, glancing at the sword.

I run my hand along the smooth wood, reminding myself why I came.

"When Awri took me to the orphanage, there was a boy there, Elian. She promised him a sword so that he could play with the others. I don't think he'll mind that it isn't from the king."

"You called it grooming," he reminds me.

"I did," I say, "and maybe it is. Or maybe it's just an act of kindness toward a little boy who wants a toy sword so that he can play with his friends."

It infuriates me to no end that he seems shocked by my declaration. What must he think of me if such a simple act surprises him? I decide I don't care and lift myself off the boulder, slipping the letter opener into the dagger sheath sewn into the thigh of my leathers, clutching the sword in my other hand.

I scold myself when his eyes follow the movement of my hand as I slide the dagger home without so much as a glance toward it. I don't give him time to ask any questions and step toward the cover of the forest.

"Now where are you going?" he demands.

I sigh, not wishing to explain myself any further. "To deliver the sword."

"On foot?" He sounds even more surprised than he had about the gift.

The male clearly finds me incapable of even walking a short distance.

"On foot," I confirm with a nod.

"You won't make it back before dawn," he says.

I shrug, relieved that if the journey does in fact keep me out until dawn, I will have avoided my demon for one more night.

"For the love of the veil." He snatches the sword out of my hand and strides toward his horse.

"What do you think you're doing? Give that back!" I yell, chasing after him.

He ignores me, strapping the sword to his saddle as he says over his shoulder, "I'm taking the sword to the orphanage, and you're coming with me."

I come to a stop behind him, my eyes narrowing on his back. When he turns to face me, his brow is etched in hard lines of determination as he points at me and says, "I'd like to get some sleep tonight, and that's not going to happen as long as you're galivanting all across A'kori, unaccompanied."

I open my mouth to protest but my breath leaves my lungs in a woosh when he grips my waist with both hands and lifts me onto the horse, sidesaddle. He swings himself up behind me, and before I can slide back to the ground in protest, he clicks his tongue and the horse leaps into the dark of the woods.

Wind tears my hood from the crown of my head, settling it between my shoulder blades. The general hooks my waist, pulling me tightly against him until I can feel the hardened cut of his chest on the side of my arm.

I'm not entirely sure he can see me glaring at him as we race through the forest, but I don't let it stop me. When the mount cuts a tight corner around the base of a towering cedar I begin tipping forward, my balance precarious to say the least.

The general's arm hardens around my waist, and he slips me more snuggly between his thighs. The act would be entirely unnecessary if he'd given me a chance to position my legs on either side of the mount. I will never understand why ladies prefer sidesaddle, dress or no.

After briefly considering throwing myself off the horse to make my displeasure perfectly clear, I decide against it. There is no need to risk an injury to make a point the male is already well aware of. Instead, I let my body settle against his. I can do little but trust his arm around me as the horse runs through the night, and remaining rigid in my seat won't serve me, it will only wreak havoc on my muscles, which I would regret in the morning.

With a light tug on the reins the horse slows to a walk when we break from the forest. Again, I debate throwing myself to the ground but smother the thought when my eyes find the orphanage just ahead. We have emerged behind the building, out of the woodland where I'd seen the children at play. I hate that I'm a little impressed that he found his way so easily through the thick overgrowth of the forest, but it isn't something I'll ever admit to him.

The general doesn't dismount when he unstraps the toy sword and leans it against the front door of the building.

"I'll send a letter in the morning, explaining that you carved it for the boy." The heat of his breath is a soft caress on the shell of my ear when he says it.

"Why not just send the sword with the letter?" I ask, as he turns his horse toward the cobbled streets of A'kori.

"I didn't think you'd agree to it. You seemed rather determined to deliver it tonight."

"You could have asked," I say, clearly annoyed despite the fact that I would have absolutely insisted it be delivered tonight.

"I'll try that next time." He chuckles, and the sound glides down my spine like a featherlight touch, sending a rippling wave of goosebumps across my skin.

I shudder at the feeling it provokes, and he wraps the length of his cloak around me to buffer me from the cool evening air. It seems we are both content to ride in silence. I take in the view of the harbor, the light of the city after dark twinkling on the rolling waves of the sea. Firelight flickers in empty windows and not a single soul walks along the well-lit stone streets.

"Why did you carve the sword for the boy?" His voice is near a whisper.

"I already told you."

"You told me it was a kindness. You didn't say why."

I keep a studied gaze on the houses as I answer, letting my eyes wander deep into the shadows of their darkened halls.

"You can't think too highly of me if you think I need a reason to be kind to a child," I say, "Maybe you think I'm incapable of kindness because I'm La'tarian, or human, but in either case you'd be wrong. I've seen enough suffering to last a lifetime. I've watched as those who could give chose not to, willing to let those who'd been born without suffer an undeserving fate."

His body tenses behind me.

"I decided long ago not to be one of those that stood by." I swallow the lump in my throat. "I chose to act instead of remaining complacent, even when that kindness was an act of futility."

"There is no futility in kindness," he says, and I huff a bitter laugh.

"Maybe not on this continent," I say.

"Did it ever occur to you that there might be something to that?" he asks.

"It occurs to me that the A'kori have more than they need and still leave those across the sea to suffer their fate," I snap.

"La'tari propaganda," he bites back, "You should know that the A'kori send regular shipments of food to the coastal villages, we've factored those shipments into every harvest since the war ended."

"That doesn't make any sense," I say, "If that were true those villagers wouldn't be dying of starvation."

"They wouldn't be," he agrees, "That is, if the La'tari military allowed them to keep those food stores."

His cloak does nothing to block the chill that settles into my bones when he speaks the last. My entire being rebels against the idea that my people would steal food meant for the poor.

Memories of my younger self surge to the forefront of my mind, memories of a small boy and an apple that helped him along to his untimely death. Isn't that exactly what I'd seen? The La'tari regime taking food stores from the coastal villages to feed their ranks and bait the starving into conscription.

"The king would never allow that," I say and as soon as it slips off my tongue, I can taste the lie that it is.

"You don't believe that," he says quietly.

I don't argue. There is nothing to say. He has no idea just how deeply this hard truth cuts into the core of the woman I am. I tell myself that it isn't without reason those food stores were taken. But what reason could be good enough to allow those people to starve?

We settle into an uncomfortable silence, the guards only offering brief nods as we pass through the gates of the palace grounds. Without the flickering light cast by the bright pillars that illuminate the streets of A'kori darkness falls like a thick blanket around us, the moon obscured by a patchy layer of clouds passing overhead.

"I never had the chance to apologize earlier." His voice breaks the silence. "For how I made you feel this morning."

"You don't need to apologize," I assure him, "You didn't say anything I don't already know."

"I know what you think you heard, but I never said the king wouldn't find you attractive." I laugh, and he adds, "I can tell you don't believe me. I just don't know why."

"Why did you laugh at me then?" I ask, pinning him with a stare, daring him to convince me he'd meant anything else.

"I laughed because your uncle does nothing to conceal his intentions. It had nothing to do with what I personally think of you. You shouldn't let it deter you from pursuing the king when he returns, if that is your wish. I've known him my entire life and I assure you; he is more concerned with the quality of a mind and the sincerity of a heart than he is about things pertaining to vanity."

"I'm not entirely sure that's a compliment," I say.

He releases a heavy sigh and a whisper muffled by my hair, "So difficult."

"Besides, I already told you, I have no designs on your king."

His gaze doesn't shift from mine, but he remains quiet, and I think he might leave it at that when he says, "I believe you. But if you change your mind, I will put in a good word for you."

I know I should snap the offer out of the air before the wind drags it away. It's everything I've waited for, but I bristle that he finds me incapable of making it in front of the king on my own merit. I have never been one to beg for help.

"I'd think if someone was worthy of a meeting with your king, you wouldn't need to speak on their behalf," I say.

He doesn't reply. The lights of the palace come into view over the rise of the land, its tall spires lost in the moonlit clouds on their ascent toward the heavens. His thumb brushes against my waist, idly smoothing the thin fabric of my gown in a wide sweep. My stomach clenches under the attention, my breath catching in my throat. His hand stills and the male glares down at it, as if he can see the hand beneath the barrier of cloaks and it somehow offended him.

The general leads his horse to a small door at the rear of the palace. Before I can slide to the ground of my own accord, he dismounts, takes my waist between his hands, and helps me down. Just as I open my mouth to scold him, a young boy bursts out of the dark door and takes the horse by the reins.

The boy dips his head when the general thanks him before disappearing into the low light cast from within the palace walls. Curious, I follow the male into a warm kitchen made of thick grey stone. A long, heavy wooden table sits at its center, the room lit by nothing but the cozy glow of dying embers in a large hearth.

A chair rocks in front of it, creaking as it sways. In it sits an old woman, a thin blanket draped over her knees, pooling around her ankles. Dark eyes peer out from under a heavily wrinkled brow and a thick mane of white hair. She smiles.

"Xeyvian, my boy." Her eyes narrow at him as she throws the blanket across the arm of the chair. "You've lost weight. Haven't they been feeding you? Come, I'll make you a bowl of stew."

"Thank you, Media, but I need to get this young lady back to her room," he says, halting her movement with the raise of his hand.

The old woman eyes me under a critical brow.

"And who might you be?" she asks.

I introduce myself, but it does little to warm her countenance toward me.

"You'll come and see me again. Soon. I'd like to know what manner of woman it is that Xeyvian is sneaking into the palace in the dead of night." She grunts and nods as if she's just confirmed my own acceptance of her *invitation*. "Now that's settled, best get the young lady back to her room before the hour becomes more indecent than it already is."

"Yes, Media." The general gives her a nod and leads me out of the kitchen and through the long marble halls. I can feel the old woman's eyes on me until I am completely out of sight.

The palace is asleep, not a soul awake aside from the guards. The only sound, the clap of the general's boots as they echo in time with his stride. The silver scar at his temple flickering as he walks through long panels of moonlight let in through the windows in the hall.

"Why did we come this way? And who was that?" I wonder.

He gestures to a hall to the right and I turn, allowing him to guide me through the labyrinth that is my current home. It is far vaster than the La'tari keep I grew up in.

"Media looked after Awri and Riesh when they were children. Like you, she is from La'tari, but came to live in A'kori when she was younger. About twenty years before the war."

"She's human," I say absentmindedly, more to myself than to the general.

"It surprises you that feyn children would have a human nanny?" he asks. He cocks a brow at me as if I should know better by now, a stray strand of ebony falling in front of his eye.

I shake my head. "It isn't that. I just assumed Awri was older."

"I won't tell her you said that."

I squint my eyes at him. All feyn stop aging in their thirties, he knows what I mean. I wrongly assumed that because Awri was in the war, she had been older when it began. If they were children when Media came, well, she can hardly be more than twice my age. To them, I assume she is still very much a child.

"I brought you through the kitchens to show you where to find our chambers, should the need arise," he says.

His room and the rooms of his companions are only a short distance from my own. Awri's and Riesh's being the closest and the general's rooms buffered from theirs by a handful of closed doors he doesn't elaborate on. Likely rooms for others that remain at court in the king's favor.

It's a quick walk to my room, and I might prefer it to the grand entry of the palace if I wouldn't have to go toe to toe with Media every time I enter the kitchen. Not that I am frightened of the woman, but she seemed rather protective of the general and perhaps a little suspicious of me. It won't do me any good being questioned by the woman every time I make my way in or out. No doubt she will report each and every one of my steps to him.

He stops in front of my room and lingers, his eyes surveying the door.

"If I leave you here, are you going to go to bed?" he asks.

"To be honest, I'm a little afraid to answer that after what happened last time you asked," I tease.

His mouth forms a thin line. "At least use the doors next time you leave."

I smile at his demand. "I make no promises."

Pushing open the door, I turn to meet his eyes before I step inside and say, "Thank you, for the pants."

His eyes flick to my legs, and he nods. When his gaze continues to my feet his brow pinches as he notes the state of my filthy slippers. They aren't ideal for trudging through the forest, but they were my only option. I'll have to throw them out. There is no bringing them back from the mangled mess they have become.

His eyes glide back up to mine and his face softens.

"I've already had a word with the palace tailor about the pants. He'll have some prepared for you within a few days."

"That is unnecessary," I protest, "I have a closet full of them at my uncle's. I will go see him tomorrow and I'm sure he will be reasonable. I'll see to it that he is."

The general quirks an eyebrow at that. "I think you just might. But don't. I'd hate for you to deprive him of all the joy of his scheming."

"We'll see," I say.

"Awri has some things to attend before she collects you tomorrow. Rest in the morning, explore if you like, and she will come find you when she is done. Goodnight, Shivaria," the general says, dipping his head before striding down the hall toward his chambers.

"Goodnight, General."

He stops a few paces from my door. "Xeyvian. You may call me Xeyvian."

I watch him vanish around the corner and slide into my room, curious about the changes I see in him. I'd thought that revealing too much of my true self would exclude me from his favor, from the favor of the feyn in general. Perhaps there is a finer line that needs to be walked between the truth and the lie of the woman I am, if I am to be fully accepted, dangerous as it will be.

Whatever changes are happening with him, I will take them all gladly, with or without explanation. Anything is better than the untrusting, brooding male I'd met on my uncle's lawns.

The sprites are still nowhere to be seen when I make my way back into the comfort of my room, and I'm glad they didn't wait up for my sake. I ready myself for bed and dip my hand into the hidden pocket of my cloak.

My fingers brush against the silky lining and the blood drains from my body in a woosh.

The small pouch is missing. It must have fallen out in the woods.

I stand at the end of the bed, staring at the covers, debating whether I should even attempt to sleep. Accepted or not, my demon will never be a part of what I can reveal to my new *friends*.

Over the years I mixed a number of concoctions after Leanna trained me in the art of herbs. After abandoning my attempts with well-known sleeping draughts when I found that they could do nothing to quell the darkness inside me, I began to trial the ingestion of poison in small doses. The latter had not always gone over well and often kept me awake into the early hours of the morning for very different reasons.

Despite all of this, I head out the door, willing to face Media after all, if it means that she might have something to keep the darkness at bay until dawn.

"Kishek." I greet the male with a dip of my head.

He seems as surprised to see me coming from my room as I am to find him lounging against the wall across from it. He smooths the line of his tunic, pushing off the marble to stand before me.

"I was just looking for Awri," he explains.

"I'm sorry, she isn't here."

The female *has* hardly left my side, but unless the male thinks we are sharing a bed, it seems an odd hour to have company.

"I see." He frowns. "Sorry to bother you."

He starts toward his room, fists bouncing gently against his thighs when he stops and turns to me asking, "Is there something I can help you with?"

I'm sure I look perfectly puzzled by his question when he continues, "I thought you might need something? If you are leaving your room this late."

"I was just heading to the kitchen for a sleeping draught," I say.

I'm not sure why, but he smiles at that and asks, "May I accompany you?"

I nod. Because what can I do? At least he might serve as a distraction for Media.

"I don't sleep well either," he says, as we start toward the kitchens. "Not since the war."

I glance at the male from the corner of my eye, wondering exactly what

visions of the atrocities he committed toward my people keep him awake at night. At least it haunts him.

"I can imagine," I say simply.

"I would be happy to help you make a draught, if you like," he offers, "It took me years to find the right combination of herbs to keep the dreams away."

I eye him curiously, when he chuckles at some unspoken thought.

"The fates have an odd sense of humor," he says, "It's part of my gift, helping others in ways I cannot help myself."

"You help others sleep?" I know I shouldn't ask, but he did bring it up, and I'm relieved when he smiles and doesn't seem to mind.

"Sometimes," he says, "Sometimes it's something else. We all have our own unique demons."

My breath catches in my throat, and I nearly trip as I round the door into the kitchen. Media is absent her chair. She'd likely gone to bed the moment I left with the general.

I follow Kishek to a small pantry at the far side of the kitchen, looking over his shoulder as he rifles through the shelves, the clinking glass the only sound to fill the room. He stacks his arm full of bottled herbs, each precisely labeled with its name and function. Many I recognize, some I've never seen.

Pushing the kettle over the fire on his way to the large table at the center of the room, he procures a cup from a nearby shelf and goes to work, dosing the mixture by sight. It's clear he's done this often enough that it's become routine, and I can't help but hope the herbs of the feyn will be the answer to my terrors.

"What is it that keeps you from your sleep?" he asks, tapping the side of a small vile, counting three petals from an unfamiliar yellow flower before replacing the stopper and setting it aside.

"Dreams," I admit.

He nods his understanding, and I note the last of the unfamiliar herbs he adds to the mixture before he sweeps the jars up and returns them to their home.

"You aren't making one for yourself?" I ask.

He shakes his head, bundling the herbs in a small swatch of gauze-like fabric and placing them in the cup, before covering them with boiling water.

"I'm afraid I have some long nights ahead of me." There is more behind

his eyes when he says it, and when I recall the reason he was outside my room, I assume whatever task he was given involves Awri.

I tuck the information away, deciding that even if the draught doesn't work, it will serve as a good excuse to venture out into the halls during hours when any lady would be fast asleep. I blow on a fine waft of steam coming from the cup, following Kishek back into the hall.

We are standing in front of the doors to my room when he says, "If it helps, tell Awri, and I will be happy to make more for you."

I won't tell her, even if it does help. But I smile and nod my thanks, the gentle timbre of his voice stopping me before I slip inside my chamber.

"She's a good friend, Awri," he says, and I pause with my hand on the wooden panel. "And a good listener. If you ever find it helpful to talk about your dreams or anything else."

"Thank you, Kishek," I reply, raising my cup to him before leaving him in the hall.

I don't doubt what the male says. I am sure the female *is* a good friend, to someone. But not to me, because she will never know me, not until it's too late.

For an hour I pace the length of my room, waiting to see if the tonic will serve its purpose. I'm beginning to doubt its effectiveness when an uncomfortable weight settles on my eyelids.

Standing at the edge of the bed, eyes lingering on the soft duvet, I debate my options and the likelihood that the tonic will keep my demon at bay. I decide in either case, I will seek out the general for his special tea recipe in the morning. Despite my experience with that particular mixture, it was effective.

Deciding I can't risk my demon, I pull a blanket onto my lap and sit by the fire. It won't be the first sleepless night I've had, though remaining clearheaded is always easier when there is a task at hand.

My eyes flick to the door and I consider finding the library or simply using that as an excuse to search the castle. Though I haven't been given a thorough tour and I'm as likely to enter someone's bed chamber as I am to find an empty room.

I'm still debating my options when my head grows heavy, a thick fog of black clouding my vision when I drift off into the void.

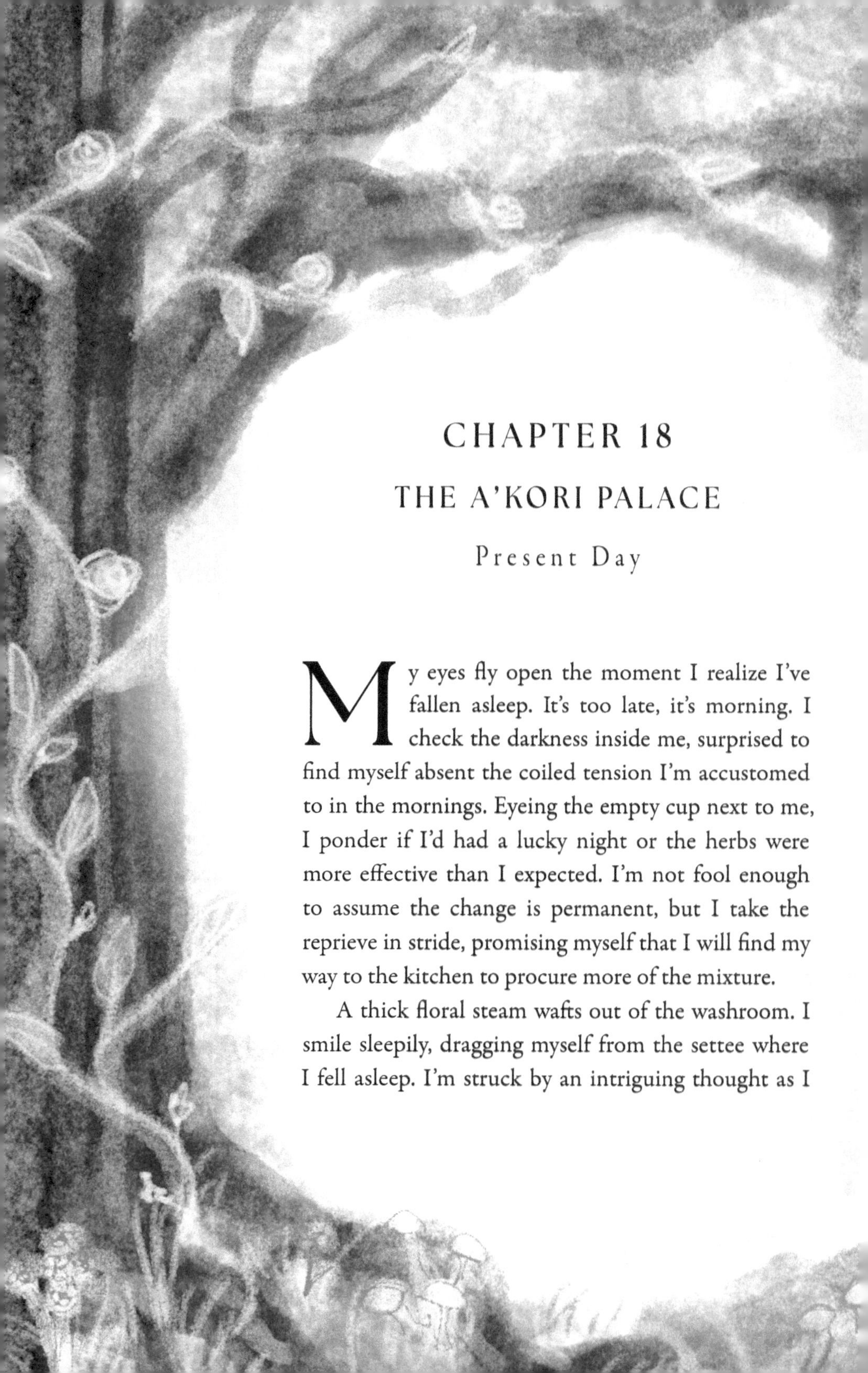

CHAPTER 18
THE A'KORI PALACE
Present Day

My eyes fly open the moment I realize I've fallen asleep. It's too late, it's morning. I check the darkness inside me, surprised to find myself absent the coiled tension I'm accustomed to in the mornings. Eyeing the empty cup next to me, I ponder if I'd had a lucky night or the herbs were more effective than I expected. I'm not fool enough to assume the change is permanent, but I take the reprieve in stride, promising myself that I will find my way to the kitchen to procure more of the mixture.

A thick floral steam wafts out of the washroom. I smile sleepily, dragging myself from the settee where I fell asleep. I'm struck by an intriguing thought as I watch the sprites plucking fragrant flowers from their hair, casting them to float about on the surface of the water.

Walking to the closet to retrieve my cloak, I turn its hidden pocket inside out, relieved when a few small pieces of debris fall into my palm. I doubt it's enough to assist in my sleep, but when I hold the crushed leaves to my nose, I recognize the unique, pungent smell of the herb.

Bending at the hip, I bring myself closer to eye-level with the sprites, extending my hand toward them.

"Do you know what this is?" I ask.

It might be a long shot, but not only are they wood sprites and well acquainted with all manner of natural things, they also contain the knowledge of the many mortal lifetimes they've lived. Tig takes a step toward my hand, eyeing the small fragments speculatively. Leaning in she gives them a sniff even as Eon pushes her sister aside and follows suit much more enthusiastically.

The sprite nods, then sneezes. The sharp puff of breath sending the remnants of my pouch into a flurry before landing scattered about the floor.

"*Ma'shai,*" she says bashfully.

My brows nearly hit my forehead as I ask, "Was that an apology?"

It is the first time her sprite words have landed so easily upon my ears, and she nods with a happy smile.

"Do you recognize the herb?" I ask.

The sisters nod in unison, Tig looking more intrigued by my question than her exuberant sister.

"Can you show me where to get more?" I wonder hopefully.

The smile falls from Eon's face as both sisters shake their heads, confirming my fear that the herb is not so easily obtained. A few breathy whispers pass between the sprites and Tig points to the flowering branches in her hair.

"Will grow." The soft echo of her voice lands on my ears.

"You can grow them?" I say in utter shock, and she seems pleased by the surprised look on my face, nodding before ushering me into the bath.

As I soak in the tub, my mind wanders to my conversation with Felias. He said there was power in the friendship of a fea, and I can't help but wonder what other hidden talents the sisters possess. Though I think it might be rude to ask them. It's clear there is a depth to their world that I remain completely ignorant of, and that is something I will need to rectify as soon as possible.

Awri was willing to answer every question I had the night I learned of the fea's continued existence in our veil. Having never pondered more about the creatures than I was told, those questions were all fairly superficial. Had I known then all that I know now, my questions would have been very different.

I remain in my room throughout the morning, content to let Awri seek me out when she is ready. I begin to question why she needs me at the palace when there is plenty of time each day for me to come and go from my uncle's manor, but I don't read too much into it. If she wants me close at hand, I'll take the opportunity it presents without question.

The sprites' voices come to me, easier than they ever have before. While Tig speaks to me in a heavily accented and somewhat broken human tongue, Eon seems to prefer the odd breathy language of the sprites. I don't ask if she knows the human language, I imagine she's had plenty of time to learn it if she'd ever cared to do so. Instead, I find myself asking the sprite to teach me her tongue, and to that, she agrees gladly.

My head is a jumbled mess of sprite speak when I finally become bored enough to venture from my room, intent on exploring the palace and perhaps finding a little food. Eon selected a silver-white dress for the day and glared at my leathers rather than offering them to me. I briefly debate wearing them, and though I would like nothing more, I decide that while the gift is a kind gesture despite who gave them to me, they may not be appropriate attire for court.

My feet take me down the same corridors the general led me through only hours before. At least I know where to find the kitchen, though whether or not I'm brave enough to face Media this morning, I've yet to decide. No doubt the woman has returned to her place by the fire.

My feet slow when I round a corner beyond the general's quarters, and I hear Riesh's voice bouncing along the walls of the passageway, "It's getting worse along the northern border. I'm not sure how much longer we can remain neutral, Xey."

"We've never been neutral. Not a single day since the sundering," the general's deep voice booms.

"Let me rephrase that. We can no longer afford to appear neutral to the La'tari," Riesh replies.

"You would do nothing?" Awri asks.

I plant my feet, willing myself not to step forward to peer behind the door.

"You know I would give anything to see this war at an end, but we need to be smart. If we anger the Vatruke, neither you nor I will suffer the consequences. It will be the people, just as it was before."

"The resistance—" Riesh says.

"I will *not* entertain an alliance with them," the general growls. "They are reckless, willing to risk the lives of the very fea they claim to protect. I will not waste the lives of the fea needlessly. The ancients would never have allowed it."

"The ancients aren't here, but they left us with a strong leader and the power to take back Terr," Awri argues, "*Valtoura—*"

"That power is in the southern kingdom, beyond our reach." The general's voice barely makes it to my ears when a throat clears behind me.

I whip around to find Kishek looking down at me, a wry smile plastered on his face. I'm not the only one he's interrupted, and I suppress a cringe when the general makes his way into the hall, followed by Awri and Riesh.

"I'm beginning to think she may be a La'tari spy," Kishek teases.

I do my best not to flinch under the general's glower as he steps forward.

"You can hardly call it spying when you're speaking with an open door," I say.

"He's only joking," Awri reassures me. "We don't hoard secrets in A'kori."

Not like the La'tari. The words she leaves unsaid feel like an unintended jab, and I want to tell her that the things they were discussing are exactly the types of secrets they should be hoarding. But I bite my tongue and thank the stars for small favors. I'm not sure what any of it means, but I tuck away the conversation to ponder at another time.

Kishek's eyes are heavy with dark circles as he eyes me thoughtfully. He looks like he hasn't slept in a week.

"Is everything all right?" I ask.

He offers me a stiff nod and turns to Awri. "I'll go and get some sleep."

Awri's eyes are tinged with worry and follow him as he disappears down the corridor. When she finds me watching her, she offers me a small smile that doesn't quite reach her eyes.

Riesh excuses himself when Awri begins toward the domed fea room and I make my way after her. It takes me a moment to realize the general followed after us. The bruise below his eye has almost healed completely and it's the first time I've ever envied the feyn. I'd known many who'd wished for their powerful gifts or coveted their long lives. If I ever had to choose from among their traits, their natural ability to heal would be mine. I can't help but wonder if the trait heals more than wounds of the flesh.

Awri walks to a large table littered with lists for the party and leafs through them. I'm not sure what she's looking for. I'm not even sure *she* knows what she's looking for. My friend seems prone to moods of whimsy when it comes to planning the masquerade.

"Your legs are bare," the general says behind me, and I turn to find him glaring at the naked flesh, laid bare by the flowing panels of my dress.

"They are." I smile at the male as if he just unearthed some great secret lost to Terr. "Have they offended you?"

I quirk an eyebrow when he meets my eyes and his jaw tenses. A quick glance at Awri tells me she's as perplexed by him as I am.

"I'll have another word with the tailor," he says, taking note of the guards stationed at both the entry and exit of the room.

"Gia." He summons a beautiful, black-haired female with a light scar on her cheek. She jogs over, dipping her head as he speaks his command. "Relieve Redik and Andrin of their posts until the masque. Auna and Kaila are to replace them."

"As you say." She rushes to dismiss the males guarding the southern door, reissuing the order for their replacement to a female standing by.

I glance at Awri and find her watching the general with great interest. Her face is contorted in curiosity and sheer confusion. The general gives her a flat look, and more passes between them than I'm able to perceive because without a word she smooths her face and hands me a sheet of paper from the stack.

"Cake?" I ask.

And why am I surprised. At the rate my indecisive friend is planning this party, I have no doubt it will take the better part of the day to have it ordered.

"We just need to decide on a shape and flavor," Awri says, as if those two decisions won't take her hours, with or without my help.

"What are the options?" I ask.

"The options are endless," she beams, clearly pleased by that fact as she bounces excitedly, listing every choice in alphabetical order.

It takes an hour to agree that the cake will be made in the shape of a woodland mushroom, frosted in a thick layer of blue with maroon spots on the cap. Apparently this particular fungi is an old favorite of the fea, eaten with lively enthusiasm and only mildly intoxicating.

Awri and I go back and forth debating flavors and when I give up on offering my opinion the female begins arguing with herself.

Even the general starts to look sorry for me when he finally offers, "Chocolate." It's all he says, but it's enough to silence Awri into short-lived contemplation before she narrows her eyes at him.

"Don't you have something better to do?" she says playfully.

"There are many things I should be doing," he admits, "but I'm beginning to doubt your ability to complete the task the king set out for you."

She levels him with a glare, and I'm proud of her when his feet shift beneath him and he begins to walk toward the door.

"Make it chocolate. It's his favorite," he says over his shoulder.

"I'm his favorite," Awri retorts.

"I'm quite sure that's no longer true," he replies.

Awri chuckles as he turns the corner, and she doesn't waste a second before writing 'chocolate' in her elegant scroll work at the top of the sheet. When Awri makes it through the rest of the stack by early afternoon, I can't help but marvel at the general's tactics pertaining to his friend's planning. Like Awri, the male is obviously a master of the craft of social maneuvering. A fact I tuck away.

Her earlier worry over Kishek never fully leaves her eyes and without a task to occupy her mind it becomes more evident that he is at the forefront of her thoughts. Rubbing her palm against her sternum, she excuses herself to check on him, giving me free reign of the palace.

Intent on taking the reprieve to bundle a few more satchels of Kishek's tea, my feet take me to the kitchens. A young human, about my age, with golden curls and dark eyes opens the door. A waft of fragrant herbs and cooked meats churns my stomach and it growls. She chuckles sweetly and invites me in.

Media is exactly as I expect, rhythmic creak following every push of her heel as her chair rocks away from the fire and back again. She doesn't turn to greet me, but casts her eyes in my direction, nonetheless.

"Glad to see you've returned so soon." She smiles and knocks the leg of the empty chair beside her with her cane. "Come and join me."

I glide into the seat, tucking my legs beneath the thin fabric of my dress. She makes no effort to hide her thorough inspection of me, her eyes dragging over my body when my stomach growls again.

"Sera, a bowl of stew for our guest, please."

The young girl is quick to bring a steaming bowl with a fat slice of heavily buttered bread. She dips her head when I thank her, then makes herself busy rolling out a thick sheet of dough on the blocky table sitting in the center of the kitchen.

"Sera is my granddaughter," Media explains.

"She has your eyes," I say, blowing on the hot stew.

The woman smiles fondly at the girl and nods in agreement.

"The general tells me you knew Awri and Riesh as children," I say.

"I did. Not as well behaved as my own children. They'd hardly begun to walk when their mother disappeared beyond the southern border of La'tari. Their father left them in the hands of the king and relinquished his title as general to go in search of her."

Her eyes fall to the wrinkled hands in her lap, and she turns them over beneath her gaze.

"He never did find her," she says sadly. "Funny, what events borne by the fates lay outside of our control. The male left to find his mate, the female he'd lived alongside for centuries, and returned instead with a ship full of frail humans, missing a piece of his soul."

I take a bite of my stew, the robust flavor lost to the bitter tale spilling from the woman's lips.

"He went back for years, so many times, always in search of her. Always returning with a ship full of mortals, desperate to flee the very shores they were born upon."

She stares off into the fire for a moment, watching the flames lick the sappy logs as they pop in the hearth.

"It took something from him, returning without her all those times. Years of hopeful searching turned bitter, and when it became clear she would never return, all we could do was hope that, for her sake, he was wrong when he assured us that she still lived."

"Why would you hope that?" I ask.

"It is better than the alternative," she says.

"What alternative?"

"What the La'tari have always done to the feyn." Her brow draws down, and she looks at me as if I just asked the most ridiculous question she's ever heard. "Hold her, break her, and force her to use her gift to aid them."

I set my bowl of stew aside, my appetite suddenly absent my body. A small ember of rage flickers to light deep inside me. They'd spent a lifetime spewing hateful tales into this woman's ears and now she believes every lie she's been fed.

"The La'tari never kept feyn prisoners," I assure her, "Not even during the war."

"According to whom? What exactly do you think started the war, child?"

I bristle at being called a child. I might be much younger in years, but it is quickly becoming clear I have more experience on the southern shores and a far greater understanding of how the mortal kings ruled La'tari in the past.

"The war started when the feyn invaded our shores, killing every soul in their path, man, woman, and child." It takes every bit of my restraint to keep the rising heat from my voice. "All so they could strip the resources from our land and bring them here, to their people."

"What resources would those be?" she asks.

"The gifted stripped the land of its fertility," I explain, "and now La'tari is little more than a barren wasteland. Crops won't grow; water is scarce. Entire families starve, unable to grow food to feed themselves."

A part of me feels bad for her. She left her homeland before the feyn came to ravage it and never saw for herself the devastation they left in their wake.

I stiffen in my seat when she cackles hoarsely. "Is that what they teach now? That land was barren long before my great grandfather was born into this world." She shakes her head at me. "Mortal lives are short, and our memories even shorter. It is a great boon to those who wish to enslave our minds and rewrite our histories."

"What reason would humans have to rewrite their own history?" I argue, hoping she can see reason.

"Not humans. The Vatruke." My heart nearly stills as the word falls from her lips.

"What are the Vatruke?" I ask, not caring if she decides I am completely ignorant.

Her eyebrows shoot up and she replies, "I never expected the Vatruke to fall from the memories of the La'tari. It is they that bleed our soil of the essence of Terr." She taps the leg of my chair with her cane, and asks, "What do you know of the sundering?"

"As much as any La'tari child."

She puffs out a dissatisfied harrumph. "If what you've shared with me so far is any indication of the rest of your education, I'll recommend that Xeyvian supply you with a history tutor, and a good one at that."

I try not to glare at the woman as she begins her tale, "The lifeforce of Terr has always been precious to the feyn. *Shivay*, they call it. The world soul. The light of all life. It is the essence they draw upon to access their gifts.

When mortals first found the feyn, they feared what they did not understand. Some things don't change much over time. No matter how many years pass, man never ceases to fear the unknown," she adds, absentmindedly.

"We have always been too quick to pass judgment, and irrational in our fear of what is new. Back then, the feyn were powerful beyond what you or I can likely comprehend. They had access to the whole soul of Terr, not the shredded bit of what's been left in this veil.

The feyn fought for years to establish peace with us, to build a world where fea and mortals could dwell happily alongside one another. But the prejudice of our kind saw them as little more than creatures and treated them as such. It wasn't long before humans began to hunt the fea."

"Humans have never been strong enough to hunt fea," I argue.

"You think not? The Drakai hunt them, even to this day."

My stomach twists at the mention of my people. She isn't wrong, but most Drakai are raised from birth to survive an encounter with the feyn and precious few make it back from such a mission.

"The fea may be more powerful than us," she continues, "but they also

have a reverence for life that mortals could never obtain in a life so fleeting. When it became clear there would never be peace between them, the most powerful among the fea gathered to discuss what could be done. The first utterance of the sundering was born that night—an agreement to separate Terr into five veils where fea could live alongside mortals, each unknown to the other. But the soul of Terr had to be divided among the five veils of our world, and it weakened the fea.

Most fea followed the path to a new world, eager to leave the humans and their wars behind, but some remained, the Vatruke among them."

"You still haven't told me what they are."

"Patience, child. I'm getting to that," she says with a tsk. "The Vatruke rebelled at the loss of their power and have done all they can to reclaim it ever since."

"The Vatruke are fea?"

"They are a small group of feyn, powerful long ago. I suppose they may still be just that, but it's hard to say what one becomes after many lifetimes of hatred and a lust for power and vengeance."

"If the Vatruke are what you claim, wouldn't they hate the humans? Why would they be working with the La'tari?" I ask.

"I've often asked myself the same question." Her eyes grow glassy and she stares into the fire, her mind lost in visions only she can fathom. "Maybe they do hate the humans. But it was the feyn that stripped them of their power in the sundering, and it is humans who now help them hunt the fea in their pursuit of recovering that power."

It is quite the tale, and I find it impossible to discern which parts were carefully crafted by the feyn to hide the true history of our world. I can't imagine the feyn giving up their power like she claims, or the La'tari working with a group of ancients.

Media's eyes grow heavy and her head bobs as she fights off the sleep that I'm sure her body desperately needs.

"Thank you for your story and for lunch," I say as I stand.

"Come back soon, child." The words hardly make it past her lips as her chin falls against her chest and her eyes shutter closed.

I don't linger, only taking time to bundle three nights worth of Kishek's

concoction before leaving. Sera offers me a silent wave as I slip out the door, back into the marble halls of the palace.

Awri hasn't returned to the domed fea room by the time I make it back to check, and the light coming through the windows is quickly growing dim. My stomach twists when I consider going back to my room for the evening. There is another task I mean to accomplish today. One I should have seen to when the general was close at hand this morning.

I find myself in front of his room, glaring at the doors as if they alone are responsible for my presence. I should have asked Media if she knew about the general's tea before she'd fallen asleep. I don't want to owe this male anything.

I tell myself that the bundles in my pocket should suffice, but there is no guarantee the tonic will continue to work. I cannot risk my demon revealing itself. And if between Kishek's brew and the general's, I can prevent my terrors, it will have been well worth my time to gather as much as I am able.

A light set of steps in the corridor behind me brings Riesh to my side.

"Are you going to knock?" he asks with an amused smile.

"I'm not sure," I admit.

Riesh laughs under his breath. "He isn't in there anyway. Is it something I can help you with?"

I cross my arms and eye the male, half relieved and half irritated that the general isn't here when I say, "I was hoping to get a recipe from him. For a sleeping draught he made me once."

Riesh smiles wryly and I suspect that unlike his sister, he knows the truth of what happened the night the general drugged me at the cottage.

"I know the one," he says, "but it isn't easy to come by. I'll send for the herbs, but it may take a week or two for them to arrive."

"A week?" I groan.

"Or two," he adds. "I'll have some ordered. There is always a chance they will arrive sooner."

I thank him and begin to debate sneaking out my window and sleeping under the stars, but I remind myself that the general somehow knew I left last time. Something I'm sure to avoid in the future with a little more caution on my part.

"Sera tells me you spent time with Media today," Riesh says, "Thank you

for doing that. She's had a hard time getting around the last few years. She will never admit it, but I think she gets a little lonely sometimes. I try to visit every day, but it isn't always possible."

"She has her family," I reassure him.

He shakes his head. "She has Sera. Her husband and three of their children died during the war."

I don't have to ask which side they fought on. I never imagined humans, let alone those born on La'tari soil, killing their own at the behest of the feyn. I pity the woman for her delusion that the feyn saved her, when all they really did was corrupt her mind until she was willing to watch her loved ones die for their cause.

"I'm sorry to hear that," I say.

He dips his head and excuses himself to put in my request for the tea with the palace courier. I hadn't had a chance to ask Media what happened to his father, but I assume by his absence, Riesh and Awri lost him to the war as well.

By the time I make it back to my chamber and sip down one of Kishek's teas, I've made up my mind to risk spending the night in my bed. There is no sign of the demon that plagues me or the lingering darkness that accompanies it.

Eon continues my lessons in sprite as Tig runs a comb through my hair. Now that I've expressed an interest, the sprite seems determined to have me fluent in the breathy language before long and isn't shy about correcting my pronunciation, which I gather is unsurprisingly poor. I'm not sure mortal tongues were meant to craft the words of the fea, at least not those of the sprites.

Tig slips me into one of the short gossamer sleeping gowns, and I slide the letter opener from the pocket of my leathers and under my pillow when I lay down. It's a far cry from my obsidian daggers, and I miss every nick and groove etched into my memory as I grasp the cool, smooth metal of the foreign hilt.

Tomorrow will be a day for exploring the options that remain beyond my lost pouch of herbs and the teas. Experience tells me that it is only a matter of time before my demon begins to grow restless.

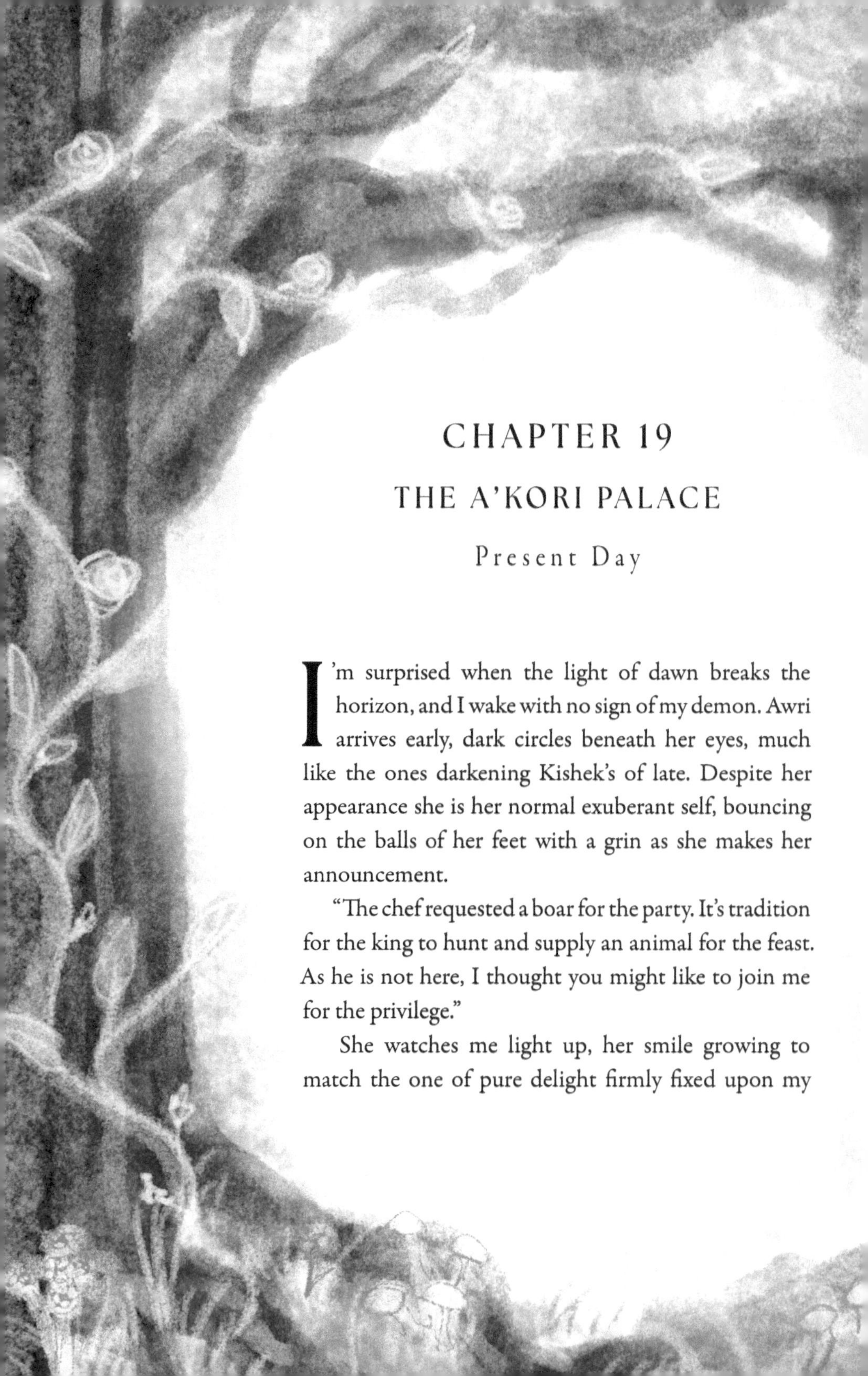

CHAPTER 19
THE A'KORI PALACE
Present Day

I'm surprised when the light of dawn breaks the horizon, and I wake with no sign of my demon. Awri arrives early, dark circles beneath her eyes, much like the ones darkening Kishek's of late. Despite her appearance she is her normal exuberant self, bouncing on the balls of her feet with a grin as she makes her announcement.

"The chef requested a boar for the party. It's tradition for the king to hunt and supply an animal for the feast. As he is not here, I thought you might like to join me for the privilege."

She watches me light up, her smile growing to match the one of pure delight firmly fixed upon my face. It's been too long since I've held a weapon, too long since I've had a chance to exercise my skills. And it feels like a lazy stretch after a deep battle worn sleep when I run to my closet and pull on my leathers. Slipping on the darkest of my grey dresses, dark enough to blend with the shadows below the forest canopy, I tie the silk panels below my hip where the fabric will not interfere with the movement of my legs.

Awri's eyes flick down to my leathers the moment I round the corner from the washroom into my chambers, my dark cloak billowing out behind me.

"Where did you get those?" she asks curiously.

"The general gave them to me," I say, walking to the head of my bed, discreetly pulling the letter opener from my pillow and sheathing it in the leg of my pants before walking to the vanity.

"I'm fairly certain I've never known a member of the opposite sex to find the female form so distasteful," I tease.

She tips her head thoughtfully. "I've always known Xeyvian to appreciate the beauty of the fairer sex."

"He appears to have found his limit to that appreciation in me," I laugh.

She looks me over from head to toe raising a brow. "I highly doubt that."

I shrug. She will never know what it's like to be anything less than what she is—feyn. Eternally young and painfully beautiful. Every pair of eyes privileged enough to take in the grace of her form no doubt desired or envied her. I can't begrudge her lack of experience with the sharp stab of rejection, nor would I ever want that for her.

I braid my hair from the crown of my brow, over my ears, and into a thick length that falls heavily down my back, before following Awri into the eerie stillness of the palace in the early morning. Guards, weary from standing watch through the night, straighten their backs when we come into view as she leads me down a series of unfamiliar corridors. Archways leading to countless marbled halls pass in a hazy blur, until the golden veins beneath our feet lead us through a wide set of doors. The thick slab of stone spills out onto the eastern grounds of the palace in the form of an ornate grand staircase, abutting the untamed lawns.

I glimpse the stables before we descend. The sight quickly lost to me below the wild hedge that lines the winding path beneath our feet. A familiar sound sends a jittering jolt of anticipation through my body and my hands begin to sweat. I already know what I will find when we round the last of the tall shrubs bordering the stable.

Riesh takes a jab at the general's side and the male sidesteps the blow with graceful ease. They've been at it for quite some time. Sweat slicks the well-defined muscles ribbing their abdomens and wrapping their arms. Both males are the epitome of the feyn of old and much like I imagined them on the fields of war.

For the first time, my eyes view the banded oaths of the fea, clinging to their sides and arms. Most are a simple line of black, following the line of their ribs from their spine. A batch of crimson bands wrap the general's forearm, Riesh's forearm bearing two in the same shade, and I find myself wondering what each of them means. Throughout my life the bargains of the feyn piqued my curiosity, though what little I know about them is hardly useful.

A small patch of fine sand clings to Riesh, just above his shoulder. He's already been taken to the ground. A clear mark in favor of the general. This time, it is the general who decides to strike, throwing his weight into a low kick. I cringe just as I see Riesh come to terms with his mistake.

His eyes fall to the ground, tracking the sweep of the general's leg. The general seizes the moment, striking high with a fist before the male can bring his eyes back to the threat before him. The blow lands with a solid thump, and Riesh staggers back. He pulled the punch, but not enough to keep a small drop of blood from forming on the feyn's freshly split lip. Riesh throws his hands up in the air in a clear concession of defeat.

"Is there a reason you felt you had to make my brother bleed this morning?" Awri asks dryly.

With the back of his wrist, the general wipes the sweat from his brow and runs his fingers through his thick mane of black. Ignoring her question, he nods in my direction, pointing to a pair of leather boots outside the ring and says, "Those are for you."

Awri raises her brows at the male, clearly shocked. She doesn't say a word but disappears into the stables. I'm sure I've misunderstood him, but when he sees me eyeing them hesitantly, he picks them up and hands them to me. I thank him, and he grunts a reply.

Kicking off my slippers, I lace the boots snugly around my calves, trying not to let on just how much I love the feeling of the leather and the familiar security it brings. Riesh elbows the general, looking over my new outfit with a wide grin, he whispers, "She really does look like she could take you on now."

I wish he would stop ribbing his friend about the black eye. He's been a little too impressed with the fact that I'd given it to his friend. The mark has all but faded and I'd prefer if the memory of that evening faded along with it.

"She caught me off guard. It could happen to anyone," the general says.

I obviously fail to keep a straight face when I bristle at the male's arrogance and Riesh taps the general on the shoulder. Pointing in my direction, he says, "That's the same look she gave you last time you said that. I really think she might like to take another stab at it and prove you wrong."

I shake my head, smoothing the lines of irritation from my face before the general has a chance to see for himself exactly what his friend is talking about.

"I'm sure he's right." The words burn like acid on my tongue. "I just caught him off guard."

I do want to prove him wrong, but there is strength in appearing weaker than your opponent and as long as he continues to underestimate me, I have the upper hand if I need it. I'm hoping to be long gone before he realizes I've killed his king, but I would be a fool not to prepare for every possible outcome.

"Please tell me the moment you change your mind and decide to humble my friend," Riesh says with a jesting smile. "I'll never forgive you if I miss it, and I have no doubt that moment *will* come."

The general scoffs, pulling his tunic over his head and picks up the bow and quiver leaning against the wooden fence of the arena. Riesh follows suit and in their dark leathers and black tunics they look very much the deadly, sinister feyn of La'tari children's stories.

Awri saunters out of the stables, donning leather pants of her own and the same knotted panels of dark silk below her hip. Her brother eyes her curiously.

"If she can wear them, so can I," she says, determination written clearly upon her face.

"*She* doesn't have any other appropriate attire," the general retorts.

I lean toward my friend and whisper, "What did I tell you? He would

bundle me up in a bed sheet and call it adequate attire if it meant he didn't have to look at my bare flesh."

I'm sure the general overhears me when his head snaps up in my direction and his brow pinches. He doesn't argue, as if I need the scalding confirmation of his distaste.

"Let's go, before we lose the advantage of the morning," Riesh says as he walks toward the edge of the woodlands abutting the estate.

I follow after, removing myself from the ever-present glower of the general. Awri steps in beside me, handing me a bow, a full quiver, and a small satchel. The bow she'd received for her birthday is already strapped to her back.

The woods are thick with foliage and dense undergrowth. What light pierces the canopy falls like shards of broken sunlight to the mossy forest floor. An unspoken silence falls over our party, the only sounds, the birds calling out into the morning and the faint rustling of leaves underfoot.

We walk for hours. The sole sign of life, the rabbit trails disappearing into dark holes at the base of the ancient trees towering overhead. Midday we stop at an old encampment with charred remnants of a fire that died long ago. The general drops his bow and quiver then slings the satchel from his shoulder letting it fall to the ground with a thud when he says, "We'll break for lunch then head east for another hour before rounding south toward the palace."

Awri and Riesh follow suit, sitting on half rotten logs, pulled around the fire many years ago. While I doubt there is a need, I can't help the urge to check the perimeter before allowing myself to relax in an exposed and unfamiliar area. I walk a small circle around the camp, making a show of looking at the early blooming spring flowers and other flora foreign to my homeland.

The general keeps a curious eye on me. The light patter of rain raises my eyes to the canopy above and thunder cracks in the distance.

"Pack it in," he says as he rewraps the dried meats he brought for his lunch, "There is a small hut directly south where we will wait out the storm."

The echoing snap of a branch draws my gaze to the forest, and I lock eyes with a boar. My heart matches the boom of thunder sounding overhead as I slowly reach back to draw an arrow from my quiver. Something shifts behind me and the boar bolts, heading deeper into the forest.

Swearing under my breath, I plunge into the trees after it. The general

swears behind me and I hear the crash of the brush as he follows in pursuit. I weave between bushes, ducking beneath low hanging branches, leaping over small creeks flowing with icy runoff from the mountains to the north. The light patter of rain quickly turns to heavy, frequent drops as I rush through an open glade. Lightning strikes in the distance and thunder rolls across the land.

The boar disappears into the forest on the opposite end of the glade and the general yells behind me, "Take the bridge!"

I don't have time to puzzle out his words as I duck back into the woodland. The dense cluster of trees begins to thin before me and a wide, rushing river comes into view. A bridge lies to the south, but I'm losing the boar, and a fallen tangle of logs spans the river in a natural crossing at my feet.

If I had time to stop and roll my eyes at him, to slow and consider the heat of my annoyance, I would. I've spent the better part of my life proving to men in the La'tari regime just how capable I am, only to have the male behind me question my ability to maintain my footing on a wide deck of fallen logs.

I don't hesitate before jumping onto the fallen trees. Midway across, I skid to a halt, quickly stringing an arrow to take my shot. Inhaling a deep breath, I set my sights on the boar and exhale, ignoring the general when he shouts my name. He calls my name again, the rest of his words lost to the rumbling peel of thunder as it cracks just overhead.

I feel it then, the icy tendril that licks up the length of your spine when hidden eyes land upon you. My heart stutters to a stop and again, thunder roils in the clouds as I whip around to face the male standing on the shore behind me. His eyes grow wide just as a chilly iron grip encases my ankle, tearing my leg out from under me. I go down hard, my head hitting the log beneath me with a sickening crack before I plunge into the icy depths of the turbulent water.

The current takes me east, frigid and swift, tumbling me over the jagged stones beneath the whitewater. Roots and debris from fallen trees litter the riverbed, tearing at any exposed flesh they find. A thin branch cuts my cheek as I'm swept by and I reach out, desperate to grasp something secure. My hands wrap around a thick tree limb, and I settle my feet on the ground, pushing off until I break the surface, gasping for air, and freeing myself from the heavy drag of my wet cloak with a pull of the clasp.

A cold hand wraps around my calf, pulling me under, and water enters

my lungs as I'm tossed back into the current. I tumble into a sunken bramble, sharp thorns cutting the fragile flesh below my breast, just before I'm caught up in an eddy and thrown against a large boulder.

My side takes the brunt of the impact, the loud snap of my rib nothing but a muffled pop under the water. My lungs ache for air as the last of my breath is forced from my chest. I free myself from a tangle of branches and push off from the creek bed, angling myself toward the shore.

I slide the letter opener into my hand, preparing for when I break the surface. I sputter a wet cough when the cool air touches my cheeks. A firm hand wraps around my calf, and I drive my dagger into the water before it can pull me under. The creature's shriek pierces the river in a deafening pitch that makes my ears throb to the frantic rhythm of my heart. It releases me, and I pull my makeshift dagger free as I quickly head for shore.

My lungs expel the frigid liquid as I drag myself up the embankment on the northern side. I grasp the thick roots of a nearby willow, wincing each time I pull myself further onto the shore. I only allow myself to roll onto my back and catch my breath after my feet are well clear of the current.

Despite what I hope, it doesn't take the creature long to find me. A cool spike of fear snakes through my veins when its head breaks the surface of the water, its eyes like dark river stones. Reaching the bank, it stalks toward me, and I only have time to scramble back a few steps before it pins me to the muddy earth.

Its hair is a stinking mass of green algae, riddled with a variety of aquatic eggs. Its skin is tinged a deep green and its teeth are every bit as sharp as the sprites'. These teeth I have cause to fear, as the creature's eyes explore the exposed flesh of my neck. A blue liquid oozes from a wound on its forearm where I'd struck it with the blade. Its eyes follow my gaze and a vicious growl tears from its throat as it widens its jaw unnaturally.

"Stop!"

I don't take my eyes from the creature when I hear the general's voice, but it seems to understand him when it pauses.

"A favor for her life," he says.

The fea tips its head at the general, as it considers the offer and says, *"Haasei'eth, kai'den vessai."*

"It's a bargain," he says without hesitation, walking toward the creature.

The fea falls to its belly and, keeping a wary eye on the letter opener, it slithers backward, disappearing into the dark rushing river.

I slide the blade back into the sheath and take the general's hand when he offers it. My left leg buckles the moment I put weight on it, and I pitch forward, headed for the ground. An arm sweeps beneath my knees, and he hooks my waist. I gasp against the pain as he lifts, settling me against his chest.

"I'm fine, I just got lightheaded," I lie and wince, clutching at the sharp pain in my side when I try to squirm out of his arms.

He pushes out his disbelief on a breath, firming his hold at my waist as he turns north, not south as I expect. The sky flickers and another booming crash echoes overhead just as the pattering of rain on the canopy turns into a fierce deluge. My body starts to tremble as the adrenaline keeping me warm begins to fade and the glacial temperature of the river seeps into my bones. I tense my muscles, willing my body to still, forcing down the frailty of my human form.

"Where are we going?" My teeth chatter.

The general glares at me. Quickening his pace, he says, "There is a winter hunting lodge close by. It will do until morning."

I don't even want to argue, and that's a bad sign. A dry place to rest while I regain my strength is the best I can hope for. My head feels like it's made of steel as it lulls and tips against the general's shoulder. My forehead rests in the crook of his neck and under all the ice of his exterior I never expected the male to feel so warm.

"Foc," he says under his breath, and a sharp pang slices through my gut, hollowing out my stomach.

I ignore the sinking feeling and his aversion to my skin against his own. I can't bring myself to care or summon the strength to fight my way out of his arms. He quickens his pace, turning up a steep incline of large boulders covered in years of overgrowth and moss. I close my eyes, clenching my jaw to stop my teeth from clacking against each other.

I'm vaguely aware of the loud crack of splintering wood as he kicks open the cabin door. The force bounces it off the wall and it swings closed behind him, latching shut. I feel a strange kinship with the latch for remaining strong in defiance of his brute strength and demands.

The cold wall of the cabin presses against my back when he eases me out of his arms and onto the floor. I immediately regret the loss of his warmth when he unthreads his arm from under my knees, only to imagine slamming my blade into that same arm when he pinches my chin between his fingers and rattles my head.

"Open your eyes," he demands harshly, "Take off your boots. We have to get you out of those clothes and into something dry. Either you do it, or I will."

I glare at the male, an act I'm not even sure he notices before rushing out into the rain. A distant and quickly fading part of me knows he's right. I need to get dry. I need to get warm.

My fingers tangle with thick laces, my hands are numb and each attempt to grasp the cords feels like a monumental effort in futility. I've never been more annoyed about knotting my laces in lieu of a simple tidy bow, a habit I picked up when I began to spar and a loose lace rarely meant anything but defeat.

The general bursts into the cabin with an arm full of dry logs, his frown deepening when his eyes fall to the boots still laced securely around my calves. He stacks the logs in the stone fireplace, produces a flint and steel from his satchel, and strikes it to the kindling. No sooner do I hear the woosh of the flame than I feel him hurriedly working my boots free of my legs.

"You'll warm up soon," he reassures me, pulling the boots from my feet.

"I'm fine. I'm not cold," I say, suppressing a shiver.

"Yes, you are," he growls, "You're freezing."

He hooks my waist, and I wince at the sharp pain in my side as he lays me in front of the fire. He's on his feet, digging through a large chest in a dark corner of the room before I realize he's even left my side. A thick quilt is in his hands when he returns and that too he places close to the flames.

He kneels down beside me, the line of his jaw growing tense as he reaches for the laces of my leather pants. My head spins and I can't even form the words to protest before he's sliding the pants down my legs. I have just enough time to grasp the hilt of the tiny blade sheathed at my thigh before he removes the leathers, throwing them over the back of a nearby chair.

He lifts me into a sitting position, gathering the fabric of my dress, bunching it around my waist. It's all too much, too fast, and raising too many memories and feelings I'd rather leave in the graveyard of my heart.

Light flickers in the window and my arm snaps forward bringing the blade to his throat before the answering crack of thunder reverberates through the dimming sky. His brows shoot up, his hands stilling at my waist. I must look like a frightened animal with claws drawn and teeth bared by the way he takes me in.

It was the first lesson I'd been taught when I learned to hunt, never approach a wounded animal. They are unpredictable, full of lethal desperation.

His face settles back into his usual glower. "I'm trying to help you."

"Don't," I rasp.

He searches my eyes and pins me with a stare. "If you fall asleep in that dress, you might not wake up."

"I'm f-fine." My teeth chatter.

"You're not fine. You're shaking so hard I can practically hear your bones rattling," he growls, "Use that blade, or don't, but I won't sit here and watch you die for nothing more than your modesty."

I make no move to take the blade from his throat, and he softens his voice. "Look, I'm keeping my eyes right here."

He holds my gaze as his fingers begin working the rest of the fabric into a pool around my waist. He slips the dress over my head, peeling the sleeves off my arms, leaving me with the dagger when he has every reason and every chance to take it from me. We both know I'm in no condition to overpower him. He unfurls the quilt and bundles me up inside it.

"I'm just checking for wounds," he says, waiting until I give him a shallow nod before he does a quick inspection of my legs, torso, and neck.

He's careful to keep the blanket draped in a way that doesn't reveal more than necessary, and he only lingers briefly by the cut beneath my breast.

"Nothing life threatening," he says as he stands.

The tremors of my body grow painful, the intense heat of the fire scalding me. Despite the cold and the pain, I've never been more desperate for sleep in my life. I lay my head against the wooden floor with only the heavy quilt as a pillow, drifting off quickly to the sound of a steady sheet of rain pelting the roof.

A cold burst of air licks my skin into gooseflesh and the chill shocks me from my sleep. I glare at the general as he pulls back my covers, relieved of his own soaked clothing.

"What are you d-doing?" I demand.

"Making sure you get the heat you need," he says, as if that will make everything all right.

My eyes flick to the dagger above my head, where I set it down when he laid me in front of the fire, and his eyes follow my stare.

"I'd rather not get stabbed for my efforts to save your life," he says, "but I would understand. Especially after this."

He wraps his arms around me, pulling me tightly against his chest, pinning my arms between us. My biceps are glued to my sides, bound by the iron band of his own. I suck in a breath, holding it as my body tenses, preparing itself for the need to defend, but the male doesn't move. He simply lays still with my chest pressed against his, and my back to the fire.

The tension slowly leaks out of my body, and I will myself to draw in a deep breath, my lungs filling with the scent of citrus and cedar. His scent. My eyes grow heavy as the heat of his body seeps into mine. I feel like an icy puddle melting in the thaw and sigh deeply as my eyes close.

"Not yet," he murmurs, his lips and a few stray locks of wet raven hair brushing my forehead. "Stay awake just a little longer. You hit your head when you fell."

"I'm fine," I whisper.

"You keep saying that. I'm beginning to wonder if you even know what that word means."

His arms loosen their hold, and he cups the back of my head, his fingers prodding the tender knotted lump I received in my fall. I pull a sharp hiss of air through my teeth and his hand falls to my back to rest between my shoulders.

"What was that thing?" I wonder aloud.

"A naiad. She guards a spring near the crossing."

I guess that means some fea *are* like the La'tari fairy stories. Though the naiads I read about as a child were benevolent creatures, beautiful and timid. Not at all like the foul thing that tried to drown me. He spoke to her, and not in the feyn tongue. I'm not fluent but I know enough to recognize it when I hear it.

"What did she say to you?" My eyes close with a weight so great I begin to wonder if I'll ever open them again.

"She named her price for your life," he says softly.

"What was it?" I murmur as the darkness comes to take me.

"It doesn't matter." His lips are so soft and his breath so warm when he whispers against my skin. "I would pay it a hundred times over."

The words are all but lost to the void.

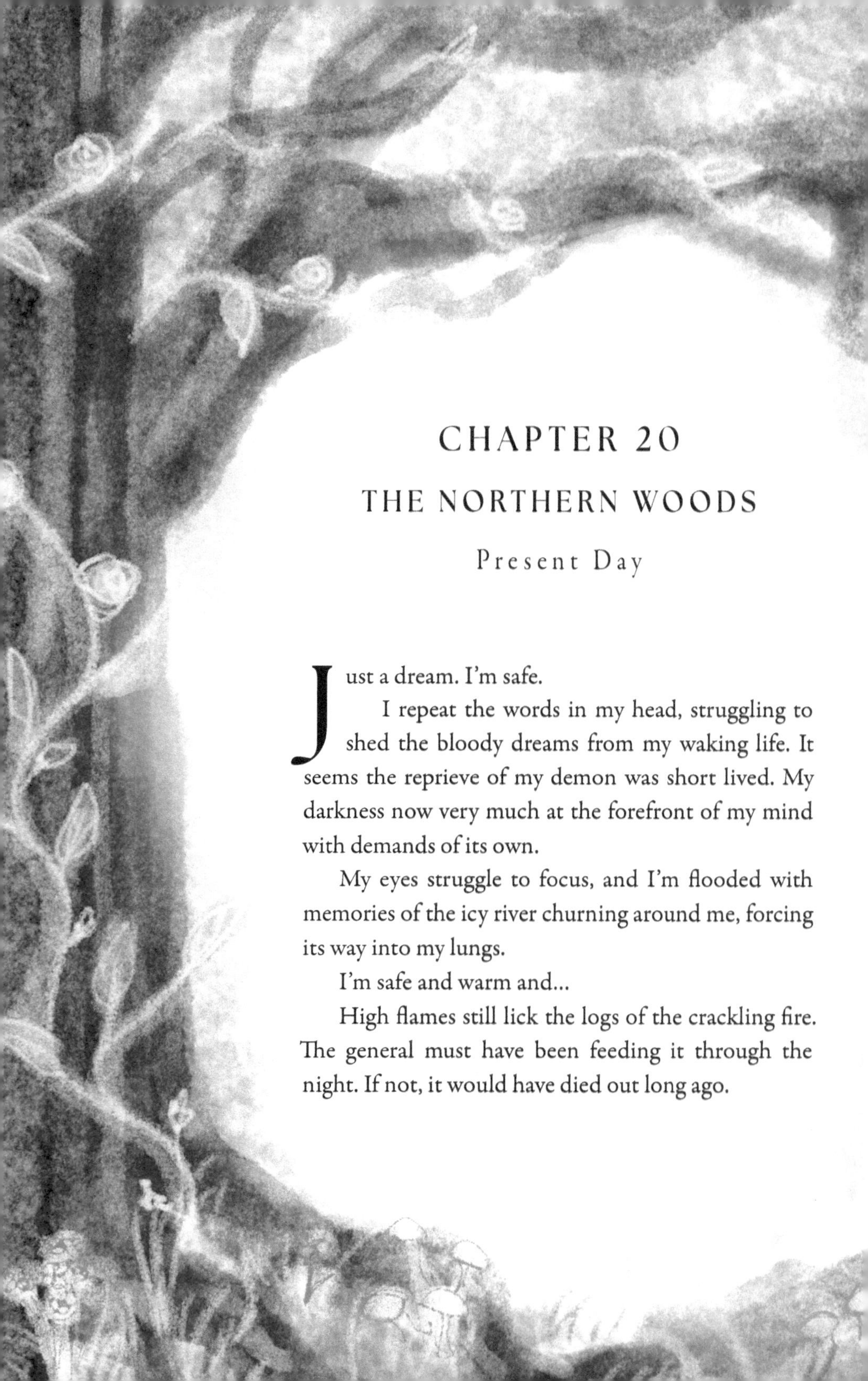

CHAPTER 20
THE NORTHERN WOODS
Present Day

Just a dream. I'm safe.

I repeat the words in my head, struggling to shed the bloody dreams from my waking life. It seems the reprieve of my demon was short lived. My darkness now very much at the forefront of my mind with demands of its own.

My eyes struggle to focus, and I'm flooded with memories of the icy river churning around me, forcing its way into my lungs.

I'm safe and warm and...

High flames still lick the logs of the crackling fire. The general must have been feeding it through the night. If not, it would have died out long ago.

The weight of his arm is draped over my hip, his thumb sweeping idle circles dangerously low on my belly. His breath is a rhythmic pulse, teasing the fine whisps of hair on the back of my neck, his rigid length pressed firmly against my backside.

My darkness uncoils under the attention of his caress, fighting to the surface to meet him. With every pass of his thumb, it yearns to be satisfied, just as it pushed me to find my release in the ring every morning. My stomach flutters, tensing as my core clenches and the gentle swirl of his hand falters. He rises from our makeshift bed on the floor, clothes rustling as he dresses behind me.

I remain frozen on the floor, too many puzzled thoughts rage in the crashing torrent of my mind. It occurs to me that he touched me much the same way the night we delivered the sword to the orphanage, and he'd been obviously displeased by the actions of his hand then. Telling myself that the touch is nothing more than a thoughtless fidget I breathe a little easier. Leanna taught me enough to easily excuse the warm press of his malehood in the morning. Some things, I was taught, are out of a male's control.

The floorboards creak beneath the heavy fall of his footsteps and he lays my clothes in a neatly folded pile by my head before leaving the cabin.

"Get dressed. We won't be alone much longer," he says.

The moment the door latches shut behind him I pull my clothes under the quilt and dress as quickly as I can. The feeling is gone the moment I slip on my leathers. They are bone dry, still warm from sitting by the fire, as are my boots when I cinch them to my calves. The silk dress is bound for the next life, torn across the back, its bodice and skirt frayed at nearly every hem. Still, it's better than nothing.

A large gash in the thin fabric exposes an angry wound below my breast. It's tender to the touch but not life threatening, barring infection.

I run my fingers through my hair, my braid had come undone in the river and I'd gone to sleep with it wet. I'm sure I look a mess. The curly nest of tangles can be unruly on the best of days. I suck in a pained breath when my hands find the knot where I struck my head. Also tender, also not life threatening. Probably.

The throbbing pain in my side is perhaps the only wound that feels much

worse upon rising this morning. Standing in the center of the cabin, I lift the dress to examine the extent of the injury when the general barges through the front door. The only door. Other than a small shelf with a lone carving of a wolf, there is little more adorning the cabin than the trunk in the corner and a small bed built into the wall.

The general's eyes flick to my bruising side before I can pull my dress down to cover it. His eyes narrow on the discoloration, and he points to the bed as he issues his demand, "Sit down." I quirk an eyebrow at him, and he adds, "Please."

I don't argue. My body feels exactly how I'd imagine if someone told me they'd been tumbled over a mile of root and stone at the bottom of a swift river. I can hardly wait to get back to the palace and sink into the hottest, longest bath of my life.

He takes a knee before me, dropping his satchel to the floor and asks, "May I?"

He waits for me to give him a small nod before lifting the thin fabric of my dress, exposing my torso. He glares at the blooming bruise, and I flinch when his hand meets with the discolored skin, a little from the pain and a little from the unexpected contact.

"It could be fractured," he says, "A healer will know more."

"It's fine," I assure him.

"There is that word again," he says with a sigh.

He produces a salve from his bag and coats his fingers with a thick dab of the pungent ointment before smoothing it over the mark until it melts into the skin. The moment the salve touches it the pain lessons considerably.

"What was it about your life in La'tari that made you feel you had to be so strong?" he asks without meeting my eyes.

"I don't know," I say, "What is it about your life here that keeps that look of eternal annoyance on your face?"

"I am not annoyed," he argues.

I hum, disbelieving, as the male settles my dress around my waist, slicking his thumb with another dab of salve. This he spreads on the cut below my breast, and blood rushes to my cheeks when I'm reminded of the idle sweep of his thumb I felt upon waking.

"Perhaps what you perceive as annoyance is simply caution," he says.

"I don't know about that. You seemed pretty annoyed the night you drugged my tea."

His brow furrows when I mention it, his eyes meeting mine briefly when he says, "I *am* sorry about that. I didn't know you then."

"And you think you know me now?"

"I'm beginning to," he says, slicking his thumb with fresh ointment and cupping my chin, running the salve across the long cut on my cheek.

"I do not take the lives of my friends lightly, and my trust in strangers is not easily earned," he adds.

"And you trust me?" I ask, knowing the answer.

"No," he admits, "but I am hopeful you'll gain that trust."

I can't fault him for his honesty, yet his confession stings when it shouldn't. He has every right not to trust me, every reason to guard those he loves. *Especially* from me.

"Do you make a habit of taking women you don't trust to bed?" I quip, trying to keep myself from the dark spiral of my thoughts.

"I do not," he says, capping the salve and dropping it into his satchel before grabbing my chin and pinning me with his gaze, "but if anyone could persuade me, it would be you."

I suck in a breath when his eyes drop to my lips. What did he just say? There is no time to untangle the messy weave of questions, objections, and emotions before his eyes fall to the floor, and he tips a pointed ear toward the door.

"They are here." He drops my chin and stands, offering me his hand unnecessarily.

I take it, because what else am I going to do? The male just admitted he doesn't trust me and in the next breath offered me a direct line into his good graces. I think.

Muffled voices filter in through the thick walls and he helps me to my feet, dropping my hand as he heads for the door. I follow him out, squinting against the blinding light of the morning sun. Awri and Riesh head a small party of mounted soldiers up the steep incline leading to the cabin.

"A little excessive," the general says.

He directs the comment at Riesh, who laughs his reply, "Be happy Toren didn't send the entire army to scour the forest for his missing general. These are

the least he would allow me to bring when I told him we lost you in the woods."

My brooding companion hardly seems surprised, turning to Awri the next moment. "Kishek?"

"Still recovering," she sighs with a solemn shake of her head.

"Have you brought a healer?" the general asks with a dipped brow.

A thick tension saturates the entire party, every back stiffening, every eye searching the general for his wounds.

Riesh waves a dark-haired male with ebony skin forward, who asks if the general has been injured. He shakes his head and motions toward me, the tension leaving the party as quickly as it came once they realize the only one injured here is the fragile mortal. I suck in an annoyed breath and glare at the general.

"I'm f—"

"Fine," he says, finishing my repetitious claim. "So you've said. You will still let Caden look you over before we head back."

Not an offer. A demand.

I manage to suppress my protests about taking orders from him. I don't disagree with the premise of being checked by a healer, but the self-important male has no right to force me to live my life on his terms.

Caden doesn't even dismount before shaking his head, offering the general an apologetic frown. "You've used the ilyandis salve on her. I can feel it."

The general gives the male a nod.

"Then you know she can't be healed until the effect of the herb wears off."

The general's jaw stiffens, relenting in his pursuit of my healing with a heavy sigh. Seeing he's not surprised by the healer's declaration, I have to wonder why he even asked.

I repeat the name of the herb in my mind until I'm sure I won't forget it. An interesting dichotomy. An herb that when applied will render pain nearly absent but prevent healing. I imagine the battles that could be waged with such an herb. A soldier that would never yield until their dying breath. I wonder briefly if the herb can be turned into a draught or tonic before the general snaps me out of my musings.

"You will ride with me," he says, tying his satchel to a riderless mare.

"That is unnecessary," I voice firmly, my eyes falling on another riderless horse nearby.

242

I want to add that I feel fine but decide to leave it at that.

He leads his horse to me, blocking the rest of the party from view, lowering his voice to a whisper. "You're injured. I know you feel better right now, but that herb will likely wear off before we reach the palace."

I don't immediately argue, but I'm sure he can see that it's in my mind when he adds, "I've ridden with a similar wound and trust me, you're likely to hate yourself if you don't rest until it can be mended."

He has no idea how familiar I am with the exact form of pain he's describing, but it will give too much away to tell him. I nod, allowing him to grip my hips and lift me onto the mount. He swings his leg up behind me, settling me snugly between his thighs just as he had the night we'd delivered the sword to the orphanage.

He pulls a dry cloak from the rucksack strapped to the mare and wraps it around us. With the click of his tongue, we begin our descent down the rocky path leading south. Awri's eyes meet mine as we pass through the soldiers, and I can't help the flush of my cheeks as she observes us curiously.

Without a single word from their leader, half the soldiers take their position at our front, the other half falling behind as we head out at a leisurely pace. I can't help but feel that the pace they set is for the benefit of my comfort alone. A small pang of guilt stabs at my gut until the contented murmurings of the feyn and their jovial conversation rise around us. No one seems terribly displeased to have been called into the woods to recover the missing general and Awri's reckless human guest.

Awri and Riesh fall in alongside us and I begin to wonder what became of them after my pursuit of the boar. Awri explains that they stayed at a shelter close to where I'd last seen them. They remained there until the storm let up, all day and a good portion of the night. With the heavy rain having obscured our tracks at the river, they returned to the palace for fresh food and mounts.

Despite my own experience in the forest, Awri tells the tale in a casual and unworried tone. Encounters with the wild fea must not be rare if they hadn't been terribly concerned.

With a wry smile, Riesh adds that they intended to come and retrieve us alone when Toren, whoever he is, insisted on an escort, a tracker, and a healer.

"How did you know where to find us?" I wonder.

"There aren't many stays on this side of the river," Riesh explains, "The next cabin to the east is below the falls. When we tracked you to the crossing, we had to hope you'd made it out before then."

"I think I would have preferred a waterfall to your green friend," I admit, and the general's arms tense around me.

"Green friend?" Awri asks.

"She had a run-in with Niya," the general explains.

The look Riesh gives me tells me he knows precisely what type of encounter I had with the fea.

"What did you do?" he asks, eyes wide.

I'm glad the general answers, because I have no idea I'd done anything. "She didn't use the bridge," he says flatly.

"The *bridge*?!" I nearly scream, "She tried to drown me because I didn't use the bridge?"

"We have agreements with all manner of fea in this forest," the general explains, "Niya is the guardian of a spring that flows into the river by the crossing. It is her territory, and she allows us safe passage across it, so long as we use the bridge."

"You could have told me," I grumble.

"I did," he says sternly.

"Hardly," I huff, "You said, 'take the bridge' and given the circumstances I would have expected more."

"Maybe if you trusted me, you wouldn't need more," he barks.

"Maybe if you gave me just a little more, I'd learn you could be trusted," I spit back.

His eyes blaze like I've just issued him a challenge, when he says, "I'm beginning to think that perhaps your trust is as hard won as my own."

It isn't an accusation like I might have assumed when we first met. Rather, there is respect in the statement and a deeper understanding than I'm accustomed to.

I tear my eyes from his and shrink a little under the continued speculative gaze of my friend. If I didn't know any better, I'd say she'd arrived at the cabin early and witnessed me wrapped up in the general's arms. I'm relieved

when Caden calls for her attention and she dips her head at me before falling behind to speak with him, Riesh in tow.

While the ilyandis salve works wonders for my pain, it does nothing to stem the weariness of my body. My mind may be unaware of my injuries, but I can tell by its sluggish drag that I need to rest and mend.

The quiet conversation surrounding us and the gentle sway of the horse below lull me in and out of a light sleep. I don't protest and in fact am only vaguely aware when, with a featherlight touch, the general rests my head against his chest and I slip into a deep and welcome darkness.

I only wake when the salve begins to wear off, the effect of the herb fading as quickly as it set in. I'm very suddenly, acutely aware of every bloody scrape and bit of bruising flesh scattered across my form. A quick glance at my surroundings tells me everything I need to know to fortify myself against the onslaught of pain. Our party has just broken through the thick under-growth of the ancient forest bordering the palace grounds to the north and it won't be long before I'm back in the comfort of my chambers.

As a young child, it was a monumental task not to groan and wince in pain after a particularly brutal training lead by Leanna. Any could easily result in a broken bone, and they often had. My lessons on exploiting weakness began early, Leanna turning my own against me in an effort to show the value of perception. She taught me well that the only weakness you have is the weakness you reveal.

Every pointed ear and sideways glance from the nearby calvary is enough to remind me what weakness could cost me now, what it will cost my people if I fail. I shove down the pain, just like any soldier is expected to do, and I don't say a word. I may not know the general well, but I have little doubt he would halt the entire procession to have me healed, and every soldier present would be reminded of just how fragile mortals can be.

The general stays behind to speak with Toren, when I make my way inside the palace on slow and calculated steps. Toren had been waiting for us when we arrived, deep lines of worry etched into his ivory brow. One look told me those lines were carved into his face long ago and he'd forgotten how to be without them. Though I hadn't inquired as to who he was before I departed, it was clear by his attire that he is one of their higher-ranking military commanders.

Awri walks me back to my chamber, leaving me at the door. She promises to check on me later before disappearing down the corridor.

It's still early, the sky just dim enough for the first of the brightest stars to announce the coming night. I draw a bath and slip in, attentive to the worsening bruise on my side. Washing is a chore with the strain of my wound, and I hurry to climb out and dry off. Combing the knots from my hair feels like a feat all its own, and I don't even care what manner of insignificant lace sleeping gown I've dressed in when I finally drag myself toward the bed.

A thundering knock sounds at my door, and I moan regrettably, seriously debating ignoring it. My eyes linger on the silk sheets. All I want to do is slip beneath them and go to sleep. I'm too tired to lend a single thought to my demon, though I wish I knew where my letter opener had gone so I could slide it under my pillow.

The knock sounds again, and I push out a heavy sigh, shrugging on a gossamer dressing robe before swinging open the heavy wooden door with a wince.

The general barges in with a rather pale looking Caden in tow.

"Do it. Now," he growls.

"Would you mind taking a seat?" Caden asks, rushing to the settee by the fire in a flustered mess as he gestures me forward, a pleading look in his eyes.

My brow pinches curiously, and I take the seat.

"May I lay a hand on your side, lady?" he asks, and I nod, yet the healer hesitates before reaching for me.

His hands are light against my skin, but an unbidden hiss of pain escapes my lips when he releases the shocking touch of his gift into my body.

"Careful," the general says under his breath.

I glare at the male watching from the door, but he is wholly fixed on Caden's hand at my side. The gift sears across the rib in a wave of sparking rivulets before it ebbs, dissipating only when the healer draws his gift from me. He repeats the action on the cut below my breast, and then my jaw.

"Her head," the general barks when the healer looks like he's ready to run for the door.

I'm better prepared for the shock of his gift when he releases it this time and I manage to school my features under the general's intense scrutiny. The

moment Caden's gift leaves my body, he turns to the general expectantly and, dismissed with a curt nod, he hurries into the hall.

I'll thank the healer later, but it is impossible to hide my irritation toward the general for barging into my room and forcing Caden to heal me.

"I said I was fine," I bark at the general and rise to my feet, "and I meant it. If I need a healer, I will find one."

"So stubborn," he says, shaking his head as if I am nothing but a disobedient child. "The rib was broken, Shivaria, not just fractured. Caden could sense the break the moment the salve wore off."

Good to know.

"He could have healed you the moment you felt the pain return. You knew that, and you said nothing," he says angrily.

"I told you, if I need a healer, I'll find one," I say through clenched teeth, fists balling at my sides.

"What happened to you?" the general asks and my gut twists with the concern overtaking the anger in his voice. "What made you so hard?"

"Those men wasted an entire day coming after me because of a mistake I made. The least I could do was get them back to their families as soon as possible," I deflect.

"You expect me to believe you did it for them?" he snaps.

"I don't expect you to believe a word I say, *General.* You've made your lack of trust in me perfectly clear."

He glares at me then, and I find that I'm a little more comfortable with this variety of the male. Brooding and hateful I can handle; it's the tender male with the gentle touch that scares me. I have no idea how to handle that version of him.

"I'm tired," I say.

It isn't a lie, but he certainly looks at me like he's attempting to discern the truth of the statement.

"Fine." The moment he says it I walk to the bed, sure that I will hear the click of the door behind me as he leaves.

"Let me check your wounds, and I'll go."

"You watched Caden heal me yourself," I argue, spinning to pin him with a stare of pure aggravation.

"As healing is never guaranteed and *you* cannot be trusted to tell me when you are injured, I'll see for myself before I leave you," he says.

I'm sure I'm turning a perfect shade of red when I reluctantly nod my consent. It's a small price to pay for his departure and I have no doubt he'll stand here brooding all night if I don't allow his inspection.

He strides across the room, and I'm suddenly wondering exactly what manner of night dress I have absentmindedly put on. He cups my jaw, and I loosen the muscles in my neck, letting him maneuver my head to the side so that he can examine me thoroughly. His thumb traces the line of my cheek where the cut was healed and his brow dips, his jaw tensing as his thumb strokes beyond the line of healing, passing beneath my lip.

My breath catches in my chest just as he looses one of his own and slides his hands down the curve of my waist until he's untying the loose knot of my robe. He slowly parts the panels of fabric, sliding it from my shoulders, letting the silk fall to the floor and pool around my ankles.

"Fates," he says under his breath as he grips my waist, taking another step toward me, "You are so beautiful."

The declaration stuns me, and my cheeks burn beneath the heat of his gaze. A quick glance down at my night dress flutters my stomach for different reasons. Two straps secure a white gossamer slip to my shoulders, the fabric so thin I'm sure he can see the pink flesh at the center of my breasts. The slip barely falls below my hip, revealing more than even the A'kori gowns. I press my thighs together, wishing I'd worn the delicate scrap of lace the feyn apparently consider reasonable underthings.

His blue eyes are a fiery blaze as his thumb traces the line beneath my breast where it was cut. Once satisfied, he continues to where I suffered the break on my side, his touch achingly slow and gentle. I flinch under the attention of that caress, and he glares at where his hand now rests above the healed break, my flesh obscured by the sheer fabric.

"You're still injured." His brow draws down when he says it.

I shake my head. "Just ticklish."

He puffs out a breath, leans his head down until his forehead rests on mine, and cups my jaw with both hands, saying softly, "I want to know that."

"What?" I ask, breathless.

"That you're ticklish," he whispers, "*Where* you are ticklish. Where you like to be kissed." I suck in a shuddering breath and my stomach tumbles. "How you like to be touched."

His hands slide from my jaw, caressing the line of my neck reverently. My eyes flutter shut with a sigh when his thumbs lightly press into the vulnerable flesh of my throat. His sigh echoes my own, full of pure contentment at my reaction to his touch.

"What else do you like, *mi'ajna?*" The moment the words slip past his lips, my gut twists.

Before I can think, he closes what little distance remains between us and captures my mouth with his own. The harsh demand of his desire, a direct contrast to his full, soft lips. Every nerve in my body responds to him, even as the sting of his words pierce my heart.

Like a beacon beneath my flesh, lightning sparks, sending a growing flame of want to my core. Who knew a pair of lips could offer such pleasure all on their own?

I'm hardly aware of myself when my hands grasp the fabric of his tunic, my mind muddled with the male before me and the man who last touched me like this. He releases his hold on my neck, letting me pull his body against my own. His hard shaft presses against my belly and he swallows the moan that escapes my lips when his fingers brush against the gossamer fabric barring him from the sensitive flesh of my nipples.

He nips my bottom lip then runs his tongue along the bite to soothe it. An action he repeats on my ear, before a set of fangs graze against the tender flesh in the crook of my neck, making me shiver. Prior to coming to A'kori, I'd forgotten the tales that claimed the feyn had fangs, and maybe they should scare me, but a larger part of me than I care to admit wants him to sink them deep inside me.

"What else, *mi'ajna.* Show me," he demands softly.

I nearly choke on the words, even as his hand follows the curve of my hip, slipping beneath the fabric of my gown, to grip my thigh. The teasing stroke of his thumb is so close to where I want him. My core clenches with yearning, a demand I struggle to ignore.

For a moment I hesitate, the ghost of a memory serving to remind me

exactly how this ends. For a moment I begin to overthink everything. And then his free hand travels up my chest, sliding across my collarbone to relieve my shoulder of the strap holding my gown in place.

The strap falls to the side of my arm, taking the thin fabric with it and exposing my breast. The nipple pebbles under the cool kiss of air, and then his mouth is on it, bringing with it a molten heat that floods my core. His tongue flicks across the sensitive skin as he nips and sucks, and I forget there is anything outside of this moment.

My hand travels the length of his arm, holding it in place, and I shift my hips, gasping when the next swipe of his thumb strums that sensitive nub of flesh between my legs. A low growl vibrates against my chest as his fingers slide between my folds, coating them in the proof of my desire.

"Foc." His breath caresses my ear as he moves his other hand to my throat, drawing back to pin me with his eyes.

I moan when his fingers slick my nub, working me in rhythmic circles. The look in his eyes gives away far too much. There is more than simple desire behind that gaze, more than want. He needs this as much as I do.

My core contracts and the tension builds until my body feels like it will tear apart from the rising pressure inside. And just like that, I break, falling against him as I shatter into a million shards of undeniable ecstasy. He catches the moan of my release with his mouth, his fingers swirling lazily until he's milked every last pleasurable shudder from my body.

I'm in a daze when he releases my neck, and goosebumps rise under the trail of soothing kisses he leaves where he gripped my throat. My stomach pitches when he picks me up by my hips and slides me onto the bed. I hadn't stopped long enough to wonder what the male might want in exchange for his efforts on my behalf, and I'm not sure I'm ready to meet those expectations. He leans forward and my breath is stuck in my lungs for all the wrong reasons.

Lifting the fallen strap back onto my shoulder and covering my breast, he grips my chin, brushing his lips against mine as he says quietly, "Tell me you'll at least consider me as a companion."

I dip my head in a shallow nod, not trusting my voice. He captures my lips with his, sweetly, softly, obviously pleased with my answer. Then he turns without another word, disappearing into the hall. I sit in a stupor, staring at the tall wooden panels of my door, trying to make sense of everything that just occurred. Tonight should never have happened, I should never have allowed it.

Why did I? Why did he?

The bliss I lost myself to fades all too quickly, replaced by the dread of what tomorrow will bring. He will want an answer, and while I might be able to delay the conversation for a few days, it will need to be had. I know him well enough to know that he won't let it go ignored.

The king's general is likely the most foolish choice for a companion, considering my mission. On the other hand, his favor will no doubt place me in front of the king the moment he returns. It's a fine line I will have to walk if I choose this, and a single slip will cost me my life.

CHAPTER 21
THE A'KORI PALACE
Present Day

Another knock sounds against my door and I groan, dragging myself from the comfort of my mattress to answer. Either the general's forgotten something or...

"I promised to check in on you." Awri's bright blue eyes sparkle in the light of the torchlit hall.

I open my door wide, and she sweeps inside with a smile, her gaze falling to the thin slip of a night dress I wear.

"Are you receiving all your visitors dressed like that?" she teases with a knowing smile, as she falls into a large chair by the fire, turning to peak over its back at me.

My cheeks heat for what feels like the thousandth

time since dawn when I deflect, "Only you." And I turn on my heel to gather my robe from the floor.

"And Xeyvian?" She quirks an eyebrow at me as I cinch the robe tightly around my waist. "I passed him in the hall on my way here."

"He was just here to check that Caden's work met with his exacting standards," I say, wishing I felt as annoyed as I try to sound, but my head is still spinning from everything that occurred between us.

"Are you fully healed?" she asks, a bit of concern reaching her brow as she looks me over.

"It certainly seems that way. Does the healing always hurt like that?"

I have never been healed by a feyn before, nor have I heard tales by others who had. While the pain hadn't been unbearable, I would certainly think twice about using it for anything unnecessary.

"Not always," she says, "the pain often correlates to the severity of the wound. But not all bodies react to gifts the same way. If you'd been of Caden's bloodline, you'd likely have felt nothing at all."

"Excellent," I snark, "As I have no feyn blood in me I'll expect it to hurt like haliel every time."

"Maybe you could simply avoid the necessity of a healer," she quips with a small laugh.

"I'll try that," I chuckle.

The fire crackles behind her and her brow dips speculatively when she says, "I wouldn't fault you, you know? If you and Xeyvian become something more. I'd even encourage it."

My feet move of their own accord across the room, without any thought or destination. This isn't the visit I expected to have with her. Though I suppose none of my visits have gone as expected this evening.

"I have wondered if there was something between the two of you," she continues even as I begin to protest. "I wasn't sure until I saw the look on Xey's face when you ran off into the forest."

"What look?" I ask, drawing the latch from one of the large windows on the southern wall, pushing it open, and breathing in a lungful of much needed air.

"Fear," she says, and my gut twists. "He was afraid of what might happen to you in the forest. If I had any doubts after that, they were all gone when

I saw how angry he became at Caden for letting you ride in pain when he could have healed you. That and the fact that he wouldn't let you out of his sight on the way back to the palace. Very unlike him. He's never been the type to fuss unnecessarily."

I fan myself with my hand, leaning into the cool spring breeze blowing in from the sea when I say, "I suppose you think I should be flattered that he'd like me as a lover for the season?"

"Did he say that?" she asks, and I turn to find a look of shock on her face that matches her tone.

"Not in so many words."

"It would surprise me if he had," she says, "Xey has never been the type to fall into fleeting friendships."

"Only fleeting bedfellows?" I quirk an eyebrow at her, and she shrugs.

"I wouldn't know. I've never known the male to take a lover. Stars know plenty have tried, and failed, in pursuit of him. Though I can't pretend to know everything about him. We all have secrets of our own."

I don't tell her just how aware I am of that simple fact.

"Call me cynical," I say, "but I can't help but wonder what interest a high-ranking, powerful feyn could have in *me*."

"Handsome," Awri adds with a cheeky smile, "You forgot handsome and well-connected."

"I'm sure you're only helping prove my point," I sigh.

She hoists herself out of the chair and strides over to the window to stand by my side.

"I didn't come to convince you of his character," she says, taking my hand in her own. "Only to check on you and tell you a little of what I know of him. And to give you my blessing." She gives my hand a gentle squeeze before letting it fall back to my side. "I like you, and I think you would be good for him."

With that, Awri walks toward the door, looking over her shoulder as she says, "He's a good male, and if you decide to accept him, I hope you don't prove me wrong."

The door clicks shut behind her, and my lungs deflate. I tell myself she can't be that good a judge of character if she trusts *me* with his affections.

Besides, it's clear from the artful way he handled my body that the male is no stranger to the female form. The fact that Awri has never seen him take a lover means nothing, and it is all beside the point. I can't afford to care.

My thoughts far too muddled to find sleep, I boil water over the fire, summoning the effort it takes to make a cup of Kishek's tea, before casting my robe over the plush chair beside my nightstand and falling into bed. I'm doubtful that sleep will find me anytime soon and maybe I shouldn't be surprised when the breathy whispers of the sisters flit past my ears. I can only hope they aren't upset by the fact that I've bathed and put myself to bed.

Tig dims the lantern I left on by the door and when the bed jostles beneath me I assume Eon is making herself comfortable for the night. I'm not sure why the sisters sometimes decide to stay with me. If given the choice, I think I'd rather live among the trees and sleep under the stars.

"*Reh'desh*," I whisper to the sisters.

The sprites, for all their complex emotions and exaggerated gesturing, seem to have a simple language. The words can be used much the same as a human might wish another goodnight or good morning only the time of day is implied by ... well, the time of day.

"*Reh'desh, Tha'haynah*," Eon whispers to my back.

The old blood. A curious title, though it is clear to anyone with eyes that long ago my ancestors were feyn. Perhaps it should, but it doesn't trouble me that the sprites make the distinction.

Maybe it's the soothing presence of the sisters, the tea, or simple exhaustion from the events of the day, but my mind does not continue in pursuit of understanding what occurred with the general. With little effort, it stills, and the void comes to take me.

"It's too early," I groan when someone knocks at my door.

Squinting my eyes open, I groan again when I find that the sun rose hours ago. The knock reverberates again, and I debate rolling over and going back to sleep. I tell myself that if it is that important, they wouldn't

be knocking. Another knock, and Eon jabs me between the shoulder blades with a bony finger.

"All right. I'm going."

I toss the covers off my body, hoping they'll envelop the meddlesome sprite, before putting on my robe and answering the door.

"Good morning, Sera," I say through a yawn.

The young woman smiles when she returns my greeting, her golden curls brushing the tops of her shoulders, shining in the morning light.

"Please, come in," I offer, but she shakes her head shyly and proffers me a basket, covered with a decorative cloth.

"I need to get back to my grandmother," she says.

"Of course." I smile. "Please tell Media I said hello and that I will come by and see her again, soon."

"I'm sure she would like that," she says, her curls bouncing as she jogs off down the hall.

I close the door with a shake of my head. I'll have to make time to keep that promise. Media may be on the side of the feyn, but she is still an elderly mortal, deserving of a visitor now and then. And though I must sift through the stories she tells me to find the truth, she still has a great deal of knowledge I lack.

I set the basket on a small table by the door, plucking off the covering to examine its contents. My stomach grumbles loudly when I'm hit with a steamy waft of fragrant seasoned butters, fresh breads, and crispy bacon. My mouth waters and I'm sure the sisters can smell it as well when I hear the patter of Eon's feet rushing up behind me.

She stands on her tiptoes, peaking over the rim of the basket just as I uncover a small bowl of berries hidden at the bottom. I hand it to her and chuckle when her delighted sprite tongue jabbers something unintelligible as she rushes the bowl to her sister.

Tearing a small piece of bread from a thick, fluffy loaf, I dip it in a soft herb filled butter before popping it in my mouth. A satisfied sigh slips past my lips as the flavors meld upon my tongue.

I'm about to inhale the entire loaf when a folded piece of parchment catches my attention, peeking out from behind a thick roll stuffed

with sugar and spice. I pluck it from the basket and admire the golden seal. The wax stamp is blank, but I don't think much of it before tearing it open.

Shivaria,

I have gone to uphold the bargain I made in the forest.

The gift of healing takes its toll on your strength, and I would have you strong. Take the day. Eat, rest, and consider my offer. I'll come to you in the morning, and honor your decision, whatever it may be.

Xeyvian

My stomach is in knots when I force myself to eat a crispy piece of bacon. Had I known what the letter contained I would have waited to read it and left my appetite intact. I can't help but consider the general's offer. It's too tempting, in more ways than I'm willing to admit.

As his companion, not only would I be well positioned to end the king upon his return, but the general is also willing, and capable, of helping me with the looming issue of my demon. I've gotten lucky so far, but I can't count on luck. Not when the solution is standing in front of me with an outstretched hand.

I spend the day with the sprites, tucked away in the privacy of my chamber, listening and learning their speech. All the while I tell myself I'll think about the general's offer later. The sun is fully settled beyond the farthest reaches of the western sky when the sisters leave me, and I dress in my leathers and a dark dress before pulling my borrowed cloak over my shoulders. Restless from the quiet of the day, and eager to better position myself to complete my mission, I blow out the candles in my room and slip out the window.

The patrols stationed near the palace are little more than lawn ornaments for all the good they do as I slip through the shadows unseen. Even the guards at the gate are easily distracted by a rustling of leaves in a tall bush nearby, and I begin to wonder if it is the reliance on their gifts that makes them so complacent or the simple fact that the palace has never seen a siege.

It is late in the evening when I climb the thick branching vines and push open my bedroom window at Felias's manor. I ponder how it is that a spy of his rank can possibly exist without being able to trust his staff. It will do me no favors if the general finds out I've snuck out again and I doubt the male will be convinced that my reasoning remains as innocent as it was before.

Snatching a purse of coins from my belongings, three bundles of herbs, and a small pouch of tools, just to be safe, I open the window facing the inner gardens and eye the brick ledge below the second story windows. Clinging to the thick vines I swing out into the night, shuffling my feet to the side as I make my way toward my uncle's room. I should have asked the man the location of Yshka's home the moment I returned from the dress shop, but I won't waste the opportunity tonight provides, even if that means waking him from his sleep.

I'm hardly surprised to find his window latched. In his line of business, you can never be too careful. Placing the small leather pouch between my teeth, I slip a thin bar from within its depths, sliding it between the frame of the window and its delicate pane. With a well-practiced flick, the bar hits the latch, spinning it open, and I swing the window wide before letting myself inside.

"Felias," I whisper.

The long drawl of his snore cuts short as he flinches awake to find me standing at the foot of his bed. "Fates!" he nearly shouts.

"You know of Ishara?" I ask, before the man can scold me for breaking into his room.

Maybe I should feel bad, but he *is* here to help me in any way he can in pursuit of my mission.

"Can this wait until morning, my dear?" he sighs, pinching the bridge of his nose.

"I need to find her father's house," I say, without further explanation.

"I see," he says, raising an eyebrow at me. "I assume you do not intend to knock when you call on him at this hour?"

I only glare at the man before he grumbles something under his breath and

tosses his thick duvet to the side. He slides his feet into a pair of velvet slippers beside the bed and walks toward a small table in the corner of the room.

"Here." He pulls a large map from a drawer at the front of the desk, unfurls it, and pins a thick finger to a large home by the edge of the sea.

The canvas is well-lit by the moonlight streaming in from the window behind him and I mark my quickest route before turning toward the window.

"Have a care, niece." His voice comes from behind me, and I pause just long enough to hear his warning. "There is very little that family would not do to take power in A'kori."

"Good," I say, swinging my foot onto the ledge outside his window.

"And nothing that will stop them from ending the lives of every mortal in this veil if that were ever to come to pass," he adds.

My back goes rigid, and I lock eyes with the man, his face heavy with concern.

"The enemy of your enemy is not always your friend," he warns.

I nod my understanding before disappearing into the night, his warnings altering the shape of my plans for the evening. It may have only been once, as we left Adora's dress shop, but Awri had not been shy speaking openly about the family's matriarch, Yshka, and her desire to hold the throne. Though my own king has not granted me permission to draw up terms that will indebt him, I would be a fool not to explore the possibility of an alliance.

I can only hope their desire to see their king dethroned outweighs their desire for the crown, as I have no doubt my own sovereign will never again allow a feyn to rule in A'kori.

It is late in the evening when I finally reach the tall manor overlooking the sea. Its walls are a deep blue and panels of firelight cast from its highest windows onto the cobbled street below. The lower rooms are dark, save for a handful of small lights illuminating the halls. The only movement on the ground floor is the silhouette of a slender female making her way up the stairs. Her thick drape of red hair gleaming in the flickering light of the candles she passes.

It is by means of a small guest cottage that I make my way toward the well-lit windows on the second floor. Stepping on a decorative stone to extend my height, I cling to the edge of the roof, grappling the porcelain shingles as they threaten to slide out from beneath my hands. Only one manages to slip past my fingers, and I thank the stars when my reflexes take over, my foot dashing out to kick the tile onto the lawns before it can shatter on the stone beneath me and announce my presence to the whole of A'kori.

I puff out a sigh of relief, pulling myself onto the roof to sneak across the ridge, positioning myself behind the chimney. I survey a gathering taking place on the second floor of the main building. It is a small group of no more than ten feyn, Ishara among them, as well as the red-haired female I'd seen below.

The muffled tones of their voices barely make it out into the night, and with every back turned to the tall glass panels of the doors, I can hardly help myself. I take a backwards step and lunge forward, vaulting off the roof to land on the balcony of the dark room beside their gathering.

It's curious that unlike Felias's window, the doors to the balcony are unlocked. The hairs on the back of my neck raise. While it is entirely possible someone simply forgot to latch the door, it speaks to the Drakai in me, stating clearly that the power contained within these walls does not require the protection of locks.

It takes my eyes a moment to adjust to the dim, moonlit room. The low hum of their voices falls on my ears, indiscernible. I find myself in an office of sorts. Books line the walls, maps on display in glass covered frames. A well-used leather chair sits behind a wide desk with a thin blade laying in the center, a letter with a broken seal beside it.

Snatching the letter, I hold it up to a small window, the script illuminated under the light of the moon.

General Xeyvian,

Reports of the resistance remain prevalent among the feyn in A'kori. Their recruitments have tripled in the last week. Many of our young pledge themselves to their cause, intent on making the voyage across the sea.

Unrelated is the activity of the La'tari navy, which has also increased significantly. We make great efforts to devise the reason and will issue another report upon discovery.

I place the missive back in the exact manner I found it, tucking away the information on its pages to ponder another time. The clear voices of the staff in the hall call me to the door, my back pinned to the wall in case anyone should enter the office unannounced.

"Where is the garnish, girl?" a female voice demands, in the hall.

"I—We don't have it."

"We do," the first female snaps. "You *must* follow the recipes exactly. I won't tell you again. The mistress is very particular. Come, I will show you where the herbs are kept."

The second mumbles under her breath and their steps fade away. I crack the door to find a blessedly vacant hall, a set of stairs at one end and a window at the other.

Opposite the room of the gathering sits a large tray filled with bubbling libations. It's hardly a thought when I pull a small pouch from my cloak, sprinkling every glass with powdered thalis. The herb has a pleasant taste, only a mild hint of almond in its scent. It is exceedingly rare where it grows on the southern border of La'tari. As our military hoards it, I imagine there are few in A'kori who are familiar with it to the point of recognition. The herb is only a mild intoxicant at this dose, though its greater purpose, the one the La'tari harvest it for, is to loosen the lips of those ingesting it.

A confident female voice with a low cadence comes through the walls, "You do yourself a disservice by underestimating the king, Yshka. He likely knows more than you believe."

A harrumph makes it into the hall followed by the melodic tones of another female's voice. "He is arrogant if he thinks he has the power to hide himself from us. He's grown far too comfortable in his seat of power."

I hear the chatter of the staff coming from the stairs and tuck myself in beside a tall buffet, disappearing into the deep cover of its shadows. The tray of crystal is lifted from the small table, and the voices in the room grow loud when the door barring me from the gathering is swung open wide.

"Let him be comfortable," the first female says, "Let him think that he has fooled you all. There is power in that deception. As long as he continues to believe he is the most powerful being on the northern continent, his defenses will remain low."

A male's voice counters, "I mean no offense lady, but it is only a matter of time before you are discovered here."

"New tides bring a call to war, old friend," she replies, "and there are many serving sentences, long overdue their reprieve that will bring allies to our cause. Let my mate and his siblings serve as a distraction while I become better acquainted with your daughter's gift. The power of suggestion is rare and will serve us well."

"I am happy to serve in any way I can." It's impossible to mistake Ishara's voice as it glides into the hall.

"Once the king is removed from power, there is nothing to hinder us from clearing this veil of the mortals that remain," a female says.

"And nothing to keep us from the fea," the female with the low voice purrs.

The thunder of the large tray tumbling to the floor and a crash of crystal stiffens my spine.

"How dare you," the same low-voiced female rumbles, "You think that I do not know the purpose of every plant that grows beneath the Braxian stands?"

"Sai—" a male says.

"Be silent!" she yells, "Which of you was bold enough to lace my drink with thalis?"

Hisht.

A whimper escapes the room, and I find my feet moving toward the safety of the exit.

"You will answer her truthfully," Ishara commands.

"I would never think to dishonor my mistress in such a way," one of the servants protests.

"Please," the other begs, "it wasn't me."

"Sai," the male says, "not a soul in this house would dare."

The rest of the debate is lost to my ears when I slip into the office, securing the low hood of my cloak to obscure my features before opening the door to the balcony. I climb up on the stone railing and perch in a low squat, positioning myself to jump and tumble onto the roof of the cottage.

My head snaps to the side when the balcony doors of the gathering swing open wide and a tall male with a thick sweep of black hair and bright blue eyes steps outside to survey the grounds. His head whips toward me, his eyes locking on mine, and my stomach pits as a chill blooms from my spine and the air is driven from my lungs. His brow creases and I don't wait to comprehend the look he gives me before I leap onto the rooftop below, tumbling off the ledge and onto the ground, landing on my feet.

I'm sprinting across the lawn when I hear Ishara's voice behind me.

"Stop!" she demands, and I breathe through the icy tendrils licking up my spine as I dart into the dark alleys of A'kori.

I don't slow to look back when the shouts pick up behind me and the loud clap of hooves pound upon the cobbled streets. Swearing under my breath, I dart toward the center of town when a mounted rider veers through the narrow alley, spurring his horse into a gallop. I slide into the shadows, his stirrups sparking against the stone walls of the buildings as he rushes past.

I puff out a breath when he turns south, weaving through the maze of A'kori, as I turn north toward the palace. It's a cautious and calculated journey toward the edge of town. The shouts dwindle as the moon crests the tallest of the surrounding structures, depriving me of the shadows that promised their concealment earlier in the evening.

I'm not sure how much time passes before I find myself standing on the edge of my cover and sheer exposure. Colorful buildings are at my back, and an expansive park sits before me, buffering the town from the road that will lead me to my bed. I take a slow step onto the grass, prepared to rush back into the labyrinth if I am seen.

A deep, feminine laugh sounds behind me, and I spin on my heel, only to be met with a female barring my entry to the narrow streets. There's no time to consider where she came from or how it is I had not seen her, before she tips her head to the side and offers me a thorough perusal. Her long white hair sweeps over her ivory skin, her blue eyes glinting with the light of the moon.

"I do not recall inviting you to attend my party this evening," she says.

My brow dips when frost unfurls on my spine yet again, my demon uncoiling to meet her with furious intent. Finally, I begin to understand the sensation for what it is. The touch of the feyn's gift. Though, no description I've ever been given of their powers was as subtle as this fleeting chill.

Her eyebrows rise as she smiles. "Though perhaps it was an invitation I simply overlooked."

 263

The hair at the nape of my neck stands on end as she begins to round me, like a large cat sizing up its prey. Eyes squinting curiously, she asks, "Who are you?"

"I *could* be an ally," I lie.

There is nothing that could convince me to make an alliance with the female after hearing the last of her declarations. At least the current king of the feyn is not intent on slaughtering humans. No. He would prefer they die by means of starvation. Perhaps a crueler death, but at least it gives my people time.

She hums thoughtfully. "You could be a spy."

"Anyone in that room could be a spy," I argue.

"Tsk." She pulls up the long white of her sleeve, revealing a number of crimson marks wrapping her forearm as she says, "I am no fool. I put no trust in words, only in the proof of the oaths I bear upon my flesh. Give me yours, just as those who have sworn fealty before you, and I will consider letting you live."

Foc.

"What oath?" I ask, buying time, considering my options, wondering how in haliel I got into this mess and more importantly, how I might find a way out.

She scoffs at the question. "You think you can deceive me? When even your king failed at such a simple task. Your oath, or your life, the choice is yours."

Her face grows dark, as she produces a long, thin blade from within the panels of her gown. When I make no move to give the female what she wants, her lips peel back, and she snarls, "Your life it is."

She steps toward me, her gaze flying to the ground the next moment, as a terrifying shriek erupts from her lungs. She bends at the waist, tearing at the thorny vines growing through her feet, piercing the flesh of her legs.

I bolt north without hesitation, my eyes catching on the thin ribbons of blood flowing from her hands as she attempts to free herself. A slender vine drives itself through her palm and she issues a slew of feyn curses. The meaning of her words are lost on me, as she levels a clear demand toward a nearby tree.

Her screams fade as my lungs burn, my legs driving me north as quickly as they can. I veer into the forest. While the underbrush will slow my ascent, there is no question that a long night is preferable to being found by the female on the open road if she manages to free herself before I'm within the tall granite walls bordering the palace.

I've hardly begun to consider all that occurred when the breathy whispers of the sisters land upon my ears. They are not the joyful tones I am accustomed to hearing in their presence. Though not every word makes it past the pounding drum of my pulse, they are clearly agitated. I'm quick to recall Felias's words about the benefits of friendship with the fea as I consider the bloody scene I fled from. Had the sisters not intervened, there is no doubt in my mind that I would not have lived to see the sunrise.

It is by means of a tall tree growing along the border of the palace grounds that I make my way onto the lawns. If my nerves weren't so rattled I would be more amused by the ease with which I come and go utterly unseen. As it is, while my legs continue to move me toward the comfort of my room, my mind is still in Yshka's home, weighing all that I learned.

Pulling myself through my window, my mind races as I make a cup of Kishek's tea and dress in a sleeping gown. Any alliance I hoped to have with Ishara's family is firmly out of the question. I had never truly considered that there were worse options for rulers among the feyn and find myself mildly relieved that their current sovereign remains on the throne. At least for now.

The tea helps to ease a bit of the tension coiled in my muscles and I do my best to set thoughts of the evening aside to ponder at a later time. I am safe, and, thankfully, still unknown to those who pursued me. There is little I can do with the information I gathered but tuck it away.

The sky is tinged with the faintest light of dawn when I crawl into bed. I should close my eyes and let sleep take me, but there are still things to consider beyond the events of the evening. Things I will shortly need answers for.

My mind wanders to the general and his proposition. I find that I am no clearer in my decision than I was when the male left my room. My eyes grow heavy, and I roll onto my back, determined to stay awake until I reach a decision, even if that means I'll be up all night. It's the last thought that floats through my quickly clouding mind when the darkness takes me.

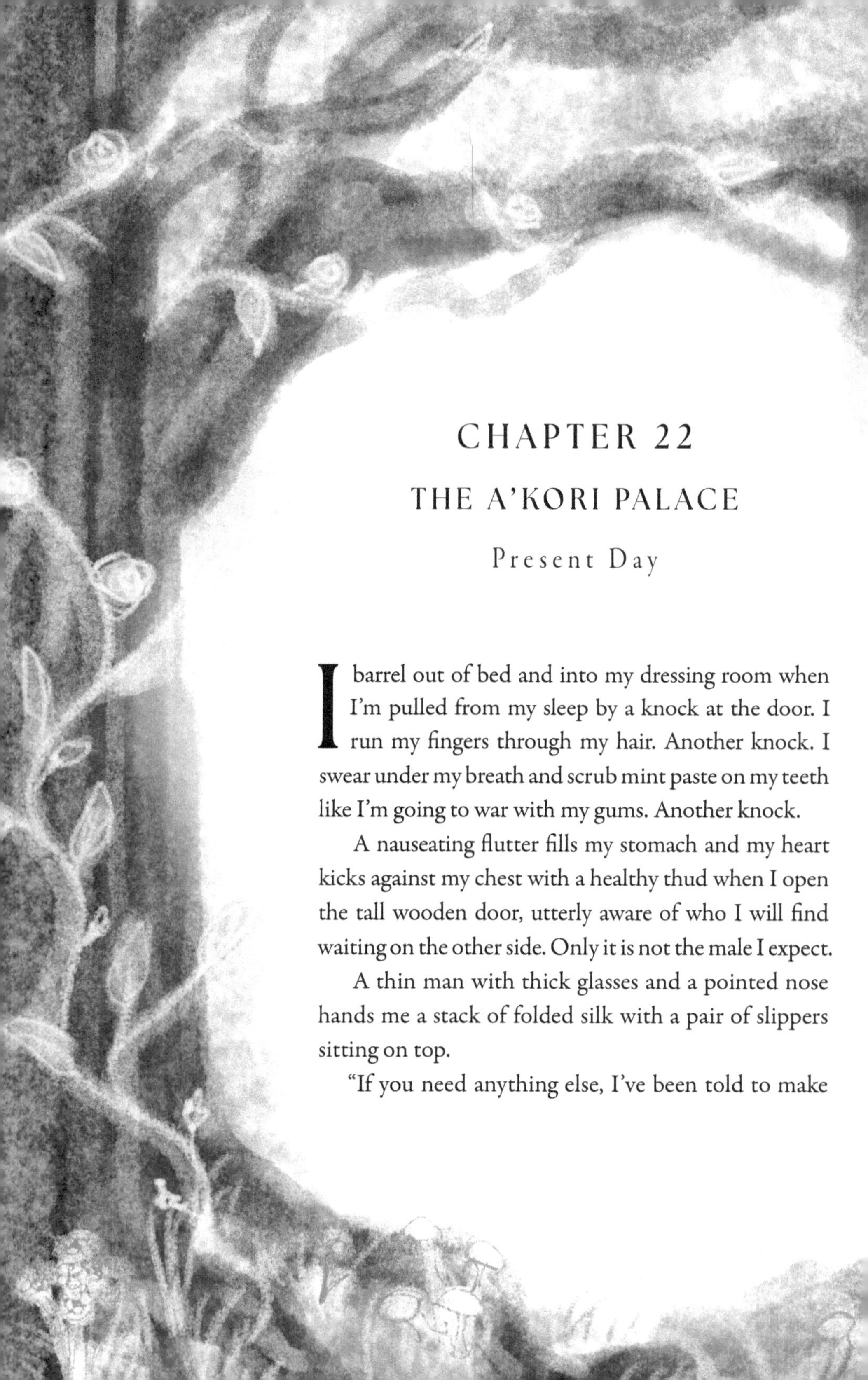

CHAPTER 22
THE A'KORI PALACE
Present Day

I barrel out of bed and into my dressing room when I'm pulled from my sleep by a knock at the door. I run my fingers through my hair. Another knock. I swear under my breath and scrub mint paste on my teeth like I'm going to war with my gums. Another knock.

A nauseating flutter fills my stomach and my heart kicks against my chest with a healthy thud when I open the tall wooden door, utterly aware of who I will find waiting on the other side. Only it is not the male I expect.

A thin man with thick glasses and a pointed nose hands me a stack of folded silk with a pair of slippers sitting on top.

"If you need anything else, I've been told to make

myself available to you," he says with a bow, then turns on his heel and disappears down the corridor.

Odd.

Back in my room, I unfold the delicate fabrics, draping them across my bed. It's clear the man is the palace tailor, come to deliver the pants the general ordered to replace the ones *conveniently* missing from my trunk when it arrived. He hadn't mentioned it, but the general thought to include two new cloaks in the order. One to replace the cloak I'd lost in the river, light enough for summer and sewn in a velvety fabric the most extraordinary shade of blue. The other, made of thick dark fabric lined with soft black fur.

If I thought the pants I'd worn before were sumptuous, the ones the male ordered are even more exquisite and unlike anything I have ever seen or felt. Beautifully beaded embellishments are embroidered into the legs of some, while lace is artfully sewn around the calves and thighs of others. The legs don't billow like the ones I had before, these will fit snuggly, showing off my form while appeasing my desire for modesty.

I eye the pair of slippers. They are a perfect match for the ones I soiled the night I carved the toy sword. The male has gone far beyond what I can relegate to being purely hospitable.

The gentle sound of running water and steam wafting from the washroom announces the presence of the sisters. They look about as lively as I feel, and there is a small pang in my gut as I consider that my actions have not only deprived them of a good night's sleep but placed them in harm's way.

Tig forces a smile and nod when I thank them for intervening with the female. I'm not sure Eon notices, when I find her leaning against a chair, cheek roughed on its arm as she struggles to keep her eyes open.

Thankfully the sisters don't seem to mind when I take my time preparing for the day. My thoughts are a jumbled mess of logic, necessity, and desire, as I ponder how the general made his way into what will likely be the most vital role of my life.

I don a new pair of blue-grey pants with beaded floral embellishments and plait my hair in a thick loose braid. It's the longest walk I've ever taken down the palace halls, my pace a slow meandering of deep contemplation. I have yet to decide what I'll say to him when I raise my fist to knock on the general's door. Maybe it's good that I don't overthink it. But isn't that exactly what I've done since I last saw him?

The door swings open before my knuckles land on the dark paneled wood. I take a step back, making room for the exquisite female letting herself out into the hall. If I'd ever been asked to describe perfection, even my mind couldn't have conjured something so lovely. She is exactly that, perfect, flawless.

No artist on Terr would ever be able to adequately portray the gut-wrenching beauty of the female standing before me. Whisps of long auburn hair shape her face and tumble down her back. The color pulls on the deep natural red of her full lips, set beneath a pair of striking green eyes that glitter in the full light of morning.

Had I not been raised among some of the most stunning mortals on La'tari soil, I might gawk. Despite having been exposed to every manor of seductive gown draped over the bodies of the Fea Dien, I have never seen anything like the slip of a dress clinging to her form. I'm quite sure not even my meddling uncle would approve of it. I'm not even sure it *is* a gown, not one that would normally be worn during daylight hours. The dark green fabric is made up of a delicate sheer lace, save for a few scraps of well-placed silk snaking their way across her body, covering only her most intimate areas.

Danger. It's the single thought the female evokes in me and without a question as to why. Though I'd only seen her at a distance, I recognize her as the red-haired female at the gathering last night. Her presence in the general's room begs the question of the male's loyalty to his king. I begin to ponder the web I am about to land myself in, if I choose to accept him. After all, I hardly know him.

I steel myself, slipping on a mask of cool indifference when she steps toward me.

"Are you here to see Xey?" she asks with a taunting smile, her voice a painful mixture of sweet and sultry.

"I just came to thank him," I lie flatly.

"I see," she says, "Unfortunately, I've just left him in bed. I'd say he's rather worn out."

She gazes at me through thick lashes, studying me. A flicker of irritation

mars her features before she smiles again and says, "I'll tell him he has company. Give me a moment and I'll have him dress."

She turns toward his room, hand reaching for the doorknob, when I shift my weight—the only sign of my discomfort. It's all she needs to withdraw her hand from its trajectory and suggest, "Or, maybe you'd like to come back later?"

"That won't be necessary." I force a smile. "I'm sure I'll run into him sometime."

She hums under her breath, departing without another word. I can't take my eyes off the satisfied sway of her hips as she saunters down the hall, disappearing down a nearby corridor. I study the handle of his door, debating what it might cost me to open it. Considering what I will find inside.

This shouldn't be a problem. It has nothing to do with me. So, what if the male already has a lover? Nothing about this is personal. It changes nothing.

I call myself a hypocrite when I walk away without knocking. I tell myself if I can't trust him then he's no use to me, knowing full well that I'm willing to deceive him to get exactly what I want. He is just stupid enough to get caught.

I don't linger on the fact that though he offered his bed, he never offered fidelity. Regardless, the female is an unknown and will be a complication at best, and a deadly risk at worst.

I crack one of the large windows in my room, grab the lighter of my two new cloaks, and leave a letter for Awri with a young page waiting by the palace doors. She won't mind when she reads that I'm going to visit my uncle. There are many long overdue conversations to be had with the man in the privacy of his gardens.

It's late in the morning when I arrive at his estate on foot. As I'm unannounced, I'm pleased to find that Felias is not only at the manor, but he also happens to have time for an impromptu luncheon. With the man's busy social schedule, I half expected to end up on his waiting list.

"So, tell me, how is life at the A'kori court treating you?" he asks around a mouthful of pastry, a knowing glint in his eye.

I only shrug, and ask hopefully, "Any word on when the king might return?"

"None that I've heard, though I expect he'll return for the masque. It would be quite out of the ordinary for the male not to attend it," he says before taking a long sip of pink lemonade from a frosted glass and pinning me with a stare. "But I don't imagine you asked me here to discuss the king's return."

Right. Straight to the point.

"Tell me about the Vatruke," I say.

His lips spread into a smile, and he purrs, "My, my. I can't wait to learn what other tantalizing secrets you've uncovered in the short time you've been away from your homeland."

He leans back in his chair and clasps his hands over his belly when he says, "I expect if you're asking, you already know that the Vatruke are a group of ancient feyn working with the La'tari?"

I gape at the man, and he chuckles, "You expected me to contradict it?"

"Of course, I did," I say.

After all, he is one of us. He knows our cause, my mission, everything. Dread knots my gut when he confirms Media's story.

"Does it really change anything, my dear? The La'tari would be fools to decline the help of any power willing to offer them assistance. Yes?"

I'm not sure the question is entirely rhetorical when I ask, "But, at the cost of the La'tari people?" I'm sure that at least this much of Media's story isn't true.

"Lives are the cost of all wars, Shivaria. You should know this. And war, like death, makes no distinction on those it takes in payment."

The sugary tart in my hand suddenly looks very sour. I place it back on my plate as I ask, "What power can the Vatruke possibly gain from our land? It's been dead since I was a child."

Felias gives me a look and I know in that moment that Media spoke the truth when she said our land had been dead since long before my birth. I shake my head, trying to rattle my thoughts around until I can make sense of them.

I can hardly find my voice when I ask, "If all that I have learned is true, then tell me how the Vatruke gain power from a land that is already barren? And what help do the Vatruke offer the La'tari that is worth exacting such a price?"

His eyes light up. I know that look, it's the same look I'd often received from Bront when I managed a perfect maneuver and blocked his sword.

"I could tell you," he says with a sly smile, "Or you could make your way to the docks tomorrow night and see for yourself. A little bird told me there was just such a ship coming in on the evening tide."

He isn't speaking of trade shipments, that much is clear. I debate asking him what I'll find on the ship but doubt he'll be forthcoming. And now that he's dangled that tantalizing bit of information, we both know I'll go and see for myself regardless of what he tells me. I settle back in my chair, a hard line etched in my forehead as I debate all that I've just learned.

"On another note, I hear you and the general are getting close." He raises an eyebrow and slips a powdered berry into his mouth, seemingly oblivious to the fact that he's just turned my entire world upside down. "I thought I told you to stay away from that male."

"Did you hear that from the sisters?" I ask.

It's a reasonable assumption but his belly bounces with a throaty laugh in reply. "Stars, no. I'm not sure how you've managed it, but the sisters' loyalty to you surpasses that which they extend to even me. They've been less than forthcoming with their information, on your behalf."

I can't help but smile at that, though the smile fades quickly from my face as I wonder what spies Felias employs at the palace.

In typical fashion, Enrik darts across the lawn to whisper something into my uncle's ear, and I speculate if these interruptions are cleverly planned so that Felias might excuse himself at his whim. He braces himself on the arms of his chair, rising from his seat beside me. With a fist resting on the edge of the table he looks down at me, sighing heavily, he says, "The La'tari people are tired of dying needlessly. I think you should know I've begun to hear rumblings from beyond the southern border. I'm not sure how much longer this semblance of peace will hold." He licks his lips, clearly uncomfortable with what he is about to tell me. "The war is soon to be reborn, and I fear for the lives of the fea. They are not as strong as they once were, and the La'tari have raised a mighty regime in your lifetime. Far greater than you or I can comprehend."

I can hardly believe the words coming from the man in front of me, and I find myself wishing more than ever for the comfort of my blades. The La'tari trust him with my life, but every word he speaks sends a ripple of warning throughout my body.

"Are you trying to tell me that that you side with the feyn in all of this?" I ask cautiously.

It's a bold question. One I'm likely to regret asking. If he perceives me as a threat, all he needs to do is expose me and my life will be forfeit.

"The fea," he admits, "I've always been on the side of the fea."

He looks as nervous as I feel when he turns his back to me and walks to the manor. He said *the fea,* not the feyn. But is it semantics or does he really see them as different species? He'd been brave enough to give me the truth, and maybe it's sheer naivete when I decide not to end him purely out of caution.

I hoped to linger in the gardens for the remainder of the day but decide that it's best to separate myself from Felias as much as possible. It's only a matter of time before the La'tari find out what he is and end him. Death by association is not unheard of in our ranks. And even if they don't, there is every chance the man will regret revealing himself to me and attempt to end me himself. Though I have no doubts about how that would end, I enjoy the man enough to regret the thought of it.

The guards by the palace gates say nothing as I enter the grounds, slipping into the forest that borders the western side. I stay close to the tree line, considering the growing pains of a world I've always lived in and never truly known, while avoiding thoughts about why I dread returning to the palace.

I've only delayed my inevitable run-in with the general by a day, and I have little doubt the male will corner me for an answer the moment he's told I've returned. Which, if I have it my way, still gives me a little time to unravel the mess of the entire situation.

Unbidden, the sprites join me in the forest. Their bodies seem to form from nothing when they step out of the tall bushes covered in wild spring blooms. Though a weariness clings beneath their eyes, the sisters exude a childlike playfulness as they follow me through the trees, disappearing and reappearing in and out of the lush foliage around us. If I'd had any hesitation about what might be lingering in the forest after my encounter during the boar hunt, the sisters' company puts it all far from my mind.

It's after dark when I slip from the forest. While my thoughts in the woods had been taken up by the reconstruction of the world as I knew it, only one thing takes up space in my mind when the lights of the palace come into view. The general will have been told of my departure, and I have little doubt he was told the moment I reentered the grounds earlier this evening.

I take my time, making my way across the lawns, learning the guards' repetitious rounds, and slipping past them with ease. A prideful glee takes over when I pass the last of the patrols unseen. Keeping to the shadows, I creep among the wild, blooming foliage until I'm under my window.

It's still cracked, and with a small leap, I snag hold of the marble lip on the first try, avoiding the male for one more day.

"The front door is open, Shivaria." I wince at the general's cool tone and after dangling for a moment, let myself fall to my feet begrudgingly. "You might try using it sometime."

I take a moment to school my features before turning to face him, his brow pinching as he observes me.

"I suppose if you've gone through this much effort to avoid me, I don't need to ask for your answer."

My back stiffens, but I can appreciate that he's being direct. Best to get it over with.

"I'm flattered by your offer," I say politely.

"That's a lie," he says flatly, and I bristle at the accusation despite the fact that he's right. I'm not flattered.

"I've considered it, and I feel very strongly that either one or both of us would regret it," I say.

"You're basing your decision off one of many possible outcomes?" he says, clearly annoyed by my reply.

"Even the best outcome between a mortal and a feyn ends in regret, General. I haven't forgotten what I am."

He looks me over speculatively before asking, "And if you weren't worried about your mortality, what would you say then?"

"It doesn't matter."

"It matters," he says, taking a step toward me. "To me, it matters."

"Then you should know, it wouldn't change anything," I say firmly, stepping back from his advance.

My stomach twists when he flinches like I've struck him, but I tell myself it's for the best.

"You mean that," he says, his brow drawing down.

I exhale a deep breath and nod in confirmation. His jaw ticks before he does his best to soften the brooding expression creasing his brow.

"I will honor your decision, and nothing of your time here will change on my account."

"Thank you," I say, dipping my head and turning toward the palace entrance.

He doesn't chase after me, and I tell myself that it's a good thing, but when I drink down the last of Kishek's tea and lay down to sleep, the room feels emptier than it ever has before. I expected more of a fight from the male, but I'm glad he didn't press me for a reason or try to persuade me. I think.

As it seems to be most every night since I've been at the palace, I toss and turn, sure I will be unable to find sleep when abruptly I'm taken by the void.

It's still early when I wake the next morning, a floral steam drifting in from the bath as if the sprites knew I would rise with the dawn. Still no sign of my demon. It should be a relief, but I'm plagued with the question of why my darkness has begun to abate. I think I preferred it when it was predictable, even if that meant enduring my demon every day.

There is a mood among the sprites this morning. They giggle in breathy whispers, the entire conversation passing over my ears in waves. After struggling for so long learning to hear them, only to find that they could simply choose not to be heard had been frustrating to say the least.

"I'm fairly certain I've already told you once before that it's rude to exclude present company from a conversation," I scold them, raising a brow at Tig.

She shrugs, resuming said conversation with her sister, their voices no clearer to me.

Cheeky.

Tig braids a thin golden cord into my hair, banding it around the top of my head, the remaining loose curls tumble down my back. It's a curious choice. The fea have shown an obvious preference for adorning me with flowers but never before gold. She plucks a handful of the last tiny, sweet smelling pink blooms from her sister's branches and weaves them into the

plait. I wonder if the dark buds just beginning to sprout on Tig are the herb she offered to grow for me but suspect that if they are she will let me know when they are ready. It can't be soon enough.

When Eon rushes out of the closet with a soft pink gown and a matching pair of pants my stomach pits. For as often as I've wished to cover the exposed flesh of my legs, I can't bring myself to wear the gift. Not after last night. Not after *her*. I should have thought to check the closet at my uncle's and decide that I will have to make a point to go back soon.

There is a different air in the halls of the palace today. Guards who usually make a point to look anywhere but my face offer me smiles and nods as I pass through the halls. Even a young feyn page slows in his hurried pace to offer me a tip of his head after raking his eyes across my body. I briefly debate returning for the pants but quickly discard the idea, deciding that the trip to my uncle's house will simply have to come sooner than I planned.

I'm thrilled when I find Awri already in the domed fea room, until she turns to greet me and her smile falters, her eyes going wide. She glances around the room at the female soldiers posted by the general, all with their heads close together, whispering near the door. She rushes to my side with another nervous glance around us, her brother sauntering up behind her, offering his own curious perusal of my form.

"What are you wearing?" she hisses in a whisper.

My brows crease, and I look down at the dress, smoothing the thin fabric in confusion. It's nearly the same as every other I've worn since the day I arrived.

"Xey said you turned him down," she says under her breath.

"I did," I say quietly, more than a little relieved that she already knows.

While I hadn't decided how I would tell her, I knew it was a conversation that needed to be had.

"Let it go, Awri. She's allowed to take a lover, even if it isn't Xeyvian," Riesh says in my defense, though I'm not sure why or what he even means.

I balk. "I have absolutely no intention of taking a lover."

"Then why are you wearing that?" Awri hisses in annoyance.

Nervously, I smooth the dress again trying to find the fault in it when I say, "The dress is the same as—"

"She's talking about the braid," Riesh says, pointing to the golden plait banding my head. "Feyn ladies have worn their hair like that for millennia to show their intent to find a lover."

The blood rushes from my face and my hand shoots to my hair, my fingers searching, desperate to unweave the mistake. I spin on my heel when I hear the loud stride of the general coming through the door behind me.

"Hisht," I say under my breath.

"Hisht," Awri echoes.

"Oh, foc," Riesh says amidst an amused chuckle.

I shoot Riesh a glare and turn for the door in an attempt to walk past the general and back to my room to correct the error. I may even take a moment to murder a sprite or two while I'm there. The general's eyes snag on the golden weave, his jaw tensing. He hooks my bicep with his hand when I make to pass by and I suddenly feel the need to explain myself, not wanting him to feel slighted. Though I'm not sure why I care.

"I didn't know about the braid," I say, "About what it meant. I'm going to take it out."

His eyes follow the bare flesh of my leg, then flick to the guards, staring. At us? At me? I'm not sure anymore.

"You look beautiful," he says, releasing his hold, "Wear the braid if you want to. Whoever he is, he'll be a lucky male."

The words land like an unintended blow, the sincerity of his voice striking my chest and sinking deep in my stomach until it hollows. I pull in a breath, and as quickly as it came, the pain fades. The façade of his sincerity shattered by the image of the female I'd seen leaving his chamber.

"I'm sure your lovers are equally blessed," I reply, just as sweetly, careful to keep any trace of bitterness from my tone.

He tips his head to the side, frowning like he hasn't quite heard me. Kishek barrels into the room, completely out of breath. He looks about as bad as the last time I'd seen him. He locks eyes with the general and tips his head toward the hall. Awri is the first to run after him, disappearing into the corridor, Riesh and the general following shortly after.

It's hard not to think about my conversation with Felias, and his warning about the coming war. There is every chance he's wrong. Fates, I hope he is.

276

But I felt the truth of it when he told me. I will see war again in my lifetime, and perhaps not because of something I have done.

Awri is alone when she makes her way back into the room, a bit unsettled. She smiles and tells me everything is fine when I ask. She does a poor job of smoothing the lines of worry on her face as we go back to planning the king's party. If I'd thought I hated all of this nonsense before, now it is nothing less than torture.

I can hardly blame them for keeping things from me. Especially if a war is coming. I'm La'tarian after all, the enemy. I remind myself I have a role to play in all of this and that maybe the death of their sovereign won't start the war but rather end it before it begins.

I make it through the day without another run-in with the general. The braid at the top of my head slips my mind until I'm reminded by the eager smiles of the guards as I walk back to my room.

Though Awri kept me past sunset, the sprites aren't waiting for me when I return. No matter, the torrent of chastisement I spent the entire day composing will keep. I waste no time changing into the darkest dress and pants I own, my only set in black. I lace my leather boots around my calves and whip the dark, fur-lined cloak over my shoulders, pulling up the hood before jumping out my window.

I half expect guards waiting for me outside, posted there by the general after my failed attempt at sneaking in. I remind myself that he has in fact been well informed of my 'sneaking' twice now and likely has little need of that sort of thing.

It's a quick descent to the sheer granite slab that walls the palace in, the guards' paths still fresh in my mind from the night prior. In my dark cloak, I vanish against the smooth black of the stone and take my time finding small imperfections in the wall to grip. The effort to scale the slab is taxing, but not impossible. I smile proudly when my feet hit the ground with a puff of loose dirt on the other side.

To walk to the A'kori port would take hours, but my uncle's home is close by and his stables well stocked. No one tries to stop me when I ride off bareback with a young midnight mare, toward the shadowed alleys leading down to the docks. It's late when I make my way through the quiet town. The only sign of life in the narrow walkways between buildings, a few scrawny cats taking up residence outside kitchen doors. Candles flicker in windows and dwindling fires crackle from within parlors, casting a warm glow upon the cobbled streets.

The saltwater scent of the ocean fills the air long before I lay eyes on the docks. A gentle breeze stirred by the current kisses my cheeks as I tie the mare to a hitching post behind the fishmonger's storefront.

My eyes rove over the shipyard, nearly as dead as the streets of A'kori. The echoing creak of the ships rocking in the harbor, the only sound to permeate the night. I will board every vessel here before morning if that's what it takes to find the ship Felias spoke of. If the A'kori are receiving shipments from the south, I want to know what they are.

A familiar voice skips off the cobbled streets and my head whips toward the sound. I'm just in time to see the general appear from below the deck of a large cargo vessel, followed by two cloaked figures. My eyes narrow in the darkness, as I try in vain to discern what they take from the ship. There is little doubt in my mind that *this* is the ship I am here to find.

The hooded figures load their cargo into a large cart, obscured by the shadows cast by the light from the streetlamps beyond. The general enters into a terse conversation with a dark figure slumped lazily against the wagon wheel, their words muffled by the evening mist wafting in from the sea.

My eyes glide back to the vessel, and I step through the shadows unseen, until I'm no longer watching from behind the fishmonger's shop but from the deck of the ship itself.

A small light flickers below, and I find myself following the waning glow of a lantern, down a steep set of stairs and into the belly. The entire space is deserted, little more than a ghost ship pitching gently on the waves that make it past the docks. Cots and hammocks of various sizes create a labyrinth from stern to bow. Open barrels of dwindling food supplies and fresh water lay scattered among the maze.

A flash of movement by the stern catches my attention and a pair of pink eyes reflect from within the dark shadows that cling to the corner. I take a cautious step forward—the motion met with a throaty growl that stills my feet beneath me. Eyes adjusting to the low light in the belly of the ship, I suck in a shallow breath when I make out the form of a wood sprite. He is the spitting image of the sisters, cut from the very cloth of the earth and knit together by the fates.

His bloodshot eyes whirl nervously, and he watches me with apprehension. The branches mingling with his green hair are snapped, caked in dry blood where they've been broken. Bruises and scrapes mar his face, and he looks as though he hasn't eaten in weeks. He cradles his arm at his side.

I take another slow step toward the sprite, and he bares his teeth at me, letting loose a loud and vicious growl that tears through the night. I glance over my shoulder, aware that we are unlikely to be alone for long, wondering if his protests made it above board.

Slowly, I crouch down, pulling back my hood and reaching my hand toward the fea in offering. The male could be feral for all I know and maybe the sisters have made me less wary than I should be, but all I feel when I look at him is pity.

"*Reh'desh*," I say softly so as not to startle him, "*Le'thay launa'hi meiur. Ty'liean vathai, vay'esh ka'ai.*"

The sprite's eyes widen. The low rumble in his chest quickly fading to a whimpering murmur and he tips his head to the side, observing me curiously.

"*Reh'desh*," he replies.

I smile, a smile he returns with a wince when he puts too much weight on an injured leg.

I remind myself that I am here to complete a task, and the male before me is not the reason I came. I tell myself that he will be all right if I leave him alone, that, like the sisters, he can simply vanish at will. But the sprites need the woodlands to become unseen, and the male in front of me is in no condition to be left alone in the forest.

He takes a wobbly step toward me, reaching out his hand to grasp mine as he nearly stumbles under his own weight. He's as light as a gentle breeze when I catch him between my hands to steady him.

His nose scrunches as he huffs a series of quick rhythmic breaths, much like a hound on the trail of its prey. His eyes saucer when they land on one of Eon's small blooms braided into my curls. He plucks it from my hair, shoving it against his nose, the petals fluttering toward his face as he inhales the scent.

He takes another ambling step toward me, pointing at the flower, repeating something I struggle to understand. I may be unfamiliar with the words but there is no mistaking the excitement in his voice when he says, *"Mah'nai. Mah'nai sa'hi."*

"What?" I wonder under my breath.

He takes another step toward me, wincing when his leg nearly falters beneath him. The pain doesn't stop him from squeezing my hand tightly and waggling the flower in my face while he continues to repeat the foreign words.

"All right," I say in a whispered breath.

Without enough time to consider all the options and potential pitfalls of a plan that I'm only now forming, I pin the male with a pointed stare. He is far too frail to walk off the ship, but all I can think about are the razor-sharp teeth behind that smile when I say firmly, *"Neh, reh."*

He gives me a hesitant nod and I pick him up like a child, popping him on my hip and sweeping my cloak over his body to shield him from view. The sentiment is one I learned from Tig, most often directed at her sister. *Be good*

Pulling my cloak over my head, I spin on my heel, ready to slide into the shadows above deck and—

"Awri." I choke out the name under my breath when she emerges from a nearby shadow at the base of the narrow stairway.

I wonder briefly how she made it below deck without me hearing but decide it's a question for another time.

"What are you doing?" she asks pointedly, with no attempt to stifle the anger in her voice.

"He needs a healer." It's all I can think to say.

Her brow drops, and she looks at me as if I've just said the single most ridiculous thing on Terr. Of course, she is already well aware that the sprite is injured. After all, I boarded the ship after she'd already departed it. One of the general's cloaked companions. No doubt her brother is nearby.

"What did you say to him?" she asks, the heat of her voice matching the aggravated step she takes toward me.

When the sprite begins to growl, pinning her with a threatening stare of his own, her brow dips at the fea and she stills. I don't have time to be impressed with him before the general glides down the stairs behind her, his feet landing firmly in front of me, Riesh in tow.

Riesh's eyes bulge when he sees the sprite in my arms. I try not to wince, try not to think about the many ways I've exposed myself.

"Put him down, Shivaria," Awri cautions me, "He's already attacked two members of the crew."

Despite what I expect, the general doesn't demand that I unhand the fearful sprite as his friend had, he doesn't tear into me, doesn't demand answers. I think I might prefer anything but the contemplative stare on his placid features as he takes in the scene before him. I can't help it when my feet shift beneath me. I disguise the uneasy fidgeting by readjusting the sprite at my hip.

The general puts his hand up, silencing any further protests or demands made by his friends.

"There is a cart by the road. Take him there," he says.

I might balk at the order if I wasn't so eager to get off the ship and away from what I'm certain will be an inquisition. I don't let myself ponder the outcome of this evening when I slide between the males, make my way topside, and begin toward the cart.

Though I can't distinguish the words, the angry clip of Awri's tone skips across the stone streets after me. Her companions' tones are much lower and mercifully more level.

I don't linger and attempt to overhear the conversation. I don't need to. I've raised a disturbing number of questions among them and shaken the foundation of the woman I portray. They will never see me the same way again. How can they?

The driver doesn't move from the front of the cart when I approach the thick four-walled wooden box and swing open the door fixed to the back. My breath catches in my throat when I take in the cargo. Fea. Many of them.

Boggles and pixies, even a satyr stares back at me. Others have names I do not recall, though I saw them all among Awri's drawings. The satyr closest to the door cradles his arm, a small bloody wound near his wrist. By the way he withdraws from the sprite, I can only assume the male on my side is at fault for the injury.

I debate the complexities of leaving the sprite in the cart, as the general ordered. Then consider the repercussions of ignoring the order and taking him to the sisters. I begin to peel the sprite off my hip, my obedience to the general the only sure way out of this. A simple claim of ignorance and unrestrained curiosity when I followed them to the docks. And the use of the sprite tongue?

I will think of something.

The male keeps a firm grip on my arm, hooking his legs around my waist when he waggles the flower at me, repeating the foreign phrase. There is no time to consider the consequences when I sigh, closing the doors of the box cart, and take the sprite to my horse.

The ride back is much slower with the wounded fea cradled between my legs. I do my best not to jostle the sprite beneath my cloak, conscious that every moment I delay there is a greater risk of being overcome by anyone tempted to pursue me. There is no lie I can tell myself to stifle the ever-growing pit that begins to form in my stomach. I will answer for this.

The guards don't stop me when I ride through the thick granite gates, though both look at me curiously. It's too early for them to have rotated shifts and I'm sure they are wondering how it is that I am returning when they never saw me leave.

Thankfully, the sprite seems content to remain tucked away as I dismount, handing the reins to a young stable hand. Making my way through the quiet corridors, I hurry back to my room. It's still early, and I can only hope the sisters are waiting for me. If not, I'll need to consider taking the male to Felias.

I puff out a breath of sheer relief when the moment I enter my room, the sisters' breathy whispers land on my ears. Their joyful laughter spills from the washroom, and the male sniffs the air before wriggling down from my side. He takes a number of painful, cautious steps in their direction, speaking into the night, his words lost to me.

A silence falls, a thick tension blanketing the air. Tig and Eon rush to the doorway, eyes as wide as I'm sure mine were when I first gazed upon him. Tig's eyes flick to me curiously and I open my mouth to explain the events of the evening.

"*Mah'nai,*" Eon practically squeals as she rushes to him.

Tig's eyes continue to grow, her head whipping toward her sister who tackles the strange sprite to the ground in a fit of giggles. He embraces her with his working arm, peppering her cheeks with kisses.

"What does it mean?" I wonder aloud.

There is a glassy sheen over her eyes when Tig turns to me, a smile tugging at the corners of her lips when she answers, "My mate."

"How?" I whisper.

A beautiful chuckle breaks from her throat as she watches her sister in the arms of her mate, a tear falling down her cheek.

"*Voh,*" she replies simply.

Fate.

The sisters insist on taking the male to the forest and I'm relieved when they decline my offer to send for a healer. I'm not sure where I would find Caden or how I'd convince him to assist the sprite. I assure myself they know much better than I how to go about healing him. I trust that if they need something, they will tell me.

Not long after the sisters depart, I answer a thundering knock. It isn't unexpected but I'd hoped to avoid it until morning. If not forever. I smooth the nervous features of my face, ignoring the pit in my gut when I unlatch the door.

Awri shoves past me, scanning the room. "You brought him back *here*?"

The general, Riesh, and Kishek crowd into the room behind her just as she's made it into the washroom, checking behind the doors for any sign of the male.

"I did," I say, calmly.

"Then where is he?" she demands, coming to a huffing halt in front of me.

"Gone," I reply.

"Gone where?" she asks.

I grit my teeth, the tone of her voice calling to the warrior inside of me, when I say, "He's safe."

It's all she needs to know.

Awri puffs out her annoyance upon my reply, and when the general snags her bicep, that annoyance trails along the length of his arm, landing firmly on his face.

"Leave it, Awri," he demands, even as she balks at him.

Sneering, she says, "Aren't you the least bit curious how a *mortal* who claims ignorance to the existence of the fea in our veil speaks the sprite tongue?"

Kishek steps up to her side and twines his fingers with hers. Her eyes soften when she looks down to their joined hands and back to his face.

"You are exhausted," he says, "Let me take you to bed. We will talk tomorrow."

She gives him a reluctant nod and leaves the room without meeting my eyes, pulling Kishek behind her. Her brother follows after them, lines of worry, and perhaps exhaustion, creasing his brow when he looks me over like he's never seen me before.

"She shouldn't have spoken to you like that," the general says from the doorway.

It takes everything I have to stifle my shock when he says it. He has every reason to be as angry as Awri, and I find that the lack of suspicion and condemnation from the male is more disturbing than anything I expected.

"She just needs time," he adds.

"I'm not sure I have that kind of time," I quip, understanding that time is relative to the immortal standing in front of me.

The general raises a brow at me before smoothing a loose piece of dark hair from his eyes.

"I only did what I thought was best to help him," I say.

"She knows that. We all do," he says calmly.

I feel my eyebrows hit my hairline in disbelief when I challenge, "Then why is she angry with me?"

He leans against the frame of the door. "Because, in teaching her a valuable lesson, you have made her feel vulnerable."

"What lesson?" I ask.

"If someone doesn't want to show you who they are, you will never truly know them." He says it as if we are having a casual conversation over polite tea.

His voice holds no accusatory tone, there is no question in his eyes, no demand that I explain myself. His words wash over me, and I feel the gentle sway of a ship beneath my feet as memories of a woman I had once been are stirred by the current. I shake my head, warding them off before they take hold, tasting the bitterness of the lesson I know all too well.

"It's a lesson we all learn," he says matter-of-factly. "Though not all who teach it to us have nefarious intentions. Your motives were obviously well

intended with the sprite." Shifting his weight off the doorframe he adds, "When her mind has a chance to puzzle it out, she will see that too."

Against my better judgment, I ask, "What makes you so sure?"

"Because we were all there, the moment you learned there are still fea left in this veil. There was no pretense in your surprise when you saw her in that tree, no deception in your curiosity when you asked questions for hours after." He shrugs. "Now you speak the language of the sprite, and the male on the ship freely gave you his trust, denying it to all who came before you."

I've given too much away tonight, and though I don't know yet what it will cost me, there will be a high price to pay for it.

"If the fea in A'kori have given you their trust..." He shrugs again, at an apparent loss as to what that might mean to him.

I have no doubt he will be piecing together every word and action he's ever witnessed from me until he has teased some deeper truth from it all. An uncomfortable silence falls over the room. I'm not sure if he's waiting for an explanation or a rebuttal but I can't give him either.

"It's late," I say, deflecting and entirely unsure if he will leave it until morning.

He nods, a flicker of disappointment passing over his features as he turns toward the hall. He grips the lever on the door, glancing back as he says, "Maybe the fea are wrong about you."

I'm not sure why my heart aches when he says it.

"Or, maybe," he adds, "you are simply wrong about yourself."

I don't reply. What can I say? Unlike the male standing before me, I know exactly what I am.

"You should know that twining your life with a fea is rarely worth their chaotic meddlings," he says, as he begins to swing the door closed.

I can't help but chuckle, remembering the golden braid still woven into my hair. But the feyn are fea, and I can't help but wonder if he is trying to warn me off the species entirely.

I quirk an eyebrow at his back and ask, "All fea?"

"I'd like to think that some are worth a bit of the chaos," he answers as the door shuts with a loud click.

After the events of the evening and even after all the general said, still,

there is a giant vacancy where my stomach should be. I refused the general as a companion, making Awri my only friend at court, my only line to the king. No matter what the male says and despite the fact that he has known her for years, I know that there is no way to truly mend the rift that settled between us on that ship.

Because even if she began to see the events of the evening in the same light as the general, she now knows a greater part of who I am and what I am capable of.

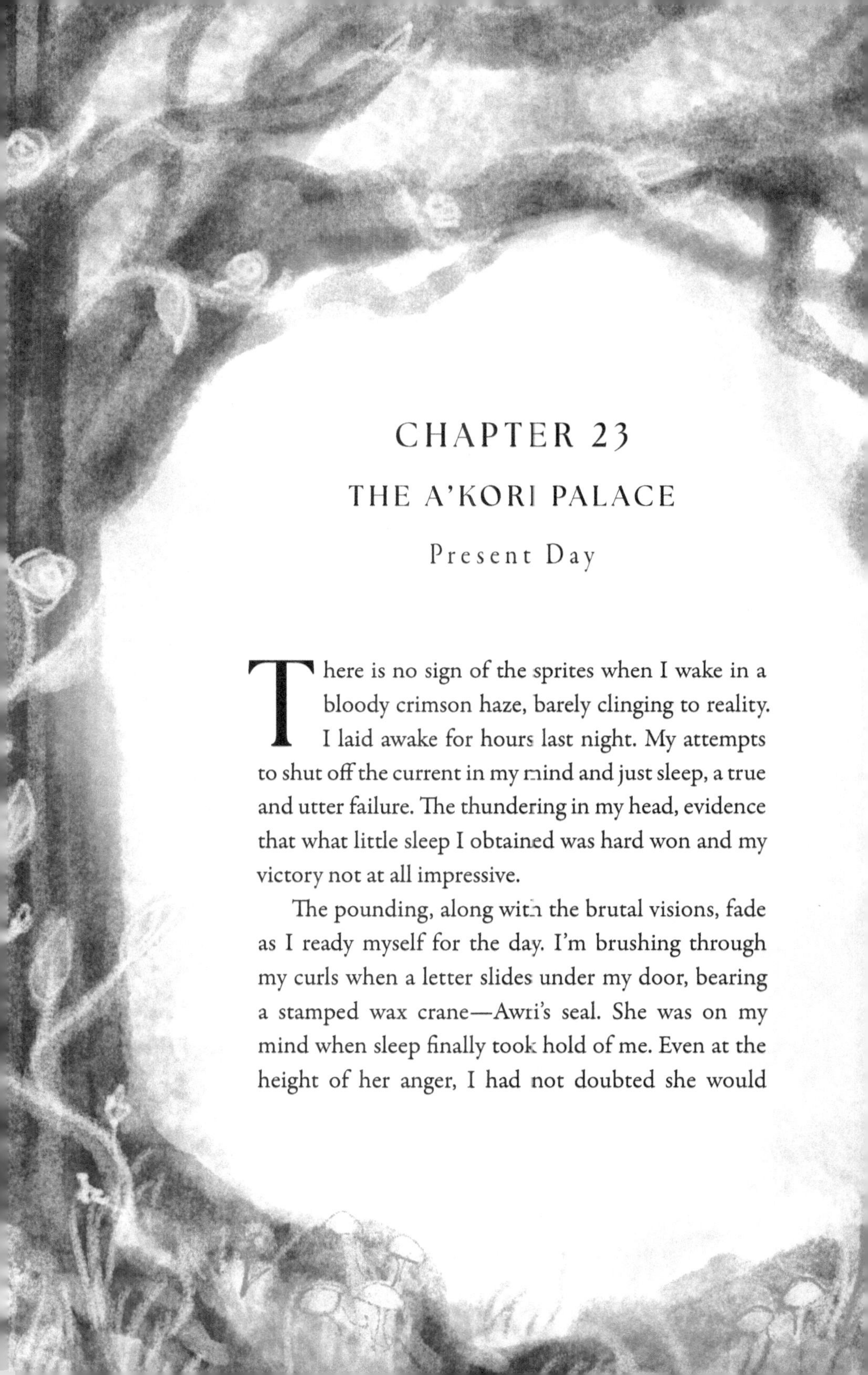

CHAPTER 23
THE A'KORI PALACE
Present Day

There is no sign of the sprites when I wake in a bloody crimson haze, barely clinging to reality. I laid awake for hours last night. My attempts to shut off the current in my mind and just sleep, a true and utter failure. The thundering in my head, evidence that what little sleep I obtained was hard won and my victory not at all impressive.

The pounding, along with the brutal visions, fade as I ready myself for the day. I'm brushing through my curls when a letter slides under my door, bearing a stamped wax crane—Awri's seal. She was on my mind when sleep finally took hold of me. Even at the height of her anger, I had not doubted she would seek me out again. I only hope it is to mend ties and not fray them further.

A curious blend of joy and trepidation twists my gut when her letter asks me to meet her at the stables. She would like me to join her for a hunt, just the two of us. I'm more than a little surprised by the invitation, and I can only hope she isn't planning my demise in the form of a well-placed arrow. I don't think so, but no one ever walks into such things without being blind to them.

The cool spring air nips at my nose. An early morning fog drapes over A'kori, obscuring the city from view. I follow the reverberating sound of blades clashing in the quiet of daybreak, every strike echoing in the dense mist. I offer my friend a small smile when she appears out of the fog, donning the same leathers I wear and an equally pensive smile.

I don't have the chance to say a single word before she embraces me. Clapping her hands against my back, she says, "I am truly sorry. I should not have spoken to you like that. Not when I call you my friend. Please forgive me."

I return her embrace with a gentle squeeze of my own, utterly unprepared for the grace she extends. While lying in bed I pondered at length how she might approach me, what she was likely to say, and what I would say in return. Of all the conversations I constructed in my mind, this had not been one of them.

"There is nothing to forgive," I say, "I understand how it looks but—"

"Don't," she interrupts, "You don't have to explain." She pulls back and smiles at me proudly. "It's a testament to your character that you honor your friends' secrets."

A dull pain strikes my chest when she says it. There is no honor in what I plan. Duty, yes. But no honor in the life I'll take and the injury her heart will suffer because of her trust in me.

I don't miss that, like the general, she seems to have her suspicions about where I learned the sprite tongue, but I take her at her word when she says I don't have to explain and leave it at that.

I force a smile, and she leads me toward the stables. I envy Riesh and Kishek as we pass by the sparring ring. They round one another with long, heavy blades, and I flex my hand, wishing I could feel the hilt of a sword again. The general watches from the sideline, his chest still slick with sweat from the rounds he'd gone before I arrived. My eyes can't help but linger, feasting on his flesh. I chide myself for looking when his eyes catch mine and his entire body tenses in recognition of my gaze.

I puff out a relieved breath when the general's stare is broken by the wall of the stables as I follow Awri inside. A quick glance around tells me that the female had this arranged since early this morning. Her grey dappled mare is saddled alongside the midnight mare I borrowed from Felias.

I'm going to need to find time to return the horse soon, perhaps when I call on him for another luncheon and to procure my pants. I can't help but wonder if the man will continue to reveal his true self to me, and if he does, what other information he might divulge.

She hands me a quiver, slinging her own across her back. I cinch the strap across my chest and, with a handful of mane, swing into the saddle. Awri notes the maneuver with curiosity, as she glides onto her own seat.

"I've ridden since I was a little girl," I explain.

The bow strapped to the saddle behind me is easy to reach, bound by a small leather strap. Adjusting my cloak around my shoulders, I give the horse a click of my tongue and she saunters forward, Awri and her mount following close behind. I'm not sure why Awri laughs when she sees the general tugging his tunic over his head, wearing his usual brooding frown, until she ribs her friend.

"We'll keep to the edge of the forest," she assures him, "And I promise to keep her far away from any of the springs."

The male pushes out an exasperated sigh that only makes her laugh louder before cracking her reins in the air, sending our mounts into a gallop toward the woodland. My cloak billows in the dragging wind and I close my eyes, happy to let the mare have her way. The crisp chill of the morning air fades into an unseasonable warmth as we near the forest. Thick tendrils of air caress the lobes of my ears before rushing down my neck and filling my bodice until my skin prickles and a wide grin breaks across my face.

True to her word, we spend the morning skirting the trees. Only delving into the dense undergrowth on foot occasionally to check for any sign of our prey.

"I truly am sorry." Her voice breaks the silence just before midday.

"Don't be," I try to assure her, again.

The quiet of the hunt is a relief, the time alongside one another easing a bit of the tension between us.

"It would be easy to blame my actions on exhaustion," she says, "like Kishek said last night, planning for the masque has taken a toll, as well as other matters I've had to attend as of late. But it wasn't any of that." She sighs, letting the conversation linger in the air until I think that might be the end of it. "You caught me completely off guard. When I saw you with that sprite it was like I didn't know you at all. Like I was looking at a stranger."

I shove down a bloom of guilt. She doesn't know me. Not really. And that is something I'm sure she will live to regret.

"But that wasn't fair of me," she continues, "you're entitled to a life unscrutinized by me or anyone else. I should have thanked you for what you did."

"You don't nee—"

"Thank you," she cuts me off with a fierce stare.

After a moment of pause, I dip my chin, and it seems the simple gesture is enough for her.

The forest is still, almost eerily so, and I find myself thinking of the naiad and other fea that might be lurking under the deep shadows cast by the canopy above.

"Why didn't the general want you hunting today?" I ask, keeping my eyes on the forest.

She laughs. "Xey hasn't fussed over me like that since I was a child. You, on the other hand," her lips kick up at the ends in an amused smirk, "bring out a very different side of the male. I think he would have sent an entire battalion if I'd allowed it."

My eyes nearly bulge from their sockets. She's joking, of course, but it begs the question, does the general really have a battalion of men hiding near the palace grounds? I have spent far too many hours indoors planning parties if it is true and I am somehow completely unaware of it.

"Does he worry about the other fea in the forest?" I ask, "He told me there were more who live there."

"There are thousands of them," she says, "The forest stretches beyond the mountains, all the way to the northern sea. The king grants any fea seeking refuge the right to live on that land."

She looks toward the snow-covered peaks as if she could somehow see the vast expanse of land that lays beyond them.

"The ship you saw last night was far from the first," she explains, "And regretfully they've become more frequent. Brax was left in the keeping of the fea after the sundering, but life for them is altered, and it is not the same home they once had. Many attempt the crossing from the south, but very few live to see the bounty of the northern woods."

"They die in the crossing? From what?" I wonder.

"The tidelands that surround Brax make for a treacherous journey. They are full of unpredictable currents and shallow reefs known as *chai'brukar*, ship breakers. Most of the ships sink before they ever make it into the open sea."

I don't have to ask what type of lives the fea must lead to drive them to such desperation. I have lived it. Seen it with my own eyes in La'tari.

"Have you been to Brax?" I ask.

"Not for many years," she answers thoughtfully, "I was last there during the war. Even then it was a far cry from what it had been before the La'tari began hunting the fea. It's only gotten worse for them since the treaty."

That gets my attention and my head whips toward her.

"How has it gotten worse?" I ask, afraid I already know the answer.

"The treaty was meant to end the hunting of the fea," she says, "but it only served to divide our people and weaken us. The fea in Brax are at the mercy of the La'tarians and their word."

"And the Vatruke," I add, watching her carefully to gauge her reaction.

She doesn't give much away when she nods. "The Vatruke would be bad enough without the La'tari military aiding them. For the fea in the south, the options are slim, risk death on *chai'brukar* or capture. If you know of the Vatruke then you understand why many might find death preferable."

A loud snap echoes in the forest, and I reach for my bow as my head reels toward the tree line. A boar roots through a pile of leafy debris below the low branch of a larch. I knock an arrow, aware of the light clack of wood on wood beside me when Awri knocks one as well. I draw, take in a deep breath, aim, and loose. Awri is a quicker shot by a second, but she misses her mark by a hand. My own arrow flies true, piercing the heart of the boar the next moment.

The sky has begun to dim by the time we've dressed and packed the animal onto the horses. Awri gives me a satisfied smirk when she mounts, a smile I return as I scan the darkening horizon, my stomach turning in on itself. The smile falls from my face, and I gasp. Awri swears under her breath when her eyes follow mine.

"Mount, quickly," she demands, "We need to warn the guard."

With a fistful of mane, I swing into the saddle, and as if the tension in my body cracked in the air, the horses bolt for the palace at breakneck speed. I glance back at the La'tari warship sailing into the cove behind us and can't help but wonder who is aboard.

Their reasons for landing here appear clear enough. If their mission involved anything but death they would have docked at the main harbor. Landing this far from town at dusk reeks of malicious intent.

It's dark when we arrive at the front doors of the palace. Awri jumps from her mare before the horse has even halted its stride. My own mare, soaked in a frothing sweat, rolls the bit in her mouth nervously.

A young man collects her horse, offering to take mine as well while Awri vanishes into the palace after exchanging a few rushed words with a handful of soldiers near the entrance. One breaks toward the stables, while the others move quickly to spread word of the intruders.

I expect to see more panicked faces, but I suppose it is only a single ship. The halls are their typical evening quiet. Though, I have little doubt as the guards eye me warily, that tonight I am nothing more than La'tarian to them. A foreign woman from a land that appears to be invading their shores.

The looks are enough to make me quickly discard the thought of procuring more of Kishek's tea. Tomorrow, when the news of the ship is not so fresh in the minds of the soldiers surrounding me, I will make enough to last the days it will take the king to arrive back in A'kori. The consistent dulling of my demon makes me a little bolder than I might have been before finding the tonic.

I walk calmly back to my room to tuck myself away for the night. Thoughts of familiar faces and war weigh heavily on my mind as I prepare for bed. What happened to make my king risk war with A'kori by sending the ship to their shores in secret? Have we ever really been at peace? I'm beginning to believe otherwise.

I pull on a dressing robe when there is a knock from the hall. The general doesn't wait for me to answer before cracking the door and sliding inside, catching an eyeful of the delicate black night dress I wear, before I close the robe around myself.

"Have you come to arrest me for being a La'tari spy?" I quip, immediately regretting the thought I might have placed in his head.

He grunts as if I've just said something ridiculous, and I can't tell if I'm relieved or annoyed that he believes me incapable.

"I'm taking a squadron of men to search for the vessel," he says, "The others are joining me. I just came to assure you that you are safe within these walls and ask that you refrain from any of your evening escapades for the time being."

"I'll do my best," I tease.

"No," he demands, "You will promise me."

I want to roll my eyes, to say something smart, to tell him he doesn't get to make decisions for me, but the look in his eyes stops me. Worry lines his forehead and creases the flesh of his brow. I sigh, telling myself to let it go. I remind myself that before he came to make his demands, I was getting ready for bed anyway.

"I promise," I say.

He puffs out a breath he'd been holding. "Thank you."

I check the grounds the moment he leaves my room, and I'm not surprised to find it littered with guards. It makes perfect sense that they would increase the patrols, but a small part of me begins to wonder if I'm now a prisoner of war. It's a question I don't have to answer tonight, and one that will surely make itself clear when I leave my room to find Awri tomorrow.

The sprites are nowhere to be seen. Between the unrest at the palace and the male they are surely tending, I suspect it may be quite some time before I see their faces again. Aside from missing the amusing presence of the sisters, I am eager to see them again so that I can speak with the male. I have questions about Brax that I only trust him to answer. If, in fact, it turns out that is where he comes from.

I sink into bed and whether it's thoughts of the sprites, my conversation with Awri, or the presence of the La'tari ship, sleep evades me. It feels like

hours that I toss and turn. My mind skipping like a flat stone across a clear lake from one thing to the next. I hate it when my thoughts settle on the image of the beautiful female I met outside the general's chambers. Even worse, her face is the last thing I see before sleep finally takes me.

I'm jarred awake when the general barges into my room at stars only know what hour. I'm going to have to find another lock for my door—a strong one that he doesn't possess a key to. I blink back the sleep from my eyes as he slips an arm beneath my knees, another around my waist, pulling me against him as he slides me off the bed.

"What are you doing? Put me down," I groan sleepily.

"We found the ship. It was empty." It's all he says before walking toward the door and I push against his chest, wriggling until he sets me down.

I suck in a small gasp when my feet meet the cool marble in the hall, only to have the male glare down at them. My toes curl in on themselves in a futile attempt to withdraw from his glower. Putting his hand on the flat of my back he pushes me down the corridor.

"Stop," I demand in frustration, planting my feet. "Where are you taking me?"

"Until we find the La'tari unit it isn't safe for you on your own," he says, "You will stay in my chamber for the time being."

That wakes me up. I squint a glare at him, voicing my protest, "Absolutely not."

"Until we find out who was aboard the warship, there is no safer place for you to be," he argues, pushing against the small of my back assertively.

I step to the side, the male nearly tripping without the weight of my body bracing his arm. Turning back toward my room, my brow is drawn in defiance and annoyance, and I'm utterly unaware of which I feel more. I say over my shoulder, "I'll take my chances. Thank you very much."

"I'm not asking," he growls, hooking my waist with his arm, hefting me off the ground, and throwing me over his shoulder as if I were nothing more than a sack of feathers.

The male is halfway through his third stride when I land a well-placed jab to his kidney and he grunts, falling to his knee. I twist out of his grasp,

my bare feet smacking against the cold stone where I land surefooted and begin marching back toward my room, a self-satisfied smile tugging at the corner of my lips.

"Enough!" he bellows. "You are coming with me and that is the end of it."

My hands bawl into fists at my sides, the heat of my anger rushing to my cheeks as I again voice my protest at the incessant male. "No. I'm. No—" The word trails off in a scream when he hooks my waist, pulling me over his shoulder.

He positions my legs to hang against his back and clasps my wrists in one large hand. Each time I attempt to kick him, he shifts his shoulder beneath me, pitching my weight enough that I lose my balance and fail in my attempt.

"What?" I sneer, the guards in the hall eyeing the spectacle, "You've never heard a woman say *no*?"

"This has nothing to do with your refusal," he hisses.

"You can't get what you want by asking, so you just take it?" I snide, as he kicks open his door with a growl, throwing me into the center of his bed.

He points toward the pillows and yells, "Go to sleep!"

"I'd love to," I spit, "as soon as I'm back in *my* room."

"That is *not* happening," he rumbles, "If they decide to attack tonight, you'll be defenseless by yourself."

I huff an incredulous laugh, scooting to the edge of the bed. He has no idea how incredibly wrong he is about that.

"If you're that concerned, I'll stay with Awri," I say.

"That isn't an option," he says, the heat in his voice fading as he latches the door. "Her bed is already occupied."

Interesting.

"Then I'll stay with Riesh," I say flippantly, as I storm toward the hall.

He's too fast and hooks my waist from behind, tossing me back into the center of the bed as he growls, "Over my dead body."

"Don't tempt me!" I snarl.

His brow pitches down and he pins me with a dark stare. Leaning against the mattress, one arm on either side of my legs, he says, "I will stay up until dawn, dragging you back to this bed if that's what it takes to keep you put. You are staying right here, where I can keep an eye on you whether you like it or not."

He doesn't wait for me to agree before he stalks off to drag a large chair in front of the door. When he plants himself in the dark velvet cushion, I give in. I've never cared where I slept before, why should I let it bother me now. If he is willing to keep his hands off me, I'm happy to let him spend an uncomfortable night awake, playing bodyguard.

I slip into the covers and put my back to him, wondering how exactly I got myself into this mess. There is a shuffle behind me before the lights dim and the room fades to black. My mind is a brutal and torturous thing when it conjures another image of the green-eyed female. I brush a hand over the silk sheets, a pit forming in my stomach when I wonder when she last slept where I am now.

It's too late when sleep finally comes to take me. I've already thought about his lips on her neck. Wondered if he touches her the same way he touched me. And for once, the bloody visions of my sleep are a welcome reprieve.

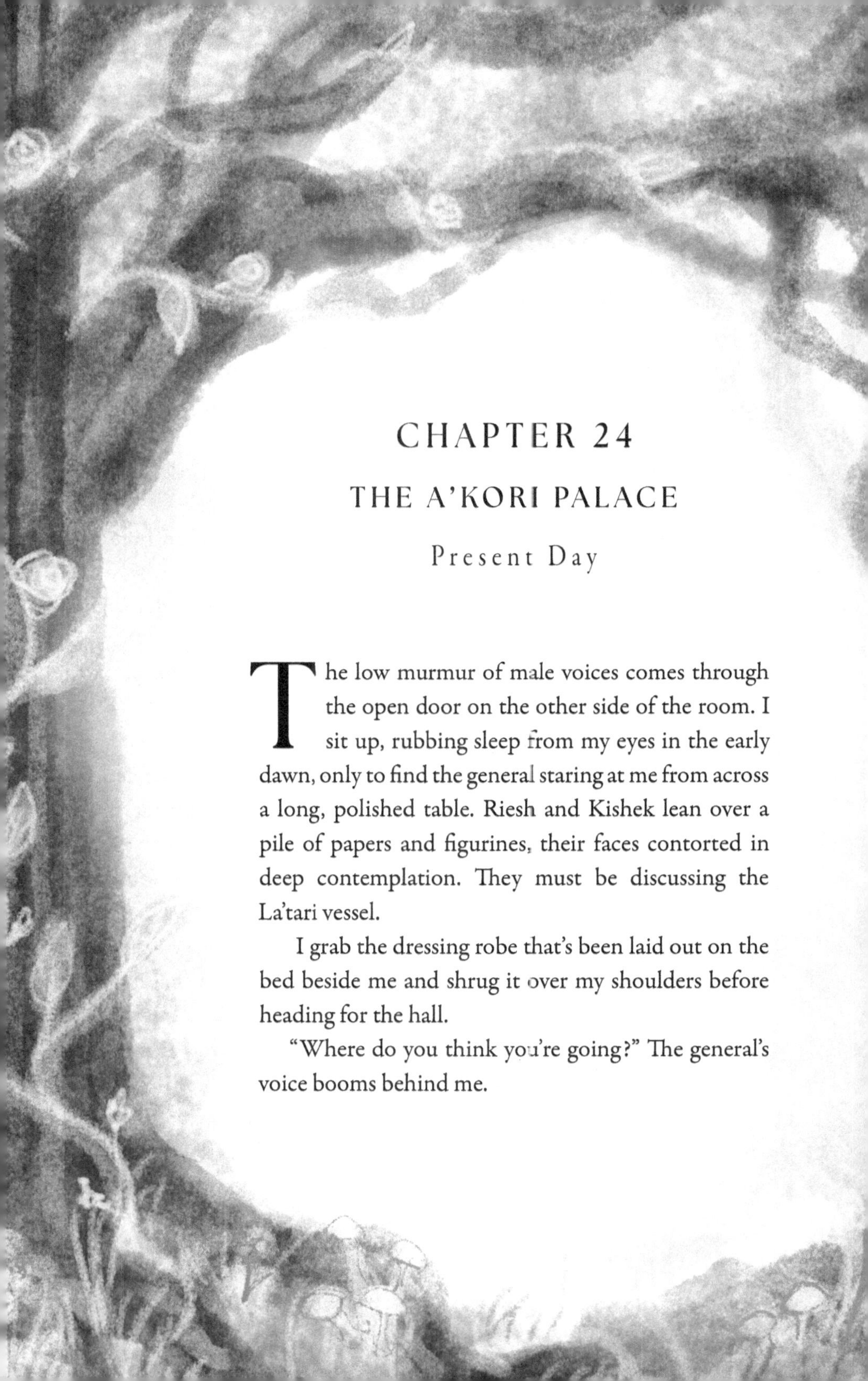

CHAPTER 24
THE A'KORI PALACE
Present Day

The low murmur of male voices comes through the open door on the other side of the room. I sit up, rubbing sleep from my eyes in the early dawn, only to find the general staring at me from across a long, polished table. Riesh and Kishek lean over a pile of papers and figurines, their faces contorted in deep contemplation. They must be discussing the La'tari vessel.

I grab the dressing robe that's been laid out on the bed beside me and shrug it over my shoulders before heading for the hall.

"Where do you think you're going?" The general's voice booms behind me.

"To dress and get ready for the day," I say, sighing in annoyance.

"In case I didn't make myself clear last night. You are staying where I can keep an eye on you." He wraps a hand around my bicep and pulls me into his washroom, pointing at a large drawer. "You should find everything you need in there. If there is anything else you require, you will let me know."

I glare at his back as he stalks toward the main room. The drawer glides open with the barest tug and clinks with all manner of oil and perfume. Trays with powders in varying shades of pink and pencils of kohl are stacked neatly toward the back. I pluck the toothbrush and accompanying paste from the drawer, narrowing my eyes on the vanity. Six drawers.

"Do you have a drawer like this for each of your lovers?" I ask, narrowing my eyes at the male, "Or do you make them share *everything*?"

He clenches his jaw. "I had these things brought here when I returned from the forest. At the time, I hoped you would have use of them."

"I see," I drawl, "Which drawer do you keep for the female with the green eyes? Or does that not narrow it down enough for you?"

The general opens his mouth then snaps it shut, turning on his heel with a growl when Riesh yells from the other room, "It isn't here Xey!"

His washroom is easily twice the size of mine. A deep pool flowing with hot water is carved into the floor, a long narrow slit cut into the marble above it, creating a steamy waterfall that fills the churning basin. I squint at a spigot inset in the ceiling and debate pulling the lever beneath it. The thought vanishes from my mind when the voices from the other room grow loud.

I round the corner in time to hear the general lie to his friends. "Other than your sister and the people in this room, no one has been granted access to my chambers for more than a week. If it's missing, someone has stolen it."

"Well, that isn't entirely true, is it?" I say with a wry smile as I lean against the wall.

My mind screams traitor as he attempts to deceive his friends right before my eyes. It's no wonder that Awri doesn't know about the female when it's obvious he hasn't told Riesh or Kishek about her either. I can't help but think that I would like to show them all *exactly* what kind of male he is.

"Would you care to explain that sentiment?" he says, looking down at me, his head cocked to the side.

I wonder just how far he's willing to take the deception and offer, "Perhaps you've changed your mind, and you'd like me to leave? So that you can have an honest conversation with your friends about who you allow into your chambers?"

"What I would like," he says, closing his eyes to steady his temper, "is for you to tell me what in haliel you are talking about."

"I'm talking about the redhead with the sheer lace gown that joined you in your chambers the morning you returned from the forest," I say, careful to keep my voice level and disinterested.

I decide the male is a better actor than I expect when he frowns and seems truly puzzled by my declaration.

"Siserie?" Kishek asks, wide eyed.

I shrug. "She failed to introduce herself when she left the general to his *nap*."

His glower deepens. "Please check Siserie's room for the missive and tell her I'd like to have a word."

His friends file out into the hall. The moment the door clicks shut behind them, his voice drops low and contemplative as he says, "Tell me why you came to my room that morning."

And just like that, I realize the mistake I've made. All I had to do was say nothing, and he never would have known I'd come.

"I wasn't aware I needed a reason," I say, deflecting.

He takes a tentative step toward me, asking bluntly, "Did you come to accept my offer?"

"That's a little presumptuous of you," I snark, willing the heat to remain from my cheeks.

"But you did, didn't you?" he asks.

He eyes me thoughtfully, piecing together every moment we've shared since that day, every conversation, every glance. The contents of my life that I wish I kept under heavy guard now coming together to tell him exactly what it was that made his offer so distasteful to me.

"You spent the entire day avoiding me before you turned me down, so why would you seek me out that morning? Unless you came to accept me, and something changed your mind?"

As much as I loathe that he's puzzled it out, that he now knows how

close I'd come to him, I don't deny it. None of it matters anyway. I break from his gaze to look out the window.

"Even if that were true, it doesn't change anything," I push out under my breath.

"I think it might," he says softly, "depending on what it was that changed your mind."

I'm not sure if he's asking, but I don't say a word. I've already said too much, given too much away. My pride won't let me voice that it was the idea of him bedding that female that made my decision for me. I won't give him the satisfaction of knowing he wounded me.

He takes my chin between his fingers and brings my eyes back to his.

"I've known Siserie for over two hundred years, and not once have I ever desired to have her in my bed."

My stomach pits and I hesitate to pull away, his eyes seem so sincere. And yet, I've seen the female, and nothing any male on Terr could say would convince me that she is undesirable to him.

"She seems entirely convinced of the opposite," I say, withdrawing my chin from between his fingers.

"I am uninterested in the thoughts or feelings of that female. I would, however, be very interested to hear of your own desires once this issue is put to rest," he says, stepping around me when a knock sounds at the door.

Resting against the edge of a sturdy desk, his posture is relaxed and somehow still every bit the king's general. His face settles into a mask of assertive confidence, and I chide myself for finding it attractive.

He tugs my arm and settles me between his thighs. Before I can protest, he says, "Enter."

His arms snake around my waist and he pulls me close, until my back is braced snugly against his chest.

"Watch," he demands.

I tense in his arms, furious at the order or the fact that he's handling me, or both. I move to pull away as the door swings wide.

Kishek enters first, Siserie following close behind. Judging by her dress, she apparently *had* considered the gown I'd seen her in perfectly suitable for everyday attire. The sheer dark green silk of her dress follows every curve of her body, artfully sewn to resemble the scales of a serpent, weaving from the

ground to her throat. A handful of scales thoughtfully placed in abundance to obscure her more private regions.

A seductive smile kicks up the edges of her lips and she casts a smoldering gaze at the general from under her thick, fluttering lashes. Her smile falls nearly indiscernibly when her eyes trace the line of his hands at my waist. But she recovers quickly, lighting up when she eyes the general once again.

Kishek steps around her and hands the general a folded piece of paper, which he immediately discards onto the desk. Unlike the one I'd seen at her mother's house, its seal is intact and the script addressing the letter to the general is written in a different hand.

"Thank you," the general says to his friend, dismissing Kishek from the room with a glance.

She takes a sultry step forward, her voice soft and alluring when she says, "Is there something I can do for you, General? You know I am at your complete disposal, as always."

If her words were not enough for me to devise her meaning, her body language leaves no doubt in my mind as to her intent. I stiffen, preparing to remove myself from between them when the general's arms tighten further. Her eyes flick to the sweep of his thumb on my belly and her face twists in disdain.

The hateful look she bears down on me convinces me to smile at the female sweetly and settle my back against the general's chest. He's made it clear that I'm not going anywhere until I've witnessed whatever this is, and the female seems like she might prefer it if I were anywhere else in the world than exactly where I am. While I don't think too much about it, I find that more than any other feyn I've come across thus far, she might be the one I'd like to disquiet the most.

"I'm glad to hear you say that," he says, his lips brushing my temple as he speaks. "I believe the two of you have already met."

"Not officially," she says, her lovely face twisting under the pressure of her clenched jaw.

"Siserie," his voice grows deadly, "this is Shivaria, *mi'ajna.*"

Her eyes go wide, even as my throat burns. I push down every memory threatening to overwhelm me when she dips her head in a shallow bow of greeting. Surprised by her response, I can't help but wonder what she has

heard about me that would explain the sudden shift in her demeanor upon hearing my name.

"Isn't she lovely?" he purrs, brushing his lips along the base of my neck.

"She is exquisite," she agrees.

I don't take the compliment to heart. It's clear that she would agree to anything the general says in this moment, and the male behind me is subjecting her to a particular type of torture that I'm loath to admit I'm enjoying.

"I'm glad you agree," he says, "Now, can you explain to me how Shivaria came to the conclusion that you and I are sharing a bed?"

The female tenses, paling notably when she says, "I'm sure I never meant to give her that impression."

The general's lips tease the lobe of my ear, and he whispers just loud enough for her to hear, "Do you believe her?"

Is he really asking me? I turn my head and meet his eyes. But he already knows the answer. I didn't believe him because of her and what she said to me.

He kisses the bridge of my nose and says softly, "Neither do I."

"Kishek," the general calls.

The male must have been waiting for the summons as he's in the room before I've even seen him coming through the door.

"Are there any empty cells in the barracks?" the general asks.

"Many," Kishek says with an all too eager smile.

"You can't be serious," Siserie scoffs, "It was a harmless prank. I am no spy. I didn't even read it!" She points at the folded paper, discarded by the general.

"You misunderstand me completely," the general assures her.

She lets out a relieved sigh. "Thank you, Xeyvian."

"I'm not sending you to the barracks for the missive you stole," he says, "Despite the fact that it is the property of the crown. I'm sending you there because you robbed me of two days I will never get back with *mi'ajna*."

What is happening?

Even Kishek looks shocked, his eyes bulging at the declaration.

"Let me make myself perfectly clear, Siserie," the general lowers his tone in warning, "If you ever break into my chambers again, I will send you to Brax. And if you ever interfere with Shivaria again, in any way that she or I find distasteful, I will have Riesh bind your gift and ship you off to La'tari."

She pales at the last and even I find it a little harsh. I have no doubt it would be a death sentence in either case. Kishek claps his hand around her arm and drags her out of the room, the thick wood of the door he closes behind them muffling her protests. I puff out a breath, rolling my shoulders. At least now I know the male isn't in league with her family. It could have proved a difficult complication considering all I learned at their estate.

The general turns me to face him, tucking a stray curl behind my ear when he says, "I'll leave the duration of her punishment up to you."

My brows shoot up and I briefly debate refusing the offer, before thinking better of it. He is making me a gift of her punishment, for the way that she treated me. It won't kill her to stay in a cell for a few days, though I'm not entirely sure whether she will be serving the general's sentence or my own.

He meets my eyes with a gentle but determined stare. "There is no one else. I swear it."

I break his gaze, my eyes falling to the floor thoughtfully and perhaps under the weight of a small amount of shame. I tell myself that he has given me plenty of reason not to trust him, then remind myself that none of it matters. My excuses are gone, and he is a direct line to the king, to fulfilling my mission.

"Stay with me tonight?" he asks.

I find my body tense as I reconsider his offer, unsure of exactly what it is he is asking for, and still entirely unsure how much I'm willing to give the male.

"I have no expectations of you," he assures me, and I wonder when I became so easy for him to read. "I'd just like to have you to myself for a little while."

"I thought I didn't have a choice," I snark, "The La'tari ship—"

"I can make arrangements with Awri if you'd rather not sleep here again." He sounds like he regrets the words even as they slide off his tongue, and I can't help but wonder if he could have made those same arrangements last night.

"Just sleep?" I ask.

He nods. "I'm not asking for more."

The thwack of knuckles against the tall panels of the door draws his attention from me.

"Just, consider it, please," he says, before reluctantly removing me from between his thighs and moving toward the door.

Awri sweeps in, offering me a cheerful smile, and my eyes snag on her leathers. Not just the leather pants she'd acquired from the stables for our hunt, but a tall pair of leather boots, the same as my own, are laced tightly around her calves. Over the top of her cobalt dress, she wears a dark cuirass. Her hair is braided and wound into a tidy spiral on the back of her head, enhancing the sharp lines of her features and the pointed tips of her ears. She looks fit for battle.

She giggles after a thorough examination of my face and waves a young man in. He offers me a stack of folded leather and my toes curl in delight, bunching up the thick furs beneath my feet. It's a reaction I don't take time to consider when I push my nose against them and breathe in the scent of home, of me.

"I think she should have been a warrior, Xey," Awri says and laughs.

"I'm quite sure she already is," he replies.

A tingle of unease rushes down my spine as my gaze snaps to his. I shrug off the shiver, relieved when I see the jest in his eyes.

"I'd like Awri to begin training with you in the mornings," he says, "At least until we solve the riddle of the abandoned ship on the eastern shore."

He ushers me toward the washroom with a hand on my lower back. "You told me you had a fighting instructor back home, and I'd like to keep those skills of yours sharp."

A sickening sheen of guilt coats the excitement budding inside me. I want this. I need this. I am a well-made tool with a single purpose, and any tool can become dull if left discarded and untended for too long. But the general has no idea of the blade he is honing or the purpose for which it was made. Like Awri's trust in me, this will be yet another moment they will come to look back on with regret.

By the time I dress in the black leathers and the dark dress that had been tucked between them, my mood has soured completely. I flip the long braid over my shoulder when I emerge from the washroom and see Awri waiting patiently by the door. The muffled voices in the war room tell me the general has resumed his earlier discussions with Riesh and Kishek. It's easy to assume they will remain there for the duration of the day, discussing the implications of the ship and the possibility of war.

Awri tips her head toward the door and my brow draws down. "The general said I can't leave the room."

"I'm sure he feels you are safe enough with me." She smiles. "Unless you'd like to train here." She scans the space, poking at a delicate vase until it tips back on the table, nearly falling over.

"I might," I huff, "If only to show the male what he's earned for his demands."

She laughs and leads me to the sparring ring by the stables. The grounds feel a little smaller than usual. By my count, the general must have tripled the exterior guard. I wonder if the La'tari even considered the difficulties they would add to my mission by all but declaring war. No doubt they expected to have more time before they were discovered.

The ring is well groomed with a deep layer of fresh sand and a wooden fence around the border.

"Why don't you show me what you learned from your instructor, and we can start from there," Awri says.

Careful.

As much as my blood heats, responding to the challenge, today will be a dangerous game of convincing them of my story without becoming a threat. The art of war is something you never stop learning, and the female in front of me has no doubt been training in the art since before I was born.

I tie the panels of my gown below my hip and take up my stance, relieved she hasn't offered me a weapon. An armed proficiency would be much harder to hide. It seems reasonable that a lady in a war-torn country would have at least been trained in the art of self-defense. So, I widen my stance and give her a nod.

She lunges forward, leaving herself open to a defensive strike, obviously unconcerned with my abilities. The combination I return is simple, something I learned as a child, and I expect her to dodge it with ease. I block the strike she throws to my face and continue my thrust with the same arm, landing a blow on her jaw. She staggers back.

"Oh hisht. I'm sorry, I didn't mean to—"

My face contorts and I issue a relieved sigh when she begins to laugh, rubbing the knot in her jaw.

"Well, my brother will be pleased to learn that he was correct in his assessment of your skill," she says.

I cringe. Riesh has been far too interested in my capabilities since I'd bruised the general's face.

"Again," she says, retaking her stance and waving me into the center.

She feigns right, but I'm not watching her feet and the blow is easy enough to dodge. She leaves herself open. This time, I don't take the opportunity to strike.

"Now you're holding back." She doesn't attempt to hide her annoyance.

"What makes you say that?" I ask.

In answer, she whips her fist out again, and this time she makes no effort to pull the punch. I barely dodge the throw with a twist to the right. She hooks my ankle with her foot, trying to throw me off balance. Against my better judgment, and despite everything I told myself when I entered the ring, my reflexes take over.

I grab her arm, twist myself out of the crook of her ankle, and use the momentum from her strike to throw a knee to her abdomen. She falls to one knee, gasping for the air I've expelled from her lungs. A small group of guards gathers to watch, and a tall fair-skinned female in a soldier's uniform studies me closely with her ice-blue eyes.

I offer my friend a hand, whispering under my breath, "I'm not sure this is a good idea."

Awri clasps my forearm, letting me help her to her feet smirking when she sees that we've drawn a crowd.

"I think it's an excellent idea," she gasps, dusting herself off. "You just need a partner with more skill than I possess. Xey will at least be happy to hear you have good reflexes. I, on the other hand, may need to join you for training." She laughs and gestures to the female soldier to join us.

"Riah, would you mind taking over?" she asks.

Riah takes me in from head to toe, a slow and thorough assessment of her opponent. Her face reveals little, and I can't help but wonder what she thinks she sees.

She smirks at me wryly. "Are you sure?" she asks, a bit of cockiness slipping into her voice.

I'm not sure who she's asking, but her eyes are still on me, so I don't hesitate to reply, "I'm sure."

Awri steps out of the ring, and I begin to regret my mouth when I see that the group of onlookers has more than doubled. The clink of silver rises above the murmurs of the crowd as coins are exchanged and wagers made. My demon stirs inside me, as if it had been waiting for this very moment. It uncoils within my belly, begging to show the female its teeth.

Riah removes her helmet, casting it aside, revealing a head of thick black hair cut to follow the line of her jaw. A thin white scar, faded by centuries, runs from the tail of her right eyebrow, across her eye, and over the bridge of her nose. She's lucky she wasn't blinded.

"Ready?" she asks, taking a relaxed stance across from me.

I nod, taking an intentionally sloppy stance of my own. I already have the advantage, but it won't last beyond this round. Her uniform tells me all I need to know about her ability to fight. I on the other hand, as far as she is concerned, am a privileged lady who had been taught a bit of hand to hand at the request of an overprotective father.

The longer we exchange attacks and counter attacks, the longer she watches me move in the ring, the more the illusion I've built will crumble. She takes her time, studying the wrong placement of my feet, the level of my arms, my fists. Just when I think she might attack, she walks across the ring.

"You shouldn't stand like that. It leaves you open here." She points to my side then her hands fall to my hips, and she adjusts my form until she is satisfied.

Her eyes follow the bend of my arms from shoulder to wrist. Examining the placement of my elbows, those she moves as well, bringing them closer to my sides. Once she's satisfied with her work, she retakes her stance, falling back into position.

I can feel my brow drawn as I contemplate the female. I expected her to *teach* me my mistakes the way I'd always learned, with a painful blow to the exposed area. That is the way of the Drakai. Painful lessons are harder to forget. Something I recently learned doesn't apply only to broken bones.

Riah throws a series of blows, some to my face, others to my abdomen, assessing my defensive skills. I watch her closely and when her brow begins to dip at the ease with which I evade her, I allow her to land a strike. A blow to the gut would be ideal, but I've already made up my mind to let her land whatever comes next. I can tell she expected me to dodge it easily when she

doesn't pull the punch and my cheek splits under the force of her knuckles.

It's far from the hardest I've ever taken, but I stagger back a step and hiss at the pain, my hand poking the tender bleeding flesh dramatically, the way I assume any lady would.

Awri rushes into the ring. "Are you all right?"

"Fine," I assure her, glad the general isn't here to scoff at the declaration.

"That's enough for today," Awri says, and I can hardly control the tone of my voice when Riah turns to leave the ring.

"No. I'm all right," I say forcefully, "Let's go again."

"Are you sure?" Awri asks, her voice full of hesitation.

"Do you really think I'll improve if I walk away every time I get hit?" I ask.

There is a spark behind Riah's eyes when I pose the question to my friend. Awri gives me a nod and retreats outside the ring. Though I can tell by the look on her face that she's not sure she should allow this.

"You attack this time, I will defend," Riah says loud enough for Awri to hear.

No doubt attempting to settle my friend's nerves.

My first strike is intentionally slow and a little sloppy. She bats my hand away like I'm little more than an annoying fly in pursuit of her lunch and makes a few minor corrections to my form. I take the opening when she lets her guard down, her attention on my stance, rather than my trajectory. Her attempt to block comes too late, and my fist connects with her face, splitting her lip.

Her eyes widen under the shock of the blow, as she takes a step back. Her tongue flicks out to sweep the blood from her lip and, despite my expectation of her wrath, a toothy grin breaks on her face.

"I guess I deserve that," she chuckles.

She rounds me in the ring and now the actual sparring begins. Voices raise on the sidelines and without looking I can tell our audience continues to grow. The strikes are a little half-hearted as we both hold back for very different reasons. On her part, I'm sure she's worried she will hurt me. As for me, I have no intention of displaying the true extent of my training.

I'm not sure how long we have been at it when she brushes a dark, sweat-slicked strand of hair from her forehead. The crowd grows quiet, only the sound of our heavy breathing fills the silence. When it's clear that our time in the ring is coming to an end, I lunge, determined to land another

blow, not willing to let this moment pass after weeks of wanting for this, needing this.

I feign to the left and she takes the bait, realizing her mistake too late. I swing, and my eyes flick to the right, snagging on the general's dark glower as he stalks across the grounds. I falter, and she takes the distraction, landing another strike, this time on my lip. It splits, and the general's frown deepens.

Riah smiles, satisfied with the strike. We've exchanged enough blows that she knows I can take it, and I've given her plenty of smug grins of my own to warrant the proud look she's leveling at me.

"Lieutenant," the general growls.

Riah pivots on her heel, her smile vanishing as her back straightens when she acknowledges the male. The onlookers disperse in a flurry, resuming their patrols or whatever other tasks they'd been charged with.

"Out." He issues the simple command clearly and Riah jogs out of the ring.

"I asked her to step in for me," Awri says, ready to defend the female.

"For what reason?" he demands, walking straight past the lieutenant and swinging himself over the fence and into the ring.

"Riah was far more suited for the task," Awri explains.

He scoffs and grabs my chin, tipping my head to get a good view of my injuries, minor as they may be.

"Go and clean up, lieutenant," he commands, "I'd like a word with you, first thing tomorrow morning."

Riah rushes off and the general puffs out a disgruntled sound. "I'm taking you to see Caden."

I raise an eyebrow. "I'm sure that's not necessary."

"It isn't an offer," he says sternly, taking my hand and leading me toward the palace.

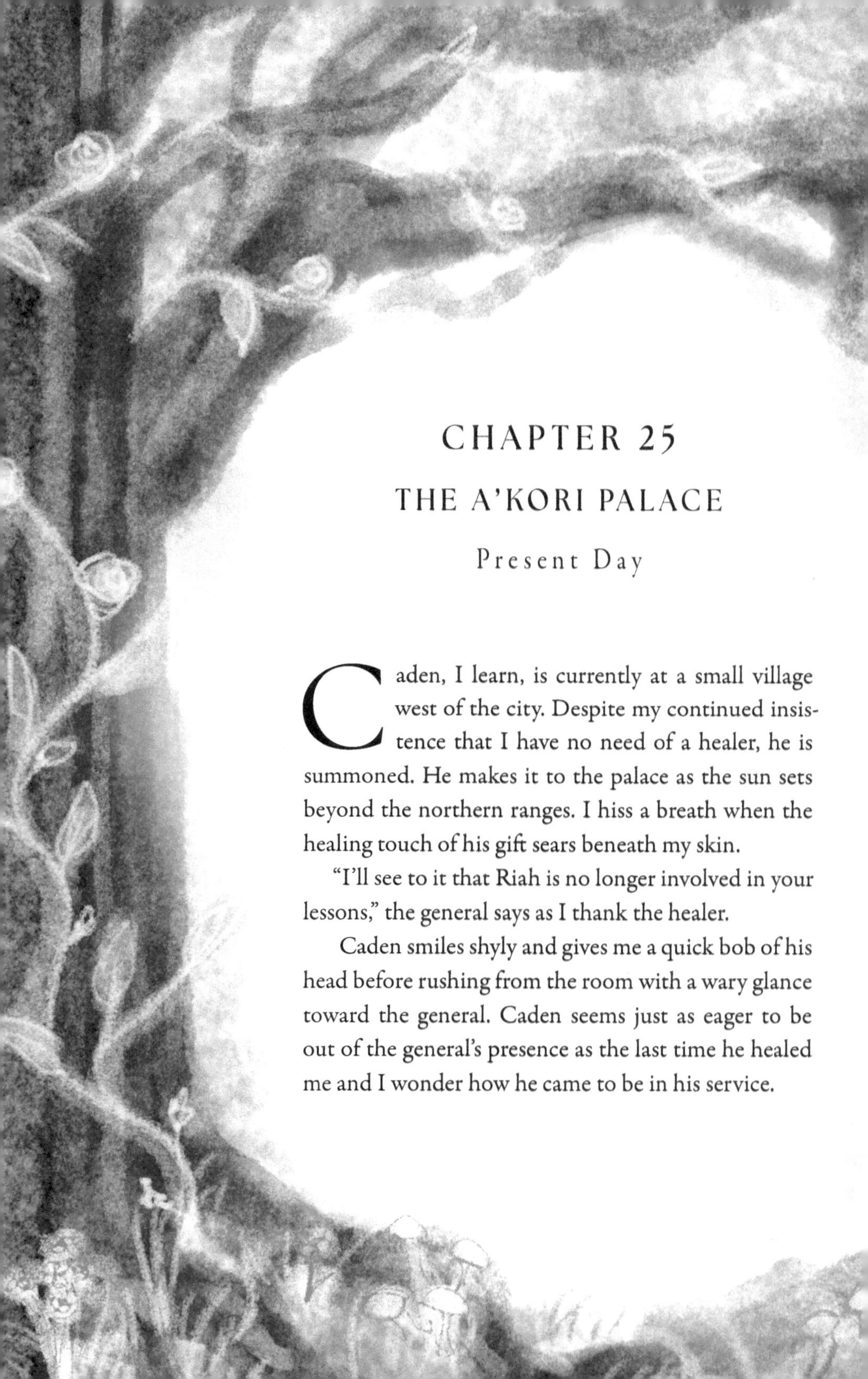

CHAPTER 25
THE A'KORI PALACE
Present Day

Caden, I learn, is currently at a small village west of the city. Despite my continued insistence that I have no need of a healer, he is summoned. He makes it to the palace as the sun sets beyond the northern ranges. I hiss a breath when the healing touch of his gift sears beneath my skin.

"I'll see to it that Riah is no longer involved in your lessons," the general says as I thank the healer.

Caden smiles shyly and gives me a quick bob of his head before rushing from the room with a wary glance toward the general. Caden seems just as eager to be out of the general's presence as the last time he healed me and I wonder how he came to be in his service.

"Did you really expect me to walk away from a training session completely unscathed?" I ask incredulously.

He gives me a look that tells me that is *exactly* what he thought.

"You did. Didn't you? That's why you sent me with Awri." I laugh. "I'll admit, I expected a feyn who fought in the war to put up more of a fight."

"Awri never fought in the war," he says matter-of-factly.

A puzzled expression forms on my face as I say, "She told me herself that she was in Brax during the war."

"She was, but not for the reasons you might think." He takes my chin and rotates my face, checking over Caden's work, though I have no doubt he decided before allowing the healer to leave the room that his work was adequate.

"Then, what was she doing in the south?" I ask.

His jaw stiffens as his eyes land on mine. I try to make my answering smile reassuring. The last thing I need is the general to assume I'm fishing for information.

"Sometimes it's easy to forget that right now I'm the enemy," I say.

Really, I have always been the enemy, unbeknownst to them. But with the recent landing of the warship, I have no doubt that they will have to draw firmer lines.

"*You* are not the enemy," he insists, "I'm just not sure you know that yet."

I should be proud that I've deceived him so thoroughly, but it isn't pride that swells inside of me when he says it.

He cups my jaw, swiping his thumb across my cheek affectionately when he asks, "Have you reconsidered my offer?"

"Not really," I admit.

What I've always loved about sparring, in addition to the release it provides that temporarily rids me of my demon, is the simple fact that in the ring, everything else fades away.

He nods. "I can speak with Awri. You can stay in her room if you prefer."

I stuff down a cringe. She'd already begun to bruise when the general pulled me out of the ring and it seems unlikely she will enjoy sharing a room with me once the pain really sets in. The general also implied she is sharing a bed with someone. Both very good reasons not to interrupt her evening.

"Caden is on his way to heal her now," he says. And I'm sure the words are

meant to be a comfort, but they only serve as a reminder that when I let my guard slip, I'm far too easy for the general to read.

He begins to draw away, taking my silence and hesitation for my answer. I surprise myself when my arm shoots out and I grip his wrist, holding his hand where it still rests on the line of my jaw. My lips curve up at the end, pleased with the shocked look on his face when he notes the reaction.

"You said no expectations," I remind him, and myself, of his promise.

"No expectations," he agrees, "If you want to talk, we will talk. If you want to sleep, we will sleep." He tips his head down until his lips brush against my own when he speaks the last, "If you desire more, it will be my pleasure to serve at your every whim."

There is time for me to push away, time for me to refuse him. But not enough time to think about the consequences and all that can go wrong before he leans in and captures my mouth with his. His hand cups the back of my neck and I part my lips in offering, an offering he's eager to accept, caressing my tongue with his own.

He doesn't press for more, and maybe I wish he would when his lips reluctantly leave mine. I should be relieved. I know I should. I would be wise to lead the male on with nothing but crumbs until I end his king and board a ship home. Now, with his encouragement that I train, I have no need of the male to keep my demon from painting the fabric of my dreams.

"I prepared a bath for you," the general says, and I quirk an eyebrow at him. "I thought you might like to wash after your lesson."

He isn't wrong. A bath always sounds like bliss after a hard day of training, I've just rarely had the opportunity to indulge.

The air is thick with fragrant steam when he leads me into the washroom, my hand in his. The pungent haze swirls about when he closes the door behind us, keeping it contained.

"Is that jasmine?" I almost moan out the question.

"It is," he says, standing behind me, working at the clasps of my cuirass.

Pink petals litter the bath, swept in lazy circles by the churning current. When he pulls the leather from my chest I suck in a deep lungful of air, my body relieved from the weight and its constriction.

The general takes a knee, unlacing my boots. The act utterly unnecessary

and completely intoxicating. I can't help but marvel at the view, wondering just how few he has taken a knee for in his long life. He strips them from my calves, throwing them toward the door as he raises himself to stand in front of me.

I'm sure I'm a mess. Dress plastered to my torso by dry sweat. Hair filled with a fine layer of dust and more than a little dirt on my face. None of that stops his gaze from tracing the lines of my figure appreciatively, lingering on the swell of my breasts before rising to my lips and falling on my eyes.

"Would you like company?" he asks.

My stomach dips and my eyes flick to the tub. It's certainly large enough for two, maybe even five or six. But what is he really asking?

"Just company?"

"You decide, *mi'ajna*. Just tell me what you want."

Mi'ajna. I swallow the words, pointed barbs that tear at my heart before sinking to my gut. With great effort, I force my mind to shed the weight of every thought that threatens to consume me. Instead, I focus on this moment and all that the male before me is offering.

I decide? I decide that I'm a coward. The idea of baring my body to him is the sole reason I want to decline. What appeal could there be in my weak mortal form when any number of females, boasting the ethereal beauty of the feyn, will gladly fall into his bed. Yet more than his words ever could, his eyes tell me that there is plenty he finds alluring, feyn or not, and I muster my resolve.

He is offering to give me something, anything, certainly more than I even know. I tell myself that despite my morning of sparring I should take him up on his offer, just to be safe. It's a selfish lie, but if I'm going to be sleeping in the male's chamber, I need to be more cautious than ever about keeping my demon in check. A weak excuse, between Kishek's brew and the privilege of sparring in the mornings, but one I latch onto desperately.

I lift his tunic over his head, letting it fall to the floor in answer. He hooks the waist of my leathers with a finger and tugs me closer, loosening the laces and falling back to his knees as he peels them off my legs. Rising slowly, his hands snake up my calves in unison, onto the curve of my thighs, over my hips, and past my waist. Slipping beneath my dress they follow my sides, up my neck, bunching the fabric over my head, the dress falling into a pile of silk at my feet.

My cheeks heat under the intensity of his gaze, the blush growing deeper when he speaks in a reverent tone. "The fates must favor me."

His voice is full of awe, and it's a wonder to me that something as simple as the female form could inspire such a thing in the male. My hands begin to shake when I loosen the laces of his leathers in turn, and he steps out of them with ease. I'm careful to keep my eyes on his face, sure I'll lose my nerve if my glance strays lower than the muscular lines chiseled into his hips.

Taking my hand, he leads me down four marble steps carved beneath the surface of the water. The water ripples at my belly when my feet land on the floor of the bath, lapping against my breasts and pebbling my nipples. The bottom of the tub slopes gently beneath my feet, growing deeper toward the cascade of water gushing from between two thick golden veins imbedded in the stone.

The general leads me toward the flowing water and all I want in the world right now is to sink beneath the surface and soak in the heat. He seems to have other ideas about how I will spend my time here when he pulls the tie from my wild mane and unplaits it with surprising ease. He tips me back until my loose spirals are drenched in the deluge of hot water spurting from the wall. The male obviously has no clue how long it will take to dry.

Before I have a chance to so much as glare at him, he's working a delicious botanical lather against my scalp, and I moan, "Stars."

I close my eyes, enjoying the feeling of his fingers against the nape of my neck, thumbs at my temples, his large hands cradling my head. He seems content to work the tonic deep into my roots until every last bubble is popped and spent. I don't try to stop him. I don't say a word. I'm not sure I could if I tried.

The only sounds coming from my mouth, inaudible sighs and throaty purrs of pleasure. Coating my hair in a rich cream with the same exuberance he'd washed it, a breathy chuckle escapes his lips as he says, "The noises you make."

"Don't get used to it." I'm not sure if I'm telling him or myself, as I rinse and wring my hair, fastening the locks in a loose pile on top of my head.

He hums under his breath, drawing me back to sit between his legs when he takes a seat on the stone ledge hidden beneath the ripples.

"And what if I'd like to hear those noises every night?" he says into my ear as he palms my back with a thick cake of floral soap, digging his thumbs in and working the knots at the base of my neck.

"Fates," I groan.

If I ever had doubts about the capabilities of the male's hands, they are all laid to rest the moment he begins patiently kneading the tight muscles between my shoulders, turning them into well churned butter. Another moan slips past my lips.

This is it. The moment I can die happy.

His lips brush the shell of my ear when he whispers, "Keep making those noises, and I'll need to excuse myself."

My stomach flutters, my core tightening with a flex when I feel the firm press of his desire against my back. His hands make their way to the dimples above my backside, and I find myself wishing for the devotions of those talented fingers elsewhere. He had, after all, made it clear that he is more than willing to offer whatever ministrations I choose to allow.

Leaning my head back to rest against his shoulder, I twine his fingers with my own and lead his hand to the tender pink flesh at the center of my breast. Pulling my body against his, he moans at the press of my ass against his length. When his free hand stills, hesitating on my thigh, I open my legs—the invitation taken the moment I part for him. His thumb rounds that sensitive bundle of nerves and I suck in a breath that gets trapped in my lungs.

My hands latch onto his thighs, and my stomach contracts. The promise of my release already swelling inside me, but it's too soon, and I want more. When he pinches the supple flesh of my nipples and I recall the way his tongue felt on my breast, the way his fangs grazed my flesh, I break from his hold and spin to face him. I'm not eager to chase after my pleasure so quickly.

The look he gives me is pensive and unsure, until I seat myself on his lap, straddling his thighs. His jaw bounces at the end and he palms the globes of my ass, pulling me against him. I release a sigh when that little nub of aching flesh is pressed against the firm proof of his longing. I rock my hips, gliding myself up and down his length, the torturous build of my release beckoning me, begging for more. I press against him harder and shudder as I writhe along his shaft.

"Foc," he groans. And there is a deadly promise behind the male's eyes when he says, "I intended tonight solely for your pleasure, but if you keep that up, I'm not sure how the evening will end."

The longing in his voice is enough to send me over the edge. I quaver a moan, peaking near his base. When I'm too caught up in my own release to continue, his hand moves between my legs, and he works me through every blissful tremor until my body stills. Too soon, it's over. I should have drawn it out. I could have. I think.

His hand cups me between my legs and he slides a finger into my folds as his breath tickles my ear. "I want to taste you."

"What?" I ask, my eyes dragging along the pointed tips of his fangs.

Another finger flicks at my overstimulated nub and I gasp.

"Let me taste you."

It isn't a demand, and I have no idea what he's asking for, but when he strums that sensitive mound of flesh again, I moan and nod. I regret the loss of his hand between my thighs immediately. Why am I agreeing to anything that stops the male from continuing in his pursuit of my pleasure? Before I know what's happening, he hooks my legs around his waist and walks us out of the pool, into the swirling mist of the washroom, his rigid length pressed between his belly and my core.

Setting me on the stone vanity he pins me with a heated stare. His lips fall against my own, his tongue flicking against them, needy and demanding. I open for him, caressing his tongue with mine. His fingers twine among the spirals of my hair, loosening the bind until the strands fall to sweep against my lower back.

His mouth drops to my neck, then my breast. My nipple teased, first by his tongue and then, by the edge of a sharp fang. I gasp in want and longing when I feel the tip of his length teasing my entrance. He brings his hips forward, brushing his shaft over that bundle of nerves, watching me quiver before sliding his hand up my belly and between my breasts, pushing me down onto my back.

Every drop of blood in my body rushes to my cheeks when he hooks my knees over his shoulders and his eyes rake across every inch of my bare flesh. His gaze falls between my legs and he goes completely still. His face a mixture of reverence and need that I can hardly stomach, much less understand. When I think it's too much, and that maybe this has all been a horrible idea, he leans down and kisses my belly. My stomach flutters.

His fangs graze the flesh of my thigh, followed by the swipe of his tongue. Every press of his lips chasing after the searing ache his fangs leave in their wake. And then, the heat of his breath is on my core, his tongue licking greedily.

I gasp, my body tensing involuntarily as I shudder. His tongue swipes at the wet heat of my passion, lapping me up like the male is dying of thirst, and I, the only oasis in his desert. His tongue moves north, and I moan when he sucks and flicks at that little bud of nerves. My back arches off the marble, fingers weaving into his hair, and my breath gets caught in my lungs when his tongue thrusts into my core. My body clenches around him and he moans into my depths, pleased by my response to his devotions.

When his tongue flattens, dragging itself north again with the agonizing promise of ecstasy, I begin to come undone. My fingers tighten in his hair as the tension builds. My breath quickens and when his tongue flicks against me again I tremble out my release in a deep contented sigh, my back arching off the marble. His tongue works me through every jolting wave that flows through my body and when I fall slack against the stone beneath me, he lands a gentle kiss on that tender, sensitive mound of flesh that tightens my core as I tremble.

I don't blame him for the self-satisfied look he wears when he leans down, giving me a chaste kiss. But I don't want chaste, and my tongue laps up the glistening proof of my fulfilled desire on his lips. He devours me and I moan into his mouth, tasting my passion on his tongue. I'm pleased when he deepens the kiss, willing to give me everything I ask for in this moment.

My stomach dips when his tip bumps against my entrance. His lips break from my own and he searches my eyes.

Sitting on the edge of the vanity with the male between my legs I tell myself not to look down. What's between his legs is none of my business. Is it? It could be. Still. I shouldn't.

I do.

My eyes widen. Not altogether unpleased by what I see, but I have no idea how the male can possibly expect it to fit anywhere inside my body. Not that I have any intention of letting him try. When my gaze wanders back to

his, I'm sure my cheeks are an unknown shade of crimson, and I look away. He just witnessed my obvious perusal of his malehood and he looks perfectly smug about what I've seen.

Gripping my chin, he brings my eyes back to his, gesturing to his body when he says, "This belongs to you. So, look as much as you like, and touch, whenever it pleases you."

My head is spinning at the declaration when he wraps a decadently plush towel around my shoulders, tying another at his waist. I pluck pink petals from my loose spirals as I brush out my hair and the general opens a large window, letting the fragrant steam filling the room waft out into the night.

He shows me to a large closet, tucked back on the far side of the washroom, twice the size of my old room in La'tari. Maybe I should be mad when I see that he's already taken the liberty of bringing a few of my dresses, but the gesture is thoughtful, if not a bit bold. I slip on a coal-colored gossamer sleeping gown and a thin scrap of lace to cover my core. In my own chamber, alone, I would have forgone it, but to crawl into bed without it tonight feels a little too much like tempting fate.

By the time I make it into the bedroom, the only light left is cast by the crackling fire. The general is crouched before it in a long pair of dark linen pants, hanging loose at his hips. His chest is bare, the flickering light from the flames embellishing the hard cut of his muscles. But it is the fea oaths, bound to his flesh in dark bands along his side and down his arm, that hold my attention.

There is a slight tick in his jaw when he rises to greet me, planting a tender kiss on my temple as he asks, "Are you ready for bed?".

"Bed?" I wonder at the implications, my eyes gliding across the dark silk sheets on the oversized mattress. "Are you joining me?" I ask, altogether unprepared for his answer.

"Would you like that?" he asks, brushing a fine curl from my eyes.

"Yes," I answer without thinking.

What am I doing?

It's not a lie, but I should be giving everything more thought. It's not unreasonable to assume I may regret every decision I've made here tonight.

"Thank the stars," he says, puffing out a breath of relief. "If I ever thought

I was strong, watching you sleep when you could have been in my arms was a greater test of strength than I ever endured before."

Odd.

I shouldn't, but I take his hand and he grips it tightly as I lead him to the foot of the bed. I crawl across the top of the silky duvet, realizing too late the view I'm offering the hungry male staring at my backside. It seems a mighty feat for the general to break his stare, but he manages with a clenched jaw. The bed dips when he crawls in beside me.

Between the heat still spilling in from the washroom and the fire, it's too warm to crawl under the covers, so I fall onto my belly when I reach the head of the bed. My body exhausted, pleasurably and otherwise, my eyes flutter shut, only to pop open the next second when he takes my hand and places it on his chest. His hand curls over mine, my fingers cupped around his thumb, and he breathes in contentedly, closing his eyes.

My gaze lingers on the male curiously until his breathing becomes deep and even. His hair parts around the nick in his ear, likely a battle wound from long ago. A small raven strand curls at the end where it falls in front of his eyes. The tension in his face relaxes and my lips kick up at the edges when I see that even in his sleep the male frowns with a pinched brow. He's handsome, so much more than I let myself admit before. And he's mine. Or so he claims.

Why? What have I done to garner his affections? I'll add it to my growing list of questions I will never have a chance to ask, things I will leave these shores without knowing. I can never be his. Not in this life, not with my mission.

Our paths will collide, but not in the way the stories describe when fated lovers meet beneath the stars. Ours is to be a very different story, one only partially told, but I know how it ends, how we end.

You'll already hate me for this. The words echo, twisting like a dagger that I can't seem to dislodge from my heart. I push them down, sealing them off with the rest of the memories I tried to leave aboard that ship. I would sink them if I could. Send them off to settle at the bottom of some dark abyss where they would never reach my ears, and the memories never cross my mind.

Pain. Regret. That is all I will be for the general at the end. A hateful memory that he will do anything to tear from the fabric of his mind. A mistake. That is all I will ever be to anyone.

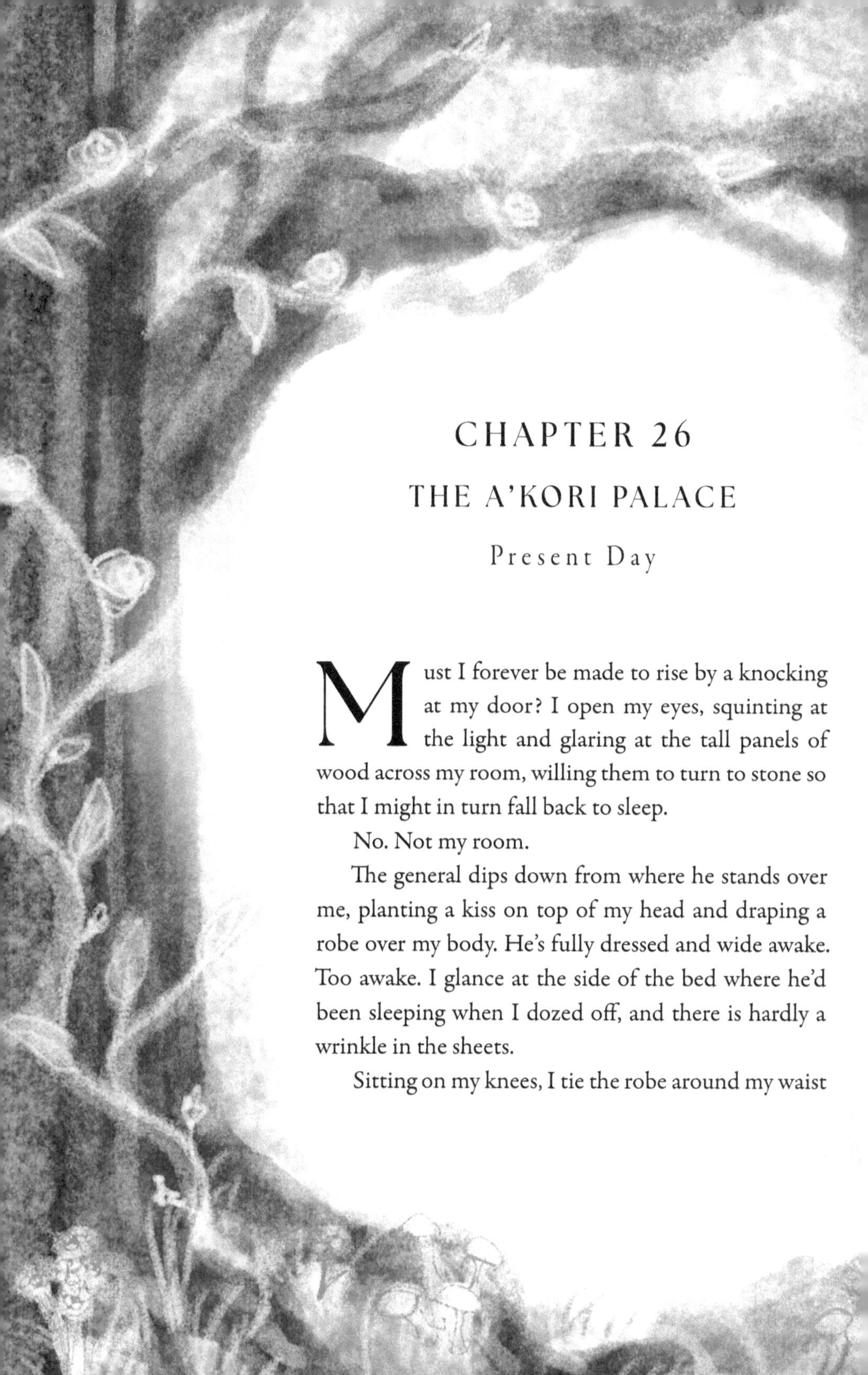

CHAPTER 26
THE A'KORI PALACE
Present Day

Must I forever be made to rise by a knocking at my door? I open my eyes, squinting at the light and glaring at the tall panels of wood across my room, willing them to turn to stone so that I might in turn fall back to sleep.

No. Not my room.

The general dips down from where he stands over me, planting a kiss on top of my head and draping a robe over my body. He's fully dressed and wide awake. Too awake. I glance at the side of the bed where he'd been sleeping when I dozed off, and there is hardly a wrinkle in the sheets.

Sitting on my knees, I tie the robe around my waist

as I stifle a yawn. I smile sleepily at Riah when she walks in, ushered into the war room by the general. The female goes ashen, her eyes bulging when she sees me. Despite the blows exchanged between us, it is certainly not the greeting I expect, and I frown when I lose sight of her beyond the doors.

I thought we got on rather well.

Wiping the sleep from my eyes, I tip my head toward the door. Even with it closed I can hear the general's voice rising behind the thick hardwood. I only catch a few words, but it's clear she's taking a verbal lashing over my unnecessary visit with Caden last night. The female had only done what Awri asked of her, and I had been more than a little willing to go along with it. I don't tell my feet to move, they just do. I'm in the war room a moment later with a stunned and still pale Riah, an angry general standing across from her.

"Is there something you need, *mi'ajna?*" he asks.

Riah groans, and I think her eyes are about to roll into the back of her head. The female doesn't seem the type to faint, but whatever he'd said to her before my arrival is certainly testing that theory.

"I just came to see what time Riah would like to meet for our morning training sessions," I say, as if it's the most natural thing in the world.

"The *lieutenant* will not be—"

"Is seven too early?" I ask and she gapes when I ignore the general's interjection. "Perhaps the afternoon would be better for you?"

"Would you mind giving us the room, Lieutenant?" The general forces a level voice when he says it.

She jumps at the general's command, keeping her eyes on the floor as she shuffles into the main room, shutting the door behind her.

He flicks an invisible speck of dust from his tunic and tips my chin up with a single finger until I'm staring up into a sea of deep blue eyes and says, "No."

The command should annoy me, should chafe against my bullheaded nature, but the word only makes my core go molten beneath the male's demanding gaze.

"I'll find someone else to teach you," he says, as if that will be the end of it.

"Someone less skilled," I say, tearing my chin from him in annoyance.

His jaw ticks. "Someone who won't send you back to me broken."

"It was hardly a scratch," I say and he huffs at the declaration while I continue to argue. "And I like her."

"You *like* Riah?" He gapes. "You hold a knife to my throat when I try to help you, but the female gives you a black eye and you *like* her?"

"*She* wasn't trying to undress me," I say with a pointed stare.

"I was saving your life," he growls.

Clearly, he isn't over it.

"So is she, by training me," I bite back, "But she can't if you won't let her."

He looks like his teeth might crack under the pressure of his jaw when I temper my stance and take his hand in mine.

"Please, Xeyvian."

I thought he might be softened by my plea, but I'm wrong. His eyes are pure desire when he lifts me onto the war table. Scattering wooden ships and infantry across the maps of Terr, he presses in between my legs, and his mouth is on mine the next second.

The passionate heat of his lips. The handful of hair he grasps at the back of my head. The press of his body against mine. The male is practically feral. He breaks the kiss, and I pull a deep breath, my heart thundering in my chest.

"Say it again," he says.

I swallow the lump in my throat. "Please."

He smiles, shaking his head. "The other part."

Now I understand what lit the fire in him. What it is he wants from me. I brush my lips against his when I repeat his name in a breathy whisper. "Xeyvian."

He swallows the sound, his tongue delving in long sweeps like he's memorizing the curve of my lips, the shape of my mouth. He wraps me up in his arms, his fingers a tangled mess in my black curls as he drinks me in. A sharp fang nips at my bottom lip, and I smile against his mouth.

Coming up for air, he rests his forehead against mine and sighs deeply. All the fight is gone from the male when he says, "No earlier than eight. I want you in my bed until then."

I nod, and nothing in the world can remove the smile from my face when he drops a kiss on the tip of my nose and heads for the door. He calls the lieutenant in and her eyes flick to where I'm sitting on the table, the scattered remnants of the A'kori military at my back.

"Have Seke cover your morning tasks," he orders, "You will be training with Shivaria moving forward."

She nods dutifully, and just when the color returns to her face the general takes a heated step toward her and warns, "Careful with her, Riah."

I roll my eyes. The male must think I'm made of glass.

"As you say, General." She salutes.

She's gone the second she's dismissed, replaced almost immediately by Riesh and Kishek. The circles under Kishek's eyes continue to darken and if he wasn't feyn I would be worried. Though, with what little I really know about the feyn maybe I should still be concerned.

Awri collects me not long after, her face as drawn as her brother's, but still, they both look better than Kishek. The grounds are quiet this morning, and my friend tells me that many of the guards have been dispersed in pursuit of the La'tari crew. She says there have been whispers of sightings near town, but so far, all of their searching has left them empty-handed.

The breeze coming in from the harbor is absent its normal morning chill, and the blue sky overhead brings with it the promise of warm summer days soon to come. Flittering birdsong fills the air with merriment, and my friend could not look less cheerful as she trudges along beside me.

"Is everything all right?" I ask, knowing it's a silly question.

She fails to muster a convincing smile when she nods. My brow pinches and she lets the façade fall with a sigh when I stare back at her in disbelief.

"Kishek," she admits.

"Is he all right?"

"He will be." She says it like a warning to the fates to let it be so. "He's never known when to quit."

"Sounds like a rather feyn trait, present company included," I say, giving her a friendly nudge with my shoulder as the stables come into view.

I cringe when her frown only deepens and she says, "Being difficult to kill does have a tendency to skew your idea of what you consider dangerous. Centuries go by, and it's easy to begin testing mortality. Millennia pass and maybe you begin to believe you truly are immortal. And then something happens to remind you that somewhere, unseen, is a tiny thread, an invisible line woven by the fates that marks the end."

Riah comes into view when we round the last of the wild hedges that border our path. She paces the ring, hands clasped behind her back, a strong

muscle bouncing at the edge of her jaw. It appears the presence of the warship is weighing even more heavily on the A'kori military than I first thought.

"I've never been much for consoling or giving advice," I tell my friend, "But I will say that it isn't a purely feyn trait to need to be reminded of your own mortality."

I shiver off the memory of icy water entering my lungs as a hand wraps around my ankle to pull me into the depths.

I continue, "Perhaps humans don't need to be reminded as often because our lives are already so short by comparison, but it really is the knowledge of our own fragility that makes the rest of life so sweet."

She hums thoughtfully as I clasp the wooden border of the ring and leap over it. Riah raises an eyebrow, and I make a mental note to use the gate next time.

"Will you be training with us today, Awri?" the lieutenant asks.

When she doesn't answer right away, I look over my shoulder to find her contemplating.

"If it makes any difference to you, training always helps me clear my head," I say.

She takes a deep breath, nods firmly, and rushes toward the stables to change.

"Who was it that saw to your training in La'tari?" Riah asks.

My head whips back to the lieutenant to find her eyes narrowed on me.

"A friend of my father's. A soldier who retired after the war." The lie slides off my tongue with ease.

"A soldier?" she balks, and I wonder if I'd been too sloppy with my form for the tale to be convincing.

The air leaves my lungs in a forced exhale when her fist strikes out toward my heart. It's a killing blow, if thrown hard enough. The force of the impact interrupting the natural rhythm of the heart can stop it altogether, ending your opponent before the fight even begins. The attack is pure Drakai, and she delivers it perfectly—her stance, the curve of her elbow, a flawless portrait that even Bront would applaud. She only makes a single error, and it has nothing to do with her form. The mistake is her choice of target.

For every deadly strike crafted by the Drakai there is an equally lethal counter. I shift my body, just enough to let the blow glance off my chest as I step into her, throwing a fist to her ribs. It's a reflex, one I'd been taught

in order to survive. The return strike will break a rib when landed correctly, often puncturing the lung. A sure death sentence on the battlefield.

My fist connects with a thin plate of steel hidden beneath her leathers. My hand crumbles, pain igniting every nerve and scrap of flesh like an arching bolt of lightning.

"Foc!" The scream slips past my lips unsummoned when Riah clasps my broken hand in hers.

The pain of every fracture is dimmed by the scorching agony of her healing gift as it knits me back together. I glare at the female warily when she slips a sheet of metal out of her leathers and throws it out of the ring. It isn't large, little more than the size of my fist. She knew where I would strike her.

"Your teacher was Drakai, wasn't he?" she asks, brows high on her forehead.

We both know it isn't really a question. The female baited me into revealing myself in a manner worthy of applause.

"You should have told me when we were training yesterday," she says.

"It didn't seem relevant," I say, my eyes on the floor of the ring.

"*Krakenhisht,*" she says. "You are more skilled than you led me to believe. Why?"

"It felt like a safe choice. Ever since the warship landed, all I am to every soldier I pass by is La'tarian. The enemy." A small amount of truth to better hide the lies.

"But you aren't *just* La'tarian. You belong to the general," she says quizzically.

"I do not *belong* to the general," I say through clenched teeth, bristling at her assumption that because she'd seen me in his bed, I am the male's property.

Her eyebrows hit her hairline, but she seems to accept my position and every explanation I've given her when the tension leaks out of her shoulders. She swipes her hand along the side of her head, running her fingers through her hair, and looses a breath. Looking down at my hand, I flex it, then ball it into a fist to test its function.

"Why did the general call for Caden yesterday if you are a healer?" I ask.

"My gift only works on bone," she explains, her eyes lingering on the fist at my side.

I catch sight of Awri running toward us, dressed in a full set of leathers, some of the melancholy already gone from her face. I step aside when she enters and takes determined strides toward Riah. The lieutenant doesn't attempt to correct her form. She just stands in the center of the ring stoically, blocking every blow Awri throws as she releases whatever she has bottled up inside.

Once Awri is spent and her brow no longer pinched down in a forlorn frown, I take her place. It doesn't take Riah long to get a truer estimation of my skill. She flows through a series of strikes and kicks I learned as a child. Each one I deflect is followed by another, slightly more difficult to evade, until I feel as if I am home, repeating my drills with Bront.

It's a relief when Sera arrives with a basket of fresh fruits and a stack of thick sandwiches for lunch. Though it's a feat to convince Riah to sit on the floor of the ring and join us for the meal. My tongue works around a mouthful of berries when an attractive male with long brown curls and blue eyes passes nearby. Awri and I share a smile when his lips curve up on one side and he winks at Riah.

"Your mate?" Awri inquires boldly.

Riah shakes her head, smiling at him as he disappears around the side of the stables. "Just a male I exchange pleasure with."

"In what way?" I ask, blood pooling in my cheeks when they both look at me curiously.

"The usual way I suppose," she laughs, before taking a bite of her sandwich.

She doesn't seem the least bit deterred by my question, so I risk another.

"You said you *exchange* pleasure. What is it you do for him?" It isn't until the words fully exit my mouth, that I feel how entirely awkward they are.

"Does that mean you've changed your mind about Xeyvian?" Awri asks, clearly surprised.

I'm not sure I want to go into detail explaining just how stupendously I'd fallen for Siserie's deception or how she was the sole reason I denied him.

So, all I say is, "I'm not sure."

"About which part?" Awri asks.

"All of it," I say.

I mean every word when it passes my lips and in the same moment realize they aren't true. I *have* reconsidered him and even though I tell myself it is all for duty, for my purpose, there is no denying my desire. Desire for myself *and* fulfillment of his own. And why shouldn't there be? It changes nothing.

"That's a lie," I admit, and Awri side-eyes me as she pulls a slice of cheese from her sandwich and pops it in her mouth. "I have reconsidered him."

The words are a torrent, released from the dam of my mind as I explain everything. The moment I'd gone to accept him, finding Siserie, when he'd taken me to his chambers in the middle of the night, and when he'd learned of my run-in with the female the next morning.

"He told her he would bind her and ship her to La'tari?" Awri asks, gaping at me.

"I hope you won't be offended when I say that I sincerely hope she crosses you again so that I have the pleasure of seeing her shipped south," Riah says with a snort, and I decide that I really do like the female.

"I'm inclined to agree," Awri chimes in, "after watching her chase after Xey for my entire life. As if he would ever consider her."

"Why wouldn't he?" I ask. "She is exceptionally beautiful."

"No lovelier than you," Awri says, and I gloss over the lie.

As much as I'm sure she's just trying to reassure me, I've never been vain enough to require flattery.

"And the female is an absolute snake, just like her sister," she continues, "She's the last feyn on the continent I'd trust with the king. I'm sure Xey feels the same."

If he does feel that way, then they are both wrong on that account. If they really knew me, Siserie would be second on that list.

I bite into a juicy apple when Awri asks around a mouthful of food, "Do you remember Ishara?"

I nod, but unlike the memory I'm sure my friend summoned, the day I met the female in the dressmaker's shop is not what comes to mind. It is her voice, calling after me when I jumped from her balcony.

"Siserie and Ishara are sisters," she explains.

I've heard of sibling rivalry, and though I wasn't raised with siblings, it's still hard to imagine why sisters would pursue the same male.

I'm trying to recall all that Awri said about their family when Kishek appears at the edge of the hedged road and she perks up with a smile. Discarding her lunch, she darts off to greet him and they disappear behind the dense bush.

Riah grins at me as she says, "The question you asked before, about pleasuring the male,"—I nearly choke on a fat thimbleberry—"I can tell you how, if you like?"

Before I know I've agreed, the female is weaving tales of long passionate nights that she's spent diligently engaged in just such a task. Exhaustive accounts of what she, in her long life, learned will bring a male to his knees. She is quite descriptive and while the lady I portray should shy away from such things, the inquisitive student I truly am hangs on every detail, supplying questions that will draw out the finer aspects of the acts she describes.

Her deep throaty laugh calls Awri back to the ring as I try to compose myself. I hack out the small sip of water I inhaled when she began to describe a long night she'd spent with not one, but two males. I'm still not sure how I would manage the general's thick length in any of the ways she described, let alone have another to contend with.

Kishek follows Awri back to where we sit with our mostly consumed meal. She is beaming, all the morning gloom shed in the ring, and perhaps behind the tall hedge where she'd lingered out of sight with the male by her side.

"What are you two talking about?" she asks with a suspicious smile.

I sputter the last of the water from my lungs, eyes watering, when Riah answers, "The art of war."

Kishek's mouth twists. "I'm not sure that is what the general had in mind for your lessons."

"Trust me," the lieutenant retorts with a wink, "The general will thank me later."

I slap her arm with the back of my hand and laugh. Not a small or forced laugh, but a laugh that makes your eyes glisten and your belly ache. A laugh that sears a happy memory into your mind. I laugh like I have rarely laughed before, my sides splitting at the look of pure confusion contorting the male's face.

The lieutenant jogs off with a wave when Kishek gathers up our picnic supplies and leads us to the palace. Awri apparently arranged for Adora to come for a final fitting before the masque, and I find that we have time to do little more than wash and dress in fresh clothes before she arrives.

Kishek waits in the main room of the general's chambers while I wash, and I smile when after a quick bath I find that the general had the rest of my

clothing brought over and hung in his closet. I pluck a colorful gown from the racks and a pair of matching pants sewn in a sheer beaded lace.

Adora sees to Awri's fitting in the privacy of her own chambers before coming to see to my own. She must be sure of her work when she binds my eyes with a thick black cloth, shielding the costume from my sight. I was wrong when I thought she would seek my approval of the gown. Instead, the female claims that while half the fun of the masquerade is revealing yourself to those in attendance, the other half lays in the anticipation of the event. She assures me that none of the ladies view their gowns until the evening of the party, and I suppose I can always discard it in lieu of a simple everyday gown if I feel it's necessary.

Awri stays with me until early evening, a stack of papers in her hands containing decisions and orders yet to be made for the party. She seems at home in the general's quarters, and I suppose she's spent many days in the war room with the others. She excuses herself when it grows dark, waving goodbye with assurances that she will continue training with me. I shouldn't press her about it, after all, she is well positioned to interfere on the king's behalf when the time comes and any skill she gains between now and then will only prove to hinder my task.

My companion is quickly replaced by an exhausted looking Riesh. He enters the room bearing a small plate stacked high with an overindulgent dinner. We sit by the fire and share the meal, the male explaining that the general is tied up in meetings of strategy.

"You are sure it was another La'tari ship they saw off the coast?" I ask, my eyebrows rising.

"I don't doubt the male who saw it, but no one else has seen the ship since it was first sighted," he explains.

It makes no sense. Why send a lone ship followed by another a few days later? There is no way to approach the shores of A'kori without being seen. Awri and I may have been the first to see the warship as it came into the bay, but more reports of the vessel came from many others, shortly after.

"What do the La'tari say?" I wonder.

"Their king claims to have no knowledge of the vessels."

Their king. A little slip on his part, but I don't correct him. Maybe they have begun to trust me more than I understand.

"And what do you think?" I ask.

He opens his mouth to reply, snapping it shut when the general's voice booms from behind the thick doors leading to the hall. He isn't alone, and whatever they are talking about, it's getting heated.

"Excuse me," Riesh says, lifting himself from the chair and sliding into the hall, the door clicking shut behind him.

I reach for a cup of robustly flavored tea, now unfortunately tepid. The click of the door latch sounds behind me, and a chill seeps into my bones. Setting the cup down before it has touched my lips, I casually stand, back stiff, forcing a façade of disinterest as my eyes survey the shadows. My feet move across the room in slow sure steps, the air exiting my lungs the only sound I hear above the argument rising in the corridor. Hair stands on the back of my neck, and I spin on my heel, too late.

"Scream and I'll end you," the stranger says.

The man holding the knife to my throat is pure La'tari. Waves of golden hair frame his face, and the rounded shell of his ear isn't the comforting sight it once would have been. For every step he takes forward, I take a step away, until my back is pressed against the tall wooden post at the corner of the bed. The tip of his knife pierces my flesh, coaxing a small drop of blood from my skin. The warm liquid flows down my neck to stain the fabric of my gown.

He's a middle-aged Drakai, judging by his leathers and the way he holds himself. With his free hand, he lifts my thick tresses, scoffing when his eyes land on the tips of my ears.

"You look like one of them," he spits the insult, "You might as well be, if you're focing one."

He steps in until his body is pressed against mine, tipping his head toward the door when he says, "Doesn't sound like they'll be coming in any time soon. Maybe I'll show you what you're missing while you're busy snubbing your own kind." He leans in close, his voice dropping to a whisper when he adds, "Before I leave you to bleed out on the floor."

His free hand fumbles with the laces of his trousers.

If I try to speak, I have no doubt the man will slit my throat rather than risk alerting the others. After all, I am not the reason he came. It's no

coincidence the man found himself in the general's room. And even if he would listen, what can I say? Very few know of my mission here.

I could disarm the man, grapple him into a hold and try to persuade him that we are on the same side. But my entire being rebels against the idea of letting him live. The man may wear the leathers of a Drakai, but his actions disgrace the name. The last merciful thought I have left for him is swallowed by my demon when he whispers the last, "I'll enjoy killing him as he watches you die."

A silence falls in the hall, as the general shouts an urgent command. As if in answer to the furnace of rage swelling inside me, Terr itself begins to shudder beneath my feet. It's too easy to disarm the man when he's distracted by the growing tremor of the land.

I grab his wrist, twist, and let the dagger fall into my free hand. Time seems to slow, and I grin, pleased with the shock overwhelming his features. He takes a step back, a mistake that will cost him his life. Not that he ever stood a chance of leaving the room alive. The simple move gives me the space I need to coil back and release a powerful kick to his chest, taking him off his feet.

The doors of the room groan and splinter in thundering cracks as the man falls against a small table, toppling a chattering vase that shatters on the floor around him. He hardly has time to collect himself before I'm sitting on him, his legs pinned between my thighs, his own knife flaying the tender flesh of his throat. His eyes bulge and my demon writhes at the sickening sound of the gurgling sputter I've heard almost every night for years.

Blood begins to fill the man's lungs, and I lean down, willing him to understand his offense before the light leaves his eyes.

"Threaten what is *mine*, and I will hunt your very soul beyond the gates of haliel."

The doors buckle and fly open, the shuddering of the earth ceasing as they slam against the walls with a force that cracks the marble. I pull the knife free of the man's throat, a warm spray of blood soaking the front of my gown as I look up, locking eyes with the general.

There are many things I expect to see on his face as he takes in the scene. Disgust, fear, caution, shock, but nothing prepared me for the look of concern when his eyes fall to mine, and the rage that follows when he takes in the body.

He moves across the room at a clipped pace, collecting me into his arms, shouting orders at the guards that file into the room behind him.

"Are you injured?" he asks, voice full of concern.

I barely hear him above the ringing in my ears and shake my head.

Riesh surveys the carnage with a clenched jaw, eyes wide. He dips his head at me approvingly before the general whisks me into the washroom, closing the doors behind us.

Time slips into a hazy semblance of what I know. My teeth begin to chatter. My body is wracked with tremors as if I'd been submerged in ice for hours. The general turns a lever on the wall and a gush of warm water flows from a spigot in the ceiling, falling on my head like thick drops of rain.

He peels the blood-soaked gown over my head, throwing it to the ground where it smacks against the floor. Discarding my pants, he pulls me under the water. He lathers a dark rag with a thick layer of soap and makes quick work of wiping every trace of blood from my skin.

Walking a small circle around me, he carefully checks every inch of my body. I bat him away when he begins to round me a second time. I'm not a child and do not need to be coddled by the male.

I snap up a jar of foaming cream and wash the blood from my hair, nearly dropping the jar when my hands begin to shake again. He makes no attempt to take over my task. He just stands back, giving me space to breathe, watching beneath a furrowed brow, his pants and tunic thoroughly soaked and clinging to his body.

I'm still filthy, I can feel it. I scour my body with another well-lathered cloth until the pale ivory of my skin begins to redden. Still filthy. I reach for another rag and he grips my wrist.

"Enough, *mi'ajna*."

I can't meet his eyes, can't stand the mournful tone of his voice. Pulling my wrist from his hand I pluck a large, folded towel off a nearby table and dry myself. He follows me into the closet, exchanging his wet clothes for a dry pair of loose linen pants and waits patiently while I change into a sleeping gown.

I walk past him into the main room, pausing under the arch of the door, glancing at the white stone floor where I left the body. Not a trace of the man remains. The shattered remnants of the toppled vase have been cleared from the room. Aside from the crack in the marble wall and the splintered wooden door closed to the corridor beyond, there is no sign of a struggle.

The general comes up beside me when my eyes linger on the ground where I left the bloody corpse. I killed one of my own people. For him. For the male beside me. I can lie and say it was for my own honor. Given the circumstances, no one would believe otherwise, but I know the truth.

I could have used this to my benefit. I could have helped him kill the male, taken out the general of the king's army, and all while maintaining the façade of my innocence. But I can't bring myself to regret the decision. I meant what I said, even now, and I would do far worse to anyone that tried to harm him. Even when I am willing to do more harm to the male than a dagger to the heart. At least he will live. I will see to it that he does.

"He came here to kill you," I say under my breath.

I brave a look at the general. His eyes are still soft and apprehensive as he nods.

"I couldn't let him," I admit.

The general nods again when he says, "I know."

How can he know? I hadn't known myself.

I stare at the vacant space on the floor, utterly unaware of the time that passes when the general takes my hand in his.

"Tell me what you need, *mi'ajna*."

How can I tell him what I need when I don't even know it myself. What do I need? The death of every assassin on that ship. The war ended. Peace between our kingdoms and a full belly for every starving soul on Terr. A safe home for the fea. How has everything gotten so complicated?

I don't have the words to begin to explain all that I need, and even if I did, they are things he can't give me. So, I lead him to bed and crawl beneath the covers. The general blows out the last of the flickering lights and crawls in beside me without a word.

I'm just getting settled in when his arm slides beneath me and he pulls me against him. He rests his chin on top of my head, and I press my nose into his chest, breathing him in. The tension leaks from my body the moment my lungs fill with the scent of citrus and cedar. I hadn't asked for this, but maybe he knew what I didn't. That this, this is what I need.

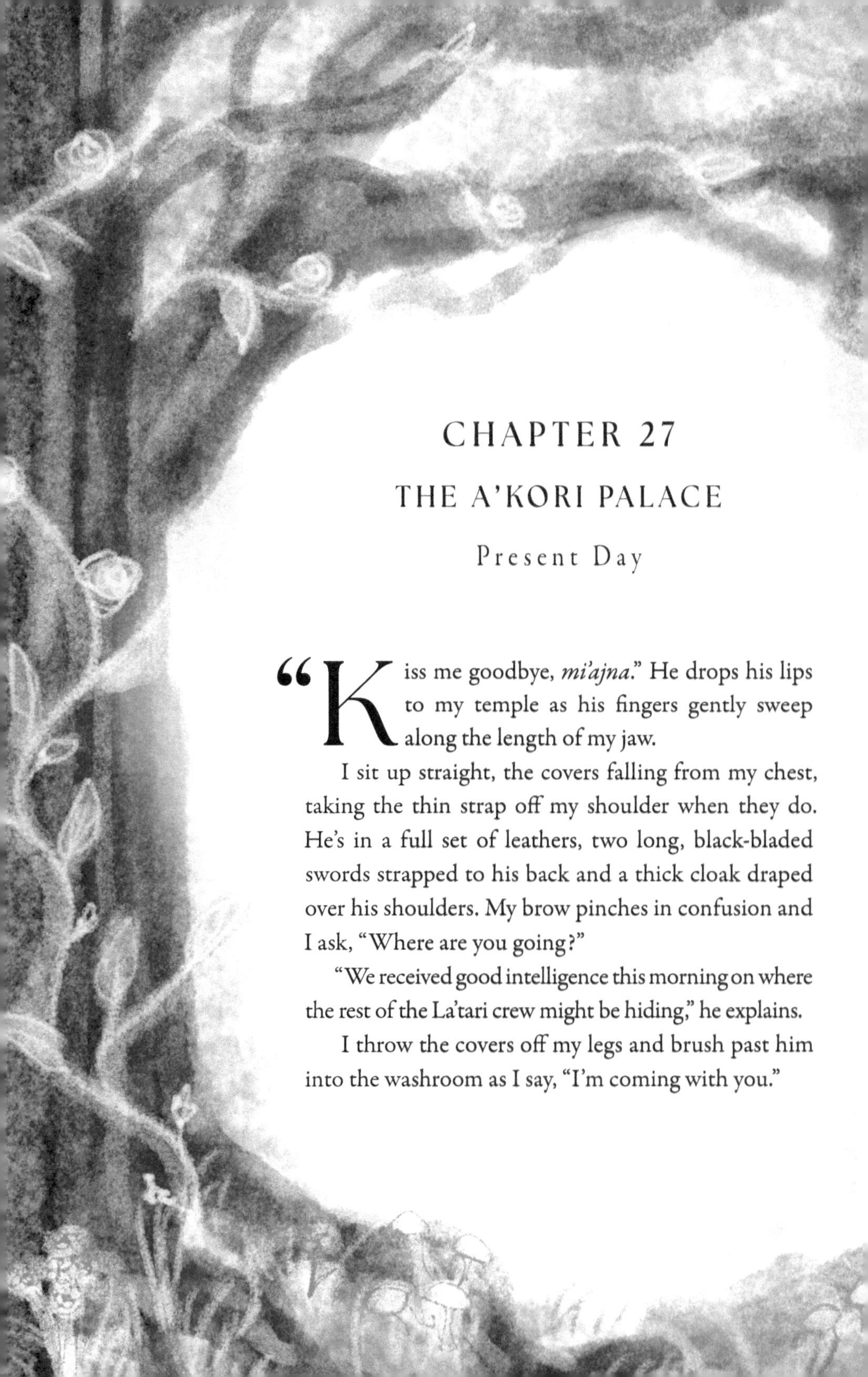

CHAPTER 27
THE A'KORI PALACE
Present Day

"Kiss me goodbye, *mi'ajna*." He drops his lips to my temple as his fingers gently sweep along the length of my jaw.

I sit up straight, the covers falling from my chest, taking the thin strap off my shoulder when they do. He's in a full set of leathers, two long, black-bladed swords strapped to his back and a thick cloak draped over his shoulders. My brow pinches in confusion and I ask, "Where are you going?"

"We received good intelligence this morning on where the rest of the La'tari crew might be hiding," he explains.

I throw the covers off my legs and brush past him into the washroom as I say, "I'm coming with you."

The male is going to get himself killed taking on two warships of Drakai. I don't let myself think too much about who might be on those ships and the La'tari lives I'm likely to end before this is over.

"No. You are not," he says, following after me.

I spit the last of the mint paste into the sink and rush for the closet to dress in my leathers.

"Shivaria, please. You have to stay here."

My pants are tied and I'm securing my cuirass over a dark dress when he makes it into the room behind me. I reach for my boots, glaring at the male when he snatches them from my hand, throwing them on the floor behind him.

He cups my face, his breath hot on my cheek when he says, "Please, stay here." My stomach twists at the plea in his voice. "For me, stay. I don't want you anywhere near them."

I *am* them.

I want to yell it. To make him understand just how horribly he has already underestimated the Drakai. There is every chance the information he received was leaked intentionally and he will be walking into a well-orchestrated trap.

But I can't tell him. Not without admitting who I am. *What* I am.

What am I doing? Ladies don't fight in wars. They don't murder would-be assassins who enter their chambers in the night. They certainly don't go running off after their generals to protect them.

I smooth the lines of my face and nod. "Of course. I'll stay."

"Don't do that," he says with a heavy sigh and shake of his head.

"What? You asked me to stay, and I'm saying I will." I fail to keep the heat of my temper from my voice.

"And I'm glad, because you'll be safer here. But don't pretend to be something you're not just to appease me. Stars help me, I love your fire. I love that you'd rather be by my side than wait idly by. But if you came, you'd only distract me from what I need to do."

I know what he is trying to say, but it doesn't make it any easier. So, I send him with a simple request. "Just be careful. Please."

He drops a kiss on my temple when he says, "I have something for you."

There's a sparkle in his eyes when he slips two black daggers out from the sleeves of his leathers. I've never seen their likeness.

The blades are slimmer than the ones I had before. And while the obsidian I'd become accustomed to was a flawless black, easy to conceal in the dark, these are something else altogether.

I pluck them out of his palms, slowly rotating them in front of my face as I examine them. The stone blades pull at the light in the room like they will draw the very flame inside and snuff us into darkness. Curious, I glance at the dark blades strapped to his back and find that they share the strange quality.

"They are carved from feynstone," he says.

"I thought feynstone was a myth?" The shock is clear in my voice.

"Rare, but not a myth."

He takes the daggers from my hands, sliding them into the discrete sheaths sewn into the leather at my outer thighs. They practically disappear from sight, so clever is the crafting, and my face stretches in a wildly amused smile.

"You seem to know your way around a blade," he says, "And I need you to be able to protect yourself. Even if I hope you'll never have to do it again."

I lift myself onto my toes and kiss the male, gripping his leathers and pulling his chest against mine. His hand cups the base of my neck and his thumb strokes my jaw tenderly. But it's his smile that catches my breath when I draw back. I've never seen the male smile like this before, and it pitches my stomach sideways, sending my heart into an offbeat rhythm.

My lips curve up in answer when I ask, "Why are you smiling like that?"

"It's the first time you've kissed me," he says.

I'm about to argue that I've kissed him many times when his meaning dawns on me. He's kissed me before, and I've returned the affection. Never have I gone to him with my lips in offering, in wanting and desire.

I crane my neck and look up at him and say with a grin, "Then come back to me quickly, so I can do it again."

He wraps my legs around his waist, pinning my back to the wall before I can take another breath. His mouth is on my neck, his hips rocking his length against my core. I don't think when my hand rushes between us and I unlace his pants.

He sucks in a breath when my hand slides down his shaft. He sighs at the contact and his mouth travels up my throat, along my jaw, and onto my lips.

I wrap a hand around his thickness, unable to close it fully as I stroke in a long, slow sweep, exploring the shape and length of his flesh.

Riesh bellows from the main room and Xeyvian's body stills against me. We linger on the precipice of ... something. Each unwilling to let this moment pass.

"I want you," I whisper.

A fist pounds on the washroom door and a muscle ticks in the general's jaw.

"When I return, *mi'ajna*. I will give you everything."

I reluctantly loose my hand from him and he sets me on my feet. There is a moment he hesitates, a moment he looks like he might tell his friend to go to haliel before taking me against the wall of the closet. Maybe I wish he would. The moment passes too quickly when he vanishes out of the room, his dark cloak trailing behind him.

"The foc happened to you two?" Riah barks from the ring.

We make a pitiful pair today, Awri and I. She looks so tired, always tired, and today she's worried as well.

"I heard the general left you in charge of babysitting," I quip, leaping into the ring.

She snorts a laugh. "If that's the case, then I think I envy the male his task."

Awri balks at the female. "You'd rather be raiding an inn full of Drakai than spending the day with us?" she says, throwing a hand against her heart dramatically.

"Yes," the lieutenant and I say in unison, and I can't help but crack a grin.

"No offense," I add when Awri glares at me.

Riah starts her warm-ups with Awri while I watch from the top rail of the fence.

"Did Riesh tell you how long they will be gone?" I ask.

"At least two days," Awri says, heaving a deep breath around her words.

Two days locked up in the palace will feel like an eternity. It's also far too long to be alone with my thoughts, considering the way I'd left things

with the general. I pinch the bridge of my nose. The things Riah explained to me are frightening enough. He promised me everything, and I hardly understand what that means.

No amount of sparring takes me from my thoughts today. Judging by the expression on my friend's face she's suffering a similar fate.

"Are you worried about Kishek?" I ask when we break for lunch.

"No. I mean, yes. But I'm also worried about Xey," Awri admits.

I suppress a shiver, goosebumps springing up along my arms when I ask, "Why would you be worried about him?"

Despite all my trepidation this morning, there is no question that the general of A'kori should be able to handle himself. Or at least be smart enough to know when to walk away.

She chews on her bottom lip and shakes her head, then bites into her sandwich. Chews. Swallows. Bites again.

"Awri, tell me," I demand.

"He's strong," she says, "and I know he'll be fine. I just don't like the idea of him going in there when his gift..."

I think I'm going to be sick, and I set down the cured meat I'd been eagerly indulging in when I ask pointedly, "What about his gift?"

I've never pressed any of them about their gifts, though, naturally, I've become more and more curious as to what exactly the general is capable of. It only makes sense that a male leading an army will have an incredibly powerful offensive gift. It is what I told myself upon his departure, to soothe the worry still lingering deep in my belly.

"You remember Niya?" she asks.

I only nod. I'm not sure how the female thinks there is any chance in haliel I could forget about the naiad who almost drowned me.

"She asked for a small part of his power in exchange for your life." She gnaws her lower lip when she says it and I wonder if the general would approve of her sharing the knowledge.

My jaw goes slack as her words set in, and I suppress every concern attempting to infiltrate my mind. I'm not sure if I'm more worried or annoyed at the male for being so rash in making the deal with the fea.

"How small?" I ask.

"Does it matter?" she says.

"No," I admit. "Will she return it?"

"Of course not." She looks confused that I've even asked.

"There must be a way to get it back," I insist, wondering if it would be wrong to suggest killing the naiad. Probably.

"Niya won't give up that kind of power, and it was a fair bargain so there really isn't anything that can be done," Awri says.

"But she could choose to give it up?" I press.

"She could, but I can't imagine what would tempt her. Naiads are protectors," she says and I huff a disbelieving laugh. Awri continues, "She has no value for gold, no need for food, or alliances."

"Can't the king make her give it back?" I ask. "If he allows the fea to live in the forest you'd think he would have some power over them."

It's Riah's turn to laugh. "*No one* has power over the fea."

"It's true," Awri agrees, "And even if he did, the king would never force any fea to give up what they'd fairly obtained in a bargain."

I know her well enough to know that she would have already gone to Niya if she felt the fea could be swayed. But I am no fea, and if the naiad will not see reason, I am fairly certain that death will render the bargain void.

I'm not entirely shocked when Awri announces she will be sleeping in the general's room with me until he returns. It feels a little presumptuous to stay in his large suite, but the male *had* moved all my clothes here without even asking. He more than doubled the guard in the hall before his departure, and there are at least fifteen soldiers patrolling the grounds outside his windows.

I haven't had the stomach to show Awri and Riah my new daggers. It feels a little like bragging, and a little like I am admitting that he and I have become something more. So, I keep them sheathed and fold my leathers into a neat pile, pushing them to the far side of my nightstand where they are not easily within reach. Despite the sparring, my mind can't seem to let go of the bloody image of the woman I scarred long ago.

We settle in for the night and only briefly do I debate lying awake until morning, before I am pulled into the dark abyss of my dreams.

Awri is in the bath when I'm stirred awake by a bony finger in the side the next morning. I don't have to open my eyes to know it's Eon. The breathy whispers of the sisters flit across my ears and Tig would never jar me awake in such a rude fashion.

I'm thrilled when I find that they have brought the male with them. He introduces himself as Rej, and thanks me profusely for bringing him to the mate he sought. The male doesn't know a single word of the human tongue, but Tig seems happy to take up the task of translating what I do not understand.

The water shuts off in the washroom before I've been able to ask the male any of the long list of questions I have for him. Before the sisters can disappear, I snag hold of Tig's wrist.

"Can you meet me in the forest in half an hour?"

The sprite nods, a quizzical look on her face.

"Thank you," I whisper, releasing the fea just as Awri bursts through the door.

I glance up and offer her a quick smile, the sisters vanishing with the male through an open window.

I slide into my leathers, tying a deep crimson gown below my hip, and pull two thin cloaks from the closet, handing one to my friend.

"We are going for a ride," I announce.

"We're supposed to meet with Riah," she says with a dip in her brow.

"She can come."

It doesn't take me long to convince Riah to saddle a horse of her own, Awri on the other hand eyes me suspiciously as I throw my leg over my mare. The less I explain, the better. All I really need is a quick word with the sisters, but they don't seem keen on showing themselves to my friends. As I'm never alone anymore, something needs to be done.

I stop at the edge of the forest and Awri is still staring at me with a pensive tilt to her head.

"I need a moment alone," I announce, dismounting and tying the mare to a nearby birch.

"Absolutely not," Awri says sternly, "Xey will kill me if I let anything happen to you."

"Nothing is going to happen to me," I argue, "The La'tari are most certainly not hiding in a forest filled with deadly fea."

Awri throws her feet to the ground and stomps toward me as she says, "Under no circumstances are you going into that forest alone."

I look to Riah for support, but the female is looking at the sky like it's the most interesting thing she's ever seen, clearly uninterested in picking a side.

"I *am* going into the forest *alone*," I point to the trees, "And you can either stand here and wait for me or drag me back to the palace and put me under house arrest."

I know I shouldn't have said it when she looks at me like it's the better of the two options, so I add, "In which case I will make my way back here the first moment you aren't looking and then you won't be standing twenty feet away if the land itself decides to devour me."

She clenches her jaw, crossing her arms over her chest, refusing to meet my eyes. I take it as a tense sort of approval, or as close as I'll get, and walk into the forest, alone. I've made it less than twenty feet through the dense brush when something grabs my arm, and I suppress a scream. I look down to see Tig's hand sticking out from inside a colorful bush.

The sprite is clearly pleased she has startled me. Ignoring her gloating smile, I tell her about the naiad, about the general's gift, and that he'd given up a portion to save my life. She asks for the fea's name, and when I tell her, I can see by the look on her face that they are familiar.

"My friend says that Niya could give the gift back if she chose. Do you know what she might accept in trade?" I ask.

The simple question is my sole purpose in meeting the sprite today. She will tell me, and I will provide it, whatever it is.

"No trade," she says simply, "We go."

She starts pulling me deeper into the forest and I dig my heels into the dirt. The sprite points north, the frustration she feels evident on her face.

"I can't leave the others," I explain, "What do you mean no trade?"

"*Sa Tha'haynah,*" she says, tugging my arm. *Take the old blood.*

"You can't take me there now. I'll meet you there before midday. I'll try to come alone, but the others may be nearby—"

"Shivaria!" Awri yells.

"I'm coming!" I yell over my shoulder and when I turn back, Tig is gone.

Awri is practically seething when I emerge from the brush and what I have to say to her is nearly stuck in my throat.

"Don't get too upset," I begin, "you'll need a little of that when I tell you where we're going."

"We are going *back* to the palace," Awri says forcefully while Riah picks at the dirt under her nails.

"We are going to see Niya," I correct.

"There is no veil in Terr in which I will allow you anywhere near that naiad again. Xey may have bargained for your life but a fea can still hold a grudge and you *stabbed* her, Shivaria."

"You *stabbed* her?!" Riah shouts.

"Thank you for joining the conversation," I quip. "Yes, I *stabbed* her, because she was trying to *drown* me."

"I'd listen to Awri," Riah says, eyes wide, "Naiads are nasty business when they're angry."

"So am I," I reply, swinging up into my saddle. "I'm going with or without you, but either way I'm not coming back until she restores the general's gift."

We ride in silence, Riah's hand loose at her side where I imagine she would have normally worn a sword, if I'd given her proper warning as to what the day would entail. Awri won't meet my eyes, and I don't blame her. I have abused the trust she placed in me, using it to get what I wanted without including her in the decision. I'm a hisht friend, and the sooner she realizes it the better.

I recognize the old camp where we stopped for lunch the day I ran after the boar. The river is just up ahead, and I need to go alone to be sure of Tig's help.

"Wait here," I say. Only to stop my mount five paces into the brush when Awri and Riah follow after me. I open my mouth to protest and Awri cuts me off.

"Since *you* refuse to have a civil conversation, I won't bother explaining why *I* refuse to simply let you wander off into Niya's territory, again."

I open my mouth to argue with the female when I hear the sprites. It's not the musical laughter I'm accustomed to, this is a chilling guttural fury,

the likes of which I've never witnessed from the sisters.

My head whips toward the sound and I click my tongue until my mare is flying through the forest and I'm dodging low hanging branches to stay astride. I jump off my mount before the beast comes to a full stop, prepared to defend the sprites from the naiad, or anything else they've come upon.

The sisters don't break from their aggression when Riah and Awri burst into the clearing behind me. I'm shocked to find Tig straddling a lovely fea with long, billowing sea moss hair. Her green eyes glint like brilliant emeralds in the sunlight breaking through the thick canopy above. Her lip quivers as Eon tugs at her hair, teeth bared in a ferocious snarl.

"*Tha'haynah vathai,*" Tig says angrily, pointing to me.

The strange fea wails mournfully reaching a hand toward me in pleading.

"Stars," Awri gasps, "Niya."

Niya? Certainly not the version I met in the river.

"*Meh'a!*" the naiad yells, "*Meh'a!*"

Tig seems pleased with the fea's reply, though the language is not of the sprites and the meaning of her words is lost to me. Tig lifts her weight off the poor creature, as Eon releases her hair. Shuffling toward me on her knees, the naiad reaches her hand up in supplication when she finds herself at my feet.

"Forgive me," the fea says softly, a weak tremor in her voice, "I did not know."

I don't bother asking what she is talking about. I've come for one reason and won't risk losing the submission the sisters have childishly tortured into her.

"What will you take in exchange for Xeyvian's gift?" I ask flatly.

Tig begins to argue in her windy sprite tongue. She doesn't want me giving her a thing, but I trust what Awri said about the fea and I can't bring myself to force the creature if I can give her something in exchange.

"My spring was dying," Niya says, "I needed the strength of his gift to make it strong again."

"What if I find you another spring?" I ask.

She shakes her head. "This spring feeds life into the forest, it guards the borders of our lands and all the fea who reside within. I cannot abandon it, *Tha'haynah.*"

"There must be another way," I insist.

"I—" she hesitates. "I can feel that which you've already given in part. A piece of the binding. Grant me a small piece as well, that is what I will exchange for the gift you seek."

"Done."

Just as it was years before, I don't have to think about it. I've already made the bargain once and it hadn't done a thing to me. Whatever these fea strip from me, it is a phantom. Nothing I've ever known.

The naiad offers me her hand and when I take it, darkness blooms between our palms, pulling at the light in the small clearing. It grows, twisting into a vortex that draws winds from afar and darkens the sky. And then, nothing. Nothing but the familiar feeling of the demon inside me. Only it's more, and it feels like home.

"How do I return it to him?" I ask.

"The gift is bound to the life it was born into," she answers, "and it will always seek to reunite with the one to whom it belongs. A simple touch will free the gift, that is all that is required."

"Thank you," I say, and her eyebrows raise in surprise.

"Anything for *tha'haynah vathai*," she says, "If you need me, you know where to find me."

My blood runs cold when the title slips past her lips, and my stomach twists itself into a knot. It takes everything I have not to ask what she means. But I can't. Not here. Not in the presence of the females who refuse to leave my side and who will surely report back to the general.

The sprites are gone when I rise to my feet. Awri and Riah look a little like they've seen the silly fairy horse in the children's books with the magical horn. The naiad slinks back into the river as I mount my horse and turn for the palace, my companions following quickly after me.

"I take it we can all agree to keep this to ourselves?" I ask, utterly aware that there is no veil in Terr in which Awri will not tell the general the moment he returns.

I'm not sure why I care or even bother asking. Perhaps in part because I still feel protective of the sisters, and I never meant for them to reveal themselves to my companions.

"I'll be the first to admit that I'm not entirely sure what just happened," Riah chuckles. "What was it that she called you? Thay nah vaiti?"

"*Tha'haynah vathai,*" I correct.

"What does it mean?" she asks.

"I don't know," I lie.

I wish I didn't. I will need to ask Tig what she meant by it, but I don't care to speculate.

Tha'haynah vathai. The old blood of the fea.

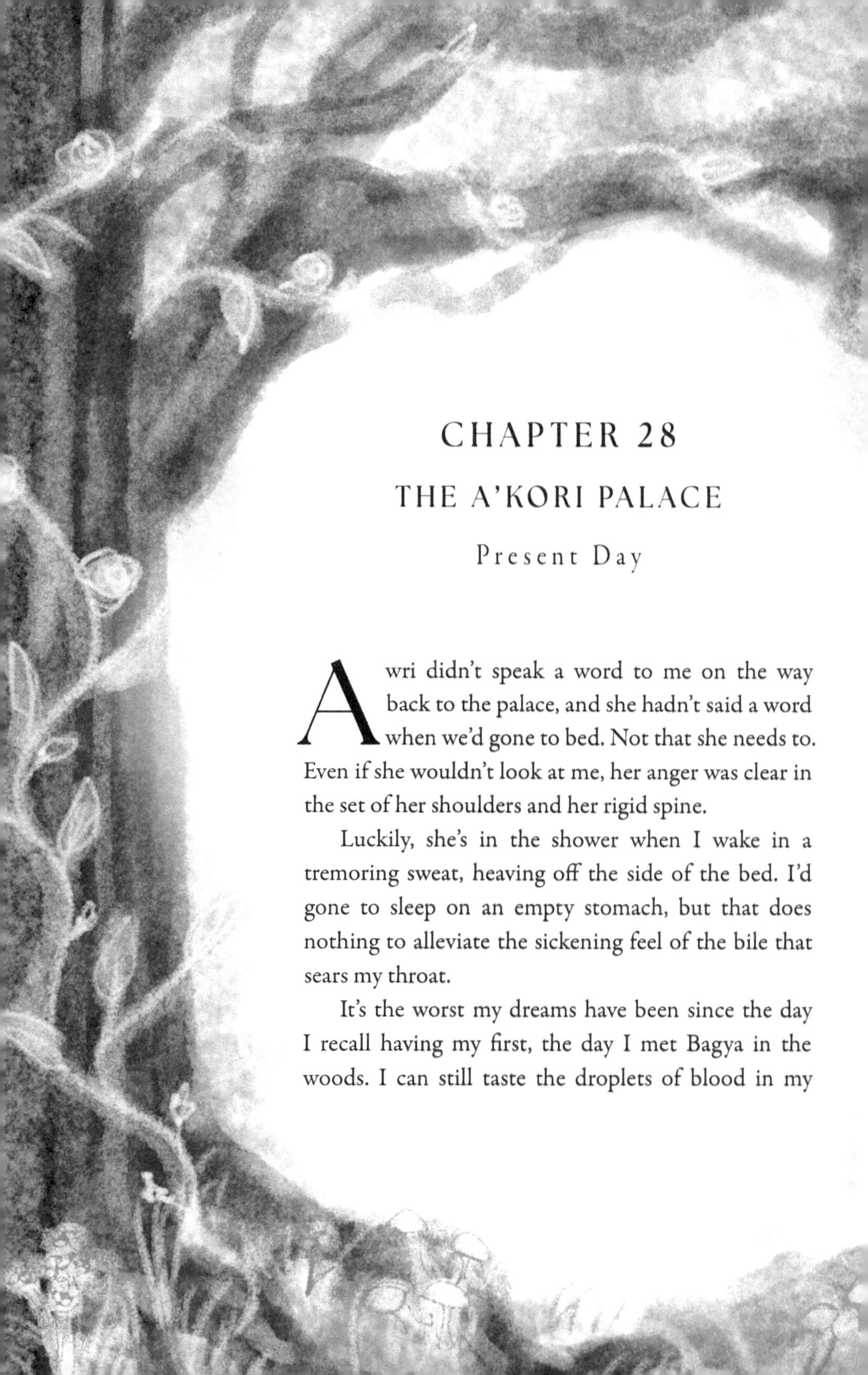

CHAPTER 28

THE A'KORI PALACE

Present Day

Awri didn't speak a word to me on the way back to the palace, and she hadn't said a word when we'd gone to bed. Not that she needs to. Even if she wouldn't look at me, her anger was clear in the set of her shoulders and her rigid spine.

Luckily, she's in the shower when I wake in a tremoring sweat, heaving off the side of the bed. I'd gone to sleep on an empty stomach, but that does nothing to alleviate the sickening feel of the bile that sears my throat.

It's the worst my dreams have been since the day I recall having my first, the day I met Bagya in the woods. I can still taste the droplets of blood in my mouth, still feel the heat of the woman's last breath on my cheek, the press of the demon as it coiled around me. I bunch the silk sheets in my fists and will them to stop shaking.

Safe. You're safe.

Taking a deep steadying breath, I swing my legs over the side of the bed, collapsing onto the floor the moment I try to stand. I grasp my head as the world spins. My ears ring loudly, the sound swelling and ebbing like a pulse, and I swipe at a tickle beneath my nose only to find my fingers coated in a thin sheen of blood.

Tig rushes to my side, her green eyes full of worry.

"I'm all right," I assure her, "Just a little lightheaded."

As usual I hadn't seen the sprite come into the room. For the first time I begin to wonder just how often she watches me completely unseen. The water shuts off in the washroom and Tig glances at the doors, then back at me.

"Really, I'm all right," I say.

My eyes flick to the tiny black blooms with the purple hue growing in her hair. Her hand reaching up to touch one when she shakes her head. I nod. They aren't ready.

"Go." I tip my head toward the window, and she vanishes with a great amount of hesitation.

I fail to regain my feet before Awri glides into the room. Her eyes begin to slide over my face dismissively, her head turning away, and I start to think she's decided not to speak to me for another day, maybe more. Until her head whips back toward me when she registers that I'm on the floor.

"What's wrong?" she asks.

I take another pass at the blood drying beneath my nose and nod. "I'm fine. Just a little lightheaded."

She bolts to the door and yells to someone across the hall, "Have Caden brought here immediately."

"That is unnecessary," I argue weakly, "It's just a bloody nose. Why would you call a healer for a bloody nose?"

I don't mention that my ears are ringing or that the spin of the room has been replaced by a considerable pounding in my head. I pull myself off the floor, making a show of appearing better than I feel. Awri follows close behind when I make my way into the washroom, and it takes everything I have to steady my legs as I walk.

"You really think I'd prefer the pain of his healing to a bloody nose that will be gone by the time he arrives?" I quirk a brow at her.

She shrugs. "Xey made me promise to call for Caden if you ever described yourself as being *'fine.'*"

Controlling ass.

I've barely dressed when Caden bursts into the room, a shade paler than he was the last time I saw him. Heaving a deep breath, he looks me over expectantly, as if he thought I might have lost a leg. Awri marches me into the main room, sitting me down on a large settee close to the windows. The look on his face when Awri describes my condition may be worth the pain of having him brought here. I can't help the chuckle that slips past my lips when he frowns.

"A bloody nose?" he asks.

Awri rolls her eyes. "Just try and heal her. Xeyvian—"

"Say no more." Caden halts her with a wave of his hand, before rubbing his palms together to warm them and laying them against my temples. I brace, preparing for the pain of his gift. Then, nothing. Not so much as a pinching sting of power. He eyes me quizzically and I shrug.

"Shouldn't it hurt to heal a bloody nose?" Awri questions the male.

"It should. Yes," he says.

"You'd like that wouldn't you." I narrow my eyes at my friend.

And I'm sure she isn't joking when she says, "A little."

"If she isn't injured, why is she bleeding?" she asks the healer.

"Maybe it's Xeyvian's gift?" I suggest.

Caden's eyes widen when he asks Awri, "He used his gift on her?"

"No," she says, "Nothing like that."

Both look at me thoughtfully as Awri explains the transfer of Xeyvian's power. Eventually, Caden agrees, "It's possible. Mortal bodies are not made to contain the gifts of the feyn. Much less a power like his. In any case, I don't sense anything that needs mending."

He looks me over once more before heading for the door as he says, "Summon me again if she gets worse." Though as he departs, I wonder why he would even bother, if there's nothing to be done.

"You should rest today," Awri offers.

I think I'd like to, but I have already risked one night without the release of my demon and find that I am quite unwilling to attempt it again, unless it is completely necessary.

As the general isn't here to assist me, I need to spar, or at least head to the kitchen and acquire more of Kishek's tea. I will need something to drive away the darkness before Awri ends up on the wrong side of one of my episodes.

"I'd like to keep training with Riah." Before she can argue I add, "If I get another bloody nose I'll come straight back here and stay in bed all day."

The promise satisfies her enough that she reluctantly takes me to train. Though after a few choice words from my friend, Riah is taking it easy on me and a training session fit for a child won't do a thing to temper the demon inside me.

Awri keeps our session short, and I can't tell if she's simply worried or if my fatigue is that obvious. She takes me back to the general's chambers without asking, and I nearly fall asleep in the tub. I haven't taken a nap in years but today feels like a good day for it.

It's dusk when Awri nudges me awake, offering me a small bowl of stew for dinner. I try to give her a reassuring smile when I note the creases marring her features. But all I can manage is a few bites before I set the bowl aside, muster the energy to slide on a sleeping gown, and crawl back into bed.

I wake to the sound of a deep, chilling shriek in the hall and my feet are moving toward the door before I've even considered what I'll find outside. Awri rushes out behind me, falling to her knees beside Kishek, who lays in a crumpled heap on the floor.

"Call for Caden!" I yell to the guard at the end of the hall.

"No, no, no, no, no," Awri cries, pulling his head into her lap, smoothing back his dark brown hair. "Not yet," she whispers into his ear, "Not yet."

I want to comfort her, reassure her, but what can I do? Tears begin to well in her eyes as she rocks the male's head in her lap, her lip quivering as she tries to coax a reply from his limp form.

"What's wrong with him?" I ask.

Her eyes are like daggers when she opens her mouth to reply, interrupted when Caden rounds the corner. I suppose, given my condition throughout

the day, I shouldn't be surprised he remained close by. It's hard to fault him for it under the current circumstances.

The healer runs to lay his hands on Kishek, skidding to his knees beside the male. A deep hiss of pain comes from Kishek's parted lips when the healing power is released into him. Awri giggles nervously, tears streaming freely from her eyes.

"He'll be all right. He's just sleeping now," Caden assures her.

Awri nods, wiping her cheek.

Caden grips her arm, a serious look on the healer's face when he says, "He needs rest."

Again, she nods, and I'm not sure the female can summon the words to reply.

"I'll watch him until morning," Caden promises, summoning four guards with the snap of his fingers.

With minimal direction they hoist the male overhead, carrying him off toward Awri's chamber, Caden in their wake.

It must take every ounce of willpower at the female's disposal to not follow after him when he disappears beyond the doors of her room. She coils her silken dress in her fists, releasing the fabric and smoothing it as she heaves a deep breath. Forcing a weak smile in my direction, she says, "Go back to bed. I'll be right behind you."

Rising from the floor, I walk back to the bedroom, only to stop the moment Awri tears down the hall in a rage and throws open a door halfway down the corridor.

"Enough!" she yells.

A long panel of light illuminates the hall where the door is open wide. The general's voice sounds from within the room.

"Awri," he says, by way of greeting.

"I will not continue to risk my mate for this, Xeyvian!" she bellows.

Mate? Kishek.

I chastise myself for not expecting it. Though I hardly understand what a mate means to the feyn.

"Tell her," she demands, "Tell her or send her away."

"I agree with Awri, Xey," Riesh interjects, "She's strong, stronger than you give her credit for. She can take it, and you can't protect her from this forever."

"She's not ready," the general says.

"Ready or not, she is weak in her ignorance," Awri spits, "and if you choose to keep her here that affects us all."

"I've received a letter from Nurai. She will be attending the masque. We will wait until she arrives and see if your gifts combined will be strong enough." There is a clear ring of finality in the general's voice when he says it.

"Nurai should be strong enough on her own," Riesh says hesitantly.

"I'm not so sure anymore," the general answers.

"You still can't access her?" Awri asks, some of the heat waning from her voice.

"A little more every day, but it has nothing to do with the strength of my gift. It's her, she's changing, trusting..."

A door swings open at the end of the hall and shadows move in the night as a fresh rotation of guards filters into the corridors. I curse under my breath, retreating to the bed before I'm seen, settling in below the duvet just as the door's hinges creak and the latch clicks shut.

I don't have to look to know it's the general. I've memorized the sound of his stride, his scent, the way that he moves. I can practically see the scowl plastered on his face with my eyes closed.

The bed dips next to me and the male collects me in his arms, pulling my back against his chest. Taking in a deep lungful of my scent, he nuzzles my hair. I roll over to face him, his form nothing more than a simple silhouette in the dark, and I capture his mouth with my own in tender greeting.

Placing a hand over his heart, he sucks in a gasp when I release his power into him. There is nothing of the whirling storm it summoned before. This transfer is quiet, subtle, the gift gladly departing to its true home.

"Fates," he gasps, wrapping his arms around my neck and tucking me against his chest. "How?" he mumbles into my hair.

"I made a bargain," I say, and his arms tense around me.

I expect a scolding, about venturing into the forest, about confronting the naiad who tried to kill me, about the sure idiocy of striking a bargain with a fea, but he only asks, "What did you give up?"

And now I understand the depth of what he said to me when I asked that very question when he first held me in the cabin. So, I answer in kind, meaning every word, still not entirely sure what it is I've bargained.

"Nothing I wouldn't give up a hundred times over."

He pulls my body against his until there isn't room for air between us and rests his cheek against my head as he falls asleep.

Dawn breaks the horizon and deep voices murmur in the war room. I splay my hand across the empty sheets beside me longingly. Just once, before I'm forced to leave this place, I'd like to wake with the male by my side. I'm not sure why. Just like the rest of it, it won't change a thing.

I prepare for training and can't help but worry about my friend. The painful sight of her crouched beside Kishek, her mate, plagues me. It was my fault, somehow. She blamed me for what happened to him and told the general to send me away.

I'm troubled by the relief I feel at the idea of the male boarding me onto a ship and sending me south before I have a chance to end his king. I would never see him again, but at least then, he would never grow to hate me.

He told her he would wait until after the masque, but by then it will be too late. The king is meant to return to attend his party, and if Awri is pushing the general to send me away for some reason, I can't afford to hesitate in my task.

There is no way I will come to be anything but a bitter regret in the general's past by the time this is over. The male might even follow me to La'tari, searching for a vengeance he should rightly obtain. I smile dryly at that. I won't blame him if he does.

'*Tell her.*' The simple demand Awri leveled at the general is more than intriguing, it's maddening. I'd never known the female to withhold information from me, though a part of me knows there is only so much she is willing to share. How much of that information I can trust is another matter entirely.

I debate asking the general what she meant by it, what he's supposedly protecting me from. Of course, then he would know I'd been eavesdropping. If the male doesn't want to discuss it, my questions will only risk creating a rift between us—right before I need the leverage of his goodwill.

A knock at the door. I answer it as I finish tying off the long braid I've woven into my hair.

"Good morning." Riah smiles warmly.

"Where is Awri?" I ask, my brow dipping. When Riah looks offended by my inquiry I quickly add, "Not that I'm not happy to see you."

She shrugs off my social blunder and motions for me to follow her.

"I believe she is spending the day with Kishek," she says.

Of course she is. I feel like an idiot for asking.

"Do you know if he's all right?" I ask.

"I'm sure we would both know if he wasn't."

I can tell she really feels that way, but I'm not so easily convinced. After what I overheard last night, it is clear just how outside their inner circle I really am.

"Don't worry." She eyes me, mistaking my troubling thoughts for worry. "The king would never let anything happen to one of his own. Not if there was something he could do to avoid it."

"That might make Awri feel better, if in fact the king were here to help her mate," I say dryly.

"I understand that things are different where you are from, but *my* king has the unquestioned loyalty of every soul serving under him. That loyalty extends to everyone he chooses to protect, fea and mortal alike," she says.

I eye her cautiously, unsure of the point she is trying to make.

She continues, "Kishek is under that protection, and there isn't a single feyn under the king's command that won't treat his life as if it were their own."

I breathe a little easier. She's right, things *are* very different in La'tari. There is no room for weakness of any kind in my homeland, and my king's favor extends to those with the strength to help him in his cause. He has always favored the Drakai for that very reason.

Lives like mine, that come with the promise of a full belly and four walls to keep out the cold, are highly prized. A vast contrast to the comfort of the A'kori. But then, I've really only seen the palace.

"Where are your barracks?" My sudden change of subject causes Riah to stumble on the stony path leading to the stables.

"To the east." She points into the distance. "Why do you ask?"

Her eyes narrow on me, and for good reason. If I were a La'tari spy, there is much I could learn from a tour of the barracks. But I'm not a spy. I'm worse. Still. Not a spy. And thanks to the general I hold the key to entry.

"Remember when I told you the general sent Siserie to the barracks?" I ask.

She snorts a laugh. "I'm not likely to forget that tale anytime soon."

"The general also put me in charge of the duration of her sentence."

She stumbles again, and I seriously begin to wonder how she is so graceful in the ring when she can't keep her feet under her while she's walking.

"And you want to pay her a visit?" she asks, a wicked curve kicking up the edges of her lips.

"I do," I say, no hesitation in the lie.

But I realize the moment the words pass my lips it is in fact not a lie. Perhaps not the true reason I intend to see the barracks, but I can't deny that I really would enjoy seeing the female in a cell.

"I only have one question." Her face grows serious and I have to force myself not to hold my breath. "Why didn't we do this sooner?" she asks, cracking a toothy grin that I happily return.

The barracks are less than an hour by horse, nestled onto a high hill with a view of the sea. It's close enough to the eastern shore to have the advantage of time if an enemy ship were spotted along the coast and brilliantly disguised as a small village. The tall beacon in the center of town, the only thing that might give away its strategic position.

A mixture of feyn and mortals bustle around us as we hand our mounts over to the stable hand. The lieutenant receives a number of salutes in the feyn fashion, a fist crossing over the chest to cover the heart. Her face takes on a deadly glower the moment her feet touch the ground, every soldier's back stiffening as we pass.

Even knowing the female, the deep crease in her brow and the half snarl she wears on her lips is enough to keep me wary of her intentions as we make our way below ground.

The barracks are carved into a long hillside. Its windows are etched into the stone of the western wall, letting natural light filter into the halls and shared spaces where the soldiers break for lunch, games of cards, and the like. The small space echoes with the screech of wooden chairs as we pass, every

soul standing to salute the female at my side. Save one.

"Toren." Riah greets the male with a stiff salute of her own.

The last time I saw him he had just sent a contingent to retrieve the general and Awri's clumsy human guest from the forest. Just as before, deep lines are etched into his face and the male looks like he's never smiled a day in his life.

He has a full head of long white hair plaited in a series of twists and braids that combine at the nape of his neck into a thick tail, falling to his midback. His hands are heavily scarred, as is what little flesh I can see exposed around the collar at his neck. The scars are unnatural, not born of war, at least not in the way one usually obtains a war wound. These are evidence of the male's torture.

Toren's eyes follow my own across the marred flesh of his hands. He holds them out and turns them over slowly, the silver-white lines catching the light coming in from the windows.

"A gift from the La'tari," he says and my back becomes rigid. "What? You don't approve?"

"Of torture?" I balk.

"Of the actions of your king."

There is no safe way for me to answer him. As a La'tari subject, the king's actions are far above my reproach, and fates know I have no idea what he did to end up in a La'tari prison. Still, there are very few crimes I personally deem worthy of torture, and it seems unlikely Toren committed any of those and still ended up in the general's ranks.

"Nothing to say in defense of your sovereign?" The male quirks an eyebrow as he looms over me.

"I'm not here for a lesson in politics," I say, forcing myself to rise to my full height, even if the male still towers over me. "Or to hear your sad war stories."

Riah clears her throat, shifting nervously beside me.

"I suppose not," he says, flicking a spec of invisible dust off his uniform. "Why exactly *are* you here?"

"I came to check in on Siserie." Not a lie.

I'm not sure how it's possible but his frown deepens. "Xeyvian did mention he'd put the female's sentence in the hands of a La'tarian."

"Tread lightly, Toren," Riah says, and I startle at the tone she takes with her superior. "*Feyn'leij ajna.*"

The male's eyes widen, and I begin to wonder if I should have asked the sisters to teach me to speak feyn as well as sprite. I'm sure they are fluent in the tongue. Whatever she said to Toren has the male reaching for a key and leading us deeper into the bowels of the barracks without another pointed word about where I came from.

Beyond the officers' quarters the halls quickly grow dark, the natural moisture from the earth penetrates the walls of carved stone and dankens the air with a musty aroma. A twinge of guilt settles in my gut as I consider the life Siserie will live if I leave her here, even if only a few days have passed since she began serving her sentence. That little spark of regret fades the moment Toren opens the door to her cell.

The lovely feyn sits in a small wooden chair in the corner of her room, a modest but comfortable looking cot across from her. Lamplight flickers on the wall where I feel the absence of a window, and a half-eaten tray of fresh fruit and cheese sits on a sturdy table beside her. *They* might call it a prison, but it is every bit the room I was raised in.

"Not much of a prison," I whisper to Riah under my breath.

"Maybe not by La'tari standards," Toren says behind me, "but in A'kori we believe that not everyone deserving of a cell should be punished as if they've committed a war crime."

Fair enough.

Siserie startles when she sees me standing in the doorway, but recovers quickly, her posture straightening. She raises her chin to look down her nose at me when she says, "Come to gloat?"

I can hardly blame her for the assumption, and perhaps it would be crueler to admit to the female that she has hardly crossed my mind since I'd last seen her.

"I came to end your sentence," I say.

A quick glance at Riah tells me that the lieutenant might have preferred if I'd decided to let the female serve out her sentence a little longer. I suppose to an immortal, a few days in a comfortable cell hardly qualifies as punishment.

"Why would you?" Siserie asks.

"Why wouldn't I?" I reply.

Is she really going to argue with me about this?

She scoffs, lifting herself from the chair in one elegant motion. I'm struck painfully by the practiced grace of many lifetimes, as she saunters toward me, a seductive sway to her hips.

"I know what you are to him, and while the very idea of an ungifted mortal sharing his bed sickens me, that is all you will ever be. *Durah.* Mortal. Fleeting." She stands so close I can feel the heat radiating off her body. "In two hundred years, you will be nothing but a distant memory. The sound of your voice, the feeling of your touch, your beauty, all too difficult for him to recall." Her lips peel back in something resembling a grin, or perhaps a snarl. "But I will remain, unblemished by the iron will of time, still beautiful, still—"

"Full of yourself?" I quip, and Riah chokes on a laugh beside me. "Pining after a male that will never want you regardless of the millennia that pass."

Her lips peel back further, and she bares her fangs. I know I don't need to say another word. She has already lost the battle between us. The general made his mind up about the female long before I ever entered his life.

Maybe it's the sting of the truth of what she said that makes me press on.

"Tell me how it feels to know that the male you've spent so many years of your long life pursuing, would rather spend his days, and nights, in the company of a woman who is, as you say, ungifted and will be ravaged by time?"

She levels me with a fearsome glare and burning embers spark to life in her eyes. I should back away. I know I should. And I might, if it weren't for the officers bracketing me on either side. Their presence emboldens me to impart one last petty jab at the female who lied to me, who tried to keep me from what is *mine*.

"How little you must think of yourself, to grasp at him with such desperation."

Siserie bares her fangs at me, loosing a growl that raises the hair on my arms. Though I have no fear of the female, ice spirals down my spine as those embers burst into flame. This is not mere rage that flickers in her eyes, but true fire that ignites, licking across her irises. Every bare patch of her flesh is licked by a white heated blaze that threatens to burn.

My heart races when I hear the woosh of fire, and my eyes flick down to the churning ball of flame that appears in her palm. To my surprise, Toren is the first to act, putting out the confrontation before it truly begins. He spears out an icy hand, grasping Siserie by the throat, his frigid embrace leeching the heat from her skin, squelching her fire with a hissing steam.

The intense rage I *am* accustomed to seeing now burns in Toren's eyes as he looks down at the wide-eyed female and growls, "*Vey'ah?*"

"Yes, *I dare,*" the female spits angrily, pointing a slender finger at me as she tears at the hand the male has latched around her neck. "*She* is nothing but a mistake."

"The fates do not make mistakes." His voice is deadly calm.

"They made one," she growls through clenched teeth, thrusting her finger toward my chest, "when they bound *that* to my king!"

"Treason," Toren rumbles, his grip tightening around her throat.

White veins of ice spread across her face, popping as they engulf what little remains of her fire.

"Toren," Riah's voice comes in warning, "leave justice to the king."

Siserie exhales a misty breath as the ice thaws from her skin, the male leaning forward to whisper a deadly promise into her ear.

"You'll wish I ended you when he hears of this. Trust that he will have questions of his own, about how exactly it is you have come to know of the lady's bond to *my liege*."

I'm hardly sure what he means, but it's a threat the female takes to heart. The blood drains from her face. Toren pins her with a stare as he asks, "Do you still intend to release her?"

I almost forgot. It *is* the reason I came, in part, but I don't have to think about it. As far as I'm concerned there is only one answer to give him.

"Keep her here until I'm dead. When that time comes, I pass her sentence on to you, Toren."

So, the male does smile.

Siserie raises her chin defiantly, but there is no mistaking the fear in her eyes or the quiver of her lip. Like Riah, Toren is obviously no friend to the female. The look on her face tells me he will be happy to let her rot for a term no mortal can fathom.

The wretched wail of her anger floods the halls when we make our way back to the light of the higher barracks. I push down thoughts of the strange exchange I witnessed below and focus on why I came.

"Does everyone under your command have a room like Siserie's?" I ask.

Despite his clear feelings on the La'tari, the male doesn't seem concerned by my inquiry when he replies, "We build homes for our officers and help provide for their families. The small village you saw above is made up of those families, for the most part. Only the young recruits live in the small rooms of the barracks, but their rooms are far more comfortable than the cells below.

As if he can see the unspoken question lingering on my tongue he says, "How could I ask them to risk their lives for A'kori and house them like criminals?"

I remain thoughtful, considering each of Toren's replies. He does not balk at my questions and in fact seems comfortable to disclose more than what I inquire about. I try to make sense of the world I've only just begun to know, unable to make it fit with the story I've been told all my life about the feyn.

When we depart late in the afternoon, Toren assures me that I'm welcome any time. I can't help but think the gift of Siserie's confinement went a long way with the male when some of the lines adorning his face smooth and he dips his head in parting.

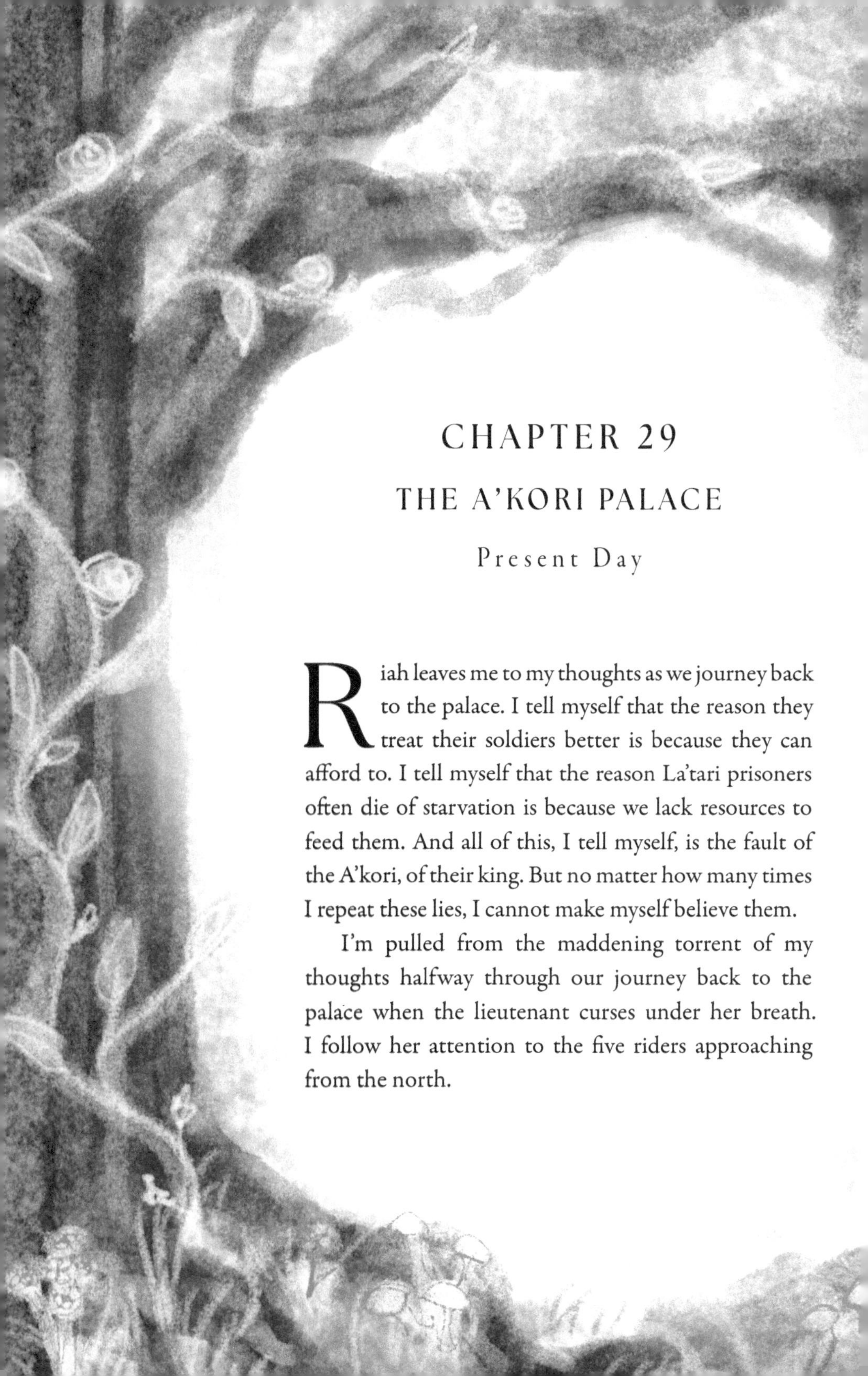

CHAPTER 29
THE A'KORI PALACE
Present Day

Riah leaves me to my thoughts as we journey back to the palace. I tell myself that the reason they treat their soldiers better is because they can afford to. I tell myself that the reason La'tari prisoners often die of starvation is because we lack resources to feed them. And all of this, I tell myself, is the fault of the A'kori, of their king. But no matter how many times I repeat these lies, I cannot make myself believe them.

I'm pulled from the maddening torrent of my thoughts halfway through our journey back to the palace when the lieutenant curses under her breath. I follow her attention to the five riders approaching from the north.

"What's wrong?" I ask, squinting in a vain attempt to make out what her sharp feyn eyes can so easily see from afar.

"Try not to fight, but if we must, try not to die."

It's all she has time to say before they nearly collide with us, halting our procession east. Four humans, three men and one woman, sit astride their mounts next to a white-haired male with dark brown skin and deep blue eyes.

"*Shivay lathrek,*" Riah greets him.

"*Shivay thien,*" he replies in a husky voice.

One of the few phrases I picked up as a child, when I was curious after my first encounter with the feyn. It is an ancient and formal greeting from a time in their histories.

Shivay lathrek. May the light of all life greet you in the morning.

Shivay thien. May the light of all life find you in the darkness.

"Perhaps you would be kind enough to offer some assistance. We've gotten a little turned around looking for the barracks," the feyn male says with a knowing smile.

Had Riah not been on edge before, his line of questioning would prickle my spine.

The lieutenant doesn't hesitate to reply, "I'm sorry, friend. I didn't know there were any barracks in these parts."

The male smirks at her, disbelieving, making a show of examining her uniform. Riah pulls on the reins, forcing her mare to step back from their party.

"If there's nothing else I can help you with, we need to be on our way," she says.

It's the tension in her voice that has me sliding my daggers from their sheaths to rest in my palms. No sooner do their hilts settle in my hands than his smile grows wicked.

"I can think of plenty of ways you can be of further assistance to me." He tips his head toward us, issuing a command to the others, "Take them alive."

Riah may as well have said nothing for all the thought I give her earlier warning. I don't think before flicking my wrist, lodging one of my feynstone blades firmly into the male's eye. I don't expect it to kill him, my entire life I've been taught just how difficult the feyn are to kill. But he falls from his horse, collapsing into a heap of unmoving flesh.

Riah doesn't spare a glance in my direction as she directs her mare into

the midst of mounted humans. She isn't armed, not with a weapon. I'm convinced she doesn't need one when she grapples one of the fair-haired men by the throat and he looses an agonizing shriek, abruptly ended by the sickening crack of his neck before he falls from his mount.

Fates.

The men unsheathe their swords, striking at the lieutenant. She goes on the defense, attempting to disarm one and procure his weapon for herself. I loose my second blade at the man attempting to attack her from behind. The knife whips past Riah before sinking into his jugular with a solid thunk. His eyes widen as he claws at the blade, but he's already dead, removing it will only quicken his descent to haliel.

"Stop throwing your weapons!" Riah growls.

A thank you might be more appropriate, but I understand her line of reasoning. I've disarmed myself, even if it was to save her from a sword to the back.

I'm too caught up in Riah's skirmish to notice that the woman dismounted behind me. A mistake that truthfully should cost me my life. She pulls my leg, pitching me off balance, sending me to the ground.

Standing over me with a cocky grin, she sneers, "You're about to wish you'd done as your friend advised. If you had any idea who we are, not only would you have remained armed, you would have run."

Her smile fades to a frown when I grin, the heat of battle soaking into my veins in a rushing wave. I sweep her legs out from under her and round back with a kick to her head just before it makes contact with the ground. With a loud crack, it bounces off a large stone half sunk into the earth. Blood gushes from the wound and her body goes limp. The woman will not rise again.

By the time I get to my feet, Riah is wiping a thick slick of blood off the blade she acquired from her opponent, the remnants of the assailant unmoving at her feet. She points it at me as I pluck my own blade from the feyn's punctured socket, my eyes lingering on the odd serrated shell of the male's ear.

"You have some explaining to do," she says.

I wipe the blade clean, sheathing it in my leathers before retrieving the second and doing the same.

"They were a gift from the general," I reply.

"I guessed that much. The only feynstone left from the sundering is in the storerooms of the crown. What I'd like to know is the name of the Drakai who trained you, and why your father thought a lady needed to learn to fight like an assassin instead of paint, or play music, or—"

"Breed?" I quip, swinging into my saddle while I do my best to deflect from her line of thinking.

"I was going to say 'sew,'" she corrects, doing her best to prevent the smile teasing the edge of her lips.

"I assume he wanted me to learn for the same reason any father would do such a thing. To keep his daughter safe."

She shakes her head, completely unwilling to believe me. "Most fathers would just give their daughter a knife and a bodyguard."

"Actually, I think most fathers would barter their daughters to a husband and charge him with their safety," I say disdainfully.

Riah lets it go for the time being, making herself busy strapping every weapon she can find to the back of her mount, saving her search of the male for last. She kneels beside him, untying a dagger from his hip when her fingers go still, her eyes widening as she takes in his face more closely than before.

"Foc," she says, jumping to her feet, scanning the edge of the forest as she rushes to mount. "Go, now," she commands me, "as fast as your horse will take you. Don't stop until we reach the palace. I'm right behind you."

A wailing shriek sounds from within the tree line, prickling the hair on the back of my neck. I don't have time to look and find the source before Riah cracks her reins in the air, sending my horse into a leaping gallop. Her brow creases as she chances a glance behind us and whatever she sees draws every bit of color from her face.

Flinging her legs over her saddle, Riah doesn't stop to tie her horse as she flies through the giant gilded doors of the palace. I rush after her as she bolts through the halls, charging into the general's war room without announcing herself.

I'm right behind her, my own brow drawn in a mixture of concern and curiosity. What had she seen that alarmed her so?

"Vatruke. On the rise, halfway between the palace and the barracks," she says, out of breath, "They are hiding with the La'tari from the warship, along the edge of the northern forest."

The general's eyes flick to me briefly before returning to the lieutenant when he asks, "How many?"

"We only encountered five in the open," she says, "Four Drakai and one of the Vatruke. We got lucky; I wasn't recognized."

"How did you escape?" Riesh asks, wide-eyed.

"We fought," she explains.

The general moves to my side, his eyes sweeping over me, checking for any sign of injury.

"You managed to kill all five completely unscathed?" Riesh says. I try not to be offended by the shock in his voice, though he directs the question at Riah.

"I only felled two Drakai," she admits, "Shivaria claimed the lives of the others."

My stomach pits when she says it, and an uncomfortable silence falls over the room. They each look me over in turn, as if they are seeing me for the first time. For once, I'm glad Awri is absent, still tending to her mate. She already looks at me strangely far too often. Not that I haven't given her good reason.

"How?" The general's question is directed at Riah but the male refuses to break my gaze.

The lieutenant gives her report, starting where our day began, the barracks. I'm not sure it's entirely necessary for her to divulge the entirety of my heated exchange with Siserie, but the pride that fills the general's eyes upon hearing my response to the female's ire is worth the retelling.

Despite the serious nature of the story, Riesh laughs a deep belly laugh when he learns I gifted the term of her sentence to Toren. Maybe I was too brash. What if the male leaves her there for a hundred years? Then again, he likely knows far better than I just how long she deserves to linger in her confinement.

But it isn't the general's approval of my decision to leave her that catches my attention. It is the fury in his eyes when Riah repeats the hateful remark Siserie spewed at me before we left. '*She is nothing but a mistake.*'

"What did she mean?" I ask, interrupting Riah's tale. "When she said I am bound to your king?"

What type of fea bargain have I unwittingly struck with their king? I

find myself wondering again if a fea bargain can be nullified by ending a life. I will need to find out.

"Fates," I say under my breath, "It's the bargain I made with Niya, isn't it? The same bargain I made with Bagya."

Of course, it makes sense that if I struck a bargain with a subject of their sovereign it might easily extend to him. Reckless. I will need to find out exactly what it is I promised Niya and how to unbind myself from their sovereign, and quickly.

"Bagya?" Riah balks. "I'm beginning to feel like I don't even know who you are," she says, pinching the bridge of her nose.

"I suggest you get used to that feeling if you intend to stay her friend. I know *I* have," Riesh quips, and I'm not entirely sure he's joking.

The general shoots them both a glare before his gaze returns to me. He brushes a stray curl from my eyes when he says, "We will handle the bargains you made with both Niya and Bagya. But first, we need to deal with the Vatruke." He looks to the lieutenant. "You say you saw more than one?"

Riah nods. "At the edge of the forest." So, that's what she saw when we fled. "It was Vos, General," she says.

His entire body goes rigid. "You're sure?"

Riah nods again. I don't know why it hasn't occurred to me that they might know the Vatruke. For all I know, they have all been alive long enough to cross paths many times over.

"Which of the males fell by Shivaria's hand?" the general demands, a subtle fear masked behind his eyes as he waits for her reply.

"Kezik." The lieutenant forms the word hesitantly, as if saying it aloud might harm her in some way.

"Foc," Riesh swears, the same moment the general asks, "You're sure?"

"Unquestionably," she replies, regaining some semblance of composure.

The orders that tumble from the general's lips are urgent and his tone even more demanding than I am accustomed to hearing.

"Riesh, inform your sister and alert the guards. Riah, get yourself back to Toren, he needs to know what we're dealing with. Leave a small contingent at the barracks. I want every remaining soldier stationed outside the palace by dawn, sooner if possible."

"As you say," they reply as one, departing from the room with haste.

"What is happening?" I ask, baffled by the exchange.

"Kezik was Vos's mate," he explains, "If Riah saw her at the edge of the forest, then she saw you both as well, and she'll be out for blood."

And just like that, as if it were a toppled piece of stained glass, my life begins to break apart at the seams. Each colored pane, a different path, a different life I've lived, or could live, but the binding holding those paths together begins to fracture. I hadn't known it then, but I can see now, that every possible future I could have known shattered the moment that blade left my hand.

All of the lies become dust. Every excuse a vapor. I killed again. My own people, *again*. I did it without sparing a single thought for their lives.

I was never in any true danger, not from the Drakai. If they captured me, I would have been freed the moment I told them of my purpose here. I could have led them to the barracks, helped them gain entry into the palace, stopped the war that is coming, the war that is already here.

But Riah's life would have been forfeit, and how many others? I can't do it. I can't sacrifice innocent lives, feyn or mortal. I *won't*.

And what is the cost of all the lives I saved by betraying my people? I will pay with my own life. If Vos seeks vengeance, and the Vatruke are working with the La'tari, can I ever return home? Will she honor the pardon the king will surely grant me for succeeding in my mission? Unlikely.

The general mistakes the reason for my concern and pulls me into his arms.

"Don't worry," he says into my hair, "There isn't a single army in this veil or any other that I wouldn't send to haliel if it meant you would be safe."

"Awri was right," I say, my face pressed to his chest, "You should send me away."

My throat burns when the male draws me closer, whispering into my ear, "There is no place for you to be, but by my side, *mi'ajna*. I swear by the fates, I will never send you away."

But he will send me away. He would do it now if he truly knew me, if he knew why I'd come, what I am, what I intended—*still* intend—to do.

I do, don't I?

My mind has never been a more chaotic clutter of unanswered questions, and my resolve begins to fray.

"Your king won't be safe here." It's as close as I can bring myself to warning him, but he doesn't understand and maybe that's for the best.

"The king is already aware of the Vatruke," he replies.

I look up quizzically. "That means—"

"He has returned to A'kori." He smiles at the surprised look on my face and drops his lips to my forehead, mumbling against my flesh. "Would you like to meet him?"

My stomach pits, my entire life dividing into two distinct paths. One planned since I was a child, formed by others and thrust upon me, and the other, new and unexplored, unconsidered, until now.

I shake my head, "Not yet."

I'm not ready to choose, not ready to let go of the male that holds me like I'm something precious. Because either path I take begins with the revealing of myself, and the male embracing me seeing me for exactly what I am.

"All right. He'll be at the masque. You can meet him then." He drops a kiss on my temple. "I need to help Riesh organize the guards. Maybe you'd like to visit Media?"

The idea of visiting the woman strikes me as odd until the general leads me to the kitchens and I survey the route like a military strategist for the first time.

It's an unlikely place to look for someone, if the palace were to be raided, and the corridors leading to the kitchens are a bit of a maze. Guards line the narrow, easily defensible halls, and as if all of that were not enough, the general leaves me in the care of a feyn by the name of Faidra.

Faidra's bright red spirals are a beacon compared to the dark auburn locks of Siserie. She touts radiant eyes in a similar shade of green, a honey complexion and a uniquely lovely freckled face. The female is no soldier, it's obvious by the brown gown she wears and her flippant attitude. I can't help but wonder if the color of her hair is any indication of the female's gift as I watch her joking with Sera on the other side of the room.

"Come back for another history lesson?" Media cackles warmly when she sees me enter the room.

She knocks the leg of an empty chair with her cane. I smile at the woman and pull the chair up to the fire, taking a seat beside her.

"I never thanked you for all that you shared with me when I came to visit before," I say.

Her eyebrows creep up her head and her lips quirk up on one side. "You still haven't."

I grin and thank the woman, appreciating her humor as much as her candor.

"Truth be told," she sighs, rocking back in her chair, "I didn't expect to see you again so soon. You didn't seem particularly convinced by my tale."

"I've seen a lot since then," I admit.

Her shoulders bounce as she chuckles. "Funny, the things that can change us in such a short amount of time."

She has no idea. Or maybe she does. Either way, she seems satisfied when I agree with the sentiment.

"What more do you know about the Vatruke?" I ask.

"Only what is written in the history books. There were eight of them, one born shortly after the sundering, one lost to the war, and one who abandoned their cause."

"Nine," Faidra corrects the old woman around a mouthful of bread, raising nine fingers in the air. "There were nine after the sundering. Then the child was born." She adds a finger. "Then Muri was killed in the first war, she was the most powerful," she says, directing the last statement at me, lowering her finger again, "leaving nine Vatruke in the veil."

Media harrumphs at the female, waving her over as she glances at me apologetically.

"It's been years since I've been asked to recall such things," Media says, "and as cantankerous as this one can be, I do trust her memory of it."

"You should," Faidra says pridefully. "My professor just covered the Vatruke during my lessons. I had to write ten pages on them."

"How old are you?" The question slips past my lips before I can pinch it back.

"Sixteen. How old are you?" she asks, completely unbothered.

"Twenty-four," I answer.

Her eyes bulge. "Aren't you a little young?"

"I'm older than you," I say, unable to stifle the annoyance in my tone, oblivious to what she might mean.

"I mean, aren't you a little young for the general?" She smirks.

My cheeks heat, and she waggles her eyebrows at me.

"Faidra, leave the girl alone," Media sighs, "You'll learn soon enough that there are some things, destined by the fates, that you have no control over." She pulls a light quilt over her legs and clears her throat. "Anyway, tell us what you've been learning about the Vatruke."

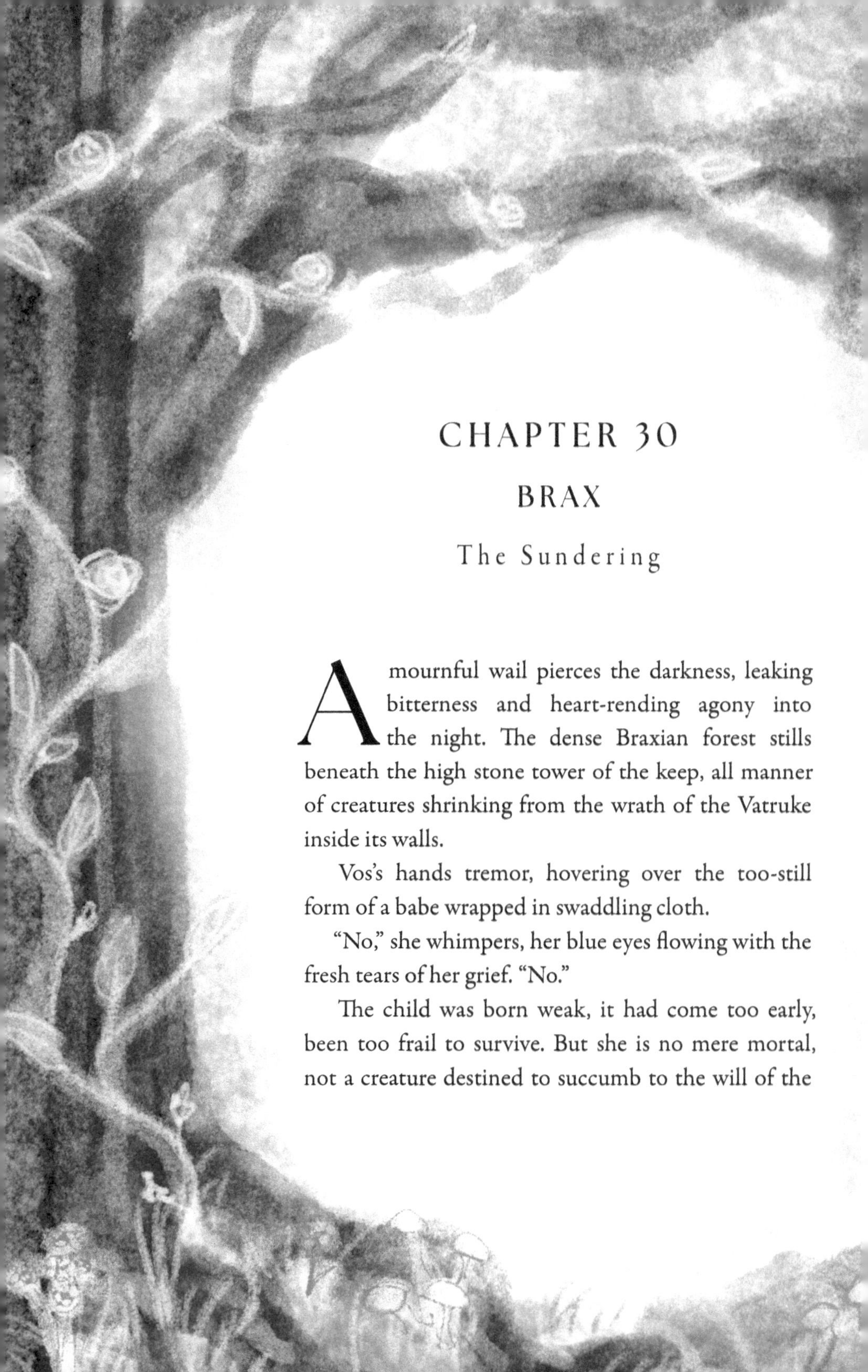

CHAPTER 30

BRAX

The Sundering

A mournful wail pierces the darkness, leaking bitterness and heart-rending agony into the night. The dense Braxian forest stills beneath the high stone tower of the keep, all manner of creatures shrinking from the wrath of the Vatruke inside its walls.

Vos's hands tremor, hovering over the too-still form of a babe wrapped in swaddling cloth.

"No," she whimpers, her blue eyes flowing with the fresh tears of her grief. "No."

The child was born weak, it had come too early, been too frail to survive. But she is no mere mortal, not a creature destined to succumb to the will of the fates. She is feyn, ancient and powerful, like the ancients who came before.

They fought to bind the fading threads of the child's life to Terr. Fought and won, tethering that life to the life force of their world. Just as its fading heartbeat began to thrum in time with the rhythm of the oceans, the veils were torn. The sundering wrenched away the tender budding threads of life they had so carefully woven.

"No," she whispers.

Her mate rocks her in his arms, his face drawn with sorrow. A vain attempt to soothe the raw, permanent ache of her broken heart.

"Let me take the child, *mi'ajna*," he begs in a near silent whisper, his lips buried deep within the long black of her hair.

"No," she pleads, rocking the child at her breast.

"Please, *mi'dair'a*," he says, "The child is gone."

"No!" A brutal wave of power tears out of the female when she screams, expelling her rage into the room.

Her mate is torn from her side, thrown and pinned against the large stone walls of the tower. Eyes wide, he groans, straining against the gift that holds him. Until her power ebbs and he crumples to the floor.

He brushes the dust from his arms and collects himself, dropping a loving kiss on top of her head as he cups her cheek. Her eyes remain glued to the tiny bundle in her arms as he says, "I'll bring the others to see the child before I take it."

Salty pools of her sorrow form on the stone floor as she dips her head in a shallow nod and Kezik slips out of the room, into the dark of the corridor beyond.

"How is she?"

He startles at the sound of Muri's voice. There is a trembling grief in her tone and a heavy weight of concern in the slow and cautious cadence of the question.

The female steps out of the shadows, her bright blue eyes ringed with red, shadows marring her fair cheeks. It's obvious she shares in their grief. Out of them all, she had always been the most tenderhearted.

Waiting for his reply, she brushes a long lock of black hair over her shoulder and crosses her arms over her chest.

 371

"Broken." How else could he describe the female he left inside.

But Muri already knew. She didn't have to ask what it meant to lose a child. No amount of time—centuries nor millennia—would soothe the ache of her sister's heart. Just as time failed to mend her own.

"Will you speak with her?" His voice is thick with pleading when he asks.

"Of course." She takes a determined step toward the door, collecting her strength, pausing to look back as she tells him, "The others are waiting."

He nods as she turns on her heel, disappearing into the chamber beyond.

Kezik departs from the mournful cries of his mate, weaving through the dark stone halls toward their gathering place. He rounds the corner and finds them unmoved, still waiting by the large fire where they had come to greet the child.

Four males stand at a thick dark wood mantle soft from centuries of wear. Every stone of the hearth carved to remind them of their history. Of a time when the feyn lived alongside the rest of the fea, deep within the forests of Brax.

He dips his head in greeting. The room seems larger tonight, absent the two females he left behind. The males greet him in turn, one with white hair and three with black, all with the striking blue eyes of the feyn. He looses a long breath, a small relief washing over him when he sees the sadness in their eyes. They already know.

Two females sit beside one another on a large and heavily cushioned chair, both wearing long, thick braids of pure white. The low thrum of their voices fades when they see him, his own sorrow reflected back in their eyes. The white-haired male, Durek, approaches him and holds Kezik's forehead against his own.

"I'm sorry, Kezik," Durek says, "Each of us feels your loss as keenly as if it were our own." It is not the frailty of grief that punctuates the quiet when he speaks. It is his anger, the pure and unrelenting hatred for the feyn who caused this. The feyn that shattered the world. "We will fix this."

"It's too late." Kezik's voice breaks.

None raise a voice to argue. For what could they say? None of them yet know the extent of their diminished power. Vos had been the first to suffer for it, but each know that, with time, such suffering will be shared by them all.

A shrill and bloodcurdling scream breaks the quiet, and every head

whips toward the hall. Mere moments pass before they've moved through the corridor and into the room where he'd left his mate to grieve.

Muri is on her knees before the child, held by a fist gripping her hair, a feynstone blade at her throat.

"Do it!" Vos demands through clenched teeth.

"I can't," Muri says, her bottom lip trembling.

"Let her go, Vos!" Durek yells over the fracturing crack of thunder, followed by a web of lightning that illuminates the sky.

"Tell your mate to do as I say, and I will release her!" Vos yells over the sudden deluge of rain brought by Durek's power.

"Kezik," Durek growls in warning, "Calm your mate, before I end her."

Kezik approaches the females cautiously. His eyes flick from those of his mate's to the dagger she fists, sending rivulets of blood down Muri's neck to pool on the white silk of her dress. He kneels beside her, cooing soothing words that soften the female's steel. She relaxes her grip on Muri's hair and releases the blade to fall clattering upon the floor.

Muri tears away from her, rushing into Durek's arms with a wracking sob of fear. Kezik alone seems unaffected by his own mate's wrath, as he bundles her into his arms, smoothing the hair on top of her head.

"You're selfish!" Vos yells across the room, her voice hoarse and weary. "The fates gift you the power of *Shivay* and you won't use it to save the innocent at my feet!"

"The gift is not without sacrifice, Vos. You know that," Durek growls in defense of his mate.

"I will pay the price," Vos says, hot tears streaming down her face. "I will pay it!"

"No," Kezik growls, silencing her.

"All we can ever do is trust the fates," Muri says weakly.

"Foc. The. Fates," Vos spits, "And foc the feyn."

The storm rages in the dead of night, thunder booming with a loud crack and flicker as the winds pick up, howling through the ancient forests of Brax.

When dawn breaks the horizon the next morning the Braxian rains finally begin to ebb. It is a new day, and life on Terr will never be the same. The ancients tore the veils to save the humans, leaving their own species to a miserable fate. Their power had been stripped from them, only a fifth of what they had known for millennia remained. Perhaps they could have learned to live with it—had it not already cost them so much.

Durek left the moment Muri began to dream beside him. Unable to find sleep himself, too troubled and plagued with sorrow. His eyes are heavy when he returns to the keep, his head clouded by the foggy haze of exhaustion. Exhaustion that taunts him with the soft ghostly echoes of a crying child.

No. These are no ghostly echoes sent to torment his mind.

His feet quicken beneath him as he rushes through the halls, through deep shadows and bright panels of light cast by the dawn. Sliding to a halt when he sees her, he gasps, wide-eyed, "How?"

Vos beams at the newborn babe nestled in her arms as she rocks it.

"Vos." He raises his voice, repeating the question, "How?"

"Muri," she coos, smiling at the child. "Muri brought the child back."

For all the joy the new mother holds in her arms, he is racked with an equal weight of dread. He rushes toward their room, breath caught in his chest, heart thundering. What price would the fates ask of his mate for the life of the child? What price would she have been willing to pay for her sister's happiness? Too much. He already knows, the price is too high.

He bursts into their chamber, collapsing onto the bed beside his mate, gripping her shoulders and shaking her forcefully.

"Muri. Wake up."

She moans, and he puffs out a sigh of relief. She's alive. He takes her hands in his own and asks, "What have you done?"

Her smile is weak. "Did you see?"

He nods, offering her a small smile in return. Not willing to admit that it was terror and not joy he felt when he'd seen the child cradled in Vos's arms.

"What was the price for the child's life?" he asks.

She turns toward the balcony, unable to meet his eyes, when she says, "Terr."

His brow pinches as he tries to discern her meaning.

"*Shivay* is in the child now," she says, her voice quavering.

"Muri h—"

"I know." Her eyes well with tears. "How many will die for the life of just one child? But how could I not?"

She turns toward him, a tear falling to stain the pillow below her cheek. "She would have hated me. Just as I hate myself for letting our own child—"

"Stop," he demands softly, wiping the salty trail from her cheek. "Don't ever say that again."

He brushes his lips against her forehead, whispering, "You are a bright light in all the darkness of this world. Your warm heart, a remnant of something I'd have forgotten long ago if you hadn't been by my side." He sweeps his fingers across her cheeks. "Let go of your regret, *mi'ajna*. There is no room in our lives for it."

She meets his lips with her own, a promise to let go of the past. One they both know she will never be able to keep, for neither time nor abundant joy can heal the wound in her heart.

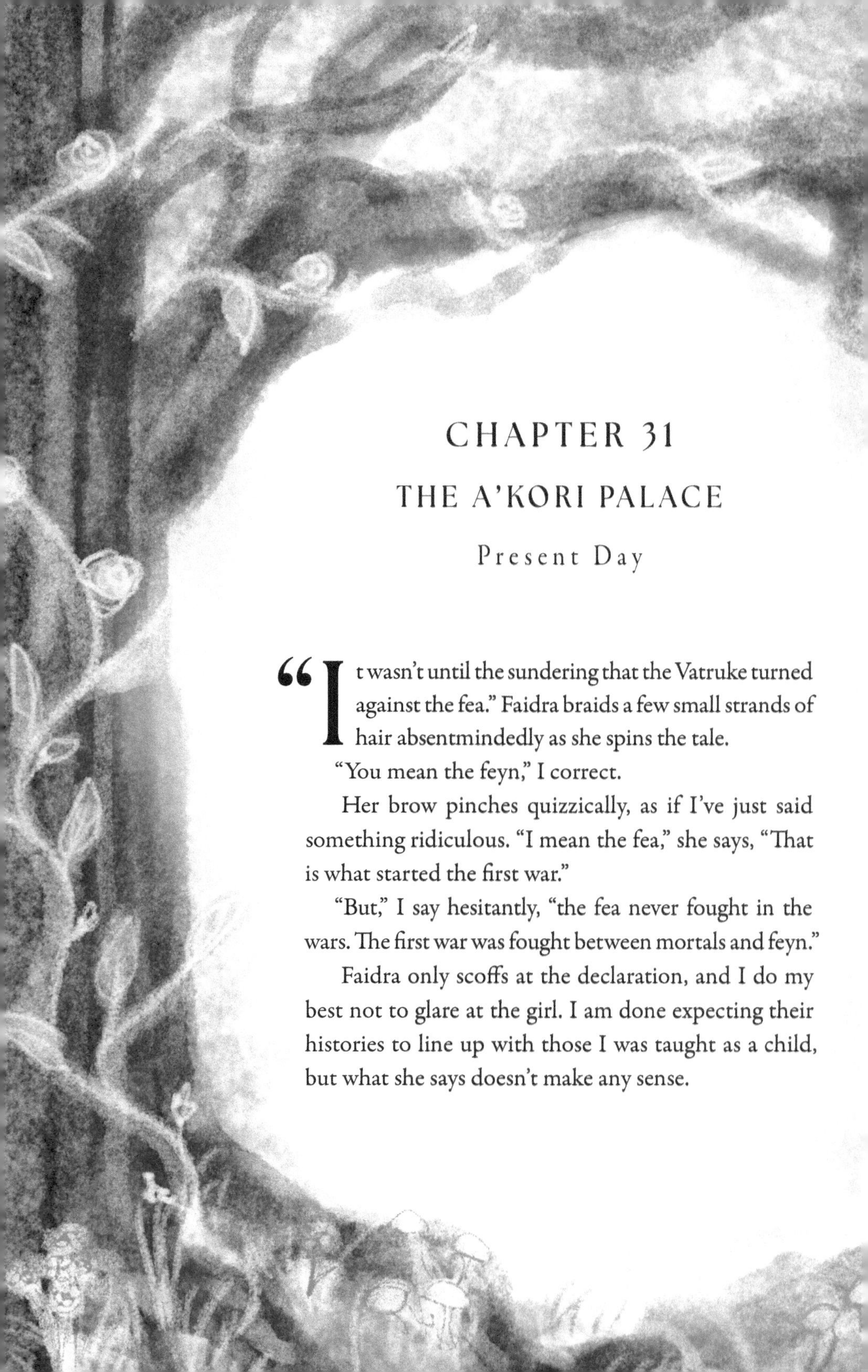

CHAPTER 31
THE A'KORI PALACE
Present Day

"It wasn't until the sundering that the Vatruke turned against the fea." Faidra braids a few small strands of hair absentmindedly as she spins the tale.

"You mean the feyn," I correct.

Her brow pinches quizzically, as if I've just said something ridiculous. "I mean the fea," she says, "That is what started the first war."

"But," I say hesitantly, "the fea never fought in the wars. The first war was fought between mortals and feyn."

Faidra only scoffs at the declaration, and I do my best not to glare at the girl. I am done expecting their histories to line up with those I was taught as a child, but what she says doesn't make any sense.

"Many mortals died in the first war, as they did in the second," Media says, "But did you never stop to ask yourself, why? After breaking the world in the sundering, after diminishing their own power to prevent more bloodshed, why would the feyn turn on the very humans they left to protect?"

I had not. Not once had I considered it. And though the stories of our history differ widely between the continents, a deep part of me knows that what she says is true.

The gifts of the feyn, despite the fact that I have seen very little in my time in A'kori, are powerful beyond what I imagined. I can't make myself believe that a veil exits in Terr in which a gifted could not easily snuff out the life of a mortal. The abundant power that the feyn possessed before the sundering is something I cannot begin to fathom.

I am still trying to puzzle it out when Faidra rolls her eyes, clearly doubtful my mind can accomplish such a feat.

"When the feyn came to the aid of the fea," she begins, "the Vatruke stood behind mortal men. They offered up your race as fodder, knowing that the feyn who had already gone through such great lengths to protect your people would rather yield than slaughter them."

My head spins as she weaves the tale.

"It was so easy for the Vatruke to convince the mortals that the feyn had at last come to destroy them. The war hardly began before it was over. The Vatruke having won the moment they retreated to Brax."

"Why would their retreat change anything? Why wouldn't the feyn follow after them?" I ask.

Faidra shakes her head, "Brax is all but inaccessible by sea. The feyn had two choices. Flee, or end the life of every mortal that stood between the northern shore and the Braxian forests."

"And the second war?" I ask, curious how she can possibly excuse the war I was born into. Even mortal memories, short as they are, recall the feyn as they burned the coastal villages.

It is Media that answers. "It took generations for the feyn to repair the rift made by the first war. Slowly, trade resumed between the continents, tenuous alliances were made, even some friendships. But the Vatruke would only allow it to continue for so long. When they saw the hearts of mortal men softening toward the feyn, they knew they had to intervene or risk our armies making their way past the southern borders and into Brax. With the support of the Drakai, they raided villages, burned homes, and took orphaned children to raise in service of your king."

Impossible. With every question I ask and every answer I receive I only become more lost in the web of lies.

Shaking my head to clear it, I tell her, "I've been to those villages, talked to the ones who survived. It was the feyn that took everything from them."

She shakes her head solemnly. "It was the Vatruke, but the race of man saw no difference between the two and the war was reborn."

I'm startled when I hear the general's voice come from the doorway.

"All that we built with the La'tari, generations of careful planning, gone in a matter of hours," he says, "as was our hope of reaching the fea that remained in the south."

"What do they do with them?" I ask.

"We still don't know," Faidra says.

I shake my head, unwilling to accept what they tell me.

"Awri told me that you were in the second war together. Tell me how that is possible if the feyn were not involved," I argue, grasping, searching for something to stop the fraying that has begun to unravel the story of my life.

The look he gives me is not the face I expect to see on a male who's been caught in a lie.

"Many of us were on the southern continent the night they started the war," he says, "Riah, Toren, Awri, and myself, among others. All for the same purpose. We sought *Valtoura*." He expels a heavy sigh. "We were there when the fires started. When the wailing of young mothers could be heard all along the tidelands. So yes, we fought in the war, against the Vatruke, against the Drakai, but never against the people."

"The villagers would have seen. They would have come to aid you," I insist.

I know they would have. Even now the hearts of the La'tari people are strong. Even after everything they have been through.

The general shrugs. "What are two monsters fighting each other amidst a world on fire as you try to flee and save your family?"

I hate every word. Hate the truth I feel in all of it. Hate that I let myself

be so deceived, so blind. What a mess we have made of our world. And how quickly this would all end if the La'tari people could be made to see the truth.

Though some know. Recalling the contingent of Drakai that rode with the Vatruke male, I can't help but wonder how many more are aware of the truth of this world. Leanna? Bront? ...Vakesh?

Had anyone who had part in forming me known the extent of the lies they fed me my entire life? Had they all? No. Not all of them. There is one, and even after everything, I can't bring myself to believe that he would deceive me.

"As a child," I say to no one in particular, grasping at the last thread binding the delicate facade that is my life, "I witnessed a group of feyn attacking humans in the forest." A small lie, and I suspect I know the answer before I even hear Faidra's voice.

"Those that sided with the Vatruke."

"Or," the general adds, "made bargains with the La'tari king, not understanding what it would cost them."

My company seems content to let me sit in silence for some time. My eyes on the fire before me, lost in the flickering heat emanating from the dark stone around it.

By the time I rise to excuse myself for the evening, Media has fallen asleep in her chair. The old woman breathes deeply, her colorful blanket slipping off the knobs of her knees. Adjusting the quilt in her lap, I thank Faidra before following the general back to our room.

"If your ancestors were trying to save the feyn, why would they leave the Vatruke behind? Knowing that they were opposed to the sundering, they had to expect something like this could happen," I ask the general as I run my fingers through the tangle of locks draped over my shoulder.

He paces in front of the fire, unable to fully relax after the news Riah and I delivered this afternoon.

"The ancients knew that the Vatruke might grow vengeful, but they would not interfere with the choice those of us made to remain behind. So, they left us with a seed of *Shivay*, a soul to guard us if ever there was need. We call it, *Valtoura*."

I tip my head quizzically. "Why didn't this *Valtoura* show itself during

the first war? Or the second? If it was meant to protect the feyn, surely that would have been the time."

"I've asked myself the same thing many times," he says, spearing his fingers through his hair.

A knock sounds at the door and the glare it puts on the general's face is comically frightening. Though I likely wouldn't feel the same if it were directed at me. He swoops in and drops a kiss on top of my head as he walks past to answer it.

"It's been a long day, *mi'ajna*. Get some sleep. I'm not sure how long this will take."

I glimpse Riah in the hall as I make my way toward the washroom. She will be briefing the general on her trip to see Toren at the barracks. Unless she came across trouble, the debrief shouldn't take long, and by the sound of her voice she isn't relaying anything terribly pressing.

I pin my hair into a pile on top of my head and twist the lever that makes water rain down from the spigot overhead. My thoughts linger on the Vatruke, on Vos and her mate. I brace myself with my arms outstretched on either side, my head tipped down between them, walls of cool, slick marble beneath my palms. Water cascades in streams between my shoulder blades and down my back. My mind spins like the endless flow of water swirling down the drain.

I am going to die. I wonder how many Drakai witness the moment the fates clip the thread of their life. I always thought death would come faster. That I would be on a battlefield and lock eyes with my fate before the end. Never did I imagine something like this. To be hated and hunted for taking what was hers.

Will she make it quick? I wouldn't.

I hardly know the male I share a bed with and have already killed for him. How much greater would that rage have been if we had shared many mortal lifetimes beside one another? How much more precious would that life have become to me?

I startle when the general's lips find the crook of my neck. "What is troubling you, *mi'ajna*?"

"Nothing that can't wait until morning," I say.

His lips linger, his hands falling to my hips, and his thumbs knead the dimples in my lower back.

"Tell me." It isn't a demand, rather a simple request for a glimpse inside my mind.

"Vos," I admit, aware that she occupies his thoughts as much as my own.

He tenses, even as his hands move to soothe my own muscles.

"She will never reach you inside the palace," he assures me.

I huff a disbelieving laugh. Tonight, I have learned enough to know that the Vatruke are nothing if not incredibly powerful.

"Even if you believe that, do you really think you'll be able to keep me here? Locked up like a prisoner?"

His hands still. "It's hardly a prison, Shivaria."

"A gilded cage," I say, turning to face him.

He sucks in a breath, swallowing whatever retort he'd conjured, and I say, "Even if I *choose* to stay here, do you truly think she will let me live out my life? Silken pillows and a full belly until I die of old age?" I sigh. "I wouldn't, not if I were her. Not if it had been..."

Too much. You give away too much. My heart falters a beat, my stomach turning inside out, and suddenly I'm back on that ship. *You're letting your guard down, Shivaria.*

I break from his touch, intent on letting the male bathe in solitude. He stops me with a hand around my wrist, before my feet can take me from the water.

"One day, *mi'ajna,* you will trust me," he says it so matter of fact. "It doesn't have to be today. And in truth, it will only ever be the day that you decide I am worth the risk of whatever it is you fear from me."

I can't trust him. Just as he can't trust me. I won't debate him and remind him that there are still things he doesn't tell me. Secrets that he is wise to keep.

A fine muscle ticks at the edge of his jaw.

"Ask me," he pleads, "I will tell you anything you want to know."

There it is. Every moment in A'kori has led me to this. I should seize it, take every speck of what he's offering. This is the way I complete my mission. But haven't I already given up every opportunity I've had to do just that?

Perhaps Vos will send me to the afterlife before I succumb to the insanity of my mind. Maybe this is it. My last chance to have every question answered

before the end. But when I think about how my life might end, and how I'd like to spend my last days, hours, minutes, I find that it isn't his answers I want.

It isn't about trust when I lean in, brushing my lips against his. It's not about my mission when I encourage the firm press of his body against my own. When he cups my jaw, his tongue delving deeply into my mouth, every fear I have of what could be is stripped from me.

"I want you." I repeat the same words I spoke to the male before he left.

"You have me." The heat of his breath tickles my lips, his hands cupping the globes of my ass as he picks me up, hooking my legs around his waist.

I think he might be taking me to the bed when he passes it altogether, laying me on the thick grey pelt splayed out in front of the fire.

His lips envelop my breast, and I suck in a breath. His teeth gently teasing before the soft caress of his tongue. His hands roam across my flesh, exploring my form. The cinch of my waist, the curve of my hips, the shape of my thighs.

When his mouth begins to travel down past my navel, my toes curl expectantly. The slow drag of his tongue as it slides across my core is *everything*.

"Yes," I whisper, my fingers tangling in his thick black locks.

I feel him smile as his grip tightens on my thighs, holding me firmly against his face. The friction of his tongue between my legs arches my back off the plush fur as I moan into the night.

He is attentive to every sigh, every shift of my hips, every sharp intake of breath as he devours me greedily. Unwilling to relent until it's all I can do not to scream out his name.

His tongue is a wicked thing. It swirls lazily over that sensitive bundle of nerves, coiling the tension as he sucks me in, before soothing me again with blissfully slow strokes and long, idle sweeps. I writhe beneath him, his tongue keeping time with the pulse of ecstasy building inside me. Every tremor of my body is met with the flick of his tongue between my legs.

I tense under his attention. It's all too overwhelming. Every sensation brings me closer to the precipice and my body shakes as I rush toward my release.

"Not yet," he purrs, as I ride the edge of ecstasy, and he slows to a wickedly teasing pace.

My breath is caught in my throat when his fangs leave exquisite trails of

pleasurable pain across my torso as he rises to meet me. He catches the tender pink flesh at the center of my breast between his teeth, and I shudder out a gasp.

"Xeyvian." His name slips off my lips in a plea and I nearly break when the male growls before capturing my mouth with his own again, the sweet taste of my passion still on his lips.

He grinds his thick length against that tender bud of nerves and nips my lip. I don't think about it when I tip my hips until the head of his shaft is bumping up against the slick folds of my core. His body goes rigid, the hesitation he feels clearly written on his face.

So, I wait, as patient as he has always been with me. Smiling at him, a smile that tells him I want this. I brush my lips against his shoulder, his neck, his ear. I let my hands explore his body just as he had mine. Every muscular curve and hard line, a map I will myself to commit to memory.

The tension leaks from his jaw as he drags his thumb down the blade of my cheek. His brow furrows further, then the hesitation pours out of the male, his lips falling to mine. There is nothing insistent about the kiss, nothing pressing or demanding. It's soft, gentle, tender. Things I hadn't known until I met him. My arms fold around his neck and I think that, maybe, if I must die, I'd like it to be in his arms.

One hand at my jaw, the other hooks around my thigh and draws it up to his side, and he sinks himself into me.

A thrum of silent thunder pulses like an echo. I gasp when a pain like nothing I've ever felt, blinding white and full of rapture, ignites my chest, searing across my torso and bicep. It brings something I can't place, like a foundation formed in the deepest part of my being. Just as quickly as it came, the force begins to settle, snapping something taut inside me.

Xeyvian's brow dips, and as if summoned by his sharp inhale of breath, a dark mark of ancient script wraps his bicep to trail across his chest, ending beneath his heart. The male rests his forehead against mine, a deep sigh emanating from his lips as he begins to rock his hips back and forth.

He is slow and gentle at first. Nothing like what I'd been taught to expect when I'd been told stories by other Fea Dien. He takes his time exploring the boundaries of our union, encouraged when I begin to move my body in time with his own.

His hands are at my waist, exploring my breasts, tenderly stroking the soft skin of my arms. His lips explore the curve of my throat, my jaw. Every bare scrap of flesh he can find he adorns with his touch.

I moan into the night, overcome with the glorious feeling of my body stretching around him. His mouth catches the sound, his tongue playing along my lips as he pushes himself in, only to retreat tauntingly. When he presses in again, I answer the slow thrust of his length by tipping my hips to drive him deeper. This time *I* swallow the male's moan, his own throaty response to the pleas of my body as I usher him inside.

He takes his time, filling me inch by inch, each gradual stroke deeper than the last, letting me become accustomed to his girth, his length, his presence inside me. My core clenches greedily, tightening around him when he finally thrusts hard, seating himself to the hilt. The achingly perfect stretch of my body as I take the male fully is rapture itself.

"Fates," he groans as he pulls back and thrusts in again, seating himself in my core. "You're perfect," he sighs. "This is—"

"Perfect," I gasp, echoing the sentiment as he slams himself into me.

With every stroke, he slides against that tiny bundle of nerves, building a tension I cannot suppress. I want this to last. I want to spend hours milking him of his passion until we are both truly and utterly spent.

But there is no denying the torrent of bliss that crashes through my body.

I gasp, when I shatter like fractured starlight, from the likes of which new galaxies are born. Each wave of my release casts me further into oblivion until I'm completely lost to myself, skating along the precipice of life, light, and utter darkness.

I'm gone, dancing along the farthest expanses of the universe when a deep murmur flits across my ears. A familiar voice pulls at a tether in my chest, and I have no choice but to follow. It's a sweet sound, followed by the tender brush of his lips against my cheek. The male purrs in my ear, breathy feyn whispers, and I loose a deep sigh of utter contentment.

More. I want more. Because what will ever be enough?

I hook my leg over his back and pitch my weight, rolling on top of him. I never expected to use the move outside of a fight, but I find that I greatly prefer it for this function. He looks surprised before he smiles and grips my

hips, encouraging me, showing me how to move. I brace my hands against his chest, sinking down on his length, moaning. I'm pleased to find that this position grants him deeper entry inside of me.

His thumb sweeps across my nub as I ride him, strumming me like a chord he's settling into perfect tune. My core tightens with every sweep of his finger, with every deep stroke of his length. A muscle bounces along the edge of his jaw as his eyes drop to the swell of my chest.

My head kicks back when he rises to capture the tender pink flesh of my breast in his mouth. With every flick of his tongue, I feel the build of a new breaking and his moan vibrates my chest with warning.

"I know," I breathe.

His hips thrust up to meet me when I slide down on him, and I come completely undone, unraveled by the male, into thousands of tiny threads that will never be knit back together. Riding out the waves of my passion, he shudders beneath me, moaning as he spills himself deep within my pulsating core.

His body goes slack against the fur beneath him, and I collapse, brushing my lips along his chest as his heart tries to break free from beneath his sternum. My hair is splayed out in front of the fire. His fingers trace idle lines down the length of my spine as we catch our breath.

This is dangerous. Because I would give the male anything in this moment.

The second he shifts his hips, unsheathing himself from me, I realize just how vacant I've always been. More than the physical loss of him pits my stomach, and I push away every thought that would take me from this moment.

Maybe I should, but I don't want to stop and ask about the feyn mysteries I was never taught. About the mark that bloomed on his body at our coupling, about what I myself felt when he entered me. Not tonight.

The pop of the fire lulls me, my skin still prickling with every rapturous release the male has driven from my body. I'm dozing off to the sound of his heartbeat, my ear resting on his chest, when his voice comes from the comfortable stillness of the night.

"Tell me that you will remain in A'kori with me." Before I've fully understood his request he adds, "Permanently."

I'm not sure if the flutter of my heart or the wrenching twist of my gut is more severe when his request finally falls into place within my mind. Why

would he want such a thing? If I were the lady I claim to be, I would have plenty of reasons to stay at his request, but what does he gain by it?

At a loss for words, I simply nod, and he runs his fingers through my hair. I expect to struggle to find sleep, with the looming threat of the war and thoughts of Vos and her vengeance still at the forefront of my mind. But it isn't those thoughts that weave into a hazy tangle as I drift off. It's thoughts of Xeyvian, and an impossible life I could have lived with the male if I were another woman. A life I find I desperately want but will never have.

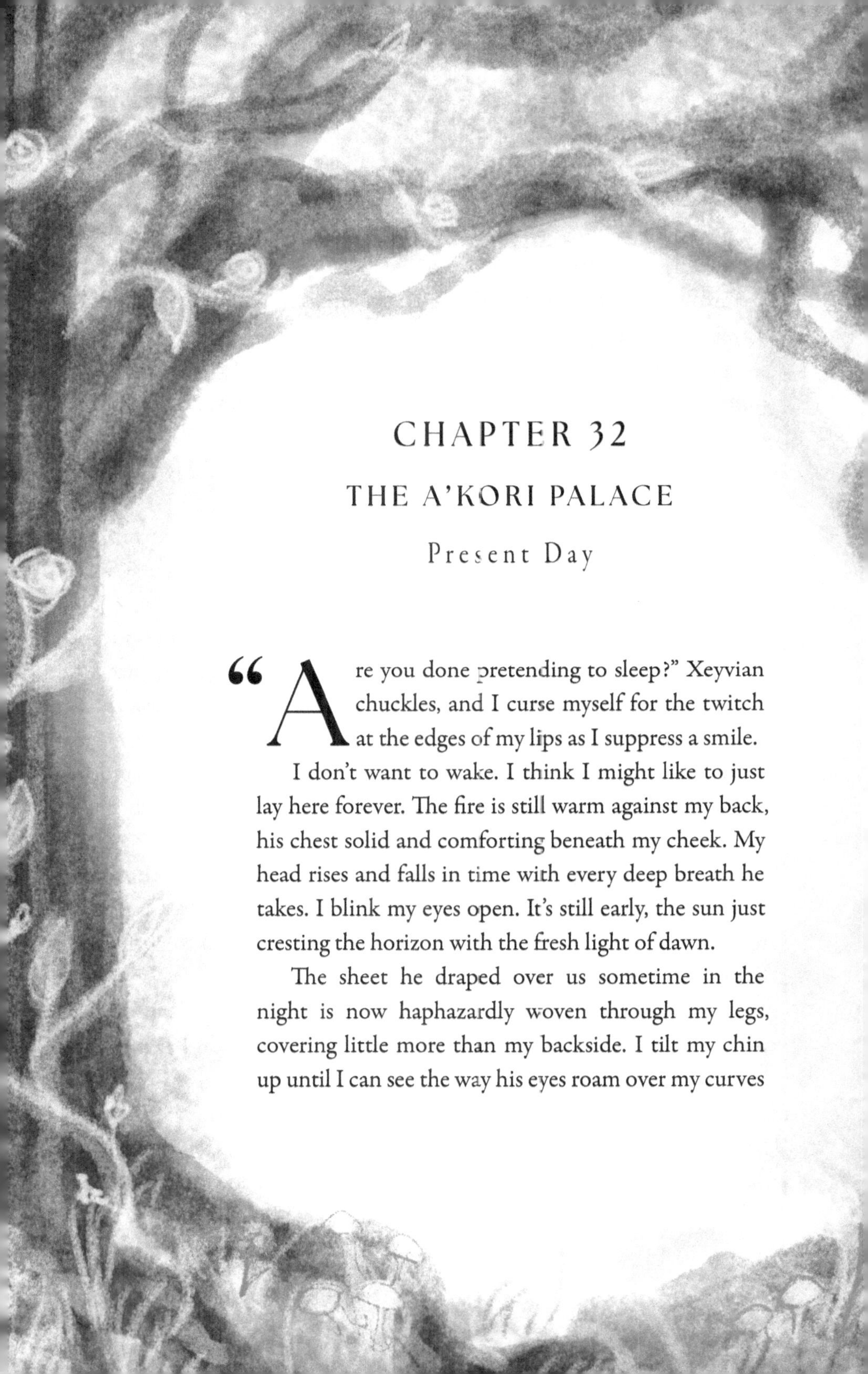

CHAPTER 32

THE A'KORI PALACE

Present Day

"Are you done pretending to sleep?" Xeyvian chuckles, and I curse myself for the twitch at the edges of my lips as I suppress a smile.

I don't want to wake. I think I might like to just lay here forever. The fire is still warm against my back, his chest solid and comforting beneath my cheek. My head rises and falls in time with every deep breath he takes. I blink my eyes open. It's still early, the sun just cresting the horizon with the fresh light of dawn.

The sheet he draped over us sometime in the night is now haphazardly woven through my legs, covering little more than my backside. I tilt my chin up until I can see the way his eyes roam over my curves appreciatively, my own eyes exploring the lines of a new bargain brandished on his skin. He smiles when he catches me looking at it, and the curve of his lips sends my stomach fluttering. The things the male can do to me with a simple smile.

"You are staying in A'kori with me." He isn't asking, but it isn't exactly a command. "Say it." Now, *that* is a command, and I chastise myself for the way it makes me squeeze my thighs together.

I break from his gaze, taking in a lungful of his scent as I nuzzle into him, nipping at the rise of flesh on his chest. He inhales sharply, tensing beneath me as he winds my hair into his fist, and I smile up at him.

"I think I'd like a shower before we have this discussion." My smile turns mischievous.

His jaw is tense when he releases me and I brace myself over him, one arm on either side of his torso. I might be enjoying this all too much when I ask, "Join me?"

That's all it takes to set his eyes ablaze. I watch as every thought is stripped from his mind, replaced with only the desire I impart through my gaze.

Rising from the thick fur, I take his hand and lead him toward the washroom. My eyes snag on our reflection as we pass by the tall mirrors lining the washroom walls. Though the feyn were more accepting of my looks than the beauties I'd been raised with, the stark contrast of the male's beauty and my own feels more evident than ever.

Maybe it's the dip in my brow, maybe the falter of my step, but he rounds on me, pinching my chin between his fingers. He looks down at me with a reassuring smile when he says, "You are the most beautiful thing I've ever laid eyes on, *mi'ajna*. Never doubt it."

I can't help but return his smile, even if my own is forced. I'm sure the male who's lived hundreds of years has seen his share of women far lovelier than I. He sweeps my legs out from under me, chuckling at the surprised squeak that vacates my lungs. He looks altogether too proud at the noise he's garnered from me. When my feet smack against the floor under the overhead spigot, I dart out from under it before he can summon the water and drench my hair.

He turns the lever and steam curls in the air. He pours an oil into a small, hollow tube protruding from the wall and it sputters a hazy mist, making the

room smell of crushed mint. Clearly, I could spend an entire mortal lifetime exploring the intricacies of the palace and still be in awe.

He's too quick when he grips my arm and pulls me under the water. My protests lost in the stream overhead as it soaks my thick spirals. It's clear he knew exactly what he was doing when I see the playful look in his eyes.

Who is this male? Where is the brooding general I've come to know?

Xeyvian lathers his hands with a thick cake of soap before spreading it across the planes of my body. His hands sweep across my back before his fingers drag out the tension locked in the muscles of my arms. The press of his fingers against my backside before they make their way down to my thighs and calves is intoxicating. He takes a knee in front of me, lifting my legs, one after the other, massaging the tight muscles he finds there before washing the soles of my feet.

Only when he's thoroughly scoured and caressed every inch and aching muscle of mine does he take the soap to his own body. My hand shoots out, grasping his wrist to still his arm as I pry the sudsy cake from his fingers. I see the moment he realizes my intent, and I'm not sure why he shifts his weight apprehensively.

It dawns on me all too quickly, and I suppress a small swell of shame. While he has been clear about his intentions and eager to see to my desires, this is the first time I am offering him any form of pleasure that is entirely selfless.

His body might as well be made of stone for all the good I do when I try to work the knots and lifetimes of tension from his shoulders. Nevertheless, he shuts his eyes and leans his head back with a groan when I slowly work my way down his spine.

I debate skipping over the muscular globes of his backside. And decide that perhaps this act isn't entirely selfless after all, when I begin to knead his firm ass, eyeing it appreciatively. My hands grace every line of the male's form before I fall to my knees, intent on washing his feet as he had mine.

Kneeling before him, my eyes catch on the rivulets streaming between the lines of his abdomen. I follow that trail down, fixated on the movement of the water until I'm gazing wantonly at his hard length. Conversations with Riah play in my mind, of how she captured the rapture of her own male on her tongue.

I look up at him, a muscle bouncing at the edge of his jaw as he stares down at me. His chest begins to rise and fall rapidly as I lean in, swiping my tongue across the salty bead at his tip.

"Foc," he sighs, my stomach dipping when he threads his fingers through my hair.

I run my tongue from his tip to his base then back again, delighted by the male's groans. I test my mouth around his girth, stretching my jaw in a way I've only done when overcome with a deep yawn. I begin to wonder what I've gotten myself into. Seeing the trepidation in my eyes, he cups my jaw tenderly, adjusting the angle, showing me how to take him in.

Breathing becomes easier, and I feel a heady rush as he slides his length deep into the back of my throat. I observe him closely as I draw him from between my lips and back again. I note every twinging muscle, listen to every deep sigh, commit to memory each twist and purse of my mouth that makes the male's pulse quicken. His hands tighten in my hair as I milk a deep rumbling moan from his throat.

My name is a whispered prayer on his lips when his hips buck, thrusting him deep. I feel his passion rise as he tugs back, attempting to draw himself out of my mouth. But Riah had been thorough in her description of how I could ensure his most exquisite release. So, I tighten my grip on his hips and pull him into the back of my throat as he tremors, spilling himself deep inside.

The taste of his ecstasy slicks my tongue as he withdraws from me. The flavor of his passion, not at all unpleasant, is well worth the fire that burns in his eyes when he draws me to my feet. He wipes the last remnant of his desire from my bottom lip with a slow swipe of his calloused thumb. Fascination, reverence, awe, all of these swirl in the storm of his eyes as he gazes at me from under the steaming water.

One step forward and he's captured my mouth, his tongue delving greedily after the proof of my efforts. His nose brushes mine affectionately when our lips part. With one hand he pulls the lever, halting the steady stream from the ceiling, and grasps a thick towel with the other.

I know what comes next, and I don't want to lie to him when he asks me again. I can't stay. I would. Gladly, I would, if I were a different woman, but I'm not. And I was born to earn this male's hatred. Maybe it makes me a

coward, but I don't think I can stomach seeing it in his eyes. I'm not sure I'd survive witnessing the moment he discovers what I truly am.

A low rumble in his chest pulls me back into the present, and I glance at him briefly, before my eyes dart away from the intensity of his gaze. I've let something slip, standing across from him, lost in my thoughts. I'm not sure what he's just witnessed but it's clear he doesn't care for it.

He wraps the towel around my shoulders and pulls me a step closer. I close my eyes when his lips land on my temple, willing myself to memorize the feel of them. They capture the lobe of my ear, and I sigh contentedly, leaning into his body. He lingers on the spot, biting gently and soothing the sting before moving down my neck with slow, agonizing strokes of his tongue. Each time he ushers a sigh from my lips or a small gasp, he stays, exploring the area until he's sure he has my pleasure perfected.

An echo of his promised intentions resounds in my mind. *I want to know that ... where you like to be kissed. How you like to be touched.*

The male is diligently working every inch of my body to be sure he discovers exactly that.

I'm not entirely dry when he drops the towel to the floor and palms my backside, hoisting me to straddle his waist. His eyes don't break from mine as he walks us to the bed. Emotions I don't recognize, things I've never known are silently exchanged between us.

The moment my back hits the bed he continues his thorough exploration of my body. A frustrating and glorious tension building deep inside me when he skips over every tender, sensitive piece of flesh he's already mastered with his tongue. He's lavishing his attentions on my ankle when I catch the glint of his fangs in the first rays of sunlight that filter in through the windows. I don't have to glance down to see that he shares the deep growing need wetting my core.

His eyes burn through me when he says, "I've already told you that I am yours." He leans over me, my breasts pebbling against his chest as it brushes against me. "Now let me show you what it means to be *mine.*"

My stomach dips at the gravel in his tone when he says it. Before I understand what he intends, the male lays down on his back, lifts me over his head, and settles my legs on either side so that I straddle his face. My cheeks burn, but before I can squirm out of his grasp his hands palm my ass and his tongue swipes at my entrance. He moans at the taste and my knees quake, threatening to collapse.

His hands move from my backside to my hips, encouraging me to partake in his greedy tongue. It only takes a small pitch of my torso and that tender nub he's been careful to avoid in his trail of kisses is being diligently teased between lips and teeth.

He smiles when I moan and, gripping my hips, he pulls me down onto his face. It's all the encouragement I need to take full advantage of the position, and I press myself against his ravenous mouth.

His. That's what he said. And I can't deny that in this moment I want to be exactly that.

His tongue delves deep inside me, as his thumb strums between my legs causing my breath to catch in my lungs. He moans into my core when I throw my head back and tremor out my pleasure, his tongue offering a caress and flick at my nub with every rapturous quake.

With a self-satisfied smile and kiss to that tender mound, he lifts me up and lays me back down, my belly against the silk sheets. He hooks my waist, lifting me onto my knees, he pulls me against him and his thick shaft slides between my legs, gliding across that sensitive rise.

His chest presses against my back when he leans over me, cupping my jaw as he whispers in my ear. "Tell me you will stay with me in A'kori."

He must feel my apprehension because before I can answer he lines himself up behind me, rises to his knees, and presses against my entrance. The slow stretch as he pushes himself into me draws a loud cry of pleasure from my lips. I clutch the sheets in my fists and bury my face in the duvet.

The male must be proficient at torture, and why hadn't I suspected that before? He withdraws each tantalizing stroke before I can find the bliss of our completion.

"Xeyvian," I beg as he teases me, "I want you."

"I know the feeling, *mi'ajna*." His breath caresses my ear. "Say it."

The demand, the withholding, the torturous promise of rapture if I give in. The male is a demon, and I can't even convince myself to hate him for it. I attempt to pull away. I won't let myself lie to him, not about this.

His grip firms on my waist and he sinks himself deep, until his hips bump against my backside and I sigh at the reprieve as he releases a throaty groan of his own. He graces my body with long, slow sweeps that send a shiver up my spine. His lips land between my shoulder blades when he reaches a hand between my legs and rounds that sensitive mound of flesh with his thumb once again.

"Fates." It passes my lips in a whispered breath as he thrusts himself into me fully. Never have I felt so complete.

My core clenches around him as I crest the rise of my release.

"Say it." His demand makes me molten, and it takes everything I have to push down the urge to give the male everything he wants.

A quiet curse slips from his lips when I peak, tightening around his perfect length, every pulse of my ecstasy drawing him deeper inside of me.

Before my body can fall slack against the silk sheets beneath us, he withdraws from me and flips me onto my side, pulling one leg between his thighs as he wraps the other around his side. I hardly have time register the position before he sheaths himself in me once again.

He cups my breast as he pulls back and thrusts himself deep, an act he repeats at a quickening pace. My back arches and I stifle a moan, my body too sensitive for his attentions to be anything but mind bending.

His hands wrap around my torso, and he pulls me back against him in the same moment he thrusts his hips forward. My head spins, my hands grasping at the sheets, my body contorting into a taut string, ready to snap. The tension builds in my belly and the male smiles down at me smugly as he repeats the motion.

With a ragged moan, every muscle in my body flexing in an uncontrolled demand for release, I spiral into oblivion. His own passion floods me as he follows after, chasing the stars and reforming the known constellations in the ripple of our combined breaking.

I'm lost among unknown worlds when he brushes a dark spiral from my face, trailing his thumb across the flush of my cheeks, bringing me back to him.

"Tell me you'll stay," he begs, "because now that I've found you, I know that whatever life I thought I had before was merely existing."

His plea guts me, and I find that more than I've ever wanted anything for myself, for my kingdom, for my king, I want to give this male everything he asks. But how can I?

Even if I tell him everything and he allows me to live—which he won't. How could he?—Even if I find out that everything they've told me about the La'tari is true, there is still more to consider.

"Vos," I say.

His brow draws down and he brushes his knuckles over my cheek. "We are strong enough to deal with Vos when she comes for you, and there is no safer place for you on Terr than by my side."

I know he believes that, and he might be right, but at what cost? I'm no fool. I know that I had gotten lucky when I felled her mate. What little I've learned about the female since then tells me all I needed to know about her strength and the impossible power she possesses.

A tick at the edge of his jaw draws my attention.

"It doesn't take an empath to see the war in your eyes, *mi'ajna*."

It isn't a question but the need to explain bubbles up inside of me.

"I want to stay," I admit, even as my stomach dips in fear of the proclamation, even knowing it won't change a thing. He wants more; I can see it in his eyes as clearly as he is reading the tempest of muddled thoughts in my own, but he doesn't press.

He simply nods and lands a gentle kiss on my lips when he says, "That is enough, for now."

He begins to push away from me, a flash of disappointment exposing his weakness. My whole life I've been trained to exploit that weakness, to use it against him to further my own ambitions. But I don't think before I thread my fingers in his hair and pull his mouth to mine.

I don't want to use the male's weaknesses against him, all I want in the world is to reassure him that I want him. That if it were just us, I would give myself to him without hesitation. With the caress of his tongue against mine, he deepens the kiss, his hand resting over my heart. When he breaks away, resting his forehead against mine, the tension leaves his body in a deep sigh.

He pulls me to my feet and ushers me back into the washroom, as he continues through, making his way toward the closet. Cringing when I look in the mirror again, I find a comb to untangle the mess of locks knotted down my back. I've barely finished working my mane into manageable spirals when he comes up behind me, ready for the day, landing a lingering kiss in the crook of my neck.

"I sent an invitation for the masque to an old friend of mine," he says, "She is set to arrive tomorrow, and I'd like you to meet her."

My stomach pits at the tone of his voice and the serious look in his eyes. But I smile and nod, considering, as always with the feyn, what her gifts might be and how a moment alone with the wrong gifted will change everything.

A knock at the door calls him into the main room and he closes the washroom doors as he leaves. Dressing in a blue-grey gown with a matching pair of fitted pants, I immediately regret the absence of the leathers against my skin. Wishing I had some way to hide my precious blades beneath the skirt of my dress, I let myself out into the room beyond.

The general stands in the doorway of the war room speaking with Riesh, his brow falling in confusion when he takes in my chosen attire. I run my fingers through the length of my hair and raise my brows. If the male has something to say...?

"You don't plan to train with Riah this morning?" he asks curiously.

I shake my head, pulling my shoulders back, well aware of the protests I'm about to receive from him.

"I'm going to visit my uncle," I announce.

Despite the fact that it is not a question, he draws in a deep breath, considering me.

"I will take Riah with me." I only say it because I'm sure that there is no veil in Terr in which the male will let me go alone, not while Vos remains on the continent.

He shakes his head, and I firm my resolve. I'm ready to go to war with him if he tries to lock me inside the palace for my own good.

"Let me send a carriage for him," he says, offering a solution.

I can't fault him for his desire to keep me safe inside the palace grounds and so I agree to his request. It might be a bit overprotective but when I recall how I felt when the Drakai came to claim his life I find that I understand all too well.

He sends a young page with a letter, extending an invitation to the palace and explaining my desire to visit with my uncle. I have no doubt he will come. A summons by the king's general is something I know the man won't take lightly.

Felias arrives by mid-morning. And as if his insistence that I remain within the palace grounds isn't excessive enough, Xeyvian directs Riah to lead a small party of soldiers to greet him. When I insist on showing my uncle the gardens the general joins us, directing the soldiers to give us a wide berth.

We exchange casual conversation until the general, sensing my need for a private moment with my uncle, excuses himself and falls back to speak with Riah.

There is no time to skirt my reason for summoning him. No time to dance around my meaning. So, I take a deep breath and let the words tumble out of my mouth.

"I saw the shipment from La'tari," I say.

Felias nods, humming under his breath before replying, "So I was told, when the sisters introduced me to Eon's mate."

I don't startle at the statement. I assumed as much.

"Why was that ship full of fea cargo?" My stomach twists even as I ask.

"You asked what the Vatruke draw power from. Now you know," he says, as if that single sentence answers every burning question the man knows I have.

"What do the Vatruke do to the fea?" I ask.

"You saw the state of Eon's mate," he says simply. "He is far from the first to arrive in such a condition."

It doesn't answer my question, but I hardly expect more from the man. The more I learn, the more I find that he's never been truly forthcoming with me. I puff out an exasperated sigh, shaking my head. He offers me a consoling smile as he says, "If I knew, I would tell you more."

"You've never asked?" I balk. Surely the sisters would tell him, even if Eon's mate remains withdrawn.

"The fea that make it to the shores of A'kori are the fea that manage to escape before breaking." A flicker of regret flashes in his eyes. "What happens to the ones who cannot remain strong? I truly wish I knew."

Larger cracks begin to spread across the panes of my world. I don't want to hear him. I don't want to believe it's true. What kind of monsters would draw the lifeforce of another being to satisfy their thirst for power?

And isn't that exactly what I am here to do for my king? I didn't know it when I came, but if I have begun to believe what I've learned in my time here, I have to ask myself if I am any better than the Vatruke for what I plan.

"Does the king know?" The question reeks of my shame.

"Both kings are well aware of the atrocity," he says, knowing full well it is my own king I am asking about.

"But the feyn king offers them sanctuary," I say, "Why doesn't he do more?"

Even after the stories Faidra wove in front of the fire I find it hard to let myself believe that the feyn are without options. So why don't they do more to help the fea they claim to protect?

"He went to war, Shivaria. What more could he do?"

"But he signed the treaty. Why?" I ask.

Surely, even if he had gone to war to protect the lives of the fea as well as the humans, he'd betrayed any good intentions when he signed that paper, giving them all over to the Vatruke.

He shrugs. "Perhaps he did what he thought was best to preserve the lives of his people."

"The feyn?" I ask.

"All of the fea," he says, intently holding my gaze as my heart thunders in my chest.

Hadn't Felias told me that *he* is on the side of the fea?

"You *are* working with the feyn," I say, a chill creeping up my spine. I curse myself for not finding a way to bring my daggers. "Why haven't you told them about me?"

Or has he?

"Because, *Tha'haynah*, as I've said, I side with the fea. And whether you've realized it or not, you are here for them."

Even if I don't want to end him for the risk he poses to my life, I certainly want to do so for the riddle he dangles like a fat bunch of carrots before a gluttonous pony.

Tell her. Tell her or send her away. Awri's voice crashes into the sudden tempest of my mind. Whatever the man is hiding from me, they all already know.

The general jogs up beside me and I flinch when he reaches for my arm, my mind caught up in the fearful vortex of all that my future might hold. His brow draws down, and I force an apologetic smile at him and squeeze his hand.

"Would you mind giving us just a few more minutes?" I ask.

He nods, falling back with Riah without another word. I shake my head and smile a small smile, pondering how the general would have responded to the same request last week.

I frown at Felias when he chuckles. "Couldn't keep yourself away from him, could you? I must say, when the fates aren't busy muddling my own life, I find that they have quite the sense of humor." He sighs exasperatedly. "Your attachment to the male is of no consequence now. I have a feeling we are all set on a course we have little control over."

I ignore his rambling, sure that what little time I have with the man is soon to end and ask, "Why do you say that I am here to help the fea?"

"Because you are," he says simply, and I have to resist the urge to strangle him.

"You know what I am," I say, a thinly veiled threat.

Drakai. The word goes unspoken, but I can tell by the disbelieving smile on the man's face he knows exactly what I mean.

"Or are you something else entirely?" He poses the question with a smirk.

"Tell me what you think you know," I demand.

He shrugs but then his smile fades and he cringes under my glower.

"I only know what the sisters told me the night you arrived. They expected you, *Tha'haynah*, they accepted you without hesitation or intro-duction, and now, even the fea in the northern woods have begun to whisper about your arrival."

"I need to see the sisters." If he can't—or won't—answer my questions, I am sure they will be somewhat more forthcoming.

He nods. "I'll tell them."

"Thank you."

I glance back at the general. His eyes bore into me and my stomach

pitches. He knows something. He doesn't trust me, he told me as much, but he's been keeping things from me as well.

Felias leaves without another productive word. We exchange a departing embrace and reassurances that we will see each other soon, though I'm not sure either of us really believe that. Everything is about to change. Not a single word he had spoken was necessary for me to know that simple truth.

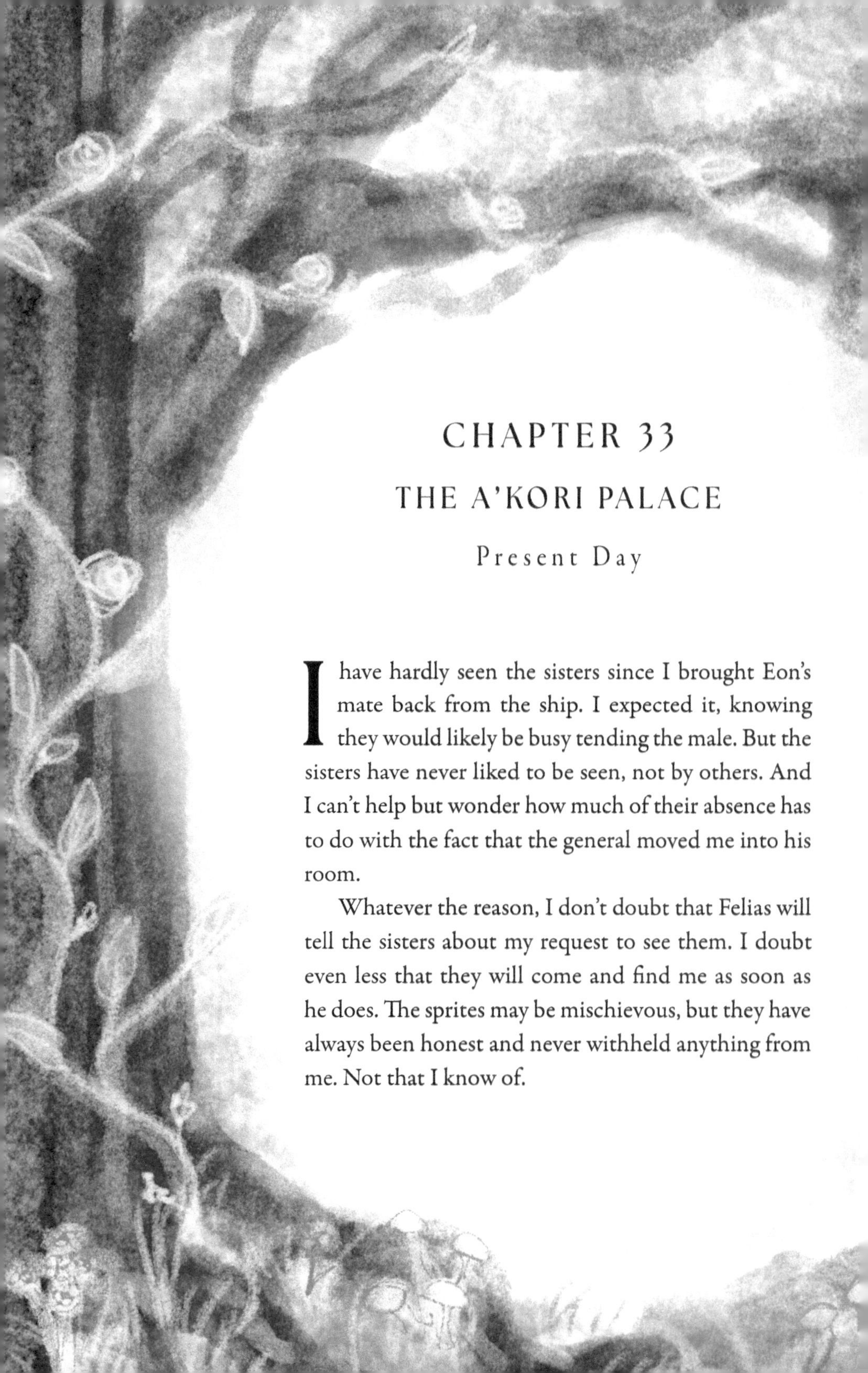

CHAPTER 33
THE A'KORI PALACE
Present Day

I have hardly seen the sisters since I brought Eon's mate back from the ship. I expected it, knowing they would likely be busy tending the male. But the sisters have never liked to be seen, not by others. And I can't help but wonder how much of their absence has to do with the fact that the general moved me into his room.

Whatever the reason, I don't doubt that Felias will tell the sisters about my request to see them. I doubt even less that they will come and find me as soon as he does. The sprites may be mischievous, but they have always been honest and never withheld anything from me. Not that I know of.

When I insist on spending the day in the garden, out of the confines of the palace, the general doesn't argue like I expect him to. He simply moves his war room meetings to the grounds nearby.

I can't help but laugh when four large males drag a long table onto the grass and supply chairs for all those that filter in and out of attendance. It's a curious sight, female and male alike streaming through the throng of blooms in full military uniform and regalia.

Xeyvian eyes me where I stand by a heavy-laden bush adorned with large globes of purple flowers. He checks the sun, noting the time of day and orders a small lunch from the kitchens. Sera arrives not long after, with plates of fruits, sweet drinks, and the like.

I'm enjoying the spectacle of what appears to be a tea party in preparation of a siege when Xeyvian hands me a plate full of berries and cheeses, cured meats and sweet breads. I smile as Toren selects a seat beside the general. There's a curious look on his face when he takes in their floral surroundings and the tall stack of neatly sliced sandwiches at the center of the table.

No one quiets when I draw near. Not a single word is hushed or a critical eye cast in my direction. While Leanna taught me that bedding someone could be a quick way to lower their guard, I hadn't expected it to work quite so thoroughly. Certainly not on the general of A'kori.

"The fea in the northern woods have been made aware of the presence of the Vatruke," Toren says, and my stomach pitches, "but none have reported seeing them."

The general's usual glower is fixed on the commander's face as he listens to his report. A small tick in his temple the only implication that the male is strained beyond what I am accustomed to seeing.

"Arda," he says under his breath, his eyes boring holes in the map beneath his flattened palms, as if he could discern the enemy's location by intimidating the colorful canvas.

Toren nods. "That is my suspicion as well. If Arda had not accompanied the others, we would certainly have discovered their whereabouts by now."

"Kezik, Vos, and Arda," the general says, pinching his brow. "I admit, I never thought they would step foot upon these shores again. This complicates things."

Toren nods, but the general's eyes are on me when he says it.

"Have any of the fea in the northern woods gone missing?" the general asks and I tense, though I'm not entirely sure why.

Perhaps it is my concern for the sisters that hones my senses on Toren as he replies, "None that we are aware of."

"If not for the fea, why would they come?" the general asks, disconcerted.

Toren sighs, replying, "That question has occupied my mind into the early hours of the morning lately. Though no explanation I can conjure feels right or settles my mind in the least."

I slip away from the table, from the small company gathered to ascertain the whereabouts of the invaders. It hadn't been the plan. When I left, no Drakai were ordered to come and assist me. No contingencies had been made upon my departure. Their presence will only jeopardize my mission, making it more difficult to gain access to the king.

My attempt to drag reasoning through the thick sludge occupying my mind is interrupted by a distant laugh on a gentle breeze. Every thought of the Drakai set aside when I head off to find the sisters. I'm sure to keep the general in sight, aware that every step I take away from the male while he remains seated is a testament to his self-restraint. I have little doubt that he would prefer if I remained within quite literal arm's reach.

I make a show of smelling and inspecting the vibrant display of flowers artfully sewn near a well-worn, cobbled walking path. A small wooden swing rocks in the wind tethered to a giant oak, a dirt path etched into the ground beneath it from years of frequent use.

Tig is the first to reveal herself to me, though she remains carefully concealed by the thick bushes beyond the border of low blooming foliage. Her green eyes are nearly lost in the sea of leaves. Eon's violet eyes and the pink eyes of her mate are buried within a heavy-laden peony bush nearby, and I find that I am curiously relieved to see the sisters again.

With a glance over my shoulder to be sure that I am still alone I ask Tig pointedly, "Do you think that I am like you? Fea?"

I'm relieved when Tig shakes her head fervently confirming my suspicions that all Felias implied was either wildly incorrect or simply said to unnerve me.

My gut hollows when Tig states confidently, *"Breh,"* the r rolling off her sprite tongue.

"What do you mean *more*?" I ask, entirely unsure I want her answer.

"*Tha'haynah vathai eh'breh*," she answers. *The old blood of the fea is more.*

"I don't understand what that means."

"*Le'sei'lie hai'voh.*"

I shake my head, squinting in confusion as I try to piece together the declaration.

"Something about promises and fate," I whisper under my breath.

Even through the thick spray of leaves concealing her face I see her brow pinch as she struggles to find the words.

"*Vey'loh hai Tha'haynah vathai.*" *Something left by the old blood of the fea.*

My brow scrunches in confusion.

"How can the old blood of the fea leave itself something promised by the old blood of the fea?" My head begins to pound as my mind grasps at her meaning.

"*Le'ru vey'loh hai vathai,*" Eon's mate says, and I'm struck by the gravel in the male's voice as it sweeps across my ears like a churning brook, chilled by the clarity he brings with his words.

The fea language still puzzles me at times, and I'm often confused by the words that can subtly shift in meaning by what was said before or what comes after. But there is no question in my mind as to his meaning right now.

You are what was left by the fea.

"And the Vatruke," I begin and Tig growls at the word before I even finish my question, "what are they?"

"*Deij,*" the male says flatly. *Evil.*

"Shivaria." I'm startled by the sound of Xeyvian's voice and spin around to find him behind me. His eyes are glued to the bushes at my back. I don't have to look to know that the sprites are gone. I begin to wonder if he had seen them when his head tips to the side and he seems to strain his ears, listening to the gentle breeze that rushes down from the northern ranges.

There is a tick in his jaw when his gaze finally flicks up to meet my own. I can see a tide of unasked questions rise and fall behind the deep sea of his eyes and my feet shift beneath me. It's a defensive stance, one I learned long ago. A position to be taken against a larger opponent that is charging you, if you happen to find yourself unarmed. It is a stance I did not intend to take with the male—one that he visibly notes.

The general looks wounded when he takes a slow step toward me, hands

splayed out disarmingly. He doesn't ask questions, doesn't demand answers. He simply runs his hand up the back of my arm and leans in to press his lips against my temple when he asks, "Are you ready to go in, *mi'ajna*?"

I was too absorbed with the sisters to note the foreboding rainclouds coming from the east. The sky quickly darkens and already the general's war table is being removed from the grounds. The military company he'd been keeping disperses into the early hours of the evening.

I nod. "I'd like to see Awri."

It's a simple request, though I'm not entirely sure why I ask. Now that the general has accepted me so completely, I have little need for the female. If I strive to keep her close, it is likely she will only complicate things further.

I tell myself that it's best to stay in her good graces, even if I don't need her anymore. Even if I won't be here long enough to smooth the ripple in the fabric of whatever we had become to each other. Not that I'm even sure what that is.

The general leads me down the corridors toward Awri's chamber, a torrent of spring rain obscuring every large window we pass. He raps his knuckles against the heavily grained wooden door, surprising me when he leans against the wall across the hall.

"I'll wait for you here," he says.

When she answers the door, taking me in without the smile I'm accustomed to seeing on her face, I find that I might prefer if he didn't leave me alone with the female.

She offers the general a forced smile from within her room. "Any word on the Vatruke?"

He shakes his head. "No, but we suspect that Arda must be among them."

She nods her head knowingly, pushing out a deep sigh. She looks tired. Not merely the tiredness that comes from long nights of little sleep. Her eyes hold the bone-weary exhaustion of events beyond her control.

Throughout my life, I have seen the same look on countless La'tari faces. On villagers who choose to surrender their lives to the king and attempt the long journey back to the keep. Even when they made the choice, some knew they would never live to see their destination.

With a wide sweep of her arm, she offers me entry into her room. The cause of such heavy weariness is laid bare to me the moment I see Kishek

asleep in her bed. His eyes are sunken deep, a sickly dark welling beneath the long lashes laying against his cheeks. His breathing is deep and even. The only sign that the male is perhaps better than he appears.

"He will be all right," Awri assures me, and I shrug off a small bit of tension winding in the fine sinew of my shoulders.

"I thought Caden healed him?" I ask, troubled.

She shakes her head regretfully. "Kishek nearly extended his gift beyond his ability, and Caden cannot heal that. The healers have done what little they can."

I've never asked about their gifts. Never danced around my curiosity in our many conversations. I know next to nothing about their world as it pertains to their power, and I grasp at the tiny thread of knowledge.

I follow as she makes her way deeper into her room. It is decorated much like her cottage. Chairs carved from gnarled roots sit in front of the fire. Rugs woven to mimic the mossy carpet of the forest floor flow between every bit of furniture. A detailed portrait of two extravagantly adorned feyn hangs on the wall between two large windows, a small table of carved creatures below it.

"My parents," she says, "The day they celebrated their mating bond."

I nod and smile politely, as if this isn't the first time in my life I've ever heard of a mating bond. I was taught that the feyn took mates but that is the extent of my knowledge on the topic. While my mind continues to sift the lies from the truths of the stories I was raised on, Awri extends her arm, offering me a comfortable seat on a plush, green velvet cushion by a crackling fire.

"You hide it well," she says as she takes a seat across from me, looking out the window.

"What?" I ask.

"Your curiosity," she replies.

When I say nothing, a smile tugs up at one edge of her mouth and she says, "I admit that when you were so inquisitive about the fea, I expected you to be more open to all the possibilities outside of what you were taught by the La'tari."

"You think I'm closed minded?" I nearly scoff, even as my mind trips over all I've learned and tried to reject since I landed on these shores.

"I'm sure there must be a reason you continue to deny any truth laid before you. And while you seem content to live in ignorance, it is not without its costs," Awri says, her eyes wilting when they land on the form of her mate.

Every defense building inside of me ebbs when I follow that gaze.

This is not the conversation I expected to have with her. I debate excusing myself and consider discarding whatever fragile semblance of a friendship still remains between us. But my feet don't move for the door when I will myself to leave her to her sorrow. As if my body were not within my control, I find myself kneeling before her instead, her hand clasped between my own.

"You said that you didn't blame me for this." It's little more than a whisper when it passes my lips.

What little hope I had in the sincerity of her claim is lost when she replies, "Maybe I'm lying to myself too."

The thin thread binding us to each other begins to slip, threatening to unravel all that is left. I may not agree with her—what could I have possibly known that would have changed this?

"What can I do?" My entire being protests the question even as I ask. It's too open, it offers too much. What price will the female exact from me?

But I can think of no other way to mend this, so I plead, "Tell me."

She doesn't hesitate in her answer, doesn't stop to think or consider what she might say. She leans forward in her chair, a challenge in her eyes as her hand closes like a vice around my own.

"Ask," she says simply. "What secrets of the feyn, of A'kori, of Terr, do you wish to know?"

Nothing. Everything.

What can the female tell me without shattering the last of the small panes that remain of my life? What can she say that will not rewrite the histories of my world and all that I know?

"What would you like me to know?" I deflect, entirely unsure I want her answer.

Awri puffs out a sigh. I asked a fair question, just not the one she wanted. I'm not even sure what that question is, but I'm sure the answer will cost me more than I can afford.

I remind myself of the weight of her offer, of all their heavily guarded secrets. How many Drakai have lost their lives in search of the information she seems so eager to share with me?

Her brow pitches down to resemble the general's glower when she replies, "Everything, Shivaria. I would have you know everything."

Her eyes flick to the door and at once I understand her. Xeyvian offered much the same. Everything I have learned since arriving has been at my request. In the cottage they answered every question I had about the fea. Media gladly taught me about the Vatruke when I inquired.

Maybe it's pure naivete, but I do not think they will force the shattering of my world. It is such a simple request, one they continue to make. 'Ask.'

I've already sought answers from Felias and the sisters. Why is it so impossible to ask the same questions of them? I tell myself that it is because there are too many lies that I have yet to unravel. But deep down, I know that it is the threat that their truths pose to my reality that stops me.

Even after everything they've told me, what do I really know? The fea are the only true innocents in this war and the Vatruke hunt them, with the assistance of the Drakai.

I swallow hard, deciding on a question that will test her without risking too much. "Tell me about the power of the feyn."

She raises her brows, tipping her head to the side, clearly surprised that I have finally given her what she wants. I expect her to balk at the question, to retract the offer, to assure me that though I may ask her anything, there are still things she is unwilling to divulge. Instead, she waves her hand at the seat across from her.

Smoothing the shimmering orange fabric of her dress resting upon her thighs she says, "Every feyn child is born with a connection to *Shivay*, the world soul. As we grow, that connection strengthens into a bond, one that *Shivay* uses to produce a gift inside of us."

"You say that like it's alive," I wonder at her choice of words.

"Do you not believe the soul of Terr is alive?" she asks, as if it's the simplest question in the world.

I'm not sure she intended to wait for my reply when she immediately continues. "Each gift is uniquely our own, some more subtly different than others, and all with differing degrees of power."

She rises from her chair, busying herself warming a kettle over the fire.

"How do you determine who is more powerful?" I ask.

"Generally, feyn who are gifted with powers of the mind are considered the most powerful. Though, that is not always the case," she says, walking to

a nearby cabinet and kneeling to rummage through it. "The power of our gifts is only as strong as our bond to *Shivay*. A gift like Toren's is physical in nature and could harm a tree just as easily as it could harm any feyn. Gifts like mine—illusion—and other gifts of the mind, while incredibly powerful, are only really effective if our target's bond to *Shivay* is weaker than our own."

Awri stands, closing the cabinet with a gentle sweep of her leg, and walks toward the steaming kettle with two small cups and a variety of teas in hand.

"When I was a child, I was often upset with my brother, and jealous of the favor he received because of his gift. One night, I entered his mind while he slept, convincing him that he had fallen asleep in the forest and risen in the midst of a wildfire." A smile breaks upon her face as she recalls the memory. "It wasn't until he threw a bucket of water onto a burning log that I released him from the vision. The log was my father," she chuckles, "and he was furious."

I've never imagined her when she was young but find it difficult to conjure the scene of the mischievous and jealous child she describes.

"Riesh never told our father. I'm not sure why."

"Why don't you ask him?" I suggest. Finding myself curious to understand his reason.

She shrugs, offering me a steaming cup of hot liquid. "I suppose I enjoy the memory as it is."

I don't tell her how much I understand exactly what she means. Memories are such fragile things. Marred not only by the passing of time but by every experience before and after they are made.

"Your gift is incredible," I admit.

Even a gift like Toren's ice would be useless if he could be convinced of a reality chosen by his opponent.

Awri smiles proudly at the compliment before dismissing it with a wave of her hand. "It *is* a very powerful gift. Rendered completely useless against a feyn of greater power."

Blowing across the surface of my tea, I stare at her quizzically as she explains. "Take Xeyvian, for example. I would be lucky to convince him that my rug is a different shade of green."

I feel my eyebrows hit my hairline before I regain my composure and ask, "He is that much more powerful than you?"

She nods, pursing her lips to blow across the beverage in her hands.

"What if Riesh amplified your power?" I wonder. "Could you do it then?"

She nods again, somewhat more hesitantly.

"Though my brother's gifts are far from secret, I hope you will understand if I don't say much about them. Knowledge about our gifts and the strength of our bond to *Shivay* can be the difference between life and death."

"I understand," I say. How could I argue even if I wanted to? I doubt there are any in La'tari who know even this little about their gifts.

"Earlier you said a gift like Toren's could harm any feyn," I say, "You mean that physical gifts, as you call them, are not subject to the same laws of power?"

She hesitates a moment before answering, selecting her words carefully. "If a feyn grows a rose bush and walks away, the rose bush remains. If a child comes along and pricks their finger on a thorn from that same bush, the finger will bleed. A gift that takes on a physical form belongs to Terr once it leaves the body, and it is no longer tied to the power of the gift of the one who made it."

I nod my understanding, though I'm not sure she's convinced when she shrugs and puffs out a breath. "I'm not sure how else to explain it."

"Thank you for trying," I say with a smile before checking the dwindling light outside the window.

Sipping the last of my tea, I rise from my seat. Awri rises to meet me, taking the cup from my hands with a small smile that seems sincere. "Thank you for coming to see me. And for being curious."

I dip my head, unsure of how to respond to the female. Tonight seems to have gone well, even if Kishek seems no better, despite her insistence that my questions would help him. I begin toward the door, stopping when my hand grasps the lever, and glance over my shoulder.

"Will you show me your gift?" I ask.

The small smile fades from her refined features and she shakes her head. I try not to let my disappointment show. Of course she won't. She just told me how important their secrets are, then baited me into asking questions to which she only gives partial truths. I feel my back stiffen involuntarily at the rejection of my request and her face wilts.

"I hope you believe me when I say that if I could show you, I would," she says.

I nod my understanding once again and slip out into the hall.

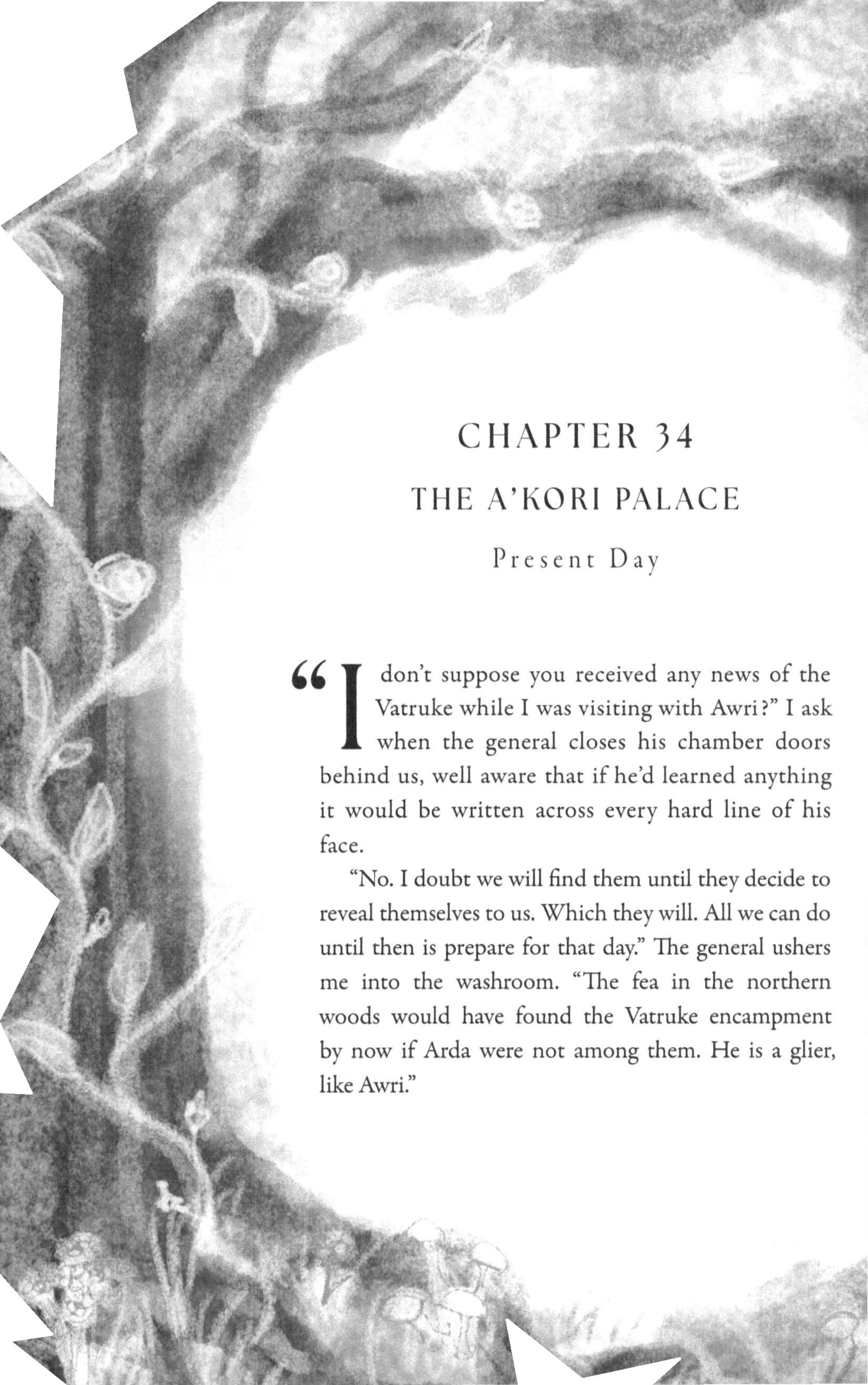

CHAPTER 34
THE A'KORI PALACE
Present Day

"I don't suppose you received any news of the Vatruke while I was visiting with Awri?" I ask when the general closes his chamber doors behind us, well aware that if he'd learned anything it would be written across every hard line of his face.

"No. I doubt we will find them until they decide to reveal themselves to us. Which they will. All we can do until then is prepare for that day." The general ushers me into the washroom. "The fea in the northern woods would have found the Vatruke encampment by now if Arda were not among them. He is a glier, like Awri."

"He is hiding them?" I sound surprised, even to myself, and I'm not sure why I haven't already drawn the same conclusion.

Of course, the Vatruke would have a means to hide themselves, along with the Drakai. Otherwise, they would never have sent so few to A'kori, not when their mission is less than peaceful. Though I still have no concept of the true power the feyn possess, I have to assume that if the Vatruke were powerful enough to go to war with their king and his subjects, they would have done it long ago.

I was not raised to command an army, but Bront taught me enough about tactics to prickle the skin on my arms as I consider their options. Too few of them have come to commit themselves to open warfare. No. This will not be a fight of skill upon an open battlefield. If they are here to take lives, it will be through strategy and cunning.

The general smooths the line of my brow with this thumb, even as he tries to keep the frown from his own mouth. He knows it too, that all we can really do is remain on guard, hope for the best, and plan for the worst.

I know I need to think about it, about Vos, the La'tari, Felias and all that the man implied this afternoon; the sprites and the claims they made, all of the questions I allow to go unasked. But when the male behind me pulls me back against his chest and his mouth falls to my shoulder, I banish every thought but the feeling of his lips on my skin. I close my eyes and tip my head to the side, giving him access to my throat, smiling when I feel his fangs slide against the shallow veins throbbing beneath them.

"Are those just for show?" I ask, a coy smile on my face. "Or should I be concerned?"

I whirl around in his arms, lowering my eyes to the slender tips of his four pointed teeth.

"I would never give you a reason to fear me, *mi'ajna*. But if another ever bared their fangs at you, they would not live beyond that moment."

I decide here and now that I will never explain to him the finer details of my encounter with Siserie. I have no doubt the male will make good on his threat, and I would truly hate to deprive Toren of the female's life sentence.

"So, they are for violence?" I ask.

"Violence," he assures me as his lips brush my temple, "and pleasure." He

purrs the last in my ear, and I shiver at the unspoken promise in his words.

"Show me," I say, leaning into him, only considering the dangerous nature of my request once it's already been spoken.

"Soon." His eyes gleam with the promise of that future, but all I feel is regret.

My time here was never intended to last and *soon* may not come soon enough.

It hasn't been a particularly grueling day, but I don't protest when the male slides my gown from my form, before undressing himself and leading me into the deep tub carved into the floor. If this is heaven, I'll take it while it's still within reach. Stars know, the barren halls of haliel are far more likely to be the accommodations of my future.

He doesn't argue when I pile my hair on top of my head to keep it dry, though I'm prepared to remove the male's hand from his body if he tries to wet it again. I lay back in his arms when he sits on the marble bench beneath the surface of the water and pulls me into his lap, both of us perfectly content to simply *be*.

The quiet and stillness should be a reprieve, but as his hands work the tired muscles in my arms, my mind wanders to my conversation with Felias. Twisting around to face him, he draws my legs onto either side of his lap, eyeing me inquisitively. I open my mouth, only to snap it shut again, my eyes catching on the new bargain gracing his skin.

I'd forgotten about it since I first saw it this morning, and I trace the marking with my finger. The ancient script winds from the side of his arm, stopping at the center of his chest, where it bends like a hook over his heart. He watches my hand exploring the strange mark, covering it with his own when it stills where the trail ends, just above the base of his sternum.

It's so entirely different than the simple dark bands that strap his sides that I can't help but ask, "What was the bargain?"

"It's a bond, Shivaria. Not a bargain."

"It looks different," I say.

"It is. Fea bargains have to be fulfilled. Bonds are given without agreement or price."

His fingers trace the same line I followed on his skin, along the bare flesh of my own, from the side of my arm, all the way to my sternum. He watches me swallow my questions as I observe the path of his hand and he puffs out

his frustration. I shoot him a glare, and he grips my waist before I can pull myself from his arms.

"Ask, *mi'ajna*. There is nothing in this world I would keep from you."

I hum under my breath disbelievingly, and I have to ask myself if there is anything he would tell me that I will let myself believe.

"You still don't trust me." There is pain in his voice when he says it and the tone is a punch in the gut.

"You don't trust me either," I argue, not willing to admit that he has every reason not to trust *me*.

Even if I could trust the male, I'm not sure what I would ask him, where I would even begin. I'm still not entirely sure if I want to know everything or nothing at all. What will his answers change? Nothing. Just as Awri's answers changed nothing.

Every possible path I could have walked in this life narrowed the moment that dagger left my hand, and of the many futures I might have had, very few remain. If Vos doesn't end me here, she will the moment I step foot on La'tari soil. I am not simple enough to believe that my king will spare me from the Vatruke upon my return. They are far too great an ally for him, and I am nothing. Little more than fodder in his legions.

The moment I received my mission from the king I had known there was a chance I would never make it back to the shores I'd been raised upon. Still, I would have left this life knowing that I was a catalyst for something greater than myself. I would have saved countless lives, or so I hoped. Now, with all that I have learned, if I am to believe what they say, I know that the death of their king will only serve to end more lives than it spares—human lives, but also those of the fea.

Bile rises in my throat as I consider the fate of the fea and the part I might play in that future. It's easy to picture the type of world I'd like to leave behind, harder to imagine, in the short time I have left, how I might help to set that course.

The Vatruke. Their end means a true end to the war. To say nothing of the fea lives that would be saved.

When my eyes meet the general's, he is examining me curiously. His own eyes soften when he brushes a finger along the line of my jaw.

"I trust you, Shivaria."

I huff a laugh at him, even as guilt twists in my stomach like a dull, serrated blade.

"Since when?" I ask.

"Right now, *mi'ajna*. This is the moment I choose to trust you."

"You *choose* to trust me?"

His deep blue eyes roam across the lines of my face when he says, "Since I cannot read your mind just as you cannot read mine, it will have to be my choice."

Maybe part of me wishes he *could* read my mind. This would all be so much easier if that were the case. Because knowing is one thing, but choice without certainty is something else altogether and as easily as he can choose to trust me, I can *choose* to trust him too.

Even my body stiffens in rebellion as I consider giving him that kind of power over me.

"I've trusted before," I admit, and a muscle ticks at the end of his jaw.

"I know," he says, and I quirk an eyebrow at his clear assumption of my past. "You are too young to be so guarded without the hurt that comes from betrayal." His eyes darken, jaw tensing as his voice pitches low and he rumbles, "If I knew who he was I would end him for breaking that trust."

I don't doubt the male when he says it, and a small part of me thaws when I find that I don't actually mind his overprotective nature when it comes to my heart. Though if the trajectory of my life could be anything other than what it is, I would never put him in a room with the shadow master. Even after everything, it would break me beyond repair to see either of them injured by the other. And, feyn or not, there is no doubt in my mind the altercation would be more evenly matched than anyone might assume.

When I don't say anything, his hand starts working the muscles of my shoulders.

"When you're ready, *mi'ajna*. I will tell you everything."

"What does *mi'ajna* mean?" I ask, unsure I really want to know, but it's a start. Something simple. Or so I assume.

He sighs, pinching my chin when he says, "*Mi'ajna* is something precious. A vital piece that is missing from the core of every feyn when they are born. Something life is meaningless without. You are *mi'ajna*, and I've searched for you for millennia. Never did I expect that the fates would be so kind when they crafted you for me. Just as I was crafted for you."

I crush his lips with my own, cupping his neck. My deep-seated longing for the male wells within me, brimming with every kind touch, and every soft word and kept promise he ever whispered into my ear. Maybe I'm a fool. But the reward of having him for my own greatly outweighs any pain I could ever suffer by his hand.

He returns all the fiery passion I pour into him, palming my ass, lifting me until he has situated me above his tip and is teasing my entrance.

"I want you, Shivaria." My breath catches in my throat when he says it.

It's a simple declaration, one that I understand well, one that I've spoken to him before. But when he says it, it tugs on an invisible thread in my chest that is firmly tethered to his own on the other side.

"You have me," I answer, understanding for the first time the promises held in the same words he said to me.

His eyes are full of that promise when he parts my entrance and slides me down his length. I moan at the perfect stretch of my body around his when he pushes himself in to the hilt.

"Say it again." His eyes burn with the desire of his request as he pumps his thick shaft in and out in long, sweeping strokes, guiding me up and down with his hands on my hips.

"You have me." My stomach hollows when I speak the words aloud, a slew of emotions clashing deep within my gut.

As much as it's a relief to finally admit to myself and to speak aloud to him, I'm gripped by the fear of what I'm giving the male. Myself, unguarded and defenseless now that he knows that *he* is what I want. Only once before have I spoken these words to anyone, and I push down the memories as quickly as they rise.

"Never, *mi'ajna*." I barely hear the whisper as his hand travels between my legs, and he swipes a perfectly calloused thumb across my nub. "I will *never* hurt you, *never* betray you."

My throat burns even as my core tightens, and he captures every moan of pleasure on his lips. With a last deep thrust and strum against that sensitive mound of flesh I unravel. Millions of small threads that once made up a whole are cast out into oblivion, to flit across tides of starlight. He meets me there, even as I dance in the ethereal beauty of the endless skies, patiently collecting those threads, binding me back together until I am whole once again. I shudder the last of my release even as he swells inside of my pulsing core, spilling his sated desire within me.

I brush my lips along his shoulder, regretting that the moment has passed. It's not enough. It never is.

His throaty chuckle tickles my ear. "Let me take you to bed, *mi'ajna*. The night is still young, and I've only just begun."

"You said you couldn't read my mind," I say skeptically, my head resting on his shoulder.

"I don't need to read your thoughts to feel the desire welling within you, it's the same as my own."

"You can feel that?" I ask, pulling back to read his eyes, speculating as to the male's gift.

He nods. "Sometimes there is a great deal I can feel from you. Other times, nothing at all."

I hum under my breath, wondering just how much of my murderous intent he'd felt at the beginning. I suppose that might explain a few of our earlier interactions. Deciding it's better to keep all those thoughts from my head, I let my eyes drop to his mouth and bite my bottom lip.

That's all the male needs to hook an elbow under my legs and carry me out of the tub. He kicks a lever by the floor on his way to the bedroom and my eyebrows hit my hairline when the gushing waterfall cuts off and the marble tub drains in a giant whirlpool. Maybe I really *could* spend a lifetime exploring the palace and all the carefully constructed inventions of the feyn.

Late into the night, after Xeyvian has driven my passion to blissful release for hours, I rest my head on his chest. My mind wanders as I listen to the beautiful sound of each breath he draws into his lungs as he sleeps. There is too much to consider, too much to ponder in one night. But there is one simple truth I can no longer deny. I have no desire to kill the feyn king.

Learning that he is protecting the fea from the Vatruke is reason enough to want him to live. But, apart from that, I know now that I could never intentionally injure the male that lays by my side. Not by ending the life of his king, not in any way that I can fathom. My very being recoils at the thought of that betrayal.

Even as I admit all of this to myself, I don't taste the bitterness of failure that I expect. I am Drakai no longer, and I will never be Fea Dien, not in the way I was molded to be.

My stomach hollows as I consider my future. I have to tell him. This is not a secret I can keep from him forever. Even if it were, the very thought of maintaining this deception between us is vile.

Despite the fact that he claims he will never hurt me, his loyalty is to his king first, and I am a threat to everything he stands for. I won't blame him if he throws me in a cell. As the king's general he won't have a choice once he learns what I am. Even as I think it, guilt swells in my gut. Guilt that the male who has given himself to me will be forced to execute my punishment.

My brow pinches when I am struck with the realization that the choice to punish me is something I can take out of his hands. I can do this for him.

I will tell the king and let him seek justice as he sees fit. I have to believe that the male is merciful to some extent, though it is entirely possible his tolerance and the sanctuary he offers the fea won't extend to a mortal sent to end him.

Tomorrow, I will seek the king and let the fates decide which of the few remaining paths left of my life I will tread.

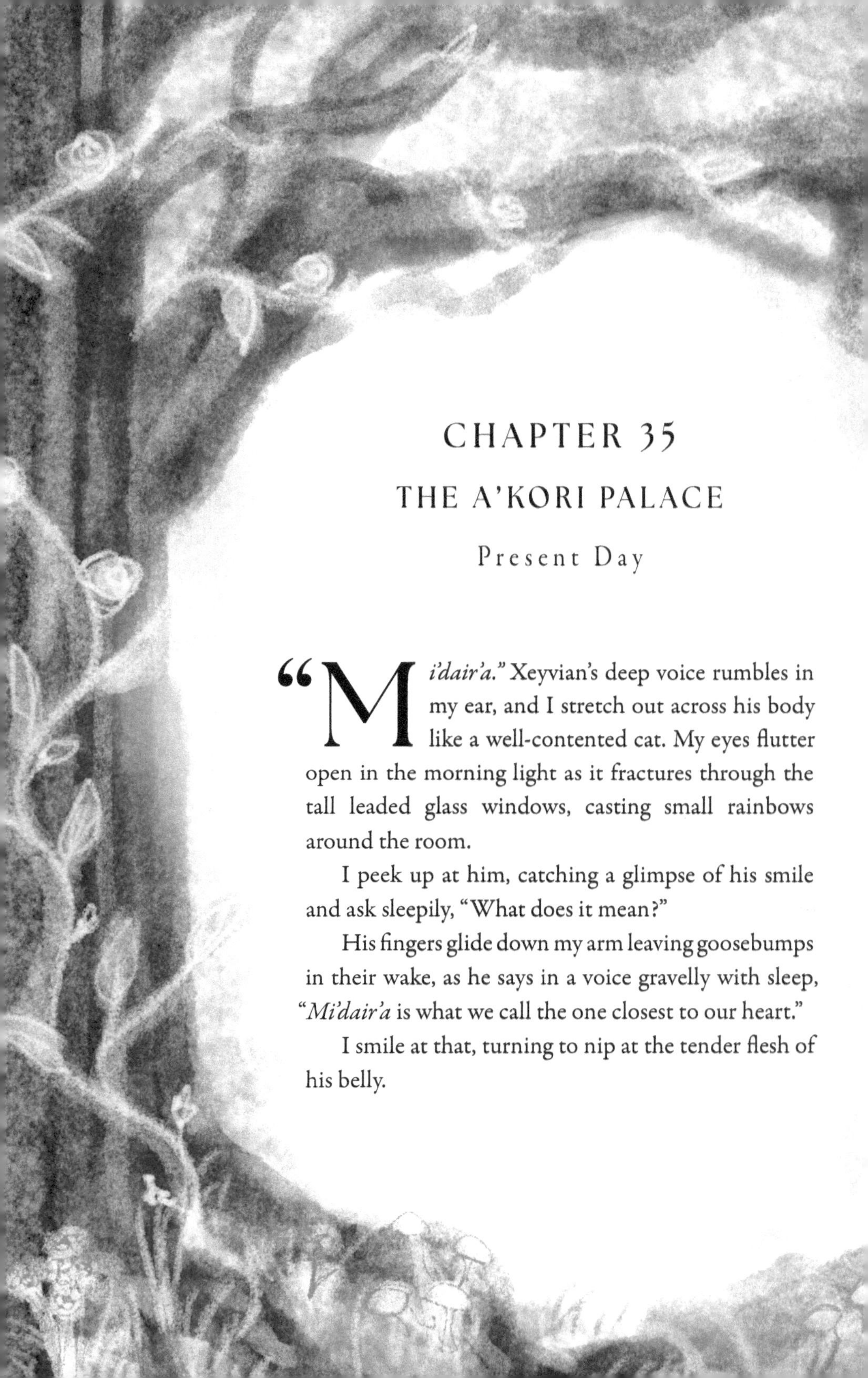

CHAPTER 35
THE A'KORI PALACE
Present Day

"*Mi'dair'a.*" Xeyvian's deep voice rumbles in my ear, and I stretch out across his body like a well-contented cat. My eyes flutter open in the morning light as it fractures through the tall leaded glass windows, casting small rainbows around the room.

I peek up at him, catching a glimpse of his smile and ask sleepily, "What does it mean?"

His fingers glide down my arm leaving goosebumps in their wake, as he says in a voice gravelly with sleep, "*Mi'dair'a* is what we call the one closest to our heart."

I smile at that, turning to nip at the tender flesh of his belly.

"I'm not sure it's your heart I'm closest to right now, General," I tease, laughing at the flash of fire igniting behind his eyes, my toes curling beneath the sheets as I squeeze my legs together.

Just as quickly as the heat rises in his eyes, his brow draws down into a frown, and he looks toward the door before the knock sounds from the other side. I sigh when he swings his legs over the bed and pulls on his loose linen pants before leaving me to answer it.

I don't recognize the voice that comes from the hall, but the tone isn't urgent. I slide on a robe of my own and head for the closet, my plans for today still forming in my mind. The king at the forefront of those plans. But it's far too early to seek an audience and spending a few hours sparring will keep my mind from the bleakness of my future.

The latch clicks when Xeyvian closes the door and he finds me knotting a dark dress below my hip, my black leathers beneath it.

"You are training with Riah this morning," he says when he sees my leathers. It isn't really a question, but I nod. "I'll have Toren station extra patrols by the stables and along the border of the northern woods."

I don't argue. I half expect the male to issue a battalion as my escort. If it makes him feel better, I'll agree happily. I plait my hair after checking that my feyn blades haven't wandered from their home, sheathed tightly against my thighs.

"My friend arrived late last night," he says, and the reason for the early morning knock at the door becomes clear. "I would like you to meet each other before the masque."

He smooths the fabric of the dress along my arms, though there is not a single wrinkle to be found.

"Would you be agreeable to meeting her at dinner tonight?" he asks. "Awri and the others would also join us."

When I don't answer right away, he offers, "I could also arrange for something more casual, if you prefer."

The male continues smoothing the lines of my dress, and though I don't understand why he's anxious, I try to reassure him. "Dinner is fine."

And it will be. I smile as some of the worry falls from the lines of his face when he hears my reply.

While my mind is focused on meeting with the king, far from thoughts of formal dinners and new acquaintances, the promise of seeing familiar faces is enough to tempt me. It eases the small amount of trepidation I suddenly feel at meeting this *friend*. I raise my eyebrows at the look of annoyance blooming on his face when another knock sounds at the door and offer him a sympathetic smile when he leaves to answer it.

The general plants a quick kiss on top of my head as I pass between the male and Toren and into the hall. The echo of Xeyvian's instructions to increase the guard follows me down the corridor as I head toward the stables.

I'm surprised when Toren catches up with me just as I exit the palace. The heavy clip of his boots quieting when he slows to keep pace beside me.

"Riesh tells me you are quite a skilled fighter," he says, eyeing me from the side.

My back stiffens, and I glance at the male from the corner of my eye. I am still in enemy territory, and until I have a chance to speak with the king, my reason for being here must remain hidden. Though I like Toren, I have a feeling that, even more than the rest of them, he is likely to throw me into a cell if he ever suspects me to be the threat that I am.

"Riah tells me you were trained by a Drakai," he says plainly.

"I was," I admit.

"It seems strange to me that your uncle, a man with such devotions to the fea, would have a brother who is willing to hire a Drakai to teach his daughter the art of war."

If I had known about Felias's true loyalties to the fea, perhaps I would have spun a different tale in regard to my proficiencies. But the time for another story has passed.

"Tell me, Toren, do you have a daughter?"

"I have three," he says, and I'm not sure why it surprises me.

Why wouldn't he have a family?

I clear my throat and ask, "And if you yourself had been unable to teach them to fight, would you have limited their ability to defend themselves by refusing the best instructor you could find, simply because she was Drakai?"

"She?" His brow draws down.

Foc. It isn't the worst slip I could make, but female Drakai have always been much fewer in number than the abundance of men who take up the profession. The proclamation drastically limits the possibilities of who my teacher could have been.

"I didn't realize you thought women were incapable of teaching, Commander," I say. It's a small jab, meant to deflect from the current trajectory of the conversation, and I'm relieved when it does.

"I have many females train others under my command," he says, attempting to explain himself, even as his cheeks flush a subtle shade of pink.

"I'm glad to hear it," I say, offering Toren a curt nod, which he returns, a little of the color fading from his cheeks.

I loose a breath, trying to hide my relief when Riah comes into view. I dip my head at Toren before veering off toward the ring. Riah tilts her head curiously when I walk to the gate and let myself in, rather than vaulting over the fence like I normally do. Hearing Toren issue orders to the guards stationed nearby, I glance back and my stomach knots when I see he has taken up a position close to the ring.

He leans lazily against a thick, well-used post, his eyes anywhere but on me. Despite his nonchalance, I have no doubt I am his sole focus, and if a threat should arise, the attacker will find Toren's posture nothing but a feigned casualness.

"Maybe we can take it easy today?" I plead with Riah in little more than a whisper.

Her brows drop, and she looks like she's ready to inspect my entire body herself when she asks, "Are you injured?"

"Just a little tired," I say.

I *am* tired, but more than that, I have no interest in Toren, of all feyn, deciding to take a closer look at me the very day I've decided to give myself up. It's a miracle Riah hadn't thrown me in a cell herself the day she broke my hand. For my part, the building of our bond has been careless, and I'm still not sure why she never asks more questions.

"Tired?" A toothy grin spreads across her lovely face, the scar at her brow pulling at her skin when she waggles her eyebrows at me.

I can't help but chuckle even as I try to school my features and keep the blush from my cheeks.

"Not like that," I insist.

"What a shame," she says, with a playful punch to my arm.

Honoring my request, she does start slow but quickly decides that I'm not as tired as I let on when I deflect each of her strikes with ease. What I intend to be a light round of simple routine strikes and deflections swiftly escalates.

It's not long before each of us is receiving well-placed blows by the other, sweat slicking our brows. I can tell by the look on her face that she enjoys the sparring as much as I do, though she still pulls her punches, likely for fear of the general's retribution.

We are nearing the end of our session, the warm sun nearly at its full height in the clear spring sky, when an icy tingle snakes down my spine, Toren's voice sounding closely behind me. "May I join you in the ring?"

I lock eyes with Riah, giving her the faintest shake of my head, my eyes pleading with her to decline. Her smile says everything as she waves the commander into the ring, thoroughly ignoring me.

"Of course. I could use a break," she says, jumping up to sit on the fence bordering the ring, looking far too pleased with herself and the unexpected turn of events.

Toren relieves himself of his leather gauntlets before rolling up his sleeves, and I huff under my breath at the male's arrogance. Whether he intends to offend me or not, he succeeds. There is no reason to remove armor when sparring unless you perceive that there is no threat. It's a clear declaration as to how he views my abilities and I bristle, my pride taking the first blow before the round even begins.

So, I do what any idiot would do in my position and remove my gauntlets as well, adding my cuirass to the pile of discarded armor shortly after. His lips quirk up at the edges as I happily imply that *he* is at a greater disadvantage in this ring. Boldly, he removes his cuirass as well, throwing it in the pile of leather.

The guards nearby begin to gather in small clusters, and I'm reminded of the first round I'd ever done with Riah. They try—and fail—to look nonchalant as they speak in hushed tones, every eye watching intently as the scene unfolds. I can only assume that the scarred male before me has hundreds of years on the measly twenty I've been training. But he's lived the last twenty years in peace, tenuous as it is. I, on the other hand, have spent nearly every waking moment of that time training for my purpose.

He doesn't begin slowly like Riah always does, testing my limitations before deciding on her next series of strikes. The male lunges at me, full force, not an ounce of hesitation in his body. Only narrowly do I avoid the fist that he intends for my jaw. It would have sent me to the floor of the ring. Maybe I shouldn't, but I can't help it when a wicked smile breaks upon my face, my blood heating as the tension builds.

This. This is what I've been missing.

Toren is quick to strike again, but he leans in too far, failing in his attempt to catch me off guard. I dodge the strike even as I throw myself toward him, vaulting off his bent knee as I twist my body, sending all the force into my knee as it collides with the side of his head. The unmistakable sound of bone-on-bone cracks in the air and the male goes down hard.

Riah swears from the sidelines, tensing as if she might jump from where she is seated atop the fence. She stifles a nervous chuckle when Toren shakes off the impact and begins to rise. Maybe I shouldn't have, but he certainly started it.

The commander grasps the hand I offer, and I help him to his feet, a little surprised when he takes a stance that implies he would like to continue. But then again, so would I.

He seems to have learned his lesson and doesn't leave himself open for another brutal attack. He doesn't pull his punches like the female watching gleefully from her perch on the fence either. If I was debating letting him land a few blows to throw him off the reality of my abilities, that time has passed. Almost every swing the male takes promises a break or fracture that I would rather not endure.

I believe we are evenly matched until the dreadful moment when his lips curve up in a sly smile. I know that smile. Words spoken to me countless times in my childhood surface in my mind, unbidden. *You're letting your guard down, Vari.*

It's too late to recover, I know it is. And my blood chills as I block a blow to my side, seeing in the last moment the knee he throws, just as it connects with my thigh. Something sharp snaps inside me. A bone, my heart, I'm not sure which and both promise to be equally painful until well-tended. I stuff down the well of emotions that flood me when the locked compartment of my memories is broken open, its contents seeping out to saturate my heart and mind.

A bone. Just a bone. Thank the stars.

I stagger back, wincing as I struggle to catch my breath through the pain, and Riah rushes to my side, a puff of fine silt wafting in the air beneath her feet.

"I'm all right," I assure her.

When she doesn't reply, I follow her gaze. The blood draining from her face is not due to the bruising she will have to explain to Caden, but the sight of the general as he rounds the last of the wild hedges that buffer the palace from the stables. The male is taking long strides toward us with nothing to slow him down.

I clench my teeth, standing tall as I force weight onto my leg that it can hardly be expected to hold for long. I have no desire to witness the punishment the general will level on Toren if he finds out that the male has broken a single part of me. I'm debating how in haliel to maintain the deception when Riah grips my broken leg and I suppress a cry of agony.

"Sorry for this." It's the only warning she gives before wrapping her hand around my side and I'm struck by the blinding pain of her mending as it reaches my bone.

My face pales as I suck in a hiss and will my mind not to lose itself to the dark that threatens in the corners of my vision.

Toren watches curiously as I grit my teeth through the brutal healing, my forehead beading with sweat as the bone knits itself back together with an audible crackling pop. The commander doesn't seem the least bit concerned, though he must be aware by now that the general is nearly here.

I wonder at his calm demeanor. If I know anything about the male stalking toward us it is that he's likely to gut anyone that so much as bruises me. I'm sure a broken bone would garner a punishment that would make a death sentence seem like mercy.

"Shivaria," Xeyvian says. I meet his eyes and smile just as Riah releases me.

Stepping toward him, I ignore the familiar sting in my leg. Years of Leanna's training has done nothing if not prepared me to ignore the pain of breaking. As Riah can only mend bone, not flesh, there will be some small amount of damage left from the blow that she was unable to heal.

I won't risk asking for Caden, not only is it completely unnecessary, but the general would want a detailed explanation as to what had happened. I let myself out of the ring, swiping my discarded leathers off the ground before the general plants his feet in front of me.

"Is everything all right?" I ask.

"Yes," he says, "I just thought you might like to change and rest before you meet our guest."

His lips quirk up at the edges as he takes me in and I'm sure I must be quite the sight, though he is kind enough not to tell me just how badly I need a bath. I've completely lost track of time and when I check the sky, the sun is just beginning its descent toward the horizon. It's still early in the afternoon. The warm spring days of A'kori getting longer with each setting sun.

Neither Riah nor Toren say a word as they escort us back toward the palace. But when I look over my shoulder the commander offers me a shallow nod in recognition, his brow drawn down as he considers me more thoughtfully than ever before. I wonder what the male makes of our time spent sparring. Perhaps in vain, I hope it isn't much.

Our companions break from our party when we enter the palace and the general leads me back to his room so that I can bathe and dress for the evening. It's a feat in itself to conceal the first signs of the large bruise where Toren landed the blow. But Xeyvian seems more preoccupied than usual, and I have dressed in a deep blue silk gown before he has a chance to notice the mark.

He strokes my hair, looking out the window absentmindedly while I apply coal to my eyes.

"I would like to speak with your king," I say. It's perhaps not the thing to say to the male in the moment, and, judging by the look on his face, the request is unexpected.

"That can be arranged," he says, failing to hide the curiosity roused by my request. "Though I intended to introduce you at the masque."

"It can wait until then." I latch on to the last night he offers me by his side.

It's a selfish delay, and I have no right to waste another day of his life knowing the likely outcome of my future. I tell myself that the party is only one day away and maybe the distraction it presents will help his spirits remain high as I lay my life at the feet of his sovereign.

"Have you decided to seduce him after all?" he asks with a teasing smile. "I'm sure you'd manage the task just fine if you chose to do so."

I glare at the male playfully. "I would like to thank him for hosting me at the palace." I pause before adding, "And I would like to ask him for permission to remain with you in A'kori." The last is not a lie, and I hope that the declaration that I *would* stay with him will soften him toward me when he finds out what I am.

It's a curious look he levels at me. Perhaps it's skepticism, perhaps apprehension. I'm not entirely sure.

"You intend to stay? For good?" he asks.

"I do." I smile, and it's a good thing that I've distanced the red lip paint from myself in that moment because the male sweeps me into his arms.

Resting his forehead against mine, he sighs his relief before delivering a kiss to my lips. It's tender, not rushed or passion driven. It's soft and sweet, a kiss for remembering a moment that will change the trajectory of our lives.

I brush my fingers down the length of his jaw. A single lifetime with this male will never be enough. I shove down thoughts of how he will watch me age, my own youth and beauty ravaged by time while he remains exactly as he is. Poisonous thoughts spilled into my ears by Siserie, but that doesn't make them untrue.

His lips brush against my temple as he murmurs, "How did I ever make it this long without you?"

It isn't really a question, and I can't help the smile that tugs at my mouth, disguising all the cracks of my breaking heart, unable to imagine the pain of our inevitable parting. It will be death that parts us, wether by the hand of Vos, his king, or time, there will be an end to this. And that is only if he doesn't learn to hate me first.

Hesitantly, he settles my feet back on the floor, allowing me to finish preparing myself for his guest.

The sky is painted in a thick watercolor of pinks and reds, the sun disappearing over the western sea when he takes my arm and ushers me toward the door.

"It's time, *mi'dair'a,*" he says, "Our guest will be waiting."

All the butterflies I've suppressed throughout the day begin to flutter

wildly in my stomach. Maybe it's only the mystery surrounding his friend or maybe it's my plans for tomorrow, but there is a void in my gut that I cannot seem to fill.

I am unfamiliar with the small and intimate dining room I find myself in. It boasts tall panels of dark wood with an extravagantly large fireplace situated between the hip-to-ceiling leaded windows I have become accustomed to seeing in every room. The small table is set with humble settings, somewhat unexpected in the palace of the king. Certainly, a far cry from the golden halls I walked through the day I arrived.

I've hardly had a chance to inspect the room when the door creaks behind me, announcing Riesh, Awri, and a tall, slender female I've never seen before. I dip my head in greeting, finding it hard to maintain a smile when I note the absence of Kishek and the concern still heavy on the features of his mate.

I wish I could reassure her, but how can I? I hardly understand what is wrong with the male. Even if I did, I'm still entirely unsure how to receive the female after our last conversation.

"Nurai, thank you for coming." Xeyvian smiles warmly at the stranger as he takes her hand in his own and bows his head against it.

It's a strange greeting, one I haven't witnessed before, and only serves to make my hesitation grow when he leads the stranger toward me.

The female moves like a cat. Her lithe body swaying nearly imperceptibly beneath the dark crimson gown she wears. Her long hair is a dense black that would be lost to shadow on a dark night, the olive hue of her skin deepening the pools of her storm-blue eyes. Her lips are perfectly pink, a natural blush adorning the apples of her high cheeks. Even among the feyn, she's striking.

She steps forward, and I nearly take a step back. Only with great effort do I school my features and force myself to step up to meet her under the flickering light of the chandelier hanging overhead.

"Shivaria, this is Nurai," the general says, settling his hand against my lower back.

She smiles a small and unconvincing smile, eyeing me from head to toe.

All my trepidation melts into a thin sheet of annoyance when she meets my eyes, her features unmoved. I know the look, it's one I endured for years, plastered upon Leanna's lovely features every day. Clearly the female finds nothing remarkable.

"Nurai, this is Shivaria," Xeyvian says, "*Mi'ajna.*"

It is the sharp intake of breath from Awri that draws my attention. Once again, she looks me over as if she's never seen me before, and I wonder if it will always be this way between us. I can tell it's the first time she's heard the sentiment spoken aloud and I wonder why Kishek had not already told her. After all, her mate was in the room when Xeyvian made the same declaration to Siserie.

"*Ajna?*" Even Nurai, who doesn't know me at all, sounds surprised, her face contorting as she inspects me more thoroughly.

It's a slower perusal, as if the female might find something she overlooked. Anything that might explain to her why the male by my side would claim me in such a way.

She finds nothing, I can see it in her eyes when she pins me with a withering stare. My spine tingles, icy shards of her gift creeping down the length of it as my heart thunders in my chest and the air is driven from my lungs.

My brow dips and I can't help considering what she's capable of. The chill weaving through my veins is unlike any touch of the feyn gift I've felt before. It grows and deepens, searching, until my demon is stirred.

Just when I think the female before me might force my demon into the waking world, Nurai's head tilts to the side, her brow pinching with displeasure.

"Interesting," she says under her breath as the ice within me begins to thaw.

I glance at Riesh and the lines creasing his forehead in confusion, but his eyes are not on me, they are firmly glued to Nurai. I puff out a relieved breath when a handful of feyn enter the room with steaming trays piled high with an array of foods. The table seems oddly wide until it looks like it might overflow with the staggering assortment placed neatly at the center.

Xeyvian pulls out one of two chairs at the head of the table, offering it to me, and I push down the awkward feeling of accepting the seat by his side. With a great deal of effort, I manage to keep my eyes on my plate, not wanting to witness another speculative onceover from Awri or the general's friend.

I am dead wrong when I think that the meal might offer some small amount of reprieve from conversation. Nurai takes her time plating her food of choice, preferring instead to engage in inquisition.

"Where are you from, Shivaria?" the female asks, scooping a modest serving of greens off a silver tray.

"The south," I reply simply, deliberately selecting foods that will take the most time to chew.

Her eyes gleam, as she cuts into a soft cheese and asks, "How far south?"

I'm relieved when Xeyvian replies, "Shivaria traveled from La'tari."

My stomach twists when I consider what feelings she might have about the declaration. A human companion. A La'tarian. Not that the female needs more than the glaring faults of my physical form to discredit my worth.

"You have the look of the feyn," she says bluntly, "Do you know your lineage?"

I bristle at the question. Maybe she's just making conversation, but I can't help but think that she might find me more worthy of the male by my side if I could claim some relation to their species. No matter how distant that connection might be.

"Yes. On my mother's side," I lie, decidedly sticking with the story Leanna crafted for me.

"Really?" she says under a raised brow.

I expect the female to be surprised, curious, inquisitive. Of course she will want to know how someone like me, ungifted and human, ended up on the general's arm. I am prepared to spill the story of my upbringing exactly as I practiced it countless times, to weave the tale to perfection. But the look she gives me dries my mouth. The edge of her lip cocks up in disbelief.

Hisht. I should have asked the general about the female's gift, unlikely as it is that he would have revealed it to me. I've let myself become far too comfortable around them, far too trusting of the general and his choice of company. I shouldn't be here.

My cheeks heat and the general's hand squeezes my leg when I clutch the knife laying at the side of my plate. I'm entirely unsure if the squeeze is due to the stream of emotions surely emanating from me or the fact that I've armed myself. I take a deep breath and smile, releasing the weapon and pointedly settling myself against the back of my chair.

Nurai's eye's glimmer at me from across the table, and I think the female perceived more from that moment than I am comfortable with. I nearly sigh in relief when she abandons her pursuit of knowing me, and instead, turns her attention to Awri.

"How is your mate?" she asks. "Xeyvian informed me that he is unwell."

"He is recovering, slowly," Awri replies.

I'm not sure why it surprises me when Nurai reaches across the table to clasp Awri's hand. It's an intimate act, something meant to comfort her, something I should have done myself. Something I truly have no business doing, not to someone I've been lying to even as I call them friend.

"He will be fine," Nurai says, offering her the assurance I could not. "There have been times, throughout the years, that I have overextended myself. Remember, our bodies were meant to live eternally. We are more resilient than you can imagine."

I might believe her, if I had not ended one of the Vatruke so easily. At least Awri seems soothed by the statement, and for her sake, I hope it's true.

"I admit," Nurai continues, "I was shocked when Xeyvian wrote to me and told me about the situation. To my knowledge, your mate is the strongest healer of his kind born since the war."

"Which war?" I wonder aloud. The female may not have given me much reason to like her, but I can't help my curiosity when she says it.

"The first," she answers.

I nearly gape and it occurs to me that the general, despite his appearance, could easily be older than Nurai, older than the first war. I'm not sure why I never asked, I'm sure he would tell me. If the male doesn't hate me after tomorrow, I will ask him. Along with a great deal of other questions.

"I was born in Brax," she says, "shortly before the sundering."

I don't ask, but the female must know, as I slide to the edge of my seat, that I am in awe of the tale of her life. Of the rich histories that live within her mind. Of a time when the fea thrived deep within the forests of the southern continent. She smiles slyly, and just when I think she might not say another word on the subject, she recounts a memory long past.

CHAPTER 36

BRAX

Three years after
the Sundering

"Muri!" Nurai shouts, a wide smile breaking upon her face as she waves her arm in the air, the wild motion near flailing.

Her cheerful exuberance is enough to draw the attention of the female standing among the many brightly decorated stalls. The market bursts with all manner of fea creatures, haggling and bartering amidst the stands full of handcrafted earthenware, farmed goods, and wild foraging's. Brownies and gnomes weave beneath the feet of satyrs, dryads, and every kind of woodland fea, shouting with raised fists when the occasional clumsy foot lands too close for the comfort of the tiny fea underfoot.

The forest of Brax sings as she breathes. Her deep lungs heave in slow and even bursts that temper the otherwise hot and humid summer day. The songs carried from deep within her lungs are those of the creatures residing within her. Many sing of new awakenings and hold the promise of hopeful beginnings, while others profess ancient tales of a time long ago.

"Nurai!" Muri beams, embracing the tall, slender female, the long tresses of her pitch-black hair shining in the light of the morning sun. "I did not expect to see you until another moon had passed."

It's impossible for Nurai to hide her disappointment when she admits, "I would have liked to stay longer, but my host seemed impatient for me to return to Brax."

A puzzled look forms on Muri's lovely face. "I thought the human king was the one who invited you to La'tari?"

"He was," she replies, taking Muri's arm and pulling her from the path of the heavy-laden fruit cart being pushed through the market. "But even the king is subject to the wishes of his people."

"Such a strange species," Muri scoffs. "As if each of them was born with the need to destroy something beautiful in the span of their fleeting life."

Nurai nods, as though she had drawn the same conclusion, and says, "Their king did ask me to return, but I'm beginning to wonder if my attempts to bond with his people are in vain. I fear that the sundering may have only fueled their desire to see what remains of the fea purged from the land. Despite my hopes, I am not sure diplomacy will change that."

Muri studies her friend carefully, piecing together all the unspoken words she holds behind her tongue.

"But you think you know something that might?" Muri asks.

"Or someone," Nurai says, her hesitation creating a palpable tension as she hooks Muri's arm and pulls her behind a large cart piled high with wild forest mushrooms.

The satyr working the cart eyes the females curiously until a gnome saunters up, producing a large bundle of red moss from a small satchel tied at his hip. The rare herb is never harvested except on the night of a full moon and only grows on the foothills of the eastern mountains. Thankfully, it's enough to entice the satyr into a distracting barter.

Behind the cart, her voice dropping to a whisper that all but vanishes amidst the lively bustle, Nurai says, "I thought I might ask my brother to accompany me, if I choose to return to the human court again."

Muri's eyes widen, the shock of what her friend implies clearly written on her face. "You would ask him to use his gift to persuade the humans?"

With a reluctant sigh, Nurai admits, "I am considering it."

"You can't," Muri says, tearing her arm from where she is joined with the female. "And even if you did ask him, he would never go along with it."

"Wouldn't he?" Nurai asks, raising an eyebrow in challenge. "You know better than most, the things we will do to help the ones we love."

Muri can't help the wince that follows the statement. She knows all too well the cost that often comes of granting such a request.

"I do know," Muri says, taking a step forward. "And I would not have either of you burdened by the guilt of such a thing."

A sadness passes behind the icy blue of her eyes, her gaze settling on a tree at the edge of the forest. It's a tall oak, and long ago had been a sturdy and thriving thing. It had been nursed by the fea as a seedling upon the fertile soil of Terr.

Hundreds of years it grew in this forest, casting its branches out to offer the protection of its shade. Its trunk is twisted, as if it spent its lifetime dancing as it spun, reaching for the sun beyond the thick canopy overhead. But its leaves are too golden in the midsummer heat, and many are cast to the ground from the gentle breeze that stirs them. A hollow in its trunk, where no doubt countless squirrels raised their broods and hid their hoards for winter, now cracked and fissured. Less a home than it was before.

"Is something wrong?" Nurai asks, her brow drawn with concern.

"No. Nothing," Muri says, with a small shake of her head.

Muri clasps her friend's hand as she pleads, "Threats are not the answer, Nurai. Don't our own histories tell us enough about the atrocities committed in the name of peace by both human and feyn?"

"You are right," she agrees with a gentle squeeze of her friend's hand.

Muri sighs, the relief she feels clear upon her face when she says, "We will find another way."

They walk about the bustling market for some time, each considering all that the other has said.

"It might help you to know," Muri says as she runs her hand down the length of an artfully painted silk panel, hanging among many in the stall of a young feyn, "that Arda, Nix, and Vos have already tried to convince your brother and failed."

With a deep sigh and the shake of her head, Nurai replies, "I'm honestly not surprised they would try. When the humans took the life of your mother, I thought we lost you all to that grief. Stars know that most of the human lives taken by the feyn have been in vengeance of such things."

Muri nods, unable to hide her sorrow upon recalling the memory. Eventually she says, "Arda and Nix mourned for many years; they still grieve her. I don't think feyn were made to endure loss the way that the mortals do. But Vos, I never saw sadness in her, though I'm sure it was there, buried deep. All she ever showed me was her rage."

"I remember," Nurai says, absently smoothing one of the silks folded neatly in the stall.

"There were days when I thought she might end the entire human race herself. She was so consumed by it. And then," Muri says, a small smile forming on her face as she recalls it, "her belly began to swell, and all that anger vanished. I could never explain the joy I felt at having my sister returned to me, how it felt to see her smile again. It was as if she forgot what it meant to live, and with that life growing inside her, she began to remember."

Muri bites her quivering lip as she continues, "If anything happened to that child, I think she might have drowned all of Terr in her sorrow."

"Luckily," Nurai reassures her, "the fates knew better than to take the child from her, and that is a world we will never have to live in."

Muri nods, her smile now seeming somewhat less.

"Now tell me, how is your sister enjoying motherhood?" Nurai asks.

"I've never seen her like this," Muri says, "Her world begins and ends with that child."

"As it should."

Muri nods her agreement, and the friends wander into the stall of a bog sprite, overflowing with bushels of rare flowers and herbs only found in the marshes deep within the Braxian forest.

The sprite shuffles forward, her short crop of fine green hair flowing

about in the air as if she were underwater. The tangle of mossy branches protruding from her head are adorned with the coveted white lilies that grow upon the marshy wetland of her home. Her skin shifts in the light as she moves. At first, it's patterned in a glistening array of scales that shimmer in the sunlight, then fades to the dull thick scales of some of the larger and less likable beasts that inhabit the waterways. Finally settling into a skin that is a perfect reflection of the weather-worn, moss-laden trees of her home.

She rummages through a nearby basket, producing a large seed from under a dense layer of flowers.

"*Rue tana hi rin thi'le meh,*" she says, handing the seed to Muri.

Muri's brow dips curiously as the feyn replies in the sprite's own tongue, "*Vareh?*"

No sprite had ever taught Nurai their language. In fact, Muri was the only feyn she knew of in the veil that the sprites deemed worthy of the honor.

It gnawed at her. For some reason, she was not enough. She could not help but think that she must lack something vital to the fea, as did nearly all feyn, or the sprites would have accepted her as eagerly as they had the female beside her.

Perhaps it is only vanity and selfishness that she wants them to accept her in such a way. Stars know that they are the most meddlesome of fea. She should be relieved that it is Muri and not herself that they had taken to. But the sprites seemed to weave the fabrics of the fates' design, carefully stitching the pattern as they went about their lives. On the whole of Terr, in every veil, there would never be a friendship more coveted than that of a sprite.

The sprite's pale green eyes flick to Nurai and the conversation shifts, the fea's words lost on the wind to all but Muri.

Nurai steps away from the pair, giving them the privacy the sprite clearly desires. She peruses each bushel of herbs, gathering up a handful of the rare and more difficult to find. She tries her best to remain distracted and to be anything but curious about the conversation happening only a few feet away—or offended by being cut off from it.

Muri nods her head at the sprite in clear agreement about something.

"I'm sorry," Muri whispers under her breath when she returns to Nurai, laying a hand on her arm, clearly concerned about how she might feel about the rejection.

"It's all right," Nurai says, offering her friend a smile and showing the sprite all that she selected from the stall.

The tiny fea folds one of her arms behind her, resting it on the small of her back, as she taps her chin with a finger, eyeing the herbs thoughtfully.

"*H'tesh,*" she says with an all too eager smile.

Muri can hardly contain her surprise as she translates, "She requests a favor in exchange for the goods."

"What favor?" Nurai asks in true curiosity.

It is rare but not unheard of for bargains to be bartered in such a way. Still, though young she may be, she is well aware that a fea bargain should never be taken lightly.

"*Ma'rei heth la'vei ma nesh ei'le,*" the sprite answers.

"She says, she will tell you when she has need of you." There is a question in Muri's voice when she says it, clearly confused as to why the small fea would demand such a high price for the bundle.

Nurai considers the small handful of herbs, none exceedingly rare, only potentially difficult to obtain. The herbs would be most valuable in trade to the humans, and she had not made up her mind about whether she would return to their court. While the pink flowers could be dried and powdered to color the mortal's faces and the others used for healing, the feyn had little use for such things.

She lowers her hand toward the basket, prepared to settle the bundle back among the rest and abandon them. An unnamed bargain is unwise and could be the highest of prices. And yet her hand falters before she can release them, a question forming in her mind. Why? Why would she ask such a price?

Perhaps it is no more than youthful arrogance when she clutches the herbs tightly, turns to the sprite, and agrees. Or perhaps it is the will of the fates when she feels the bargain etched upon her skin, weaving her into the loom of their design.

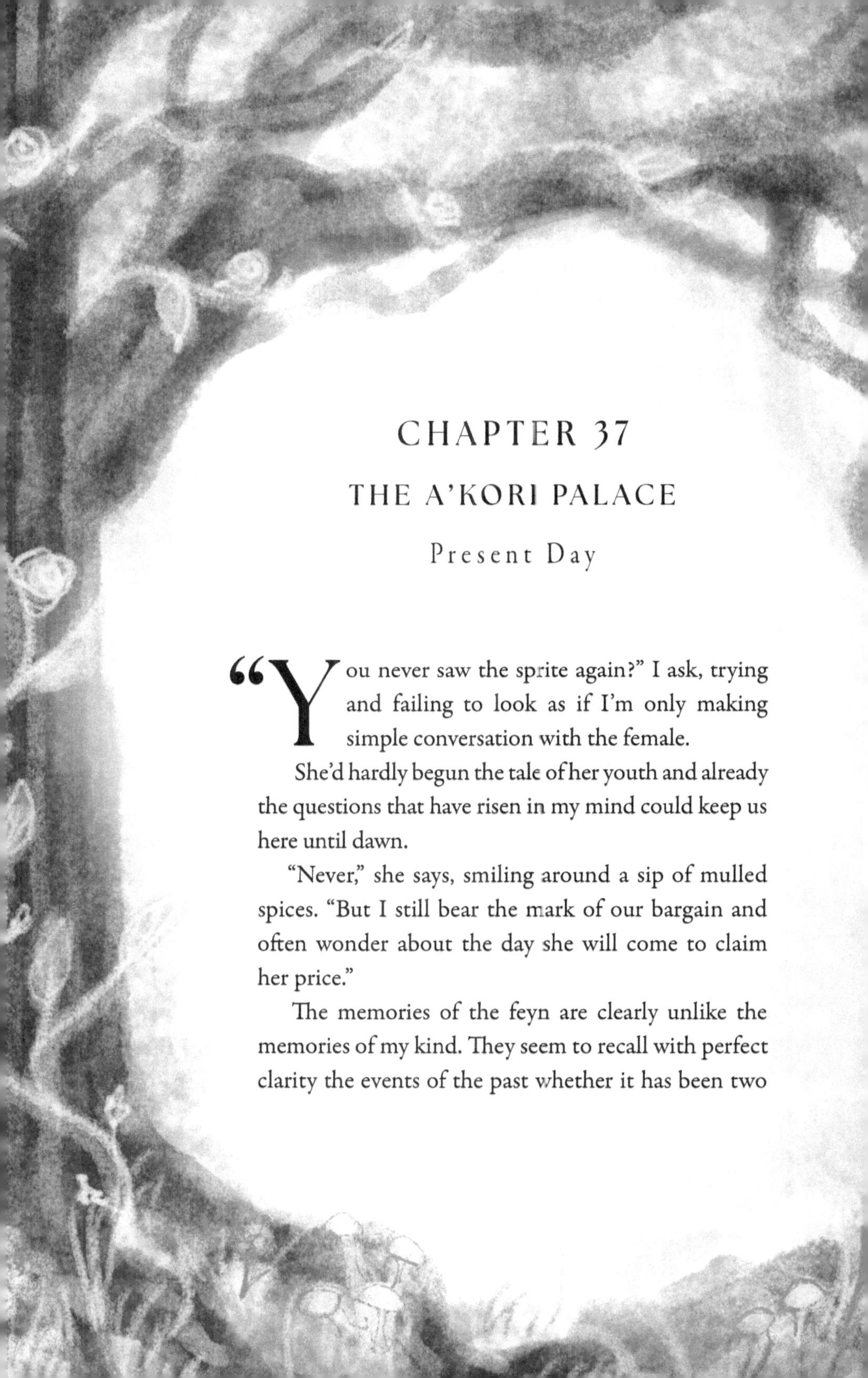

CHAPTER 37
THE A'KORI PALACE
Present Day

"You never saw the sprite again?" I ask, trying and failing to look as if I'm only making simple conversation with the female.

She'd hardly begun the tale of her youth and already the questions that have risen in my mind could keep us here until dawn.

"Never," she says, smiling around a sip of mulled spices. "But I still bear the mark of our bargain and often wonder about the day she will come to claim her price."

The memories of the feyn are clearly unlike the memories of my kind. They seem to recall with perfect clarity the events of the past whether it has been two days or two hundred years. I have no doubt the sprite will always remember the bargain, even if it were not etched upon her skin. How the fea will find her to exact that payment is another matter entirely.

"And ... you are close with the Vatruke?" I ask.

She nods, and I'm relieved when she answers, "I was close with them, back then. Before they were known as the Vatruke. Divisions among the feyn only began after the sundering. I think many of us would have liked to maintain those bonds, but the Vatruke made it impossible. I was either with them or against them. As were we all."

"How could you maintain friendships when they were ending the lives of the fea?" I ask heatedly, and Nurai raises an eyebrow at my tone.

"That, child, is the reason I am not with them."

I try not to bristle. To her, ancient as she is, I will be a child until the day I pass into the next world. Perhaps even then.

"After the sundering, the siblings became very guarded, very selective of those they kept close," she says.

"Siblings?" I wonder aloud.

It is Xeyvian who answers from his place beside me. "Arda, Vos, and Nix."

"And Muri," Nurai adds, a flicker of sadness distorting her features.

Xeyvian nods. "For a time. Though Muri turned on them during the first war."

"Faidra said that Muri was killed in the first war," I say. It isn't a question, but I'm pleased when Nurai explains further without making me dig for the answers I clearly seek.

"Muri was always close with the fea, and the others must have known that she would never agree to harm them. I believe they kept it from her as long as they could, and when she found out..." Nurai trails off, unable to speak the last of it aloud. "She came to me just before the war and told me of the conversation she had with the sprite at the market. Fea were disappearing, ancient stands of trees had begun to die, and none of the fea knew why. The sprite was sent by the fea to ask her for help and offer aid."

"What aid?" I ask.

Nurai shrugs. "I wish I knew. Muri never told me, and then, she was gone."

"And you never sought out the sprite so that you could ask?" I wonder incredulously.

Nurai raises a hand to her ribs, absently stroking where I can only assume the fea bargain is concealed beneath her gown.

"If there was anything she wanted me to know, she would have found me long ago," she says. "I, on the other hand, have no doubt I could spend a feyn lifetime searching Terr for the sprite and never find her if it is her intention to remain hidden."

I can't argue with that. Even Tig and Eon can be difficult to find, and they seem to seek my company eagerly. Still, there is a question sliding off my tongue before I know I'm asking it. "What did you do to the fea to make them mistrust you?"

Riesh's fork clatters against his porcelain plate when it slips from his hand, and the general tenses beside me.

Her face is far too calm when she answers, "Why would you assume it is anything that *I* have done to them? When the fea began to go missing and our world descended into war, they fled into the forest of Brax and have had very little to do with the feyn since that time."

"But they seek sanctuary in A'kori?" I ask, wondering at the dichotomy of what she tells me.

"When they are desperate enough, yes." She takes an elegant bite of food as if she hasn't just proven my point.

The fea are willing to risk *chai'brukar*, the ship breaking seas off the Braxian shores, yet the sprite who bound Nurai has not sought her out. Why?

Nurai covers a yawn with her silk napkin, before using it to blot the side of her mouth.

"You must be tired," Xeyvian says to her, his hand brushing against my thigh. "It was a long journey."

"I am," she replies with a smile, sliding her chair out from under the table and rising from her seat.

"It was lovely to meet you, Shivaria. I am sure we will have more time to talk again soon." She dips her head the slightest bit, her eyes traveling the length of my form once more, before raising an eyebrow and turning to let herself out.

"You know," Riesh says around a mouthful of meat as he points his fork at me, "the fea really have distanced themselves from the feyn since the first war. It isn't just Nurai."

I know that. I have seen it myself. Though I hadn't exactly tried to hide my skepticism as the female wove her tale. Still, I find that I am mildly annoyed when Riesh speaks up in her defense.

"You weren't even born yet," I say.

Everything he knows about that time he either read in the histories or was told by someone else. While I hate to admit that it's a lesson I'm beginning to know well, unless he witnessed it himself, he should be open to questioning the validity of the story.

"True." He stabs a piece of breaded fowl and pops it in his mouth. "But I believe what Xey tells me about that time."

Because Xeyvian was alive then.

I don't miss the unspoken meaning of his words, and why hadn't I suspected as much? The male *had* already told me he'd known Siserie for two hundred years. How old is he? More questions, always more questions.

He seems pleased at the expression he's put on my face when I slide my chair out, the general following suit as he thanks his friends for joining us. Riesh seems content to remain behind as we depart, apparently committed to a valiant attempt at devouring every morsel of food before bed. Awri doesn't linger, flowing out of the room behind us, she heads toward her chambers, toward her mate.

I can hardly imagine what it might take to repair the rift between us, but it's one more thing I may not have to consider after tomorrow. She may never speak to me again. Though I might harbor some regrets about that, I certainly won't blame her for it.

It isn't a long walk back to our rooms and I can't help but wonder where Nurai is sleeping. Not that I can do anything with the knowledge. It's just that I might prefer if it were on the other side of the palace, if not outside the grounds entirely.

I'm running my fingers through my hair, already dressed in a richly colored sleeping gown, when I eye Xeyvian through the mirror that sits across from our bed.

"How long is she staying?" I ask.

Apparently, I failed to make the question sound casual when he chuckles before replying, "You don't like her."

It's not even a question and I wonder what kinds of emotions the male felt from me over the course of our meal.

"I don't trust her," I tell him—even if it doesn't matter, even if by tomorrow any trust he's ever laid at my feet is broken beyond what I can repair.

He raises an eyebrow at me. "I'm not sure you trust anyone, *mi'ajna*."

There is one. But for the most part, he's right. I was raised not to trust, but to question everything outside the La'tari regime and to seek the inevitable outcome of every situation. I was taught to plan for each possibility as I tried to force the course of my choosing.

But this is not the same. There is something about the female, something about her story. And as much as I try to tell myself that maybe it is only my own ignorance causing this feeling in my gut, I can't make myself believe it.

Eyeing his reflection in the mirror, I watch him step up behind me and wrap his arms around me. He buries his nose in the crook of my neck, taking in my scent, and mumbles into my hair, "Should I have her thrown out now, or should we let her sleep until morning?"

I puff out a laugh, though I'm not entirely sure he's joking. Tempting as it may be, I won't bristle any more feyn until I know my fate, not if I can help it.

"Maybe after she's told me all her tales about Brax," I say.

"She does have plenty of those." He smiles.

I shouldn't ask, but it's too tempting when the male holding me begs for my questions. With a single finger, I stroke the long muscle of his arm, braced around my waist.

"But not as many as you." Curiosity rings in my voice when I say it.

He shakes his head. "No. Not as many as I do."

Ask. His unspoken request begs of me, and maybe there are some things I can know, even though they will change nothing.

"Were you alive for the sundering?" I finally ask.

He nods, slowly, as if he's afraid the answer might frighten me.

"Like Nurai, I was still young when the veils were formed," he explains.

"I think humans might have a somewhat different idea of what *young* means," I tease.

He shrugs, his mouth turning down thoughtfully. "I've known feyn of two hundred years that I would consider children, and some as young as thirty that I would let advise me. When I say that I was young, I mean I lacked the sound mind of a male who understands the weight of his choices."

I can't help but hope that the grace he extends to his younger self is the same he will extend to me once he learns what I am. Perhaps his king will be lenient, given my honesty and my upbringing, just as Awri was when I first arrived. A hollowness wells in my stomach when I'm reminded that the female seems to have met her limit in what she is willing to accept about me. I decidedly give up pondering my future and the general's past, until I know what path the fates will set my feet upon tomorrow. There are no promises of what the days might hold after tonight. It doesn't matter if these moments are my last with him or just the beginning of many more; they will always be precious.

"What is troubling you?" he asks.

I hadn't noticed his brow drawing down with concern as he examined my reflection. Shoving everything I feel into a well-guarded corner of my mind, I lock it away. He sighs.

"You are a fortress, *mi'ajna*." He brushes a stray curl from my eyes. "I only wish I lived inside your walls."

How can I tell him that the walls that keep us divided are for his protection and not my own? Maybe one day he will let me explain, but that conversation isn't for tonight. Tonight is for us, and all that we could have been.

I offer an apologetic smile through the mirror and spin to face him. I trace the hard lines of his face with my fingers. Rising to my toes, I brush his lips with my own. It's a small gesture, a beckoning, one he answers sweetly.

Cupping my jaw reverently, he leans into a deep kiss. Ballads are born of such kisses, full and deep with longing. The passion the male pours into my being has a life of its own and could bear entire worlds if I dared to let it free. These are moments I will treasure. When I recall them, they will remind me of how, even as the sun sets beyond the farthest horizon, she ignites the darkening skies with colorful wonders before ushering in the blanket of night.

I grip his shirt tightly, pulling his chest firmly against my own, unwilling to let even the air divide us. His hands are in my hair the next moment, fisting my curls, as if he too might capture something that can never be taken from him. Something that, unlike myself, will always be his.

Lifting his tunic overhead, I drop it to the floor. His hands move slowly across the exposed flesh of my neck, down my side, and onto my thighs until in one fluid motion he is hoisting me up, hooking my legs around his waist, and carrying me to the bed.

Light from the fire dances in the deep sea of his eyes when he lays me on the thick duvet. He takes a step back, taking his time as his eyes wander across the landscape of my body. The thin gossamer gown is bunched at my thighs, a single strap falling from my shoulder, but Xeyvian looks at me as if I am completely bare before him. As if he has already memorized every curve and dip of my body and can recall it at will.

I tense when his eyes land on the blooming bruise Toren left upon my leg. It's not the eyesore it will be two days from now. Still, I worry that he will abandon me to find Caden, or worse, in pursuit of the knowledge of who dared leave a mark upon my flesh. Perhaps it is the heat of his passion, or maybe it is the pleading look in my eyes, but he drags his eyes away from it and meets mine.

He drops to a knee at the end of the bed, his intent written clearly on his face as he hooks my ankle around his neck and nips at the sensitive skin of my calf.

The sharp inhale of air passing through my lips garners his attention and his mouth tugs up at the edges, his fangs glistening in the low light of the room. My breath hitches in my throat as his tongue slides up my inner thigh, my stomach dipping with anticipation.

I should be wary of the male and the precarious position I'm in, but it isn't his fangs I feel when his mouth lands upon my core. It's the slow slide of his tongue across my folds as he laps up my passion.

I gasp when he hooks my free leg over his shoulder, just as he positioned the other. His tongue delves into my depths. Like a predator, he watches me over the rise and fall of my chest as my pulse quickens with every stroke from the male. I clutch the sheet when he works his way toward that sensitive bundle of nerves, grazing it with a sharp fang, before soothing it with the flat of his tongue, and sucking me between his lips.

I lose sight of him when my head drops against the bed, the weight of it suddenly too heavy to hold. My back strains as it arches, a pleasurable need coiling within me. He is a master of this craft, and he works my body to perfection with every sweep across that tender peak of flesh. He builds the tension like a rising tide drawn by the moon to break upon the shores. And when I do break, my back hitting the bed as my body tremors out a rasping moan, his hands find my waist and he pulls me against his mouth with a desperation I understand well.

His tongue moves in time with the rhythm of my quaking. The male between my legs unwilling to allow the heights to which he brought me to diminish in the slightest. He toils between my thighs until I cry out into the night, breaking anew, my whole being eager to meet the demands of his tongue. Only when my entire body writhes uncontrollably under the intensity of his attention does he withdraw.

He meets my eyes, a fiendish smile on his face as he drops a kiss against my inner thigh, my body shuddering. Every nerve is on fire, my cheeks flushed with the rushing blood of my pounding heart. He looks truly pleased with himself when I find that I am unable to summon the strength to move and I wonder if this had always been his plan.

Lifting the fabric of my gown, he drops a gentle kiss on my belly. My nipples are already peaked when he eyes me through the valley of my breasts, relieving me of the thin gossamer sheath and discarding it.

I've regained enough of my strength to meet his lips when he brings them to mine, delighting in the taste of my pleasure upon his tongue. My hands travel along the lines of his back, tracing the muscles below his shoulders, down his sides and onto his firm ass. The fates certainly took their time when they chiseled his form and tonight, I am determined to memorize the feeling of his body as he presses it against my own.

He slides his thick shaft across the slickness of my core, retreating tauntingly when my hips rise, encouraging him to enter. He smiles against my throat, fangs grazing the surface, and I arch my neck to the side in invitation.

I don't have to look to know that the smile has fallen from his lips. The tense stillness of his body says everything, a low rumble forming in his chest. He hesitates, the heat of his breath caressing the crook of my neck.

"Don't make me beg," I whisper.

The words are meant to tease him, but I find that I might do just that if the male continues this pleasurable torment.

"I will give you everything," he puffs out against the base of my neck. "But only when you understand what it is you are asking for."

Before I can comprehend the movement, he snakes his arm under my lower back, grips my hip, and flips me onto my belly. Pulling me back until I am on my knees, he kneels behind me, my ass cradled in the seat of his lap, his chest pressing down against my back. His hand slides up my throat until he cups my jaw and turns my head to face him.

"If you understand nothing else, understand this," he says quietly, my core stretching around his length as he slides into me, filling me from wall to wall, "your pleasure is my pleasure, and you will never have to beg me for that, or anything else."

He seats himself fully, capturing my moan with his mouth before retreating from my body in a painfully slow slide as I clench around his girth. Every stroke of his tongue against my own is echoed by the stroke of his shaft, his hips rocking back and forth lazily as if my body was made for his pleasure, just as his was made for mine.

His hand cups my breast, and a vibrating rumble grows in his chest as his fingers round my nipple and it hardens in response to his touch. He rises onto his knees, his hands gripping my hips as he pulls back, only to plunge himself into me to a depth I've never known. I gasp, and my body explodes in a myriad of tingling sparks.

My mind grows hazy even as the rest of my senses heighten. My knees begin to tremble when he slams into me again, deeper still and more eager than before. His pace quickens with every thrust he drives into my core, pulling my hips until I'm seated firmly in his lap.

I think he might find his release. The thought of the male's passion spilling into me, enough to strain the tension already coiling in my belly. He groans when I clench my legs together, my body tightening around him. The slick of my passion coats his length anew and he swears under his breath as he pulls himself from within me and rolls me onto my side.

There is a desperate look written on his face when he settles his feet on the floor and slides me to the edge of the bed. Wrapping his hands around my torso, he pushes himself between my legs with a deeply satisfied groan, my knees nearly nestled against my chest. His eyes roam across my flesh, taking in the pinch in my brow and the sway of my breasts as they keep time with every thrust. They wander toward the curve of my backside, his pupils blown wide when they finally travel to where we are joined.

It's the aching desire on the male's face that finally pushes my body to crest the wave of my building passion. It's too much, the intensity of the rise, the swell of my core as he pumps himself inside me.

"Xeyvian," I plead on a shallow breath and it's all he needs to lose himself, pouring himself into me.

His body stills, his breathing a mere shudder as his shaft throbs within me. I'm not sure I can continue but even so, when he parts himself from me, I struggle to bury the loss of our joining. His breathing is hurried and deep when he collapses onto the bed. His arms wrapping me up, he pulls me to his chest, laying my ear over the thundering of his heart as he sighs contentedly.

A sweet silence fills the room, and for a while, I'm able to keep my mind from wandering from this moment.

After a time, the rise and fall of his chest becomes more even, and he traces invisible pictures across my back. These precious seconds I tuck away, unwilling to let the memory fade from my mortal mind. I breathe in his scent, take note of the way his arms curl perfectly around my form, of how I've never felt more at home than I do cradled against his chest. I memorize the sound of his breathing, the woosh of the air as it exits his lungs, and the sound of his heart, beating in time with my own.

But these moments are not made to last and even in the midst of this comfortable perfection I cannot stanch the flow of thoughts threatening to overwhelm me.

I've nearly made up my mind to lay in silence until sleep finds me when the question passes my lips. "If there are things you wish to tell me, why make me ask?" I say quietly into the dim night.

He spools a lock of my hair around his finger and looks down at me.

"Because, *mi'ajna*, I believe you will ask when you are ready, and I trust you to know when that time is right for you."

None of it matters if the king sends me away or locks me in a cell—or worse. But I smile and say nothing, kissing him sweetly before resting my head on his shoulder and closing my eyes.

It is the one outcome I hadn't let myself consider, if the king is truly a reaver, he could take my mind from me if he chose to do so. Dark thoughts of a ravaged mind are the last that filter through me when the void comes to take me, regretfully. For tonight is a night I wish to live in forever.

Blood pools by my feet and a shiver snakes up my spine at the rasp of the demon's blade sliding across the floor. My heart slams against my ribs. Every ragged inhale of smoke swirling in the air burns my lungs. Blood soaks the hair of the still form of the woman reaching for me.

The demon steps toward me. I scream, a dark storm tearing through the fabric of the veil, spearing the demon with a black blade etched in starlight. It gleams, as the demon falls to his knees with a wail, dark blood weeping from its chest to drip upon the floor.

An old woman in tattered rags rises from where the demon falls in a crumpled heap, a black toothed smile adorning her wrinkled features. She is wrapped in rags, a large hood obscuring her face. She reaches a gnarled hand toward me.

"Give up the lie, child."

In the distance, someone calls to me and the crimson world shudders.

"No," I beg the crone.

"Shivaria!" A black scaled demon rushes through the door. Its eyes lock on mine. There's nowhere to run, every wall of the building around me set ablaze. I rush the demon with fearful determination. I will not die, not like this. Slamming my shoulder into its abdomen I send it to the ground with a grunt.

"Shivaria!"

The crimson world fissures. I shake my head, clearing the fog, and bare my teeth as two strange demons flood into the small space.

"Hold her!"

I land a blow on one and it staggers back, the crone cackling behind them.

I take the break in their line to rush for the door, halted by an arm, like a steel band hooking my waist, pulling me back into the fray.

"Shivaria, stop!"

I strike at another demon closing in on my right, landing a well-placed kick to the knee of the demon diving at me from my left.

"Enough, Xeyvian. She's too strong. Do it, now!"

The crimson world breaks around me, consumed by darkness, and the last sound upon my ears is the scream of my own raging fury as the void takes me.

CHAPTER 38

THE A'KORI PALACE

Present Day

Gasping for air, hands shaking, I drag myself from the thick sludge of oblivion. My heart races as I claw my way to the surface, sure that if I falter it will pull me into its depths and I will sink down, never to reemerge.

Safe. You're safe.

At last, my demon came to claim its portion from my dreams. My hand glides across my throat, soothing the tender muscles. My eyes fly open, a deep panic welling within me when I recall where I am.

I clutch the empty sheets beside me, sighing my relief when I find that the general is absent his usual place on the bed. The sky is tinged a dark shade of grey, only the faintest of proclamations that the sun is set to rise, and there are still hours before dawn.

My senses still dull from the clouded visions of my nightmares, it takes me entirely too long to notice the murmur of muffled voices beyond the doors of the war room. If not for the time of day I wouldn't think much of it. The room is, after all, well trafficked by those he trusts.

I can't help but wonder if the Vatruke have been sighted and find it difficult to conjure little else that would rouse the male from my side in the small hours of morning. Pitching the sheets from my body, I cinch a thin dressing gown around my waist, curiosity pulling me toward the flickering light spilling from beneath the doors. I raise my hand to the lever, my body stilling when Nurai's voice comes from the other side.

"What you are asking is impossible, Xeyvian. There is not a feyn alive that still has the power to unbind her."

"There is someone," he growls angrily, "Or she would not be as she is."

"The Vatruke?" Riesh offers.

"Muri was the only one left with that kind of power after the sundering," Xeyvian says.

A thoughtful silence falls over the room before Nurai offers an inconceivable option. "Take her back to La'tari. Surely if that is where she is from, that is where you will find the answers you seek."

"It's a good plan, Xey," Riesh says, "And it will get her out of Vos's reach."

"Vos cannot easily reach her behind these walls," the general argues.

"You underestimate her if you think that's true," Nurai says flatly, confirming all my fears about the female that hunts me.

A hush falls over them, the general considering all they have said.

"I will accompany you," Awri offers, "A glamour to hide what you are, and you will be free to move about the southern continent unhindered."

The general's voice is full of far too much hesitation when he answers, "All right. We will take her to La'tari. Riesh, you will come with us."

"I will join you as well," Nurai says, and I really wish she hadn't.

"I will alert Toren," Xeyvian says, "Awri, tell Caden that he will be joining our party and send Riah to my chambers. Have a ship prepared for the crossing and well stocked with supplies for our landing. We leave tomorrow, on the earliest possible tide."

There is a moment I am a coward. A moment I tell myself maybe there is a life to be had in the midst of this lie. I can leave with the male, put myself far from any harm I could cause his king. Savor whatever time it allows us to share.

But it wouldn't be real. Not any of it. Not until he truly knows what I am.

It is Riesh who first exits the war room into the general's chamber. I don't try to pretend I haven't overheard them. The pause the male gives me when he meets my eyes only speaks of the relief he feels in that knowledge. With a shallow nod he leaves to see to the general's orders. Awzi follows shortly after, a relieved smile adorning her face as well when she rushes out to see to her task.

"Take the *glier* if you must but leave the others," Nurai says, and I bristle at the demand in her tone. "A small party will be far easier to conceal."

"If that were not the case," the general responds, his voice low in warning, "I would have Toren beside me as well, a fleet of ships sailing south, and a legion aboard them. Trust me when I say that this is the least I will allow to accompany us, and far from my comfort. Where she is concerned, I have not found my limit, and I would give everything to see her safely through this."

"Careful, Xeyvian," she says simply, "The fates may choose to test that declaration."

She smiles at me when she leaves the room and I'm not sure why it feels like a taunt. I tell myself that it is only that I do not like the female and push every thought of her from my mind.

The general is the last to join me in the main room, cloaked in gloom. It's clear by the look on his face, he is not at all surprised to find me awake. I, on the other hand, am unaccustomed to seeing him with dark circles beneath his eyes. As the others had, he offers me a smile but only looks worn out as he pulls me against his chest, resting his chin on my head.

"Did you sleep?" I ask, knowing that nothing as simple as a night awake would be enough to wear on him like this.

"A little," he says, dropping a kiss on my head before taking a seat on the edge of the bed, pulling me between his legs.

"So, *mi'ajna*, will you travel to La'tari?" he asks without pretense.

"Do I have a choice?" I ask.

It's a fair question. After all, he made his plans without consulting me, and all the arrangements are well on their way to being complete.

"I will never take your choice from you, *mi'dair'a*." His brow dips as if he can hardly believe he has to explain it to me, and maybe I shouldn't make him. "If you want to stay, then we will stay, and find another way."

Another way to what? To unbind her. To unbind *me*.

I remind myself that he promised to help me undo the bargains I hold with the fea, but I don't ask him what Nurai meant when she said it, afraid of what his answer might be.

Today is for us, tonight for the revealing of myself, and tomorrow, a new beginning, no matter which threads of my life the fates choose to pull upon.

"You've only just asked me to remain in A'kori," I tease, a small deflection.

He pins me with a hard stare and says, "Allow me to make my intentions clearer. It would please me to have you by my side, always. A'kori, Brax, continents unknown to the feyn. Let your home be here." He grasps my wrist, placing my hand over his pounding heart and I want to choke on every lie I have let the male believe. "Your heart is my home. Every piece of what you are decorates the halls of my life in a vivid splendor I never dreamed to possess." He cups my jaw. "You are so much more than I ever hoped for."

I hide my sorrow in a kiss, savoring the taste of him as my throat burns and my chest aches.

"If you still feel that way tomorrow," I say, "ask me again."

A frown flickers across his face, but he nods slowly in agreement.

"I have a gift for you," he says, producing a small box from within his pocket, carved from knotted wood. "I have wanted to give you this since the night you fell in the river. There was a time, as you slept, that I was sure you would never rise." His brow creases as he recalls it. "To have found you, only to lose you…"

He shakes off the memory, unable to speak life into all that he feared that night. More than ever, I wish we lived in a world where I could reassure him that he would never lose me. But I won't lie to him. Not anymore.

He composes himself and with the swipe of his thumb unlatches the box, settling it into the palm of my hand.

"I think I know you well enough by now to know that you prefer the blades I gifted you, but you can't take them everywhere," he says.

I raise an eyebrow at the male, but I don't argue. It's true that the flimsy dresses of court would do little to conceal them, but I'm sure if I put my mind to it, I could manage.

He chuckles. "Well, for my sake then, consider wearing it."

Holding back the lid he reveals a feynstone ring, simple and lovely, nestled in a thick clutch of black velvet. Just as my blades do, the stone has an odd way of pulling at the light as if it might gather up every flame, snuffing us into darkness. The kite shaped stone is set in a thin band of delicate gold and, though the jewel wasn't crafted to be a weapon, the pointed shape of its tip begs to be used in such a way.

I can't help the smile that breaks upon my face, a pleased grin forming on his own as he plucks it from the box and places it on my finger.

"It's beautiful," I say, never having thought I would ever honor a jewel with such words.

"It is nothing compared to you," he replies, and for the life of me I can't understand why, but I know he means it.

He rises from the bed reluctantly, the exhaustion he feels lingering upon his face when he says, "I need to speak with Toren and help him fortify the grounds before the guests arrive."

I nod. "I will come with you."

"You will stay here," he says. And when he sees I'm about to protest, he adds a simple, "Please."

He's lucky when a knock at the door grabs my attention. Luckier still that it is Riah on the other side. If the male won't let me join him, at least the female he's leaving me with is likely to offer some form of entertainment I can truly enjoy.

The general plants a kiss on top of my head, his fingers twisting the ring on my hand affectionately, before he leaves. A pang of sorrow resounds in my chest when he walks out. I should have been more diligent in capturing the last moments I was assured with him. I should have left him with words he could remember as he had done for me so many times. The fates promise no tomorrows, and I'd been careless with precious moments that could easily be our last.

Riah eyes the ring, a broader smile than usual taking over her features. "That is quite a gift. I don't suppose you will tell me how you got it."

She waggles her eyebrows at me, and I turn toward my closet before she has a chance to see my cheeks flush. She follows close behind. When I reach for my leathers, she places herself in front of me and puts up a hand to stop me.

"What are you doing?" she asks, a confused dip in her brow, though she is obviously aware of my intentions.

I frown. "Sparring."

"Not today," she says flatly, "The general wants the grounds clear when the guests arrive."

"Then we have plenty of time," I say, making to reach around her. "The party doesn't start until the sun goes down."

Riah snorts. "And every noble with an invitation will be here by midday. I assumed it was the same in the La'tari courts. Every feyn and mortal privileged enough to be invited will be eager for the opportunity to work themselves into the good graces of my liege." She bows dramatically with a wild flourish of her hands, and I can't help but roll my eyes at the image she paints.

"We can spar until midday," I argue, but she gives me a look that says nothing in this veil will tempt the female to join me in the ring this morning.

Her eyes fall back to my ring when I cross my arms over my chest and her face grows dark as she considers it.

"Did you know that the feynstone blade would take down Kezik when you threw it?" she asks, deadly serious.

"No," I admit, eyeing the ring myself, suddenly very curious about the rare stone it holds.

"I didn't think so. There really isn't much on Terr that will so easily end the life of a feyn, much less one of the Vatruke."

And the general of A'kori put that power in the hands of the enemy. My hands. My entire life I'd been taught how to end the life of a feyn. And despite the ease with which the shadow master dispatched them when I was young, nothing I'd ever been taught was as simple as a blade.

She grins, clearly amused when she says, "I admit, I am looking forward to seeing the faces of the nobles when they see that ring on your finger."

"Why?"

"For a number of reasons." She shrugs. "The rarest stone on Terr, taken straight from the king's hoard, one that can easily end the life of a feyn, on

the hand of a mortal." She whistles at the implications. "The general certainly wants to make a statement to anyone that might find you…"

"*Durah,*" I supply, clearly annoyed.

She rolls her eyes. "Vulnerable, was the word I was looking for."

My brow draws down thoughtfully when I ask, "Why would the king give him the ring, only so that he could give it to me?"

"You would have to ask the king that question. I'm not sure how it is in La'tari, but in A'kori, the king does what he wants," she teases.

Maybe I *will* ask him. Maybe. There will be plenty to occupy my conversation with her sovereign and though I am truly curious about his motivations as they pertain to the ring, I know we will both be far too preoccupied with the topic of my life.

I glance at my leathers once more before puffing out my frustration. "If we aren't sparring, what do you intend to do all day?"

I decidedly hate chess. How Riah ever thought this would distract me from our usual morning routine I cannot fathom.

"Again?" she asks gleefully, as she swipes my king off the board.

"No," I say flatly, "Thank you."

The sun finally crests the eastern sea and even I have to admit that the staggering number of patrols set upon the grounds seems excessive.

"He's worried," I say absently, surveying the uniformed soldiers sweeping the grounds.

"Tonight *would* be the night," Riah says, confirming my unspoken fear, and I'm sure everyone else's, "if the Vatruke want to make trouble."

"I didn't get the feeling it was trouble they were after," I say.

Leaning back in her chair, she shrugs. "They gave up the element of surprise when they revealed themselves to us. No doubt they thought a single feyn escorting her lady would be an easy enough mark."

"They must be incredibly powerful if they're willing to risk that kind of mistake," I say as I reset the board.

She nods, "They are," then frowns as she considers. "The Vatruke *have* grown

comfortable in their power, but they are not foolish. I do not think they will risk revealing themselves among the powerful allies attending this evening."

What she says makes sense. But then I recall a single moment of their failed ambush that nags at my mind before the memory can fade.

"Why was Kezik looking for the barracks?" I wonder aloud.

It is something I should not have overlooked. I chastise myself for being so wrapped up in the tangled web of my own life that I had not asked myself the question until now. I can tell by the look on her face that she failed to ask herself the same. There is a moment that her eyes drift off in thought, and when her eyes snap up to mine, it is a moment I wish to never relive. The full weight of her own dread fills me as she pushes up from her seat, rushing into the hall without a word.

Before I know where my feet are taking me, I'm standing in the center of the general's room watching the door latch shut behind her. It is more than the look upon her face that prickles the hair on the back of my neck. Whatever conclusion she'd drawn is concerning enough that she abandoned her post to report it. I'm alone for the first time since the assassin broke into the general's chambers.

I wait in the quiet stillness of my room, my fists bunching at my sides. Clearly, it's been too long since I've been alone. I struggle to stop the fraying of my nerves as the minutes pass by. With greater effort than I'd like to admit, I collect myself, deciding that the best use of my time is in fact *not* staring at the tall wooden doors, waiting for my companion to return.

I remind myself that it is not cowardice to be cautious as I gather my feynstone blades, keeping them nearby as I bathe. I'm opening a tall window in the washroom, letting the steam out into the late morning air when the door of the main chamber clicks shut. The hair raises on my arms. Well aware that it is unreasonable to be concerned, I snatch one of my blades and settle it behind my back. Pinching the sharp tip between my fingers I round the door into the main room. Better to catch an intruder off guard than allow myself to be cornered.

I tell myself that no one coming to end my life would use the door off the main hall. Still, my blood sings, *caution*. Arm tensed to throw the dagger, I puff out a relieved sigh at the sight of Riah.

Pausing in the entry, her eyebrow lifts as I drop the blade to my side. It's a look I return. What does she expect?

"I'll be sure to announce myself next time," she teases.

"Not a bad idea," I quip.

While I'm certainly curious about the thoughts that took her from the room, I don't ask. She might not tell me, and even if she were to, I'm sure her king would not look favorably on a human with knowledge of their secrets. I likely already know too much, and the more he finds within my mind to displease him, the more certain my fate will be.

I head back to the washroom when Riah turns to answer a knock at the door. I'm tying a robe at the waist, heading back toward my companion, when my eyes catch on the fresh bundle of dark glossy flowers sitting on the heavy stone slab under the mirror. They are bundled with a pliant vine, and I recognize them at once by their smell.

A small breeze drifts in from the window, and I tilt my head to listen. With all that happened, I nearly forgot about the flowers Tig offered to grow, the ones that will help keep my demon at bay. While it is unlike the sisters to come, only to vanish before I've seen them, I don't think too much of it. With Riah close by, I can hardly blame them for remaining distant, even if I would like to see them again before I find myself locked in a cell.

I find Riah standing at the edge of the bed. She's eyeing a large black box tied with shimmering lace, marked with the golden script of Adora's dress shop. Beside it, a small envelope signed in the general's hand.

"I see the general has you right where he wants you." Riah chuckles as I walk to her side and reach for the letter.

"What do you mean?" I ask, cracking the blank seal.

"I've known enough well-bred ladies in my long life to confidently say that most would have reached for the box containing their gown before reading a letter from their male," she explains.

My nose crinkles in disgust when I say, "Then I feel just as sorry for the ladies you've known as I do for the males who have attempted to entertain them."

She laughs as I slide the note from within the folds of the envelope, plopping down on the edge of the bed with a heavy sigh as I summarize aloud,

"He apologizes that he won't make it back before the party and says that you will escort me there."

It isn't how I imagined my last moments with him but there is little to nothing I can do about it now. I set the letter upon the bed despondently, eyeing the black box. I tug at the lace, in a half-hearted attempt to unravel it when my eyes snag on a black velvet fold sitting on top. Unclasping the center and folding back the thin fabric reveals a delicate necklace of black shimmering stone.

"I guess you've got him right where you want him too." Riah smiles.

I don't tell her that if that were the case he would be here now, beside me. I simply lay it back against the velvet and turn my attention to the gown.

Adora has outdone herself. And though the gown is a far cry from the memories I hold of the crone I met in the woods, it will certainly serve its purpose tonight.

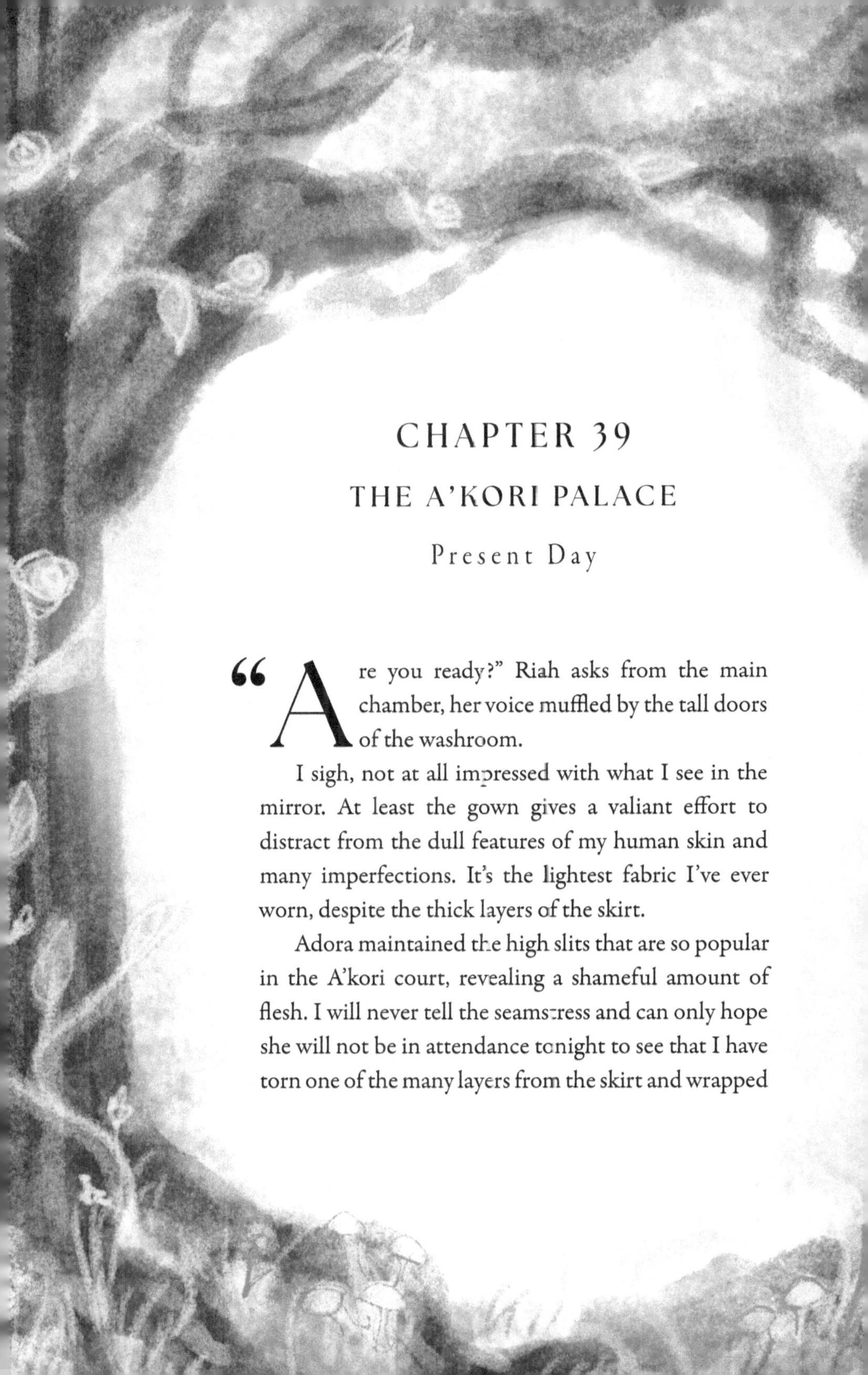

CHAPTER 39
THE A'KORI PALACE
Present Day

"Are you ready?" Riah asks from the main chamber, her voice muffled by the tall doors of the washroom.

I sigh, not at all impressed with what I see in the mirror. At least the gown gives a valiant effort to distract from the dull features of my human skin and many imperfections. It's the lightest fabric I've ever worn, despite the thick layers of the skirt.

Adora maintained the high slits that are so popular in the A'kori court, revealing a shameful amount of flesh. I will never tell the seamstress and can only hope she will not be in attendance tonight to see that I have torn one of the many layers from the skirt and wrapped my legs to conceal them. The binding is perhaps a better representation of the crone in all her tattered rags and serves a purpose I had not initially intended. The same long strips of fabric that wind about my legs serve to conceal the feynstone blades strapped to my thighs.

The seamstress constructed the bodice well and the deep blue lace of the gown sets fire to my eyes., though the neck plunges lower than I would have designed for myself. The flesh below the rise of my breasts and down the length of my arms is obscured by little more than a sheer panel of lace.

I've never been partial to the gowns of court or the extravagant adornment that accompanies them, yet I can't help but appreciate the unparalleled beauty of the fabric when it moves. I suck in an appreciative breath when thousands of tiny crystals sewn into the fabric shimmer as if I were wrapped in a blanket of starlight.

"Shivaria?"

"I'm coming."

I place the last of the precious flowers left by the sisters in my long cascade of thick spirals. I hadn't planned for them and find that after everything, I am completely unwilling to let them out of my sight. If I leave them here, I may never return to his chamber to claim them. It is pure luck that the waxy petals gleam a dark blue and purple when they catch the light. They are all but lost in the depth of my curls, glinting subtly as if my tresses contain a secret of their own.

I'm struggling with the clasp of the necklace when I push open the door of the main room. I glare down at the ridiculous heeled sandals Leanna taught me to walk in. While I have never been fond of the strain they put on my body, I can at least appreciate the pointed tip of each heel as a make-shift weapon. I expect Riah to mock me and prepare myself for the shocked look on her face when she sees me like this. But she only smiles, nodding her head as if this is the most natural thing in the world and at last every-thing is set right.

"Bagya was a brave choice," she says.

"I'm not sure choice is the right word," I tease.

Her head tips to the side curiously when she asks, "What do you mean?"

"I certainly hadn't planned on picking Bagya until the general explained the custom of that choice," I say, "that it should be the last fea I had dealings with."

My stomach sinks with her eyebrows raise suspiciously and she asks, "The general told you there is a custom?"

I nod, managing to find the clasp of my necklace.

She raises her hands in the air and smirks, shaking her head as she says, "I've never heard of such a thing."

I know the truth before the question leaves my lips. "He lied to me?"

"*I* did *not* say that," she asserts, a single finger pointed in the air, "And I trust you to make sure he knows that."

I can hardly hold it against him when I recall how we were with each other at the beginning. Before Niya. Besides, Adora's hard work and imagination created a masterpiece that is utterly unique in its own right. I can't imagine anyone else made the same selection. Even if none of that were true, I am in no position to judge the male for anything he has done. I won't let myself hope that it is a grace he will extend to me after tonight.

My steps are hesitant when Riah takes me into the halls. I'm not sure what I expect. Surely the guests who have arrived this evening are barred from this portion of the palace. She takes up her place beside me, the jovial face I'm accustomed to seeing on her transforming into that of the military commander she is. The general certainly had a vision of the way he would have me presented to the feyn this evening.

The guards are far quieter than I've seen them before. All are tense. Not one nods in acknowledgement as we pass. The only noise in the halls, the faint laughter and easy conversation drifting in from the party above the clinking of crystal and the hum of the quartet.

Clutching the last of my costume, I bring up the thick piece of sheer lace, tying it tightly at the back of my head as I situate the mask over my eyes. Riah tracks the movement, my hands rushing to hover over the blades at my thighs when she gasps.

"Focing fates, Shivaria," she gapes, "Is that shadowbane?"

Her eyes are glued to the small flowers strewn about my curls. She plucks one out, presses it against her nose, and takes a long drag of the bitter citrus scent before asking, "Where in all of Terr did you find these?"

I open my mouth, unsure of what story will spill from my lips. I only know whatever it is, it won't involve the sisters.

"Stop," she says with a hand in the air as she squints her eyes shut. "I don't want to know." She repeats the last to herself, as if it might somehow make it true. "I. Don't. Want. To. Know."

She pockets the tiny bloom and levels a commanding gaze at me when she says, "Just promise me you won't slip them into anyone's meal."

I think she might be joking, until I'm suddenly very certain she will remain here all night until I do just that.

"I promise," I say, my brow drawn in confusion.

I can tell that it's barely enough to convince her as she hesitates and, with a deep sigh, resumes toward the domed fea room.

The coiled tension of the ring before a sparring match is nothing compared to what I feel when I round the corner into the party. Hundreds of feyn glance up from their conversations. They gaze across small plates of delicate morsels and over the rims of etched crystal full of bubbling libations. It is only with great effort—and the hand that Riah places on the small of my back to usher me forward—that I continue into their midst.

Awri commissioned a handful of feyn that she considers artists of the highest caliber, and I will never argue that artists they most certainly are. Some have grown a stunning array of flowering vines, creeping toward the twilight sky painted overhead, the shape and color of the blooms unlike anything I have ever seen. Subtly, they alter the magnificently painted walls with astounding depth.

Living vines weave along painted trees as if they were bound one to the other. I imagine the artist's attempt to mimic the lush forests of Brax, the true home of the fea.

I'm lost in wonder when Riah jostles my elbow, pointing her chin toward a large table. Riesh piles delicious fair onto a wide plate, as Awri and Nurai speak with a group of feyn nearby. A few of the strangers disperse as I approach, eyeing me warily as I pass.

"Shivaria." Awri welcomes me warmly, and I can't help but wonder if the small glass of red in her hand has anything to do with the improvement of her mood.

Her costume is made of a fine green tule, artfully sewn to portray the concealing leaves of the sprites. For a moment, I find myself wishing for the company of the sisters and can't help but think they would enjoy the festivities that honor their kind.

Awri's eyes shine as she looks me over with approval and appreciation. Nurai stands beside her, the female's smile clearly hiding a frown. I'm not surprised to find her dressed as a naiad. Though, if anyone asked my opinion, I would have suggested the more terrifying version of the fea and happily supplied the mossy fish eggs for her hair.

One of Awri's companions steps toward me, and my gut pits. It is not the wrathful fire in her eyes that has me steeling myself as she dips her head, unable to hide the disdain she clearly feels for me. It is the memory of the last time I saw the female, and the command she issued as I fled.

Though she does wear a dress resembling a water nymph, it is not the image of the nymphs of Kator the female threatened the general with when I first met her.

"I don't believe we've met. I am Ishara."

My brow draws down in puzzled confusion and I reply, "We have met. At Adora's."

She recoils when I say it, hissing, "I told you to forget that."

Icey tendrils of her gift skate up my spine as she levels an expectant glare at me before her brow creases. She schools her features in a practiced way when she looks to Awri and says, "I suppose you thought it would be amusing to deceive all of A'kori into believing the general chose the company of a human over mine."

"I have done nothing, Ishara," Awri insists.

But it is Nurai that manages to settle the female by grasping her arm and warning, "Let it go, dear. The general made his choice. Now, I suggest you leave, before the king finds you here."

There is a moment that something passes between them, an understanding that cools the fire of her rage. Ishara nods once that she understands, departing without another word.

She is not the only one affected by Nurai's threat, and I brush a chill from my arms when I recall that, for me, tonight has a single purpose. I

glance around the room, my search for the general interrupted when Awri introduces me to the other strangers standing nearby. My eyes follow Riah when she excuses herself to speak with Toren.

The male is in a neatly pressed dress uniform, one hand resting on his lower back, his hair swept up in its customary braids, plaited into a single thick column. My breath catches in my throat when she produces the small flower she'd taken from my hair. My spine tingles as she leans in and whispers into Toren's pointed ear. In a flash, the cold steel of his eyes are on mine, stiffening my back.

The gesture itself might not be alarming, if it weren't for the female's insistence that I not feed the tiny bloom to anyone in attendance. But when Toren gives the lieutenant a curt nod and excuses himself from the conversation he'd been having with some of the more important looking guests, I can't help but question the potential uses of the flower beyond what I know.

Hisht.

With every step he takes toward me, I feel the web of the fates binding my future, until he's standing beside me, offering me his arm.

"Shivaria, I was told you requested an audience with the king," he says.

Even as I drape my arm over his, making my excuses as I depart from the others, I remind myself that this was my choice. This *is* my choice. That of the few and narrow paths my future holds, only one is a path I desire to live, and it starts with this.

There is no time for goodbyes as he leads me through the room, my eyes lingering on Awri until she disappears beyond the throng of dancing guests. A pang of regret wells in my gut when I consider what this truth will cost her. My actions as her friend have made her cautious of me, and rightfully so. After tonight, I can imagine no way to bridge the rift that will swell between us.

The time for any mending has passed. And friendship is a skill I was never taught—after all, Drakai have no use for anyone beyond their use as a tool.

Maybe it is only my nerves, but I swear every eye in the room is upon me. I straighten my back, head held high as I pass through the midst of them all, trying to keep my thoughts from my future.

I expect to be led through a tall set of doors, brilliantly carved and inlaid

with gold. The doors of a king. The doors to a throne room. But the door he opens, swinging his arm in as he offers me entry, is humble and plain.

My stomach dips when I walk inside, each breath requiring a monumental effort to draw. I think my lungs might like to give up, to let this be the end. They burn in clear opposition to my chosen steps.

It's a large room. In many ways, much like every other I've visited in the palace. White stone, thick veins of gold beneath my feet, tall windows lining every wall. Unlike every other room, however, it boasts a large array of plants. Some in large pots strewn about candlelit paths, others planted into the ground where large swaths of stone have been removed, revealing the soil below.

Much of the foliage is in the throes of early spring bloom. The colorful flowers fade in and out of the darkness with every passing firebug drifting about on the breeze coming in through the open windows.

"The king will be here shortly," Toren says, following me down a path winding north.

I nod my understanding, full of wonder and dread, hope and fear, my entire being raging a silent war within itself.

"May I ask, why you have requested this audience?" he asks flatly.

"To thank him," I say, the same lie I gave to Xeyvian.

"You could have done so at the masque," he prods.

"And to ask him if he will allow me to remain in A'kori," I add.

"Again, something you could have asked outside of a private meeting," he says.

My feet still beneath me when the path breaks into a large clearing, the glass dome roof offering a stunning view of the brilliant stars looking down upon Terr. A single star tears itself from the heavens, my eyes following its path as it crosses the vastness of our skies. Until it falls below the northern mountains, lost to my sight.

"Tell me," Toren's low voice bounces off the stone, "are you here to kill him?"

My gaze falls to him, his eyes darkening as he studies me. My blood chills when he looks at me like he knows every secret I've ever harbored, every lie I've ever told, and every truth I've ever left unspoken. My palms begin to sweat as I'm reminded of the tales of their king, of his gift, and it takes every bit of my willpower not to reach for the feynstone blades strapped to my thighs.

I eye the male before me as if I've never seen him before, asking myself questions that should have surfaced in my mind long ago. What if the king of A'kori was here all along? There is a moment I doubt myself as I recall the icy touch Toren set upon Siserie, but hadn't Awri told me that their gifts are all unique? I should have asked when I had the opportunity to understand all that she meant.

"What do you want with my king, Drakai?" The menacing tone of his voice is matched by the promise of wrath in his eyes.

My entire being begs to remain hidden among the lies I practiced for so long when I insist, "I am not Drakai."

"Lies," he growls.

"I am *not*. But I was," I admit.

"Clever," he smiles, "to twine your lies with the truth. But a Drakai cannot unbecome Drakai, just as there is no gift on Terr that can unmake a feyn."

He rounds me like a lion, on slow and silent steps. Each stride a sure testament to the male's restraint. His breath comes out in a puff of icy mist, as bright veins of blue reveal themselves on every inch of his exposed skin.

The truth then, all of it. For there is no question in my mind that I will not leave this room alive if I cannot make him believe me.

The truth spills from my lips in a torrent. That I was raised Drakai, of the day I received my mission from the La'tari king, of my intentions to end the life of his own. He lunges at me, fangs bared, and I fall to my knees, raising my hands over my head, palms up in supplication just as Ishara had done with the general.

He stands over me, a low rumble in the back of his throat. I swallow hard, keeping my eyes nailed to the vein of gold beneath me. Dropping a hand in front of my face, he spins the small flower from my hair between his fingers.

"Brazen," the low vibrato of his tone is near a growl, "to cover yourself in shadowbane, strap those blades to your form, and meet with a male you've been sent to end, all while claiming innocence."

A quick glance and I find the high slits of my gown have fallen, revealing the feynstone blades. It's a mistake, one I will surely regret for the rest of my life. The shimmering panels of the dress drape between my thighs, pooling on the marble beneath me.

"I swear, I only brought them to defend myself if the Vatruke came," I say.

"That was wise." A female's silken voice caresses my ears and the flesh on my arms prickles.

Risking a glance up, I find Toren's body rigid, facing a tall silhouette as she glides into the low light.

"Useless, but wise." She smiles.

"Vos," Toren says in a low warning. The air is driven from my lungs when the name finally finds meaning within my scattered mind.

Her lithe frame sways as she walks, the long black of her dress melding with the shadows, her dark hair glinting as it's pushed over her shoulders on a gust of wind coming off the northern ranges.

"Toren," she says in greeting. "Forgive me for eavesdropping, but I couldn't help but overhear."

She clicks her tongue at me when I risk rising to my feet by Toren's side. Sliding the blades into my hands, I conceal them from her view, resting them against the back of my forearms.

"Leave, Vos. I will only ask you once," Toren threatens, and I can't help but wonder if his gift is enough to match the power of her own.

I think not when she laughs. Waving her hand at the male dismissively, she says, "Give me the girl and I will. She is the only reason I came here tonight."

My stomach pits with dread when she offers Toren a simple solution to his problem. Give up the Drakai. A life already hanging at the precipice of his mercy—my life—as an offering to his enemy. One that will appease her, if only for tonight.

"I cannot," he says plainly, startling me when he places himself between us.

"Really?" she purrs, "In that case, I'm sure you will understand."

With the flick of her wrist, Toren grunts and in the next moment the male is careening through the air. He stops when he collides with the thick stone wall of the keep, a sickening crack resounding through the night before he lands upon the ground in a crumpled mass.

She tips her head to the side as she observes me.

"I thought your death would make me feel better," she admits, "But you are nothing, and even I will have forgotten your face in the span of a few short years."

I will my feet to remain beneath me as she steps toward me.

"I would like to make this last longer," she says, "to take my time with you. I would enjoy watching you suffer as I have, but vengeance is vengeance, and I *will* have mine."

She waves her hand toward me, and I can't help the coiled tension of my body when I flinch, my eyes remaining fixed on the female. If I am to die, I will not let her see the fear that bleeds within me, staining the very essence of my being. Ice snakes up my spine, even as my veins ignite as if they will be set ablaze and the air is driven from my lungs. The female frowns, lowering her hand to her side, and my demon unfurls within me.

A wicked smile takes over her features, the look on her face truly pleased when she says, "*Shivay lathrek, Valtoura.*"

She chances another graceful step in my direction. I move to the side, unwilling to turn my back to the female. I work my way toward a larger clearing amidst the vegetation, where I can more easily defend myself if it comes to blows.

"I thought I might have to burn down every forest in Brax to find you," she says gleefully, "And all the while, Xeyvian hid you here. Clever."

Her words have no meaning. Every thought that exists within me, homed in on one simple task. Survive. I round the courtyard defensively, searching for an exit, for any way to escape the certainty of my future if I end up within her reach.

"Had I not sought you out after you killed my mate, I might have over-looked you in this form," she says, "A mistake I won't make again."

The loud click of a solid door at the far end of the room draws her attention and I bolt. Ducking beneath low branches heavy-laden with a myriad of blooms, I round tall bushes covered in thick waxy leaves. I head toward any of the open windows that will allow passage to the northern lawns. My stomach wells with dread when her laugh chases after me, the female following close behind.

Each window slams shut the moment I reach for it. Every attempt to dart toward an opening and claim my freedom only ends up costing me precious inches of what little space remains between us. Until I am standing face-to-face with Vos, my back pinned against the cool stone wall of the palace.

"Shivaria!"

I want to weep when Xeyvian's voice comes from the farthest side of the room, just as I hear the skirmish begin between the male I treasure and what I can only assume is a squad of Drakai. I won't let myself consider his fate if it is the Vatruke and not the La'tari assassins he faces.

"So disappointing," Vos says softly, her face contorting in mock sadness. "Will you only run? Or will you show me what the ancients would have me fear?"

I lunge at the female, swinging the pointed tip of my blade into my palm as I strike out at her chest. She doesn't flinch, doesn't blink, as I thrust the dagger toward its mark only to be halted the moment it pierces her flesh. A single drop of blood beads and falls between her breasts.

Her head tips to the side curiously, her eyes squinting in confusion when she asks, "Why do you hold yourself back, *Valtoura*? You know as well as I do that your human form is not strong enough to wield those blades against the might of my power."

Her eyes fall to the blades. Icy tendrils spread through my body, her gift threatening to tear the blades from my hands. My brow pinches down as they begin to slip, and I struggle to hold my last defense. It is no use to fight the might of her power. I know I've lost even before the blades fly free, one slicing a deep gash into my palm. They clatter, bouncing upon the stone path that I hoped would lead to my freedom, until they are lost to my sight, tumbling into the darkness.

Even as I think it, I know it is only a vain hope that the general will reach us before Vos ends me. Any hope I hold of making it out alive dissipates with the seconds that pass by. He won't make it in time, if he makes it at all.

It is panic or madness, I am not sure which. Though, only madness can explain the thoughts that cross my mind when I strike at her with nothing more than a closed fist. Not a single lesson I'd ever received about warring against a feyn leads me to believe that this is a good idea. And yet, when my fist collides with her nose, there is satisfaction in the way it bends unnaturally. The fragile bones within give way to the battering ram of my arm with a loud *pop*.

A slurry of feyn curses come from the female as her hand flies to her nose, attempting to stanch the heavy flow of blood gushing out. It is enough. The moment her eyes flicker shut I dart away, sure that I can hide myself somewhere in the dense foliage around me until someone more equipped for this battle comes to aid me.

"You *will* live to regret that, *Valtoura*." Her voice comes from behind me, and in it I can hear the blessed distance I have put between us.

"Sleep well," she says. A pang of dread wells deep within me when, in the flicker of a windswept flame, a large stone slams against the side of my head and my eyes shutter into darkness.

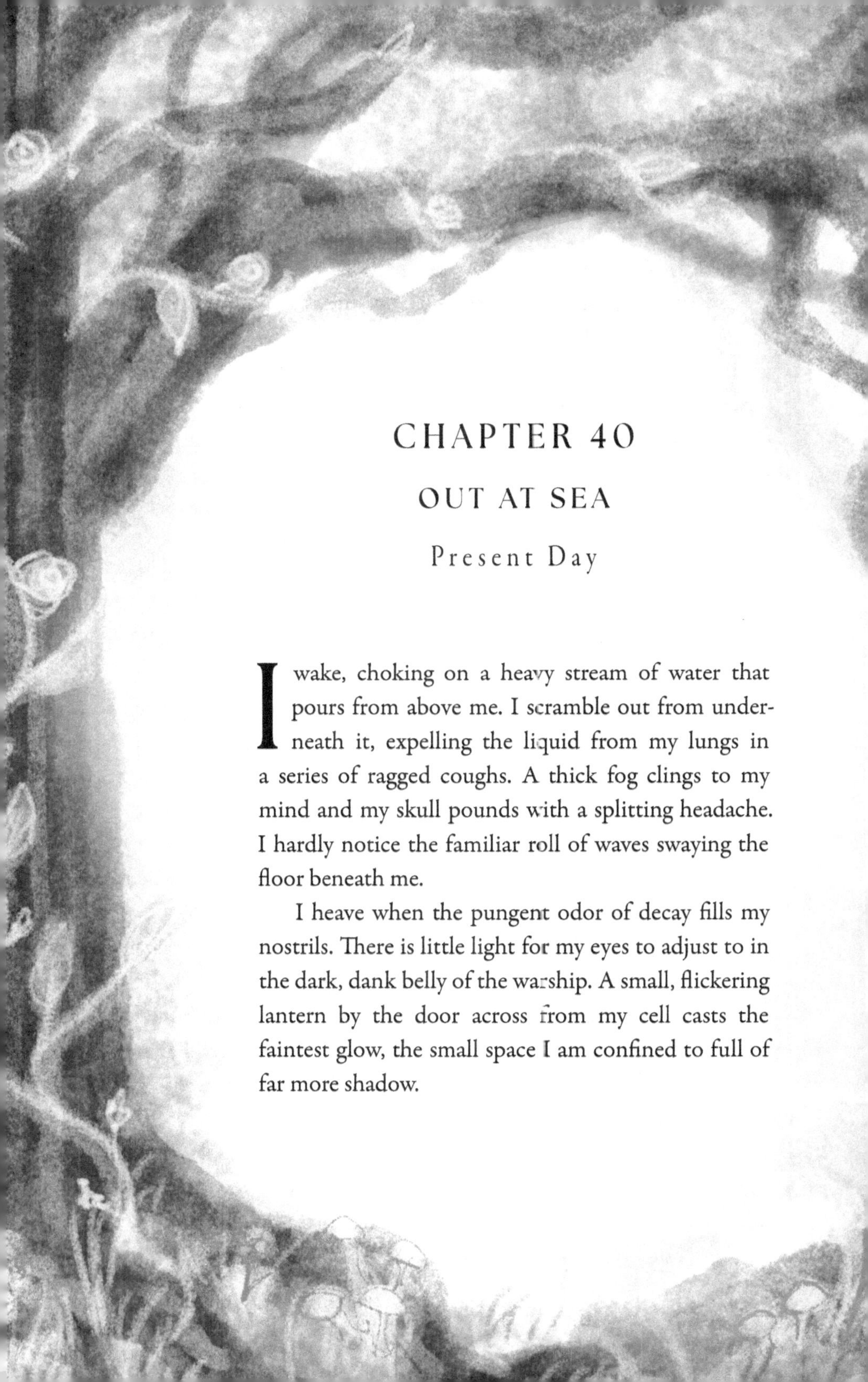

CHAPTER 40

OUT AT SEA

Present Day

I wake, choking on a heavy stream of water that pours from above me. I scramble out from underneath it, expelling the liquid from my lungs in a series of ragged coughs. A thick fog clings to my mind and my skull pounds with a splitting headache. I hardly notice the familiar roll of waves swaying the floor beneath me.

I heave when the pungent odor of decay fills my nostrils. There is little light for my eyes to adjust to in the dark, dank belly of the warship. A small, flickering lantern by the door across from my cell casts the faintest glow, the small space I am confined to full of far more shadow.

"Awake at last, *Valtoura,*" Vos purrs from where she stands over me.

She is bracketed on either side by two male feyn. Both with black hair, both sharing her features, and both graced with the same strange shape of Kezik's ears. The larger of the two holds an upended jug, setting it aside when he kneels before the bars dividing us.

My current position, splayed out on my belly, is far too vulnerable, and the world spins as I attempt to rise, pushing my torso off the floor. I falter in the upward motion, remaining on my knees, my hand cradling my head tenderly where a sharp pain emanates from my temple. There is no mistaking the slick of blood I find there, but all my lessons about tending wounds are far from my mind.

"*Valtoura?*" the kneeling male says in mock surprise. "I expected more from the ancients."

"Have a little caution, Nix," Vos warns from behind him, her finger sweeping across the small stain upon her chest where I nearly ended her with my blade. Or so she allowed me to believe. "She may be caged, but she still has claws."

His head tilts to the side, a small bit of loose hair falling from where it's partially bound to hang before his eyes. The male, Nix, is cut from the granite of Terr, far larger than any feyn I have ever seen. His is not the toned, nimble form I am accustomed to expecting from their kind, but the thick, brawny mass of the warriors I had been raised alongside in La'tari.

"Are you sure that this is *Valtoura?*" asks the male remaining by her side, clearly skeptical in the tale the female wove about our meeting.

The curious face he levels at me sparks the memory of the last and only time I've ever seen him. It was upon Yshka's balcony, the night I'd sought out Ishara's home in search of allies. The hair on my arms stiffens, a world of revelations crashing into my mind. The Vatruke have been in A'kori longer than I or anyone else realized, working with the only house with the name and power to usurp the feyn throne.

Vos looks me over, hesitating to answer. I know the look, I have seen it countless times in my life, resting upon my own face every time I look in a mirror. The female is unsure of herself, and I grasp at the moment it reveals.

"I am not *Valtoura,*" I say weakly, and maybe I shouldn't because I'm sure

it is the only thing keeping me alive. Though the fate I might have among the Vatruke if I claim to be what they say is enough to raise the bile in my stomach.

"I *was* sure," Vos says, and I can hear the question in her voice, no longer convinced of what she believes.

"If you are not *Valtoura*, then what are you?" Nix demands.

"Drakai," I admit, the truth of it and the lie it has become coating my tongue in a thick film of bitterness.

Nix rises from where he is crouched before me, huffing an incredulous laugh. "A feyn Drakai?" His eyebrows lift disbelievingly. "Such a thing does not exist on Terr."

Feyn.

I find my palm rubbing my sternum absently, unbidden. As if it might soothe an unknown ache lingering beneath the surface of my skin. The male remaining next to Vos looks at me from beneath furrowed brows, his eyes tracking the hand at my chest.

"Mated? Perhaps she is just a feyn." The last he directs at Vos as she steps forward to observe me more closely.

I grip the fabric of my gown, willing my hand to still.

Mated.

"Perhaps she *is* only feyn," she says, the smile returning to her face. "But mated she most certainly is. Arda, why don't you go and see if the captain needs any assistance."

The male by her side pales, his jaw tense as he departs from the room.

"He's never had a stomach for these things," Vos explains, but it is the excitement adorning Nix's face that chills me when he unlocks the door to my cell.

There is no hesitation when he steps in front of me. One large hand fisting my curls, he lifts me until I meet his eyes, my toes sweeping against the deck in a futile effort to find footing. My hands clasp around his wrist, pulling to free myself. But he only laughs as I struggle, his grip like soldered iron.

"I could ask," Vos says as she slides into the cell, "What you are. The name of the mate I will rend from your bond just as you have done to mine." She glides in front of me, a smug smile on her lips. "But even if you tell me everything I want to know, you owe me a debt of pain, a debt I will spend the rest of your long life collecting."

It's the only warning she gives, before revealing the jagged blade she conceals at her side as she places it against my ribs and begins to carve.

The scream tears at the tender flesh of my throat as the blade finds its home near my spine. Piercing the skin at my back until it drags upon the rib beneath, severing tendon and nerve as it flays the flesh open wide. Vos takes her time, slowly slicing through the muscles. Each fiber on fire as the sinew slowly separates, her knife working its way around to the flesh of my side.

My head tips back as the last of my strength leaves me. Nix eyes the exposed flesh of my throat, his fangs protruding wantonly.

"Show me your true form," Vos says, the same demand she has issued after each of the five ribs now boasting the bloody evidence of her attention.

But my arms are slack at my sides, weary from struggling through the four attempts she delivered to my side before. My body is heavy with a mixture of hot and cooling blood, drying to cake against my skin, and my mind is hazy, unable to form the words I offered at the beginning.

I can't.

When the iron of Nix's hand finally releases its hold on me, I smack against the floor in a nauseating puddle of my own blood and vomit.

I'm vaguely aware of footsteps when Vos's voice comes from the other side of the small space. "Leave her, brother, she is too fragile to continue in this form."

His stride is too reluctant when he departs. I shudder to think about how far the male might have persisted if not for his sister. For the first time since I woke aboard the ship, I feel relieved, listening to their steps as they leave the dark room.

There is nothing to stop the slow trickle of blood as it leaks from my ribs. I can't help but think that this is a better end than what I might have endured at their hands if my body were made of something stronger. I'm hardly aware of the door when it opens again, or the patter of nimble feet when they venture into the growing pool of my blood.

A petite female kneels by my head. The tips of her long swath of white hair soak up the deep crimson on the floor, the fabric of her snow-white dress doing the same.

She glances toward the door and a larger part of myself than I'd like to admit suffers an excruciating loss when she slides the feynstone ring from my finger and into her pocket. Her hands wrap about my torso and a blinding pain courses through my body the next moment.

I loose a scream straight from the depths of haliel. The familiar agony of healing melds with the terror that rises within me when I see clearly the vision Vos has for my future. I have no doubt that once I am healed, the torture will begin again. A cycle that will repeat until she is satisfied that I have endured a punishment she deems worthy of the male I've stripped from her life.

I grasp the healer's wrists in fury as much as in fear, the demon that lives within me roiling in rebellion of the female's gift. Death. I choose death over the life they have in store for me.

"No!" I scream, my voice rasping and shrill even as her gift attempts to mend it.

Small as she is, her brow pitches down in terrifying determination as she presses her weight against my chest, forcing her gift into me. I grit my teeth, glaring at the healer. The boat creaks and groans as it shudders beneath us. I'm only vaguely aware of the alarmed shouts that rise overhead.

"Stop it," the female hisses, her forehead beading with sweat, as she glances behind her.

I suppress a sob when the door slams against the interior of the room, Nix ducking beneath the doorway as he enters. The healer parts from me. The ship ceases its turbulent rumble, as she rushes to stand before him, head bowed.

He brushes her hair over her shoulder. An act I might consider tender if I could not see the dark thoughts lingering behind his eyes when his gaze falls upon me in the same moment.

He brings his fangs to her ear and whispers, "Would you like to watch, *mi'ajna?*"

She glances back at me, a mournful look on her face as she offers him a single nod.

"Good," he says, sweeping wide around the female as he strides toward me.

His eyes cross over my wounds, and he frowns. "You were told to heal her."

The female shrinks from the wrathful pitch of his tone.

"She fought me," she says, the timbre of her voice wavering.

"Bring the surgeon," he demands, waving her away, a chilling smile spreading across his face. "If you think my sister will allow your life to end so easily, you are mistaken," he says, wrapping a thick, calloused hand around my throat. He drags me off the floor, and I suck in a gasp as the weight of my body tears at my broken flesh. "And if you think the damaged state of your form is anything but appealing to me, allow me to correct that assumption."

I can't help the whimper that escapes my lips when he pins me against the wall of the ship with his hips. The promise of every desire the male harbors within him pressed between my legs.

"Your mate should have marked you when he had the chance." It's the only warning he gives before breaking my necklace in his fist and casting it to the floor as his fangs find purchase in the fragile skin at my throat.

His tongue laps at the blood, a contented rumble in his chest. I claw at his face. A sad and desperate attempt to part him from my flesh. He bats my hands away before raking his fingers through the open skin of my side and I loose a scream of utter agony and rage that makes the male smile against my throat.

"Enough!" Vos shouts from the doorway and he drops me back to the bloody deck beneath his feet.

I stifle a sob, the feeling of the male's fangs beneath my skin more repulsive and violating than could ever be put into words.

I don't hear the harsh words exchanged between them when the surgeon pours a vile smelling solution on my wounds. My eyes grow wide when he produces a small wire brush from a black bag and takes it to my side. I heave up bile as he scrubs the exposed muscle at my ribs, surely scraping the bones that lay beneath.

The waking world shutters as my vision blurs. I watch the small female drenched in my blood fall to her knees and pocket the necklace. If only the void calling to me were death, I would have peace when it finally comes to take me.

If the frequency of my meals is any indication of the passing time, it's been a week since I came to in the brig. A week of near solitude, save for the surgeon who attends me daily. He had washed my wounds that first day, stitched and bound them, before I woke in the darkness and wept.

Two days later I woke with a fever and a dreadful ache in my side. I screamed when he broke the sutures and washed the wound again, much more thoroughly than he had the first time. He wrapped my ribs in a poultice after that, the green of the herbs melding with the fresh flow of my blood to stain the bandages.

My fever broke three days later, and today Vos joined the surgeon to see for herself the state of my condition. Though the surgeon assured her it is too soon to continue my torture, it's clear the female's patience is at its end. I can only hope it will be the blade and not her brother that leaves its mark upon my body when we begin again.

Long after the surgeon's visit this morning, laying in the near dark of the brig, I note the creaking of the ship as it begins to tilt at the whim of the harsh gusts overhead. Large waves batter the sides, and my stomach has wound itself into a tangle of knots.

I've hardly moved from where my blood has dried into the deep grooves of the wooden floor. With only my thoughts to keep me company, my days are filled with misery as I ponder the mess I have made of my life. The solitude of the dark and the memories I cannot purge from my mind are perhaps a more acute torture than what Vos laid bare upon my flesh.

Ask.

An echo resounding within me day and night. The sound of his voice, the first thing I hear upon every waking. I am a fool, for not asking the male who offered me so much, for not trusting all he laid at my feet. And I am a coward, for running from a truth that would have shattered all that I am, as much as it would have freed me from the shackles of my upbringing.

A tear falls from my eye, wetting the crimson stain beneath me. It isn't the first. There have been many, and I have no doubt there are more to come.

Where once there were numerous paths I might have tread, now it seems only one remains. One that I find no pleasure in pondering.

My palm rests on my chest, a futile attempt to soothe the ache I fear will plague me for the rest of my life. What little might remain of it. Another tear falls, and I wonder if the male I am bound to will find a way to shed the bond between us. I would, if I were him, just as I tried to shed the ties of my past life when I set foot upon the shores of A'kori.

I eye the poultice, wishing to strip the mesh from my skin and let the wounds fester until I meet death at last. But they would only be replaced, and I have little doubt I would find myself shackled to the wall for my efforts. Another tear falls to the floor, and I wince at the pain in my side when I jump at the voice coming from the dark.

"Foolish," she rasps from the shadows, "You or I, I know not which."

My eyes strain to find the source, hidden in the darkness.

"Bagya." I suck in her name on a painful and shallow breath.

Unchanged since last I saw her, the crone sits atop a box of cargo, hidden in a dark corner across the room. Wrapped in tattered rags, a large hood further obscuring her face, she cracks a hideous and broken smile.

"I suppose, *Bagya* will do for now," she says simply.

I should fear her, I know I should. The general's warning resounds in my mind, and yet, what price would be too great to be free of this cage? I cannot help the hope that rises within me, matching all the dread I feel at seeing her again.

"Have you come to make another bargain?" I rasp out, unwilling to grasp at hope if she only came to taunt me.

"That depends," she says, "are you done with the lie, child? Or will you hold it with you forever?"

I huff scornfully. Only briefly considering the riddle of her question.

Focing fea.

"I *am* done with lies," I say, my voice weak. I stifle a small quiver in my lip, brought on by the deception I've held close for far too long.

My honesty came too late and at too great a cost. I stanch the flow of memories, unwilling to consider the lives that may have been lost as my limp body had been dragged from the palace.

"Then a bargain we will have. The lie, for your freedom," she says.

I want to end the crone, to tell her that her words are as twisted as the deceit that kept me captive to a life built upon lies. But what can I do? As long as Vos still lives, my future is assured, and it is not a future I look forward to living. Just as she had when I was young, the fea sitting before me holds the power to grant me the only thing I truly need.

Why am I worried? Hadn't I already given her the same? And never for a moment in my life have I regretted that exchange. To remain aboard this ship is death, and if I do remain, that death will be a welcome reprieve when it finally comes.

"It's a bargain," I say quietly, swallowing my defeat, still unsure of what I'm giving up.

Ice fills my veins, my heart beating wildly within my chest as I struggle to breathe. It ebbs, and I suck in a deep breath, wincing at the agonizing pain of my side.

"Then it's done." The crone's voice is a whispering echo as she fades into the shadows surrounding her, vanishing, while I remain behind the cool steel bars of my cage.

Moments pass, as the ship continues to pitch from side to side. All alone within my cell, a fire begins to build within me. I want to forfeit myself to haliel. To scream in the faces of the fates and demand that they explain the joke they have made of my life.

I grit my teeth, and with great effort rise enough to grasp at the door of my cage and rattle the bars. It stays firmly latched, and I collapse with a wracking sob. Rage fills me, my ears pounding with the beating of my heart and—

No. Not my heart.

Banishing the fresh tears of my wrath, I listen to the waves of Terr beating upon the belly of the ship in a rhythmic pulse, familiar and sweet. I'm rocked with every sway. Moved in time by the waves, like a child is swayed by her mother as she clings to her breast. Wind like the filling and freeing of lungs bursts in a timing all its own, sweeping across the deck overhead.

Clutching the bars, I struggle to pull myself to my feet, letting my rising senses swaddle me in the strange feeling that is the life of Terr. My eyes linger upon my hands, upon the newness of my own flesh, my fingers gently scouring the unfamiliar shape of my form.

My stomach pits when my fingertips brush the newly pointed tip of my ear. Not formed like that of the feyn, but with the uneven edges of the Vatruke.

The fall of heavy footsteps calls my attention to the door across from me. Shadows beckoning, I back into the dark corner of my cell, the pulse of Terr consuming me, until we meld together and our pulses beat as one.

Nix ducks into the room, his hesitation evident in each step when he fails to discern me. I sway, lost among the thick drapes of heavy darkness clinging to every corner of the small space. The strength of my legs threatens to give way beneath me.

Too arrogant in his own strength he unlocks the door of my cage, stepping inside. It's hardly a thought when I travel between the shadows, finding myself behind him. Before I've even considered what I've done, my quick reflexes slam the cell door shut, locking him inside. He whips around to face me, a slow smile spreading across his face, not at all concerned with being confined.

"There you are," he says softly, dragging his eyes from the elegant and bloody legs beneath my torn gown to the oddly shaped tips of my ears.

The latter widens his eyes and his smile grows. "I think I prefer you like this," he admits, his hands grasping the thick steel bars between us. "Much harder to break."

He tightens his grip and the metal bends, groaning as it concedes to his might.

I don't think when I bolt out the door. A patrol spots me from the stairwell leading topside and I swear under my breath. I burst into a sprint, hand bracing the wounds at my side as his voice rises above the storm to alert the others.

The ship pitches violently as I make it to the upper deck. I swallow a scream of pain when I slide into the railing, the only thing keeping me from the turbulent seas below. Rain pounds the ship, a deafening roar to my newly heightened senses. Lightning illuminates the dark seas in short flickering bursts, allowing me a momentary glimpse of the A'kori vessel in pursuit of the Vatruke.

Relief. For a moment. Until my eyes widen when I see for myself the massive rocks jutting from the shallow reefs of *Chai'brukar*. White water breaks violently upon itself. Thunder booms even as lightning flickers over

the shore of the Braxian coast, the dense forests of the fea swelling with light, only to dim the next moment.

"*Valtoura!*"

I spin around to face Vos, certain that the only end to this will be paid for with her life or my own.

She stands outside the door of the captain's room, Arda at her side. Nix creeps up from below deck and begins rounding on me slowly.

"There is nowhere for you to go!" she yells over the crashing of waves as they break against the bow. "Let us put this behind us."

She takes a cautious step toward me, her eyes ravenous as she takes in every bit of my new form.

Another step. "Come with me, and I will show you what true power is."

Another step. "Let me free you from the bonds of your fate."

Nix is nearly at my back when I step toward her. She smiles, reaching out her hand. When I level her with the heat of my fury, her face falls.

The ship pitches beneath us. While she struggles to keep her footing, I clutch the rail, using the momentum of the waves and the leverage I've gained to throw myself off the side. The wounds on my torso tear themselves anew.

The cries of Vos's rage are lost to the icy water as I plummet into the sea. The calm of her womb is a stark contrast to her violent surface overhead. Dark waters surround me. Only the distant, flickering light over the forests of Brax declares where I might find air. Air my lungs should desperately need. Yet, there is no burning in my chest, no gasping urgency.

My dress weaves among the current, thousands of tiny crystals shimmering in the sea. I find that I am content to remain in the quiet darkness, and I close my eyes, letting myself rest for what might be the first time in my life. After everything, I've found peace in the stillness and quiet of my end.

A thrum in the deep, and I open my eyes. Lightning streaks across the sky, dancing upon the waves that ripple overhead. In the darkness that surrounds, tiny lights flicker into being. A beautiful hum in my chest rises to meet her

song. I can feel her now, my demon. Dancing in the midst of the starlight that encompasses me. So familiar, and yet...

She greets me as never before, shattering the last of the fragile panes that divide us. She pours herself into me, filling the deep void in my being, sharing in every sorrow, every joy, and every fear. She sings to me sweetly, tenderly, enduring the pain of our breaking until bound together we are knit anew.

A murmur from the depths of Terr. Her name is a soft caress as it skates across my ears, only a whisper in the darkness.

"Shivay."

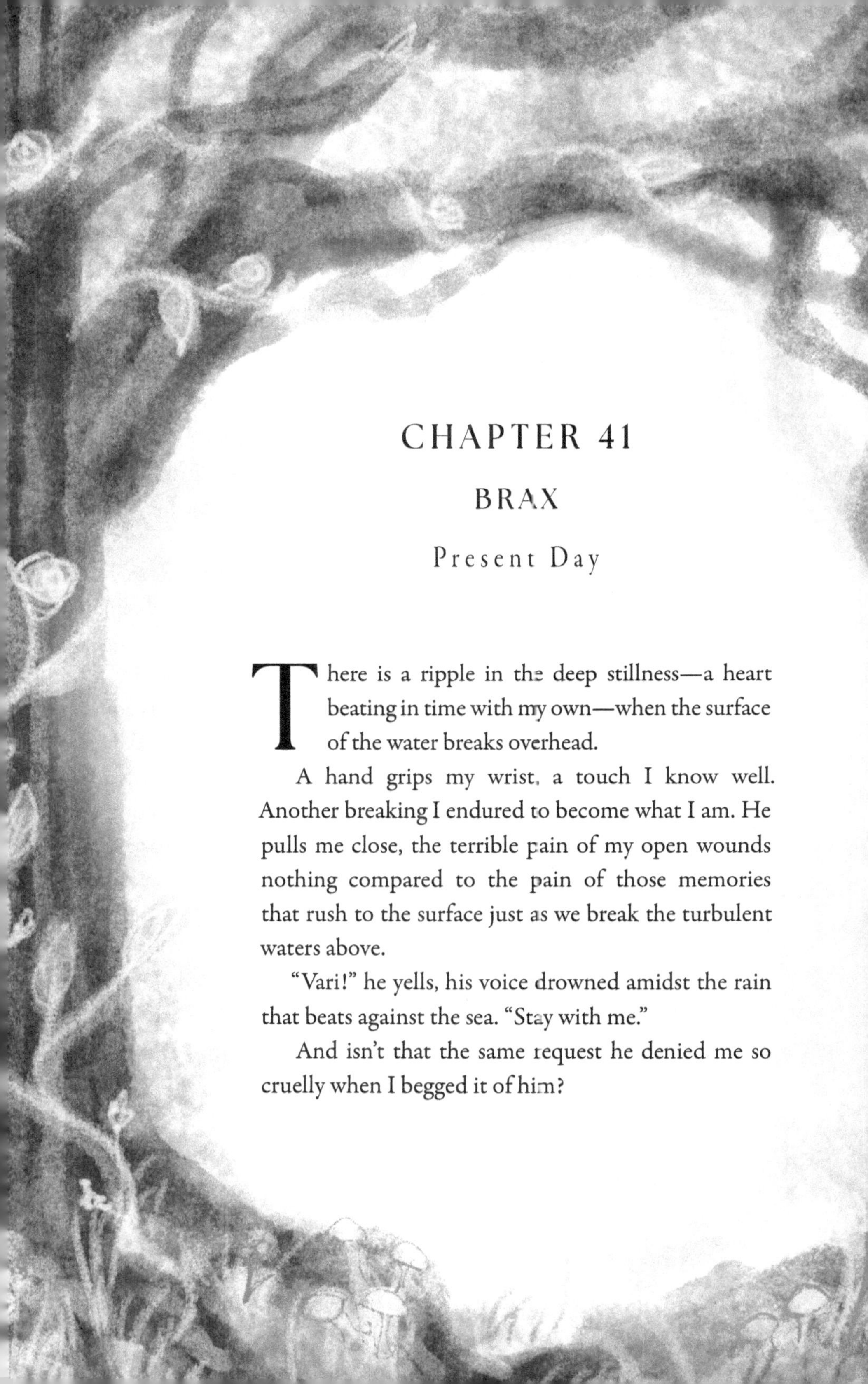

CHAPTER 41

BRAX

Present Day

There is a ripple in the deep stillness—a heart beating in time with my own—when the surface of the water breaks overhead.

A hand grips my wrist, a touch I know well. Another breaking I endured to become what I am. He pulls me close, the terrible pain of my open wounds nothing compared to the pain of those memories that rush to the surface just as we break the turbulent waters above.

"Vari!" he yells, his voice drowned amidst the rain that beats against the sea. "Stay with me."

And isn't that the same request he denied me so cruelly when I begged it of him?

My lungs burn, but not for lack of air, when he hauls me to the sandy shore of Brax. His hands are at my side, a swear on his lips as he attempts to rebind the gauze falling from the bloody lacerations.

But it is the warship I watch in the distance, the flames that lick up its bow as lightning continues to strike it in an unnatural fashion. The mast cracks, splitting in two as it falls upon the deck, the ship lost to the arching fire of the fates. As if Terr herself willed an end to the lives of those aboard it. I don't blame her.

Wrapping an arm around my waist, hooking the other beneath my knees, he pulls me to his chest. He breaks toward the A'kori ship that made it to shore. The rain pounds the ground around us, a small break in the clouds above offering a momentary pause to the deluge stealing the heat from my bones.

Though there are many voices on the ship, they all slip past my ears as he races to the captain's quarters, laying me in the center of a large wooden table as he yells, "*Bri'vek eh hiven*!"

I'm hardly aware of the heavy blanket he drapes over the wracking form of my body. A young feyn with a kind, freckled face barges into the room the next moment. They share a quickly whispered exchange in feyn speak before, with an apologetic glance, the young male clasps my side, releasing his gift.

I scream as the parted sinew of my side knits back together. Though the pain of healing is nothing compared to the disgust I feel at Nix's mark searing itself onto my neck. My vision turns to a blinding white before shuddering to black.

"You're safe, Vari."

It's the last thing I hear before I let myself drown in the void of my agony.

Safe. You're safe.

The gentle light of morning is a stark contrast to the heavy blanket of dark I've lived in for the last week of my life. The windows of the captain's cabin, a welcome sight for someone who wasn't sure they would ever see the sunrise again.

Gingerly brushing my hand along my side, I test the healer's work. He did

well. Only a small amount of scarred flesh is left to remind me of the crossing. Not that I could ever forget it, even without the marks upon my skin.

Swinging my legs over the table's side, my feet smack against the wood of the floor. Perhaps it is vanity that leads me to pass by the large doors of the cabin when my freedom waits behind them. But I find myself in front of a small mirror hanging above a basin of fresh water, fearfully curious of the creature the crone freed.

It's still me. Only different. Only … feyn. My features are sharper and more defined. The blue of my eyes like the icy waters in early spring, dark hair like soft spirals of silk, capturing the light as if they might contain it.

The odd leaf-like shape of my ears, the only thing to declare that I am, as Felias warned, *something else entirely*.

"Vari?"

Had I not memorized his voice when I was still too young to be called to the service of the crown, the smell of storms gathering would announce his arrival. He doesn't seem surprised when I turn to face him. Not horrified like I expect. Maybe it is only that he has had all night to come to terms with what I am.

His gaze doesn't wander. It stays firmly glued to my own. An apology I do not understand written in the lines of his eyes.

Eyes that I treasure. Eyes that, like his voice, I thought I memorized many years ago. Now different. Now … feyn.

Eyes that are now the brightest of blues, icy like my own. The pointed tips of his ears peek out from within the thick drape of his white hair. He begins toward me, his brow drawn and jaw tight as he approaches. I find that I hardly know this male. There is no hint of the pleasing smile that settled me so often when I was young. No hint of the man who broke every barrier I'd been taught to maintain.

Each step is cautious, as if he fears I might run. Maybe I should. Maybe I'm only fooling myself, thinking I know *any* part of the male that stands before me. The *man*, I trusted. With my life. With my secrets. With my heart.

He was careless with all but one. My stomach twists itself into a knot I can never unfasten when I realize that the secrets of mine he kept, were not secrets I had known.

"You lied to me," I say. The words bite at the quiet stillness, and I refuse to let the sheen of my sorrow reach my eyes.

Better to face him with anger than to allow him to break me all over again.

"Only to protect you," he explains.

I nod, a sarcastic rendition of my understanding. "Protect me from what? From Leanna?" I ask in mock curiosity. "Or was it the feyn? Or the fea? Vos? Nix?" My voice cracks and he swallows hard, his eyes softening.

He reaches for me, his hand stilling the moment my back stiffens in response, a vacant mask falling over my features.

"Don't do that," he pleads.

"Isn't this what you taught me to be?" I ask coldly, as if I am completely unaffected by it—by him.

"I came to La'tari to find you, when you were young." The words spill out of him as I move to step around him, uninterested in the tale he weaves. True or false, it makes no difference to me.

He places himself in front of me as he continues, "I wasn't sure it was you until the day you met Bagya in the woods, and she frayed the threads that bound your power. She told me—"

"Bagya told *you*?" I spit the question.

Traitor.

"What did Bagya tell you, Vakesh?"

As if the clouds themselves feel the rage building within me, they blanket the morning sun and the room darkens.

"Did she tell you to lie to me? Tell you to train me? To gain my trust? To use me? To *foc* me?!"

Fists balled at his sides, this time he doesn't block me when I walk around him. His mouth hangs open as if he'd gone to speak only to find that all the air had been let out of his lungs. I don't look back when my hand falls on the lever of the door, but for a moment, my feet still beneath me.

"You can blame all of Terr, Vakesh. But they were all *your* choices. Every single one of them. And maybe you did what you did to protect me, but as fates would have it, *you* are the only one I ever needed your protection from."

Every step away from him unravels a binding that I hadn't realized

tethered my very soul. Every breath I draw into my lungs, an entreaty for a new life, one without the weight of longing and fear.

The deck of the ship is busy with the crew rushing to do as they have been commanded but it is Felias that catches my eye as he dips his chin toward me in recognition. I turn away without a word. Everything I had to say to the man has already been said.

Long and determined strides find me upon the shores. There is no path that will take me to the dense forests of Brax but the one I make. I set out heading east, determined to become lost among the ancient stands.

All I know about myself is what I have been told. Drakai, Fea Dien, lady, *mi'ajna*. All names I was given by others in place of the name I should have called myself. Perhaps lost upon a foreign soil, with no home and no one to tell me who and what I am, I might finally begin to know her. The woman, the female, the stranger, who faced me in the mirror every day of my life and never left my side.

"*Tha'haynah?*" Tig's gentle voice quiets the violent raging of my soul, and I pause just long enough to answer. The sprite is lost among the wild and thorny bushes growing upon the dunes, when I say into the wind,

"*Launa rek'hi meiur. Rin'nik voh rei thai'es.*"

Come with me, friend. To where fate will find us.

I don't wait for her reply. There is no need. For as surely as the sprite is my friend, she has worked to weave the web of my fate, twining it with her own.

Thank you for traveling with Shivaria on her journey, and for spending time in Terr. It means more than I can say that your heart found a home in these pages.

This is only a first glimpse into the Veils of Terr and the journey is far from over. It would be my great honor to share what comes next.

Unlock exclusive lore, ancient languages, and a secret scene from Xeyvian's POV by joining my reader circle at www.SmuttyBuddies.com

And come say hi on Instagram and TikTok: @jrcathers